THE CITY IN THE DAWN

THE CITY IN THE DAWN

by Hervey Allen

Containing:

THE FOREST AND THE FORT

BEDFORD VILLAGE

TOWARD THE MORNING

RINEHART & COMPANY, INC.

New York · Toronto

NOTE

Because of his deep interest in and knowledge of American history, Hervey Allen undertook to write a saga of colonial times—in Pennsylvania, the Ohio country, and New York State. It was to be called *The Disinherited*. The protagonist was one Salathiel Albine.

Mr. Allen finished the first three volumes of this great novel: *The Forest and the Fort, Bedford Village,* and *Toward the Morning.* He had written a section of the fourth volume—*The City in the Dawn*—when death cut short his labors. Fortunately the completed chapters bring Salathiel Albine at last from the forest to the city, the symbol of man's pilgrimage from savagery to civilization.

To make this single-volume edition possible, much careful and judicious editing has had to be done in order to retain the vitality of Mr. Allen's fascinating story and of his deep insight into life and people. This editing was done by Julie Eidesheim, who worked closely with Mr. Allen throughout the writing of these books.

The Publishers

CONTENTS

The Forest and the Fort

1. Genesis

IN THE BEGINNING was the forest. God made it and no man knew the end of it. It was not new. It was old; ancient as the hills it covered. Those who first entered it saw it had been there since the beginning of habitable time. There were rivers in it and distant mountains; birds, beasts, and the mysterious villages of red men. The trees were vast, round, and countless; columns of the roof of heaven. The place beneath was endlessly aisled. There were green glades where the deer fed and looked at the buffalo; trails that went back into the animal time. There were valleys where the clouds lay and no man came there; caves where the wolves mated; peaks where the panther screamed.

But the forest itself was silent. It slept and dreamed of something in a perpetual grey-green shadow in the summer. The lightning flashed at evening and the thunder echo rolled. In the fall the leaves fell and the stars looked down through a roof of sticks. The snow sifted and glittered. Winds heavy with the silver breath of winter smoked on the mountains. The trees burgeoned. Red flashed into the green flame of spring. The grey-green shadow brooded in the forest again, gestating sunlight.

Birds, those free spirits of the weather, were the only beings who saw the spectacle entire. As the earth rocked, every spring and autumn their blood burned. They rose, trillions of them, feathered nations with innumerable tongues and various languages, and took to the air. Their nests and their love songs followed the tilting ecliptic like a pæan of time. They also sang the praises of the Almighty One with innocent, unthinking hearts. High in cold atmospheres, they beheld the grandeur and beauty of His thought.

Northward a necklace of great lakes glittered across the breast of the continent. Eastward the tabled plains of the Atlantic flashed lonely to the unbroken water rim. Not a sail gleamed. Only the steam clouds over the warm river in the ocean cliffed towering into heaven. The moon

rose out of them at the full and looked at the sun setting beyond the
Appalachians into a sea of western grass. Between lay the forest, green,
gladed, unbroken, beautiful; riding the still waves of the long mountains, stretching from ice blink to palms.

The fingers of innumerable days trailed across the roof of the forest,
while spring and autumn ran up and down it countless thousands of
times. The stars shifted in their houses. Eastward over the waters the
wings of gulls wheeled; gleamed and vanished; vanished and gleamed—
prophetically. Until in the fullness of time something whiter glinted
there; held the sunlight steadily; discovered the tracery of sails. Man-
made thunder saluted the land.

Then harbours reflected the lights of ships' lanterns; the windows of
gabled houses gleamed orange in the dusk. Broad plumes of smoke arose
from capes and along the estuaries by day. Fire and steel axes ate the
forest away, thinning it westward. Field patches and road scars began
to show among the trees. The haze of wood smoke gathered over towns.

Generation after generation the ships kept coming. From one century
into another the white man increased his town bases behind him. The
tentacles and network of roads began reaching out for the hills. Vainly
the silent stone-tipped arrows flitted from the forest at twilight. The
flash and roar of musketry replied. Manitou and Jehovah wrestled in the
valleys together—and the tasselled corn-god lost. Death like a mist out
of lethal nowhere fell upon the red man until he vanished. The forefathers he left behind him slept in quiet mounds beside the east-running
rivers. Only tobacco smoke lingered like a memorial incense scenting
the breeze.

Beyond the cloudy rampart of the mountains the Indian gathered his
surviving tribes. In the years numbered 1700 he and the forest stood at
bay together. And for a while the forest prevailed. In the quarrel between the two houses of the Great White Fathers lay the Indian's chief
hope of continuing to exist. Now on one side, now on the other his
hatchet rose and fell. What he fought for was to preserve the forest
beyond the Alleghenies. If the trees and the game went, if the white
man came there, the Indian must go, too.

He knew that. His great men and prophets arose by the secret council
fire and said so. The wampum strings of alliance flitted from tribe to
tribe. Many laid hands upon them and promised never to let go. Meanwhile, with sonorous oratory, he smoked the peace pipe or exchanged
the war belt with the French or English—always on the side of the trees.

And for a while, for a long time, the forest stood there. It stemmed
the onrush of the colonists of Europe. The frontier ceased to flow westward majestically. It blundered against the barrier of the trees, the tribes,
and the mountains. It recoiled. The inflow of its peoples pooled like the
trickle of waters rising slowly behind a dam head; fanned out northward; flowed notably south.

Beyond the mountains lay the Valleys of Eden. But to go there was to slip one's finger out of the handclasp of mankind. To go there was to go lonely; to defy the forest, the Indians, and the lawful king. To go there was to move westward without the baggage or the impedimenta of the past. It was to drop everything, except God, language itself, and the memory of simple numbers. It was to begin all over again, to become a something new and unique in time.

But that was the fascination of it. That was the lure. That was at once the refuge, the opportunity, and the goal.

The American did not begin by overthrowing society, by reorganizing an old civilization. He left all that completely behind him. He disinherited himself. He reinvented and reincarnated society. For the first time in memorized history man was free to act entirely on his own responsibility. He was back in the forest again. He had nothing but himself, the animals, and the trees to contend with. There liberty was not a dream and an idea to die for; it was a state of nature to be successfully lived in. In the Valleys of Eden, west of the Alleghenies, that was where and how new America began. The seeds of it were scattered in lonely cabins, lost apparently in an ocean of trees.

Out of them genesis.

2. A Scriptural Prelude

ANCESTRALLY it is sometimes, although not always, well to go back as far as one can. In North America the Atlantic usually provides your easy eastern limit of the past. And that is convenient even when it is not actually final.

All that it is necessary to know here, then, is that in the next to the last year of the seventeenth century there appeared in the vicinity of Norwalk, Connecticut, a forceful individual by the name of Abijah Albine. He came from England. He was a doctor of divinity out of some university, a disciple of St. Augustine through Calvin, and a mighty preacher of the word of God. In the course of a decade he gathered about him a scared, troublesome, gossiping, but withal faithful flock. He died in 1742. And that is about all that can be known with rigid certainty about the Reverend Abijah Albine.

He eventually married one Abby, or Abigail, Belding. Abigail's brother, by the way, was postmaster at Norwalk, and probably her sole support in her widowed old age.

The Lord blessed the Reverend Dr. Albine and his Abigail, and they had two sons. Benjamin, the older, was small, slight, but with great burning eyes and the hectic face of a young seraph; Lemuel was tall, well built even as a boy, and later on dangerously powerful, for he took after his father, who was a huge man with a great golden beard and arms like flails.

The Reverend Abijah yearned over his delicate older boy, whose mind was as remarkable as his body was sickly, and he laboured with him and prayed over him and taught him so well, or so ill, that at the age of eight Benjamin not only could read from the Greek testament, but could also expound it movingly.

Now, this was all well enough for Benjamin, though it turned out *not* so well later on. But it was misery itself for the younger child, Lemuel, and for his mother. For the good doctor lavished all his attention and affection on his first-born. And he was so proud of him, and so crotchety about him, and so absorbed in preparing him to be the wonder of the coming age in the ministry that there was nothing left over for Abigail or Lemuel, except perhaps cautions to be quiet and cold bursts of rage that they were there at all.

Lemuel was a lad of spirit and stood up to his father, comforting his mother as well as he could secretly, and fetching and hewing wood and drawing water for her and the others. As a result of which he grew tall, active, silent and strong. And his father hated him. And thus the days went on while Mistress Abigail's heart was nigh to breaking. She taught Lemuel his A B C from her own hornbook, and how to read and figure a little. This was all the education he ever got, since his father took him into the study only to admonish, or even to whip him.

This state of affairs was well understood in the congregation and the village, where it began to be whispered about that young Benjamin might not be altogether divinely inspired. That sceptical rumour coming to the ears of Abijah Albine made life even harder than before for Abigail, upon whose family her husband laid the blame for the talk.

Yet he acquiesced readily enough in allowing Lemuel's uncle Belding to arrange to apprentice him to the blacksmith on the square at Norwalk when the boy was only fifteen years old, though already growing rapidly into a great lout of a young man.

And so Lemuel left home and began toiling over the anvil just across the village square from his father's meetinghouse. And he throve at it, and grew mightier every day. But Mistress Albine was left alone at the manse, her only music the distant clinking of the iron under the hammer of Lemuel and the memory of what he was like when a child.

Then the Angel of Death came through the green lanes of the village of Norwalk, looking for pious young souls and bestowing the gift of smallpox. And in the deep nighttime, the Dark Angel touched Benjamin and he arose and left his body behind.

Then the eyes of the Reverend Abijah Albine were opened for a while. His wife comforted him, and he wept with her until they were together again in spirit for a time. And he sent for his son Lemuel and humbled himself before him also, begging him, for his mother's sake at least, to come back again under the roof.

But Lemuel was a grown man now, although a young one, mighty in body and firm in mind. He looked about his father's study, smiled slowly, and turned over in his mind how he could speak to his father so they should understand each other. Finally he rolled up the sleeve of his huge right arm, pointed to it, and said quite simply:

"You and my uncle and the Almighty have conspired together to make me a blacksmith. I am already a good one. I have only one more year to serve. That is your bargain I shall keep. When I am free I shall find me a woman, follow my trade, and go west. I hear there is both land and freedom to be had in Pennsylvania."

"It is a nest of malignants," said his father. "I am told that every error is at liberty to flourish there."

"So I have heard," said Lemuel. He pulled down his sleeve and tied the wristbands slowly.

"I have a mind to go there," said Lemuel, and stalked out.

Which might have been the end of him, so far as we would ever know, had it not been that he got himself into a rather notable scrape soon thereafter. Or rather his father got him into it. The incident was sufficiently grave and tragic to be mentioned in passing elsewhere as well.

Whether Lemuel found his woman before he served out his last year as an apprentice is not clear. The exact timing of events is more than difficult to make out, but the sequence of happenings is fairly plain.

It seems probable that Lemuel did complete his year as an apprentice. And that afterward he continued with his employer. Or else he took his place and set up for himself as the blacksmith at Norwalk in the same smithy on the square. Also he found his girl. In a letter she was described as dark, Irish, and Roman Catholic. Her name was O'Moore. We do not know her given name or whether he ever brought her to Norwalk or not. Probably not, one can guess. He was not there long after his marriage, to judge by what followed. And the cause of his sudden leaving was notable.

One beautiful Easter morning in the year 1740 a party of British officers and provincial gentlemen rode into Norwalk, going "down east". What their errand was and who they were, there is now no way of telling. They appeared. And the disturbance they made in the town was considerable.

Every soul in the place whose body was not either that of an infant or bedridden was at church. Everyone, that is, except Lemuel. He was the only comfort the strangers appear to have found. The road they had just passed over was one of the worst in the king's dominions, outside of Ireland, and what they all wanted was two things: liquor, and a blacksmith to get their nags reshod.

There being no drink to be had for love or money until church was over, and that might be hours yet, the whole party, after having thundered at half the doors in town and disturbed every watchdog into a foaming delirium, gathered before the forge across the square from the chapel and began to clamour for the smith.

The Reverend Abijah Albine was just entering upon "secondly" under the third head in his sermon on the Resurrection when this clamour arose across the square and came rolling in through the open doors of the meetinghouse, for it was a warm spring day.

The spell the minister had laid on his congregation was lost, and with it the fruits of many weeks' work on his Easter sermon. He stopped, prayed silently, and then went on again. Finally, he began to beat the Bible frantically and to roar sonorously, because that was the only practical defence he had against his rivals for attention, those devil's minions across the square.

The effect he produced was notable. It caused even the most urgent and strident of the gentlemen gathered around the blacksmith shop to look across at the little white building with the steeple, which seemed to be a church but was apparently the stable of a lion. A moment's silence fell on them, produced by sheer astonishment.

The Reverend Abijah smiled grimly in his pulpit and reversed the hourglass. Then there was a sudden burst of laughter across the square, and immediately afterward the mellow clink of his son's hammer on hot iron.

Now, this was more than the minister could bear. His eyes burned in his head. He closed the great Book with a bang, and sailed down the aisle with his gown flapping behind him. Most of those in the chapel crowded to the door to see.

The minister strode furiously across the square, and there was that in his face which caused the gentlemen who were crowded about the smithy door to step aside hastily and give him room. Although one of them did laugh, and would have tripped "the damned Whig" up as he passed, if one of his companions had not prevented him. Perhaps it might have been better if he had succeeded, since the path was now cleared to all of the mischief which followed.

Abijah found himself confronting, or confronted by, his son Lemuel, who stood with his leather apron on, hammering away merrily over the anvil at a red-hot horseshoe with a *clink* and a *clang*. The horse for which the shoe was being readied was standing close by in the shed, held by her owner, a calm, middle-aged man in the gorgeous scarlet and gold lace of a colonel of Royal Light Infantry. Abijah was not so possessed but that he recognized the officer's rank and breeding instinctively, and it gave his native English heart to pause. Lemuel, however, went ahead working at the horseshoe.

"I forbid you!" cried his father at last, standing and pointing a long arm and finger at him imperatively. "Cease! Would you profane the Sabbath in the presence of God's minister and your own father?"

And at that Lemuel did cease working the iron and looked across the anvil at his father, while several of the gentlemen crowded into the shed to see whether they would be getting their horses shod now or not.

Seeing the iron was turning cold, the colonel spoke up, hoping to save the day.

"My dear sir," said he to Abijah, "here is no question of profaning the Sabbath. We are a party of travellers in need of assistance. We are bound for Boston on government business. I have demanded your son's help to shoe the horses in the king's name."

"No king rules here save Jesus," replied Abijah sullenly.

"I take it you are mistaken, sir," said the colonel coldly. "This is part of his Majesty's dominions, and I opine he reigns even in Connecticut by the grace of God."

Someone outside laughed. Abijah went black in the face and towered up to his full height. He pointed upward.

"I forbid it," he said. "In God's name."

By this time the shoe on the anvil had gone cold. The issue had been put squarely to Lemuel, and all stood waiting tensely to see what the big smith would do.

He turned and thrust the iron back into the fire. It was the colonel who worked the bellows. Finally the shoe came out white-hot again with little sparks flashing along it. Lemuel laid it on the anvil and looked calmly at his father, who still stood there. Then he raised his hammer to strike.

The Reverend Abijah Albine rushed forward and caught the hammer arm of his son Lemuel in mid-air. The hammer crashed.

Then something quite astonishing happened to the Reverend Abijah.

He found his own hands pinioned behind his back in the iron grasp of the mighty blacksmith he had fathered, and he found himself lifted into the air and being carried across the common like so much lumber on the shoulder of Lemuel.

The minister was a hulk of a man himself. It was a great feat of strength on the part of Lemuel, discussed for miles around for many a year. But across the square Abijah went, despite his struggles and hoarse shouts. The amazed congregation stood aghast on the chapel steps, or peered out the door horrified. Not a man moved, not a woman screamed. It was all over in a few seconds.

When he got to the church Lemuel suddenly set his father on his feet again. Then he twisted him about and looked into his face. In the steely eyes of his son, Abijah saw the result of twenty years of tyranny glaring back at him.

"You attend to your trade and I'll attend to mine," shouted Lemuel, so all could hear.

"Back into your shop you go!" he roared. And picking up the older man by the arm and knee, he heaved him into the chapel through a window sash, with a violent shattering and rending sound.

The Reverend Abijah Albine sat on the floor of his church, where he had been pitched by his son. A piece of broken window glass had cut his forehead. He bled freely, but was otherwise bodily uninjured. He sat there groaning for his life in ruins about him, while his wife and some of the faithful tried to comfort him. But in vain, for across the square the sound of the hammer rang triumphantly, shaping the secular iron into horseshoes.

Lemuel finished his work, surrounded by the now silent and entirely respectful gentlemen.

It was an hour at least before the selectmen of Norwalk could meet. What was the outcome of their deliberations, no one knows. Lemuel hitched up his wagon, threw his tools and put the anvil into it and rode off with the strangers. No one suggested following him. Probably the situation was held to have solved itself by his departure, as well as it could.

Lemuel, we know, drove north. The gentlemen were going to Boston. Perhaps Mrs. Lemuel was still in Rhode Island.

3. Flight into the Wilderness

THE PAST is the Land of Missing Persons, and it is only by a combination of diligence and good fortune that anyone who is not monumentally remembered can be found there.

As for those in America who wandered beyond the utmost borders of the wilderness, neither their lives nor the resting places of their bones were too often noticed or conveniently marked. Oblivion dogged their steps and ate the last one. The silent trees of the forest finally closed over their heads. They vanished, drowned in a green nowhere, leaving a crumbling cabin, a few stones arranged in the dancing basin of a spring, a cellar hole on a hillside, with an apple tree or a rosebush in ashes to scatter petals in springtime, as though they remembered something lovely, tragic, and secret that no one else knew.

So it would seem almost a fruitless task to ask where a blacksmith and his wife went. They have wandered out of time; how find them again in space?

One might easily fail in such a self-appointed search. But with Lemuel Albine there are some signs still in our favour.

He was a blacksmith. He was a huge and remarkably powerful man. He had a peculiar, if not a unique, family name. His character seemed fated to get him into trouble. All or any of these items might have been deliberately or accidentally noticed sometime, somewhere, and set down.

Also the search is narrowed a good deal; that is, it is not hopelessly continental. Lemuel had once told his parents he had a good mind to go to Pennsylvania—that he would find him a woman, follow his trade, and go west. All that somehow got itself into the record and, what is more, preserved.

Let us go to Pennsylvania, then, and go west. But how far?

Far enough certainly to find free land and freedom. Probably Lemuel wanted a good deal of both, like a great many other people who had been oppressed and found themselves disinherited both from property and from the past. We know he must have left Norwalk with a disgust for village life, and a burning indignation against tyranny, books, schools, ministers, authority—perhaps even religion. That might carry a young man quite far. And there is something else.

In 1740, at least, one did not heave one's father through his own meetinghouse window just for the sheer, blithe joy of the thing, even if one were a powerful blacksmith. There were bound to be serious mental as well as physical consequences. One would have liked to leave both the scene and the memory of such an act extremely far behind. If one were going west, for example, it might be well to go as far west as the direction held. That is not evidence, of course, but it is fair human and historical reasoning. And the inference in this case is that, if any evidence of Lemuel's whereabouts can be found, it would be as far west in Pennsylvania as he could go—if not farther!

Now, in 1740, or thereabouts, the farthest west attainable in Pennsylvania was by river, and at Harris's Ferry on the Susquehanna. It is true that some had gone even beyond there into the Kittatinny Mountains or the far-flung coves of the hills nearer the Juniata. And there were traders who went every year over the great ridges as far as "Allegheny". But it was a question if they were still in Pennsylvania, because no one knew precisely how far into the sunset Pennsylvania extended.

So those who had been ferried over the river by Mr. Harris had actually embarked with a sort of Charon for a trip into the vague and misty beyond. They were sojourners rather than settlers in a kind of no man's land, tenants of what landlord no one knew. And if a person were to be found far west in Pennsylvania, he might either be at Harris's or he would probably have passed over the river there into the free beyond.

Let us see, then. How will this do?

Here is an entry on a page of an ancient account book kept by Esther Say, the able wife of John Harris, trader and ferryman, early in 1741:

> £1–2s–4d, to ye Smith L'Albine, for forging and furbishing ye
> gun locks of Robin Patterson's company, who came here to ride
> ye Borders, this same Patterson having been killed by a bolt of
> thunder whilst watering off against a lone tree, owing ye said
> smith.   Paid.

Now, it is impossible not to exclaim immediately over the severe tax on the renal powers of Mr. Patterson, and to observe, if a male, how not to behave in a thunderstorm.

As to who Mr. Patterson was, and why his company was riding "ye Borders", it is not now easy to say. There appear to have been seven in the party up until the time Mr. Patterson tried to compete with the storm. For the rest, it looks as though this might be Lemuel. "L'Albine" could be a Frenchman, to be sure, but that is not likely at Harris's in 1741. It also might be, and probably is, meant for "Lemuel Albine", who we know was a smith. That is especially convincing, since any blacksmith would readily enough take to repairing gun-locks on the frontier.

But there's nothing more to go by. Not an item in the whole book, and it covers over a year, that can be fathered upon Lemuel. We do not know for certain whether Lemuel's wife was with him, or exactly what he was doing at Harris's beyond repairing gun-locks.

There is, however, a good deal in these accounts at Harris's about one Garrett Pendergass, or "Pendergrass",—the man probably spelled his own name two or three ways,—and as we hear about Lemuel from him later, and at some length, it is possible to infer that Mrs. Albine was with her husband, that they tarried at Harris's about a year, and that during that time Lemuel plied his hammer whenever he could. We learn he also became interested in trading, largely through his acquaintance with Garrett Pendergass, who, it appears, had his own designs upon him. These, to do Pendergass justice, were quite right and forward-looking for both himself and Lemuel, who might have been better off in the end if he had listened to them.

One can pick up a good deal about this Garrett Pendergass and his family here and there. Some years later he is to be found at Raystown, or Bedford, on the Juniata, running an establishment next to the fort there, a kind of combination inn and trading post, by far the best on that frontier. Where he came from, there is no certain record. Probably from about Colchester in England. But he appears, from a variety of indications and testimony, to have been an able, upright, and educated man.

At the time he ran across Lemuel Albine at Harris's he seems to have been acting for old John Harris and his wife, as a kind of factor or advance agent with the Shawnees. Probably he transported trade goods from Harris's Ferry, distributed them to the Indians then in the hunting grounds just east of the Allegheny ridge, and gathered up the furs and skins in return. His reward was likely to be allowed to do some trading on his own. Also he was interested in patenting land.

At any rate, about this time he had gone up the "Conedogwainet Branch", past the most outlying cabins there, and settled, or camped, in semi-permanent form in the Path Valley beyond. He even maintained a "lodge" or some kind of trade-meeting place in the Great Cove west of the Blue Mountains, possibly not far from where Fort Lyttleton afterward was. Thence it was only a short and fairly good path for horses by the old Indian trace through the water gap of the Juniata to the Shawnee hunting grounds.

In any event, Pendergass's cabin was at the extreme border of things in those days. Only the licensed traders had pushed on farther west. Some of them, in that comparatively quiet and peaceful time, before the Indian and the French troubles broke out, had penetrated to the Allegheny and built cabins in the vicinity of Chartier's Town. But they were itinerants rather than settlers; they came and went with the seasonal trade in furs. So when Garrett Pendergass wrote something in his "diary" in Path Valley beyond the Blue Mountains he was setting down a record of how the days went at the very verge of the world.

His "diary" is a curious old book. Not a diary in the strict sense of the word, rather a commonplace book, the last third frequently blurred by some leak in a long-vanished roof, maybe. It has the smell of dusty leather trunks about it; something of the air of a century's sojourn in a garret. And it is a memorandum of many things: births, deaths, accounts paid and unpaid, moves and removes, who came and went, receipts and simples, the state of trade, and the weather, an occasional piece of hearty male gossip, hints for planting, little plans and sketches for forgotten things, a map of the country about what was later Bedford—what not?

We can put together certain passages concerning Lemuel, really, when assembled, quite a peephole backward into time. The day dates are not certain, however. Even the months rest frequently upon internal evidence of things done. The "diary" was not kept for our convenience.

This entry is evidently sometime in the spring of 1742. April? Wheat had been planted about a week or so before, and new clearing was going on at the Pendergass cabin in Path Valley:

Thursd'y—Came the big Yankee smith and his pretty Irish wife from Harris's. She being made much of by my Rose and both our girls. Is a mighty help about the cookery . . . Had a bull ox about the High Springs of the Conadog' branch mauled bad by a painter. The smith about building the forge tomorrow without loss of time, he hasty in work yet patient. Hope to persuade him in on the trading. These are the first draft cattle came over the ridge into Path Valley.

Sab'th—We five to hear the Reverend Jms McArdle at the Conadogwinet log meeting at McCombs' in the vale. A pert young minister, he, has a call to preach to the Indians like a mad Moravian. Dissuaded him. Returned to find the little chimney finished and the smith's bellows agoing. His wife, a Catholic, said her prayers in the woods on beads. I remonstrated working Sabbath. Albine says he is tired of the Christian calendar. A strange, determined man.

Fri—Albine worked on the wagon irons all day, and nigh finished. Horses all shod again. The Lord be praised.

Sab'th—Passed through, riding west, six Shawanees in the rain, squaws and young, leaving their Wyoming grounds. Albine very curious about these wild people. Fear he has a secret mind to follow them.

Wensd'y—Must persuade Harris to buy the valley from the Penns as they offer, so I can get land warrants. Albine and I to the ferry tomorrow for the trade goods.

Sab'th agin—We all singing hymns together when came Mrs. McQuiston's girl Maggie tapping at the door and in a great way, she having been driv into the woods and about to bear. Her mother won't abide her. Thought it might be my Charlie, he being a big boy now, and she walking nine miles to our cabin, but found out not. Thankful.

Mond'y—Rounded up the hogs. Mrs. Albine of much help with the McQuiston girl, who cried out terrible. She and Rose brought her through with a lusty baby girl for their trouble. Albine gone to Harris's again with one wagon.

Wensd'y—The smith returned.

Satd'y—Albine laced Charlworth, Harris's man, till he roared like a bull o' Bashan. This for having a loud mouth and a bawdy tongue. The smith and his wife like our own now. Have persuaded him to stay, I think. Preparing for trade at the lodge in Great Cove. Will leave Monday, weather moderating.

The following items occur about a year later, apparently about the beginning of summer, 1743:

Sab'th—Long talk with my wife Rose today. She not so averse from my long projected journey as I supposed. Apprehensive I desire to move her to the Great Cove, and she so comfortable here. Promised not. The time has not come for that yet. Mrs. Albine makes ready. All here cast down at thought of our parting so soon.

Tues'd—Came the western hunter, Tingooqua, or Old Catfish, with his lame squaw and three horses to show us the trace from Great Cove to the crossings, and be fed at our fire. The half-king will let Albine tarry at the Turkey Foot if he trades. Thence about eighteen leagues to the Oio, or to Shirtees. Have a mind to see the new country myself, but Lord the women! Albine gone a week now.

Sat'd'y—The smith back today from Harris's. Has laid out well, and nearly his all. Three pack horses, a brindled ox, and a red one, iron nails aplenty, and some bar iron. Nevertheless, I tried again to dissuade him from going so far, his wife being three months along, Rose says. Did urge him to stay, or set up at the lodge in Great Cove instead. Too many people here he avers. Was rather grim, but thanked me.

Wensd'y—Nothing will hold Albine here. Says he wishes to be reborn again, but not in the Lord. Asked me to urge him no more. I promised. Owe him more than shillings and pence or trade goods can repay. He much touched by my Rose's gift of the old cradle from home. Will pack it along, carrying fine meal till the time comes. Trust they be settled by that time. Says he has promised to furbish guns for the half-king for his land at the Turkey Track. A doubtful holding, I fear. The Lord be with them.

Thursd'y—Leaving young James and Tom, Delaware Joe, Charlworth, the McQuiston girl and her brat, and the useless negar with Harris's new man, Barber, a factor that he lent me for this year's trading. He to live in the house here at Path Valley. Barber an honest and careful man will keep things going. Warned him about Charlworth and the McQuiston. We ride tomorrow through the peacefulest woods where is no man. Albine expects the Shawanee guide at the Juniata crossing. Thence about four days ride to the Turkey Foot of the Yogaginy. Weather and the women permitting, I will go as far as the crossing with him and spy out the land.

June entry—(going back)—'Twas the last Friday of last June, if I recall rightly, we left to ride with the smith Albine and his wife as far as the Juniata crossings. Of my family along was my wife Rose, my grown son Charlie, and my two big girls, Polly and Bella. Took six pack horses, one loaded with presents for the Shawanees to the tune of £3, 8s. The rest with supplies and gear. Albine and his Mrs. had two pack horses and the two oxen laden, not drawing.

Camped in the Branch Gap in the mountains the first night, where a glade for pasture, and on to the lodge at Great Cove. All well there from last winter, but a scaffolding broke down by the bears and the old smoked hog meat et. Albine came up next day, delayed by the oxen. His wife manages his two pack nags beautiful. Rose, to my great comfort, pleased with the prospect and the land here at Great Cove. Stopped for two weeks about.

Off over the old trace to the Juniata, about the middle of July, as I reckon. Trail good, but for one mishap below the water gap where we came near losing Albine's brindled ox. Through the water gap the fourth day, and on to the Shawanee grounds. A mar-

vellous beautiful valley I covet dwelling in someday, God pros-
pering me. Camped, and made the dale with the stinking spring in
it by noon next day.

Purged ourselves at the spring on the north side of the Branch.
This brought the pains on Mrs. Albine, but she recovered, scared.
Did bathe in the stinking spring, too, which proves fine for the
hair.

About the first of August, as I reckon, the guides came from the
half-king to pilot Albine to the three forks of Yohaginy they call
Turkey Foot. Many tears among the women. Albine silent, and I
much cast down at our parting now after two good friendly years.
His Mrs. very heavy with child now, and will be her first. A brave
pair withal, but he a mite determined. Rode with them as far as the
crossing of the Juniata, and the Injuns from the village all with us.
They over the river with many calls back and forth of sad farewells, and so off into the woods to the west-running waters. And I
doubt we see them again. . . .

4. In Which a Little Boy Turns Turtle

THE FIRST THING he could remember was lying on a pile of soft
twigs and looking out over a sea of treetops in early leaf. In the distance
the silver vein of a river gleamed, but there was no end to the treetops.

It was somewhere on the side of a steep hill and he was basking in
the new warmth of the spring sun beside a tremendous stump with great
gnarled roots.

On the top of the stump sat his mother, cross-legged like a Tartar.
She was a dark, hawk-faced woman with a tender, smiling mouth. Her
smooth raven hair, brushed straight back, was caught about with a
snood of some scarlet material in which a sprig of red berries had been
thrust. The little boy felt that she was strong, wild, and comfortable. He
thought her name was Emma, afterward, because he could remember
his father calling her "Em". That, and a few tones of her voice, was
about all he ever could remember about her.

Curiously enough, he could never recall her face any other way than
just as it was at that moment. It must have been about noon, for there
were no shadows upon her. And it must have been one of those rare
moments of early childhood, when the eyes open to fix irrevocably and
brilliantly a fleeting moment of time in the mind's eternity. For the
moment he was completely happy, utterly comfortable, and serene as
only a child can be. From the vantage point of complete well-being he
looked at his mother.

On a gentler slope, not far below, his father was ploughing. He could see him, the man in a sweaty deerskin shirt, striding along behind the plough and the brindled ox. He was a huge, tall man, with a golden beard. It wasn't a field he was ploughing. It was a rough new clearing on the hillside, with blackened tree trunks sticking up all over it like fire-scarred posts. The ox and the plough and the man went on and about and around.

After a long while the man stopped ploughing. It was cooler now. The man came up the hill carrying the plough, and driving the ox before him. The ox came and breathed in the child's face. He always remembered the wide flare of its horns, the shining brown eyes, the soft wet nostrils, and the sweet hot breath in his face. He cried out, half with terror and half with delight, at being intimately noticed by such a wonderful brute.

"Shut up, boy, or the Injuns will git ya," said his father, laughing.

Then his mother reached down to comfort him, as though out of the clouds. He could hear the reassuring tones of her voice. The vague, soft comfort of her presence always remained, palpable, warm, and physical, even in his dreams, but he could never remember, never hear just what it was she said to him as she reached down. If he could only recall her words, get her to say them again, he knew he would be at peace once more. But it was best not to try to do that, because if he tried to remember too hard, he heard her scream. The scream came from underground, and wakened him. Somehow the comfort of his mother and nightmare were always close together.

But that day, after his father finished ploughing, they all went down to the cabin together quite happily. It was a dark, one-room cabin. It, and the shed where the anvil stood and the ox looked at you, sat in a small valley not far from the running spring that bubbled all night long. The water made a noise like little owls. When you were sleepy you could hardly tell the difference.

It was the great fireplace in the chimney at one end of the cabin by which he chiefly remembered it in years to come. That was necessarily so, for there were no windows in the cabin. Light, warmth, and comfort streamed from the hearth. When the door was open in the summer it made an oblong of light, and the green forest glimmered beyond. Afterward, when he first saw the sea, it reminded him of the forest beyond the door. His mother was like a shadow about the hearth. He could never see her face there even in the firelight. She was always crouching over the fire, cooking, with her back towards him.

In what years had these things happened; how old was he?

All he knew was that he was so young he still thought the fire was alive. It ate the sticks his mother fed it. It cracked them with its yellow teeth as a dog cracks bones. But the fire belonged to his father just as the ox did. His father "made" it. His father had made everything they had. He could make anything.

There was another fire in the shed, by the anvil. It ate little lumps of black things. His father made things out of iron there. Sometimes tall red men with feathers in their hair came and stood by the shed while his father worked on their guns. The hammer rang and sang. The sparks flew. Then the red men would grunt, take their guns, and go back into the forest again. They moved like shadows. They toed in. When they came his mother always closed the cabin door.

He could never entirely recall his father's face. Only the grey-blue eyes under the fur cap, and the yellow beard. Sparks flew into the beard from the iron. Some of the deep tones of his father's voice remained. "Em," he would call, "Em." They were deep and kindly then. "Lem" was his father's name. "Em" and "Lem".

But his father remained chiefly a vast bulk, the sheer height and the width of him, a shadow full of mysterious strength. Out of the shadow came quite clearly, as though thrust from darkness into light, his long, sinewy hands with heavy veins. They made things. They grasped the handle of the hammer, or an axe. He could remember that.

And he could remember those hands making a bow for him with a long knife.

That was after he had been so ill, a terrible stabbing pain under his belt. Hot and cold cloths had been laid on him. He recalled his mother crying out something to his father, and the comforting tones that replied. He had taken new confidence from them himself. They had often called his own name to him then. "Sal, Sal, little Sal—"

When he got up again and was well his father made him the bow and the arrows to shoot with. Then he knew all of his name. He was proud of it. When he wandered too far, shooting arrows at the trees, his mother would call him back. "Sal, Sal—Sal-*athiel* Albine, you come back here. Stay out of the woods." Those were among the few words he could remember his mother saying. She was always saying them. There were painters and bars in the woods. It grew darker as you went farther in among the great trees. There were Injuns there. They'd get ya! Sometimes he could hear his father's gun shoot away off in the woods. That was for meat.

Less and less he went into the woods. His father was away often now and his mother kept him near her. She was lonely, and gradually he became aware that she was afraid. He helped her, doing a thousand small chores. He was a big boy for his age, and strong. He spent hours shooting his arrows at the mark on the big sugar tree near the cabin. The arrows went straight now. The bow twanged. Someday he would have a rifle gun to shoot, his father said.

Once his father came back in the night quietly and mysteriously. He heard him and his mother whispering together. Something in the forest had gone wrong. Menace hung about the cabin like an animal. The wind in the nighttime made sinister sounds. The song of the anvil was heard no more. No Indians came to have their guns worked on. His mother and father never laughed together as they used to. They were waiting for something. The boy felt that.

One day a strange white man and an Indian came to the cabin. They emerged into the clearing quite suddenly. The white man wore a white coat and tight breeches. He had a sword, and buttons that twinkled in the sun. There was gold lace on his hat and sleeves. He rode a horse, but the Indian walked. It was the first horse the boy had ever seen. It seemed to hold its head in the sky.

"Lem, Lem," called his mother, as though trouble had come.

The white man took off his hat with a plume and gold lace on it and made the boy's mother a bow. He was very pleasant, and smiled. He talked in a strange language that made the boy laugh. To his great astonishment his mother replied in the same tongue.

His father had come hurrying from the shed with the rifle gun over his arm. His mother was telling his father what the stranger was saying. It made his father angry. His voice boomed when he replied. The stranger shrugged his shoulders so that his epaulets danced.

At last the boy grew tired listening to what he could not understand. He went out to look at the horse. The Indian lifted him into the saddle. He was scared. It was very high up there on the horse, but how fine! He sat with the reins in his hands looking proud. Finally he shouted. The horse stamped. The white stranger looked out of the cabin and laughed.

After a while the Indian picked up the boy's bow and started to show him how to shoot. He said nothing, but he sent the arrows straight. He rearranged the boy's hands on the bow. It went better that way. The Indian knew.

The Indian was a magnificent fellow. A great knife hung down on a thong before his breast, and he had a red turtle painted over his left nipple. When you put your hand on the turtle you could feel the Indian's heart underneath go *thump, bump.* It was not long before the boy was not afraid of the Indian any more.

There were long eagle feathers in that Indian's hair. His nose turned in toward his mouth, and his eyes looked out like a hawk's. He smelled of wood smoke and bear's grease. He played with the child roughly. He took him by the hair of his head and almost lifted him by it. His mother called out, but the white stranger laughed again and reassured her.

There was nothing to be afraid of. It was fun to be wrastled with, and lifted up by the hair. The boy wanted to go away with the Indian when he and the stranger left. His mother had to stop him. He stood, watching the Indian loping along beside the horse. Then his father called out something in an angry tone after the white man. It was something about snails and frogs.

The horseman wheeled suddenly and made partway back. Then he stopped and shouted, "You are crazee man. I ride ze woods for tell your wife. She ez couzen mon bon ami Dillon. I say all ze Anglais chez Chartier—" Here he rose in his saddle with excitement and made a circular motion around the top of his head. "You see? C'est la guerre, monsieur. You have bébé là! You go? No?"

In the flaring sunset the long shadows crept across the clearing, pointing from the woods towards the cabin. The boy never forgot that tense moment. His father leaned against the doorpost with his rifle across his breast, muttering. His mother had thrown herself against him and kept hold of the gun. "Lem," she kept saying, "Lem, Lem!" For a minute the Englishman and the Frenchman looked at each other. The brass housings of the officer's harness and his weapons and buttons twinkled and gleamed. At the edge of the hill by the clearing the feathered silhouette of the Indian stood dark and menacing, waiting against an angry sky. The silence spoke.

Then the Frenchman took off his hat, bowed from the saddle and said, "Adieu, madame." He wheeled and rode off into the forest. The Indian was gone.

Not knowing exactly why, the boy rushed into the cabin sobbing. His father hushed him sternly. . . .

They were going to have to move. The French king had said so. It was the king's land. That man had come to tell them. All the English must go back over the mountains. All the land and the woods belonged to the king of France and the Indians. The Indians were the friends of the king of France. They had already killed some English traders and taken their goods. All this was not very clear to a small boy. He heard his father talking.

God lived in the sky. The king of France lived across the great water. The king had said they must go. Sal's father said God didn't want them to move. They would disobey the king. They would ask God to help them. It was now that his mother taught the boy to pray. Every night they said, "Our Father who art in heaven." But a great fear had come to the cabin. Sal's father hunted at night now. Sometimes he brought back only fish. There was another reason why they couldn't go, Sal soon discovered. It was something that was a secret between his father and mother.

The leaves fell from the trees. It began to turn cold. There was a new baby by the fire. It had come in the night while the boy slept. So had the first snow. He looked for the baby's trail in the snow, but it was not there. It couldn't walk. An Indian had brought it. He showed the marks of the moccasins to his father. They came close to the door, and went away again. His father said, "God damn," but he patted the boy on the head.

Afterward, he couldn't remember whether the baby was a boy or a girl, but he could remember the bundle squirming by the fire, and squalling. He remembered a small red hand about his finger. His mother gave the baby milk. The weather was terribly cold now. His father went out only to get meat and feed the ox. He always went out at night. He opened the door carefully and crawled out into the starlight with his rifle gun.

It was the ox that went first. An Injun cut its throat in the night, while his father was away. They heard the ox die, groaning. His mother stood at the door with the gun and shivered.

The boy cried when he saw his friend the ox next day. His father made meat out of it. The ox would never come and smell him friendly any more. He felt sad, and it was dark in the cabin. The winter was long. The snow drifted. They needed salt. Then his father didn't come back.

They waited. His mother prayed. The boy never saw his father again. He was alone now. He thought about that. His mother had the baby.

Salathiel helped his mother. He knew he must do that. The ox meat and the big logs were gone. He went into the woods and dragged in branches for the fire. It was getting warmer again and they managed. There was only a little meal and some small potatoes left. The boy shot some rabbits and a bird now and then with his bow, when they came into the clearing. He grew skilful and patient. His mother praised him. But she always called him back anxiously. She said, "Salathiel, Salathiel Albine," when he went to the spring to get water. The spring was "far away". He cut branches for his mother with the small axe. The fire looked cheerful at night, but the door was always close barred, and his mother never sang any more. They both missed his father, but said nothing. She sat by the fire and listened. She sat with the gun and the baby. Outside the owls sang. The leaves were coming out again. Soon it would be summer. The boy slept. He dreamed that his friend the ox came and smelled him.

Then one day it was all over.

In the very early morning he went to the spring. A frog jumped into the water. As he reached down to fill his bucket a brown arm with a copper band around it came out of the bushes and grasped him by the hair. He stopped breathing. The arm lifted him up to his feet by the hair, and he found himself looking into the face of the Indian with the turtle on his breast.

The Turtle had a knife in his hand. He looked fierce. His eyes glittered, but the boy hoped it was only fun. He had been lifted up that way by the hair before. He was big now. He wouldn't cry. He managed to grin in the Indian's face, because his hair hurt him. He clicked his teeth together because it hurt. The Turtle grunted and put up his knife.

Then he lifted the boy up and threw him on his horse, which was hidden in the bushes. It was the same horse the French king's man had been riding the summer before, but it was blind in one eye and looked thin now. That was all the boy had time to notice before he heard his mother scream. . . .

He never forgot that scream as long as he lived. Somehow the scream came to live with him on the inside of his head. . . .

Suddenly the little clearing was full of racing forms with blackened faces. They streamed across towards the cabin from the trees, closing in like shadows.

The boy gave one whooping, strangled cry before the Turtle clapped the bucket down over his head, and rode off with him. He held the boy's wrists behind him and put a thong on them. Salathiel Albine knew better than to cry out. He knew what had happened. The Injuns had got him. Inside the bucket the blood roared in his ears. His little heart pounded fearfully.

Presently there was nothing to be heard but the breathing of the horse and the muffled thud of its hoofs on the leafy floor of the forest. The bucket banged Sal's nose, and wore soft furrows on his small shoulders, but he said nothing. He could look down his bleeding nose and see the ground and the horse's feet, under the bucket. They rode on. They forded a large stream. Presently they were passing over some grassland. They rode on until evening, he thought. About twilight the Turtle rode into an Indian village and gave the death helloo twice. A chorus of exultant yells answered him. The Turtle's loot from the raid was an iron-bound bucket and a man-child. His squaw, Mawakis, might value the bucket. When he took it off the boy's head, the white child sat with a masklike face. Two ribbons of blood streamed from his nostrils. His heart and brain were frozen with terror. He scarcely breathed. He sat on the horse waiting to be killed.

Some squaws and a crowd of young Indians and children surrounded the horse. It stood with its head drooping. The Turtle had gone off somewhere.

The crowd began to hoot and shout and to poke sticks at the white boy. He said nothing. He sat. A big boy jabbed at him viciously with a pointed stick. The French officer's horse, a present to the Chief Big Turtle, had lost one eye that way not long before. It took the Indian boy's forearm in its teeth and began to crunch the bones. The lad screamed. The horse bit. The squaws and children shrieked with delight.

Just then the Big Turtle came back, seized the horse by the nose, and kicked the Indian boy in the jaw. The crowd scattered.

The Turtle led the horse to the door of his hut, and tied it. It grasped a post with its lips and teeth and began to inflate itself with air. It made a noise like a saw. "Wind Eater" was that horse's name.

Big Turtle lifted Salathiel off the horse, untied his hands, and pushed him before him into the log hut half sunk in the ground. This served the Turtle and his squaw for a lodge in the winter when they stayed to trade with the French.

The Indian woman waddled towards them through the smoke. There was a chimney, but she had built a small fire in the center of the room on the clay floor. Through the reek she peered at the child and the Turtle with brown, thoughtless eyes. She was fat, and she wore a brocaded court gown that, minus its hoops, swathed her in enormous grimy folds through which the original pattern of damasked gold and silver butterflies still glittered here and there. The place stank of Indian, wood smoke, rum, and urine. The white boy choked, and looked about him. He began to feel the blood in his hands and feet again.

The Big Turtle began an angry, guttural discourse to his squaw Mawakis, who swayed and grinned at him. He picked up an empty leather rum bottle and tossed it into the chimney. Then he pointed at the fire and gave Mawakis a hearty kick. At that she began to move. She seemed to realize he was there. She picked up the burning sticks from the floor by their ends and threw them into the chimney, where they began to blaze merrily. The Turtle assisted her by hitting her between the shoulders from time to time with small smouldering chunks. She shrugged them off. Finally she put a kettle of venison and hominy on the new fire to boil.

During this performance the boy stood leaning against the wall by the door, listening to the horse, Wind Eater. He was sick at the stomach and he retched violently. Afterwhile, the smoke began to clear and he felt better. But he slumped down on the floor shivering.

The Big Turtle melted some bear's grease on his hands, and, dragging the boy close to the fire, rubbed him with it. Then he put him under a buffalo robe on a pile of skins in the corner. The boy kept shivering and his teeth chattered, but he gradually grew warmer. His eyes followed Mawakis moving about the room. She was smoking a pipe about three inches long, filled with dried sumach leaves and tobacco. The smoke smelt sweet. Suddenly the boy went to sleep.

It was night when they wakened him. He could hear the owls and night birds. The fire was a heap of glowing coals. The meat and hominy were ready. They gave him a bowl of it, and the hot, thick soup revived him.

In one corner the Big Turtle sat on some dressed deerskins and fed his mouth with a wooden spoon out of a pumpkin bowl. He sucked the marrow out of the deer bones with a *plop*, and tossed them into the chimney. Then he took a long stone pipe out of a deerskin bag. He polished it with his hand. He filled it out of two other bags with the killikinick and tobacco. He lit it with a coal from the fire, and smoked. He blew the smoke out through his nose. The boy watched, fearful and fascinated.

How long the Turtle sat smoking, Salathiel had no idea. He was sure that the Indian was thinking about him. As a consequence he held his breath in order to be completely still and attract no attention. Then he had to breathe again with a long sigh. Now the Turtle really was look-ing his way! He said something to Mawakis sharply. She built up the fire again till the shadows danced. Then she brought the Turtle a small, copper pot with two sticks in it. When he lifted the sticks they dripped scarlet. There must be blood in the pot. The boy felt himself lost. The Turtle was coming for him now.

It was true.

The Turtle walked over and pulled the boy from under the robe. He stood him up in the middle of the floor. He put his face close to the boy's, looked into his eyes, and scowled at him. The child was certain now that his time had come. He didn't care. He looked at the Indian, and hated him. He scowled back—fiercely.

The Big Turtle laughed.

He pushed the boy to the floor, sat down beside him, and began to stir the pot. Certainly there must be blood in it, it was so red. Salathiel closed his eyes now—the Turtle had taken out his knife.

He began by pricking the boy on the chest with it. The child shud-dered. His skin seemed to have dried up. It was sheer terror. He could scarcely feel anything on the surface of his body. Then everything went black, and he thought he heard his mother scream. She had done that for him. There was no use screaming himself.

Presently he became aware of the yellow firelight again. He opened his eyes a glimmer. Now he could see the hands of the Turtle still busy over his breast with the bright knife and one of the red sticks from the pot. He watched, breathing slowly. After a while he saw the picture of a turtle begin to stand out over his left nipple. It was a little turtle. Red.

The Big Turtle smiled at the Little Turtle. He began to breathe more easily. Mawakis made a consoling noise in her throat. She understood. This child would be counted someday as a warrior she and the Big Turtle had given to the tribe. There had never been any children in their lodge. The Shawnees were a hard-pressed people and needed war-riors. Her husband finished and pointed sternly and proudly to the sign on the boy's breast. She saw—and gave a grunt of grateful assent.

The Big Turtle motioned to her.

She picked the Little Turtle up and wrapped a fine, new trade blanket about him. She put a warm bone filled with marrow in his mouth. Then she squatted down on the floor beside him and began to rock herself back and forth on her hunkers and croon.

The Big Turtle crawled into the pile of skins and went to sleep. Mawakis continued to croon and rock a little. Outside the door the horse Wind Eater made noises like a pipe organ in pain. The fire died down. The boy gradually grew warmer, content with a full stomach, and an incapacity to feel any more. As he slid into an exhausted sleep, once again and far off, he thought he heard his mother's scream. That sound was still more than he could bear.

He hastened to leave the bad neighbourhood of reality. He seemed by an effortless desire of the will to throw himself backward into the oblivion of darkness. Why not? Why remain Salathiel? The worst had happened. The Injuns had got him. Salathiel had turned into a little turtle. He slept.

Thus, sometime between the ages of five and seven—he never knew exactly how old he was—he had tasted despair. Afterward, it seemed to him that he had died and awakened still living, but in another world. Nothing worse or more final could ever happen to him. The red turtle was at his heart. His opportunities for fear had all been exhausted in advance. In the real world outside he was never afraid of anything animate or inanimate again. What was left of terror remained sealed up in some dark cells of his brain to which only one bad dream had the master key.

Towards morning he half wakened. The fire was low and dim. Yet he could see the figure of Mawakis, leaning against the wall. She still squatted there like a bronze image of Patience, her face maternal and composed in sleep. There was something about her that comforted him. He felt safer. He relaxed and slumbered deeply.

Light was streaming into the lodge through the open door when next he opened his eyes. A wisp of smoke from the fireplace curled slowly across the ceiling. He awakened gladly into life again.

And into a matchless early May morning.

The misty face of the sun peered into the lodge of the Shawnee Chief Kaysinata, known as the Big Turtle, and of Mawakis, his barren squaw. It was in the Indian town of Sacunk, near the junction of the creek called Beaver with the Ohio, or Beautiful River, about a day's journey down from the Great Forks. French militia and fur traders had helped build the huts for their Indian allies and customers only a short while before. They were anxious to keep their enemies, the English and the Iroquois, out of these virgin hunting grounds, and they had been at some pains and expense to induce the wandering Shawnees to settle there when they abandoned Pennsylvania. Kaysinata had already received much gear and finery from his new Great White Father of France. The lodge was piled with miscellaneous gifts and the recent loot of some unfortunate Pennsylvania traders, who had been driven away from the Ohio country or murdered.

The Little Turtle propped himself up on his elbows and let his curious, young eyes slip from an officer's cocked hat with a medal on it, over piles of matchcoats and new blankets, broken rum bottles, flints, a staved-in keg, a bundle of axes and an array of powder horns, to a fine English saddle with the pistols sticking out of its fringed holsters. All this meant little to the boy. He was ravenously hungry.

Beyond the door the sun glittered on a magnificent expanse of the Beautiful River gliding along with sunny streaks in its current between misty islands and towering, forested banks. In the chimney, which the French had so kindly built, the backlog of the night before finally collapsed and burst into flame.

Kaysinata, the Big Turtle, grunted and rumbled. Mawakis rose and began to bestir herself. She put a great dried salmon on a cleft stick before the fire. The Little Turtle, alias Salathiel Albine, sat up abruptly.

A ravishing odour of broiling fish filled the lodge.

5. Of Old Forgotten Things

TIME to a child is heavily alloyed with eternity. And where Salathiel had come to dwell there was nothing but the long flow of the seasons to mark the calendar of earth. Life was like the course of the Beautiful River that came out of the forest, ran through the forest, and disappeared into it forever.

In another place and century, Salathiel Albine thought he could count at least ten, and perhaps a baker's dozen of winters that the Little Turtle passed in the lodges of Kaysinata as they moved about. But there again he could never be certain.

He was certain, however, that it was spring when Kaysinata first brought him to the cabin at Sacunk, for the days between the time of his advent and the departure of the tribe from the village for their summer hunting were numbered, literally, by the hairs of his head.

Mawakis took a sharp knife, and laying his long yellow hair on a log, she cut it off as short as she could. Then she dipped her fingers in ashes and began to pluck him bare as a fowl for the pot. Afterwhile he was bald except for one lock that grew from the middle scalp, which Mawakis greased with bear's fat and wrapped about near the base with twine. It looked like a little sheaf of wheat left alone when the field had been gleaned. After that, when the fuzz came, Kaysinata shaved his head. That hurt at first, and so he remembered.

And one thing more about that time or later. Kaysinata put him in a canoe and paddled up the Ohio to Logstown. Logstown was an even bigger village than Sacunk. There were many Indian children there from various tribes and he played with them and swam in the river. They spoke several tribal tongues. Their people had come to get powder and little rolls of lead for the summer hunting from a French half-breed trader named Chartier. But there was an Englishman there, too. His name was Gist. He stayed for two days only. He was afraid. The French would have had him killed or taken prisoner, but he was a messenger from the governor of the Long Knives, and Kaysinata would have none of it.

Gist spoke secretly to the Little Turtle. The boy was glad to hear his own tongue again. Gist asked him his name, and who his parents were. Salathiel thought awhile and told him. Gist bade him remember them when he said his prayers. He would have ransomed the boy from the Big Turtle, if he had had any goods with him. He was on a mission from the governor of Virginia to spy out the land for the Ohio Company. He went across the river in a canoe in the night. But Salathiel remembered. For a long time he secretly said the prayer his mother had taught him, and told the names of his parents to God. After a long while the words grew dim. At length he thought he forgot.

The Big Turtle was angry when he learned that Gist had talked with his "son". He took him to the river and ducked him. He held him long under the water. Then he had him painted brown, blue, and red. He put a fine new doeskin shirt on him that Mawakis had made, and he showed him at the council fire. All the Indians, and he himself, saw that he was now indeed the Little Turtle, and one of the Sawanos, the people who came from the south. This was after they returned to Sacunk.

Soon after that they went hunting. It was the first time. They hunted beaver that summer. The Little Turtle learned all about beavers. He was badly bitten by a pup. The scar on his thumb remained.

Every summer the tribe scattered. They left their winter cabins in the trading villages by the river and became separate lodges, hunting where they listed, as long as they didn't interfere with one another.

For the most part the Shawnees wandered west, or south into the great empty country south of the Beautiful River, empty of men, but full of game. They sought buffalo and elk there in the bluegrass glades. Once they were ambushed by Catawbas. Kaysinata killed two of them and took their scalps.

One summer the whole tribe went and camped at the DeTroit. The Little Turtle saw many white men's houses there, and the great barns along the river between the two lakes, like the street of a town. He saw an ox again.

The French officers at the fort kindled the council fire often. Their chief was called de Bienville. There were many speeches, and much rum flowed. There were drinking clubs amongst the lodges, and people ran about screaming. They shot guns off and wounded one another. They fought with knives and several were killed. It was hard for the chiefs to keep the peace among the tribes.

The French were persuading the Shawnees to take up the hatchet against the Dawn Land people. Kaysinata was gloomy and sad. He had once grasped the hand of the English at the great council fire at Philadelphia. There were too many of them to fight, he said. Let them trade. Their goods were cheaper and better than those of the French. Many gifts were showered upon him by the French to make him change his mind.

That was a bad summer for old people and children at the DeTroit. Mawakis was drunk most of the time. She grew blear-eyed and fat. Her teeth loosened. She beat the Little Turtle often, until the Big Turtle beat her. Kaysinata hated the firewater and the wars that the French would kindle against the English and the six fires of the Long House. He was a hunter. His half-brother Nymwha was a prophet. Nymwha made medicine with tobacco, killikinick, feathers, and the shoulder blades of deer. He foretold disaster to the Shawnees from the wars of the palefaces. He tried to persuade his people to leave the DeTroit, to give up guns and firewater, to hunt with bow and arrow again, and to use the fire sticks. They laughed at him.

The tribes from the north across the great lake danced the war dance. They danced all summer, and drank. They often went mad and killed one another. There was no hunting. There would be no food in the fall. The French would have to feed them, and they would have to take up the hatchet for the French.

Kaysinata believed Nymwha. It was a bad summer. Even the children ran wild. The squaws drove them from the lodges. They shifted for themselves, all but the very little ones, whom Father Bonnecamp brought to the fort and baptized.

It never occurred to the Little Turtle to take refuge with the French. He remembered in the back of his mind he was once an Englishman and the French were his enemies, although he now thought of himself as an Indian and was proud of it. He was a big boy, and strong. He spoke the chief's Shawnee well, and he could talk in several other tongues, and the sign language. He and some other youngsters stole a birchbark canoe from the Ottawas. There was a hole in the canoe, but they repaired it. They spent the summer fishing and gathering berries. They camped on islands in the lake, and built fires. Rattlesnakes bit two of them and they died. Once the woods burned while they slept and they took to the lake just in time, with their eyebrows burned off. A Huron boy called Speckled Snake was drowned.

Before autumn came Kaysinata and Nymwha took their squaws and lodges away early from the DeTroit. They took the fine clothes, the brass kettles, the paints and vermilion, and the wheat flour and lead they had received from the French, and headed south across country for the Beautiful River. All their furs and skins were gone. The horse, Wind Eater, had died.

They stole horses from the Mingoes, and hunted to lay in food for the winter. There would be no corn that year for hominy. None had been planted. They smoked fish, and dried berries. They took bears and fat raccoons. They worked the squaws hard. They struck the stream called Beaver and followed it south till they came to the Beautiful River again. They settled for the winter at Logstown on the banks of the Beautiful River. The French soldiers came soon after and built them log huts and stone chimneys, and they lived there that winter on the bounty of the French.

Kaysinata had at last been persuaded to take up the hatchet against the English. Nemacolin, the Delaware, who lived near the fort of the Old People at Red Stone, came and told him he had shown the English the Old Buffalo trail over the mountains, through the Great and Little Meadows. The English were coming. They had sent horses and soldiers to Red Stone. The Long Knives were already there. Next year they would build a fort at the Great Forks. The Six Nations had sold the English land south of the Ohio.

Kaysinata was very angry at this news. He feared the English more than the French. When the English came they cut down the trees, made houses, and stayed. Soon the hunting grounds would be full of English all along the Beautiful River. So the Big Turtle listened to the French.

The Little Turtle heard all this talk, sitting in the cabins at Logstown. He filled the pipes of the chiefs. He blew smoke in their faces to be polite. He was growing tall now. He listened with open ears.

In the chief's hut there was always much meat, gifts, and food. Kaysinata and Nymwha were the best hunters of all the Shawnees. They remembered most of the old lore of their fathers. They spoke of it together at night. The Little Turtle listened. He grew tall and fierce. His hands and feet were large. He played with Indian boys older than he was. He made them afraid of him. He was the chief's son. The Big Turtle taught him how to wrestle and strike out with both hands and feet, like the half-breed Frenchmen. He taught him how to skin beasts, and how to throw the knife and the hatchet. His bow of arc wood had once been a warrior's. It came from the Illinois. The Little Turtle was the only boy who could bend it. He was taller now than the bow.

That winter two Englishmen came to Logstown. Shingas, the Delaware chief, brought them. One was a tall, young man with a pink face and his hair tied back in a queue. He was a Long Knife and brought with him an interpreter called "David's son". Four French deserters also arrived, with whom the tall, young man talked. He also sent for Tanacharison, the half-king. He came and talked with the tall man secretly in his tent.

Then there was a great council of the Delawares, Shawnees, and Mingoes held at the council house. The Little Turtle heard English talked again between David's son and the Long Knife. He told all that passed to Kaysinata, who sat and said nothing. The Long Knife wanted guides and an escort to the French captain at Venango. He had come to warn the French to leave the country. Kaysinata laughed. "It's lead will do the talking," he said to Nymwha. He would not let the Little Turtle speak to the Englishmen. Shingas, Tanacharison, Jeskakake, White Thunder, and the Hunter went with the Long Knife, Wash'ton, and David's son to Venango. They were not seen again.

"There will be war now between the palefaces," said Nymwha. "We will wait till they are weary and then drive them out. One paleface is as bad as another. Let the hatchet bite deep."

In the early spring Kaysinata needed horses. He stole two from the English at their fort near Red Stone. He stole another from an Englishman named Frazier at the mouth of Turtle Creek, on the Monongahela. The Little Turtle lifted that horse. First he went close to the cabin. He heard the man Frazier saying goddamn to his wife. She was angry, and poured water on the fire. Then the Little Turtle caught the horse and just rode away while no one was looking. He said goddamn to the horse, like Mr. Frazier, and it went faster. He named the horse that. The French laughed, but not for long, for Nymwha stole three horses from them at Venango. He cut off their manes and dyed them with walnut juice so that they would not be recognized. The two lodges went far up the Beaver and made sugar from the big maples near its source. Then they all rode west on a great hunting.

They ranged along the Ohio, clear out to the Big Miami. They caught catfish and shot ducks and swans. They ate beaver and buffalo and venison. Kaysinata and Nymwha hunted together. They pitched their lodges side by side. There were four squaws in Nymwha's lodge. All his children had been daughters. They were strong. That was why Kaysinata hunted with Nymwha.

Kaysinata wanted much dried fish and jerked buffalo meat. He brought in many animals to skin. There must be dried berries and pemmican for the winter. The corn must be ground, and the hominy stamped. The fires were to be tended. Nymwha's squaws could do the work. He and the Big Turtle still insisted on laying in supplies for the winter. They did not wish to sell themselves to the French and the traders just for a little food.

Nymwha watched his squaws carefully. He would not let his daughters marry. He made bad medicine and prophesied they would give birth to snakes. He scared the young men and drove them away. The three big girls bothered the Little Turtle. They once caught him in swimming and found he was not a full man yet and made fun of him. He hated them. When he grew larger he made them afraid of him. He beat them with Nymwha's stick. He never spoke to them again, except to tell them to bring him something. They made moccasins for him, and grunted. They were named after the three winds.

It was different with Mawakis. The Big Turtle did not abuse her. He simply disregarded her as she grew old. She stumbled after him through the forest when they made a march, carrying what she could on her back. Sometimes she was too late to kindle the evening fire for Kaysinata. The Little Turtle would do that. He also brought her things to eat and she gradually became quite dependent upon him. Once he was gone a week and stole a little horse for her from the Twigtees. Nymwha praised him for going far away to steal. Kaysinata said nothing. Sometimes he gave Mawakis tobacco to smoke.

There was an affection between the Little Turtle and Mawakis. She was the only being who loved him for himself. She had tried to be a mother to him. Had it not been for her, he might have forgotten his own mother entirely. Sometimes Mawakis would squat close to him in the half-lodge at evening while Kaysinata smoked and they looked into the fire. She would stroke his cheek with her old, roughened fingers. Then he would think of the fire in the cabin and the old days that were now like a dream.

At such times Nymwha made medicine and talked with his great-grandfathers. Animals looked at them from the trees with red, glowing eyes. The owls sang. Pictures would come upon the white shoulder blades of the deer with which he prophesied. They clicked together in the ancient box of hardwood that had come from the south. There were other things in the box. Once a year Nymwha blew upon the conch shell, which was also there, and burnt tobacco to celebrate the day the Sawanos had come from their far island in the south. All the voices from the past were sad now, he said. He drank the bitter drink, and dreamed dreams. Sometimes he danced and once he frothed at the mouth.

To all this Kaysinata said nothing, but he listened to Nymwha and believed him.

Many evenings Mawakis sat looking into the fire and told the Little Turtle of her girlhood in the happy valley east of the mountains. Those were good times, she said. Kaysinata agreed, and told stories himself. He, too, longed to return to the good valley between the long mountains, where his forefathers had hunted by the Juniata.

But for the most part the Little Turtle was lonely in the forest on those western huntings, even when Nymwha's lodge was along. There were no companions for the Little Turtle, no young men or boys in the party. Kaysinata and Nymwha worked him hard. All day they taught him many things. But they would not let him go to the villages of other tribes alone. Nor would they smoke with him. "Women and tobacco are for men," they said. "You are tall, but you are not yet a man. Hunt. Grow strong. Listen to us and become wise. War is coming."

So, because of that, the forests and the long stretches of the Beautiful River were lonely to the boy. He was grave and sad in the summer. He was glad when they turned back as the first leaves began to fall. They had wandered far. They marched back eastward under the great trees for a score of days.

They came back to the Beaver Creek well and strong that year. They had much food and piles of beaver pelts and deerskins. Even Mawakis was better. There had been no firewater.

On the banks of the Beaver Creek the tribe gathered. There were

many villages there of several tribes. In the autumn the traders came
with goods and rum. And it was then that the fun began, and the
trouble too.

Kaysinata, however, would buy no firewater that year. He traded all
his deerskins and the beaver pelts for guns, powder, flints, and clothes.
Then he took the best horses and went away with six other warriors to
raid the English east of the mountains. It was good raiding weather. It
was fine Indian summer. And Nymwha's saying had come true. There
was war. The French had struck the English and finished the fort at the
Great Forks, which the English had begun. They called that fort "Due-
kane."

That was the year the bad trouble began. The tribes began to break
up. Many warriors who went to raid never returned. Many more were
away loafing at the fort at the Great Forks most of the time. Few cared
to hunt while the French fed them. There was small work done in the
villages by the squaws. Sometimes even the fires went out. The squaws
sold themselves to strangers and French soldiers for a little food. The
chiefs were at the fort talking with the French. They were going to
drive the English into the salty lake, they said.

Nymwha had foretold all this. He had seen something like it happen
before. He removed from Logstown to the high rocks on the south side
of the Beautiful River, just a little downstream from Fort Duquesne.
There he camped in an inaccessible gorge which led to the top of the
cliff. There was a hill near by that swarmed with turkeys. Only officers
could land near the rocks. The commandant issued an order about it.
Nymwha would rent his daughters to none but those who wore a sword.
He required considerable gifts for them. His daughters were happy, and
there was great plenty in the lodge, and no trouble.

Nymwha hid an English trader near the rocks and kept him till he
could go east. That man's name was McKee. Nymwha gave McKee
wampum to take back to the English and told him consoling speeches to
say to their chief men. He saw many bad pictures on the shoulder blades
of deer when he made medicine now, but he said nothing about them to
the French.

"Let the hatchet fall on many," he said. "Who would be a paleface?
They live only to feel themselves. They are right when they kill one
another. Let the hatchet fall on many of them."

The Little Turtle found life in the village on Beaver Creek difficult
while the Big Turtle was away. He took a canoe and went to see his uncle Nymwha, at McKees Rocks. He told him that Kaysinata had returned from raiding, but was still at the fort. Mawakis was hungry and
there was little game to be had. Life was bad in the villages. At first
Nymwha said nothing. He smoked for a long time. He looked at the
boy keenly. Then for the first time he passed the pipe to his nephew, the
Little Turtle, who also now blew the smoke out through the nose.

6. How Nymwha Blew on a Conch Shell in the Moon of Full Leaves

NYMWHA was a man who listened to his own voices. He believed in his medicine whether it promised him good or ill. Through all the great war between the French and English he lived in the high gorge near McKees Rocks in the way his ancestors had lived before him. He hunted. Save for a few French officers who came for a while to visit his daughters, no one else had come there. The country to the south of the Beautiful River was deserted now because of the war.

At the fort at the Great Forks the tribes gathered to help the French meet the English. All the warriors were gone from the Beaver. It was lean times there in the villages of old men, women, and children. A great army of the British, Red Coats and Long Knives with cannon, were coming over the mountains. The banks of the three rivers there, and the islands, were lined with the watch fires of many warriors. The Little Turtle climbed the high rocks near Nymwha's camp to look at them. At night he could look upriver past an island and see the red glow of the fires of the warriors pictured in the water and the sky.

Mawakis and the Little Turtle had come to live with Nymwha while Kaysinata was on the warpath. There was quiet, much food, and contentment at his snug bark lodges in the gorge. Even the French officers did not come any more as battle drew near them. And two of the squaws had babies now. The papooses hung strapped to boards under the trees. They hung there silent, and looked about them with big brown eyes. They were as fond of honeycomb as young bear cubs. They would suck it from your finger.

Mawakis made much of them. She grew better after she had once been chased by snakes. There was nothing to drink in Nymwha's gorge but cold water from the spring. Many canoes passed up and down the river far below, but none landed to speak with Nymwha. He was content. "They will find trouble both ways," he said. He and the Little Turtle smoked together, while the women chewed deerskins. Nymwha once spoke at night of the far-off past:

". . . In my family," said Nymwha, "the words have been handed down from mother to son with the conch shell. It was to the totem of the Turtle that the conch and the words were delivered. I have the conch shell. Only I and Kaysinata, my half-brother, know the old words. In my lodge is nothing but daughters. Thou art the only son of the Big Turtle. When thou art a man I will deliver thee the words. The clan of the Turtle had no children at all. Now the paleface comes again. Soon it will be the moon of Full Leaves. Kaysinata and I will smoke a pipe and make medicine together. Whether we shall blow once or thrice upon the conch shell, who knows? We shall see."

Nymwha was very grave when he said this. He touched the Little Turtle on the shoulder with his pipe and looked at him. Of the days to come he would say nothing at all. . . .

In the month when the British were cutting a road through the forest over the mountains, and the French and Indians watched for them at Fort Duquesne, Kaysinata came to visit his half-brother Nymwha at the gorge near the high rocks. He came secretly by night in a canoe from the fort, and alone. The Big Turtle was a famous warrior now.

"Dost thou still exist?" said Nymwha, and held out his hand.

"I do," replied Kaysinata, "and here is my hand."

Kaysinata and Nymwha said nothing to the women for fear the bad ghosts of their mothers might follow them when they made medicine. They fasted for a day, drank the bitter drink, purged themselves, and went into the forest. They bade the Little Turtle keep the squaws tied in the lodges until they returned. They gave him a gun for the first time, and said, "Watch."

After two days they came back.

A deer was then killed. They had venison and roasted the first ears of the young corn for a feast. All by now were very hungry, but the feast was a sign that Nymwha and the Big Turtle had made good medicine. The two chiefs sat together in the same lodge and smoked fine tobacco. They invited the Little Turtle to come and sit with them.

"Does he learn?" asked Kaysinata.

"He does," replied Nymwha.

"It is well," said the Big Turtle. "Let Mawakis fetch him a coal for his pipe. Let him begin."

So the Little Turtle smoked with the two chiefs before all the women, and he was both happy and proud. Nymwha had praised him greatly.

As for Kaysinata, he returned to Fort Duquesne by night as secretly as he had come. And it was high time he came back there, for he found that nearly half the warriors were gone. As the English drew nearer, and the strength of "Bladock's" army became known, canoe after canoe had slipped down the Beautiful River, or up the Allegheny, filled with warriors, with the gifts which the French had given them, with the loot and prisoners from their raids on English settlements. There were a number of white women and children among them who were thus spirited off into the wilderness and were seen no more.

The Shawnees were no exception to what was going on. Although amongst them the authority of their chiefs was great, many had left while the Big Turtle was away. More were preparing to go. It took all of his persuasion and oratory, the promises and presents of Monsieur de Beaujeu to detain the remainder. For that purpose Kaysinata held an assembly of the Shawnee warriors. He taunted those who had left, with panic and cowardice. He lauded those who remained. He promised them that when the English approached nigh the fort a messenger should go to Nymwha, who would make medicine just when the battle was about to be joined. Nymwha would blow upon the ancient conch shell three times, said Kaysinata, and ask the help of their grandfathers' ghosts. Never again would there be so many scalps, guns, and prisoners to be taken. "Bladock" was a fool. The hatchet would surprise him and find him out.

Thus, by arts and promises, the Big Turtle persuaded them to stay.

There was a great war dance at the fort. Their father, the commandant, Monsieur de Contrecœur, sat in his chair and gave his children new guns, lead, blankets, and powder. An English boy named Smith, who had been captured near Raystown, was made to run the gantlet. Afterward the French nursed him back to life in the fort. All was ready. The place of the ambush was decided upon near the lower crossing of the Monongahela. The English were only three marches away. The sound of their cannon could be heard in the forest at sunrise.

At the beginning of the moon of Full Leaves a messenger came down the river to Nymwha. "Make ready," he said, "the time has come. Speak to the grandfathers."

Then Nymwha arose from the lodge where he had been singing and fasting. He put the women in one hut and tied the door fast with wolf gut. He threatened them, and told them not to watch or follow him. He took his box with the medicine in it, his best blankets, his feathers, a copper kettle, and his paint pots. He caught the two best horses out of seven that fed in the long glade at the top of the cliffs, and bidding the Little Turtle to follow at a respectful distance, he set off southward into the forest, singing a powerful song to his grandfathers. After a day the Little Turtle knew that song, for the words went the same way over and over again. He joined in, and Nymwha was pleased.

The trail south was a good one. It was narrow and it led along the crests of the hills.

On the third day Nymwha and the Little Turtle came to a tall hill in the midst of the largest stretch of meadows the Little Turtle had ever seen. Once there must have been cornfields there.

The next day they made ready to make medicine. They cleansed themselves, and fasted.

First they uncovered an old hearth of stone under the deep pine needles. Nymwha knew exactly where it was. They built a fire on it until the stones were hot. Then they put out the fire, swept the stones clean, and built a frame of saplings over them which they covered with blankets. After the stones cooled somewhat, Nymwha threw upon them dried bundles of herbs which he had brought with him, and the tender end-shoots of the pines gathered on the spot. They packed the floor thick with these, and every cranny of it.

Next they went down to the river together and drew the brass kettle full of water, after washing it clean with sand. Then they took it back slung on a pole between them to the top of the hill. Nymwha now removed all the wire from the long gristle loops of his ears. He took off all his clothes, even his breechclout, and ordered the Little Turtle to do the same. He plucked leaves from the bitter drink bushes and made a strong, brown brew that was rank. They drank this. After a while they became dizzy. They fell down, and vomited.

Then Nymwha dumped the water from the kettle on the hot stones in the hut covered with blankets. He and the Little Turtle crawled in and sat in the aromatic steam. They sat there till the paint and the grease and the sweat ran out of them. Pretty soon balls of wax fell out of their ears. They sat there till Nymwha was through chanting the cleansing song. Then they darted out of the hut and plunged into the river. They drank deeply of the cool water. They felt well. They were clean inside and out.

The Little Turtle saw when he came out on the bank that he was a white man. Only the mark of the red turtle remained very clear over his heart. It was bigger now. It had grown with him. Nymwha looked at how white he was and grunted. Then they went back to the hills, wrapped themselves in their blankets, and slept.

In the nighttime the Little Turtle dreamed. He heard his mother scream. It seemed to come from underground. He remembered again what had happened to him and to her. He awoke shivering. He was very hungry. He had not eaten for two days. The owls sang. He was an Indian again. He said nothing to Nymwha of his dream for fear Nymwha would know the ghost of his mother had followed him. He went to sleep once more. Nymwha awoke him at sunrise. He would not let him eat.

"This is the day," Nymwha said. Then he began to make big medicine.

He painted himself carefully, then he faced south from the deer thong that stretched between the two pine trees. He walked south for as many paces as he had fingers and toes. On the spot where he stopped he built a pile of big stones with a flat one on top. On that he laid dried pine cones, the heart of a deer, and lumps of the sweet gum which had gathered in the marks he had made on the two pine trees. Over these Nymwha laid clean, dry twigs. He sang a loud song, kindled a fire with his fire sticks, and fanned it with a fan made out of eagles' wings.

"O, ho," he said, "O, ho, ho."

The fan made of the wings of eagles scorched slowly on the fire and poured forth a dense white smoke. Nymwha stood before it, tall and waiting. His blanket drooped from his shoulders to his feet. He raised his hands three times before the fire, saying the secret words.

Suddenly the feathers sublimed in an intense, clear flame. They crackled. Nymwha drew the old conch shell from under his blanket and blew on it.

All the woods echoed back as though a bull buffalo had bellowed.

He blew on the shell a second time.

While he filled his lungs for the final effort, the echo answered back. Nymwha smiled. He raised the shell and blew on it a third time. Not a sound came forth. Only some white dust and a few grains of sea sand. Shattered by the vibration, the ancient shell fell to pieces in his hand.

The Little Turtle saw that the big medicine of Nymwha had failed. But he was surprised not at that, but at how he felt about it. He was glad. He felt like a white man. He wanted to laugh. When the shell fell apart Nymwha had grunted.

A ghost of smoke drifted down into the meadows from the dying fire. On the pile of stones the bones of the eagle wings covered the last embers like the fingers of a skeleton hand.

Nymwha fell forward on his face, groaning. He was a man who had believed in his own medicine.

The return to the camp in the gorge was a quiet one. There were no songs along the way going back. "What you saw, you have not seen," said Nymwha to the Little Turtle.

But the Little Turtle turned all these things over in his mind as he rode along. He was glad he had said nothing to Nymwha of his dream. It was no time to remind Nymwha that he was a white man. But the Little Turtle had certainly been reminded of it.

What was going to happen? Was it really better to live in the forest than to live like a white man? Kaysinata said so. How did he know? Someday I will talk to some of the captives, he promised himself. I will do so secretly. I will try to remember the words. I will tell them my name is Salathiel—Salathiel Albine. They will be glad to see me. I will ask them.

So he pondered and tried to comfort himself as he rode back to the lodges by the Beautiful River. When they got there they were met by the tremendous news of Braddock's defeat.

Curiously enough, it was that news which confirmed the Little Turtle in beginning to ponder the ways of being an Indian. He was ashamed. And he was afraid now they would begin to remember he was a white man, after all. He became more than careful for one of his years, although apparently he was reckless. He began to consider carefully the consequences of anything he did.

Now the youth called Little Turtle or Salathiel Albine—he did not yet know which—was not alone in his predicament.

No battle fought in North America has ever had such far-reaching and permanent effects as Braddock's defeat. On the sunny afternoon of July 9, 1755, in the ravines of a forest meadow along a river whose name most Englishmen have never heard, General Edward Braddock lost quite definitely and permanently the empire of Marlborough and Queen Anne, in the reign of his Majesty, George II.

It was the first day on the white man's calendar which Salathiel could be absolutely sure of. It was, of course, irrevocably fixed in his memory. Consciously or unconsciously, like most other Americans of his generation and time, he arranged the years of his life as before and after Braddock's defeat, as time wore on.

The French and the Indians at Fort Duquesne went crazy. They could hardly believe themselves. The British Red Coats had been beaten! They had been massacred and stampeded. There was a way to stop them. The Indians and the Americans remembered the way. The French straightway forgot.

Salathiel remembered to his dying day the fierce red glow in the sky by night above the river gorge about Fort Duquesne after the battle, the constant firing of cannon, and the fusillades of joy that went on day after day; the passing of canoes down the Ohio filled with prisoners with blackened faces, and their Indian captors howling like demons. It was a full week before the place quieted down. Those who had run away before the battle returned to take scalps and trophies from the stricken field. He and Nymwha beheld all this at a distance, from the high rocks above the river.

"Let them go by," said Nymwha; "this is the end."

It was not until many years later that Salathiel thought he knew what his uncle, the Shawnee, meant.

Seven days after the victory Kaysinata came to see Nymwha. He was still quite drunk. He was still dirty and bloody; covered with fringes of scalps that he had belted about him. He never knew himself how many he had taken.

Kaysinata boasted himself to Nymwha. He vaunted his brave deeds, and the success of the great medicine.

Then Nymwha laughed. He told Kaysinata what had happened. He showed him the fragments of the broken shell.

Then the English began to come over the mountains again.

Nymwha was right. After only three winters the English were back at the fort at the Great Forks. The General Forbes was a sick man, but he had himself carried in a blanket bed across the mountains. That general died, but the English stayed. The General Stanwix came next and started building a fort at the Great Forks out of brick. They called it Fort Pitt now. The French had gone. They would never come back again. They had given the Indian lands to the English. What was a man with many English prisoners going to do? The times were terrible. Kaysinata raided, and drank. Finally he made peace with the English at Fort Pitt.

Meanwhile, the Little Turtle had been forced to shift for himself as best he could. He was what the older warriors called a "young scalp". He had gone secretly to Nymwha, and taken his advice. It was good advice, well suited to the times.

7. How They Found Moses in the Bulrushes

THERE were four of them, all about the same age. There was the Little Turtle, Locust Mouth, Whippoorwill Hill, and Black Hawk. They were not quite young braves yet, but old enough to be free of the squaws. When the firewater and the English traders came now they had learned to flee the lodges on the Beaver and live to themselves.

It was usually sometime between the first fall of leaves and the coming of ice on the waters when they stole a canoe and lived on the islands up and down the Beautiful River in the fat season of the year. As time went on, and their tactics improved, they returned only at longer and longer intervals to the village, and they gradually increased the scope of their depredations.

The Little Turtle was now much taller than his bow. He was "high as the head of a horse", and he shot long, straight, and hard. He was not cruel; he simply had no qualms at all. He was like a young male panther in its third year, long, muscular, and lean.

He was always hawk-nosed, and he was now burned, tanned, and smoked a fine even copper color. As he grew older his frame became larger and more powerful than an Indian's. Fluff appeared on him, which he carefully singed off. It was an embarrassing distinction not to be tolerated. His skin thus became hardened by fire. He promised to be a young giant shortly. His senses were as keen as the others', and his mind gave him a wider and more certain play of thought.

He saw that when one thing happened another must follow. That was the chief difference between him and the other Shadows. "Now" was enormously complete to them; night was more like the passing of a cloud than the passing of time. The forest was eternity—but not for the Little Turtle. He dreamed of something and somewhere else. He wondered. Gradually the four of them came to have but one will and purpose. It was by mutual, almost by unconscious consent that both were supplied by the Little Turtle. Black Hawk, the son of a chief, was his only rival. But he was the youngest Shadow of all.

They learned to take the deer in the water. An exhausted doe about to make a landing found four topknots swimming beside her at twilight, and her throat cut. An unerring stone, a loop in the grass, or a twig trap was the death of any small thing they fixed upon as prey. For birds—an arrow came flitting from the thicket and struck the drumming partridge from the log. They marked down what they needed and took it. There was always something for the pot. On the Isle of Chestnuts in the autumn they were even like to become fat.

They kept coming back there often after the first year, in spite of a difficult landing. The river was narrow on either side, deep and swift. There was a fall not far below. Most people went around, and the place was their own for quiet keeping. That was why and where they caught the Reverend James McArdle.

From a certain point of view the arrival of Mr. McArdle on the Isle of Chestnuts might be regarded as a sheer physical accident. That was the light in which the Shadows looked at it. He came like a fish from the stream. And from the standpoint of Mr. McArdle himself, his sudden advent on an island in the Ohio was a beautifully special act of God. He was left there, like Moses, in the bulrushes.

James McArdle was a self-constituted missionary, Scotch-Irish from Belfast, fanatically learned, and as hard to root out of the land as a dock weed. He insisted that God had called him loudly to preach to the Indians. He had played apostle to five eastern tribes in three Algonquian dialects in ten years. A sermon to the Munsees on the circumcision must have been misinterpreted by them, for they had removed both his ears instead. He had borne this with patience, however, since his vital organ, the tongue, still remained intact. And with it he had continued to preach his novel doctrine, to the effect that the Indians were the ten lost tribes of Israel, a remnant of God's chosen people condemned to wander in the wilderness again until the news of their redemption was brought to them.

Mr. McArdle was by no means alone in this opinion. Many of his more discreet, reverend, and regularly licensed brethren concurred—but for the most part in writing. It was only natural, then, that his rather unwelcome news of the alleged partiality of the Deity for Indians, or lost Hebrews, should not be received by the harried and burnt-out laity of the English settlements with a helpful burst of sustaining glee. Quite the contrary.

Martyr and rebel to the core, no human pressure could straighten out his spiritual eccentricity. Finally, he was carried bodily out of the Conococheague settlement on a fence rail. And he was then forced to look on while some miserable squaws, three little children, and two old men of the Delawares, whom he had harboured and comforted, were quietly knocked on the head in the year of grace 1759.

Earless and disillusioned, sick at heart but indomitable, he set out westward over the new "Glades Road", lately cut by General Forbes, and for some months cobbled for the garrison and teamsters at the new Fort Ligonier on the Loyalhanna. Opportunity serving, he then joined an ammunition convoy, and the late autumn of the same year found him mending shoes on weekdays and souls on the Sabbath at Fort Pitt.

The king's deputy Indian agent, George Croghan, was an Irish Catholic. It was rumoured that on the previous St. Patrick's Day he had openly drunk the health of the Pretender, in the fervour of his cups. However that might be, when sober he looked with a jaundiced eye upon the efforts of Orangemen to evangelize the "king's Indians". Once again

Mr. McArdle was prevented. Nor did he fare much better in his efforts among the Welsh, Swiss, and Pennsylvania Germans of the Royal Americans in garrison.

Their commander at the time was also a Swiss, an impoverished officer, but a cultivated gentleman, who had been nourished at the very breast of Calvinism in his native Geneva, as a child. Yet—as he himself put it—when he became a man he thought as a man. He went in for mathematics, and he read Voltaire.

Thus at the very outset Mr. McArdle's dream of a Theban Legion at Fort Pitt, as well as his hopes of a harvest of souls amongst the lost tribes of Israel, were murdered, as it were, in the cradle like holy twin innocents. And when the Reverend James went in unto Herod to protest— eloquently—he found instead a dapper and dangerous little soldier, who occasionally smelled at a verbena-scented handkerchief, while he rocked the foundations of Mr. McArdle's faith seriously. It was a terrible, almost a soul-shattering experience for the Reverend James, who was finally dismissed with a glass of neat brandy and the military courtesies of the gate.

And so to pastures new.

That was the only alternative to cobbling. The unknown and unconverted wilderness lay westward before him. This was, he felt, the crucial test of his faith. He obtained a "small shallope", and, despite the fact that winter would soon be coming on, he set off down the Ohio, remarking that the Lord would provide. The Beautiful River did all the rest.

It was three days later when necessity and the current drove him ashore at the Isle of Chestnuts. It was twilight, and he was weak and cold from exposure and little food. He caught his foot in a crevice of rock as he stepped ashore, and snapped his ankle painfully. He lay for a moment groaning among the rushes. Instantly four young Indians were upon him like a pack of wolves.

His dugout slowly floated off in an eddy.

Possibly because he lay perfectly still, they did not kill him immediately. They scarcely knew what to do with a perfectly inert "enemy". This was submission itself. So they stood around looking at him curiously in the last grey twilight. He had fainted, more from the pain in his ankle than from the beating they had given him. Then he came to again and said something in the Onondaga tongue. There was no reply. He tried several other dialects, with no result. Then he began to pray, for his pain was great and he thought his time had come. He said, "Our Father".

"My mom say that," said a young voice out of the darkness, with a strange thick accent.

"Who are you, then?" demanded McArdle hopefully.

There was a pause. "Sal—Salathi-el Albine," the voice replied presently.

The Little Turtle could remember his name, but it had taken him some time to frame the syllables satisfactorily when he tried to speak them. For him it was a momentous reply, as well as for Mr. McArdle.

The sudden question out of the darkness, "Who are you?" had forced an issue, which, deep in his being, the boy had been asking himself over and over, and getting no answer. Now an instant reply had been demanded from the outside. There was no time to adjust the balance nicely and reconsider. The weight of the stranger's question had unexpectedly been thrown into the scale. The Little Turtle was forced to speak up, and he found it was Salathiel Albine who stood there, after all. He had simply been disguised as the Little Turtle. It was Salathiel who found himself. Now he knew.

As for the Reverend James, he felt that he was saved alive. His prayer had been answered. Hope was like a drink of strong cordial to him. He revived. He sat up, and managed to make a sign of friendship which Nymwha had taught Salathiel. He even made it understood that his dugout was floating away.

Salathiel gave the word and two of the boys plunged in and eventually returned with it. It was a long, cold swim in the darkness, and they almost missed it. McArdle had the presence of mind to reward them with a knife and spoon. Things went better after that. Meanwhile, he had been able to tell something of his predicament to young Albine.

He and the boy called Locust Mouth finally picked up the Reverend James between them and carried him to a hollow behind the bank, where they built up a fire and laid him beside it. Albine wrapped him in his blanket and they gave him some roast squirrel and hot, baked chestnuts. He sent them back to his boat for a little corn meal and salt, and they baked cakes on a stone. McArdle's foot was numb now. He strained every nerve to make himself welcome. Some iron fishhooks from a small box in his pocket brought even the young Black Hawk around. Also he found that by talking slowly, and by using simple words and gestures, he could make himself understood in English by the big boy with the turtle on his breast.

Thus the evening wore away with McArdle as an object of considerable interest. Curiosity and novelty had apparently been substituted for hostility. Nothing, however, finally allayed the pain of a broken ankle, and in spite of the risks the minister was at last forced to do something about it.

He was a man of iron nerves, and after explaining as well as he could to Albine, he gave directions for setting his leg. They hauled and pulled him until he fainted again. Once the "fun" became fast and furious, and if he had groaned or cried out the young savages might have found it too interesting to leave off. But he kept silent, and he finally got them to bind his leg in a piece of heavy bark for a splint—and stop. It was an ill job, of course, and as a souvenir of the occasion Mr. McArdle limped all the rest of his life. His foot turned in.

They remained at the island for nearly a fortnight.

Through the long hours of the night the Reverend James talked to the white boy. He talked of the white lodges in the Sunrise Land beyond the mountains, where the people were more numerous than the trees of the forest. The Little Turtle listened while Salathiel within him awakened and dreamed. The glimmering vocabulary of his childhood began to come back. They said their prayers together while the others slept. The Reverend James began secretly to teach Salathiel many things. He began with the watch, which was magic and a speaking thing. For the first time, and suddenly, Salathiel became aware of the audible and visual passage of time. Where was he going, and what would he be?

Gradually the boy felt the pride of his race stir within him. It was his people who had made the watch. All that McArdle spoke of belonged to him if he should claim it. Greater than being the son of the Big Turtle was being one of the white men.

One morning the season changed suddenly and there was a skin of ice on the shallows about the island. It was time to return to the lodge of Kaysinata. They felt confident in the white man's "big canoe". They laid him in it and paddled back two days to the mouth of the Beaver. That year the Shawnees had gone farther up the creek. Near the old huts at Logstown they killed two wolves and took their skins. Every winter there were more wolves now. Wolves followed war.

The Big Turtle was proud of his son for the prisoner he had taken. He let McArdle lie by the fire in the lodge. Mawakis was pleased and happy that the Little Turtle had come back. Things would go better for her with him around. McArdle made himself useful. He made things with his hands and spoke of the Great Spirit. They soon respected and feared him. Sal Albine began to regain the use of his English tongue. Once resumed, it came back, and it went on with a rush. Hitherto, the Little Turtle had felt it beneath him to converse with white captives. But this man was different, and he was his own prisoner. He began quietly to try out his talk on some of the other captives. There were many that year. There was a certain white girl he had noticed. He spoke to her. He liked her, but she was afraid of him. She still thought he was an Indian. It was best not to tell her that he wasn't. Kaysinata might be angered. He was jealous for his son.

Meanwhile, the Reverend James McArdle's leg was slowly healing and he talked at night of many things. Mawakis would go to sleep, wake up again suddenly, and grunt. Then they would laugh, conscious that the difference between her sleeping and waking existence was merely an unpleasant surprise. The fire flickered and smoked as before. But there were new pictures in the embers for Salathiel.

8. Shadows of Indian Summer

THE YEARS were at hand when for all the English frontiers, but especially in Pennsylvania, the terrible expression "Indian summer" took on an even more deeply sinister meaning than it had had before. It was the renewed and extended terror of the delay of winter that made the paleface paler. The Indians were summer fighters. Winter brought surcease to the settlers. Indian summer meant more Indians longer in the fall.

After the French were driven north, and westward down the Beautiful River, there was a brief pause in hostilities. The hot embers of French resistance smouldered, flared up, and finally died away at Montreal. All men waited to see what the English would do.

When General Stanwix left Fort Pitt in the early spring of 1760, thirty-five chiefs accompanied him eastward. Kaysinata and Nymwha went along. Some turned back at Raystown, but the half-brothers went clear to Philadelphia, leaving their horses at Lancaster.

In Philadelphia they saw the great town and the endless numbers of the Broad Hats and English. They saw the canoes with cannon that sailed upon the rivers and over the great salt lake. They saw them come from and depart into the sunrise. They saw the streets swarming with people, horses, and wagons. The Governor Hamilton shook hands with them. The general hung a gold medal around their necks with the English king's face on it. The honourable house gave them a few stingy presents. Then they were dressed up like British majors all but the wig, packed in wagons, and sent off. They were kicked out at Lancaster to get home as best they might. A Broad Hat there had sold their horses to pay for the corn.

Nymwha and Kaysinata had seen. They understood. They saw that the English increased mightily; that nothing could withstand them. They traded their gold medals for horses at Harris's and fled home over the mountains. At Fort Bedford a white man named Garrett Pendergass fed them, warmed them by a huge chimney in his store, and gave them new trading blankets after they had made the sign of amity. He understood the Old Medicine. He belonged. He treated them as chieftains of a great nation. It was the only kindness and real courtesy they received on the way west.

It was early summer when they got back to the Ohio.

They avoided the English at Fort Pitt. The place was made strong with brick and stone now. It bristled with cannon that looked into the three rivers and the moat. The English were not going.

They agreed to act secretly together, come what might. Nymwha went back to his lodges in the gorge near the fort. Kaysinata returned to the Beaver.

Kaysinata moved his lodges that summer clear out to the Wabash. The belts of Pontiac and his brother, the Prophet, were going around. Many had laid hold of them and promised not to let go. Kaysinata had not yet held one in his hand. He was hunting. He moved often. He took the Little Turtle, McArdle, Mawakis, and three of the "captivated" English women along. Black Hawk and Locust Mouth followed. They were made welcome by the fire.

Kaysinata permitted the young men much freedom now. In another summer they would be made braves of the tribe. He also listened to McArdle when he spoke of the Great Spirit. But he smoked his pipe and said nothing. He had heard from the French about Maly's Son. This was another medicine. But the words were good. McArdle was a wise man. He kept peace in the camp. He made it possible for the three captive white women to exist. Kaysinata would permit no one else to speak to them. Kaysinata respected McArdle. He let him come and go as he liked.

That summer the Little Turtle, the Reverend James, Black Hawk, and Locust Mouth rode westward, clear out of the forest. They came to the prairies that belonged to the Illinois. They rode at last to the place where the trees came to an end. An ocean of grass stretched away into the sunset. Locust Mouth was frightened, heaven was so vast. But McArdle wrote a book about this country on strips of bark. He bound it together with deer sinews, and two slabs for covers. He had taught the Albine boy how to read out of his pocket Bible.

He and the two Indian boys and young Albine hunted buffalo together on the prairies. It was a good summer. Salathiel learned to make the marks that spoke on the bark. McArdle made him write most of the book about the Fox Indians and the prairie. They made pens out of the feathers of wild geese. Salathiel wrote down what McArdle would say. He had to spell every word correctly. They used many strips of long bark.

Out of his Bible McArdle began to demonstrate the meaning of words. He taught God and language at the same time. He explained and explained. He acted and gestured. He even drew rough pictures. In two years he taught Salathiel how to count and cipher.

In the winters McArdle went from one Indian village to another through the Ohio country, administering to the captives and preaching to them or the Indians whenever he could. He and the Little Turtle wrote the names of these captives and where they came from upon bark tablets and concealed them.

The smallpox came walking through the forest in '61, and in many a village where there had been songs there was silence. McArdle bound the scabs of the spotted sickness on the arm of Sal Albine. The boy was sick, but he soon recovered. It was a light case, and he was never troubled again by the spotted sickness. This "cure" tended to cement the bond between Salathiel and McArdle, when they returned to the Beaver again in the early autumn after the great hunting westward.

That was the last fall that the Shadows hunted together as a free band of young scalps. That year they ranged the forest northward to the great lake called Erie.

Kaysinata was very angry when they returned. Ganstax, a Seneca chief, one of the Mingoes, had complained to him. The Shadows had been recognized at Venango. It was time such foolishness was over, said the Big Turtle. Next year they must be received as full warriors, take squaws among the Shawnees, and have their own lodges.

In these days Kaysinata and Nymwha were both much troubled. Secretly, they wished to remain friends with the English. But Kaysinata had been forced to lay hold of the war belt sent by Pontiac. He had sent blue wampum in return. Nymwha was not a great warrior. His actions were not so jealously watched. He promised to make medicine and spy on the English. He left the gorge and moved upriver nearer to the fort on a stream called Sawmill Run. The English had built a lumber mill there and posted soldiers near the mouth of the creek. The place was almost opposite the fort. Nymwha felt safer there. He warned his friend McKee of the trouble to come. The commandant began quietly to prepare. . . .

In the spring all the tribes were to rise as one man and at one time. They were to surprise all the English forts west of the mountains and massacre the garrisons to a man. They were to fall on the settlements at the time of the spring corn planting. All the cabins and little villages west of the mountains were to be burned. There was to be no mercy. The hatchet was to speak to the English from the Great Lakes to the Potomac.

Unfortunately, some could not wait. Raids began even in the autumn before. Many prisoners, women and children, were brought back for hostages. Sickness came with the white captives. The winter was long, fierce, and bitter. White children with the Little Spots had been brought to the villages on the Beaver.

That new trouble ran through the lodges of the Shawnees, the Mingoes, and the Delawares for miles back into the country like fire through a dry pine forest. Few entirely escaped. Many strong, old warriors died. Locust Mouth and Whippoorwill Hill were stricken. They built a sweat lodge, and threw water on the hot stones, and sat in the steam. They died the next day, speechless and swollen. The Little Turtle and McArdle buried them. Measles was the English name of that death.

The Little Turtle buried many friends. He was not sick with those spots either. All who crawled into the sweat lodge died, but that made no difference to the others. It was the thing to do. Mawakis died. She gave the Little Turtle the two gold coins on a bar that hung about her neck, medals that had come from her grandmothers. She patted his hand, and her eyes turned back in her head. The Little Turtle wept. McArdle said it was right he should do so.

Salathiel grew impatient. He heard of the plans for attacking the English. Many rumours flew about. Salathiel Albine began to think it was time to run away. "Wait," said McArdle, "the time to do that will disclose itself."

Kaysinata was alone in the lodge now with the Little Turtle and the Reverend James McArdle. The fire often went out. He sat with his head leaning against a keg of firewater. He drank from it with a wooden spoon. The snakes came for Kaysinata, and McArdle and the Little Turtle held him down. They put a stick in his mouth and tied it there. In a few hours, they were able to take it out and he talked to them again of things everybody could see.

The traders had been murdered or warned away. Cloth and food and blankets were very scarce. Clothes wore out. That winter many dressed in wolfskins, and all but starved. Many captives died. Spring, it seemed, would never come. At the fort the English feasted and celebrated Christmas, 1762. The commandant kept his powder dry and handy.

9. Witchcraft and Deep Snow

MARY CALAHAN was a white witch. She was a poor Celtic bog-trotter sold out of Ireland into the plantations by some London snatchers, and later "captivated" by the Indians along with her American mistress and her daughter near Frederick, in the province of Maryland. It was she, and her mistress and *her* daughter, who had gone along to do the squaw work for Kaysinata on the western hunting of the summer before.

"Malycal", as the Indians called her, could neither read, write, nor speak much English. She spoke Erse as though it were a living liturgy, and her life mostly had been bright, age-old misery. But for all that she was a wisewoman from the hills of Munster with half an eye at times into the past or the future. She foresaw the death of her mistress in detail, and foretold it with tears. But to no avail. For Mistress Jessica Lloyd was a proud, tireless woman, who despised the Irish even more than the Indians. Mary was left behind for her trouble when Mistress Lloyd and Miss Eva tried to escape in a bark canoe to Fort Pitt. They were drowned on the falls in the Beaver, and wolves tore their faces after they were dead.

The next day William Wilson, a trader, came from Maryland and offered to ransom the Lloyds from the Shawnees. Wilson then wanted to take Mary back to Maryland, and offered Kaysinata four hundred blue wampum shells and his tow bag for her, but Mary did not want to go. She had five years to serve yet at Lloyds'. She said the work was easier with the Indians, and that she hated the bloody English, who were cruel and cold as the Western Sea. Kaysinata let her have her way and refused to part with her. So she stayed on to make hominy for his lodge and foretell the weather and the hunting and certain select deaths.

That had been in the early fall and Wilson was still able to get back to the fort. He was the last trader to visit the villages on the Beaver till the war was over, and his scalp prickled, for he felt the hatchet raised in the air over his head.

When Mawakis died at the beginning of winter, Malycal had taken her place and did all the chief's work for him, taking better care of the lodge than any squaw, though she would sleep in no man's blanket. Her fleas did their own hopping. She preferred to scratch alone, she said. No one troubled her.

All the other women in the village were afraid of Malycal, both white and Indian. She knew when they were going to die. Sometimes she laughed to herself, and sometimes she told them. People gave her tobacco when she needed it, so she would not think ill of them. When she drank she sang long songs in Irish. She sang the "Cattle Drive". She was afraid of McArdle because he spoke Latin like a mass priest. He forbade her to mutter at him. On the whole, and considering, they got along together in the lodge not badly. And it was well they did, for it came on to be one of the worst winters ever known.

Malycal foretold the great snow that lasted nearly a month.

It was her business to inform Kaysinata of the weather and he valued her much for it, because it helped the hunters. She would go out into a clearing, lie down, and look up at the sky for a long time. Presently she would stop winking and her face went dead. In the evening she would come back into the lodge, eat, and speak of the weather.

Salathiel learned to believe her. He wrote down what she had said would happen on certain days, and it came out her way. Even McArdle was half convinced. Before the great snow came they roofed in the lodge of Kaysinata with pine slabs, and Malycal stuffed moss and clay between the logs of the walls like sod in a Munster shebang. She also brought in some coal which she had dug out of the streambank, like peat. It made the first coal fire Salathiel ever saw. It was so hot McArdle had to build a clay and stick chimney to contain it.

Then the snow came.

Great black clouds of ducks and other wildfowl from the lake regions, flying south, began to darken the sun the day before. Next the sky came down close to the forest and turned pearl grey. The third day it grew dark as evening. Then it began to snow. It snowed for nineteen days.

There was also an earthquake that winter before the snow went. It broke the ice on the river in places. The ground rumbled. Frozen catfish were thrown up out of the mud. It was a great help to those on the Beaver Creek, for no one could hunt in the soft drifts, and the fish saved many from starving. They came alive on the fire. Large, white horned owls came from the far north and sang to the villages till men's blood froze. Some people went to the fort to beg from George Croghan. They got salt beef there, but no powder. The commandant, Captain Ecuyer, said he would give them plenty of powder and shot when they came in the spring. He laughed when he said it.

When a hard crust at last formed on the snow, it was Salathiel and McArdle who did most of the hunting. What little fresh meat there was that winter they brought in. They took sleeping bears out of hollow trees. The deer had gone over the river. Even rabbits were scarce, for the owls and wolves lived on them. They shot grey wolves for their coats, and trapped otters. One day about midwinter they killed a young elk. It was great luck. But they had ranged far to find him, and it took them two days to get the carcass home over the snow. They hung it on trees at night and stood the wolves off with a leaping fire. At that they were nearly frozen, but the meat was desperately needed. In fact, it came in too late. When they got back to the village they heard Malycal keening, giving the Irish death howl.

Most of the white captives had been done away with in the massacre. There was nothing for them to eat and they would have died anyway, said Kaysinata. It was a measure well meant, to save trouble. The useful and strong had been saved. Now there would be enough meat to go around. Those who had been done away with were stuffed into the river through a hole in the ice. If anyone came looking for them they would not be found. Kaysinata was anxious the news should not be taken to the fort.

McArdle listened sadly to the chief and then went outside of the lodge to weep. He crossed off eleven names on his bark tablets and put a little hatchet after them. Salathiel saw there was now quite a bundle of these bark tablets with prisoners' names, wrapped in deerskin. It was the record of most of the Indian captives held west of Fort Pitt. McArdle had been at great pains to get the names set down. Salathiel had helped write down many of them himself. He could remember the lists, too. McArdle and he had memorized them together. The Little Turtle made a singsong of all the names. They were to go sometime to the fort. McArdle was afraid he would be killed and the names lost. If so, young Albine and the song would remember them. It would be time to take the list to the fort in the spring, McArdle said.

Salathiel had made up his mind to go to the fort in the spring, anyhow. He would tell them that he was English and sing the song of the lists to the captain-commandant. He was tired of the gloomy life in the lodge. He would leave and go clear back to the inhabitants. Maybe he could find him a girl there. He was beginning to be much troubled under his breechclout.

When the snow finally went there was a great flood. Half the low country along the Beaver was like a lake. But it was better for the Indians that way. The game was driven to take refuge on high ground and hilltops that were now temporary islands. There was a great slaughter and everyone had plenty and to spare.

Kaysinata called in the Shawnees up and down the Beaver. He wished to delay the attack until the time appointed. Two bears were killed, and he gave a feast. He also gave out the firewater. As a consequence nothing was decided. This suited Kaysinata well, for he was a much-perplexed man.

McArdle saw to it that the whites who were still left alive had pickings from the feast. There were still seven of them in the vicinity, four children and three women. They had been afraid to call attention to themselves by asking for food. It was the sight of these captives which finally enabled the Big Turtle to make up his mind what course to take.

He decided he would use the remaining captives to stay friends with the English by sending them safe and sound back to Fort Pitt. The commandant there, the Captain Ecuyer, was always demanding return of white captives. Now the Big Turtle would return them and so gain favour. And he would send the Little Turtle and McArdle along with the captives to guard them, and to take wampum to the commandant. The Little Turtle could make the speeches to the Captain Ecuyer that would go with each belt of wampum. McArdle could explain away the massacre of the other prisoners, if they asked him. He could say they had been drowned in the flood. He was a man of God, whom the English would believe. Also he was an important prisoner himself.

All this, of course, was to be done quite secretly. If Pontiac or his own people objected, he would explain it as a crafty move to lull the commandant into security before the attack. The more the Big Turtle smoked over the problem the better he liked what his pipe told him. One thing he liked especially. No one could say now that his son, the Little Turtle, had run away to his own people. If he stayed on at the fort, Kaysinata could blame the English. He, himself, would not lose honour.

Kaysinata hoped that the Little Turtle would stay at the fort; that he would return to his own people, and never come back. It was not that in his own way the Big Turtle was not fond of the Little Turtle. He was a good son, he admired him for his courage, wits, and strength. But the ritual reason why Kaysinata had shot the big, yellow-bearded smith in the back, stolen his boy baby and adopted him, had lapsed; it no longer held good. Nymwha's big medicine had failed. The Clan of the Turtle could cease.

It was for this, and not for sorrow of personal parting, that Malycal one night saw the tears run down the cheeks of Kaysinata, as the chief sat in his own corner and smoked bitter stems.

Nymwha agreed that the plan for the captives was a good one. Still it was hard for Kaysinata to come to the point. He began to feel like an old man.

At last he called the Little Turtle and McArdle to him and explained his scheme. He let them see many things for themselves. He put matters so as to save his own face. As for Salathiel and McArdle, if they saw their own opportunity, they also remained silent. And that, too, was understood.

Kaysinata gave the Little Turtle four strings of wampum. These he was to take with him along with the captives to Fort Pitt. Then he was to lay the strings across the knees of the commandant and say his say. The first string was to wipe away the captain's tears, another was to open his eyes, the third was to renew the ancient friendship of Kaysinata and his fathers, the English. The fourth belt was to cause the captain to remember it. Kaysinata made the Little Turtle learn the speeches solemnly. Once more McArdle had to go out of the lodge to hide his emotion, but this time it was to laugh. The pains the good minister had taken with Salathiel Albine would not be in vain, he saw. The youth would be delivered out of the hands of the heathen with his soul and mind alive. "Blessed be the name of the Lord, whose ways are inscrutable."

It was spring now, but there was yet a chill in the air. The great flood had gone down the river leaving ice behind it. Part of the works at Fort Pitt had been caved in along the riverbanks. The commandant laboured desperately to repair them. The Indians gathered their tribes for the attack. Still Kaysinata delayed. Almost a month went by.

One day word came by an Ottawa runner that nearly all the English forts westward had been taken. The hatchet of Pontiac had fallen. The surprise was disastrous and complete. All the English were cut off from their friends beyond the mountains. There could be no holding back now.

The war belts passed through the forest and the tribes from the west and north closed in on Fort Pitt. The Shawnees rose like one man. Soon the road to the fort would be completely closed. Already the commandant was firing great guns at the canoes that tried to pass up and down the rivers. Kaysinata sent for the Little Turtle and McArdle in frantic haste.

He called the seven captives into his lodge and explained. McArdle made a prayer to the Great Spirit. Kaysinata gave them new blankets and a little parched corn. He also showed them a long canoe concealed in the bushes, and gave a musket and powder to McArdle.

They waited in the lodge till night fell. At the last moment, parting from his son was not so easy for Kaysinata. He gave the Little Turtle a curious thing to remember. He told him never to eat turtle meat of any kind, lest it be the end of him. Then Kaysinata put his hand on the sign on Salathiel's breast and Salathiel's on his own, and made him promise solemnly to return if ever he or Nymwha sent for him. Then he gave him his ancient tomahawk and they shook hands both with the left and the right hand. This was a warrior's dismissal into the world, and Salathiel felt that Kaysinata had been a great chief. Now he was old.

They went down quietly as a cloud passes in the darkness to the banks and the black water of the Beaver Creek. The ice had now long passed away. The trees would soon be in full leaf.

They began to embark.

10. A Marriage Is Recorded on Slippery Elm Bark

THE THREE WOMEN wrapped the four young children in blankets and put them in the bottom of the canoe. The women sat up. McArdle paddled in the bow; the Little Turtle in the stern. They slid out onto the dark waters of Beaver Creek. For a moment they stayed with paddles poised while the current swung the canoe. The Little Turtle looked back. Kaysinata stood on a high point of land with a single pine tree on it. The eagle feathers in the chief's hair spread out raggedly against the sinking moon. He wrapped his blanket about him with both arms and stood there darkly. The paddles dipped and the canoe slid forward. Presently it glided around a bend into the forest.

Sal Albine could see the dim figure of the woman who sat facing downstream in the forward part of the big canoe, the silver flash of McArdle's paddle in the bow. But immediately in front of Salathiel was the blanket-draped shadow and dark head of a young girl. Her golden hair was done in braids and he could see the white glimmer of her neck in the V between her pigtails. That winter he had noticed her several times moving about among the lodges, helping one of the squaws dress deerskins. He leaned forward between paddle strokes, humming a song he had heard her sing. She looked back at him startled.

"What's your name, girl?" he asked.

"Jane Sligo," she murmured.

"Mine is Salathiel Albine," he whispered.

"I thought you were the Little Turtle, the chief's son," she said.

"I'm white, like you," he replied.

There was a pause while they paddled around the bend. The howling of the wolves was much nearer now.

"Take me with you to the fort," she whispered eagerly. One of the women looked back. They were both silent awhile.

"In my blanket?" he asked in a low tone, between paddle strokes. She did not reply.

"Jane!" he pleaded, whispering her name. The woman in the bow of the canoe looked back again.

"Your mother?" he asked, after the woman had turned and was looking ahead again. She shook her head and made a circular motion about the top of her head. He understood then that her mother had been scalped.

"I'll take you," he promised.

She put her hand behind her back and gripped his. Her hand was warm and soft, with little pads of calluses on it from grinding corn. He leaned forward and kissed her between the braids of her hair. Her hair smelled of pine smoke. They both sat silent now. The woman ahead did not look back again. They were nearing the great river.

The canoe went forward into the night with sweeping strokes. The Reverend James McArdle began to breathe hard. His young companion in the stern was suddenly setting him a strong pace.

They floated out onto the calm bosom of the Ohio. Here and there the gaunt outline of a great tree with writhing branches drifted by, for the river had recently been in flood. On their right was a long sand spit that ran out like a white leprous finger into the black water that poured from the mouth of Beaver Creek. Five or six wolves were growling over something there. Their eyes dripped like molten coins. It was necessary to pass close by that place in order to avoid an eddy. McArdle and Albine plied the paddles rapidly. The dark bundles on the sand spit that the wolves were dragging about were the bodies of those massacred weeks before. They seemed to have gathered together at the mouth of the river. One of the women moaned.

"Oh, God," said she, "why did we'uns ever leave Lancaster? It's them there now."

The canoe shot by.

They turned its bow into the current and felt the slow drag of the mighty stream against them. McArdle began to repeat the Twenty-third Psalm. The women turned to quiet the children who had been scared by the wolves. Far ahead there was a great wavering red light in the sky. Perhaps the fort was burning. A storm was brewing over in the east. The light of the flames beat up under the thunderheads.

The little company crouched low and wrapped their blankets about them as the chill night wind sang past their ears. There must have been a hailstorm somewhere. Luckily there was no rain. On that reach of the river it was as clear as a new mirror. The dark mass of a forested island began to loom up before them. They would hide there all day and go on the next evening. The lodges of Nymwha were at the sawmill built by the English soldiers just across the river from Fort Pitt. They had agreed to go there first. It was at the mouth of a little stream called

Sawmill Run. It would take them at least another night's paddling to get there. The loom of the island seemed to float slowly down upon them.

They beached the canoe and hid it carefully. Albine made sure they were alone on the island. They went inland into the forest under the great elm boughs that hung down over the banks. There was a high bank that leaned forward at an acute angle hollowed out by some ancient flood. It was dry there now and the ledge beneath was deep with half-rotted leaves. They sank down into the leaves thankfully. Dawn began over the river. The exhausted voyageurs slept.

Sal Albine took Jane Sligo by the hand and led her off into the thicket. He knew a deep hollow under the roots of an ancient catalpa that had outweathered more than four hundred seasons. There was no wind now. The morning sun beat into the place gratefully, and bathed the erect column of the tree with pale golden light. The girl stood patiently, hanging her head in confusion while he spread his blanket for both of them. He pulled her down to him. They sank into a great depth of dry leaves that gradually covered them like the sands of time.

It was hours later, and midafternoon, when, quietly raising his head above the surface of his forest covering, the boy beheld the stealthy, alert face of a startled vixen looking at him fixedly over a neighbouring tree root. Her barking had wakened him. Jane was reluctant to leave her bed where the warmth of the sun had penetrated. It was delicious among the fragrant leaves. They rose unwillingly, and shook them off.

They returned through the woods and found McArdle and the two women and young children sitting about a smokeless fire of chestnut burrs in the shelter of the bank. They were picking bare the bones of a wild turkey. Something about them reminded young Albine of the wolves on the sand spit of the night before. He and Jane stopped for a moment, standing hand in hand.

"There they are," said the woman who had kept looking back at them the night before in the canoe. "I told you so! She's nothing but a blanket girl. I heard'm whisperin' last night. Jane Sligo, ye young slut, I'll have the hide off'n yer." She raised a branch angrily.

"What's the matter with the white squaw?" Albine asked McArdle in the Indian tongue. The face of the woman reminded him of the face of the fox that had recently looked at him. "Is she angry because no one has slept with her?"

"Her husband's dead," replied McArdle.

Jane tried to smile at the children and the other women by the fire. "We were only bundlin'," she said apologetically.

"Ye lie!" shrieked the woman, waving the branch threateningly. "Look at your blanket. Ye lie! I know ya!"

She advanced on the girl and would have beaten her, but Albine snatched the branch from her hand and shoved her away. He looked appealingly at McArdle. Meanwhile, the other woman shoved Jane from the fire when she tried to approach it.

"Keep your hands off them children," she said. "There's no place for the likes of you here. I'm a lady. I've got a juty toward them pore innocents whose mar was murdered, and I won't have no trash from the settlements that beds down in a Injun's blanket in the woods tryin' to pretend t' mother 'em."

Jane had turned pale now. She covered her face with her hands and wept.

"The young man is white," said McArdle.

"What!" said both women. "What!"

"His people must have been from Connecticut. They're good old stock there," insisted McArdle.

The women sniffed. "Why don't you make it right then?" said the lady. "You're a minister, ben't ya?"

McArdle nodded. "I'd thought of it," he admitted, "but it seemed sudden."

"Not soon enough," sniffed the lady.

"That's what I say," added the Fox. Jane sobbed. The boy with the Indian topknot stood looking on, puzzled.

"Salathiel," said the Reverend James McArdle suddenly, "you'll be after getting married! Are you willing, Jane?"

The girl rose slowly from beside the fire where she had been crouching. She looked her tormentors in the face.

"I'll not be pushed away from the fire by no old women like you," she said. She came over and stood beside young Albine. McArdle took out his tattered Bible and joined their hands over it.

The Fox took a thin ring from her finger. "Here," she said, and tossed the ring to McArdle. "I'll not be needin' it much longer. I'll never see the settlements agin. I've got a lump in my breast. The crab's eating into my heart." She began to weep. The children looked on, wide-eyed.

Both the women cried while McArdle married Jane and Salathiel. He married them with a broad Scotch-Irish accent, with the Presbyterian service, and the sick woman's ring.

After it was over Jane gave Salathiel a peck on the cheek and went and sat down by the fire. The Fox moved over for her now. She took the girl's hand and fondled it. She looked at the ring on Jane's finger and wept again.

"It brought me good luck oncet. That's why I guv it yer," she choked.

Jane tried to thank her. McArdle sat on the end of a log reading his Bible. He felt he had done a good morning's work. Salathiel busied himself baking some corncakes on hot stones. There was no salt, but they broke the marriage bread together thankfully and with friendly smiles. McArdle traced something with his fish-gall ink on a piece of his precious bark. The "lady" signed it, and the Fox made her mark. The minister also signed it and gave it to Jane, who could read. After she spelled it out she put it carefully in her bosom.

What was it all about? wondered Salathiel Albine. What had been wrong with Jane that the women had worried her so? She was a good girl. She had been happy with him. It had all gone very well and easily. He knew he was a man now. He felt contented and satisfied, but not a little puzzled. White ways were curious. He went down and drank his belly full of river water and washed the paint off his face. Let them see he was not an Indian.

Jane was delighted with him when he came back. She put her arms around him and kissed him. He smiled at her and held her hand. She would make him a good squaw.

On the whole, he liked her.

11. Outside Looking In

AT NIGHT, after the moon sank, they launched the canoe and pushed on up the river again. There were not so many wolves now. Miles ahead, as they swept around a bend, came a new sound, distant but unmistakable. It was the barking of European dogs at the fort.

Daylight overtook them before they could reach the fort. It lay only a few miles farther upriver, but beyond an island. In the darkness of the morning hours they heard rifle fire. Once the river gorge echoed to the bellowing of a great gun. The point between the two rivers, where the fort stood, was overlooked by towering cliffs. Another hour of darkness and they might have made it, but there was a clear reach of water ahead and the dawn was upon them. It was plain that if they tried to make a dash for it they would be fired on by the fort. In the fog, before the sun rose, they saw the bright flash of hand grenades being thrown into the ditch on the Monongahela side.

They were also aware now of many canoes making across both rivers away from the fort in the mist as the light grew brighter. All night the Indians crept close to harass the garrison. With the day they retreated to the opposite banks or lay concealed in hollows close under the walls of the fort. There were already hundreds of them concentrated in the country about the Great Forks.

Once a canoe came drifting downriver and quite near them in the mist. It came near enough to hail, and Salathiel replied in the Shawnee tongue. They gave the death helloo twice and passed triumphantly westward down the river. It was a close call. The women cowered down in the canoe. The children whimpered. The mist had saved them. McArdle encouraged them, telling them their journey was near its end.

Presently they turned aside toward the south bank and made their

way into a deep creek that came down out of the hills. A brief distance
behind, the land towered up in a series of cliffs to the plateau above.
A short reach of level bank hereabouts was covered with huge and
ancient trees. It was here that the English had built their sawmill at the
mouth of the creek. The lodges of Nymwha and his squaws lay a half
mile farther upstream on the banks of Sawmill Run. They arrived at
the camp shortly after the sun began peering into the river valley and
licking up the mists. The guns from the fort spoke. They were firing at
any canoes they could see, and spraying the banks opposite the fort with
grapeshot. The commandant was a careful man. He began each new day
with a fusillade as a matter of routine.

There was no one, besides the chief himself, but the three squaws
and the two papooses at the lodges of Nymwha. He received the message of his half-brother Kaysinata with approval and regaled the party
with dried venison and hoecake. Nymwha also had recently sent wampum to the fort to make his private peace. The English, he said, would
soon be coming over the mountains with an army to relieve the fort.
Already they were gathering at Carlisle. Of what use, then, to howl
like wolves outside their palisades?

It would not be easy to gain admittance to the fort. By day they fired
the cannon at canoes that tried to pass it or that approached it too near.
At night they fired from the ramparts at the slightest noise in the ditch
beneath. The Indians all about were lying in wait for refugees trying
to gain the fort. Nymwha assured McArdle that the matter of getting
their little party into the place would have to be well planned and considered. Nymwha advised Salathiel to go and see the lay of the land
about the fort for himself. Also, at the sawmill, he said, there were two
English soldiers still hidden in the loft. There was, too, a sunken boat
concealed at the mouth of the creek. Nymwha had burned neither the
soldiers nor the mill. He had even sent food to the soldiers. Let the Little
Turtle tell the Commandant Ecuyer that when he reached the fort.
Meanwhile the white captives would be hidden and safe.

Albine went and slept with Jane. He slept all morning, rose, and ate
heavily. Then he put the paint of a Shawnee warrior on his face again.
That afternoon he and McArdle climbed the hills above Sawmill Run
and looked along the three rivers and down on the fort. The place lay
nearly a thousand feet below them, spread out like a green map. The
Allegheny and the Monongahela swept together just below them to
make the broad Ohio. The rivers were about half a mile wide.

Just at the point of the Y stood the fort.

The English flag flaunted brightly in the sun from a mastlike flag-
pole with spars upon it. The bronze and brasses of the cannon glittered.
The place swarmed with people. They were driving the cattle out to
pasture into the fields east of the fort with strong supporting parties of
soldiers scouting before them.

The houses about the fort had all been burned. You could see the fresh scars of the burning upon the riverbanks. That had probably been done by the commandant's orders, for in the upper town that stood farther away up the flat at the foot of a high hill, some houses were still left standing. There were cultivated fields there, roads and tracks that led eastward.

Women were going into the fields with sickles, with a company of riflemen before them, to cut spelts. A wagon raised the dust with a small party going out for firewood. Smoke rose from the chimneys of the barracks and hung there like a pall in the still air of the gorge. In a garden along the Allegheny side of the fort the lacy white of appleblossoms stood out against the tender green of the leaves and lay scattered like snowflakes on the ground. Salathiel had never seen fruit trees before. It was a warm day.

On an island below the fort, on the other side of the Allegheny River, the skin tepees of an Indian encampment lay hidden from the ramparts, behind a small hill. Canoes were pulled up there on the beach. At a distance they looked like a row of black teeth. All of this, from the top of the cliffs south of the fort, where McArdle and Salathiel were standing, was like looking down on an ant heap. It was a view in miniature of inch-high horses and pea-sized men. But the surrounding country was gigantic.

The heart of young Albine leaped within him. The fort at the end of the long point seemed to be aimed like the head of an arrow, pointing straight westward at the heart of the Indian lands. What would happen when the great king across the water loosed that arrow from his string?

Salathiel laughed. He despised his savage childhood now. Spread before him at his feet was the scene in which his manhood should begin. Down there was his white heritage. All he had to do was to cross the river and enter into it. Indeed and indeed, Kaysinata and Nymwha were right. They were wise in their own way and time. Well, he would take their wampum to the fort, deliver their message, and have done with them. He would take Jane there, too. Later, when the siege was over, they would go back over the mountains to the settlements. All this came into the boy's mind with a rush and an invincible determination.

McArdle was excited, too. It was many years now since he had seen a white settlement. He explained, and talked, and answered a thousand questions. Secretly he was sad. He also longed to return but his conscience, he knew, would force him to stay with the Indians and the captives.

So they stood together, well hidden, in a thicket at the top of the cliff. Salathiel watched, fascinated, until evening came. The bland, smooth song of the bugles rose, echoing up out of the gorge. The sunset gun crashed. The flag came down. The dogs in the fort howled. Twilight descended. The fires of the fort, its yellow windows and little lights, began to shine and twinkle. The cressets along the parapets flared. Finally, Salathiel turned away reluctantly to follow McArdle back to the lodges of Nymwha.

Later that evening they went down the stream together to the sawmill and conferred with the soldiers. At the mill they found an English sergeant by the name of Jobson, and one Murphy, an Irish recruit. McArdle talked long with them both. He and Salathiel had a good plan to get into the fort. So they raised the sunken boat by moonlight and bailed her out to be ready to start.

Salathiel was to go alone with the soldiers when the moon sank. He was to take the Big Turtle's wampum, and McArdle's bark tablets with the names of the white captives on them, and give them carefully to the commandant.

It was finally agreed to make a dash for it after the moon went down, row across the river, and get into the outer ditch on the Monongahela side. Then they would carefully crawl up the glacis and call out. They would have to take their chances of being fired on in the dark or of meeting hostile parties of Indians prowling about the fort. It would be an advantage to have the two soldiers from the mill along. Their voices would both be known to the sentries.

The commandant was to be asked to send back as soon as opportunity served for the women and children left at Nymwha's lodges. A green flag was to be hoisted at the fort the day of the night before the commandant would send to fetch them. McArdle promised to stay until the boats came. Then he would go westward again into the Indian lands, he said. There were still many captives to see to. His release was not yet.

Salathiel saw it was no use to argue with McArdle where his conscience was involved. Instead, he went back to the lodges to say goodbye to Jane. She took the parting calmly.

"I'm a married woman now," she said. "I can wait." She showed him the bark writing with the marriage record and signatures on it, proudly. She rubbed her wedding ring for good luck.

Salathiel kissed her, and returned to the mill.

While he had been gone, the soldiers had been busy muffling the oarlocks. When full darkness came they intended to row up an eddy in the Monongahela and cross over to the fort along a sand bar that choked the river near its southern side.

Slowly the moon dropped towards the western hills. The soldiers chewed tobacco and spat into the water. As darkness became more complete, a chorus of wolves began farther down the Ohio. At the fort the dogs barked and barked.

The evening wore on.

12. Inside Looking Out

SIMEON ECUYER, gentleman, captain in his Britannic Majesty's 60th Regiment of foot, the Royal Americans, and commandant of Fort Pitt, sat near the door of his quarters and contemplated, not without military interest and a Gallic eye for the picturesque, the scene in the interior of the fort that lay before him.

He had moved that day into the "Governor's Quarters," as it was called. It was the new brick building near the southwest bastion, which Colonel Bouquet had occupied some months ago, and reserved for his use, if and when he should return. The colonel had even left his camp bed behind, with a good mattress. But, as there seemed small chance that Colonel Bouquet would be able to return from the eastern settlements and lead the remnants of his sickly West Indian regiments over the Alleghenies to the relief of Fort Pitt for some time to come, Captain Ecuyer had taken advantage of a state of siege, and the excuse of necessity, to move into his colonel's quarters.

The good captain was tired of America. He would have liked nothing better than to sell out his commission in the Royal Americans and retire to spend the remainder of his days enjoying the excellent wines and the no less cultivated and elegant conversation for which the shores of Lake Geneva and his native city were so noted.

But he was still a mere captain, and as yet too young to retire. Only thirty-six, in fact, although he looked much older. And there was small chance of his being able to sell out. No one with money, and the influence that went with it, wanted to buy a commission in the Royal American regiment.

Colonel Henri Bouquet, whom the captain had first met when in the service of the king of Sardinia, had lured his friend Ecuyer from a minor but promising post in the electoral household troops at Munich, by tales of the opportunities for active service and swift promotion to be had with the Royal Americans. Ecuyer had finally succumbed. He trusted and admired the genius of his friend Bouquet. They had been together at the battle of Coni, and besides that, the colonel was a Swiss himself, a native of Rolle in the canton of Vaud.

Only part of the colonel's great expectations for America had come true, however. There had been a great deal of active service in the bitter school of Indian warfare, and little more. Promotion, apparently pay itself, had all but ceased. Nevertheless, it was still a distinction and a joy to serve under Colonel Bouquet. He succeeded where "great generals" had awfully failed. Indeed, he was the prime reason why Ecuyer still employed his own not inconsiderable talents in the service of King George, despite wounds, hope deferred, and growing poverty.

For the rest of the officers in the Royal Americans the captain did not care—particularly. They were well enough. Some were professional soldiers like himself, foreigners in a foreign service. They at least obeyed orders carefully for the sake of professional reputation. But it was not always so with the bulk of the English officers who had come out to America with visions of easy garrison duty on a colonial post, only to find an Indian war on their hands. A certain lack of enthusiasm among the older English officers was therefore understandable, but to Ecuyer's professional mind none the less exasperating. The subalterns alone he regarded as the grand hope of the regiment. They came from good families both in England and in America. They were the most promising material for soldiers the captain had ever seen.

As for the rank and file, they had been raised as the act of Parliament forming the regiment had required—in America. As it so happened, mostly in the province of Pennsylvania. They were made up mainly of immigrant Swiss, Welsh, Pennsylvania "Dutch", Irish, Scotch-Irish, Germans, renegade Quakers, a few frontier riflemen, escaped servants, and quite a number of mariners picked up along the water front at Philadelphia, men who would rather fight Indians and be scalped than linger to be flogged to death in the king's floating hells.

There were a great many unfavourable things that could be said about the Royal Americans. The English officers and the War Department constantly said them, but there was one thing that outweighed all the rest. The Royal Americans had *esprit de corps*. Thanks to Colonel Bouquet, Captain Ecuyer, and a few others, they were at that moment the hope of the frontier, and of Fort Pitt in particular.

There was an exceedingly simple, personal reason for this then vital military fact. In times of great crisis the "administration of events" tends to fall into the hands of a certain few persons. In the month of May, 1763, it so happened that the defence, in fact the very existence, of the western frontiers in America, depended upon two individuals primarily: Colonel Henri Bouquet and Captain Simeon Ecuyer. They met the situation not only zealously but ingeniously, and they were followed and obeyed even by rascals and masterless characters, because by no means could either of them be bought, cajoled, flattered, frightened, or betrayed into doing anything less than his whole duty at any moment.

All this was more or less in the nature of things. For even if his mother had been a French noblewoman and left him a small pension in the public funds, Captain Ecuyer was a thorough Swiss, a professional soldier of fortune from Switzerland. Born a republican, he served the monarch to whom he had sworn allegiance with skill, honour, and a professional zeal that might have touched King George to the heart, if he had ever heard of it. But there was small chance of that, or of promotion, and the captain knew it. He accepted what fate had thrust upon him, but he had his personal feelings just the same. And he cursed quietly and fluently, but resignedly, as he ran his professional eye over the barbarous scene before him. Pittsburgh, as the settlers now called it, was indeed a long way from Geneva.

Also the captain's claret had given out. He was now reduced to native, Monongahela corn whisky. Even the issue and the trade rum was exhausted. He took a reluctant sip of the perfectly white, slightly oily liquid from the glass poised on the arm of his chair, and shuddered. No wonder the Indians rose against the English! This was a drink fit only for some hostelry in inferno.

Thanks to the allegedly triune God, he still had Johnson! Johnson, that invaluable combination armourer, valet, barber, cook, washerman, and groom. And to think that they were going to hang Johnson in England for stealing a pearl-set pin! But, thank God, they had transported him instead to the colonies. What life on the frontiers would have been like without Johnson, Captain Ecuyer shivered to think.

For the captain was now quite literally at the end of the world. Just over the Ohio bastion on the point, and across the Ohio River, began the pathless forests. No one really knew where they ended. Apparently, they were inhabited illimitably by the same kind of merciless devils as now surrounded Fort Pitt.

To the mind of Captain Ecuyer, a thoroughly cultivated and European mind, the Indians constituted a ponderous problem in extermination.

Personally, they annoyed him. Their manners were bad. Also they were the enemies of the sovereign he served, and, as a good soldier, he was being thoroughly practical about doing away with them. In this policy General Amherst himself concurred. In fact, he had already written Colonel Bouquet suggesting the use of Cuban bloodhounds, if they could be obtained, and the introduction of smallpox-infected clothing amongst the tribes.

In any event, Fort Pitt was not going to be surprised or easily taken by the savages. Captain Ecuyer was the warrant for that assumption. Should Fort Pitt fall, the English might well be rolled back to the eastern seaboard.

Meanwhile, the hope of English advance and perhaps the fate of an empire lay in the hands of Colonel Bouquet, who was gathering his expedition at Carlisle, and in Ecuyer's hands at Fort Pitt. Both the colonel and the captain were keen enough to know that. They were also Gallic enough to laugh wryly in their letters to each other over the fact that the English empery in America depended, for the time being, upon two Swiss gentlemen whom King George had hired to fight for him, and that no one in London would ever know it unless they lost.

Night after night Captain Ecuyer poured out his thoughts in such letters to Colonel Bouquet at Carlisle and Fort Bedford, and the colonel in like manner replied.

On the rough pine desk in the headquarters room just behind Captain Ecuyer the papers, pen, and wax had already been laid out by Johnson, and a well-snuffed candle lit. A bright fire of large square lumps of soft coal glowed incandescent in the chimney. Johnson himself, a middle-aged man with a sleek bag wig, the bulging contours of an old servant, and a kindly face rendered expressionless by suffering, was starching and ironing his master's lace jabots, spreading them upon an ingenious little rack placed before the fire.

A greasy cloud of coal and wood smoke hung over the fort continually. Soot fell in flakes. Consequently, the process of laundering the captain's linens, lace cuffs, and stocks was continuous; the polishing of his boots, buttons, and weapons, endless. And Captain Ecuyer had three wigs.

To these labours Johnson devoted himself, and to the grooming of his own equally immaculate exterior. The captain, or rather his physical appearance, had become religion with Johnson. It was the last check of duty, devotion, and responsibility which still held him to the European world from which, in reality, the current of events was sweeping him farther away every day. He was being made over from an Englishman into an American, rapidly.

Already he was thinking of acquiring land and settling down. He was engaged to a young woman of property, Amelia Hart, a Pittsburgh trader's daughter.

If and when Johnson could find someone to take his place, he had made up his mind to retire from the fort. But, under the circumstances, a satisfactory substitute was not likely to turn up. Johnson had been one of the best valets in England and the captain was fully conscious of his good luck in having retained him. He had paid his passage money when he arrived at Philadelphia, and thus saved Johnson from five years of indentured slavery. And Johnson was grateful for that. He found himself in a predicament between a comfortable servitude and the prospects of a fearful but fascinating freedom. Meanwhile, Amelia was having a child.

That was the reason Captain Ecuyer was able to sit on the edge of the Western world dressed with all the precision and attention to immaculate detail that would have admitted him to a levy at St. James's.

All this was not without its effect on the garrison. The fact that he was a gentleman of steadfast courage and shrewd policy had already been made abundantly plain to both the traders and the Indians. Perhaps the final element which implicated his successful defence of Fort Pitt was a tact which arose from an understanding of certain democratic principles then in actual practice in Switzerland alone.

At that moment the official guardian of the gate was being carefully and fearfully observed by three little girls in pigtails, who held hands and whispered. A smile from the captain was sufficient to send them

scampering back, scared but happy, to the bedlam of a casemate near the
flag bastion which then constituted their home.

"Scared but happy" might, indeed, be said to describe the general
spirit abroad in the fort. Rather happy tonight, for after a cold spell and
a flood the weather was unusually pleasant.

13. A Stone Souvenir Descends from Heaven

CAPTAIN ECUYER had permitted his coat to slip down off his shoulders, and across the back of his chair. The moon, whose setting young
Albine and his companions, at a distance of only a mile or two, were
awaiting so eagerly, still obstinately poured its feeble light over the Ohio
bastion. The interior of the fort was illuminated by it with a kind of
unearthly grey light.

There were five hundred and forty "mouths", men, women, and children, including the garrison and the refugee population of Pittsburgh,
crowded into the fort. Every casemate in the walls was occupied and
glimmering with candles, torches, or lanthorns. The square windows of
the barracks looked at him from all sides with rows of yellow eyes. Now
and then a door opened, revealing a scene of crowded confusion within,
and a glimpse of glowing coal fires. These fires went day and night,
summer and winter. They were both the curse and the comfort of the
place. Its inhabitants were almost fanatically prodigal with fuel. People
took coal out of the hill across the river and used it like madmen. There
was no end to the coal.

A military forge across from the gate was also in full blast. The hammers of the smiths and the muted ring of glowing iron on anvils seemed
to fill the place with a clashing of harsh bells. Stacks of hay and proven-
der rose everywhere like little hillocks, furnishing at once a perfect fire
menace and the assembly points for cows, horses, and poultry. The loud
flapping of cow dung on the flagstones, the pissing of cattle, the interminable trumpeting of geese and crowing of cocks provided merely the
comparatively hushed monotone accompaniment for the constant staccato of humanity that arose from the casemates where the families of the
unfortunate settlers of burnt Pittsburgh now sheltered themselves.

Somewhere an Irishman was apparently beating his wife to death.
Babies squalled. Mothers screamed the names of their strayed offspring.
Little boys played leapfrog. Lines of people were waiting to get corn
meal and whisky from the storehouses turned over to the traders. From
the commissary rations were being issued to the garrison. Against the
silent loom of the dark forests across the river the Americans were unconsciously raising a defiant human shout. It was the outstanding characteristic of the inhabitants, a constant disorderly and complaining noise.

Not infrequently it became surly in tone. The garrison of Fort Pitt boomed and yelled at the moon.

It would be better when the planet sank. Darkness would come and some of them would *have* to go to sleep then, thought the captain. In the early morning the Indians would creep in upon them. They attacked with fire arrows and hysteria. Guns, with them, were largely something with which to make a noise. Most of them were vile shots, even worse than the English regulars. Only the Americans could use a rifle. They always fired it at something or someone in particular. The Indians fought with hatchets and knives. Hence, a stockade stopped them. The captain rearranged his stock, and sighed audibly. It was his task, with only a modicum of authority, to bring order into all this chaos.

"Tomorrow," said the captain, *"allons nous en!"*

On the walls the cannoneers stood with smoking linstocks beside their loaded cannon. He could see the glow of their matches in the gloom of the bastions. Beyond, over the moat, the sentries of the Royal Americans walked to and fro along the platform of the stockade which Captain Ecuyer had had built all about the glacis. Just at that moment he listened somewhat sceptically to the announcement that all was well, repeated twenty-seven times, one after the other by each sentry. The consoling thought was thus enunciated clear around the walls. At least the sentries were alert. The captain counted the voices. He stood there, and finally crushed the fire out of his cigar while he leaned forward listening intently.

The moon sank, and the shades of night engulfed the pentagon of Fort Pitt. The place gradually became quieter. The captain rose and wrapped his coat about him.

Inside, Johnson finished and folded up the little mangle he had brought from Philadelphia, to put it into the chest which held his valet's kit. The starch on the jabots was dry. He began to fold them neatly and put them into a small drawer in the captain's military chest. Then he stopped, standing for a moment as though suddenly frozen. Captain Ecuyer also was still standing just as he had risen with his coat wrapped about him. For at that moment a curious and demoniacal wailing began in the fields beyond the fort.

The women camping in the casemates and lean-to huts arranged against the walls clutched their children to their breasts. It sounded as though a pack of wolves was being slowly burned to death out there. A graveyard chill crept along the spines of the sentries, who stood transfixed, peering over the pointed stakes of the parapet about the glacis.

Ghostly glimmers of fire twinkled amidst the grass in the meadows about the fort. From these points, soaring up like rockets, streaks of flame mounted into the sky. Some of the sentries shouted. Captain Ecuyer saw the fire arrows fall like shooting stars into the fort. They plunged, hissing faintly. Instantly the shingle roofs of the barracks were

alight with little spluttering tongues of flame. A babble rose from the
fort. Captain Ecuyer roared. The deep roll of drums began to thunder.

Under the penthouse roof, by the gate, the captain could see the
drummers in dim silhouette against the lanthorns, moving their arms
like automatons. The garrison turned out. Ladders were rushed to the
roofs. Women formed a line and began passing buckets from the wells.
The swish of water on the roofs became rhythmic. The tongues of flame
spluttered and went out.

A pile of hay burst into lurid smoky flame, and was quenched. A
crackle of rifle fire began from the opposite banks of the rivers. The
bullets whizzed and moaned into the fort. Here and there wood splintered. The tinkle of a smashed window light sounded ominous. Three
wounded men plunged, with sickening crashes, from the roofs. The
Indians wailed like lost souls. The fire arrows finally became fewer. Now
and then from the stockade the sullen bump of a musket thudded into
the night. The Royal Americans were being careful of their precious
powder. The crack of the settlers' rifles was more frequent.

Captain Ecuyer mounted the ramparts and took his stand by the cannon on the flag bastion. To the eastward, on rising ground near Grant's
Hill, a house had burst into flame. A crowd of Indians could be seen
about it capering against the fire, and driving off cattle. They were
nearly a mile away.

The captain gave an order. Twice, under his direction, the matross
corrected the elevation of his piece. Its thundering explosion shook the
fort. At the foot of Grant's Hill, the house, the Indians, and the cattle
disappeared in an intense white flash and a rocking shell explosion that
re-echoed from the woods. The burning timbers of the house hurtled
into a near-by thicket and set it on fire. The red glow, framed by the
frowning forests, threw a kind of infernal dawn over the valley. From
the parapets of the fort several cannon began to spray the country about
with grapeshot. The rifle firing and demoniacal yelling died away. The
cannon ceased. Over the fort hung a low, dun-coloured cloud of choking
powder and coal smoke.

The captain made his rounds. Finally he stood watching the dark lines
of the forests across the rivers that swept away, rocking along the cliff-
tops into the slowly paling eastern sky. There must be nearly a thousand
savages concealed there. He had estimated their rifles—hundreds of
them. The prospect of a long siege was by no means a delightful one.
He hoped Colonel Bouquet at Carlisle would hurry. Perhaps by this
time he had been able to advance to Fort Bedford. Perhaps? There were
only a few weeks' provisions left at Fort Pitt. The captain stood pondering that solemn thought. A retreat through the forest would mean
almost certain death for all. An arrow from the nowhere above suddenly
plunged viciously into the muscle of the calf of his left leg.

It was exceedingly painful, and the wound bled profusely. It was a nasty gash. He retired to his quarters to be bandaged. The men on the stockades began to throw hand grenades down the glacis as morning approached. They exploded in the ditch with a crimson splash and a bump. The captain tensely watched Johnson and the surgeon cut a stone arrowhead out of the calf of his left leg. That arrowhead would be the most cherished item in his souvenir collection, he reflected painfully.

Suddenly he could see himself at Geneva, exhibiting it to his neighbours. The faces of many people he had forgotten surrounded him. He was sitting in a small summerhouse near the lake. The vision was extremely clear. He began to hear familiar old voices. Then he fainted.

Johnson completed the work of the surgeon, who had been called hastily elsewhere. He poured *eau de Cologne* into the wound. The smarting brought the captain to again. Johnson wrapped his master in a cloak and laid him upon Colonel Bouquet's camp bed. He poured the blood out of his boot, washed it, wiped it, and lay down himself on the floor. After a while Johnson began to snore. The captain shuddered feverishly now and then. It seemed to him he could see the future in the dark. Finally he slept exhaustedly. Outside an occasional hand grenade viciously punctuated the early morning hours.

14. Portrait in Oils of a Young Scalp

THE ARROW which struck the captain was also like to have been the death of young Albine and his two soldier companions. The news of Captain Écuyer's being wounded caused the garrison to keep a doubly sharp and vengeful watch from the platform. The slightest sound from the riverbank, or the least suspicion of something moving in the shadow of the glacis, brought spurts of rifle fire from the loopholes, or the earth-shaking splash of a grenade.

It was nearly morning, therefore, before the little party of three dared even to leave the cover of the deep overhung riverbank by the point, where they had landed and taken shelter about midnight.

There had been no trouble in crossing the river after the moon had gone down. They had simply rowed up an eddy to the bar, and then poled across. It was just their bad luck to have chosen a night when an attack was on to try to enter the fort. When they were halfway across, the Indian rifle fire had broken out viciously from the cliffs on the banks above them. Also they were afraid they might be seen in a cannon flash from the fort. For that reason they abandoned the boat, and, crouching low, waded in on the bar that ran out from the point.

Under the deep bank it was safe enough till dawn came. With daylight, however, they would inevitably be seen by the Indians on the opposite bank, and picked off. Yet if they stuck their heads above the bank now they would be killed by the sentries on the parapet. So it was the devil and the deep sea. They stood shivering in the mud for two hours, occasionally conferring in whispers. Jobson, the sergeant, eventually decided to try to make the foot of the parapet by crawling around the point into the "King's Artillery Garden" on the Allegheny side of the fort.

They started, having to swim once, and proceeded with infinite caution, for as they wormed their way through the rows of lettuce and red cabbages toward the deeper loom of the slope of the glacis they became aware of other forms crouching here and there in the darkness. Once Albine whispered something in Shawnee as a crawling Indian overtook them from behind. The Indian crawled on. Presently a shot rang from the palisade and the Indian sprang into the air and crashed into the ditch. That was warning enough. After that they kept still for an hour. Murphy, the other soldier, stuffed himself with parsley, like a rabbit. It was his last meal.

The sky began to turn grey. The lurking forms on the glacis slipped back through the bushes to the riverbank. They heard canoes being quietly launched. Presently the three white men felt they were alone. Morning was coming on fast now. They could occasionally see the head of a sentry sliding along the pointed stakes of the palisade. Between them and it lay the slope of the glacis, and the ditch. It was still pitch-dark in the ditch. They were on the western side of the fort. Jobson wriggled up the slope without being seen, and called out. Young Albine and Murphy followed more slowly.

"Don't shoot!" cried the sergeant. "It's me, Sergeant Jobson, from the sawmill. Is that you, Leftenant Francis? I know your voice. For God's sake, call your men off!"

A cultivated young English voice replied. The lieutenant assured himself he was really talking with Sergeant Jobson. He took a terrible time doing so. Then he sent for a rope. It also was a terrible time coming.

The three men on the glacis could now be seen from the parapet. "Hi, Murphy," said a soldier from the platform, "have you still got your har? Who's that wid ye?"

"It's a young white bhoy tryin' to escape from thim red divils, and mind ye don't tike him for one. An' fer Christ's sake, git that rope or we'll all be moithered out here entirely, you with yer blatherin' mouth in there."

"Shut your own," growled Sergeant Jobson, "and get you ready to make a rush. Here's the rope now."

It came wriggling over the parapet, and fell into the ditch with a splash. The sergeant went first. He picked his way through the ditch, tied the rope under his arms, and was drawn up, not without a good deal of difficulty. The rope came dangling down again.

"It's your turn, me bhoy," said Murphy. "You're a spalpeen. I'll tarry."

A couple of bullets droned across the river and splashed against the parapet. Someone had brought a lanthorn onto the platform. Everyone on the palisade ducked, and cursed the man with the light. It went out.

Sal Albine rose clutching his bundle of bark leaves to his breast. He put the thong that held them together in his mouth, and rushed for the rope. Out of one corner of his eye he saw the Indian in the ditch, wriggling, but he couldn't call out. He had the thong in his mouth, and he mustn't drop that precious list. He went up the rope hand over hand, bracing his feet against the wall of the palisade. He stood on the platform and began to shout a warning to Murphy.

"Good for you, young'un," said Jobson, clapping him on the back. Then they heard Murphy scream.

"Jasus! Jasus! I've caught me fut in a baver trap. Howly Mither of God!" The party of ten soldiers on the parapet stood looking down at him helplessly.

"I'll go back," said Albine, and started. But it was too late.

A form, painted black and green, with animallike red stripes on its face, rose out of the shadow of the ditch. It rushed upon Murphy where he was struggling helpless in the trap, and gripped him by the hair. A knife flashed. A horrible floundering and moaning followed while the Irishman's scalp was torn from his head. He shrieked. The Indian rushed down the glacis and the death helloo rose triumphantly from under the riverbank. It was answered and reanswered eerily from the opposite bank. On the parapet Salathiel Albine, Sergeant Jobson, Lieutenant Francis, and eight soldiers of the Royal American regiment dressed in scarlet coats and white leather cross belts, stood shivering in the lethal dawn. They seemed stunned. It had not been possible to fire at the Indian without killing Murphy. Then someone threw a hand grenade. It blew Murphy to pieces.

"You God-damned idjit!" piped the lieutenant. A young soldier began to vomit. "Git back to yer posts," roared the sergeant. "Do you think it's a quiltin' bee?" The men scattered.

Young Albine stood on the platform and looked out over the inner moat and roofs of Fort Pitt. In his nostrils for the first time was the faintly fecal odour of civilization mixed with coal and powder smoke. He was never to grow quite used to it.

"Come on, me lad," said the lieutenant. "I'll have to enter all this in the orderly book."

They walked along the stockade platform in the growing daylight, and descended a ladder opposite the music bastion. The musicians were gathering there and the cannoneers preparing to fire the sunrise gun. They crossed a hand bridge over the fosse that fed the moat from the Allegheny, and found themselves at the guardhouse at the outer gate of the fort.

The guard was already drawn up awaiting the morning relief. In the increasing morning light their burnished arms and scarlet coats gleamed cheerfully. The water of the moat reflected impressively the frowning dark ramparts and cannon looking out from the embrasures of the wall. The place seemed armed to the teeth. From fifty chimneys the black coal smoke announcing breakfast rolled threateningly into the air, and drifted down the Ohio. The sun peeked over the eastern hills, its first beams saluted by the thunder of the morning gun, and a ruffle of fifes, drums, and trumpets. The echoes rolled grandly up the river canyons as the Union Jack rose over Fort Pitt.

The heart of the young man dressed in muddy wolfskins, with the bark bundle under his arm, expanded with pride, hope, and astonishment. To the youth from the wilderness this bare outpost of civilization, the ragged panoply of European war thrust into his native forests, had the effect of an explosion in his imagination. His white heritage fell upon him at one swoop; left him dizzy. He rallied to it with the phlegm of the savages he had been raised among. Inwardly he was amazed and excited; outwardly he was calm and apparently contemptuous.

"Can you speak English?" asked Lieutenant Francis, for so far Salathiel had made no reply to anything he had said.

"Better than you," replied Albine proudly. "I can even repeat all the psalms by heart."

"Every Scotch rebel in these mountains can," said the lieutenant wryly. Most of the people, he noticed, had the accent and manners of the former age. They were all Covenanters except the Catholic Irish, and they were nearly all runaway servants.

"What's that under your arm, a Bible?" the lieutenant asked.

"It's a list of white captives now in the western woods," replied Salathiel, "and it's for the chief here. How do you call him?"

"The commandant," said Francis. He looked at the youth in wolfskins now with more curiosity and respect.

"I have wampum from the chiefs for him too," added Salathiel.

The lieutenant nodded. In these parts you could never tell who or what a man was. There were no certain signs of class distinction. He thought it best to take Salathiel to his quarters and give him some clothes and breakfast. There would be some wild tales of the forest in him at least. The lieutenant was bored. He missed the excitement of routs at Bristol, and you couldn't bed with a girl in America without catching fleas at least. Eventually they gathered under one's wig. He scratched thoughtfully.

They were waiting for the drawbridge to fall. It soon came down with a crash, and the relief in the scarlet of the Royal Americans marched across. The drums banged. The lieutenant saluted and dismissed. Then he led the way onto the little island barbican in the moat and across the second drawbridge into the fort. The smell of corn mush, frying bacon, boiling pork, humanity, and cattle filled the air. The fumes from the chimney caused Salathiel to choke. Astonishment once more filled his mind.

It had never occurred to him that buildings could be built of anything but logs. He had never seen anything but a log cabin or an Indian hut. The fort was a mass of solid dirty grey brick and stone. There seemed to be enormous numbers of people in it. The cattle also were amazing. He remembered his father's ox that had once breathed in his face. All these animals looked monstrous. And the chief sound that marked the presence of the white man was the crowing of cocks. It sounded delirious.

The lieutenant paused to unlock the door of his quarters. Salathiel stood lost in admiration over the ingenious contrivance of lock and key. He even stooped to examine it.

"Come in, come in," said the young officer impatiently.

For the first time in his life young Albine entered a civilized room.

It was a simple enough place. There were three deal chairs, a bed, an officer's chest of polished wood with a brass lock, and a painted table. A shelf of books, containing nearly a dozen volumes, hung on the wall. Across from it a small cupboard displayed some pewter and a few pieces of china and crockery. There was a ragged woollen rug on the floor. Into this place, through a spotlessly clean window, poured the level rays of the newly risen sun, which seemed to Salathiel to gild the apartment with a kind of palatial splendour. He stood obviously lost in wonder and admiration until the lieutenant laughed.

Lieutenant Francis was a young gentleman of talent and small income. The second son of a rich and titled English family, his commission in the Royal Americans had been bought for him in lieu of a lean living in the Irish church. Baggage, even some effects of elegance, had accompanied him. He actually painted a little. Two oil landscapes and a portrait of his sister, by no means despicable, adorned the walls. There were iron candlesticks, long clay pipes, and bottles on the mantelpiece. A white cloth with a set of military silver and steel knives was laid out on the table, and his servant just at that moment knocked on the door, entered, and began to prepare breakfast over a bright coal fire in the little chimney place. To cap the climax, the walls were plastered and a ray of sunshine, focused by one of the bottle panes, illuminated charmingly the white face of the young lady in court dress smirking at them all.

All this at once assaulted the senses of Salathiel. The young man in gold lace and scarlet, hanging his gilt-hilted sword on a peg in the wall, might have been the sultan of Golconda, or the king of England. It had never occurred to Salathiel that a room could be smooth and white inside. He ran his fingers along the plaster in amazement, and left a smudge on the wall.

"Sit down," said the lieutenant, laughing. "No, no, in the chair!"

So that was what they were for!

"Hawkins," continued the lieutenant, addressing his servant, "set another place for my guest." The soldier grinned and coughed. They settled down to tea, rashers of bacon, corn bread, and eggs.

It was now that young Albine, perhaps by sheer native shrewdness, hit upon a scheme which was to lead him to whatever modicum of success he achieved in life. Imitation was his only hope and defence. He began to copy the actions of Lieutenant Francis' eating. He mimicked him precisely. He poured his tea into his saucer, blew upon it carefully, and swallowed it. It was to him a nauseous dose, but he downed it. He watched every move the lieutenant made with his knife, fork, and spoon. He managed not to spill anything. He thought butter was wonderful. He ate six eggs and a half pound of bacon.

"That's all we have, sir," said Hawkins, rising, with his face a beet color, from before the fire. "It's the week's supply."

"Buy some more," said the lieutenant, tossing him a coin.

Salathiel blushed under his paint and mud. But what did these English live on? Eggs? The lieutenant made some hot toddy. He plied his guest, and both their tongues were loosened.

They began to talk with instead of at each other. In the half-Biblical, half-learned jargon of the Reverend James McArdle, mixed with the idiom of the frontier and some Indian words, Salathiel began to reconstruct his life in the forest in reply to the amused, but searching, questions of Lieutenant Francis. He did surprisingly well. Then he began to ask questions, too. A feeling of friendliness sprang up between them as the toddy neared the bottom of the bowl. The young Englishman began to tell Salathiel about Bristol and Bath. Francis grew enthusiastic about Bath. "It would do you good to take a plunge in the hot springs there," he said. "I believe you'd come out a white man. Lord, I'd like to spend the morning in the bath, myself!" He scratched his wig dolefully. "Now then," said he, "if you're going to the commandant, you will simply have to have some decent clothes. Ecuyer dresses like a courtier. He's the only man on the frontier who's not hoppin' with fleas. But before you dress up, I'd like to catch you just as you are. Do you mind?"

Albine, of course, hadn't the faintest idea what he meant.

"Sit over there in that streak of sunlight," continued the lieutenant. "Here, try a pipe." Although he was still completely puzzled, Salathiel complied. The tobacco was excellent. The lieutenant took out his palette, a small piece of old tent canvas stretched on a frame, and some oil paints. He began to daub rapidly. The sunbeam shifted slowly down the wall. Outside, a trumpet sounded, making his subject jump, and the tramp of marching men passed the door. The lieutenant painted on. This fellow, he knew, would never look like that again. And he *was* a specimen, a type!

He sketched in the head against a tangled background of dim forest and branches. Across it fell streaks of sunlight, high-lighting the big shaved head with its prominent ears, the topknot with an eagle feather tied to it. The face he did rather from the side. The large, piercing grey eyes, wide apart, the nose that swept down and finally curved in a little at the mouth. That was the really astonishing feature. Or was it the hatchetlike lines of the lower jaw that gave him so much character? It would have been a grim face if it were not for the mouth, the fine, big, white teeth, slightly pouting lips parted in a happy, manly young smile. That smile was ingratiating, whether it was unconscious or not. Certainly it was natural.

On the costume Lieutenant Francis let himself go. He draped the wolfskin over one shoulder and put in the little red turtle over the heart. "And we will suppose it is summer," he said. "The background shows it." He put a rifle gun in his subject's hand. The lieutenant drew guns well. And he seated his subject on a stump whose roots wreathed themselves into the base of the picture.

"No chairs down the Ohio?" he asked.

Salathiel shook his head, and laughed.

"Hold that," said Francis. He worked rapidly.

On a stump in the forest his young hunter sat, smoking between shots. "Rest in the wilderness," said the lieutenant. All that was needed was a wild turkey lying at his hunter's feet. He would put that in later. He stopped, rather breathless and tired. A fit of coughing shook him.

Salathiel could not admire the picture enough. He kept going backward and forward between it and a bit of looking glass on the chest. The picture, he saw, was how he looked to the young Englishman.

"I like your likeness better," he said.

Francis laughed. "I see you will probably get on in this world," said he. The lieutenant was pleased.

"But I will have to stop looking like that if I do," Salathiel added.

The lieutenant laughed again.

"I opine you will," he admitted. "Perhaps you had better begin the metamorphosis now."

"What?" said Albine, looking puzzled.

Francis gave his new-found friend a piece of soap and poured out a basin of hot water. He showed him how to use the soap, and persuaded him to wash his face. The lieutenant sat back enjoying all this immensely. His friend was white, after all. Looking in the glass again Albine could scarcely recognize himself. He looked at the picture half regretfully. That was me, he thought.

Just then Hawkins came back with some clothes from the quartermaster, where the lieutenant had sent him. All this reminded young Francis of amateur play-acting at home. It made him a bit homesick, but he liked it all the better for that. He now contributed an old linen shirt, tied at the wrists.

Salathiel then stepped out behind the quarters and had Hawkins dash several buckets of water over him. He left the muddy wolfskin lying on the ground and returned to dress in the new clothes: a pair of soldier's boots, knitted socks, half-leather breeches, and the lieutenant's shirt. An old green coat, provided by the province of Pennsylvania for its militia, completed the costume. Only the boots were unbearable. He finally took them off and put on his moccasins again.

"That's better. They go with the topknot. But I'd let my hair grow," said Francis, who never cracked a smile. "Put the feather on again. It gives you a more respectable look."

Hawkins would have guffawed but, even in his moccasins, the young man stood six feet four, with narrow hips and broad shoulders. The muscles in his arms were pantherlike. Also he looked intensely grave. It might be a mistake to guffaw. Anyway, at that moment the lieutenant sent Hawkins along with a message to headquarters. He returned shortly with the desired answer.

Salathiel picked up the bundle of bark and his pouch with the wampum in it. Then he and the lieutenant set out together to see the commandant. Lieutenant Francis was filled with a kind of schoolboy curiosity, bordering on mirth. He wanted to see Captain Simeon Ecuyer confronted by young Albine. It would be something to tell at mess, where his reputation as a wit had suffered somewhat of late for lack of new material to embroider upon.

15. Shaving as a Fine Art

ECUYER was in a back room of headquarters, where he slept. There was a large window there. There was also the largest mirror west of the mountains. It had been sent by Governor John Penn to General Stanwix when, for a brief time, the English commander in chief had been at Pittsburgh planning the building of the fort. Despite the window, there was a candle burning in a sconce on each side of the mirror, and Johnson was shaving the captain in a chair placed before it. The captain's wig was off. His wounded leg lay stretched out on a stool. The lather covered his face, and his eyes were closed.

"Come in, gentlemen," said he. He spoke with a clear voice and scarcely a trace of accent. "Do sit down, please."

They took the bench by the door.

The lieutenant began to relate the events of the night before, while Johnson continued to shave the captain. He shaved slowly with short, brief strokes. Young Albine watched him, fascinated. He had never seen anyone shaved that way before. Shaving an Indian's head was quite a different process. The captain did not open his eyes even when Lieutenant Francis recounted the incident of Murphy's death.

"Arrange to punish the man who threw that grenade," he finally said.

"The men must learn to think before they throw grenades, and to aim at what they shoot at with a rifle. What is the message the newcomer you speak of brought?"

Francis nudged Salathiel. He stepped out into the middle of the floor and drew the wampum strings from his pouch.

"Father," said he. Johnson stopped shaving.

The lieutenant put his hand over his mouth. This was going to be magnificent.

Captain Ecuyer opened his eyes.

A strange, tall, hawk-faced young man was standing before him holding out strings of wampum that wriggled on his wrists like snakes. Captain Ecuyer wiped some lather away from the region of his mouth. A small ironical smile was revealed under the lather.

"Go on," he said, without sitting up.

"Father, I am the mouth of Kaysinata, the Big Turtle, and the tongue of the half-chief Nymwha," continued Salathiel. "The mouth opens and the tongue in it speaks for your children, the Shawanees. Father, the commanding officer, by this string of wampum we open your ears, wipe the tears from your eyes, and remove everything that is bad from your heart." He laid a string upon the knee of Captain Ecuyer, and went on:

"Father, with this string we renew the ancient chain of friendship with Our Great Father, the king across the seas. We would bury the hatchet and ask that his gifts be renewed; that powder and shot, horses, and white flour be sent to us. We have listened to lying tongues. Our hearts are sore. The children of the English who tarry in our lodges we will return to our father . . ."

"Enough!" said Ecuyer, sitting up. Even with lather on his face he looked impressive. His eyes shone with indignation.

"Go back to your friends and tell them when they deliver their captives and come here themselves to ask peace, we will smoke the calumet with them. Do not lay any more strings on my knees, young man. I accept those you have given me to open my eyes. My eyes are open. Go back and say so. Here, Johnson, take these trinkets and put them in the chest where we keep the rest of this stuff." He sank back in the chair. Johnson took the belts of wampum and went out.

"Go back"—the words rang in the ears of Salathiel with a doleful sound. The forests seemed to be closing around him again.

"But, captain, the commandant, I don't want to go back," he said.

"What!" exclaimed the captain. "What! Then why do you come here?"

Salathiel began to explain as best he could. The fervour of forest oratory, that had sustained him and made him stand up to deliver the wampum with savage bravado, deserted him. The mouth and tongue of the Indian chief was silent. It was with his own voice and for himself that he pleaded now.

The captain opened his eyes again, very wide indeed. From a mouthpiece the young man before him had suddenly turned into an individual. The captain would listen to such a man. With mouthpieces he had little patience. His leg hurt him, but it was a young white man speaking to him now, and he was sympathetic and patient.

The story Salathiel poured out interested him. "Good!" he exclaimed when he heard about McArdle's list of captives. Then he lapsed into silence. From time to time he raised his hand in assent. Otherwise, Salathiel soon seemed to be speaking to a man asleep. The captain had closed his eyes again. The lather dried on his cheeks. Finally he opened his eyes and looked at the speaker.

"I would advise you to stay here. You might even enlist," he said. "Lieutenant Francis, look after this fellow for me. See that he is started in right. He seems to have brought valuable information. Also go and tell Captain-lieutenant Shay to take the guard mount for me today. I can't get about now. My leg's horrid stiff. Tell Johnson to hurry back. The lather's drying. Damn it, where's that rascal gone to? As for the prisoners on Sawmill Run," he added, as though they were an afterthought, while he glanced at Albine, "I'll send for them as soon as I can. Now sit down, young man, I want to ask you certain questions about those captives."

Lieutenant Francis departed. Salathiel sat waiting.

He could hear a watch ticking in the captain's vest, but Ecuyer said nothing. He was very tired. Johnson did not return, for some reason. The captain lay with his eyes closed, waiting for him. The wound in his leg crawled. He felt faint, and Fort Pitt seemed far away. Five or six minutes passed.

It was then that young Albine made the most important move of his career. He rose quietly on his moccasins. There was something fascinating about the captain's half-shaved face; something alluring about the little brush that made the foam.

The soap cup and the brush lay beside a case with seven razors marked with the days of the week. The one for Tuesday was open. Johnson had been using it. Salathiel picked the one for Wednesday. It looked keen. He began to stir the soap with the brush. The lather creamed anew. That settled it.

Copying Johnson, he began to spread the lather carefully on the captain's cheeks. Ecuyer threw back his head, thinking Johnson had returned.

Very carefully, just as Johnson had done, with quick, careful strokes, Albine began to shave Captain Ecuyer. It was just like carefully scraping a fine, thin doe's hide. He finished the cheeks and under the nostrils. Captain Ecuyer had a long upper lip that he stiffened against the razor. The chin Salathiel was most careful about, and he ran the razor over it lightly. But he had the hang of it now. The captain threw back his head even farther, exposing his throat. The shaving went on. Johnson stepped into the room, and gasped.

The captain opened his eyes.

He saw a young savage with a feather in his hair, standing above him, with a razor resting at his throat. He said nothing. Neither did Johnson.

Salathiel Albine finished shaving the commandant of Fort Pitt. . . .

The captain sat up and felt his face critically. He ran his hand over his cheeks, and especially his throat, thoughtfully. Then he began to laugh.

"There you are, Johnson," said he. "You've found an assistant, and a damned good one. What's your name, young man? Are you honest? At least you didn't cut my throat, and I've never been sure that Johnson wasn't going to do that, ever since I paid his passage money."

The scandalized Johnson protested loudly.

"Tut, tut!" said the captain. "You've been talkin' about leavin' me ever since you got sweet on that trader's daughter and married her. I know! And now here's a natural from the forests, with a sartorial gift. What more can you ask in this howling country? It's a special act of grace!"

For a moment Johnson had been both angry and jealous. But now the captain's suggestion seemed to pull a trigger in his brain. He *had* been thinking of leaving the captain—next year. Maybe there was something in what the captain said. Johnson looked at young Albine keenly.

"Come," said the captain, "help me over into that camp bed. It's Colonel Bouquet's. But he isn't here, and I am. God help me," he added, and touched his leg ruefully.

Johnson and Albine together lifted the commandant into the cot.

Johnson began to curl the captain's wig. He gave directions to Salathiel how to put away the shaving things, and watched him closely. Pretty soon Salathiel was washing one of the captain's shirts at the fireplace. He was most careful. He did everything exactly as he was told. He moved quietly on his moccasins, and said nothing. Johnson nodded.

An obedient assistant would make life easier for him, anyway. The idea *might* work. The captain had a good eye for a man. Of course, he would have to show this young savage everything. But it was easier to teach than to work. Anybody knew that.

Salathiel went back for supper to Lieutenant Francis' quarters. Johnson had told him to report again in the morning. The young Englishman congratulated him.

"You're on the way up," said the lieutenant. "But I can't have you eating here at the table with me any more if you are going to be the captain's servant. That won't do, you know."

"Why not?" asked Salathiel.

"Oh, afterwhile you'll find out," replied the Englishman. "But in this country that doesn't need to prevent us being friends quietly on the side.

We will go hunting when the woods are safe again." They shook hands on it.

"I'll need a gun," said Salathiel wistfully. A gun was something he had never been able to obtain, even from Nymwha.

Lieutenant Francis looked at the picture of his new friend on the mantelpiece, where he sat with a nice shooting iron in his hand, and pondered.

"I'll give you one!" he said impulsively.

He rose and gave him his own fowling piece. It was a double-barrelled hunting gun of small caliber, and quite beautifully chased. "Wilson, London, 1752" was under the mark.

"My God, she's a fair beauty," exclaimed Salathiel, flushing with pleasure.

"She's all that," said the lieutenant. "But that piece belonged to my older brother, and I never liked him, or anything he owned. Maybe it will bring down good fortune if I give it away. Anyway, keep it, and go shooting!"

"Thank you with all my heart," replied Salathiel.

"Well, well, good luck," said the lieutenant, almost as though he were glad to be rid of the gun. Then he smiled.

Salathiel understood it was time to go.

He stepped out into the night and the confines of the crowded fort. He had no idea where he was going to sleep. Overhead was a pall of coal smoke, but he could see the stars through it. They winked at him blindly.

16. How Salathiel Slept with a Widow

SALATHIEL stood before the door of Lieutenant Francis' quarters with his blanket and his new gun over his arm, but in a quandary. No one had said anything about where he was going to sleep. As far as he could see, every nook and cranny in the fort was pre-empted, and he still had a feeling of faint hostility to all the noisy crowds of whites gathered about the fires and those swarming in and out of various buildings. There seemed to be something indecent about so many people being crowded together in one place. He hesitated.

An occasional shot from the parapet confirmed the state of siege. He wondered what Jane was doing over in the lodges of Nymwha on Sawmill Run. It would be cold sleeping without her. He was alone again! This was the first night of his new life—and there was no place to sleep unless he found one.

He began to walk about quietly, looking for a bit of shelter or a soft place to lie down. The only result was to disturb a number of people,

who complained. Evidently his accent and appearance were not reassuring, either. He enquired for his friend, Sergeant Jobson, only to find
he was on duty at the outer barbican. He persisted. But growls, surly
replies, a blast of profanity or ironic abuse was all he got from those he
approached on the subject of a place to sleep.

He was wary, anyway. He was a very strange stranger in a strange
land. No trees, nothing but brick and stone—not a pile of leaves to lie
down in. Even the ground was covered with cobbles.

At last he found himself in one corner of the fort near a line of casemates. Unlike the other casemates, these were not occupied by people.
They looked like caves in the wall. It was dark under them. He entered
one, thrusting his hands out before him. That casemate was full of hay.
Some officers' horses were being stabled there. There was also a sentry
on duty, he discovered, who warned him away.

The hay belonged to the king. No, he couldn't sleep on it. It was
orders.

He sat down nonplussed and weary on a wagon tongue. The sentry
passed on. His back was turned. Albine slipped noiselessly into the
shadow of the casemate and climbed over the pile of hay that went up
nearly to the roof. It smelled sweet. It was the new "English grass". He
had never smelled grass like that before. There was a space of a couple
of feet between the top of the hay and the arch of the casemate. He
crawled through. Behind, at the far end, was a hollow. He discovered it
by sliding down. It was warm, silent, and dark back there. A grille in
the rear wall let in a little moonlight and air. A few mice rustled. He sat
quiet, listening to the futile tramp of the sentry outside. Then he heard
someone breathing. Whoever it was seemed to be asleep. He settled himself in a soft spot, dug in deep, and wrapped his blanket about him.

It seemed that no time at all had passed when the clamour of the
reveille wakened him. The cold light of early day was coming in dimly
over the top of the hay and through the barred grille behind. Outside
there was a great bellowing of cattle and a distant popping of rifles. At
first he could not recall where he was. Then he remembered, and
stretched himself luxuriously. He had had an elegant sleep on the king's
hay.

"Whist!" said a voice in a half-whisper. "Who be ye?"

He sat up and brushed the hair out of his eyes. Not ten feet away,
sitting where the ray of light fell upon her from the grille, was a red-
headed girl looking at him with wide-eyed surprise. As the light from the
slanting ray grew more intense, her hair flared. There were dried leaves
and wisps of grass in it. She was chewing a straw quizzically and squatting cross-legged.

"Arre ye a man or a kelpie?" said she. It was probably only his topknot she saw, as his head alone stuck up out of the hay.

"Kelpie?" said he. "Kelpie?"

"Aye, I thought so," she continued. "No man would leave a young widow like meself to perish of cold the night, and him with a blanket. It's not Christian."

"You're a widow!" he said. He looked at her now closely.

He had never seen a widow, he thought. He remembered they were mentioned in the Bible. There was the Widow of Nain, for example. What he saw now was a handsome girl apparently about sixteen, a magnificent head of auburn hair, freckles, a sprightly turned-up nose, and large grey eyes. She was dressed in ragged linsey-woolsey with a bedraggled shawl wrapped about her firm young body and shoulders. She had neither shoes nor stockings.

"I'm a married man, myself," he said at last. Certain things had reminded him of that.

"You're not tired of it, are you?" she asked.

"No, no," he replied. "I'm not tired of it! I was only married a few days ago. I've left her with the Indians across the river at Sawmill Run."

"That was hasty of you. You'll never see her again," she said.

"I'll fetch her as soon as I can cross over to git to her," he retorted.

She shook her head. "Me husband was moithered at Toitle Creek a month come Tuesday. Injuns. It was only a little stream and he was tryin' to cross that to fetch me. But he was just a bhoy, and I never got much good from him. So I buried him and came on to the fort meself. I ain't got nobody to do for me. I'm alone. Gawd, I wisht you wasn't married!" She looked as if she were going to cry.

"I'll get you something to eat this morning," he replied. His own stomach reminded him. "Stay here till I come back."

"Mind the sintry," she whispered. He nodded. The light was coming in over the top and through the hay now. He wriggled through it and peered out cautiously.

There was no sentry in the daytime. Anyone stealing hay could be seen from the ramparts. He stepped out and brushed himself off. Now for breakfast.

That was not so easy. He passed down the line of settlers huddled against the wall, camping and cooking in the open. Once or twice he stopped. A family was gathered about a kettle, eating mush.

"You're a lone wolf, aren't you?" said one old woman, eying him suspiciously. "Be off."

A lone wolf! That was it. Somehow that tickled him. But there was no place for him by that fire. He went on to one of the barracks and asked for Sergeant Jobson. In the barracks there were long tables, and a great smouldering coal fire in the end chimney. They roared for Jobson, who came looking sleepy.

"It's the boy I was telling you of. Make a place for him," said he. He seemed glad to see Salathiel.

"It's rations you want, I suppose," he added. Salathiel nodded and smiled with relief. Some of the men were still eating at the table near the fire where Jobson led him.

"It's not regular rations, but it will do," said the sergeant.

Salathiel sat down and filled himself up with bacon and fried mush. There was plenty. The soldiers at least had that. He began to put aside something on a plate surreptitiously.

"So you've got someone you're feedin' already," said Jobson, and clapped him on the back. "You're a fast worker, me lad. Sure, you can have it, if you bring back the pannikin."

A few minutes later he was back in the casemate behind the hay, watching the girl wolf her food. She sighed with satisfaction and lay back on his blanket. Already she had appropriated that.

"Will you be here tonight?" he asked.

"I'll wait for you," she assured him. "Don't forget me. You're the only friend I've got."

"I'll be here, sartin," he promised. He gave her a tentative kiss. She made no objection. "What's your name?" he demanded.

"Bustle—Bustle McQuiston. Missis," she added. "It's me married name." She threw one arm sleepily about his neck.

"All right, Mistress McQuiston," said Salathiel. "But I've got to go now. They promised me work at headquarters."

She didn't believe him, of course, but he didn't care. He crawled back through the hay and made for Captain Ecuyer's quarters.

All the troubles at Fort Pitt, at least for young Albine, were now on the outside of the walls. He felt like a young panther in the spring, trying out its claws on new bark.

17. A Nice Bundling Arrangement

AT HEADQUARTERS Salathiel found the captain out and Johnson fuming. After this, he was told, he was to report early, immediately before reveille. He was to make up the captain's fire, start his breakfast, and lay out his boots and clothes for the day. Also, he was to be damned quiet about it.

Johnson grumbled on.

Actually, the cause of his being disgruntled was that he had come to the decision only the day before to train young Albine to take his place. Once the siege was over, Johnson had finally decided to cast his lot with his wife's family, to go entirely American. The cloak of valet and general factotum was then to fall on Salathiel. When the young fellow had not come on time, Johnson had been anxious. Yet it would never do to let Salathiel see that.

As a matter of fact, there was no one else to take Johnson's place, if young Albine would not. The personnel of the Royal Americans was such that only the roughest kind of orderly or officer's servant could be had from them at best. That might do for the subalterns, but not for the commandant. And among the frontiersmen, farmers, traders, and workmen of Pittsburgh, now crowded into the fort, Johnson could think of no promising candidates for the post of valet to Captain Ecuyer.

He had been quick to realize, however, that in young Albine fresh from the forest, raw though he was, lay a virgin field for cultivation free from the tares of any civilized prejudices. He determined to reap his own harvest from that field even though he would have to clear the ground and dig out the primeval stumps. In fact, for various reasons he preferred it that way. He wanted to have a faithful and competent successor.

For in deciding to set up for himself as a trader or farmer, Johnson could not bear to see the captain left neglected. Both a professional pride and a personal obligation to Ecuyer forbade. Indeed, he had rather a poor conscience about leaving the captain at all. But he couldn't go back to England and a break would have to come. He intended to trade or take up land. Everything grew out of land. The shaving incident of the day before had, as though by a natural mandate, appointed the person of his necessary substitute. To Johnson, young Albine now seemed to have been indicated as though he had been chosen by lot.

Of all this Salathiel, of course, had no inkling. In drawing the line about eating with a servant, Lieutenant Francis had merely puzzled him. Salathiel regarded his chance of being useful to Captain Ecuyer as both good luck and an honour. In his eyes it was as honourable to brush the captain's shoes as it would have been to fill the pipe of Pontiac.

Not until years afterward did it even occur to Salathiel to think there was anything incongruous in having begun his experience of civilization by being taught by one of the best of English valets the intricate mysteries of the European male toilet in a frontier fort besieged by howling Indians. On the contrary, at the time it seemed not only natural, but inevitable.

So he began that morning on the captain's boots, shoes, straps, saddles, and other leather accoutrements. On the care of leather, on the nature of saddle soap, on the mixing of polishes, on lampblack, pipe clay, and their application, Johnson enlarged, demonstrated, and put his pupil to work.

As a teacher Johnson had the essentials. He was enthusiastic, he was patient, and he knew much more than he taught. He did not smile, therefore, when Albine polished the sole of one of the captain's boots. He merely explained. And both time and the brushes flew. Salathiel was fascinated by a glimpse into the chests and the complicated valet kit. And, in addition, he could see that it was ingeniously made for its intended use. He asked questions, but Johnson insisted on one thing at a time.

"It's leather now," said he. "Next we'll take up the care of clothes and the linens."

There was also the horse, but he said nothing of that yet. It had always hurt him that in America he had had to be a stableboy too. He had lost caste with himself there. So the morning flew.

Pretty soon the captain's leatherwork was impeccable. All his boots, his holsters and saddles shone.

It was then that Johnson began to show his pupil how to go to work on himself. In half an hour Salathiel was a changed man. He looked at himself in the glass, amazed. There was only one thing he would not do. He would not wear a wig. Indeed, in Johnson's third best wig he did look ridiculous. Johnson sighed. He plaited a pigtail onto the boy's top-knot. He felt that was as far as he dared to go.

"When your hair grows," said he, "we can powder it."

Salathiel shook his head.

"But you *will* let it grow?" asked Johnson anxiously.

He agreed to that.

"It will take months," said Johnson. "Until then you'll look like a sailor."

"What's a sailor?" asked his pupil.

"Oh, Lord!" said Johnson. But just then Captain Ecuyer came in.

The captain, despite his stiff leg, was in an affable mood. An express with encouraging news from Fort Bedford had crept in only the night before with tidings of Bouquet's advance to that place. The captain himself had made unexpected progress that morning in reorganizing the affairs of the garrison. He therefore sat down, removed his wig, and leaned back contentedly. Secretly, he was not a little pleased to find his domestic arrangements already on so comfortable a basis. Ecuyer was not an altogether well man. He had received a wound at Quebec some years before which had never healed satisfactorily, and he needed to recruit all the energy he could in the comfort of his own quarters. Albine shaved him under the direction of Johnson, while the latter rebandaged the new wound in his leg.

The new wound from the stone arrowhead had already begun to heal. That, too, was an immense relief. One could never tell. He was good enough to praise the new barber and to commend him for having brought in the lists of white captives on the bark tablets. He enquired about McArdle and for some reason, not evident to Salathiel, seemed amused. But he was also obviously pleased. Those lists were going to be of immense help. He told Albine he had already written to Colonel Bouquet about them. The tribes would no longer be able to fool them. He and the colonel could now name the captives whom they demanded. The chiefs would think they must be mystically informed. A complete copy of the lists should be forwarded to Colonel Bouquet that very night, if a messenger could be found willing to take the risk.

Albine volunteered to go.

"No, no," said the captain, "that was not what I meant, decidedly not." And then, "Can you write?"

"Not very well," Salathiel replied truthfully.

"But well enough, no doubt," insisted Ecuyer. "No, no, we shall keep you here, by all means. A secretary-orderly and a valet-apprentice," he continued, winking at Johnson, "that, and all in one. It is not lightly to be sent out to be scalped." He leaned back luxuriously while Johnson sparingly applied some precious cologne water. There was not much left of it. An odour of verbena filled the room. Salathiel sniffed audibly, and the others laughed at him.

Striking while the iron was in so pleasantly glowing a condition, Johnson suggested the terms of Salathiel's hire. He was not to enlist. He was to remain as the captain's personal attendant. He was to have tuppence a day, his food and clothes. If they moved, the captain would provide a mount. To this, Salathiel eagerly agreed and Ecuyer consented.

"But le bon Dieu only knows when you will be paid, young man," he said ruefully. "I have only ten shillings left in my purse now. I haven't been paid for a year myself, and I had to borrow fifty guineas for my journey here from Quebec. You'll touch no coin until we get back over the mountains. If we ever do," he added.

But to young Albine this was perfect. Money meant nothing to him. He had never seen any coin except the two guineas of Charles II long treasured by Mawakis and now in his pouch. They were soldered on a silver bar and chain black from a century of wear by Indian squaws.

"You can sleep in the back room here," said Johnson to clinch the bargain.

"Oh, I don't think I'll want to do that," he replied. Both the captain and Johnson grinned.

"No?" said the captain. "Why, I thought your wife was across the river!"

"She is," said Salathiel, and wondered why they laughed at him.

"Very well," said Ecuyer, "but I'll want you any evening now to help copy. We'll see if you'll do as well with the quill as the razor."

Johnson nodded significantly. It was a bargain.

Johnson himself clinched it later by presenting his apprentice with an old, but as he said, respectable coat. It had tails and was to be worn only about headquarters. It could be altered to fit.

The captain lay back for his midday nap. He slept soundly from twelve to one. Then he ate. It was his invariable custom. It was one of the secrets of his success. Only a pitched battle could prevent his nap.

Johnson began to lay the table for lunch in the next room. There were four places. The table furnishings came out of a separate kit. A stream of whispered instruction from Johnson kept seeping into Salathiel's ears.

He tried to memorize the process. The little bowls in the big bowls, cup and saucer. The round dishes, soup plates. The knife, fork, and spoon. The napkins remained a mystery until he saw them used. The cloth-covered, neatly set table looked magic. Great chiefs would eat there! At first he regarded setting places as pure ritual. He learned the movements and arrangement by rote. That was why he did so well. Later he saw the meaning of his acts, the end in view. But he was never able to improve on Johnson.

That day at one o'clock precisely the captain stood beside his chair. The three invited officers arrived. Ecuyer drank to the king, apologizing for the whisky. They sat down, and the meal proceeded. Salathiel watched, sitting in a corner. Johnson made occasional explanatory gestures. He cooked at the open fire and served.

There was soup, cabbage and chicken, a plum duff with lighted brandy. Salathiel thought it had caught fire by mistake. Then he was lost in admiration. The white chiefs ate fire, he thought, and smiled at his own lingo. The discharge of a cannon outside, in reality fired at a canoe attempting to pass downriver, nevertheless seemed to the boy from the forest a fitting close to the meal.

The meal, however, continued. The whisky of the three officers was replenished. It was really a council of war. Ecuyer was planning to incorporate all of the militia in the regular companies. The discussion was lively. The boy listened. Then he began to think of Bustle McQuiston. Presently Johnson used him to help wash the dishes. The officers had departed.

Immediately after lunch there was a great blowing of bugles and banging of drums. The entire male population in the fort, except those on actual watch, was assembled. The captain even made a short speech. During the siege he was going to draft all of the militia, and that was every able-bodied man, into the regular garrison. Heads were counted and the men were divided equally amongst the various companies. Those who would not fight should not eat. This applied to Quakers too. Captain Ecuyer was not very patient with Quakers.

"Thou shalt not number my people," muttered one of them.

"Then thou shalt not be numbered among those eating," was the reply.

Necessity and not Scripture was now the basis of authority.

Albine and Johnson found themselves tolled off to the company of Lieutenant Francis. They went on guard that afternoon. There would be drill every morning thereafter. All those under arms were to draw pay and the king's rations. Arms and accoutrements were issued. Many found themselves in boots for the first time. Among them was Salathiel.

A particularly vicious attack on the Monongahela side of the fort, followed by the driving off of some of the cattle still pasturing near Grant's Hill, amply proved the necessity of Captain Ecuyer's strict measures and stiffened the backbone of discipline.

Confident of general consent now, the commandant began to clear up the mess which the interior of the fort presented. Hay and powder were moved under shelter. Families were consigned to regular quarters. Cattle pens were hastily erected. Traders were moved into casemates with all of their goods while boards were laid across the doors for counters. The amount of provisions, particularly the meal and dried meat in private possession, was carefully registered. All the liquor was piled in one shed and put under guard, despite the protests of Mr. Croghan, the Indian agent. Mr. Croghan's remonstrances threatening to become violent, he was put under guard with the liquor, thus becoming at once the object of envy, disciplinary example, and repartee.

Salathiel found himself stationed on the platform of the stockade nearest the point where the two rivers met. From there he could look directly across the Ohio to the mouth of Sawmill Run. There was no activity there whatever. The firing came from the cliffs along the Monongahela south of the fort. The sharpshooters replied. Salathiel longed to be able to use his new gun instead of a musket. It would carry across the river, he was sure.

The rifles of the Pennsylvanians were relied upon for long-distance work. They were uncannily accurate. He watched these riflemen crouching here and there along the ramparts, waiting for the telltale puff of smoke that advertised the position of their enemies. Then they would draw a bead on the spot, wait—wait quietly with the long patience of the hunter—and shoot. But they shot only when they saw something.

Captain Ecuyer came walking along the ramparts commending them for that. He insisted that the Royal Americans should follow the example of the Pennsylvanians. He had a cane and hobbled a little.

Salathiel watched this display of skill with the rifle gun and a desire was born in his heart to be a fine shot. It was like the desire of a musician to have and to master a fine instrument. The Pennsylvanians treated their rifles as though they were fancy girls. They cherished them and pampered them. The long bows of their ancestors had at last found an adequate and a more powerful successor. Their rifles, each made separately by a cunning smith, were individual works of art. They were the most deadly weapons in the world.

Just before twilight a hail of lead descended upon the fort from the heights to the south. There was only one reply from the fort. A rifle cracked. From the top of the high cliff on Coal Hill an Indian sprang into the air and hurtled downward. They heard the crash of his body in the thicket below. A roar went up from the flag bastion. Somebody gave the death helloo. Soldiers could be seen pounding the fortunate marksman on the back. The shooting from the cliffs had suddenly ceased.

The bugles called to mess. Fires leaped in the twilight, suddenly turning a golden colour as darkness fell. The relief appeared, marching along the rampart. A few minutes later Johnson and Salathiel were back at headquarters, preparing supper for Captain Ecuyer.

Afterward the desk candles were lit, and, for the first time, Salathiel sat down that evening to copy out dispatches. He wrote a long flowing hand with wide gaps between words. It was like a lesson set by the Reverend James, only he was writing on paper now. Captain Ecuyer looked at the copy and was satisfied with suggesting a closer space between words. Paper was scarce. The candles burned low. Johnson snuffed them twice. Then he nodded to Albine. "Tomorrow," said he, "on time, you know." Salathiel promised, and once more found himself outside headquarters and alone.

He longed suddenly for the quiet of the forests, the noise of the night wind through the trees. A guard was going about gathering up the innumerable loose dogs. There were lamentations and argument from their owners. Presently the dogs were all thrust together into a closed lean-to against the wall. They began to eat one another with hideous clamour.

Pressing his hands to his ears, Salathiel made his way to the casemate and crawled through the hay. It was quiet and dark in there. The place still smelled sweetly of fragrant grasses. A couple of horses stabled at the front could be heard crunching away. They were eating their way inward. But their threat of disturbance was extremely remote. Now and then the steps of the sentry could be heard slowly passing. Salathiel laughed and stretched out. Someone giggled.

"Are you there, McQuiston?" said he.

"I am," whispered the girl. "Did you bring me my fixin's?"

"I did," he said. "Come on over and we'll eat." He undid a cloth around some fragments from the captain's table he had put aside.

Bustle sat leaning against him, picking a chicken bone. She sighed with contentment. His arm went about her and she laid her head against his shoulder. They talked on in low tones. She had been out only briefly that day, she said. The women about the fires had seemed rather hostile. "I didn't belong to no family," she explained. "I washed up, and I borrowed a comb off a lil gal, and a Mrs. McKee give me somethin' to eat. Then I come back in here. 'Pears more homelike back in the hay with the horses munchin'. Hit's like Pendergasses' old barn back to Raystown. Ain't you goin' fer yer gal?" she enquired with a catch in her voice.

"Soon as can be," he replied. "She's safest acrost at the sawmill now. When I can git a boat acrost, I'll go. There's more Injuns around the fort than you think, and the captain says he won't risk it yet. If I went myself, happen I couldn't get back again. There's other women and children with her, you know. It wouldn't do to jes get 'em scalped. It's best to wait."

Bustle considered this for some time. "I reckon you're right," she said doubtfully.

"If we're agoin' to keep house in here," she said after a while, " 'pears thar's somethin' I oughter tell yer."

He waited.

"I'm agoin' to have a baby, and you'll have to leave me alone. It ain't that I don't like yer," she went on breathlessly. "I know how men are. I'd like to play 'Gallop the Mare to Shappinstown' with you right well. But I've been athinkin' it over, and that don't seem right. He's just daid. And I think I ought to hev me baby before I take me a new man. Anyway," she said, clutching him tightly, "ef you're agoin' to sleep here, you've got to promise to let me alone. I thought I'd be fair and tell you fust off. Maybe you'll go for Jane now?"

"I tell you I *can't* go for Jane now without getting her or me, and maybe a lot of others, to have their hair lifted," he said vehemently. "It ain't you that's keepin' me from goin'. Hit's common sense. Ef'n you don't want me to sleep with you, I'll promise to let you alone. I'm no renegade. I'm jes lonely. I never had no folks sence I was little. It was nice findin' you here. I'll take keer of you ef'n you'll let *me* alone," he said, trying to gain some moral prestige.

She giggled.

"Hit's a bargain then," she said. "I'll try to look after myself in the day. You bring me some fixin's here at night, and we'll not tell nobody. It's nice here," she added after a while. "I hope them horses don't eat their way through from the front. There's no tellin' how long this yere siege is agoin' to last."

"It can't last after the hay and grub gives out," he said. "Bouquet's men will be here from Fort Bedford long before that."

"Aye," she said, "ef'n the Injuns don't stop 'em."

"They're comin'," he said softly but with a kind of doubtful assurance. "Captain Ecuyer says so." They arranged their blankets and lay down together.

"Mind," said she, "hit's only a bundlin' arrangement."

"Jes bundlin'," he said.

She gave him a peck on the mouth. He laughed and they were soon asleep.

A furious fusillade from the Ohio bastion roused him about four in the morning. The whole garrison stood to arms. There were many moccasin tracks seen in the ditch next morning. One of the sentries was dead, shot clean through the heart.

Salathiel and Johnson served the captain's breakfast. The work of the day went on. It was absolutely quiet. The Indians seemed to have withdrawn. Johnson began to show his pupil how to launder linens.

In the afternoon Salathiel had a talk with one of the gunsmiths. He showed him the fowling piece Lieutenant Francis had given him. It was beautifully chased. "Mighty purty fer shootin' lil birds," said the gunsmith. "I *could* fix it fer business, maybe," he admitted after a while.

"It's Spanish steel by the look of it. I ain't never seed a gun with two barrels afore," he added. Then they brought four of the king's horses in to be shod, and he returned to the bellows.

Salathiel began to ponder about the gun. "It could be fixed." He remembered that. For the first time the desirability of money occurred to him. How much would it cost? he wondered.

18. A Mercenary View of Affairs

CAPTAIN ECUYER was a Swiss mercenary—but to suppose that that phrase was adequately descriptive of this Homeric little man would be an ignorant indictment of language. Ecuyer was naturally addressed as "your Honour" by discerning men of virtue and paid the compliment of being called a son of a bitch by villains.

But even that gamut was insufficient, for he was not so easily tagable or to be had in a word.

To both his superiors and his inferiors there was never anything elusive, but there was always something mysterious about the man; the impact of his personality seemed invariably to produce an effect greater than its visible cause. And it was that, plus a kind of radiation of invincible courage, which awed savages and made even the sophisticated respectful.

Those who came in contact with him at all intimately sensed in the indescribable flavour of the man's presence and the pleasantly ironical pitch of his talk a humorous ripeness of experience, a poised consideration and affability, combined with a latent capacity for anger which it might be terrible to evoke.

Both he and Colonel Henri Bouquet looked forward to retirement, when the wars were over, to cultivate their own gardens in neighbourly companionship. And for that purpose they had together secured adjacent plantations on the borders of Maryland near Frederick, situated in some extremely pleasantly wooded and kindly watered land.

Now, the strange thing about this plantation where the captain expected to pass an amiable old age was that it did not, at least in his own mind, interfere at all with his equally cherished plan of spending his old age in Geneva. Apparently the captain was going to have two old ages to spend. He was not unaware of this little difficulty ahead, he even regarded it whimsically. But he was not at all unwilling to have two strings to the rainbow of his future, and there was also the consideration, always present in the mind of the soldier, that he might not have any old age to spend anywhere. The captain's nice balancing of this matter was, indeed, somewhat complex.

It was a good thing to have land. Everybody who was anybody, even nobodies in America, took up land. Johnson, the valet, was going in for land. Colonel Bouquet had finally persuaded Ecuyer into the arrangement of the plantation. It was an intimate arrangement, helpful even now. The prospect of being neighbours and veteran friends in the future made his association with the colonel more pleasantly personal in the present. And if Ecuyer could once "seat himself" on his plantation, if he became the master of a house, servants, and acres, he could write "esquire" after his name with a good conscience. And that was a consideration not to be sneezed at even in the colonies. Major Simeon Ecuyer, Esquire, was the style he looked forward to and fancied. Possibly colonel, if he had luck. Of all this, naturally enough, he said nothing except to Bouquet, who always encouraged him. But the mere prospect of thus solidly settling down tended to enhance the captain's prestige in his own eyes. This was not mere vanity. It seemed to promise some tangible reward and comfort for years of hazard and barbaric hardships innumerable.

As for Geneva—that was another matter. There was a lady there. Lucille was her name. The captain had been formally betrothed to her as a youth. His father's prospects had been brilliant then for a city advocate, particularly after the ancient suit about the city wall had been settled, and the family of Lucille had condescended only a little for substantial reasons and because of friendship in betrothing Lucille to Simeon. The tragedy was that the young people had actually fallen in love with each other later on.

There had been one wonderful winter in Palermo, where Lucille's mother had gone for her health, accompanied by Lucille and the Ecuyers. The odour of orange or lemon blossoms was still moonlight and music to the captain when he thought of that time. Then reverses had come. His father had died suddenly. His mother was left with nothing but a small pension secured in the English funds. And Simeon had gone for a soldier of fortune to fight for the king of Sardinia. In the end, he comforted himself by thinking it was not Lucille but her parents who proved unfaithful.

Lucille had promised. She said she would wait. She loved him. But the campaign in Piedmont and the Islands had been long. Letters at best were difficult, and the lustre of foreign laurels doubtful. When he had returned after nearly four years on a lieutenant's stipend, Lucille was married to the richest and most eloquent minister of the largest church in the canton of Vaud. They lived in a beautiful chalet by the lake in the summer. And Ecuyer had seen her once there, a distant view from a boat, walking in her garden. And he had seen her once again in church, where she had got up precipitately and walked out when he gazed earnestly at her.

That was all, except for a small, ebony box which the captain cherished. In it was a miniature set with small brilliants, a withered spray of lemon blossoms, and a wisp of straw-coloured hair. If these had once been too frequently bedewed by the tears of anguish of a young soldier, they were now looked upon dry-eyed by an older one only semi-occasionally—yet still, as the years went on, with a growing sense and maturer realization of the loss of what might have been. His disappointment was abysmal, his affection final, and the small ebony box was in reality the coffin in which reposed the still darling image of his stolen love.

Dreams that arise from, that hover about the fountain of life, and are forever forbidden, die at best but lingering deaths. And it was some compensation to the captain to garb his little tragedy with at least a consoling cerecloth of hope—hope that the doctor of God who had married Lucille might be called by his Maker to an accounting in heaven. Many an accomplished soldier has married a widow after the battles of both are over. And even the thin probability of it was balm of Gilead, recalled forcefully to Ecuyer's memory by the scent of verbena in his nostrils, and to his anticipation by the word "Geneva" on his lips.

For the rest, Ecuyer was content. He had not been soured even by so bitter an experience. He was too essentially strong and clear in nature for that. He had his profession, his mind, and his honour. He solaced his loneliness by a certain well-concealed sympathy with others, which brought him companionship. He was prone to relent, sometimes at the last moment, from inflicting extreme penalties. And he had gradually discovered that to agree suddenly with an obstinate opponent is quite frequently to take him at the unexpected disadvantage of his own terms.

As for the rest?—Well, the rest was not silence. For the living it was something more salutary. The rest was conversation and routine.

All the captain's conversations, however, were not held aloud. He had his mind and his books. There was a small chest of the latter, well filled, and a large library in the former arranged conveniently for reference. Both accompanied him wherever he went.

Fully to understand the captain's wide opportunities for silent conversation, to glimpse his intimate routine, and to appreciate why he was always a bit mysterious even to his friends, could best be accomplished, perhaps, by stepping into the small bedroom back of headquarters at Fort Pitt some evening when the captain was alone.

At Fort Pitt it was his habit to retire fairly early whenever he could. After young Albine had finished copying out the last orders and dispatches and left, Johnson would light the large brass, sperm lamp in front of headquarters, lock up the desk, chests, and cupboards, and rid up. He would then help the captain pull off his boots, bring his small shoes, and build up a brief fire in the bedroom to take off the chill. He would leave one candle burning by Ecuyer's bed, snuff out all the others, and say good night.

The officer of the day, seeing headquarters darkening, would immediately report to receive his instructions and the parole and countersign.

Ecuyer prided himself in always referring in these countersigns to something loyal and English, and in never writing them out until the last thing at night. Thus there was no means of learning them in advance by anybody.

On Friday, June 3, 1763, Lieutenant James Francis reported a little after ten o'clock and found the captain in a cheerful mood with the prospect of a possible night's sleep before him, since there had been a lull of two days in any attacks in force.

Tomorrow would be the new king's birthday and Ecuyer gave orders that the men were to receive a dram that evening for their good behaviour, and another the following day to mark the royal anniversary. Since all the rum was exhausted, it was understood that the drams would have to be whisky. That, to tell the truth, worried Ecuyer more than it did Lieutenant Francis.

"And," said the captain, opening and reading directly from the orderly book, as he often did—

> ". . . the commanding officer desires his thanks to be given to the garrison in general for their assiduity in carrying on this work with such good spirit and dispatch, and for the future orders that but one-half of the garrison off duty be ordered for work in the forenoon and to be relieved by the other half in the afternoon."

The lieutenant looked pleased, and the captain nodded, for they both understood that this curtailing of constant labour would be even better news to the garrison than the extra drams.

Ecuyer then remarked that the parole for tomorrow would be "the king," and the countersign "George", that it was still strangely cold for this time of year, but fine clear weather and no excuse for a surprise. To which proposition the lieutenant carefully agreed, saluted, received the commanding officer's hearty good night—and retired.

A cannon exploded violently on the music bastion and a red glare washed the windows of the room. Francis had probably poured train oil into the moat and lit it. They could pick Indians off the banks by rifle fire in the glare of the flames. The captain listened. Several rifles popped. Probably they wouldn't have to call him. It was just the routine procedure during a minor attack. Undoubtedly the noise tonight was unusually vociferous.

Ecuyer smiled and blew out the candle. For some time he continued to look wide-eyed into the darkness. Just now the dogs had it. They were barking, wailing, and yapping at the moon. There was also the undiminished noise of the garrison and the "inhabitants". It slowly grew less in Ecuyer's ears after he closed his eyes. Deep down in himself, almost on the borders of sleep, Ecuyer knew what that noise was about. It was a protest against loneliness. The fort not only was besieged by savages, it was ringed about, positively threatened by the eternal silence of the forest. At any moment that silence might close in.

He struggled for a moment against it and succumbed.

There was no attack that night. Captain Ecuyer slept soundly. In the morning Salathiel awakened him. He was always on time now. There was a great deal to do.

19. How Salathiel Lost an Ear

IT WAS an enormously fortunate accident for young Albine that he had come to headquarters at Fort Pitt when the remarkable team of Ecuyer and Johnson were still working together at their professional best.

To the youth raw from the forest, the transition to civilized life might well have been purely aimless. It might have left him without any point of reference, lost in a chaos of new and confusing impressions. Salathiel was given a way of life and a direction by stepping into the old shoes of Johnson.

To be devoted to one thing and to make all other things subservient to it, to persist to the finish although not necessarily the logical end, is to become something and someone; to acquire a character adequate and necessary to master circumstances. Finally, it is to be able to steer a course through the otherwise mysterious fluid of events, because there is a constant point of reference in view.

Ecuyer and his valet, Johnson, afforded a nice illustration of this. They differed greatly in degree, but not actually in kind.

The captain's singleness of purpose arose largely from a simple, yet a complete professional loyalty to his chosen sovereign. Monarchy has long been an effective lodestar for individuals as well as for tribes and nations of men. It is, in fact, difficult to find a better one. To Captain Ecuyer the interests of the British crown were, while he served it, his own. And in thus following his profession completely he was also satisfactorily loyal to himself.

Johnson's point of reference was much simpler, but essentially similar. He aimed to be a perfect valet to the man who had hired and befriended him. Like Ecuyer, he did not have to stay permanently hired. Yet while he was serving he was completely and professionally detained.

The three small headquarters rooms at Fort Pitt were the abode not only of men, but of the fixed purpose which they embodied. Order, neatness, and a vast organized intention lived there. To step out of those rooms was to step into a barbaric chaos frightened by its own confusion. Yet during the comparatively short time that he stayed at Fort Pitt, particularly during the days of the siege, young Albine saw order, neatness, and organized action spread from the three rooms at headquarters until they completely embraced and included all of the fort and its environs. That he had an intimate and direct part in this process was good luck in education.

For Salathiel at least, the lesson was conveyed only in personal terms. It was "Captain Ecuyer and Mr. Johnson". He was not so dull as not to understand the difference in the importance of the parts they played. But he also saw that they both played them well. The models he began copying made him ambitious to act well himself, and in that lay his salvation from savagery. Captain Ecuyer became his hero; Johnson his tutor in how to serve him. Thus the siege and Salathiel's education, the larger containing the smaller experience, went on. And it was much the same for a great many others.

The siege of Fort Pitt was what in European parlance would have been described as "a desultory investment of a fortress". There were no siege lines strictly drawn by the enemy, no scientifically constructed approaches that closed in by degrees until the wall could be breached and the place overwhelmingly assaulted. Indeed, it was that kind of attack that Captain Ecuyer most desired. But the Indians were too cunning, far too naturally informed, to provide the good captain with so convenient an opportunity for thus slaughtering them en masse.

To begin with, there were not enough of them. They produced an effect of numbers by strategy. In reality they were always much fewer than the English thought. They preferred, and they had to fight, the kind of war where every man and every shot counted. Attrition, treachery, surprise, unseen menace was their game. In besieging a fort they always awaited that not impossible opportunity, that moment of unconscious relaxation on the part of the garrison or some of its sentinels, that would open a closed way. To bring this about they perpetually resorted to incessant cajolery.

Scarcely a day passed when some Indian did not appear singing and without weapons, calling upon the name of Mr. McKee, Mr. Trent, or Mr. Croghan, and claiming to bring news. Captured letters seized from murdered messengers would be brought in by them, after having been opened and read by white prisoners. For these, which they pretended to be delivering as a matter of courtesy, they demanded tobacco, bread, and vermilion. Traders' supplies were running low. Plunder from the inhabitants did not make up for the lack of steady trade. At first Mr. Mckee or Croghan would go out to meet them. At last they were admitted to see only Captain Ecuyer himself.

His stern demands that they must prove their friendship by delivering up their prisoners, his threats of the armies approaching to relieve the fort and chastise them, above all his refusal to provide them with lead and powder or weapons and food, amazed them. They were not used to being given tongue lashings by their white father, followed by no presents. To some chiefs who still demanded gifts Ecuyer passed out the blankets and handkerchiefs from the smallpox hospital.

Finally, a party paraded with English colours and a stolen drum before the fort. Then they crossed the river and kept crying out for an opportunity to talk. Two soldiers who were sent across in a boat to parley with them were attacked suddenly and knifed. They barely escaped, one nearly knifed to death. A load of grapeshot at last scattered the band.

That night several houses were set on fire up the Allegheny valley in revenge. Croghan's fine establishment some miles up that river disappeared in flames. A sentry was stealthily murdered. After that there was no further pretence of making talk.

All day, all night, and the day following, a steady stream of rifle fire from the heights and hills about was poured into the fort. It cut the roofs to pieces. Everyone, man, woman, or child, who became careless and conspicuous, brought a swarm of bullets about his ears. The hospital began rapidly to fill up with wounded. The dead were buried at night. The garrison stood continually to arms. The casks along the ramparts were filled after dark by women. Those who would not carry water were refused rations. Fire arrows fell and were quenched. Every morning the signs of the enemy having been in the ditch and along the riverbanks, even in the Artillery Garden, were numerous. There was no relaxation.

Then the attacks ceased as suddenly as they had begun. The woods and hills all about were silent. At night only the owls hooted. There was not a sign of an Indian. The settlers began to drive out their cattle to pasture again. They cut spelts and even brought in unripe ears of corn from abandoned fields. Nothing happened.

The quiet was menacing, but to Salathiel a relief. He began to long to go hunting. For even the people in the fort were quiet now.

A great change had come over Fort Pitt and all its inhabitants. The days of attack had enabled Captain Ecuyer to enforce the stern discipline which he professed. It was enforced even upon the dogs. Nothing sounded now but the bugles and the call of the sentinels every hour all night, post by post. "All's well."

It was during this lull that young Albine finally went across the river to get Jane.

He went alone. He could get no one to go with him. Captain Ecuyer would not permit it. He would not refuse Salathiel's plea to fetch his wife, but no one else was to risk his scalp. And, indeed, that was the best arrangement. For there might be several others with Nymwha who would wish to return to the fort in the canoe. Salathiel took a canoe. He could manage that best, and it was silent and swift.

Late on a dark night he glided out of the moat, kept in the shadow of the riverbank, and then drifted out into the stream past the point. Word had been passed, but a nervous sentry fired at him and the bullet

whistled close past his head. Despite the possible alarm to lurking enemies he decided to push on.

There was no trouble at all. In the deep shadow of a long cloud that
floated across the stars he drifted noiselessly into the mouth of Sawmill
Run. The skeleton of the mill, burnt now, stood gauntly against the sky.
There was not a sign of a dim fire or a sound. Presently against the stars
he saw the prongs of a stag feeding upon the fresh herbage along the
millrace. Certainly no one was near. Nevertheless, he took no chances.

He beached the canoe in a thicket and made a silent crawl through
the woods upstream to the encampment of Nymwha. The lodges were
gone. Everything, even the poles, had been removed. The ashes of the
fires were many days old. He ran his fingers through them and could
feel the small blades of grass coming through. Gone, many days ago! A
sudden longing for Jane, stronger than he had supposed could possess
him, came over him. He had a feeling she was lost.

He lay still with his cheek on his bare arm listening to the stream. It
spoke sorrowfully to the forest. It seemed to lament its loneliness softly
but eloquently. He lay and listened.

A twig snapped somewhere. Now he saw the green eyes of a small
night animal watching him. They caught the glimmer from the water
and reflected it. He felt relieved. Then he saw something else. A white
blaze on a near-by tree. He got up and walked over to it. There were
marks on it but you could not read them in the starlight. And only the
remnant of a moon was beginning to rise. He had better not wait. Soon
it would be bright on the river. Bright enough to see a canoe.

He poured some powder out on a chip of bark and snapped his pistol
lock into it. There was a flash that made the shadows jump away. On the
blaze he saw an arrow pointing south, four big marks and three little
ones underneath. The darkness jumped back.

Almost at the same instant there was a blinding report and the side of
his head seemed on fire.

He streaked for the stream and plunged in. His left ear had been shot
away. He swam underwater as far as he could. When he looked back he
could see the shadow of a man working himself along the bank. It would
be slow going there. He dived again and swirled down the stream. He
was leaving the man behind. The cold water was balm to his wound, but
his head roared like a waterfall. If they had seen him hide his canoe he
was done. But they hadn't. He reached it and shot out into the river.
Someone came crashing through the thicket behind him. It was half a
minute, however, before a shot rang out.

He swept the canoe upstream with powerful strokes, calling out as he
neared the fort. The salty blood ran into his mouth. They let him in
through the small postern. They thought at first he had been scalped.
Salathiel was furious at the surgeon for laughing as he bandaged his ear.

"A close call," said the surgeon, admiring his bandages. "You're lucky."

"I'm a damn fool, sir," said Albine bitterly. "I ought to have known better than to flash that powder. Only an Indian musket would have missed me. He must have heard me and been waiting there all the time. It ain't only my ear I've lost. It's my wife."

"I still say you're lucky," said the surgeon.

Salathiel held his hand over his ear and wondered.

So Jane and the other women and children had gone south. Probably they'd make for the settlements. Where? Virginia? Maybe he would hear if they ever got there. Maybe? His ear was gone.

He went and bundled in with Bustle. She was kind and kissed him and kept cold cloths on the side of his head. Next morning he showed up to help Johnson, as usual. Captain Ecuyer listened to his story and said nothing except "Mind you keep a patch on your ear." That afternoon Johnson let him leave work to go to sleep. Salathiel was surprised to find that he no longer missed Jane. He thought less and less about her. She was gone—south.

20. In Which a Casemate Proves Unkind

SOME DAYS there would be no attacks on the fort at all. A seeming peace would settle down on the whole region. There would not be a sign of the enemy. Not even a distant smoke plume rising above the forests.

From the brick parapets on the east stretched a series of gardens and meadows as far as the foot of Grant's Hill a quarter of a mile away. They were full of tall trees dotted about the meadows, of sweet English grasses which had just begun to appear in that part of the country. They were full of cellar holes with here and there a field of German spelts and the remains of the settlers' corn planted the year before.

Those east-lying meadows, and the Artillery Walk on the north, or Allegheny, side of the fort were a constant temptation to the confined garrison and the inhabitants of Pittsburgh.

Let there be the slightest encouragement of the return of peace, and they would drive out the cattle to graze in the fields. They would scatter to gather spelts and the Indian corn for meal and roasting ears. Or in the Artillery Walk the women would be seen doing their washing about great kettles and tubs, sousing their white things in the river, making soap, and hanging up fluttering garments, while the children looked for green apples under the trees that General Forbes had had planted some years before. When a week or ten days of such a lull occurred, discipline was invariably relaxed. It was such times that Captain Ecuyer feared most as the opportunity for a surprise attack.

He did all he could to ward off the ill effects of false security. Those who went to work in the fields or to graze cattle were protected by a screen of troops. And these were not too scattered. After a near riot he met a committee of the women and arranged for a Monday washday, and no other. So on Monday the artillerymen stood by with lighted matches and the riflemen watched.

A parade of the troops was sometimes held in the late afternoon outside the walls. The scarlet-and-green uniforms, the weapons flashing in the sun, the roll of drums and the squalling of fifes carried defiance to ears attentive in the forests.

The effect of parade, drill, and obedience without argument had already brought about a new spirit among the militia incorporated into the regular ranks. It fell to Salathiel and Johnson's company to go out into the thickets and watch while the work went on behind them in the fields.

Albine enjoyed these occasions greatly. To be beyond the walls in the sunshine and free air raised his spirits, and made him feel free again. And it was amusing then to talk to Johnson. The little valet became a different man. He would lie behind a log scanning the countryside for enemies and the near-by hills for a likely place to fix upon as his future farm. They would talk over this farm and the kind of life to be lived there, by the hour. Johnson would contrast the ways of the New World with the Old.

Then he would suddenly fall silent, look sidewise at Salathiel, and remember presently to praise the advantages of being a perfect gentleman's servant, and the brilliance and luxury of life in England, even when seen from the servants' hall.

It was such glimpses of the great world which most interested and intrigued the boy from the forests. He could never ask questions enough. At least, at the very least, he would go downcountry and see the settlements.

It seemed as though the Indians themselves would at times come to the aid of Captain Ecuyer. Let a lull last a few days and the inhabitants would inevitably begin to grumble at the restrictions which he so rigorously enforced. Some woman would insist upon washing on Tuesday, or someone would wander too idyllically in the Artillery Walk, or stray too far after a cow.

Invariably a murder then took place. The cow and the man would be missing. A bullet would zip through a pair of breeches just washed by Mrs. Jones. And then suddenly, quietly, without any warning, the ditch would be full of devils with fire arrows all night. A fusillade would break from the cliffs. The death helloo would announce the return of a successful scalping party from the settlements.

For a week the riverbanks would be full of howling enemies waiting for a lucky shot at a sentry as he passed a loophole, or to scalp a bather. The gates would be tight shut, the forage would run low, and fuel would give out. Terror and secret despair would descend again, and with it discipline, always a little stronger and a steadier increase of discipline, enforced by the enemy more drastically than Captain Ecuyer himself could have dreamed of doing.

Those who disobeyed perished. The obstinate individual who smartly evaded some rule he felt to be beneath his dignity to observe contributed a scalp. As time went on the garrison became not only willing but even mentally smart. As their uniforms grew faded and worn, their weapons shone the brighter, their aim became surer, and their spirit more certain.

"Hammer the Americans hard enough," said Captain Ecuyer, "and you forge the best weapon in the world." The strategy of the Indians was making a keen and beautiful weapon. "The best of the provincials are better than the regular troops," wrote Ecuyer to Colonel Bouquet. "But hurry your arrival here. I boasted of provisions for three years to the chiefs instead of the three months that I have."

"Patience, in the autumn," replied the colonel. "Hold out, hold hard. I am trying to gather provisions to feed my own troops and to let the West Indian regiments recover from their fevers. The general sent me every last man he could sweep out of the hospitals. I am bringing some on wagons. Not a single one of the country people here has joined my ranks."

Meanwhile, the savages harassed the frontiers. DeTroit and Niagara alone held out, all the rest had fallen. All but Fort Pitt. And, meanwhile, there was much time to pass there, many things to be done.

For Salathiel day after day the quiet instruction of Johnson had gone on. He was now, so far as Captain Ecuyer was concerned, a satisfactory military servant and a good man. He did all the leather, looked after the captain's horse, washed, furbished the weapons, barbered, and helped wait on the table. There his progress was slower.

The mystery of cooking, cooking in a civilized way, came slowly. Johnson taught him dish by dish.

It was really quite simple at first. A few chickens, some eggs, a rare green snatched from the neglected gardens by one of the settlers, potatoes, onions, and salted beef and pork were the staples. And there were beans, bags of them brought clear from England and hauled over the mountains on the backs of horses. The officers had a little fine flour but it, too, finally ran out. After that they lived on corn bread, johnnycake, "maize", as Captain Ecuyer called it.

In one thing Salathiel excelled. He could bake corn bread and Indian pudding beyond compare. Johnson was seldom successful there. Like most Europeans he simply couldn't take maize seriously. Or he treated it like wheat flour. Salathiel took considerable satisfaction in Johnson's flat failures with corn bread, and the captain's remarks about it, while Johnson sighed for wheat flour and wine.

Wine! How could one cook without it? This to Johnson and the cap-

tain was the chief hardship of the siege. Some precious brandy obtained
at a great price from Mr. Croghan was eked out. It saved resorting to
whisky. But to the inhabitants the absence of wine was no hardship.
Most of them had never tasted it. There was lots of whisky, the good
Monongahela corn or rye. It could be had for credit at a frightful price
or wheedled from the soldiers. One way or another it was to be had. It
made life tolerable, evenings merry.

On Monday and Saturday evenings the officers held a club, "The
Club".

"Club" was a fresh word that held a combination of snobbery, exclu-
siveness, and conviviality about it. Not everyone could have a club. Not
the "mob", also a new cant word. Gentlemen might form a club and invite the "ladies". They were invited at Fort Pitt, all the gay Molls. The
respectable wives of traders were not invited.

The club made a good deal of hard feeling in the garrison. Most of
the girls were Irish. Their finery was both weird and pathetic. Hoop
skirts were decreed. No linsey-woolsey would do. The traders' stores, Indian fancy goods for vain and childish squaws, were drawn upon and
selected from with considerable rivalry. A half-breed French packer
bound for old Vincennes was discovered to have some lace. The chief
difficulty was shoes and stockings. It was curious to see a girl with her
hair powdered, rouged with Indian vermilion, but with bare feet.
Beaded moccasins were the usual compromise. "One thing," said Captain Ecuyer, "you colonial officers will have to learn now not to step on
a lady's feet in the dance."

They used the big storehouse nearly empty now of rations. It had a
plank floor. There were three fiddlers, artillery lanthorns and Lieutenant Francis' candelabra for illumination. There was much stamping, a
tall cutting of capers. Now and then came a quadrille for the sake of eti-
quette. These were always languid. The country dances were popular
and jigs by the Irish girls, while the rest of the company sat around on
bales and chests.

At midnight by special dispensation the colour guard came for the
colours and the whole "rout" paraded behind fife and drum as the flags
were returned to headquarters.

Johnson and Salathiel served supper there with the captain as official
host. The jugs of Monongahela made up for any lack of sillabubs. The
girls sat around on the officers' knees. The absence of stockings seemed
to worry no one, even to be appreciated.

All in all, the club was a success. Its midnight parade brought out
all of Pittsburgh there was in the fort. The procession aroused venomous
comments, and maledictions from the pious. Quakers pulled their hats
down over their eyes. A few ministers pronounced the girls lost, in
audible tones, as they made behind the drums for headquarters. Some of
the older women complained. But cheers for the pretty girls from the

soldiers, the asides and comment on the finery by the ladies not invited, a good supper, whisky, and ardent officers prevailed against respectability and hell's fire. Candidates for the primrose path comprised nearly every unmarried woman under fifty. Those under twenty were chosen.

What was the surprise of Salathiel one Saturday club night when Bustle McQuiston appeared at headquarters and sat on the knee of Lieutenant Francis. Somehow he felt Bustle belonged to him. Also she did not look as though she were having a child at all. She wore an old, white velvet bodice that Mrs. McKee had given her. It was trimmed with black. She managed her hoop skirt made from old flag bunting and barrel hoops a little awkwardly, but somehow delightfully. "The black is because I'm a widow," she explained. Young Albine wondered why a roar went up from the officers at this.

But she and Lieutenant Francis got on very well. Everyone congratulated him on his widow. Bustle didn't return to the casemate the night of that first dance. Salathiel slept there alone. He was enraged at first, and thought of shooting Francis with his own gun. It seemed a remarkable revenge, so good that he decided to talk it over with Bustle first. But she didn't come back the next night either. Salathiel observed that the horse on the outside had almost eaten his way inside. He missed Bustle. On the third night she returned. She sat eating the fragments of the captain's dinner he had brought her in silence. The darkness seemed a barrier between them.

"Like it?" he said.

"Lieutenant Francis has a better cook," she replied. "I'm more partial to his chicken."

"Maybe it ain't jes his chicken you're so partial to," he countered.

"Happen it ain't," she retorted.

"So all the time you were lyin' to me about yer baby, eh?" he drawled.

"All the time," she admitted.

That hurt.

"What made ye do it, Bustle?"

"Oh, I jes wanted fer to see what you'd do," she answered.

It was so unexpected and casual that he sat amazed and silent. That seemed to worry her.

"You didn't do nothin' about it," she continued afterwhile half accusingly.

"I kept my promise," he shouted angrily. "That's more 'en you did."

"I didn't promise anything. I jes hoped," she giggled.

"And got the captain's fixin's every evening and a warm sleep. I didn't think you were jes a blanket girl."

"The fixin's kinda come in handy, afore I got to know my way round the fort."

"I guess you know yer way around pretty God-stricken' well now, don't ye?" he rejoined.

"That's why they call me Bustle," she said quietly. "I bustle around and I gits thar."

"Oh, you do, do yer!" His hand shot out in the darkness and grabbed her arm. She gave a frightened little shout. He drew her close to him.

"How about playin' 'Gallop the Mare to Shappinstown'?" he whispered. "How about bustlin' around with me?"

She lay quiet in his arms, her head against his breast. But he seemed to be supplying all the warmth. Not like Jane, he thought. The McQuiston was saying something. He lost the first part of it.

". . . and I don't need the captain's fixin's no more," was the last. A surge of fury came over him. He threw her down on the hay.

"I'll *fix* you," he said. She laughed under him. Her arms came about his neck.

"Wait, Sal. Wait till I kin slip out of me things," she pouted.

That was all right. He let her go. He could hear her rustling in the hay.

"It's me bustle," she whispered, "it's tied on." The rustling continued. Then it ceased. He lay waiting.

"Well?" he said, and reached for her.

But Bustle and her bustle had both gone.

There was dead silence. Outside the horse suddenly resumed champing hay. A rush of fury brought flashes of light to his eyes in the darkness. He sprang up automatically under the surge of it and rushed out.

There was no one outside the casemate. Only the stars overhead and the narrow brick alley down the side of the main wall behind the barracks, with marks of Bustle's bare feet in the puddles. The horse snorted at him. He gave it a great slap on the behind just as the sentry came around the corner.

"Did you see a gal pass ye?" demanded Salathiel.

"No, I didn't see no gal," said the sentry witheringly. "An' who are you loiterin' around slappin' the leftenant's mare on the arse. Git along wid ye, or I'll turn you in. Let's have a look at you."

It was then that young Albine discovered that God had given him great strength.

Without meaning to do so, he spasmodically took the sentry by the belt and the coattails and threw him, musket and all, clear up onto the parapet. He was a small man, to be sure. But it was about a twelve-foot throw. On the parapet above, the man landed with a tremendous clatter. His musket flashed in the pan. The guard came running.

"Here, here," said the boyish voice of Lieutenant Francis, "what the devil are you doing up here off your beat, Number Four? How the hell did you get onto the parapet?"

"A young giant come out of the dark, sir, and threw me up here out of the alley!"

"He's drunk," said the lieutenant. "Put him in irons for desartin' his post. I'll prefer charges tomorrow."

The man was led off protesting; getting into deeper water with every explanation.

Salathiel stood below in the shadows, listening. It gave him satisfaction that someone was in trouble. He patted the mare's neck and laughed grimly. He wasn't the only one that could be fooled, it appeared. The sentry would get twenty-five lashes at least, maybe fifty. Good!

He crawled back into the hay and lay down in his blanket alone. Passion, disappointment, and anger made him shake as though he had an ague. Afterward a kind of torpor ensued. He slept exhaustedly. In the morning he was wakened by a whinny. The mare had finally eaten her way through. Her head protruded through the hay into the little compartment behind. He patted her and laughed. "There's nothing here, darling," said he. "The place is bloody empty." He shook the grass out of his hair and left to start the day at headquarters. Romance had died in the casemate for Salathiel Albine.

From then on he began to acquire the fanatical devotion of Johnson to his work. The older man noted it and was pleased. As soon as Colonel Bouquet relieved the fort he was going to go and live by the riverbank and trade. The farm would come later. He could leave the captain now with good conscience. All that Albine had to learn yet was the care of digs, the dressing of hair.

For Salathiel the mystery of curling irons, the way to mix pomade with candle wax so that it would stand up in a hot climate, the nice art of powdering and tying the hair in a bag, took the place of worrying about Bustle and Lieutenant Francis.

He had given up his idea of shooting the lieutenant. Instead he was going to have the lieutenant's gift made over into a Pennsylvania rifle.

Rafe Carmichael, the gunsmith, was a powerful and ingenious man. He had never seen a "carbine gun" with two barrels before. How to make a rifle out of it aroused his ingenuity. He and Salathiel struck up quite a friendship discussing the problem. Rafe agreed finally to do the work for one guinea the barrel. That, indeed, was why he decided to keep the gun double barrelled. He found Salathiel had two guineas. He took them off the bar by which they had hung about the neck of Mawakis and polished them up. The long bewigged countenance of Charles II gleaming with a slightly red tinge from the good Guinea gold fired his avarice and ambition. He would make a good long rifle out of the English carbine piece for the "Injun boy", as he called young Albine—or he was no gunsmith.

They worked together at night after the long labour of the day was over. It took nearly two weeks.

The gunsmith was proud of his work. He insisted that young Albine must do him credit by using the gun right. They spent hours before the summer was over in the ditch of the fort shooting at a mark. Old hunters sat around drawling their advice. Salathiel became a marksman. He had a steady hand and eye. He fell in love with the gun. He was so proud of it he took it around to show to Lieutenant Francis. They became friendly again. The lieutenant was extremely decent; ". . . so I reckon I won't shoot you with it, after all," said Salathiel, grinning.

"What d'ya mean?" said Francis, who was not entirely reassured by the grin. Salathiel explained. He was now able to tell how Bustle had fooled him as a good joke on himself. The lieutenant was not entirely amused, however.

"So you left me to ride both horses, by Gad; the lady and the mare you slapped, and had the fowling piece made over into a rifle with homicidal intent. How about the sentry? He's posted for fifty lashes!" The young officer looked serious.

"That's what I really come to tell you," said Salathiel. "I wanted to get him let off, and you'd have to know why."

"Quite," sighed Francis. "Here," said he, suddenly turning less thoughtful, and pouring out a nip of brandy, "here's to a narrow escape from murder and a warning to you, you young American scalp. You're getting along in the world now, a little too fast maybe. You're the captain's man. Don't let it go to your head. Let the king's sentries alone and don't plan to murder your officers. Treason is imagining the death of the king, you know. The guilt lies in the thought."

"I've been thinkin'," said Salathiel.

The lieutenant nodded. He wanted the interview to be over.

"What I came to say is that when I heard your voice on the parapet that night I got kind of shamed and I thought I might jes say that maybe Bustle will get tired of your fixin's, too."

"Just you leave that to me," said Francis, grinning himself now.

"I'll do that, sir," replied Albine, "good luck."

"Damn his cheek," mumbled the lieutenant, and then thought better of it as he wrote out a release for the sentry. "I'll take another Moll to the next dance, though." He wrote his elder brother in England a long letter that night.

. . . the lieutenant's pen ran on, discovering a rather homesick and lonely young man sitting quite solitary by a candle in a small room at Fort Pitt. London was astronomically distant.

There was a tap on the door and Bustle came in. He doused the candle and took her in his arms. She lay quiet and let him do what he liked. There was some comfort in that. Maybe he'd take her to the next club, after all.

But he never had to make up his mind about that, for the last "club" had been held at Fort Pitt. Colonel Bouquet was preparing to move forward from Fort Bedford for its relief. The Indians gathered from the far west and the Great Lakes region to ambush him when he set out. It was to be another Braddock's defeat.

Meanwhile, they gathered about Fort Pitt too, and a constant day and night harassing of the garrison went on.

Salathiel was kept busy copying dispatches at headquarters in the evenings. Now and then an express would slip through from Fort Bedford and then the same man would take back Captain Ecuyer's replies. It was near the end of July. Ecuyer ceased work on his defences, which were now satisfactory even to him, and turned his attention to building boats to carry Bouquet's men down the Ohio, after they should arrive. The war was to be carried into the enemy's country. Meanwhile, they were using cannon now to keep the Indians at a distance. The gunners grew more skilful every day.

Then again there was a complete lull. Only this time people waited breathlessly for news from Colonel Bouquet. Would he be able to cross the mountains or not? That was the question.

21. The Last of the Siege

ONE FINE AUGUST MORNING a procession of Indians, mounted and on foot—there were even a number of squaws—began to pass across the peninsula between the two rivers at a safe distance from the fort. The procession continued with interludes all day long. No one had ever seen so many Indians before. Indeed, it was suspected that this was an old stage trick, that the procession was in fact continuous because it was circular.

Careful watching proved this to be so. A piebald horse that had been stolen from Mr. McKee, the trader, was seen to reappear five times. By this, and other signs, the captain concluded most of the besiegers had left the vicinity of the fort and had gone eastward to ambush Colonel Bouquet.

The anxiety at the fort was now intense. Everyone was kept at work to keep down panic and discontent. Under a screen of troops the inhabitants were permitted to return to their fields and gardens. Every remnant of corn was picked, hay made, the spelts reaped, fodder and fuel brought into the fort. A small party was even sent across the river and brought back several boatloads of coal from the thick seam near the top of the cliff. They reported all quiet there, not a sign of the enemy.

Inside the fort, the carpenters and guardsmen built a bateau a day and sank it in the moat to swell. Even the children were kept busy pegging down sods and grassing the ditches. All went well. The cattle were grazing again all day in the fields. Not a shot rang out. The only discontent was from the women. Captain Ecuyer had refused to let them "smooth" (iron) their clothes, as it took too much fuel.

Johnson and Salathiel worked the little mangle with charcoal. They were engaged in just that one morning when a wounded messenger staggered into headquarters with the news that Colonel Bouquet and his relieving force were ambushed at Bushy Run about a day's march from Pittsburgh. Then there was no more news for two agonizing days.

It was the sixth of August when the first messenger came and was sent to the hospital. On the eighth a number of canoes ran the fire of the fort in the darkness and disappeared down the Ohio. Everybody had been called in. The sentries were doubly cautious. If Colonel Bouquet had been turned back, the canoes they had seen might be Indians dropping downriver to summon further numbers to surround the fort for a final onslaught. Still no word came. Captain Ecuyer, his face drawn with anxiety, which he explained as "the pain in his leg", dictated the general order as usual.

The captain stamped out, leaning more heavily than usual on his cane. The old wound he had at Quebec was beginning to trouble him badly again.

It was a blustering, rainy night. While Johnson put dry blankets on the captain's bed, Salathiel built a small fire in the grate with a few of the massive coals. Presently the captain returned. He smiled at the warm room and the nightshirt laid out on the bed. He had not put one on now for some days. Johnson and Albine removed his boots with great care. He took a swig of precious brandy, the last of the flask, and wrapped himself in a warm blanket. The wind and rain beat fitfully against the small, square window. Johnson departed.

"Can you play écarté, Albine?" asked the captain.

"No, sir, I don't know the cards. The Reverend McArdle forbid them. He destroyed those he found among the captives."

"They are a solace the devil has provided to comfort us for acts of God," said Captain Ecuyer, apparently speaking to himself. "Now sit down. I'll show you. This king is David, this Pharaoh, this Cæsar, and Alexander . . . suppose we try loo, it's simpler to begin with."

The world outside was forgot. Salathiel finally won a hand.

"Wrap my legs in a warm blanket," said the captain at last. "Even if I am going to lose my hair, I might as well keep my feet warm. How does your scalp feel, young man? A little itchy?"

Albine ran his hand over his growing hair now about an inch long.

"There's not much to get hold of yet," he said.

"No," mused the captain, dealing another hand. "It's going to be a close shave. Isn't that what you say?"

"Yes, sir, they do say it. But the Injuns don't always scalp you."

"We'll not go into that," said the captain. "Your play."

They went on for hours.

"Open the door," said Ecuyer toward morning, "it's stuffy in here. You're getting sleepy."

Outside lay the calm promise of a beautiful morning. Lieutenant

Francis came across the little green, his rapier clicking against his boots.

"Sir," said he, "Birnam wood has come to Dunsinane."

"What, what!" said the captain. "You're drunk?"

The lieutenant coloured violently. "I mean, sir, there's a party of Indians with branches stuck in their muskets, howling and singing in the dawn on Grant's Hill."

"Admit them two at a time," said Ecuyer, rising. "Tell the commissary to kill a bullock and start it roasting. Bouquet will have sent some troops with the news."

"Dress me," he said to Albine.

The door closed on a glimpse of Lieutenant Francis running toward the main gate.

The captain put on his best uniform and an order. He fingered for a moment in the box where he kept his few medals, some family relics, and trinkets. "Young man," said he, "there has been a great English victory. Your hair will grow longer. You are in the service of a fortunate man. Here is something to remember the greatest moment of his life." He stalked out dramatically with a peculiar French fling to his shoulders, leaving a small, silver watch in the hand of the astonished Albine. The captain had set it exactly by his other timepiece, probably to mark "the greatest moment of his life". It was 4:55 on the morning of August 9, 1763.

Fort Pitt was relieved.

To judge by the noise outside everybody in the fort including the cattle knew it already. Albine never forgot that day. In a sense time began then for him, European time on the captain's watch. The eternity of the forests and the Indians was over. He put the watch to his ear and heard it ticking. Yes, his time had come alive.

Ten friendly Indians were already in the fort shooting off their muskets and being feasted. Every inhabitant of the place had come out to take part in the general rejoicing. Men, women, and children mulled about, laughing, crying, and whooping. Indeed, the scene was one of such confusion and general abandon that Captain Ecuyer had the drums beat and the entire garrison called to arms and sent to their posts.

In which condition of "alert", with a guard of honour drawn up before headquarters, he and Major Trent of the militia received the small advance party bearing the news of Colonel Bouquet's hard-won success at Bushy Run.

In particular the exhausted survivors of the West Indian regiments, many of them fit only for the hospital, were made much of. The news they brought was indeed stirring.

Colonel Bouquet had been attacked in a dangerous defile, where, in order to protect his convoy, he had been forced to encircle his wagons and supply train with his entire force. All forward movement had, of course, ceased. The attack went on for two days. There was no water.

It looked as though the defeat of Braddock would be repeated, when the colonel ordered the circle to be opened as though part of his men were in flight. The Indians rushed in and were surrounded in turn by a ring of fire. Many warriors were shot down among the several tribes and the rest put to flight and scattered all over the country. Those scattered Indians would continue to harry the settlers, but the fort was relieved. That fact was immediately patent. The enemy had evidently abandoned the neighbourhood entirely. Scouts sent out could find no sign of him.

"Now," said Johnson, "we shall get some wine for cooking. With a little sherry we can have the Queen of Scots soup to celebrate the arrival of the colonel, and white flour!"

All that, and Colonel Bouquet himself, arrived on the tenth.

It had been necessary to rest and reorganize the troops after the battle. They came marching down from Grant's Hill over General Forbes's old road with the band playing, the Highlanders' tartans and the scarlet uniforms and accoutrements of the 76th and 77th foot making an astonishingly bright show against the green of the fields and forest.

Behind them followed the dark green of the Pennsylvania provincial militia, then a long train of wagons on which rode many a drunken, friendly Indian along with the wounded, then pack horses, a herd of sheep, cattle, and hogs, finally some artillery and the rear guard of hardbitten men in hunting shirts. Trouble, if any, could now be looked for from the rear.

The entire garrison of Fort Pitt was drawn up outside to receive them. Volleys were fired and the river valleys echoed to the discharge of muskets and salvos from the ramparts. Colonel Bouquet and Captain Ecuyer embraced, which seemed strange to all the English and Americans. Nevertheless, their hats went high in the air.

That evening the fort was full of the red glare of torches and bonfires, drums, music of all kinds, roasting sheep and cattle, Indians capering in Indian finery, fights, and official feastings. The captain moved out of headquarters to make room for Colonel Bouquet.

More important to Salathiel, the colonel borrowed Johnson from Captain Ecuyer. In two small rooms near the music bastion Captain Ecuyer and Albine now conducted their establishment alone. Johnson, in fact, had foreseen this. It would only be courtesy for Captain Ecuyer to offer to lend his man to the colonel. Johnson had simply assumed that he would, and had acted accordingly. It would in the end be an easy way to part with the captain. For after a brief service with the colonel, Johnson intended finally to depart.

It was some days before Captain Ecuyer fully realized this. He was considerably annoyed at first and sent for the chests with Johnson's valet and barber kits. They belonged to the captain, having been purchased by Johnson for him in Philadelphia.

Salathiel went for them and took them away as part of the captain's private baggage. Before the colonel, Johnson could say nothing. Later he came around and struck a bargain. He was to have the loan of what items he needed from the kits, provided he should continue to help Albine when necessary.

It galled Johnson to have to ask this and to find that his pupil was smart enough to drive the bargain. Yet in the end he laughed. It was easier than having had to give the captain notice. When Colonel Bouquet went down the Ohio into the Indian country, Johnson intended to stay behind. Already the inhabitants were beginning to plan where they should rebuild their houses when they were released from the fort. Already they were quarrelling about lots. The colonel settled that. No more houses were to be built near the fort. He had one of the royal engineers re-lay a plan for the streets of Pittsburgh. Among the first lots to be pre-empted was one for Johnson and his Amelia near the Diamond.

22. The Captain's Man

THE REMAINDER OF THE SUMMER and all of that autumn were an intensive period of apprenticeship for Salathiel. For the most part it was pretty lonely, too. More and more of his friends kept departing, while the captain remained at the fort. Captain Ecuyer was in charge of the surrounding neighbourhood and of communications as far back as Fort Bedford, while Colonel Bouquet prepared for his coming move down the Ohio into the Indian territory.

Despite the all but desperate activity of the garrison in building bateaux and collecting supplies, the population of the fort gradually thinned out. Even the personnel of the garrison constantly shifted. A few days after the place was relieved all the refugees from the mountain settlements, and the captives of the Indians who had escaped or been delivered to the fort, left for the eastern settlements under a strong escort.

Among them were Lieutenant Francis and Bustle. The lieutenant was taking her to Philadelphia. She said good-bye to Albine shyly but with a quiet triumph, for she was mounted on a good horse and in a town gown with a wimple. Uncommonly pretty, Salathiel had to admit. She secretly was in hopes the lieutenant was going to take her to England, and had already assumed a certain condescension to colonials. She said, "La, la"—and rode a side-saddle the saddler had especially made. And she had learned to "simper under her wimple," as the lieutenant said.

"Be careful how you use that gun I gave you, Albine," he shouted, as they rode off along Forbes Road for the Alleghenies.

Most of the captives, who were being returned to the settlements, set up a great outcry of farewells and not a few lamentations. There were many orphaned children among them and they were leaving the only friends they had. The orders were strict that none should be concealed or remain behind, for the crown was evacuating all the country west of the mountains. With the exception of Pittsburgh, which was to be a trading post about the fort, that region was to remain Indian lands.

In spite of the danger of a renewed Indian attack, the inhabitants of Pittsburgh were soon out of the fort and engaged in rebuilding their houses on the new plan provided by the engineers. They resented the plan. They wanted to put their houses anywhere. They insisted on carrying on an illicit trade with the savages which continued to provide the Indians with whisky, guns, bullets and powder even in the unsettled and warlike condition of the frontier.

All gratitude for the defence of the fort was soon forgot in the petty irritations of rules imposed by the royal officers. Colonel Bouquet and Captain Ecuyer remained personally popular, but the class they belonged to was more and more hated and held in contempt. Their red coats were the symbols of the crown's veto on the growth of the settlements. They and the garrisons were a dam behind which a flood tide setting westward rapidly backed up and accumulated.

Salathiel spent the rest of the summer at the fort. He was kept intolerably busy. That was the way he felt about it at first. Gradually he grew used to a day that was a constant round of work and routine from reveille to sunset. In fact, the evenings and nights too were frequently taken up by work for the captain. Fortunately, he soon found that he had the capacity to lose himself in his work. And the departure of his friends and companions made it all the easier. Also fortunately, Captain Ecuyer was an extremely exacting man.

Salathiel rose before the sunrise gun and groomed and fed the captain's horse. Then he took a plunge in the river or the moat and returned to quarters and dressed himself most carefully and neatly. Then he laid the captain's uniform and weapons out on a table at the foot of his bed: polished boots, knee breeches, carefully pressed, a fresh laundered shirt with shirred lace neckpiece, a set of buttoned gold-lace cuffs and linen armbands to cover them.

All this, including a pair of long silk stockings that must be fresh and darned, was made ready for him, with one of his three cocked hats, kept in a press-box, laid out on the top with the gold-lace edging hooked on.

Next to the pistol holsters lay his gorget and spurs. These he put on last. The gorget was all that remained of what had once been the complete body armour of a knight.

After all this equipment was complete and every item accounted for, Salathiel brought a bucket of hot water from the kitchen and filled the captain's silver ewer and laid out the shaving kit beside his basin.

At the first note of reveille the captain sat up. He took a French book and read several verses. He looked at a locket in a small ebony box, and stepped out of bed and was shaved. He then dressed himself, had his hair dressed or he put on a wig, depending on the state of the temperature. After that, he went over to Colonel Bouquet's quarters for breakfast. This was served to both the gentlemen by Johnson and Albine together, until late in October when Johnson left. After that event the colonel dressed in his own quarters with the help of an orderly. Albine cooked and set the table.

After breakfast Salathiel swept out the quarters, made up the bed, rearranged the captain's papers from the night before. Then he washed, starched, and ironed, curled the wigs when necessary, cleaned the pistols and leatherwork, and looked after his own clothes.

He now had two good suits, thanks to the captain. He wore moccasins whenever he could, but when he heard the captain coming he slipped into boots. Usually he was through by eleven o'clock. That gave him an hour in which to read.

The captain had a small chest of books. Some of them were in French. Others were military texts and novels in English. Before he left Fort Pitt Salathiel had read all the novels. He then took to borrowing books from Major Trent, the militia officer, who had a nice little "library", as he intended to settle in Pittsburgh.

At noon the captain came to his quarters for lunch. He usually brought some other officer with him. Lunch was a light meal hastily eaten, soldier's fare with a glass of wine. Captain Ecuyer then slept for an hour, first giving instructions as to what uniform to lay out for evening wear. Salathiel would rid up, lay out the captain's clothes, and go to the stables. The afternoon was his in a sense, provided he could share it with the captain's horse.

There was very little use for the horse while in garrison. He was expected to give it exercise. It gave him an excuse to return to the forests. It was not safe to cross the rivers yet. But just east of the fort between the two rivers was a tangle of high hills and ravines, glades and thickets that teemed with game. Here and there was an old clearing abandoned now. The cabins were burned.

In such a little clearing near the Monongahela he once came across the body of a child lying near a spring. The face was nearly eaten away but the fair hair remained. He could see it had been scalped.

This incident brought back to him forcibly the memory of his own early life. He began to ponder much over it. He remembered he had had a brother or a sister. A savage moodiness, part of his age perhaps, and so natural enough, began frequently to obsess him.

Sitting in a thicket once, waiting for a doe to come to investigate his lure, suddenly he thought he heard his mother scream. She seemed to scream at him from underground.

He missed his shot.

Suddenly he was furiously angry. He longed to kill somebody—Indians! How he hated and despised them now! They had made him what he was. The Big Turtle had carried him off. Probably it was he who had planned the attack on his father's cabin. He looked at the turtle over his own heart, felt it as though he would like to rub it away. It was there, indelible. Well, it should remind him. Remind him to kill!

He went back the next afternoon to the spring where the child's body lay, and scraping a shallow grave with his hatchet, he buried it.

He had a violent headache when it was over. Someone would have to pay with blood for what had happened to that dead child. It smelled. He could smell blood!

And so many a time, wandering the woods in the afternoons of that August and September, these black moods came upon him. When other young fellows were thinking of girls till grey spots swam before their eyes, Salathiel remembered, remembered, and remembered. He was waking now. He was beginning to think. Sometimes on these afternoon excursions he would find himself weeping. He loathed himself for that. Why he wept, he had no idea.

These moods gradually turned from ones of extreme feeling to a long-lasting hardness. They were rare moods but they tempered his metal as extreme heat followed by a plunge into cold crystallizes steel. It was that summer that his face began to take on the narrow planes and angles of a hard-wrought hatchet. Perhaps the siege had not helped to soften the metal any. It was now more malleable, to be sure, but not exactly flexible.

No one who looked into the face of the boy who returned to Fort Pitt nearly every afternoon about five, riding the captain's horse without a saddle, and with a long double-barrelled rifle over his arm, would have described him as a pliable youth. His hair, which had curious streaks of steely grey in it from the time when first it grew out from his shaved head, was now long enough to be tied back into a queue. The eyebrows were appropriately raised, just enough to convey a disconcerting irony of expression that went well with the piercing blue-grey eyes and eagle's beak beneath. Yet there was something decidedly humorous and pleasant about the chin, and his bright flash of a smile set off by firm straight lips and big white teeth.

Salathiel seldom returned without something for the captain's pot: a rabbit, a turkey, or a young deer. His aim became more and more unerring as practice trained his eye. Twice he shot wolves. And once a young bull buffalo that had somehow wandered across the river near Croghan's burnt cabins. As for foxes, beavers, and other pelt-bearing animals—he was collecting a bale of furs for trading.

Thus during August and September he managed to lead a double life. He was the captain's man at the fort, cook and valet-secretary; in the forests and wild hills about Pittsburgh he returned to his former wilderness self.

Yet there was no conflict for him in these two widely contrasted modes of existence. They were all of a piece. Things had just happened that way.

He did discover, however, an unusual and steadily growing strength of muscle and limb. The early years in the forest of alternate feasting and starvation, of hardship and lazy timelessness, had left him with an iron frame, an unbelievable power of endurance, and a deftness of movement and keenness of sense alien to most civilized people.

In particular, he used his legs and feet as though they were meant to walk on and not as though he were lame. He could bound, leap, and turn handsprings. Few could wrestle with him. He was quick, and to lay hands on him was like grasping an eel. The favourite sport many an evening was a bout between some champion of the garrison or the militia and "the captain's man".

One older man from Devonshire, one of the grenadiers, threw him again and again. In the end Salathiel made friends with him and got him to teach him all he knew. It stood Salathiel in good stead all his life.

Evenings were usually as busy, if not busier than the day. The horse was put up after Salathiel returned. He had to see it groomed and fed. Then he hastened to dress the captain at six o'clock. Every evening the captain dined in full-dress uniform. When it was his turn to take a parade or guard mount he did so in a wig or powdered hair. That, with pomatum, took time. Then there was supper, either to be cooked—or Albine helped Johnson serve it. Sometimes a full dinner with wines had to be prepared and served. Bouquet had brought a cart of wine along with him, including Burgundies and sherry. And on many an evening there was the captain's correspondence, which he was expected to indite or to copy, and not infrequently a game of cards or chess, providing no one dropped in.

Then suddenly the whole order of his existence dissolved and took on a new and absorbing aspect.

23. The Ark

MILITARY LIFE, which so often gives the appearance of being permanent and well settled, is in reality, and of necessity, most changeable and ephemeral. Soldiers are like jinn who serve the master of a compelling cup. At any moment the new Aladdin who has the cup in temporary keeping may rub it and send them off to the world's end on impossible or even captious errands. It is the part of the jinn to salaam and obey. Young Albine was now about to learn this by experience.

He had taken the routine of existence and labour during his months of sojourn at Fort Pitt as part of the order of nature. Much of it, indeed, he had had to learn by rote. He had therefore carried on his work as a kind of ritual in which the reason for what he did was not always fully understood. He had performed as he had learned, by rote. In fact, it was this exactitude in an unvarying and faithful performance that had finally impressed even Captain Ecuyer. Consequently, when there were humorous incidents or he made ludicrous mistakes, the captain had condescended to explain. Errors were never repeated.

Now all this round of habit was completely changed. Albine was thrown on his own resources under difficult and ever-shifting circumstances, for Captain Ecuyer was ordered away from the fort and put in charge of speeding up reinforcements and protecting the transport of supplies over the difficult mountain roads from Fort Bedford westward.

The success of Colonel Bouquet's projected expedition into the Ohio country in the coming year would depend mainly on his receiving these supplies, and Ecuyer was the only officer the colonel could wholly depend upon.

When Ecuyer finally had decided to remain, he called Albine into his room one night after he had gone to bed, and had his first intimate conversation with him. Captain Ecuyer was troubled by his great responsibility and growing weakness. He needed personal help.

"Sit down," said he, "I want to talk to you. You seem to be a *garçon* of considerable natural common sense, and you have been faithful and held your tongue since you began to serve me. I have even thought you might care to go back with me to Switzerland if I resigned. It could have been arranged."—Here he raised a candle for a closer look at Salathiel's face. "Good! I see that would have pleased you. But we shall not be going to Switzerland now," he continued. "The good God only knows whether I'll ever see my own country again. It is beautiful!" Here he caught himself up rather sharply.

Salathiel was surprised at the softness that had suddenly crept into the captain's harsh features. "*My* country!" the captain exclaimed again, and went on.

"No, I rather think I'll never see it except in my dreams. Instead, we shall be traversing these American mountains, and winter is coming on. I wonder if you will care to stay with me and look after me. You are not enlisted. You have never taken the oath to the king. You do not have to follow me. Perhaps you would rather return to the forest? But I shall be needing you more than ever. My wound is not so good. Yet I would not command you to come. You understand, I think.

"I shall be needing something more than blind obedience. And much more than my personal comfort will depend upon you, because all of the success of the coming campaign will in a way depend upon me. If we can't keep the supplies coming forward over the mountains, there will be no Ohio expedition next year. So I shall need someone like yourself, someone that knows these forests, who can help keep me alive long enough to do what I have to do. Yet I am wondering if the disappointment of not going to Europe will not make you feel like running away. Like—how do you Americans say it?—'going over the hill'. Isn't that it?"

"Yes," said Salathiel, unconsciously answering the literal question first. "But *no*," he cried, seeing the captain's face, "I do not mean I will go over the hill. I mean I will stay on with you. I will go over many hills with you. It is you and not the king I am serving."

"Tut, tut," said Ecuyer, "no use talking treason. There is too much of that about in these hills now." Nevertheless, he looked pleased.

Salathiel later on was not able to conceal his own satisfaction when the captain told him that Lieutenant Francis had also asked to take him along, nor his disappointment that Captain Ecuyer was not going to Switzerland, at least immediately.

The captain understood. He knew that Salathiel was anxious to learn, and see the world. He had noted, and secretly approved, his interest in books and his struggle to learn the ritual of European ways and manners.

"I'll take you along when I do go home," he said at last. "But it is only fair to say that I may not live to get there. I am really an ill man. Yet if I do go, you'll come along?"

"I will," said Salathiel. He rose and shook hands with the captain in solemn Indian fashion. Ecuyer grinned. He knew the customs of the country, and that shaking hands after a council meant a solemn bargain, a pledge of friendship, something more binding between man and man than even the military oath. "*Bon!*" said he.

"Now here is what we shall have to think of first," the captain continued. "I am not going to be able to ride my horse—much. You must contrive with me some sort of wheeled vehicle, a chariot, for these hills. Not only for me, but for our supplies, papers, and medicines, and for feed for the horses. There will be five horses, four to haul and one to ride. There will be three of us. For I shall also need a man who is a good soldier, a driver, and a combined blacksmith and carpenter; a good shot, too! A man of high heart," said the captain, "and of calm courage, and patience. Do you know him?"

"Rafe Carmichael," exclaimed Salathiel, thinking instantly of his friend the blacksmith.

"Excellent!" replied Ecuyer. "But wait—the colonel will never let *him* go. He is the only competent arms smith he has."

"No," agreed Salathiel, "old Buckey would never let him get outside the fort."

"Well, then?" said the captain, overlooking the familiar term for Colonel Bouquet, which all the Americans used. "Well, then?"

Salathiel shook his head, at a loss.

"How about Burent?" he finally suggested.

"I believe that is our man, if we can get him!" exclaimed the captain, astonished that he had not thought of Burent himself. "He's not enlisted, but he's been invaluable all during the siege at every kind of work."

"Which he hasn't been paid for," added Salathiel.

"I know, I know," said Ecuyer, "but maybe I can have that rectified now. I'll take it up with the colonel tomorrow. Meanwhile, here is what I want you to pay attention to now—the *voiture*, the chariot, the wagon —what is it you call it? Maybe your friend Carmichael can help with this?"

Shuffling among his papers, the captain drew out a little sketch on a piece of torn paper and handed it to Salathiel.

"You will observe," said Captain Ecuyer, "that my machine is to be made from a heavy ammunition wagon drawn by four horses, and behind this is to trundle a chest on two wheels, a *caisson*, as the French call it, for carrying extra supplies.

"Over the main wagon is to be stretched a piece of stout canvas on a ridgepole, for shelter, the end flaps to be fitted carefully. And also observe this: the whole concern must be painted dark green, canvas and all. The gunner has that paint in stock for his iron cannon. You see, it is not my wish to be observed moving around the mountains in a white tent, ten miles away.

" 'Tis most important that you should see that all the ironwork is doubly strong, the axles of hickory, and everything double bolted; the tires of new iron, thick, cold-shrunk on. And I shall need, too, a small stairs both to mount into the wagon and to get up on mine own horse, which is to follow behind. My leg is getting stiff. My horse can follow behind, or you can ride her.

"Now I think in this *voiture*," said he, tapping the sketch, "we can get around in these mountains. Since they have brought hundreds of wagons and heavy artillery over the new road from Bedford ever since General Forbes cut his way through, and was carried over on a litter, another sick man may follow where he went. No, it is not impossible, not with four or five horses.

"Well, here are the requisitions on the quartermaster and master gunner for the wagons and their parts, and the supplies. And here is a list of what is to be taken along. I have already made arrangements with Colonel Bouquet for the horses. We must leave here shortly. Before the weather breaks, if possible. So see to it tomorrow, and have everything perfect. Now, good night. I'm glad you will be along."

Captain Ecuyer blew out the candle, put a pad between his knees to ease the wound in his groin, and settled himself for sleep.

Seated by the coal fire in the next room, for it was now frosty autumn,

Salathiel looked at the sketch, and the list the captain had given him. Small tongues of gas flames licked out of the lumps of soft coal, flickered, and seemed to impart a shadowy movement to the wagon and its imaginary teams. He could see them jolting along the rough road through the mountains.

Doubtless there would be trouble with the Indians. He was surprised to find how much he looked forward to stalking them. What a satisfaction it would be to have them at the end of his gun sights!

He began to turn over in his mind the difficulties that must be met, and what they would need to meet them with. The *voiture*, he had to admit, was a good plan. He turned to the captain's list. Unlike the sketch, there was nothing artistic or romantic about it. It was the neat, hard thought of a soldier, carefully set down.

Accordingly, the last days at Fort Pitt were busy ones for Salathiel. Grateful for the hardships which Captain Ecuyer was about to undertake for his sake, "Old Buckey", as Colonel Bouquet was affectionately called, gave the captain's man the run of the storehouse, the services of the carpenters and blacksmiths, and the pick of men, wagons, and horses. This was fortunate for Albine, since Captain Ecuyer was now all but penniless, not having touched his pay for over a year. And in the English service little was done for an officer personally that was not furthered by gold. Most important of all, John Burent was secured to accompany the wagon.

Burent was not a soldier. He was an English master cooper who had been brought to Pittsburgh a year previously by Bouquet. He proved to be a minor genius in all kinds of construction. Most of the bateaux for the coming expedition down the Ohio had already been built by him, and in the defence of the fort his aid and ingenuity had been simply invaluable. He was devoted to both Bouquet and Ecuyer, particularly to the captain. But the combined ingenuity of both these officers had not sufficed to get him paid.

He was therefore ready to leave the fort and return to Philadelphia in order to take up his trade again. But he agreed to stay awhile with Ecuyer as his "military servant". There was a page ruled in the paymaster's book for that, and he worshipped Ecuyer.

Burent was a dapper, brown little man, powerfully built. He had brown hair, brown eyes, brown eyelashes, and a brown deerskin suit beautifully made. He was all brown, even his boots. And he was unfailingly cheerful and had a carpenter's laugh, as Carmichael the blacksmith said. Burent and he were brothers in energy and in work, and Carmichael had taught Burent as he had taught Albine to be an excellent shot. With the three of them collaborating on the captain's *voiture*, it fared well.

One of the great wagons of a Pennsylvania trader who had followed the 42nd foot as a sutler was seized upon for the king's service. That wagon was rapidly made over. Burent entirely took apart and rebuilt the wagon body so that it was tight as a boat.

There were no springs. The bargelike body was simply bolted to the axles reinforced by iron plates and to these plates the singletree was chained. It was long enough for the first team only. The front team was to pull against collars. A brake, made from hickory planks sprung like a bow, and worked by a sprocket wheel and chain from the front seat, was the great innovation and was due to Burent.

It was the news of this brake "contraption" which first began to gather spectators about the wagon while it still stood before Carmichael's forge. The smith worked late into the night. Soldiers and settlers stood about while the chests were lashed along the sides, and their contents and storing eagerly watched and discussed. Impassive Indian faces, their owners wrapped in ragged blankets, stood like columnar shadows in the background, black eyes glinting as the flames leaped at the forge. The news went about, "The little captain's leaving, and you had ought to see the cabin on wheels he's going downcountry in. It do beat the ark." And so Captain Ecuyer's *voiture* became known as "the ark".

The "trundler", a tremendous chest mounted on two wheels with a tongue shaft, something like an artillery caisson, was trundled up and hooked on behind.

Inside the wagon the chests were already lashed firmly along the sides. A lanthorn was hung from the ridgepole, the captain's folding chair set out next to his desk constructed as he had directed, and the straw and robes spread out on the floor. The crowd peered in and grew silent at so much luxury and ingenuity. All their quips by this time were exhausted. Old Buckey, Captain Ecuyer, and some of the other officers of the garrison strolled over from headquarters, where Johnson had outdone himself on a farewell dinner. They, too, were eager to inspect the wagon.

"Exceedingly snug bachelor quarters, *mon ami*," said Colonel Bouquet. "I think I'll be going along with you myself at this rate." He and Ecuyer entered the wagon and sat down. "My present to this house on wheels is a dozen of Burgundy and a jug of brandy." He sent Albine to get it. Ecuyer looked his gratitude. With a little wine, existence would still be possible. The two officers sat down under the tarpaulin and drank to Ecuyer's success.

Outside the crowd became denser. An impromptu but all the more touching farewell was being staged for Captain Ecuyer. The news and noise of the gathering spread, and a number of the settlers from the little town of huts and cabins clustered about the walls without, men and women who had gone through the siege with Ecuyer, came trooping in while the sentries looked the other way. For once the general hostility and coolness towards a king's officer was suspended, and both Ecuyer and Old Buckey received a rough-and-ready but hearty ovation.

The inevitable keg of liquor appeared. This time conveyed from the king's storehouse by command of Old Buckey himself. And good black rum it was. Hot water, hot irons, and cider and rum hissed in can and pannikin and disappeared like hot lightning down a hundred throats. Carmichael piled the entire remainder of his coal high in the forge and plied his bellows until an incandescent pyramid lit the casemate where the forge was, throwing a warm glow of heat and light about its arched door. Indians came forward rubbing their stomachs for draughts of rum. These being forthcoming, two of them began to shuffle and "woof-woof". The crowd jeered them good-naturedly. A couple of bagpipers appeared, and a fiddle with a voice like a hoarse buzz saw.

Albine and the man from Devon staged a final bout. Salathiel understood the compliment when he was permitted to emerge on a draw.

Johnson shook Salathiel's hand and presented him with a book of receipts copied out by Mrs. Johnson, whose heart overflowed with rum and happiness that at last Johnson would be hers and not the captain's man from now on. Her "God go wid ye" was perhaps the most sincere of all. The captain had presented Johnson with a horse. It was an old one, to be sure, but a great gift nevertheless.

Colonel Bouquet and the captain now shook hands all around. There was a cheer and a health for them, and one for the king, after which they walked off together.

Salathiel slept in the ark that night for the first time. That is, he stayed in it to watch the captain's property. The celebration about the forge went on until the small hours. It ended about three o'clock by a gouging fight in which a Welsh soldier lost an eye before the guard interfered. Then the pile of glowing coal fell away suddenly to ashes. The drink was out, and all except Burent and Carmichael went home.

Salathiel collected his own small bundle of belongings and his cherished double-barrelled rifle and stowed them in the wagon. Then he caught a wink of sleep. It was still dark when Burent awakened him.

The horses were being brought up to be hitched on.

He went and roused the captain and dressed him in quarters for the last time. They had a breakfast of sizzling rashers and fresh eggs. "The last for many a day," said Ecuyer, wiping his plate with a piece of bread as only a Frenchman can, and sighing as he rose to make ready for the road.

24. The Road

OUTSIDE a few snowflakes were drifting down. The dawn was breaking clear, cold, and without a breath of wind. There was a sudden heavy trampling of many hoofs and a rumble of iron wheels. Captain Ecuyer picked up his cloak and threw open the door.

The ark had drawn up before his quarters, long and dark in the half-light. The horses' breath smoked frostily. There was an occasional glint and gleam from the brazen harness mountings. Burent was riding the off wheel horse, his rifle slung over his shoulder, and the handles of two heavy cavalry pistols bulged out of a pair of holsters before him. Carmichael had come to see his handiwork and the captain depart. To his disappointment the captain did not enter the wagon but called for his horse and mounted it.

"I'll leave here as I came," he said.

Salathiel hastily fitted the last of the valet kits into Johnson's portmanteaus, took a final look about him, and then poured some water on the fire. He stowed the portmanteaus in the chest under the wagon seat and took the reins. The captain handed the key of his quarters to the sergeant of the guard as they rumbled out over the drawbridge across the moat. The gate of the stockade swung wide, giving a broad glimpse of the empty, misty fields before the fort. The chimneys of a few newly built cabins rose above the morning fog here and there, rolling out black coal smoke. Over Grant's Hill the eastern light showed a silver streak through the woods along its crest. The heavily rutted and boggy road twisted away in that direction. At a cabin on the Diamond just beyond the fort a figure carrying a jug halted them. It was Johnson.

"I wanted to say good-bye, captain, and this here's a jug of the Queen of Scots soup triple strong I brewed ye. It'll do your fixin's good. Captain Ecuyer, I'm much obleeged to you. I wish ye God's best luck."

Then to everybody's amazement he reached up to the captain on his horse and shook hands. There was no longer even the trace of the air of a servant about him. He looked like another man.

Captain Ecuyer shook hands and blinked.

"*Bonne chance*, Johnson," he said. Then he lifted his hat and rode on. The wagon followed.

"If ye ever git to England," roared Johnson at Salathiel, as the heavy wheels ground past, "tell me Lord Bishop of Exeter to go to hell." He waved his hand and strode off into the mist.

"What's come over the man?" said Burent to Captain Ecuyer as he rode up beside him.

"It's the New World running in his veins," replied the captain, and beat his gloves together to warm his hands.

Salathiel heard this reply and pondered it as they started up the breast of the first steep hill. Climbing, they came suddenly out of the mist of the river valley onto the crest of the rise, where only a few years before Major Grant and his Highlanders and some Virginians had stood to be slaughtered by the French and Indians. As they stood on the height the red sun rose smoking and curling with frosty mist out of the endless folds of the forest ahead. They stayed for a moment to breathe the horses after their short but wicked climb.

"She drags sore heavy," said Burent.

"It will go better when the road freezes," replied Ecuyer unconcernedly, and turned to look back at the fort he had saved for the British crown. They all looked.

The mists in the river valley were rolling. The forests all about blazed with the last strident purples and yellows of the North American fall. At the point where the two rivers met, the star-shaped mass of the fort loomed redly through the thinning mist, the morning light playing along its moats and brick ramparts.

From the music bastion the sunrise gun dirked a scarlet splash of fire and smoke into the fog and set the echoes rolling. The Union Jack rose suddenly into the upper sunlight and clear air above the fort, and stood out boldly for an instant in a brief breeze, and then fell listlessly back against the staff. A fanfare of drums and trumpets began to shout the reveille.

The blood came surging to Ecuyer's face. His mare neighed, pawed the stones, and gave his wound a painful wrench.

"My reward!" he muttered.

But there were tears of pride as well as pain in his eyes. He dismounted slowly and motioned to Salathiel to ride the mare. Burent at this left the lead horse and took his place behind on the big wagon seat to drive.

"Ride forward and keep your eyes open for everything ahead, Albine," said the captain as he climbed into the wagon again. "I'll watch from behind. It's all I can do for a while. I think you'll be riding the mare most of the time this campaign, you know. Use her sweetly, mind! She takes a good grasp with the knees, and I've lost that." He sat down on his chair and began to bind himself into it with a long handkerchief.

Salathiel slung his rifle and rode on ahead. The ark, the trailer, and the four horses splashed, rolled, and jolted after him. Burent tooled his two teams along with great judgment and skill. He had driven from Carlisle to Fort Pitt several times and he knew the road exceedingly well.

"We'll make Turtle Creek tonight, captain," he said. "We might even get to the Loyalhanna if we don't cast shoes."

"Good," muttered Ecuyer, his eyes glassy with pain. He wished now that he had resigned.

The wagon lurched on through Penn's *sylvania* towards Fort Bedford one hundred miles or so eastward. A light snow began to fall. The road froze and the iron tires of the wagon and the horses' shoes rang in the keen, frosty air and crunched along more easily. The captain mixed a dram of brandy with a cup of Johnson's soup, which was still warm. He felt better.

He began to wonder in what shape he would find the garrison at Ligonier. Affairs went badly there, according to Colonel Bouquet.

Well, he would see. He hoped young Albine would keep a keen lookout ahead. For his part, he would never take his eyes off the road and the hillsides as they slowly closed in behind him.

This new military road, Forbes Road, the "Glades Road", led from the forks of the Ohio, mounting wave after wave of the Appalachians clear back to the inhabitants, clean to Carlisle, and then on into Lancaster County and the peaceful, fruitful meadows of Penn's grant along the Delaware. To point out its more important direction, it passed in one way or another right through from Philadelphia to Pittsburgh. And it was the only road over the mountains into the west, into the valley heart of the continent. Its opening was the most important continental event that had yet stirred the colonies.

As yet only a few people had come over the new trail, and they were mostly the military. As Salathiel rode along it that morning on the best horse that he had ever had between his legs, it was vacant of all except a few curious or startled animals. It was just a great sword cut through the forest, a swath cut by the might of Britain's fighting arm, and the day was a beautiful winter day in the lonely American woods.

"It will be all right for the horses as long as they're new shod and the calks stay sharp," said Burent on one of the infrequent occasions when Salathiel returned to the wagon for a while and rode alongside. "I'll git a smith at Ligonier to keep the shoes sharp," he insisted.

"Good idee," agreed Salathiel, and clapping heels to his horse, he rode on ahead again.

He and the mare were both in fine spirits. She seemed to know she was going east once more; home along the trail she had travelled before. She pawed the ground when he stopped to reconnoitre.

As for Salathiel, he was surprised himself to find how delighted he was to be out in the forest again; to be at home. A load seemed to have left his mind and even to have relieved his muscles since they had left the fort behind them. He filled his lungs with the clean, smokeless air. The intolerable stench of quarters, intolerable to one whose scent was so keen, no longer affected him.

Once off the slopes of Grant's Hill, they began to move over a succession of wooded rises from the crests of which an occasional glimpse of the gorge of the Monongahela and its islands was to be had. Then the road left the vicinity of the river tending northward and emerged from an area of tangled thickets and ravines onto a plateau where there was a long vista of natural open meadows and majestic oak thickets.

No more handsome stretch of country could be imagined. There was a great bald, craggy hill to the northwest and an amphitheatre of rolling blue hills to the east towards which the road ran. And there, dark and sombre, extending without end, the wall of the forest once more began. Those hills, in fact, were the outliers of the mountains whose main ranges lay two journeys to the eastward. But they were the highest hills

Salathiel had ever seen. Unconsciously, a certain sense of exhilaration was already taking hold of him. To be high, to be up there, and away!

Enough snow had now fallen and lain sufficiently long to provide him with a printed page of the recent events of the neighbourhood. To judge by the tracks, there were more deer that year than usual. It had been a lush season. There was also an extraordinary number of foxes and wolves. Salathiel had never seen so many wolf tracks and he drew the captain's attention to them. They were timber wolves, evidently big grey wolves that had come down from the north.

"Battles," said Captain Ecuyer simply. "In Piedmont, after the late wars, wolves swarmed in the hills and mountains one winter, I remember. Here, too, most of the settlers' stock had been turned loose into the forests when the inhabitants fled to the fort."

It was true, thought Salathiel. There must be a good many lost domestic animals wandering about here and there. That fact, indeed, was soon confirmed and led to the only incident of the morning.

An unusual trail attracted Salathiel's attention. He recognized it as that of a pig. Following it, towards the thickets and young oaks, he finally aroused an enormously fat and ferocious old boar. With timber wolves and bears about, that boar must have been unusually able to take care of himself. There was no doubt of it, for he soon made a vicious charge at the mare's legs, rushing unexpectedly out of some scrub where he had been champing acorns. His angry squeals, the surprised snort and neigh of the mare caused the wagon to stop to watch the conflict.

The boar chased Salathiel and the mare some distance, while the captain and Burent shouted mockingly. Salathiel had never encountered a pig. When he chased it, it would turn on him and charge. This little game continued for some time. Finally the boar turned at bay. It meant business. Its small eyes were bloodshot. The mare was sweating. The pig charged her, slashing wickedly. Suddenly in mid-career it turned and made for the wagon, which apparently it now saw for the first time.

Burent now shouted in alarm. There were sixteen of his horses' legs on the road. Tired of fooling, Salathiel unslung his rifle and dropped the animal, shot clean through the head. It expired to a chorus of unholy organlike squeals.

The captain and Burent kept laughing at Salathiel. Somehow he felt ashamed, especially when he looked up and saw on a neighbouring crest a stag with a fine pair of antlers. It, too, had been watching curiously. Now it gave its white tail a jerk and left in long, soaring leaps, scared away by the rifle shot. He fired the other barrel and missed.

"Never mind," said Burent. "Pork's better nor venison any day, if you'll listen to me. And here's enough fresh pork for the trip, prime mast fed, and cold weather to keep it."

He and Salathiel attacked the carcass with tomahawk and knife. They worked as fast as possible. Head, hams, and sides were soon stowed away in some extra bags, salted, and swung high to the ridgepole of the wagon.

After an hour they were under way again. Captain Ecuyer produced a long-cherished Havana cigar, somewhat battered, but a parting gift from one of the gallant 42nd, late from the West Indies. He felt better than he had, although laughing had hurt his wound. But it was a relief to him to feel that the responsibilities of the fort lay behind him. The *voiture* worked even better than he had hoped. On a long level section the horses broke into a trot. They smoked and steamed in the winter air. The ark jounced along, curls of the captain's cigar smoke leaking from under the canvas. Burent coughed. He could scarcely abide smoke. He chewed, but secretly and rather daintily. Even the stains he made then were brown.

25. In Which Hospitality Spills Over

SALATHIEL continued to ride on ahead. It was after midday now. The snow had ceased. Presently he came on some moccasin tracks mixed with the trail of many horses. Heading through the woods, which were now beginning to close in about them, he saw smoke rising, and then the black walls of a large cabin. There was a branch hung out on a pole over the door. A short, stout man with a rifle taller than he was himself came to the door and peered out.

This place Salathiel knew must be Frazier's tavern, or the "Bill Pens", the first tarrying east of Pittsburgh. He was rather curious to see the man he had stolen a horse from years ago. Frazier had moved since then from his old cabin at the mouth of Turtle Creek to the crossroads, where a horse trail led southeastward down a densely wooded valley towards Braddock's Field on the Monongahela. It was the same fatal trail the French and Indians had taken to ambush the British eight years before. Now an occasional trader from Virginia drove a string of pack horses over it, but only with much difficulty. Yet, bad as it was, it was the only negotiable trace between the end of Braddock's road and Fort Pitt, and Mr. Frazier's tavern had been built just at the forks of this trail and Forbes Road in order to catch all the trade there was.

At that moment Salathiel noticed a large number of moccasin tracks in the snow, converging upon the cabin from all directions, both going and coming. He reported these to Captain Ecuyer, who was evidently not pleased at the story they told.

"Frazier is an old rascal," said Captain Ecuyer in a low tone, for they were now drawn up before the door, and Salathiel had come to help him out of the wagon. "Burent, *you* remain by the wagon, and keep a sharp eye on the horses while we're here. I'm going in to have a look about and find how the wind blows. We'll stay just long enough for a bite by the fire. That'll be our best excuse."

Salathiel fitted the pair of little steps to the wagon and the captain descended with some difficulty.

"Fresh pork for lunch, captain?" asked Salathiel loudly, so that Mr. Frazier leaning by the door could hear.

"Why not?" said the captain, winking.

Up until that moment Mr. Frazier had remained by his doorway, the most indifferent and oblivious of hosts. If he was consumed with curiosity and speculation about the strange conveyance which had just halted before his cabin, he was not the man to discover to others that anything could ever be new to him. However, when a king's officer in full uniform walked down out of the wagon on a pair of steps he was not entirely able to restrain a look of cunning surprise.

"How d'ja dew, captain," said he, for he had seen Ecuyer at the fort often enough. "Be ye fixin' to stay with us? Ef'n so we're pretty durned packed." With this he closed the door, that was open a crack, behind him. Then, remembering he was a sergeant in the militia, he turned and gave the captain a solemn rifle salute. There seemed to be something a mite surly or mocking in this. The captain smiled and touched his hat with his cane in reply.

"All I need, Mr. Frazier, is a bite by your fire, a touch of warmth before we drive on," he said.

"But we've no fixin's, I tell yer," replied Frazier, now leaning on his gun. "We're clean et out from crib to garret."

"I'll provide my own meat," insisted the captain, hobbling towards the door painfully, but with a determined air. "Come," said he, suddenly getting red in the face, "why do you think Colonel Bouquet granted you licence to remain and keep tavern here? Or is it only the king's officers that must stay outside in the snow?"

Frazier mumbled something that might be taken for an apology, leaned his rifle against the cabin, and with obvious reluctance opened the door at the same time roaring out, "Sabiney, Sabiney, build up the back log and put a kittle on. Do you hear, woman? It's the commandant from the fort comin' in on us!"

A complete silence followed this warning, except that the crackling of a fine fire already roaring up the chimney could be heard and its tall flames seen in the dark cavern of the place as the door swung open on squalling hinges.

"Thank you," said the captain. And he walked in, motioning Salathiel to follow him.

Once inside, it was immediately patent why Mr. Frazier's constipated welcome had been both hesitant and constrained. Eight or ten Indians lay sprawling drunkenly about the floor in helpless and grotesque postures, wallowing in a welter of vomit-soaked blankets, bedraggled and trampled headdresses, loose feathers, muskets and tomahawks upon which some of them had cut themselves and bled freely. They were a war party, their eyes painted green with surrounding circles of red, their faces and bodies smeared black. There were blotches of vermilion designs on their naked chests. Their scalp locks nodded sickly and helplessly. Some of them gurgled and others snored. One or two, at the entrance of strangers, tried to crawl towards the door, but gave it up when that, the only entrance to the place, was banged shut and barred by Mr. Frazier.

"Take the bar off the door!" said Captain Ecuyer.

Since Mr. Frazier seemed not to hear, Salathiel unbarred the door and stood by it. As his eye became used to the gloom and shadow he looked about him in the firelight.

The captain was now standing directly before the fire, warming his back, and pulling his coattails aside to do so or to keep his hands on the pair of small pocket pistols he carried over his hips. There was certainly an indescribable feeling of hostility about the place, although a giant shadow of the captain was thrown across the logs of the ceiling and seemed to dominate the room.

Behind him in the chimney the long right arm of a bear with outstretched paw hung flayed and roasting, dripping grease into a pan underneath and occasionally twisting in an agonized manner in the draught of the fire.

At the extreme end of the cabin, farthest from the fire, and also in semi-darkness, the magnificent figure of an Indian chief arrayed in a scarlet, hawk-feathered bonnet with his blanket wrapped stoically about him sat cross-legged on the only table of the establishment. He was sober, silent, kinglike. His features as though coined from bronze or carved from mahogany now and then glinted or sprang into sharp relief when the fire leaped. His silver armbands glittered, but he neither moved nor spoke. Salathiel saw that he was a Seneca, a chief of the Long House, and that the party sprawled on the floor beneath him were Delawares.

Except for a ladder, which disappeared into the mysterious gloom of the loft above, there was nothing else on that side of the room. It was into these higher regions that Mr. Frazier had ascended and he was now heard stumbling about aloft, evidently trying to arouse his wife to the importance of the visitors below. He and she soon seemed to be trying to quarrel in grumbles or whispers.

The chief on the table and the Indians on the floor were, however, not the only occupants of the room.

In that part of it which extended to the right of the fireplace, stretched out on a bench against the wall with his head on a bundle of beaver-skins, lay the lanky form of a white man sound asleep. Despite the stench and foul air of the place, his mouth was wide open and he snored. Occasionally he wrinkled a livid scar down the exposed side of his face. He had on a coonskin cap drawn down over his eyes, a deer-hide shirt with filthy red fringes, and worn riding breeches of heavy English cloth tucked into a pair of cowhides provided with rusty spurs.

Judging by a bundle or two from which bottles protruded, a strong smell of whisky, and a number of bales tucked under the bench over which his lanky form seemed to be draped in sinister guard, the man might be taken for a trader or trapper, one of those inveterate purveyors of firewater to the savages whom neither proclamations nor menaces could stop.

Behind him, in sober and decent contrast, sat a quiet grey-haired man clad in butternut and a Quaker hat, the fine beaver nap of which he smoothed with a pair of fat, satisfied hands while it reposed on his knee. From time to time this rather tight-lipped individual from Pennsylvania, for he was obviously that, looked at the captain a bit apprehensively with a couple of wide-set, innocent blue eyes and smoothed the hair back from his forehead. When not smoothing either his hat or his hair, he would smooth the front of his coat.

Captain Ecuyer took both these gentlemen in at a glance, and commencing to whistle silently, continued also to twirl his stout cane. Not entirely comfortable under the captain's continued scrutiny, it was the Quaker who spoke first.

"Art thou by any chance returning home?" he asked in a tone that somehow conveyed a deal of effrontery.

"Alack for me and for thee, *no*," replied the captain. "Art thou by any chance peddling powder and shot?"

The Quaker solemnly shook his head.

"Whisky?" persisted the captain.

"I am not acquainted with the personage asleep beside me. I am Samuel Japson of Philadelphia," said the Quaker, and moved a little farther from the man asleep on his left.

The man lying on the bench, hearing the sound of voices, now opened his eyes under his coonskin cap and carefully looked about the room without moving a body muscle. Under the cap, and in the firelight, his eyes glittered like those of a hawk.

"Yer a damned, hypocritical liar, Friend Japson," he finally drawled in a southern voice, "and furthermore I kin prove it."

"*Vraiment!*" exclaimed the captain, suddenly lapsing into French at so illuminating and satisfactory a turn to the conversation. But further revelations were suddenly cut short by an outbreak, or rather by an accentuation of the scuffling upstairs.

"Stop pinching," shouted a girl's voice. "Stop it! Ouch! Oh!"—a slap followed.

"Drat ye, git yer carcass out of bed," said the husky voice of an older woman. "Git the mush kittle on. Thar's company. Up wid ye, down wid ye! Tie your hair, ye slut." Another hearty slap was followed by a sob, and at this juncture the legs and rear quarters of Mr. Frazier were seen descending the ladder.

"There'll be victuals in a jiffy, yer Honour," said he, rubbing his hands with satisfaction.

An exceedingly good-looking Irish girl, despite the fact that her dark hair was in tangles, her face red from slapping, and her body concealed in a sacklike linsey-woolsey, now came nimbly down the ladder and started to fill a kettle with water, corn meal and a handful of salt. There was something about her slim, young movements that reminded Salathiel of Jane. The girl looked at him, the tears still standing in her large, grey eyes, and was instantly aware of his interest and sympathy.

Salathiel was not the only one whose glances followed her about the room. The trader on the bench sat up and tipping his cap back gave her a yellow-toothed grin. Mrs. Frazier, who had now managed to lower her dowdy bulk out of the garret, was also aware of the glances which followed her maid. That, or something else, enraged her and she lost no opportunity to assert her authority and call attention to herself by chivying the girl about the room. Her most pleasant epithet was "Frances, ye bound-out slut."

"Aye, they'd follow ye even when ye go out to squat in the snow," she muttered.

The nimbleness of the girl in avoiding now and then a well-placed kick brought a grunt either of surprise or of disappointment from the chief on the table. As the preparation for the meal progressed, he was seen to be solemnly filling a long ceremonial pipe with tobacco and killikinick. Two red feathers and one white one hung on a string of wampum shells from its black stone bowl.

Meanwhile, Salathiel had brought in a roast of fresh pork, which he now proceeded to divide into chops, spit on a ramrod, and place before the fire. A barrel chair was rolled up to one end of the table occupied by the chief. The captain spread his handkerchief out on a corner and selected two plates from his kit which Salathiel had brought in. One of these he placed before the chief. By this time the Indian had almost completely filled his pipe. The two little piles of tobacco and "cabbage" had been well crushed between his palms and nicely packed into the bowl. He now reached down with one foot and kicked one of the sleeping Delawares on the floor.

"Go, dog," said he in the Delaware tongue, "and fetch a coal for your betters." The Delaware rolled over and belched. Salathiel seized a coal, tossed it in the air, and brought it to the chief.

"The ears of the white man are as swift as his legs," said the chief gravely in the Shawnee dialect to Salathiel. "Was it not at Logstown on the Beaver that I saw thee before?"

"At Logstown at the council fire of Kaysinata three winters ago. I am the son of the Big Turtle."

"Thou hast crawled into a larger house," said the chief, smiling with his eyes as he dropped the coal, which he had been tossing up and down in the air, directly into his pipe.

"I follow a greater chief," said Salathiel, looking at the captain significantly. "He it was who defended the fort at the forks of the three rivers."

"Is it he?" said the chief. "He's English but he talks French?"

He looked keenly at the captain, and leaning over his pipe bowl, thrust the stem in his lips and emitted a cloud of fragrant smoke.

The meat was done now and the Irish girl came forward and placed a crackling chop on the plate of the captain and one before the Seneca. A baked potato and a spoonful of corn mush followed. Captain Ecuyer made a gesture of invitation to the chief.

"Et iss de honoul to sup wide soo gleat solda," said the chief in guttural but passable English. He presented his pipe.

The captain leaned forward, and taking a long whiff, exhaled slowly through his nose. He and the chief then began to eat, the captain using his three-pronged fork and the Seneca the clean blade of a long, sharp scalping knife with equal dexterity.

"See that the distinguished company is served, Albine," said Ecuyer, looking about him with an ironical smile. "There is enough fresh hog flesh for all."

Mrs. Frazier needed no further encouragement. She seized the remnant of the large roast Salathiel had brought in and began to cut it up into a mountainous pile of chops. The trader looked towards the fire hopefully. The Quaker put his hat on his head and took a slab plate on his lap. From time to time he smoothed it expectantly with his hand.

In the chimney mouth Salathiel and Frances, the Irish girl, hung over the spit together broiling chops as fast as the pork would sizzle in the flame. Some of the Indians, smelling roasting flesh, sat up and gulped.

"The bear paw's for them," said Frazier. He took the handlike object off the hook and began to chop it up with a tomahawk. "Can't spare no hog drippin's for Injuns."

His wife sniffed her agreement.

"Reckon it was one of Bert McCallister's hogs they got," said she to her husband, and sniffed again.

"Hope it hain't been eating no corpses," said Mr. Frazier.

"Fresh killed meat at the fort last night, ma'am!" said Salathiel, lying indignantly. He was not going to let the old woman be right about anything or have the old man spoil his meal. She glanced at him and carried a chop over to Mr. Japson.

"Yer a foin lad," whispered Frances, "git me out of this for the love of Jasus."

Salathiel shook his head.

"If you can get yourself to Ligonier I might be able to help you there," he whispered.

"Ligonier!" exclaimed the girl. "And how would I be gettin' meself to Ligonier?"

"I'll Ligonier ye!" exclaimed the old woman, who had come up behind them quietly. She tossed the hair out of her eyes with the hand holding her pork chop and glared at Salathiel.

"Don't ye be foolin' with me gal, young man. She's legally bound. Mr. Frazier give six pounds for her at Lancaster a year ago come June, and she's two years to sarve yet. I'll have the lawr on ye ef ye go foolin' with her," roared she, putting her hands on her hips while the greasy chop dripped down her skirt. "I'll Ligonier ye!"

The Irish girl shrank back into a corner by the chimney, her face going pale. Mrs. Frazier's voice rose suddenly from a husky roar to a hoarse scream. "I'll have the lawr on ye," she screamed again and again.

"Speaking of the law," said the cold voice of Captain Ecuyer in the peculiarly clipped and faultless English which he assumed when annoyed, "speaking of the law—you, madam, and your husband"—he pointed his fork at Frazier—"are harbouring drunken Indians here and selling them whisky."

"Not me," shouted Frazier. "No, sir. I wouldn't sell them a drap, nor the old woman neither."

The captain turned his fork like an accusing finger in the direction of the man with the coonskin cap.

"Right, sir! It's him. He came last night, and the ten Delawares with him," cried Frazier.

" 'Twas an honest swap," said the trader, his eyes narrowing as he looked at the captain. "Ten bottles for these hya bales of peltry." He kicked the purchases under the seat emphatically.

"What's your name?" asked the captain.

"Reynolds, Tom Reynolds of Virginia. At your service, me lud," he added surlily. "Damn the lobster backs, is what I say, says I." His hands began to move nervously towards his belt.

"I'll trouble you for the knife," said Salathiel, swooping over to the bench and sitting down beside him.

The captain nodded.

Ready for any move, Salathiel took the knife from its sheath in the man's belt and held it behind him. The man tensed. But the captain's fork was pointing at him again.

"You sold liquor to a war party," said Ecuyer. "You know what that means."

"They're going south to fight the Creeks, south to Car'lina. They're not bent for no settlements. I'd not sell 'em a drap, ef'n I knowed they was on a raid 'gin our folks. Not a bottle b'God!"

"Not a bottle!" said the captain icily. "Not if you were sure, eh? What a careful man you are. Have you a pass, Mr. Reynolds?"

"Two of them, Mr. Soldier," said Reynolds. He raised his feet in the air and wriggled them in the captain's face.

"They will pass you back to Virginia," said the captain, his face darkening. "We are keeping all the bottles. Don't come trading this way again without a licence, sir, or I'll see you hanged. This country is closed to trade and settlement by his Majesty's proclamation, and it is a capital offence to bring aid and comfort to the enemy. Tell all your friends we are having the Virginia road watched."

"That'll interest quite a few back in Virginny," drawled the trader, "especially them as give their time, taxes, and blood to make and keep the road open. I'll tell 'em! Do I lose my nags and the rest of my plunder too?"

"I said we would keep the *whisky*," said Captain Ecuyer. "You have still several hours of daylight for a good start, Mr. Reynolds," he added significantly.

"Dost thou wish to part with thy plunder for a fair price?" interjected the Quaker. "I'll give thee what it cost," said he.

"And me with the trouble and danger of totin' it over the big hills! Nothin' fer that?"

The Quaker shook his head and smiled.

"I have just said there would be no trading here," remarked the captain. "Get yourself gone and be about it, Reynolds. Now, Mr. Japson, what, for instance, have you brought into this interestin' wilderness besides your pious insolence? Any powder or lead, for example?"

"No powder, my friend," replied Japson.

"Go and see what are in his bales, Albine," said the captain, "and give the knife back to the Virginian."

Salathiel stepped out and made his way rapidly to a lean-to shed behind the cabin. Mr. Reynolds was already saddling the horses, his own and two pack animals.

There were five other horses crowded into the place, milling around, and a pile of bales on which a young Delaware buck was sleeping. Salathiel rolled him over. He then took the knife and started to prod into the cloth of the bales.

"Thar's lead thar, all right," said the Virginian, grinning. "It 'ud be a shame to make holes in all that cloth with *my* knife."

"Catch," said Salathiel. He spun the knife four times in the air. The man caught it by the handle unerringly, and returned it to the sheath in his belt.

"Glad you and me ain't tossin' it one at t'other, Mr. Man," he said.

He swung into his saddle and led off with the two pack animals stringing behind. The young Delaware followed at a lope. The horses, Salathiel noticed, were well laden. Two of them had bales lashed in ex-

actly the same way as the Quaker's. Mr. Reynolds took the trail south
through the forest towards the Monongahela, going fast. The figures of
the two men and their horses were rapidly lost amid the darker outlines
of the trees.

Salathiel returned to the cabin. He noticed Burent had the wagon
ready to move and the feed bags off the horses' noses.

"How long they going to be?" asked Burent. "The sun's westing
now."

"Just hold your horses awhile," said Salathiel, grinning at the little
Englishman, who looked cold and for once impatient. Then he stepped
in through the door.

The tremendous sour smell of the cabin caught at his throat. Frances
was putting more wood on the fire. The Indian chief was orating at Mr.
Japson. Between sonorous periods in Algonquin he blew out tremendous clouds of smoke. Mr. Japson looked most unhappy. He had ceased
smoothing anything at all. His hands lay passive in his lap. His hat sat
squarely on his head, pulled down firmly. He might, indeed, have been
taken as the perfect likeness of the Pennsylvania House of Assembly refusing to vote supplies on a military bill.

"There's lead in the bales, captain," reported Salathiel amidst the silence of all present. For even the Seneca had subsided at Salathiel's entrance. Everyone was waiting to see what Mr. Japson did have in the
bales, and what he would say for himself. Also what the captain would
do.

In addition it was certainly an uncomfortable moment for Mr. Frazier.
From his standpoint Captain Ecuyer could not have arrived at a more
unfortunate time. A roomful of drunken Indians, a Virginian on the
loose selling whisky, and now Mr. Japson with his shot metal—all this
was not calculated to cause the authorities at the fort to renew his licence to keep tavern on a disturbed frontier. He therefore sat down
heavily on a log puncheon and looked helplessly across at his wife, who
was wiping her hands on her skirt and standing by the fire. It was a time
when a man needed an able partner to support him.

But what a fool his old woman was! She had no eyes for anything except that jade of a servant girl, who was actually going to pile more wood
on the fire, and they were already roasting. God knows, he had worked
like a Turkish slave building the place! He wanted it kept decent. And
now look at it!

The Quaker was speaking.

"As thou knowest," said he to the captain, "the Friends do not countenance the use of lead and powder in warfare. They are opposed to strife.
I have brought only enough shot metal in trade to enable the savages to
seek their meat from God."

"Friend Japson," replied the captain, with as near a sneer as his fine
countenance could show, "your solicitude for the heathen of these devas-

tated parts touches me to the quick." He made a motion with his hand towards his left side. "Laws, I'm desolated at having to curtail such charity. You will, however, have to leave the lead here with Mr. Frazier and return to Fort Bedford, where I shall expect you to be awaiting me when I arrive in the course of the next few days. The metal is confiscated and you are under detention. Take your horses with the remainder of your goods and start immediately. Do not fail our rendezvous. It might go hard with you." He waved the man out, and Mr. Japson went meekly enough.

"Frazier," continued Captain Ecuyer, "get that lead out of the Quaker's bales and into your wagon, and take it to Fort Pitt tomorrow morning. You will be paid for your trouble. And take this note with you to Colonel Bouquet. It shall be your warrant and something more." He scribbled a message on a page of his notebook. "Now go out and see to that rascal's leaving. I have said nothing to the colonel about what I have seen at this house today," he added, "but let me tell you, you must be more careful."

"I must sarve who comes, sir," said Frazier.

"But not too well," said Ecuyer.

The man scuttled out.

"We'll be left alone with these red varmints tomorrow. Do you hear that, gal?" cried Mrs. Frazier nervously. "The maister will be off to the fort, and us here alone!"

The Irish girl continued to rock herself slowly backward and forward where she was sitting in warm ashes near the hearth. She nodded but looked at her mistress balefully.

"Ask the chief where his war party is going, Albine," said the captain.

Salathiel spoke to the chief in Shawnee, in which the Seneca replied. The Indian spoke another tongue than his own, slowly and with immense gravity. Salathiel translated literally. A short question from Salathiel brought a long reply from the Indian—who was Chief Ganstax, of the Senecas.

"Tell him, Albine," replied the captain, who had learned to bargain with the savages, "that he can ride to the fort in Mr. Frazier's wagon, provided he sends these Delawares home now."

Salathiel translated, putting the matter in more flattering terms in order to save the chief's pride.

"Let the white captain also give me a writing to Buckey at the fort," countered the chief, "and I will set the feet of these drunken children upon the homeward trail."

The captain nodded and complied.

The chief rose slowly and stiffly to receive the paper. He shook hands solemnly with the captain. Then, equally as solemnly, he gave the nearest recumbent Delaware a tremendous kick on the rump. As the Delaware scrambled to his feet confusedly, the Seneca hoisted him again towards the door. The chief spoke harshly as the man rose and glared at him. The Delaware grunted sullenly, but finally assembled his sadly scattered effects and stood outside the door, waiting as he had been told.

The Seneca sat down again on the table edge, rubbed his foot, and then got up to continue the process. He was saved further efforts, however, by an accident at the hearth.

It was really Mrs. Frazier's fault. She had given the Irish girl a pinch on the arm to remind her to replenish the fire. It was a vicious pinch. The girl dodged, caught her skirt on the handle of the bubbling mush pot, and dumped it so that it slushed out several gallons of boiling contents into the middle of the floor.

The girl screamed and jumped. Mrs. Frazier, who found herself standing in a pool of boiling mush, screamed and jumped, with hot mush in one of her shoes. Hopping on one foot like a strange wading bird, and hobbling, she took after her servant with a stout stick, stamping upon several dozing Delawares in the pursuit. That, and a thin coating of steaming mush as it spread quietly but surely among the Indians, proved an effectual reveille.

They got up one by one and rushed out with strange guttural or whistling noises. In their various scrambling exits they were assisted either by the feet or the rhetoric of their father, the Seneca. Towards the last he was reduced to the use of his mouth alone, for his table was now surrounded by a film of hot mush, and he was forced to sit there, grave but isolated, looking down with grim satisfaction at the steaming confusion of the room.

Ecuyer had not laughed so heartily for years. Even the painful stitches it gave his wound could not prevent him from shaking with laughter. And Salathiel scarcely knew which was funnier, the Indian or the scalded spryness of Mrs. Frazier, whose pursuit of Frances had finally resulted in the capture of that unfortunate girl halfway up the ladder to the garret into which she had foolishly tried to climb.

A squalling struggle took place at the ladder, Frances trying to ascend, and Mrs. Frazier attempting to drag her down. A loud scream and a ripping sound announced and accompanied the departure of Frances' linsey-woolsey into the hands of Mrs. Frazier, leaving a rosy young figure of Mother Eve standing on the ladder.

"That's the way I want ye!" screamed Mrs. Frazier, who now seized the girl about the waist and tore her by main strength off the ladder rungs.

No one was laughing now. There was something exceedingly grim in the expression on Mrs. Frazier's blowzy countenance. Her bangs had come loose and flowed down over her face like the hair of a terrier. Behind these Medusa fringes her eyes glinted red and green. A sudden frenzy of strength possessed her. One big arm clasped the kicking girl about the waist like a child, and she was yanked to the bench by the fire and thrown over the old woman's knees like a big frog.

Mrs. Frazier then seized a short-handled, twig broom used for sweeping ashes, and began to belabour her over her bare buttocks with a merciless and iron strength.

The girl screamed and struggled furiously. Finally she went limp and simply screamed. But the old woman continued to beat her. At last, driven frantic by stinging pain, the girl managed to sink her teeth into the arm that was holding her.

At that Mrs. Frazier shrieked like a huge parrot. The screeching attained a shrill climax. Frances bit hard, refusing to let go even under a hail of blows. Finally Mrs. Frazier reached for the iron poker. But at that instant the door burst open and Mr. Frazier entered.

He took in the situation at a glance, seized his wife by her front hair, and rammed her head against the wall with a *crack*. The girl slipped from her tormentor's clutches and shrank back into a dark corner, rubbing her bare flanks and moaning. Mr. Frazier gave his wife's head another solid bang.

"I'll larn ye, ye murderin' old bitch ya," he said furiously.

His wife made no attempt to fight back. Her head drooped down on one shoulder now and she looked at her husband through her hair with one eye that had gone cold. The other was half shut and bloodshot. Mrs. Frazier drooled. A sudden silence fell on the cabin. Some of the bedraggled feathered heads of the Delawares came peering in through the door. The firelight glittered on their incurious, black-brown eyes.

"I'm right sorry, captain, 'deed I am," said Frazier shamefacedly. There could be no doubt from his expression that the man's chagrin was genuine. "It's a turrible thing to be jined with a mad thing," he muttered, and mopped his face with his sleeve.

"See to it she doesn't murder the girl," replied Ecuyer.

The Seneca grunted and spoke.

"Two squaws one lodge heap bad. Use'm big stick," he said sententiously, and smote his hands together. Then putting his feet to the floor, he felt the mush tentatively to see if it was cool enough to walk on in his moccasins.

The girl in the corner gave a shivering sob.

"Come," said Ecuyer. "Enough of this. By God, it's worse than Italy!" He walked out past the Delawares at the door, twirling his cane. Half of them were squatting in the snow.

"Get something to cover that poor wench with," said Ecuyer, pausing for a moment to look at the Delawares.

Salathiel dived into the wagon and took out a spare blanket from the chest under the seat. Then a thought struck him. He also took one of two small pistols from the arms chest and loaded it. He thrust this in the folds of the blanket and returned to the cabin.

Frances was still sitting in the corner. She looked up at him unashamed and unafraid, but with so much misery in her eyes he scarcely knew how to speak to her.

"Here," he said roughly but kindly, extending the blanket.

She rose and draped it about her nakedness with great dignity.

"Thanks for that much," she said.

Then he pressed the pistol into her hands. She understood instantly and laid it under the blanket folds in her bosom.

"It's loaded," he whispered.

"I'll not be after shooting meself with it," she said. "But I'll be after you as soon as I can walk. She's nigh cut the behind off'n me."

"I know. I saw," he said.

"Aye," said she, "now that you've seen so much of me, young mon, you'll not be like to forget me soon."

"I'm not likely to," he agreed.

"Albine," called the captain sharply.

He patted her hand with the pistol in it and left. She was holding it next to her breast. The eyes of the old woman followed him witchlike as he went out.

She sat, still dizzy, with her head against the logs. As the door closed behind Salathiel she got up and with her arms hanging before her and her hands working advanced slowly upon the Irish girl.

"So you'd be leaving me after all," she muttered, keeping her eyes on her.

Frances said nothing but sat watching her intently.

"*Give* me that blanket," said the old woman, leaning forward, "or I'll strip it off yer!"

It was then that out of the folds of the blanket close to the girl's neck Mrs. Frazier saw the small round eye of the pistol looking at her. She straightened up. Her hands fell by her side. She went back to her seat by the fire without saying a word.

Outside, Burent had the steps of the wagon down and was assisting the captain to climb in and strap himself into his swinging chair. One of the Delawares was examining the brass mountings on the harness with a disconcerting admiration and was inclined to be surly when Salathiel crowded him towards the cabin door with the shoulder of the mare. His father, the Seneca, and Mr. Frazier took him in charge.

An harangue by the chief, Mr. Frazier's sturdy bulk obstinately planted in the doorway with his rifle leaning conveniently by, the fact that the supply of whisky had departed—all this at last got the badly battered party of Delawares headed home. They went northwest instead of off on the war or horse-stealing path to the southeast, where temptation lay. They departed gloomily in single file, disappearing at last in a dense thicket about a half a mile away, apparently headed towards the Allegheny River.

Burent was now waiting only for the word to depart. He had already broken the wheels loose from the frozen ground, and the horses pawed impatiently. The old chief and Frazier stood looking on with lacklustre eyes. The wagon to them seemed a machine that might have descended from the skies, a contrivance whose perfection and ingenuity might at least have been the work of some minor deity. But their expressions were both noncommittal.

"Get the lead to the fort tomorrow and be sure to take the chief with you, Mr. Frazier," called the captain, who had at last bound himself with a broad kerchief and to his own satisfaction into the chair.

Mr. Frazier promised.

"I'll be passing by here now and then," said the captain significantly.

The chief grunted.

"Get on with you, Burent," said the captain.

Burent's whip cracked twice like a double-barrelled pistol. The horses threw themselves against the traces, and the heavy wagon drew away from the gloomy cabin at the crossroads at a steady trot, leaving two broad ribbons behind it in the snow. The back wheels were set a little wider apart than the front.

Half a mile ahead they began to breast a hill. Salathiel rode several circles about the slowly moving vehicle. The mare was delighted to be going again. Then the forest began to close in on them. Salathiel set himself to rein in his horse in order to keep just far enough ahead of the ark to be in sight, while as much as possible of the road ahead on both sides was in his constant and unrelenting view.

There were still about three hours of daylight left. He wondered where they would be camping that night. The shadows of the trees were long now. And the red tinge in the light began to beat levelly from the westward in open aisles of the forest, where there was a clean floor of snow.

26. In Which the Dead Arise

IT WAS uphill and downdale, about as tumultuous a bit of landscape as Salathiel had ever seen. This, indeed, was the foothill country of the Alleghenies, covered with an undisturbed forest from the beginning of time. Then the road would swing down to follow the valley of some stream amidst sumac thickets, whose black branches, with great red torches and remnants of scarlet leaves upon them, illuminated the way. The road was in good shape here.

Suddenly they came to the edge of their hilly plateau and plunged down into the valley of Turtle Creek just as it began to grow dark.

At the bottom of the long grade he splashed through a ford. His horse started to gallop ahead through the open glades of the valley, but he turned her about and waited in the twilight for the wagon on the bank of the stream near the ford. Open spaces lay ahead. The going would be good.

The wagon came over the stony bed of the creek, water rising nearly to the horses' bellies. They came up out of the flood, breasting the slope and pulling all together against their collars like one team, the water curling against their breasts and falling away gleaming. The brass points on the harness twinkled with a hundred sunset glints, and the great, dark bulk of the ark loomed behind, its wheels washed suddenly clean.

The mare snorted impatiently at her mates, and they were off again.

All at once they were out of the forest, taking a winding course through a long valley with all but perpendicular sides. In the sheltered valley the stream ran in wide, sweeping curves through a succession of wild meadows where the buffalo grass was still green near the roots and stood nearly waist-high. There were green leaves here even on the bushes, as though summer lingered regretfully in this retreat. The place swarmed with rabbits and wild turkeys. The thickets were alive with crows. Salathiel saw that, except for the wagon, there was nothing in that long valley of the Turtle Creek of which even a crow need take notice.

Yet they would not camp here, he guessed. The horses had enjoyed a long rest at Frazier's. In the valley the road made a smooth, clear track on a gravelly soil, good clean going; and they passed on, winding in and out for miles along the meadows while the night fell, the stars came out in a cloudless frosty sky, points of steel caught in a gauzy net that shimmered like wind-ruffled water against the black vault overhead.

Yet it was a white night. The starlight alone was enough to drive by. On the heights the wolves howled. At this season the night birds were ominously still. Here and there a scream from a rabbit told where a silent owl had drifted down.

Then there was a long, heavy haul up onto the heights again.

Salathiel stood waiting again just below the crest, seated easily on the mare, his rifle in the crook of his elbow. It was a great night, he thought. A storm of high-flown and half-glimpsed happy thoughts and sensations flowed through him.

In the valley he had let himself dream. There was the unknown and alluring world of the settlements ahead of him, a desire to see and find out akin to hunger increased by expectation, yet already in process of satisfaction by his being on the way. There was also the warm glow, the pleasing pity, of having helped the girl at the cabin. He would like to take her across his knees—that way—for a more pleasant pastime. Perhaps she would get away from Mrs. Frazier? Maybe she would make it to Ligonier after all?

But he had no luck with women. It was best to let them alone. They disturbed everything else that he was doing.

Did he wish he could find Jane again?

He began to think of her affectionately with a certain sorrowful yearning. In the vast night, in the forest that ran between the rising and setting of the moon, where was she? But, he reminded himself again, he must *not* think of such things. He must not give himself up to these pictures that glowed inside him and seemed to have a life of their own.

The noise of the mounting wagon, still some distance below, recalled him. It brought him back to the world that was outside, that was real. It was a world so vivid and dangerous, one that needed such constant and careful attention that to be caught "mooning", as he called it, might mean the difference between life and death. And what were dreams? What the past or the future compared to now?

It was winter, and there were enemies about. His eyes must look keenly outward to fit the puzzle of the blue shadows, the trees and the snow; of starlight and the vague loom of the country into a bright, clear, true picture of the way, the way they must go!

Here were the horses and the heavy wagon now.

He gave a low call to Burent, and heard his hail in reply. Then he turned and rode on again, aware of everything about him.

Surely the captain would be camping now—soon. But neither Salathiel nor Burent had yet learned the iron nature of the man in the wagon; the will in the weakening body that grew stronger as the body grew tireder. That night they rode on, and eternally on. That night they began to learn what, in the estimation of Captain Ecuyer, serving the king meant. So did the unfortunate horses.

In another hour they were up on the heights that lay between the Turtle Creek and Bushy Run, a long stretch, some of it bare and comparatively treeless from fires and weather. A wind from the northwest piped about them bitterly. It bit through clothes and slowly benumbed their feet and hands.

Burent swung his arms ceaselessly against his chest. In the wagon the captain stifled the groans that the constant motion of the vehicle was like to drag through his chattering teeth. He lit a small charcoal foot warmer and endeavoured to beat back the sleepy feeling in his leg, a numbness which threatened to ascend to his wound. He bitterly regretted now that he had set out without a sufficient escort. There should have been someone to ride behind as well as ahead. When he got to Ligonier he would rectify that.

From all accounts things were at a pretty pass with the garrison at Ligonier. Bouquet had gone into the matter with him at some length. Ligonier was important as the halfway post between Bedford and Fort Pitt. He might have to take stern measures. In this naked wilderness it was hard to be strict with the men. Poor devils, they suffered! And they seldom got paid. He would write Colonel Bouquet for the love of God to release him. He couldn't go on in this way. He needed surgeons, a rest. Geneva! He closed his eyes to see the snow peaks mirrored in the water. Lucille, how had you found it with the reverend doctor? If you had only waited, Lucille!

He stopped his mouth, and a groan, with his handkerchief and inhaled the verbena scent. Lucy, Lucy, how dainty you were, smelling so! Sicily! God, what a road! What a slide into the pit was that which the wagon had just taken! Enough to disembowel a man. They were stopped. He drew back the rear flap. A hundred yards behind, four fiery eyes were dripping molten silver in the moonlight. They stood watching with a sinister steady glare. Then two shadows faded into the brush. Wolves!

"Albine's riding back, sir," said Burent. "There's something ahead not quite right. Hosses lyin' down, it seems like."

Salathiel came trotting back rapidly.

"It's the Quaker Japson and his string of pack horses," he explained. "He's alone, and he's made a fire in a pit to keep him from freezing. Some of his beasts can't get up. I saw the glow of his fire and rode right over into his camp. That's what's bringing the wolves around. The man's scairt and wants we should camp here. He says we'll freeze if we don't. There's a blizzard-snap comin' on. It does feel like it."

The captain listened without comment. "Tell him if he wishes to come with us he may do so," he said finally. "Help him rouse his horses and let him follow behind. We'll camp at Bouquet's old battleground tonight. It can't be over an hour's going from here. There's a small stockade was built there this autumn by the convoys. It will give some shelter from the wind at least."

"And from the Injuns," added Burent, who made no disguise of his feelings. "I keep athinking of those Delawares."

"There'll be no Injuns tonight," said Salathiel. "It's now so cold they'll have stopped to make pit fires like Japson. You can't walk the ground in moccasins on a night like this."

"Maybe so," said Burent doubtfully.

"Get your horses going or they will be down, too," said the captain, impatient at the talk.

They stopped again abreast of where the Quaker had camped. With great difficulty Burent and Salathiel managed to get the Quaker's horses on their feet, all except one beast whose legs were paralyzed and already rigid with cold. They piled its pack into the wagon where Japson had promptly climbed. He seemed to take his welcome there for granted. One of his hands appeared to be frozen. His constant talk of the terrible cold made them all realize for the first time how extraordinarily cold it really was.

"The coldest night of my life," said the Quaker, "and I've traded through these woods twenty years come December. Thou hast caused me to lose three horses today, friend Ecuyer, two to the Virginian at Frazier's. He made off with them. And the one that can't rise."

"Thou wouldst lose all of them if Burent were not tying them behind for thee now," replied the captain. "It is fortunate we found thee here or the wolves would have by morning." He handed the man the charcoal burner.

"Aye?" said the Quaker, and began to smooth the mysteriously warm little box with his half-frozen hand.

Salathiel and Burent hastened the fastening of the string of pack horses behind the wagon as best they could. The wind was now pouring itself out of the northwest, arctic, clear, and steady. They wrapped themselves Indian fashion in extra blankets and put the horse blankets on the wagon teams and the mare.

Salathiel took a lead horse by the cheek straps and started them off. Burent ran alongside the wagon. The horses seemed to sense shelter ahead and strained forward. Luckily the string of pack horses "towing" behind was too tired to make trouble. Mr. Japson continued to ride in the wagon and let them take care of themselves, even though his precious goods were involved.

It was that which made the captain realize how cold it was, more than anything else.

Five miles, which took nearly two hours, brought them between two and three o'clock in the morning to the ford at Bushy Run. It was frozen smoothly solid. There was no sound in the valley and the still, dead cold of the place was appalling. A noise like a musket shot just ahead caused the front team to rear and everybody to handle his arms. It proved to be a chestnut tree split open halfway along its trunk by the frost. From time to time that night such reports continued to come to them out of the forest.

"Cheerily now," said Burent. "The stockade's just under the rise of yon hill ahead. Another mile will do it." He began to soothe and coax the lagging horses along.

Salathiel rode ahead for a careful look about. There was no one. The heavy wagon, its trailing caisson and string of horses came up slowly behind him. It was nearly three o'clock by the silver watch that Captain Ecuyer had given him when Salathiel saw the ark blunder through the gate into the small, entrenched stockade that had been erected for the protection of wagoners close by the battlefield of the summer before.

It lay, as Burent had said, just under the crest of the hill. The rise and the twelve-foot barrier of logs provided a grateful shelter from the paralyzing sweep of the blast. There was a rough lean-to shed and a well with a sweep.

The captain emerged from the wagon and began to call urgently for a fire. While the horses were being driven into the shed, he himself began to drag the remains of logs from old fires together, and to try to nurse along a blaze started by his flint and steel. The flame finally started up, revealing the black, log walls and frozen, mud-trampled interior of the place; the horses' rumps sticking out dejectedly under the shed.

Salathiel recalled afterward that they worked with a certain desperation that night. All were aware that in a few minutes more they would be stopped by the cold. It kept getting colder even inside the still stockade.

"Have the goodness to assist us, Mr. Japson," said the captain, "to preserve yourself."

"Me hand's frozen," said the Quaker.

"My foot isn't yet," said Burent, and approached him menacingly.

He gave in, muttering something, and began to help drag the logs towards the fire from a near-by pile. Albine knocked the ice and snow off them with his tomahawk, cut off the dry branches, and in a short while the fire had taken hold the length of several good-sized trees. They dragged up more wood, and the sparks soon soared up towards the stars.

"That will give notice to every savage within ten miles that we're here," said the Quaker.

"They'll think there's a large force then," said Salathiel. "The more fires we make now the better."

He and Burent started another blaze between the shed and the wagon. The horses were fed and lay down on piles of old leaves under the shed. They fed the Quaker's horses with corn from their own chest behind the wagon, out of mercy to the half-starved beasts. Burent forced Japson to bed down in the leaves under the shed near his horses, pointing out that if the fire reached the leaves, Mr. Japson would perish along with his property. Then a few collops of meat were roasted, which all ate ravenously.

The captain cut three straws of different lengths. He and Burent and Salathiel then drew lots for keeping watch. Burent drew the first watch and the captain the second. No one thought of trusting Japson.

"Two hours' sleep apiece," said Ecuyer. "That will get us under way late in the morning, but the horses must have some rest. If it comes on to snow, whoever is on watch must wake me. We'll leave, for we can't risk being snowed in here. Keep your eyes open, Burent."

The captain and Salathiel crawled into the wagon. Burent kept himself awake by keeping up the fires and bedevilling the Quaker.

Two hours later the captain took his watch. The fires died slowly. When it came Salathiel's turn there was a great bed of glowing coals. Japson snored. Some of the horses were beginning to struggle to their feet, although it was still dark. The wind had completely died away. A more than usual stillness reigned. The tremendous cold had laid a hand of death on the country. It was the coldest Salathiel could ever remember. In fact, it was the coldest night, save one, he was ever to know.

He built up the fires again carefully, and stood listening.

It was in this desolate open tract of country, waterless, and hemmed in by the eternal woods, that Bouquet had been ambushed the summer before. A long line of clay scars in military order showed where his dead had been buried just off the road. The gaunt, black arms of the forest seemed to be tossing despairing hands over them towards the sky.

Despite the cold, Salathiel stepped out of his boots and hid them by the gate. His fur-lined moccasins would do, and he would be gone only a little while. He intended to fetch a circle around the stockade. It would be just as well to do so.

He faded into the shadows silent as a wolf. It was the old hunting stride, the rifle at a long trail, and he crouching a little. He went back as far as the ford, never losing sight of the stockade. There were no tracks there but their own. He felt the ground and the snow now turned to a crisp ice crust, where every track was frozen like a mark in stone. He came crouching back through the woods up onto the crest of the hill and looked down over a chaos of tumbling hills and forest.

There was a trail there that led off to the northward, but nothing but a few deer tracks were on it. Half of this scout he was doing for sheer enjoyment, half from an excess of caution. But it *was* sheer joy to be back in the wild again, to hear the silence, to be rid of smells. The cold air seemed immortally clean. He came down the hill just behind the sky line and struck the road again. A faint light was beginning to dull the stars in the east. There was a hazy overcast, a kind of premonition of dawn in the air, and it was in this blue-greyness against the crest of a little rise that he saw them.

He saw them before he heard their stealthy sounds, a rustle in the weeds, the crack of a twig, or a loose stone now and then. There were only two of them, a man and a squaw, and most curious of all there was a pony. It was that which had made the noise.

His first impulse was to shoot. But the thought that there might be others about restrained him. And as the grey dawn grew gradually a bit brighter, and he could see the movements of the couple more plainly, curiosity overcame him.

He crawled forward to a fallen log and then down a small gully to a considerable clump of bushes. They were quite close now. They were searching for something. He saw it before they did. It was marked by a branch sticking up with a long white feather tied to it. One of the horses at the stockade neighed. The Indian grabbed his pony about the nose and looked back anxiously. He couldn't be seen from the stockade. He was just below a ridge in the hill. They waited. Morning grew brighter.

The squaw began to poke and scoop in a hollow full of leaves and pine needles below the feathered stick. She began to make a low noise of mourning. It was the beginning of the death song. The man with her struck her. She fell forward into the hollow place on her knees. When she got up a tall, rigid Indian with a chief's bedraggled war bonnet seemed to rise up out of the ground with her.

Salathiel's rifle came poking through the branches instinctively. He drew a bead on the head of the chief who had so suddenly appeared as though out of the earth. He could just see the end of his rifle well enough to aim. Then he saw that the man he was aiming at was dead, frozen stiff as a board; that his face had fallen away and the white cheek-bones showed through.

For some instants Salathiel found himself looking down the long barrel of his rifle at the two pits of darkness under the chalky brow. The dead chief was too bedraggled, too covered with leaves and debris, to tell to what tribe he had belonged. It was plain he was one of the dead from the battle of the summer before. Salathiel guessed that it must be his brother and sister who had come for him. It would not be the duty of the man's squaw. They had come from beyond the Illinois, perhaps. The western tribes made much of their dead.

While he watched the squaw, memories of Mawakis returned to him. He lowered his rifle. These were the last Indians who should ever pass safely before his sights, he vowed. But there was something moving and pitiable about the three before him. He watched them fascinated.

They took the dead chief, forced his legs apart, and bound him on the pony. One of his arms, from the hand of which the flesh had slipped like a glove, extended behind him. The woman trudged before, the man behind. He stopped once and looked back. Then the forest swallowed them.

Salathiel rose, conscious now of the cold that had begun to stiffen him. The metal of his rifle burned through his jacket. All the eastern crests of the Alleghenies were outlined with grey light. The horse at the stockade neighed again. It was probably one of the Quaker's.

The cold was colossal. He started to run up the hill towards the stockade to send the blood through his numbed extremities.

In the frozen, wheel-rutted interior Burent was up and had a huge fire of piled logs going. The captain, wrapped in a long cloak, was seated before the flames, toasting his shins. Japson was tending the horses in a way which met even with Burent's approval. From time to time the Quaker came over to the fire to dip his frosted hand in a kettle of hot water.

The captain looked relieved at seeing Salathiel again.

"Our friends the Delawares, for example?" he said, raising his eyebrows.

"They have not followed us, sir," replied Salathiel. "I have been out looking for them since before dawn. We'd have heard of them before this if they were on our trail."

"Thou wilt *not* be followed," said Japson emphatically, and went over to feed the horses, his own included, with corn from the caisson. Burent said nothing but looked annoyed.

"I think Japson is right," agreed Salathiel, "and the road will be like iron at least as far as the fort. We should make good time."

"I have certain plans about the road," said the captain, and smiled enigmatically. "I don't think we'll be following the road all the way. Get a file out of the tool chest, Burent," he added. "No, I'll not shave this morning, Albine. The lather would freeze on my face, I think. But the file is not for that."

They sat down and ate heartily of bacon and fried corncakes. The captain shared a dram of brandy with them and looked longingly at the mare, shook his head, and climbed regretfully into the wagon. Salathiel wrapped him up as best he could and blew into the charcoal hand stove until it glowed. Ecuyer prepared himself for the day's ordeal. Ligonier was still many hours away from the standpoint of a man in pain. Perhaps the cold would help to numb it some.

"When we come to the first crossing of the Loyalhanna Branch," he said to Salathiel, "let me know. Waken me then, even if I am asleep."

It occurred to Albine forcefully as he looked at the captain's face, which had begun to have a peaked and wasted look, that there might come a time when he would not be wakable. The captain's mouth trembled despite his firm chin.

"Never mind," said Ecuyer, sensing something of what was passing in Salathiel's mind. "I'll pull through. And there will be a good surgeon at Bedford. I hope it's Boyd."

Just then the clatter of Japson leaving ahead of them with his pack horses and the shadow of the man himself passed by between the sun and the canvas walls of the wagon. The captain noticed it.

"But I think we'll get there before you, my friend, for all that," he said, signalling Albine to hasten the wagon's departure.

Burent and Salathiel linked the horses to the trace chains rapidly. In a few moments the ark rolled out of the stockade over the frozen ruts and took the road eastward to Ligonier. Japson had already disappeared ahead.

"Keep the horses at it," said the muffled voice of the captain inside the wagon. "Trot when you can. Never mind me."

Surprisingly enough, they *were* able to trot from time to time.

From Bushy Run the road went over a succession of low ridges with an occasional stretch along a brief plateau. It ran into the densest thickets, while the hills kept getting longer and steeper. Once Burent caught a glimpse of Japson and his string of horses crossing a crest ahead. He was going fast. The wagon also was making time, and quite steadily, for at least there were no ruts or holes to negotiate. The water in them had frozen level with the ground and hard. They came lurching down the hills, the horses slipping and stumbling, the wheels sliding, brakes on, and Burent performing miracles with the long reins.

Then they would stop, breathe for a few moments, and breast the inevitable climb ahead with the backs of the two teams stretching out in two parallel lines, shoulders thrust into the collars.

At such places Salathiel rode forward, and passing a toggle with a canvas collar on it that had been arranged for the mare, he made fast to rings in the forward trace chains and threw the weight of his own horse into the haul upward. It was funny how soon the team horses came to expect this. They would snort and whinny for the mare to come when they started to climb. And they followed after her and her rider eagerly. In this way they would come up over the crests famously and Salathiel would whip aside as the wagon plunged recklessly down.

And so hour after hour with an occasional rest, and then the cold for a spur at the start again.

It was at one of these times of brief rest, when all was silent, except for the breathing of the horses, that Salathiel managed to shoot a deer.

It came peering at them suddenly out of a thicket with the fatal curiosity of its kind. Then it flirted its white tail, jumped aside on a log, and was about to bound away when Salathiel's bullet struck it down.

There had been just time enough to unsling his rifle. He began to ponder that. In his estimation it had taken far too long, fifteen counts at least. He would have to learn to do better. It would not always be a deer that awaited his shot. Yes, undoubtedly, he must practice. And it was irritating how long it took him to reload too.

The deer was strapped on the caisson. It was a young doe and its head, that had at first flopped at him, speedily stiffened in the cold. It seemed now to be looking back at him steadily and reproachfully. *It* had not been quick enough, he thought. *He* would not like to be caught—for the same reason.

A ridge now lay ahead, the most mountainous they had yet crossed. From its summit there was a brief, splendid glimpse of the Laurel Hill and the Alleghenies far off and up, cloudy, marching parallel north and south in long, undulating solid walls of trees. For a moment Salathiel stood looking at them uplifted, astonished, and amazed. The clouds were low and the mountains seemed to drag at the bottom of the sky. Then Burent shouted something at him, and they plunged down again. He understood him to say that this was the Chestnut Ridge and that Ligonier lay on the other side.

At the bottom, in a wide valley, was a dense tangle of sycamores and the silent, broad, frozen levels of the Loyalhanna Creek stilled in full winter flood.

Here they stopped and cooked a brief meal, which the deer furnished. Then they watered the horses. It was necessary to chop a hole in the river, and Salathiel noticed that the heads of the horses disappeared almost to their ears when they drank, so thick was the ice.

It was not necessary to waken the captain as he had ordered. He had emerged himself in considerable distress. The wound in his groin had broken and it was necessary to wash and rebandage it. The icy water they dipped out of the Loyalhanna, he soon discovered, gave him great relief. For some reason his fever also abated. At any rate, he now insisted upon dressing himself with some care, assisted by Albine. Except for a day-old beard, he soon looked himself again and very much the king's officer in a fresh wig and a gold-laced three-cornered hat, cockade and all.

While this combined surgery, tailoring, and toilet was going forward, the captain directed Burent to take the file and sharpen the calks on the shoes of the horses. The mare was included. Japson, they saw, had scrambled up the far bank across the ford and continued along the road, as the marks left by his horses plainly showed.

"But we will not follow him," said Ecuyer. "It is about eight miles by the road, which is quite bad here, to Ligonier, and only some three or four miles by the creek. If this little sketch map of mine is to be trusted, the stream curves here and cuts across through the forest, and you know the Ligonier stockade is on its banks. So we will take the river, since nature has paved the way. Burent, do you see that the horses do not fall."

Salathiel and Burent were both lost in admiration at this simple stratagem, particularly that even that morning the captain had remembered to take the file out of the chest. They would not have to drag the chest from under the wagon now. They might even make the fort ahead of Japson. Burent chuckled.

With a little coaxing they got the horses to trust themselves upon the ice. Then they tied the wheels together and the ark slid on its iron tires along the creek like a sleigh. The horses walked gingerly at first, but with more confidence as the iron points on their shoes continued to hold. Only once were they in great difficulty. It was where the river ran a brief stretch of rapids before a low falls. Two of the horses fell, one on either side. They wrapped blankets about their heads and got them up again.

"Only the blind can be persuaded to get up and go on again, sometimes," remarked the captain. "Perhaps that is why the future is always kept dark to us? Go on! Get on with it! Don't gape. Take the blankets off!"

They dragged the ark by main force over a small rocky island at the falls whose spill made a kind of ramp. The removal of some saplings with an axe made the way just negotiable. Then they resumed, sliding ever so smoothly again. The river wound in and out like a serpentine canal. The captain lit a cigar. His wound was delightfully numb again. The discharge had seemed to improve it. At least it was no longer throbbing, and the motion of the wagon was silken. No one would be expecting him to arrive at the fort, especially when he came by "water". His welcome was bound to be exquisitely informal.

The trample of the horses on the ice made a kind of low booming sound at certain places. It was windless and appallingly still in the deep valley. It was many degrees below zero. Salathiel was slapping his legs and thighs to keep the blood going. Burent from time to time beat his feet on the wagon floor.

Yes, they would certainly arrive as a surprise, thought the captain. He would be able to see what was really going on at the fort. Ligonier was such an important link, the main outpost between Fort Bedford and Fort Pitt. It had nearly been lost once last summer, reinforced just in time. Good discipline must be kept, and at all costs a strict watch, or the frontier to the west would fall for lack of supplies being able to reach it. Ecuyer leaned back for a moment, easing himself in his swinging chair.

At that moment the thud of a musket and a hole that seemed to appear simultaneously in both sides of the canvas roof about a foot above the captain's head confirmed his opinion that the arrival of the wagon at Ligonier would be a "surprise". The horses reared and Burent burst into a stream of profanity surprisingly sustained for so quiet a man.

"It's the fort, sir. We've just raised it through the trees," said Salathiel. "The sentry post at the bridge across the creek must have fired at us. I can see some of them making up the road for the fort now."

"Ride forward and tell them this wagon is not a moving Indian village," replied Ecuyer. Salathiel took to the west bank and galloped forward along the road to the fort, shouting and waving his cap. Captain Ecuyer dusted a little powder off his hat and looked up at the holes in the canvas thoughtfully.

A drum began to roll.

"Move on, Burent," he called. "Get the wagon up that patch of low bank at the landing, take the road straightaway, and get under the walls of the fort. They can see what we are then."

A few minutes later, and ahead of the wagon, Salathiel rode out into the large clearing before the stockade. It was high land here and overlooked the valley southward. The clearing was large enough to serve as a rough drill ground, and for that purpose the stumps had been removed. A party of Highlanders in red kilts scrambled and ran before him towards the gate, which was open. Inside the fort he caught a glimpse of a frantic dashing around. The drums crashed again. Somebody was trying to close the gate. Someone else with a plumed Highland bonnet came out of a barracks door, drawing a claymore.

Salathiel rode through the gate and drew rein on a little cobbled space. For a moment all the garrison that was visible, including the sentries on the galleries, stood looking foolishly at him.

"Weel, young mon?" said a sergeant, the man in the plumed bonnet,

coming towards him and sliding the claymore back into its scabbard.
"Weel, what is it ye have to say?"

27. Mr. Yates Introduces Himself

SALATHIEL announced the arrival of the captain, and suggested that
no more loaded salutes should be fired.

The Highland sergeant's face turned dark with anger when he heard
what had happened. A furious conversation in Gaelic occurred between
him and the sentry who had fired the shot. The man came forward
reluctantly at the sergeant's order and gave up his musket. The rumble
of the wagon was now heard coming along the walls.

In urgent haste the sergeant formed what men he could literally lay
his hands on into a guard drawn up at the gate. They were a motley
crew, three Pennsylvania militiamen in tattered green watchcoats and
six Highlanders in red and black crossed kilts. None of them were armed
except the sergeant, who still had the rifle of the sentry he had disarmed.
This was duly presented as the wagon came through the gate, but not
without delay. For having once been dragged half-shut, the gate was
now to be opened again only by violent measures. Finally, it slipped off
its upper hinge and sagged inward drunkenly.

The ark drew up before the barracks in the fort with rather a professional flourish on the part of Burent, who saw that the horses were
reined in and stepping high. Salathiel fitted on the small pair of steps
and Ecuyer came limping down them, his heavy cane under his arm.

A deep silence, broken only by the grunting of an extraordinary number of pigs, fell upon the interior of the outpost. The captain walked
over and took a look at the "guard". He also glanced sidewise at the
sagging gate. The sergeant's face turned as red as his tunic.

"You can come to the order, sergeant," the captain said. Another moment of even more intense silence ensued.

"What are these?" asked Ecuyer finally, pointing to a pile of curious,
flat round stones with iron handles on them, which the guard had piled
hastily in a heap behind them.

"Curlin' stanes, your Honour," gasped the sergeant.

The captain's brows went up in enquiry.

"It's a game the Scots do be playing on the ice, sir," countered the
sergeant. "And it's fine curlin' weather, the noo . . ."

"So no trivial duties have been allowed to spoil the sport," concluded
Ecuyer, bringing out his handkerchief with an irritated flourish, and
looking the sergeant in the eye. He observed, however, that alone among
the garrison, the sergeant was properly turned out. "And you are the
only one on duty here?"

"Your Honour has stated it aboot correctly," said the sergeant, returning the captain's level gaze. "You will find the post in a dreadfu' way.
You're a sight for sare eyes, sir. I'd gladly git oop and tastify so at the
auld kirk. The Scots are verra loyal, but—"

"Dismiss your curlers, sergeant," interrupted the captain impatiently.
"Tell them to arm themselves ready for a general muster. Post some
sober sentries. And, sergeant, before you do anything else, rehang the
gate and close it. By the way, where *are* the officers?"

"Lieutenant St. Clair has gone back to Fort Bedford. Him and Ensign
Erskine couldn't get along, sir. The Pennsylvania officers have whusked
off to Bedford, too. You see, the ensign has a king's commission whilst
the two militia lieutenants were only of the provincial line. The men
have a' been takin' sides. Half the Pennsylvanians are locked up the
noo i' the old hay byre. Meestir Erskine is dootless aboot."

"Thank you, sergeant, that will do," said the captain. "Have Mr.
Erskine report to me at once. Dismiss the guard."

"Curlers, dismissed," said the sergeant, a look of sly triumph on his
face.

A cackle of loud talk burst out in the fort as the guard scattered.
Hoots and catcalls mingled with the shrill voice of a woman here and
there.

Disregarding this disrespectful welcome, but burning with indignation, Captain Ecuyer made for the blockhouse in the centre of the
stockade from whose stone chimney, the only one in the fort, sparks
were soaring high into the still air. Evidently it was the headquarters
of the place.

While all this was going on, Salathiel had been looking about him
at the interior of Fort Ligonier and at the strange assortment of his
Majesty's subjects, armed and unarmed, male and female, who might be
said to infest rather than to inhabit it.

Fort Ligonier was by no means a large one. Perhaps an acre had been
enclosed by a log stockade set in the midst of much more spacious outworks, trenches, rifle pits, and artillery emplacements thrown up hastily
by the troops under Forbes, and later on by Bouquet, as they had moved
forward to Fort Pitt and made their base here for the time being. These
outer works enclosed an area of several acres of fairly level ground lying
at the foot of a small knoll upon which the stockade itself had been
erected. But it would have taken a small army to man these outworks,
and they were now abandoned, full of water, and lying in great raw
gashes around the clearing.

In the middle of this tangle of rutted roads, camp pits, entrenchments, the stockade of the permanent post rose on its knoll in the centre
to a height of nearly forty feet. About the whole encampment, except
in the direction of the Loyalhanna Creek, and at a distance varying from
a few hundred yards to a quarter of a mile, swept the black arc of the

forest utterly impenetrable except in single file by an Indian trail northward to Venango, or by the military road which passed immediately in
front of the stockade and disappeared not far away into the rolling hills
eastward towards Fort Bedford.

There was nothing remarkable about the stockade at Ligonier, except
that it had been provided more than usually generously with cannon.
There was a small defensive tower rising a story above the gate, which
could accommodate at least ten riflemen, and this, together with the
more permanent buildings in the interior of the place, was roofed with
cobbles and pebbles held together by puddled clay to ward off fire
arrows. The last had been Captain Ecuyer's own suggestion to Colonel
Bouquet, and he was very proud of it.

Salathiel was greatly disappointed as he looked about him while the
captain had been inspecting the guard. He knew, of course, that Ligonier was only a way post and could not hold a candle to Fort Pitt as a
fortress. But he was expecting that the inhabitants, if not the garrison,
of Ligonier would begin to discover some of those traits of elegance and
refinement of which he had read in the novels of Captain Ecuyer's small
library. Was he not already almost a hundred miles nearer London—at
the least, fifty!

Alas and alack, there was not a single refined novelty to be seen anywhere as he gazed eagerly about him. The inside of the fort consisted
of a double-storied blockhouse with overhanging, loopholed eaves and
a massive door with some stone steps leading up to it. Between it and
the gate was an area paved roughly with large, smooth boulders from
the creek, and this in turn was flanked by two long, low, windowless
log barracks, slab-roofed, that looked at each other with a blind, uncom-
promising, bulldog stare.

Behind these barracks a foul, muddy area stretched to rough sheds
and storehouses which ran along both sides of the fort close to the walls.
They also were windowless.

Beyond the centre blockhouse or headquarters were two lines of some
twenty huts facing each other. Most of these huts had chimneys of
plastered clay and sticks which smoked away abominably, filling the
interior of the fort with a reeking haze through which the long rifle
platform, that ran all around the place like a continuous gallery, could
be seen with difficulty.

Crouched here and there along this platform was a sentry trying to
warm his hands over a pan of coals or striding up and down beating
his arms while his musket leaned against the parapet. These sentries,
with the pigs moving below them, and the sooty folds of a flapping
Union Jack would have been the only signs of animation about the
place had not the alarm given by the recent firing of the outpost at the
bridge set the garrison to scurrying about and brought the inhabitants
of the huts to their doors, where they now stood coughing and shivering,

wrapping tattered blankets about their shoulders, and calling shrilly to one another.

Among the population of this miserable "village" were a number of women with soot-smutched faces and elflocks flying in the wind. They now began to pick their way from one hut to another, driving the pigs before them up the narrow street, and lifting their skirts above their knees at the worst mudholes. Evidently the news had spread that the occasion of the alarm was not an Indian attack, but something much more serious, the arrival of a king's officer. Visits and gossip were in order.

Captain Ecuyer, accompanied by the sergeant, whose name Salathiel soon learned was McLaughlin, now came across the cobbled space towards the blockhouse before which the wagon had drawn up.

"Send for the drummer," said the captain to McLaughlin; "we will have a general muster here in a few minutes. This is where you usually assemble, isn't it?"

"Aye," said the sergeant. "It's the only spot free of pigs in the establishment. Lefteenant St. Clair is verra fond of swine."

"We'll take that up with Mr. St. Clair later," said the captain. "Albine, it looks as though we'd be here for a day or two, unless Lieutenant St. Clair does return sooner. Have Burent stable the horses. Keep the wagon here, and carry in all the necessaries for cooking and comfort. Sergeant, put an honest sentry on this beat before headquarters and see that he is relieved by another honest man. No pilfering from this vehicle, or out of your own pay it comes."

Sergeant McLaughlin looked serious. "There be sax Alexanders i' the coompany," he said, "twa of thim—"

"Will do," snapped the captain.

At this moment a woebegone young drummer boy of the militia appeared in a green watchcoat that stretched nearly to his heels. He had been crying, to judge by the smears on his face, and looked apprehensively about him.

"Cheer up, my child," said the captain. "Can you beat the general?"

"Yis, sor. Thot I kin!"

Tightening the snares on his drum, the boy struck an heroic stance and the drum began to roll its loud summons, filling the stockade with reverberating waves of sound. A look of rapt, urchin pleasure, of a trancelike delight fell across the boy's features, causing Captain Ecuyer, the sergeant, and Salathiel to smile. The drum ceased.

"Well done!" cried the captain. "You're a true soldier!"—and without thinking, he tossed him the next to the last sixpence he had. It fell in the snow, and as the lad stooped to pick it up, his cap, much too large for him, fell off.

"Great God!" exclaimed Ecuyer.

The top of the boy's head was one hairless, red scar. Only a fringe of hair remained like a tonsure. It also was carrot red.

"Aye," said McLaughlin, "thot's why they call him the 'Monk'."

Salathiel suddenly remembered a copper-coloured arm that had once come out of a bush and caught another boy by the hair. It might have been this way . . .

"Come on, *you*," said he gruffly but kindly to the young drummer, "lend me a hand unlading this wagon."

While Salathiel and the Monk addressed themselves to getting the captain's things moved out of the wagon and into the blockhouse, the garrison of the place was rapidly assembling in the paved area before the barracks, the Highlanders on one side and the militia on the other.

"Careful now," said Salathiel, as he and the drummer swung one of Johnson's old valet chests up the short flight of icy stone steps that led to the blockhouse door. "It won't do to stumble with these." He reached for the latchstring.

Just then the door was flung violently open, revealing a small, dark young man with a pair of blazing eyes that seemed to be starting from his head. He carried a half-pike, or "spontoon", threateningly. He was dressed in filthy white officer's breeches, a pair of magnificent London boots with green tops, and a vest from which a fine cambric shirt, also filthy, protruded. In addition he had on a gorget, and the remains of a leather stock. His handsome face was flushed a dull red and subtly swollen, so that his expression was like that of a mask of extreme exasperation and sullen anger. In fact, about the short, dark young man there was an air of sleepy menace and malice, and he was now glaring directly into Salathiel's eyes.

"God damn it!" roared he. "Who's the bloody zaney gave orders for the drum to be beat?" And then, noticing Salathiel for the first time, "Who, by God, are you? What are ye trying to bring that blasted coffin in here for?" He flourished the spontoon.

"Out of my way," he screamed.

Then he seemed to be flung by some force from within him, for he cleared the doorway and steps in one nimble leap, jumping clear over the chest, and landing gracefully enough on the cobbles only a few feet behind the spot where Captain Ecuyer and the sergeant were standing awaiting the assembling of the garrison.

But something else had happened during the jump. As he passed over the chest, Salathiel had twisted the spontoon out of his hand. It had been a simple instinctive move on his part.

Disturbed by the clatter of boots behind him, Captain Ecuyer now turned around. The angry, dark young man came slowly to attention, the anger in his face giving way to a blank expression of surprise.

"It was *I* who ordered the drum to be beat, Mr. Erskine," said Captain Ecuyer. "Do you usually attend formations with your coat off?"

"I sometimes attend them with nothing on at all, sir," replied the ensign.

"Losh!" exclaimed the sergeant, a look of alarmed disgust on his face.

"So I have been informed by Colonel Bouquet," replied the captain. "But it is now extremely cold weather, and I would advise you at least to put on your coat, Mr. Erskine." He smiled at the dark young man enigmatically. "And your hat, likewise."

Mr. Erskine apparently considered this advice carefully. "Yes, sir," said he at last, humbly enough, and started to return to get his missing garments.

"A sad case but a *verra* brave young mon, sir," ventured the sergeant. "His mither was a Featherstonehaugh."

"*Vraiment!*" said Ecuyer.

"Oh, aye!" said the sergeant.

"Is he always as drunk as he is now?" queried the captain.

"On the Sabbath it's much warse. He has a braw breeth on him then would be like salvation to the saints. I hae been here sax months the noo, an' I hae niver seen him sober aince."

The captain nodded impatiently. The garrison seemed to be all assembled.

"Call the men to attention," he said.

Salathiel and the boy called the Monk were now well along with unloading the wagon. Burent had stabled the horses and returned in time to give them a hand. They brought in the captain's desk, his cot, all of Johnson's valet supplies, and the cooking utensils.

The blockhouse main room was a large one. It occupied the entire lower floor of the building. It had an immense chimney at one end and was lit now by a roaring fire, three lanthorns, and a surprising number of candles stuck in an even more astonishing number of rum bottles. Except for the door, and the loopholes stuffed with rags, there were no openings. Nevertheless, with the fire, lanthorns and candles, the room was warm, inviting. In each corner was a double-decked bunk and there were several barrel chairs and a ladder leading to the rifle loft.

At a table drawn somewhat back from the fire sat a dapper young man in a smart bag wig, a beautiful suit of grey clothes, and scarlet stockings. His buckled shoes were cocked up on a chair under the table, and his head was leaning on his elbow in such a manner that his hand shaded his face. Writing materials, a pile of legal papers, and a pack of cards disposed in some intricate game of solitaire lay spread out before him. There was also a bottle half-full with a tumbler turned down over its top.

When the door had first opened to admit Salathiel and the Monk with the captain's chest, and to permit the egress of Mr. Erskine, the young man had put a weight on the pile of papers with a gesture of annoyance, and one arm across the arrangement of cards.

"Shut the door," said he, with a peculiarly stark accent. "Keep the winter wind and that damned madman out of here if you can." Then he looked up, suddenly aware that strangers were entering.

Salathiel was instantly confronted by a pair of as determined and disconcerting eyes as he was ever to see. They were Scotch grey with green flecks in them here and there. A powerful but finely moulded face with a broad brow and hard pointed jaw seemed to stamp itself as if by a blow on his mind.

"Hello, Mr. Giant," said the young man to Salathiel. "Excuse me for beginning our acquaintance by offering you good advice. But, even if I were twice as big as you, I'd put that spontoon back in the rack there by the door. Its owner will be after it in a few minutes, I can promise you. Unfortunately I know him to be quarrelsome."

Salathiel nodded amicably enough. He lowered the end of the chest he was carrying and put the half-pike back in the arms rack by the door. Then he returned and took up the chest again. But for the first time he was suddenly aware of how very big he was. A giant, eh? It seemed to him quite suddenly that his height and his shoulders crowded the room. How could the small man at the table be so disconcerting? Maybe it was because he, Salathiel, must make a ridiculous figure, a large awkward oaf at one end of the long, black chest with the small, scalped drummer boy tugging at the other handle. The Monk's large cap had slipped down over his eyes. The man at the table was grinning. His smile was good-natured but patronizing. A wave of anger swept over Albine. He couldn't stand there with the chest forever!

"I'll trouble you to move your table, Mr. —?"

"Mr. Yates," said the gentleman obligingly, but making no effort to move. Salathiel put down the chest ponderously and took a step forward.

"Oh, very well," said Mr. Yates, "I'll give you eminent domain." He helped Salathiel to move the table to one side of the room and sat down at it again, gathering the disturbed pack of cards into one hand with a peculiarly deft motion. "Who's the nabob?" said he, nodding at the chest.

Salathiel had never heard of nabobs and he failed to reply. He and the Monk put the chest down in the corner near the fire, which he had determined the captain should occupy. He turned about . . .

"I say," said Mr. Yates, returning to the charge, "who's coming in on us? Who's your master?"

"No one," said Salathiel. "I'm neither a soldier nor a servant, my friend. The chest, however, belongs to Captain Simeon Ecuyer, if that's what you want to know."

"No offence, no offence!" cried Mr. Yates. "Ecuyer's one of the finest, even if he is a Swiss. You might well be proud to sarve him."

"I am," replied Salathiel, "but just because I'm doing something useful, I'm not a slave."

That had been one of Johnson's pet contentions, and it now came pa
to his pupil's tongue.

"Demme, I like your spirit," replied Mr. Yates. "This is America an
you can suit yourself." He flipped the pack of cards from one hand t
another in a continuous stream. The Monk was fascinated, until his ca
slipped over his eyes. "Demme, what you said is exactly the phrase
want for my letter home," remarked Yates as an afterthought. He pu
the cards down and made a note. "I'm much obleeged to you, Mr.-
what-did-you-say-your-name-was?"

"Salathiel Albine."

"There's a fine rebel sound to that. It hath a Roundhead twist." H
laughed, picking up the cards again. The Monk took off his cap to watc
him shuffle them. Mr. Yates started back in surprise.

"For God's sake, boy, put that cap on again," he yelled, stopping th
cards in mid-air, as it were. "I can't stand the face of a cherub topped o
by what looks like an African monkey's behind!" he exclaimed. "This i
a terrible country," he insisted, bringing his fist down on the table. "
say, boy, *put on your God-damned cap!*"

At that precise moment the door burst open again and Ensign Erskin
entered and began a frantic hunt for his coat and hat. He eventuall
retrieved them from under piles of his belongings and the bedclothes
Then he stopped and seemed to recollect something.

"My spontoon!" said he, advancing menacingly on Salathiel. Mr
Yates pointed violently at the arms rack and managed to attract hi
attention.

"Hurry up, Malcolm," he said. "The commandant from Fort Pitt i
here."

"Chreest, don't I know it," cried the disturbed young officer, an
seizing his spontoon from the rack, he stumbled out through the doo
and down the steps with a curious drunken gravity and agility.

Salathiel, Mr. Yates, and the Monk found themselves laughing hear
ily together at this performance. Mr. Yates was full of quips at th
expense of the confused Mr. Erskine, but good-natured and merry ones
He and Salathiel soon found themselves talking. The captain lingere
outside, and the talk went on while Salathiel sat on the big chest, an
from time to time Mr. Yates spun the cards from one hand to anothe
out of sheer nervous energy.

It was surprising how from the time of their first meeting a definit
understanding, what might even better be termed a "working agree
ment", came into being between Salathiel and the young lawyer, fo
such he was, found sitting at the table piled high with legal papers an
cards before the headquarters chimney at Ligonier.

Like any other enduring alliance national or personal it was, of course
based principally upon a mutual sympathy and understanding, uncon
scious at first, and only to be tested later on by events. It so happene

there were enough basic likenesses and interesting differences in the real characters of both men to provide the grist for an enduring association. It was not precisely a friendship. That would have been too warm and human a word to describe it. "Working agreement" is the more apt expression.

That evening in the room at Ligonier each of them sensed immediately and instinctively that the other was a lone wolf. Afterward they drifted into hunting as a pack of two. The dual advantages were soon obvious and enormous. They found their strength enhanced by the square.

Mr. Yates continued at the table to shuffle cards with a professional dexterity punctuated by remarks of admiration at the ingeniousness of the captain's provision for comfort. In particular, his hearty approval of the preparations for supper begun by Salathiel in the great fireplace was hardly surpassed even by the Monk, and that is saying a great deal, for the boy was half-starved.

The conversation went on.

Mr. Yates presently got up and took an active and skilful part in the preparations for dinner himself, producing a large plum cake from his own baggage and anointing it with raw brandy. The fact that the cook was a giant, that anyone so large could or would cook at all, continued to intrigue him.

The young lawyer had arrived some years before in America. He had from the first made up his mind to remain permanently in the colonies and to enter into the spirit of his new environment as naturally as possible. Albine was a native specimen and a puzzle to him. Here was something to be investigated. Yates began, and with great skill and tact, to cross-question Salathiel about his past. And to Yates, at least, the story was amazing. There was nothing like this in London or even in Thurso! They went on talking and laughing.

Salathiel on his part had not had a talk with anyone his own age so interesting since the disappearance of Lieutenant Francis towards Philadelphia with the ever-memorable Bustle. But this time he did not feel himself at a disadvantage. Yates was friendly, was a gentleman, and yet somehow they stood on the same floor together. If he asked personal questions, he also replied frankly when questioned himself. He helped get the supper instead of ordering a servant to bring it in. Between them, in about an hour, the meal was ready. The table was set for four.

What had become of Burent, Salathiel could not imagine. He had disappeared shortly after helping them carry in some of the chests from the wagon. Perhaps he was having his own troubles at the stables?

And in that surmise Salathiel was not far wrong.

28. In Which Poetical Licence Is Taken

THE INSPECTION of the garrison conducted by Captain Ecuyer was not, as Sergeant McLaughlin confided to one of the "sax" Alexanders, "a braw succiss."

The condition of affairs at Ligonier was even worse than Ecuyer had supposed, and he had had no roseate expectations. The company of the 42nd Highlanders were all present or accounted for, but they looked dirty and depressed, and some had "lost" their muskets, although they all still retained their claymores.

The captain was aware, however, that the Scots were genuinely relieved at his arrival and would welcome the prospect of a return of order and good discipline, if for no other reason than that guard duty would not fall entirely on them.

Ecuyer, Sergeant McLaughlin, and Ensign Erskine with his spontoon —which was rusty—stood about twilight in the middle of the little paved square at Ligonier, making a gradually dimming splash of scarlet, while the Highlanders lined up on one side and the provincial militia, a thin line in ragged green watchcoats, were drawn up on the other. The dark barracks lay behind them. On the pared sapling which acted as a flag-pole the remnant of a Union Jack flapped and tugged in gusts of bitter wind, as though it were trying to yank itself clear of the halyards. Without ceremony, when darkness came it was eventually taken down. The Highlanders were dismissed to their quarters and Captain Ecuyer then turned his attention to the shivering militia by the aid of a couple of smoky lanthorns that threw grim and wavering circles of light upon the unhappy scene. For it was now that the true condition of the affairs at the post began to become fully manifest. The roll was called.

"Captain Edwin Anderson."

"Died of the pox at Raystown," shouted a voice from the rear ranks of the militia.

"Lieutenant Arthur St. Clair."

A burst of laughter, catcalls, a derisive cheer, and guffaws greeted this name.

"Lieutenant Neville."

Silence.

"Ensign Willum Aiken."

"Ahoorin' at Bedford, both on 'em," shouted a peculiarly insolent voice followed by some salty chuckles that ran along the ranks.

"Hold your lanthorn up, sergeant, so I can see these men," said the captain sternly. Silence ensued.

Then a respectable-looking man with iron-grey hair and a certain clean-liness stepped forward and saluted properly.

"Beggen your pardon, your Honour, but all our officers have left us, desarted, or gone off on their own affairs," said the man firmly but respectfully. "We've been left to take the darty end of the stick. Mr. St. Clair has been selling us rations on our pay and trading for our equipment, powder, and guns. He and his man Japson have et up the substance of all of us at the fort. It's the custom, you know, sir, but it's shameful, I say, nevertheless. So we're half-starved and naked, and nigh the quarter of us are locked up now in the stable shed next the pigpen. If I may say so, sir, those poor divils must be about perished with cold."

"Is this true, Mr. Erskine?" demanded Captain Ecuyer.

"Aye," said the ensign, "yon mon's corricht. It was Lieutenant St. Clair's orders." The captain looked at him witheringly.

"What's your name, my man?" asked the captain, advancing to the soldier who had just spoken.

"Pollexfen, your Honour."

"*Mr.* Pollexfen," said Captain Ecuyer, raising his voice so all could hear, "in the absence of your officers, I appoint you in the king's name commander of this company."

A murmur of approval rose from the ranks.

"None of that now," said the captain. He walked down the ranks rapidly, looking each man in the face and holding up the lanthorn now and then to examine a more than usually ragged individual. They all looked both starved and neglected.

"Now dismiss, go to your barracks, and see that some large logs are dragged in for fires. Sergeant McLaughlin, take five men and issue rations to Mr. Pollexfen from the king's store. Issue enough for tonight and tomorrow. There *are* rations, aren't there?"

"Aplenty, sir. Mr. Erskine has the keys."

"But these men are provincial troops, and the king's rations . . ." said Erskine doubtfully.

"Feed them for *all that,*" said the captain sardonically. "And, Mr. Erskine, tell my man Albine to report to me, and do so yourself directly after you have got me the keys." He turned curtly and walked off in the growing dark in the direction of the stables, where an intolerable din of pigs', horses', and men's voices had broken out.

"Captain Ecuyer," called McLaughlin after him through the darkness.
"Well?"

"An' you let yon colonials loose from the pen the nicht, thar'll be little short of a mutiny. They're a neefarious crew."

"It's the sober truth, sir," said Erskine, who had lingered, hoping the captain might change his mind about the rations.

"What! The sober truth from *you,* Mr. Erskine?" The captain chuckled. "Give me leave to doubt it, under the circumstances."

Mr. Erskine said nothing but departed for the keys.

"Sergeant," continued the captain, "a gentleman of the Quaker persuasion may appear shortly at the gate with a string of pack horses. His name is Japson. Admit him. But under no circumstances permit him to leave the fort before I do. See to it!"

"I will," said McLaughlin. "I ken the mon weel."

The captain then limped off in the direction of the stables, where in a few moments he was joined by Salathiel. Mr. Yates, when the captain's orders had been received at the blockhouse, had obligingly promised to stay and see that the dinner did not burn.

"I've been given the lie direct by the captain," said Erskine to Yates, as he searched for his keys. "He denied that I was sober."

"You'll not call him out for that, will you?" asked Yates, laughing.

"Na, na!" said the ensign, affecting his native Scotch. "I'll no deny thar's a mite of truth in his conteention." He took a swig from Mr. Yates's bottle, and went out, slamming the door. The fire leaped, sending a world of sparks up the chimney.

Mr. Japson arrived about this time at the gate and clamoured for entrance. Half-frozen, he drove his exhausted beasts toward the stable. His troubles were not over yet. At the stables to his consternation he found Captain Ecuyer and Albine standing together just outside the shed, conducting a parley with various persons inside, but invisible in the darkness. The captain had also been confronted by a surprise.

The "stables" at Ligonier was a long, slab-roofed shed. Down the middle of it ran a row of heavy, log stakes about six inches apart. These set off that part of the shed where horses were tied from the other half which had been built to contain forage and hay. The stakes had been continued all around the portion set off for hay. They made, in effect, a barred stockade exceedingly staunch through which an arm, a hand, or a horse's nose could be thrust, but that was about all. This, of course, was to prevent the pilfering of hay.

Behind this stable and its stockaded wall was the muddy and straw-littered area in which the swine kept at the fort were supposed to be confined. Most of the pigs did go there to lie on the straw at night. But horses and pigs were not the only animals confined in and about the stable.

The heavily barred and staked portion set off for forage had been turned into a convenient prison. The day before he left Ligonier to go to Fort Bedford, Lieutenant St. Clair had locked twelve of the Pennsylvanians into the now nearly empty forage crib. He considered the men he had thus incarcerated to be mutinous, and perhaps he had his reasons for thinking so.

But Lieutenant St. Clair had now been absent for five days. There was bad blood between the Highlanders and the Pennsylvanians, and the terrible cold had come on. McLaughlin had given them their blankets but, by instruction, scarcely enough food to exist on, and they were now desperate.

Some had frozen hands or feet. All were ready to desert at the first opportunity, and two or three were quietly determined to murder St. Clair when occasion might serve. Also there were leaders and men of resource among them. A dark-browed and memorable Irishman by the name of O'Neal occasionally brought poetry to their relief by masterful descriptions of the details of the projected murder of Lieutenant St. Clair.

Burent, of course, had known nothing about the plight of these men. He had not even suspected their existence. And they had kept entirely quiet when he had first brought his horses into the shed. It was quite dark in the stable, and Burent could see nothing between the bars of the haymow. He had tied up his horses and returned to help Albine unload the wagon.

The prisoners, however, had watched his every move, and from the Scot who later brought them their meagre rations they had learned who had arrived at the fort.

"I'll tell you what, bhoys," said O'Neal, "the little brown booger that stabled his bastes here must be the captain's mon. Did ye notice the airs of him, the gintility of the tilet and the rubbin' doon he give the harses? Oi, there's hot mush and blankets for the Sassenach mare but niver a dacent bite or a koind word for the likes of us! Ef I had me knife, I'd reach through the bars and slit the throat of the mare. Listen to her champin' away at her carn, and me own belly grindin' at nothin' at all!"

A gruff growl of approval met his remarks. He rose, and going over to the line of stakes, looked out between them at the contented horses beyond. The mare snorted at him, but was presently accepting small wisps of hay from his fingers.

"Whist, bhoys," said he, "I have a foin schame, I have."

"O'Neal, ye damned fool, don't ye hurt the hoss. For-by she's the apple of the captain's eye. Ye'll only get some of us hanged belike," said one Williams anxiously.

O'Neal chuckled. With a wisp of old hay he managed to get the mare's nose in the air where the bars chanced to widen, and he finally enticed her to put her head through a space higher up. She then lowered her neck for the dainty. When she tried to back away again she was caught. The Irishman began to laugh quietly.

"I tell ye, *lay off* that horse," said one of the older men, getting up anxiously and approaching O'Neal. "Williams is right. You'll be getting your empty head in a noose for nothin'."

"So me head's empty, is it? Listen, ye poor blatherskites. Did ye raley think I'd be so wake-minded as to waste me time on the harse? It's bait I'm using her fer. Now if you'll kape quiet and crooch down in the straw there, I'll git ye out of the misery ye haven't the brains to git out of yourselves. Here you, Jepford, lend me the rawhide belt off you, you fat guts. Be God, ef you aren't a fathom around, praises be!" With the man's belt he made a running noose, and then borrowed two others with the comment, "They're not so long, but they'll do." They watched him anxiously.

"Now mind ye, no nonsense," continued O'Neal. "I'm only going to taze the baste and bring that little brown booger back arunnin'. Then we'll see what we'll see."

With that he reached through the bars and lashed the mare over her back with a belt.

Unable to pull her head back, and caught as though in a trap, the mare began to kick and whinny. In a short time she had the four wagon horses frantic as well, and the stables resounded with the alarmed snorting and wild neighing of the half-crazy animals. Burent heard it at the blockhouse and came running. In the dark shed it was hard to see what was wrong. At last he made out that the mare had caught her head between the bars.

"*Soo, soo,* gal," said he, stroking her, and trying to quiet her panic. "It does beat all, lassie, the trouble you can find."

The mare finally responded and the other horses gradually quieted down. The mare quivered and waited to be released. On the other side of the posts O'Neal crouched low in the shadows. Presently Burent thrust his arm through the bars to try to lift the mare's head up. At that instant a leather noose was slipped around his neck, choking him. The world went black.

When he came to he had been turned about with his back to the posts and his arms strapped around one of them behind him. He was looking out into the stable where the dust motes danced in the air—or was it specks over his eyes? He had no idea what had happened to him or why.

"When they come to git you," an Irish voice finally explained, "say what I tell you to say, and don't say nawthin' more. There's a noose round your gullet and a sharp stake at your kidney behind." A painful dig below the ribs confirmed the latter fact.

So Burent waited. It seemed hours, and he did spend a good part of the afternoon there. It was mortal cold and he shivered from chill and shock. O'Neal had released the mare's head and she now nosed Burent from time to time quizzically. The horses, however, were quiet enough now, reassured by his presence. Finally darkness fell. Shortly afterward a lanthorn approached the shed. It was Captain Ecuyer and Albine. The Monk held the light.

"Stop! Stop where you are, Captain Ecuyer. Don't come into the shed," called Burent desperately. "I . . ." His voice ended in a choked gurgle.

"Who's that?" said the captain, stopped in his tracks by the obvious urgency of the warning.

"Tell him," whispered O'Neal, loosening the noose again.

"It's me, Burent! They have me tied up here. There's a noose around me neck and a stake at me back. Don't come in for the love of God, sir. Or they'll murder me, they will!"

"Who are *they?*" demanded the captain, who had the good sense to remain standing where he was.

"Oil tell you who *they* are, ye domned lobsterback," said the voice of O'Neal. "We're twelve good men and true locked up by the tyranny of Liftinint St. Clair, God wither his bawdy heart, and if ye don't lave us out I'll drive this sharp stake clane through the bowels of your little brown man, captain. Won't I now?"

An agonized scream from Burent confirmed the fact that he probably would.

Just at this moment Captain Ecuyer was joined by Mr. Erskine, Sergeant McLaughlin, and Japson, who came up out of the darkness.

"You've only a short time to make up your mind, captain. It's a *nice* little mon I have here. You'd be after missin' him. And think of his wife and childer," called O'Neal.

"I haven't any," shouted Burent. "Never mind . . ." He was choked off.

"Bring the light," said the captain in a low voice to Salathiel.

"I'm coming down to parley with you," he shouted towards the shed. "I'll come alone, except for the boy with the lanthorn." He and the drummer advanced into the shed.

"Stop there," said O'Neal.

In the dim light of the lanthorn Captain Ecuyer could now see the five horses, and Burent trussed up against the wall with the fear of death on his white face. Out of the darkness behind again came the voice of O'Neal.

"Let us out of here. Open the door and take us out of this dom pen. We're devoured by flays."

"Very well," said the captain, "I'll do that."

"You'll do what!" said the amazed O'Neal.

"Let my man go, and I'll let you out," said the captain.

"Will you give us a fair trial?" demanded O'Neal.

"I'll give every one of you a fair trial—and tomorrow. Do you hear that in there?" shouted the captain.

A number of voices began to shout at O'Neal to take the offer.

"Let us out first, and I'll let your man go," said O'Neal.

"You heard my offer," said the captain. "You'll have to take it or do murder and hang." There was a moment's silence. In the lanthornlight in the quiet stable Ecuyer stood looking Burent in the face.

"Oim lettin' your little brown man go," said O'Neal finally. "Kape your word like a mon, captain."

Suddenly Burent, who had been turned loose, fell forward on his face.

"Mr. Erskine," called Captain Ecuyer, "bring an armed guard with some lights and open this pen door. Suppose you carry Burent to your quarters, sergeant, and get some strong liquor in him. He's had a bad time."

"A verra bod time," said the sergeant, picking Burent up like a sack. "And will your Honour be sindin' the liquor over to my quarters for him?"

"Yes!" said Ecuyer and swore to himself. The Scotch never lost an opportunity.

Erskine appeared shortly with a portion of the guard and more lant-horns. They opened the door into the haypen and flashed the light on a miserable group huddled against the far wall in terror and doubt as to what might be before them. By common consent the prisoners had all withdrawn from O'Neal, who now stood alone, armed with the sharp stake with which he had lately been threatening Burent.

"Step this way one at a time," said the captain. "No need to tie them," he added, as the first of the prisoners came up and submitted themselves humbly enough. "They're weak from starvation, poor devils. March them up to the barracks, Mr. Erskine, and give them something to eat directly, king's stores or anything else."

"This way, you," said Erskine to O'Neal, who, now left completely alone, still stood fingering his club.

A panic seized the man.

"You moitherin' bastards, I'll niver submit to ye," he roared, and with marvellous agility for so big a man leaped for a rafter, climbed on it, placed his back against a slab on the roof, and buckled it loose with his shoulders.

Before anyone could get to him he was through the hole and they could hear his feet padding along above them.

"Quick, Albine!" exclaimed the captain.

Ten seconds later Salathiel was out on the roof, too.

It was a moment before he could get the lanthorn's shine out of his eyes.

Then he saw that the escaped man had not really bettered himself much. The stable roof was completely cut off from all other structures and surrounded by open ground. Salathiel could see his man crouching near the edge at a far corner. The whole building was surrounded by this time, and the man was covered by the sentries standing on the galleries above him.

Mr. Erskine called to the sentries not to shoot. Evidently the ensign was just below the point where the man was crouching. O'Neal looked over the roof and began to curse him vilely.

It was now that, from Salathiel's standpoint at least, an amazing thing occurred. A figure in a pair of white trousers was suddenly seen coming down on the roof, apparently right out of the stars. It landed next to the fugitive.

O'Neal gave a howl of surprise and started running back to jump off into a strawstack in the pigpen near the end of the shed. He did not know Salathiel was on the roof and he did not see him, for he was still prone. All that Albine had to do was to reach out and grab the man's ankle as he passed. He fell with a smash and his impetus shot him off into the hands of the guards waiting below.

"You disappoint me," said the voice of Ensign Erskine, somewhat breathless. "He was mine. Mon! Did ye hear what the loon called me? Did it come to your lug?"

"No," said Albine, "it didn't."

"It's just as weel," said the ensign.

They climbed down through the hole in the roof together and dropped into the dark shed below. Outside the prisoners were already being marched away.

"Do you mind saying how you got on the roof, Mr. Erskine?" said Salathiel.

"I vaulted oop. There was a nice long pole by the wall, as God would have it."

Salathiel looked at his companion with considerably more respect. It was a tremendous vault.

"This Johnny captain of yours seems pretty sooft-hairted. Will he be coddlin' these rascals, do ye ken?" asked the ensign as they walked together towards the blockhouse.

"They'll get exactly what's comin' to 'em," replied Salathiel. "You can be sartin of that, sir."

"Aye," said the ensign, "so I thought. I am glad he's here. I'll say this to you, and you can pass it along, after you forget who told you. Leftenent Blane left this post in magneeficent order last autumn. Since then it's been in the hands of our fawncy macaroni, Leftenent Arthur St. Clair. And so—God save the king!" There was a concentrated bitterness in Erskine's tone which carried his own conviction that something was rotten in Denmark.

"Aweel," he sighed, "losh! Let's have a bite and a nip aboot the fire. That's your captain Johnny and the Monk with the lanthorn gain' intil headquarters the noo. Come on," he called.

They raced each other to the steps at the blockhouse.

29. Court-Martial by Firelight

THE LOW-CEILINGED ROOM of the blockhouse provided at first glimpse something of the appearance and the same feeling of security as a large ship's cabin, except that at one end blazed the immense fire. Mr. Yates had just piled it high again, arranging the supper before it on the hearth to keep hot. A number of candles stuck in bottles cast a wavering, saffron glow so that the apartment presented that rarest of all appearances on the frontier, a room well lit at night, at once warm and cheerful. So used was everybody to conducting existence in a deep gloom after sundown that the captain was betrayed into giving a groan of relief followed by a sigh of contentment as he sat down by the bunk in his chosen corner, looked about him, and stretched out his legs to have his boots drawn off.

"Upon my word," said he, "you gentlemen treat yourselves damned well here, don't you?" His eyes twinkled as he noticed that the table had been set for four. "I trust I shall have the pleasure of your company, Mr. Erskine, and of your friend here, if you'll be good enough to introduce him." Who the other guest was to be did not appear.

"Mr. Edward Yates, sir," said the young ensign in some confusion at having overlooked the formality. "Mr. Yates is an attorney representing the interests of the proprietary family in these parts, I believe."

At this Mr. Yates arose from a haunch which he had been basting by the hearth and bowed with the spoon still in his hand.

"Your courtesy is an honour, sir. To keep the records straight I should say that, while I *do* represent the Penns, my present business here is with the survey of certain lands that have been granted to Mr. St. Clair."

"No matter who your clients are, I am quite content, Mr. Yates. Since you have saved the dinner from burning, the least I can do is to invite you to share it. My God, Albine, don't pull that boot on my wounded leg so!" The captain turned white and sick for a moment. "There, it can't be helped, I know. Gentlemen, your pardon." He slipped his feet into a pair of furred shoes and hobbled over to the table.

"Your chair, sir," said the ensign, drawing it up.

"Are you sure you will put it back under me, Mr. Erskine?" asked the captain, a mischievous smile framing his lips.

"Oh, really, I was only a bit fuddled, sir, when you first came in. It was sleep as much as anything else. And the room was hot . . . stifling, if I may say so."

"And since then the Irish mutiny has sobered us all, I am sure," said Ecuyer, seating himself. "What a leap you made onto the roof! Are you circumstanced to pole vaulting, Mr. Erskine? It seems to me to be an unusual, and yet possibly a valuable military accomplishment. Pray do be seated!"

The young ensign, being a Scot, was not entirely unaware of an amused gleam in the captain's eye. But he scarcely knew as yet how to take it.

"When we made the attack at The Havana," he replied, "there were a great many moats and ditches to cross. The Spaniards in Cuba go in for dirty ditches, sir. Well, some of us in the Forty-second took to jumping them on poles to get at the foot of the walls during assaults. I wasn't so bad at it. We used to do a lot of pole vaulting at Almondel in Linlithgowshire." Here Mr. Erskine stopped himself and blushed.

"But it was hotter in Cuba than in Linlithgowshire, I suppose," said the captain.

"Och, aye! Och, a fiery climate I'd call it!" exclaimed the ensign.

"Possibly then *that* was where you formed the regrettable habit of holding guard mount without any clothes on," continued the captain. "You see, Mr. Erskine, that unfortunate incident here was reported to Colonel Bouquet and he has requested me, before calling a court-martial, to look into it. What is your explanation?"

At this unexpectedly serious turn to the conversation the entire room grew silent. Salathiel placed the remains of Johnson's Queen of Scots soup on the table noiselessly, but it lay untouched and smoking while Mr. Erskine considered his reply.

"Shaw!" said the captain after an interval. "I was in hopes that there were ameliorating circumstances. Drink your soup!"

Mr. Yates stopped a desire to guffaw by a fiery draught of liquid essence of chicken and boiled eggs from his soup plate, and choked a little. His eyes opened widely. The captain had winked at him.

"Excellent soup, sir! Very remarkable! I never guzzled the like."

The captain nodded. "I cherish the secret formula for it," he said to Yates. "Well, Mr. Erskine?"

"It was like this, sir," said Erskine, who had now recovered his voice. "It was last summer when this fort was sore beleaguered. I was drunk. At least I had been drunk the nicht before. Airly the morrow morn there was an Injun alarm and I turned oot in turrible haste. And there I was, sir! There I was with the guard lined up by the gate, and somehow I'd forgot to fetch my kilt and jacket along. But I wasn't naked, sir. That's a gross exaggeration. I had my boots and hat on, and I had my spontoon!"

"Your spontoon!" said the captain. "You had *that?*"

"Aweel, I *did* have it," insisted Mr. Erskine, quite shocked, for Captain Ecuyer had put both elbows on the table, his face in his hands, and begun to laugh. And Mr. Yates joined him.

"Aweel," insisted Mr. Erskine, quite annoyed now, "I did *have* it. My friend Mr. Yates here will corroborate me—when he stops laughing."

"I'll be glad to," said Yates, suddenly turning quite sober. "I'll gladly act as a witness, but I'd rather appear in Mr. Erskine's defence and make a plea for him, if I may."

"Why," said the captain, "since you already represent the whole proprietary family, I see no reason why you shouldn't represent an ensign, Mr. Yates. It's a little unusual, of course, for officers in his Majesty's service to be provided with civil counsel—perhaps you can explain that later. But—go on. Be eloquent though, Mr. Yates! I have no use for arguments unless they are eloquent ones."

"We have only had soup so far, captain. Excellent as it was, may I remind you . . ."

"Bring some Burgundy, Albine, one of the dark-red bottles out of the case the colonel gave me just before leaving. And put the meat on.

"Mr. Erskine, I hope you will exonerate me from any desire to prejudice your case by asking the defence to proceed on soup alone. This, I think you will agree, should inspire even a dull advocate." He held up a bottle that turned ruby in the light. "May you be ingenious as well as eloquent."

They drank the toast.

"Well, sir, proceed," cried the captain, signing to refill the glasses. Mr. Yates cleared his throat:

"On the night of July the twelfth, last, the accused here was involved in a series of strange circumstances over which he had no control and which he cannot explain himself without seeming to be desirous of impugning his commanding officer. I refer to the late commander and present proprietor of this post at Ligonier, Mr. Arthur St. Clair."

"Proprietor? What the devil do you mean by *that?*"

"By your leave and patience I will directly explain," continued Mr. Yates.

"Be pleased to recollect that up until the second of August, last, this fort was being constantly attacked and harassed. It was then under the capable command of Lieutenant Blane. Mr. Erskine here was the only officer left with the Highland detachment. He and Lieutenant Blane, therefore, were the only commissioned officers at the fort, and they defended it well and gallantly until Colonel Bouquet relieved it on his advance to Pittsburgh and reinforced it with the militia that you now find here—and the officers of the militia whom, sir, you do not find here."

Mr. Yates, now finding himself got going, drank off another glass and rinsed his mouth as a refresher.

"Colonel Bouquet, as you know, then passed on to relieve Fort Pitt, scattering the savages on the way. He took Lieutenant Blane along when he left, and Mr. Erskine as the only king's officer present was thus in command of this fort. Even after the battle at Bushy Run there was still an occasional alarm in this neighbourhood and great vigilance was necessary. And there was much trouble with the militia officers, who disputed both their rank and the command with Mr. Erskine.

"This dispute eventually caused factions in the garrison. Each command would obey its own officers only. The militia shirked, and all the guard duty fell upon the already overworked Highland detachment. A crisis finally occurred when, upon the occasion of an Indian alarm, the militia refused to turn out to man the rifle galleries. It was then, sir, and not before, that Mr. Erskine lost his temper and attempted to settle the dispute with the two militia officers by means of his claymore."

"Was he successful?" asked the captain.

"He was. You should understand that all three of the militia officers were quartered in this room and that when Ensign Erskine entered commanding them to their posts of duty, and they refused, he drew his sword. And he was then attacked by two of the provincial gentlemen at the same time. It was Lieutenant Neville and Ensign Aiken. Captain Anderson, who has since died, sat still and looked on. Mr. Erskine disarmed Neville and cut Aiken across the forehead so that he staggered around, howling out that he was blinded. The gentleman who was disarmed, after consulting with his gallant captain, consented to join his men on the galleries, apparently for the reason that it was more dangerous to remain here than to go there. Captain Anderson finally buckled on his sword and went out too. Now, I don't think that any of these fellows were really cowards, they were just in an obstinate and mulish state of mind. I might add that I was a witness to all this, as since my arrival here I have been quartered in this room."

"What did you say the names of these two gallants were?" demanded the captain. "Albine, get your pen and write this in my red memorandum book, the one with the brass clasp."

"Lieutenant Neville and Ensign Aiken of the Pennsylvania line," repeated Yates.

Albine wrote this down and the captain signed to Yates to go on.

"It was probably a mistake on the part of my young client here to have lost his temper and to have drawn blood, but . . ."

"Tut, tut," said the captain, "during a war one is sometimes forced to resort to violence. Pray continue."

"Well, as you see, the provocation was great and the safety of the garrison had been compromised. Such considerations, nevertheless, were too subtle for the gentlemen who had been worsted to concede gracefully. They obeyed Mr. Erskine, perforce, from then on, but most sullenly. And they determined at the first opportunity to complain and if possible to ruin him. And now, sir, I am forced to inject another consideration into this affair. I refer to the arrival at this place on the eighteenth of September, last, of Lieutenant Arthur St. Clair. If things had been difficult before the arrival of Mr. St. Clair, they were thrice as confounded afterward, for he brought with him three papers:

1. A Commission as lieutenant in the 60th Regiment, your own, the Royal Americans, but that commission was resigned in the year '60—three years ago.
2. A memorandum from General Stanwix ordering that all provincial forces on the frontiers should respect and obey Mr. St. Clair as though his commission were still in force, until further notice.

3. A deed of purchase of one thousand acres of land from the proprietors of the province of Pennsylvania, transferring in fee simple, subject only to certain quit rents, the land upon which this Fort of Ligonier now stands and all the buildings and other works of man found upon it to Arthur St. Clair, his heirs and assigns forever, all duly registered and passed upon by the Land Office at Philadelphia.

"By the terms of that purchase Mr. St. Clair was also authorized and required to bring in and settle as many people as possible upon his land, and the licence for doing so was attached."

"The damned self-serving scoundrel!" exclaimed the captain, bringing his fist down on the table. "As if things weren't difficult enough in this naked country without his trying to strip us to the bone. But the king's use and possession here is paramount, isn't it?"

"Undoubtedly," replied Mr. Yates, "but when the royal garrisons are withdrawn, captain?"

"Why, then 'all the buildings and other works of man' left at Ligonier will belong to our friend St. Clair, I take it."

"You have an apt ear for phraseology, sir," said Yates. "That is the point exactly. And from the time that Lieutenant St. Clair arrived here until the present moment, I hesitate not to say that he and his henchmen have been extremely busy and most ingenious in transferring every known 'work of man' from the possession of the garrison into the hands of the agents and to the warehouse or store of the said Lieutenant St. Clair, including firearms, powder, garments, and even the preserved rations of the garrison, which he has managed to purvey from Bedford and in some cases to trade in for the equipment of the troops stationed here. The colonials have been half-stripped. In some cases forced to trade even their muskets for food. And when they have had the spirit to complain he had them locked up and half starved. There's scarcely a man in the place, to say nothing of the women, who isn't in debt to Lieutenant St. Clair."

"I suppose he established himself here as commanding officer," said Ecuyer, turning to pose the question to young Erskine.

"It was impossible for me to stand against him, Captain Ecuyer," said the ensign, speaking up for himself. "There was that order from General Stanwix, and . . ."

"Yes, yes, I can see," said the captain.

"I did manage to keep the Highland detachment under my immediate orders, but the militia were quite out of control. And their officers were, as Mr. Yates has explained, enraged against me."

"Was that the way you managed to lose your clothes, Mr. Erskine?"

"Yes, sir, it was."

"But you were drunk, you said?"

"I was the nicht before," the ensign hastened to explain. "You see, Lieutenant St. Clair had returned from Fort Bedford, where he goes quite often. Weel, he returned thot nicht and in honour of the birth of his first cheeld, sir,—he had the news at Bedford,—he invited us all, that is, Mr. Yates and me, and the three militia officers, to a high celebration in this room. Now I don't say Mr. St. Clair planned to undo me. But I was put off my guard by it, and he prevailed on us all to shake hands and let bygones be bygones on accont o' the nature of the supper thot nicht. Aweel, we did shake hands, and I meant it. And I got masel fuddled and had to be helped to bed."

"And when the alarm came you couldn't find your plaid and jacket, could you?" said the captain.

"Exactly," chimed in Mr. Yates.

"And if I hadna appeared at me post they'd have had me oop for coowardice, sir. So I went oot in me skin and took over the guard despicht the scandal."

"Were you sober then?" grinned the captain.

"Sober enough to lead a sortie and cut off some savages that had been harassing us for days," said Mr. Yates.

At this point Mr. Erskine excused himself, and walking over to his bunk, rummaged among his effects awhile and returned with four scalps nicely stretched on cord webs. These he exhibited with a certain artless pride which he could not entirely conceal.

"Some of your old playmates, Albine?" asked the captain.

"They're Mingoes I'm sartin," said Salathiel. "That's the way they braid their scalp locks, four strands to the end knot."

"You see," said Ecuyer, "there's nothing like having a well-informed valet on the frontier. Suppose, Albine, you light the brandy on that pudding Mr. Yates has contributed, and bring it on. And put a finger or so of the same spirit in our glasses all around."

The pudding and its flaming halo were much admired.

"A fitting close to the feast," said the captain. "To me at least it has been a most illuminating occasion." He raised his glass.

"Gentlemen, the king."

Ecuyer had risen with considerable difficulty.

"Mr. Erskine," said the captain, turning around to look over the back of his chair, "do me the favour of making the rounds this evening. Indeed, I'm not able. But *see* to the sentries! And there's a Quaker here by the name of Japson. He's not to leave the fort for any reason. Can you trust your men?"

"Aye," said the ensign, "the Heelanders."

"And, Mr. Erskine, consider yourself confirmed in your opinion that you are in command of this garrison. You have nothing to worry about on that score. Depend upon it."

"Thank you, sir," replied the young Scot in tones of genuine relief and gratitude. He saluted and walked out firmly—a different man.

Salathiel now prepared the fire for the night, bringing in a tremendous green ash backlog and bedding it firmly in the ashes against the white-hot throat of the chimney. Beside this at the distance of an inch or so he laid another log not quite so large. The latter was of wild cherry green, not dried. The space between the two he filled with dry oak chips, called hunks. The woodpile of the fort had evidently been cut by the colonials, who knew what they were doing. In a few moments, kindled by the heat of the stones, a clear sheet of flame ran up the back of the chimney, which was about nine feet wide. A long, steady sighing sound told of the strength of the draught. The room streamed with a flowing, yellow light, and a genial heat beat back along the floor and the walls.

It was still so cold outside that even the brief opening of the door for the exit of Mr. Erskine and the bringing in of the logs had thoroughly chilled the place and the captain had called out impatiently at Albine. He now sat back, however, some distance from the chimney, his wound freshly dressed, basking in the grateful warmth and relieved of his wig, stiff boots, and uniform. He was wrapped in a heavy flannel nightgown and stocking nightcap, and thoroughly comfortable for the first time in several days.

Mr. Yates, who had returned to his table after supper, was much amused by all this. It had especially intrigued him that the same man who brought in the immense logs, without so much as staggering slightly, had also bound up the captain's wounds, undressed him, and was now curling his wig and preparing deftly to put it away powdered in its right box for the night. The curling irons heating in the fire and the double-barrelled rifle leaning in the corner by Salathiel's bunk formed a variety and contrast in capacity Mr. Yates had never seen before.

"In Europe they haven't made fires like this since the Dark Ages," commented the captain. "There are chimneys like this in the castle at Blois, for instance, and elsewhere I remember. But there hasn't been the wood to feed them for generations. In Savoy I nearly perished of cold at the duke's own headquarters."

"No," responded Yates. "I never really saw fires till I came over. It's a lost art in England. They sell coals by the basket there, and bunches of twigs like bouquets. It's worse in Scotland. A peat fire, it's like trying to warm yourself before the painting of a sunset. But over here the true mark of your native inhabitant is that he regards a tree as his enemy. The more he can burn, the better patriot he is. I'm afraid the trees are doomed."

"Twenty journeys westward from here all trees come to an end," said Salathiel, who was now seated in the corner polishing his rifle. "A sea of grass begins. And I have seen flocks of pigeons there like great storm clouds. They pass for hours, darkening the sun, and the sound of their wings is like summer thunder. You can get out of the trees if you go west."

He went on polishing his gun.

Perhaps it was because he was beginning to be sleepy that he had spoken solemnly, like a voice in a dream. Something in the quality of his voice conveyed a sense of distance, of things remote.

"I think, sir, I'll go and have a look at Burent before turning in. He said to thank you for the brandy."

As Salathiel opened the door the distant, savage music of a hunting chorus of wolves trailing a deer on the Chestnut Ridge to the westward yelped into the cabin. The door closed and the sound with it, leaving the two inside alone by the fire.

Outside, Salathiel stretched, pausing at the top of the steps for a moment to fill his lungs with the sparkling, bitter cold air. A draught of new life raced through his veins. There was moonlight on the snow.

The chorus of the wolves on the ridge to the westward suddenly attained a frantic crescendo and ceased. They have him! he thought. He could see them leaping in and worrying the kill, the flash of white fangs in the starlight. God, it was good to be alive on a night like this! He wished he were out there now, moving silently along the ridge, looking down over the black treetops into the silent valleys, gliding with his rifle from tree to tree. Well, it was time to have a look at Burent and see what he could do for him.

"Nine o'clock, and all's well," sang the sentries, one after the other.

Inside the room the captain listened. There were seven sentries and they were all awake. That would do, he hoped.

"Mr. Yates," said he, "do me the favour of bringing your chair over here by the fire where I can see you. I want to talk some things over. Tomorrow I have certain moves in mind, and I should like to discuss them."

Remarking that he was flattered, Mr. Yates complied.

30. In Which Mr. Yates Draws a Bill of Credit on His Own Account

"YOU SEE, it's like this," said the captain. "I must press on to Fort Bedford as rapidly as possible. A heavy snow in the mountains might delay me for weeks. But this is also an important place at Ligonier. Our chain of communication is no stronger than the weakest link, and I must strengthen this one before I go. Now is it really your impression that Mr. St. Clair is the main cause of friction here?"

"Candidly, that *is* my impression," replied Yates. "Before the advent of the gentleman alluded to, Mr. Erskine had the garrison in good fettle, despite the opposition of the militia officers. But St. Clair's arrival changed all that. He brought with him some twenty-odd people, men, women, and children, as settlers, and he opened up a store for trading and supplies. These people are now quartered in the cabins which they have built as best they could. Their presence in the fort has been demoralizing. By the way, didn't I hear you mention the name of one Japson?"

"Yes, the Quaker; a pious rogue if there ever was one."

"But Mr. St. Clair's agent," explained Yates. "He it is who has been bringing goods and supplies over the mountains and even trading farther westward from here. St. Clair and he undoubtedly have in mind a little traffic in furs with the Indians."

"It's a pretty kettle of fish, no doubt," said the captain. "And this fellow St. Clair has colour for everything he is doing."

"A specious reason for every act! You would be well advised, sir, to move circumspectly in his case. Mr. Arthur St. Clair is a man of native ability, powerful connections, wealth, and impenetrable pride. He is one of those men for whom, once a thing promises to be of benefit to him, all the means to bring it about become automatically correct and in good conscience. *Dominus* is the word, sir. Nothing short of that will do for him. He has come into the wilderness to dominate, to avoid any opposition, something which he cannot understand or abide."

"You speak feelingly, Mr. Yates," said the captain.

"I have good cause to do so," replied the lawyer. "I confess, sir, to an abiding dislike of Arthur St. Clair. I am being candid, for I know him only too well. You should know that and perhaps make allowances for the sentiment in anything that I have said."

"From all I can see, your feelings do you credit," answered the captain.

"I value your opinion, captain," said Mr. Yates, flushing. "I am flattered you have asked for mine. Your situation at Ligonier in regard to Mr. St. Clair is about as follows, I think: he has, as you know, only a specious pretext for having insisted on acting as commanding officer of this post. General Stanwix's memorandum required, 'all colonial forces to recognize his commission as though still in force'. That did not and could not apply to the king's regular troops, such as the detachment of the Highlanders stationed here. Actually, Mr. Erskine, being a king's officer, was still in command. But since he was only an ensign, and, as the colonials outnumbered his men and their officers adhered to Lieutenant St. Clair, he was in effect put down. I might say that Erskine was most miserable under this tyranny and drank a good deal even for a Scot. He knew St. Clair was writing letters calculated to get rid of him. The colonial officers are in fact St. Clair's agents for trade, acting with Japson. They expect to settle here on St. Clair's property and prosper. Just now they are at Bedford to meet a train of pack horses bearing Mr. Japson's goods in order to guide them over the mountains. St. Clair is, of course, too clever to own these goods openly himself. They are probably the legal property of Japson. Only a few years ago he married a niece of Governor Bowdoin of Massachusetts Bay, and 'tis said she brought him fourteen thousand pounds sterling in her own right."

The captain whistled. "And so," he said, "he is now laying out his wife's money in a little lucrative trade with the savages. And the caravans are on their way. Well, at least I have Japson in the net. As for St. Clair's being commanding officer here, my own commission will take care of that. It's in force, and I am a captain in a king's regiment. But what about these settlers he's bringing in? The king's proclamation, as I understand it, absolutely forbids it."

"I'm not so sure," said Mr. Yates. "A certain number of people are permitted to settle at a government post, if licensed. Just by whom is not clear. Also in this case Mr. St. Clair has a grant of land from the proprietors of Pennsylvania with a proviso for settlement. And under their charter, you know, the proprietors of Pennsylvania have sovereign and feudal rights, which might hold even against the king's officers. To evict these people might subject you to a civil process, and one tried in the proprietors' own court."

It was now the captain's turn to flush—angrily. If there was one thing that as a soldier he hated, it was the processes of the civil law.

"The grant of land is for four thousand acres, the largest west of the mountains, providing settlers are brought in. If not, for one thousand on the present purchase," added Yates.

The captain whistled again.

"Just what is your own position in all this, Mr. Yates?" he finally demanded. "That you don't like St. Clair is abundantly clear, but not much else."

"I was hoping you would ask that," replied Yates. "Frankly, I wish to ask a favour of you shortly, and in view of that I should like you to understand just who I am, what I am doing here, and why. May I draw a bill of credit on your patience then, in order to make myself completely clear?"

"I'll honour it," said Ecuyer, "but it must be on my own terms of discount, provided"—he smiled—"you put another chunk or so on the fire. Albine's not back yet."

"Agreed," replied Yates. "I hope we shall mutually profit."

Under his care the fire began licking up the chimney again. Captain Ecuyer drew nearer to its warmth and prepared to listen. There was a certain sincerity and matter-of-factness about the young lawyer that had greatly impressed him.

"Probably the easiest way to show you my position here and to explain a number of other matters will be to give you my brief personal history," remarked Yates, seating himself and dusting off his hands some small splinters and pieces of bark left from the firewood.

"My rightful name is Hamilton," he began. "Unfortunately I am not able to prove that. I am the second son of James, Sixth Duke of Hamilton and Brandon, by a chapel marriage with a Scotch-Irish girl named Margaret Yates. It was an early love match, surreptitious on the part of his Grace, a union which he never acknowledged for cogent reasons of his own. Perhaps, as you know, in such cases neither the Church of England nor the English law recognizes the validity of marriages performed by unlicensed dissenting clergymen not holding under any of the establishments, and the duke took full advantage of that fact, in addition to keeping the proofs of his living with my mother in his own hands.

"What I say to you, therefore, rests on my own assertion alone. It is proper to insist, however, that my mother was an honest woman, although a comparatively poor girl, and that I have seen from Antrim the record of the marriage and talked with the old field preacher who performed it. The record has since disappeared.

"After the birth of a first child, my elder brother, in Ireland, the duke became more than ever anxious to conceal his adventure as he was then about to marry the present dowager duchess, a reigning beauty with a quixotic mind. For that purpose, and for various other convenient reasons he brought my mother to the town of Thurso in Caithness. Some of her maternal relations still resided there, who were ready to take their Irish relative and her little family into their care, the dull edge of their Scotch charity being no little whetted by a generous allowance discreetly bestowed on her by an agent of the duke.

"It was at Thurso, shortly after my mother moved from Ireland, that I was born. And it was in that place that I spent my infancy and boyhood. When I tell you that Arthur St. Clair was also born in Thurso, and that we were playmates and went to the same dame school together, you will no doubt begin to see that my knowledge of the gentleman is not entirely documentary."

"Go on!" said the captain. "I confess to a curiosity to know by what a ravelling of fate we find ourselves tonight in the same room at Ligonier."

Mr. Yates laughed. "It is, as you say, sir, quite a ravelling, and of many curious strands." He began a long and detailed history of his life in Scotland—from birth to the time of meeting Thomas Penn.

"So that is how and why I came to America.

"I sailed in October, 'fifty-nine, and the only person in the world to see me off was old Cousin Harry Ferguson. He came down all the way alone from Edinburgh. He embraced me warmly when we parted and told me to write him, and he wept. He is the only human being in Europe that I can say I love, and he's probably dead now, for he was an old man, and that was all of four years ago."

Mr. Yates paused and looked gloomily into the fire that was beginning to burn low again.

"And so we find ourselves at Ligonier," said the captain. "Well, the colonies are full of strange stories. Take this fellow Albine, for instance, you must get him to tell you his tale. It *is* curious that you should run across your friend St. Clair again, and here of all places. Isn't it?"

"Damme if it isn't," said Yates. "I *am* a bit superstitious about it. And he isn't happy about my being here and surveying his land. He has received his one thousand acres and *no more*. I've seen to that. And I've made him pay up. He was willing to compound matters to gain a little time. It's a pretty kingdom he's got with his wife's money, the lucky dog! I envy him. I would like to do likewise, I admit."

"Land?" said the captain.

"Land!" said Mr. Yates. "Precisely that."

"So you'll be staying on in the colonies, will you?"

"Permanently," replied the young lawyer. "I am going to find my ideal spot and seat myself there. But I shall look far and carefully first. It must be like Scotland in some ways. Something that will remind me of home."

"Your lost dukedom regained?" laughed the captain.

Mr. Yates smiled but did not reply.

"Bouquet and I both have some land in Maryland," continued the captain. "The colonel has built him a house and found a nice wench to put in it, too. That makes a difference, you know."

"I suppose so," agreed Yates, apparently indifferently. He looked up in surprise as an odour of verbena came to him. The captain was using his handkerchief. The perfume was faint but it was almost as though the ghost of a woman had walked into the room.

"Well," said the captain, "since we've eventually got round to the wenches, I suppose bed is next in order. After your confidence, Mr. Yates, I'll be inclined to consider the favour which you have forgotten to ask me. It's been an interesting evening, and in these parts one should be grateful for finding an enemy of *ennui* to be one's friend."

"The compliment is delightful from you, sir," said Mr. Yates. "May I return it only in part by not asking you my favour until later? It is too late tonight for further explanations."

"It is," exclaimed the captain; "a half after one o'clock! That rascal Albine must be making a night of it with Burent and his friends in the barracks. I don't blame him. What humanity needs is an innocent debauch about every ten days. But will you give me a hand to my bunk, sir? *Bon Dieu!* I'm stiff. It's been a long journey and a devilish hard day."

Mr. Yates helped the captain to his bunk, threw a chunk or two in the chimney, and after hastily undressing climbed into his own corner. The candles had long ago burnt out. In the headquarters room at Ligonier, the steady breathing of the sleepers blent regularly with the soughing of the mighty logs in the fire. Salathiel entered noiselessly towards morning, and wrapping himself in a fur rug, lay down near the hearth and slept like a panther on the warmed floor.

31. In Which Friend Japson Returns

THE PROFOUNDEST SCHEMES of statesmen and the high strategies of soldiers are at the mercy of such things as fatigue and temperature. Because there was a log of wild cherry in the chimney at Ligonier, and because it burned warmly and long, trouble came upon that humble outpost of the king's dominions while Captain Ecuyer slept.

But it was no wonder that he slept. The sheer exhaustion of the day before had reduced him to a state of coma in which even his will power lapsed. His tired body lay recovering itself, trying to heal its wounds; and Colonel Bouquet's plan for an advance down the Ohio in the early spring hung in abeyance. In fact, although nobody knew, it quietly slipped over into the late summer or autumn of the next year, while the captain softly snored.

Mr. Yates, too, was doing full justice to the soft occasion, after a certain relief of mind and frame that had followed his "confession" to the captain of the night before. The room was delightfully warm. Just the right temperature for late sleeping. The gradually penetrating cold of the early morning hours had suddenly been dispelled when the green cherry log, dried out by hours of baking, had burst into a vigorous flame towards six o'clock in the morning.

And it was about this time that Mr. Japson, released from durance vile by some of his many friends in the garrison, quietly loaded his pack horses and drove out of the gate of the fort headed for Fort Bedford.

A glorious sunrise greeted him an hour later as he pressed on smartly, using switches and a certain strained vocabulary of Biblical language to hasten his horses.

Mr. Japson was joined about five miles from Ligonier by two Indians who were trotting beside him before even he was aware. He drew up in a small valley near a spring from which his horses drank, while he and the two Indians went into council. Tobacco and one small flask off Mr. Japson's person were exchanged and the business at hand was soon settled. The Indians might easily be recognized as old acquaintances of Mr. Japson by a film of mush which still clung to their unusually filthy blankets and trousers. To tell the truth, they were also customers of Mr. Japson, and a short conversation in muskrat-Delaware soon served to conclude the business at hand. What this was, was soon quite evident, for as Mr. Japson pressed on merrily in the direction of the Laurel Hill Mountain, the Indians disposed themselves thoughtfully behind a log

on a small eminence which overlooked a stretch of road to the westward. At the same time they carefully reprimed their muskets and ad-
justed their flints.

Back at the fort Salathiel had been awakened by the cherry log not
long after it had burst into flame. The heat had nearly blistered his
shoulders and brought him up standing. A glance showed him that both
Mr. Yates and the captain were still sound asleep, and he saw no reason
to disturb them. In fact, after the evening of the night before with
Burent he had no idea what time it was at all. Going quietly to the door,
he stood outside on the stoop watching the slow approach of dawn and
chewing a piece of dried beef from his pouch. He washed it down with
a handful of fresh snow. This preliminary "breakfast" was scarcely swallowed before Burent and Ensign Erskine came hurriedly around the
corner of the militia barracks to say that Japson was gone.

A hasty conference took place on the steps as to the best measures to
take. O'Neal and some of his friends had been released at the same time
by the sympathy of the militia. They had overpowered the Highland
sentry posted to watch Japson, managed the man at the gate—and the
bird had flown. The curious thing was that O'Neal had undoubtedly
remained in the fort.

"He's loose now down in the inhabitants' quarters, no doubt hidden
in one of the huts waiting to make further trouble, and it's that which
worries me," said Erskine. "St. Clair, you know, was expected back last
night. That's what the fourth chair was set at the supper table for. He'll
probably be along today and the two militia officers with him. All hell
may break out when they ride in. I hate to take this to the captain as my
reveille report. He'll wonder if I was drunk again."

Salathiel shook his head. "I doubt that, Mr. Erskine," he said; "at any
rate, you were sober up to two o'clock. Both Burent and I can testify to
that." He smiled slowly at the nervous young Scot. "I'll tell you what
we'll do. I'll take the captain's horse and set off after Japson. Rely upon
it, I'll bring the varmint back. And you can tell that to the captain when
you report. Give me a few minutes now until I can get me gone. A little
more sleep won't do the captain any harm. I'll not exactly dally."

He strode back into the room and silently gathered up his pouch and
rifle. He also snatched a piece of bread and cold meat from the supper
remains of the night before. Two minutes later he was feeding and
saddling the mare. That took a bit of time. Both Burent and Erskine
were still standing on the steps as he rode for the gate of the fort. The
ensign saw him out.

"Habeas corpus," he called after him and waved hopefully.

The trail of Japson's horses led like a plain line of print straightaway
into the dawn. Here at one place one of the horses had stumbled. At
another Japson had dismounted and cut a good-sized hickory switch.
From there he had gone on faster. Two Indians had joined him at an-

other place. Their pointed moccasin slots accompanied him along the road ahead and on around a curve. It was precisely at this point that Salathiel pulled the mare aside and skirted through the forest. Thrice he crawled back to read the record on the highway. The third time, he came to the place in the little valley where Japson had held his hasty conference near the spring.

It was all quite plain. There was even a little tobacco spilled on the ground. Best of all, there were only the same two pairs of moccasins.

So Mr. Japson had then gone on without them!

Salathiel paused to consider. Presently he tied the mare near to the spring, scraped some snow away to give her a brief patch of forage, and took up the trail of the moccasins carefully, holding his rifle handy, and gliding from tree to tree.

The Indians had made no attempt to conceal their trail. Once they had run along some logs and leaped sidewise off into a patch of snowless ground. But it was all sufficiently plain to the eyes of the Little Turtle.

He had forgotten everything now but the joy of the hunt. He laughed silently.

It was quite light now. A faint breeze drifted with the sun, slightly warmer, carrying a message to Salathiel through the silent forest. He sniffed it eagerly. Away off somewhere a branch cracked. It was a magnificent day. He shivered slightly, not from cold. It was the shiver of a hound absorbed in and thrilling to its life's business. In the breeze was the faintest but absolutely unmistakable tang of tobacco smoke.

They must be crazy to smoke now, he thought. And they must be someplace fairly near. He had his plan. He must shoot one of them first. That would inevitably bring out the other. Most guns had only one shot in this country. He smiled and instinctively patted his rifle. It mustn't miss. Presently he came to the sharp declivity of a deep ravine.

He crawled along the edge stealthily and came to a clifflike formation topped by a thicket. He wriggled through this, covered his face by a branch with brown leaves on it, and peered out.

A considerable panorama lay stretched out before him. The road crossed a stream in the valley just below and then wound upward through a tumble of small foothills to the shoulder of the high ridge beyond. Then, almost at the same instant, he was rewarded by a glimpse of exactly what he was after, both Mr. Japson and the "moccasins".

He crawled back from the edge of the ravine and then ran along it rapidly. He went noiselessly, although he had no fear of being seen. He skirted the edge for nearly a mile. Presently the land levelled out at the headwaters of the little valley. He took a drink from the spring there, and still in good cover, crossed around it. In another half hour he was on the other side of the ravine coming up on the watchers of the road from their rear.

The last quarter of a mile was a brief masterpiece of stalking. At last he could hear them talking, a guttural remark now and then. But it was some time before he could see them. They were just over the ridge of the hill, looking down on the road.

Another ten minutes of inch by inch movement and he could see them. From behind a log they were both intently watching the road below. Someone must be coming, for their muskets were both brought to the ready. Then he understood. He heard the mare neighing at the spring, where he had tied her, a mile away. Probably she was lonely by this time and was trying to pull off her bridle. It was a bad habit she had when left alone, but the acme of fortune now.

The two Delawares waited tensely, all their senses and attention directed towards the road. One of them had a good rifle, and he drew a long, careful bead on the ford. His head slowly came up above the log to do so.

Salathiel shot him through the back of the neck from behind.

It was a windless straightaway over brown leaves and snow at about one hundred yards. He had meant to catch him between the shoulders. So the right barrel fired a little high, eh? That was what he thought as he watched the other Delaware roll over and down the ridge, clutching his musket, and out of sight instantly. There had been no time to draw a new bead, and it would never have done to risk an unaimed shot.

Instead, he leaped back into a dip in the ground behind him, away from his own powder smoke, and crouched down. At that instant the surviving Delaware came racing back over the slope.

Salathiel shot him through the heart.

He fell, and his musket went off with a dull bang that echoed in the valley. Just for old times' sake, for several minutes Salathiel kept absolutely still. After a while he heard the mare neigh again. She seemed nearer now. Very carefully he ascertained that both the Delawares were really dead, but only after he reloaded both barrels and before crawling too near.

Then he went over them both rapidly. He took a fine French knife, five louis d'or, and a rifle from the first Indian. He also took a letter from his pouch, and his powder and shot and tomahawk. Then he scalped him with the French knife neatly and quickly.

There was nothing on the body of the second Delaware. He looked to be scarcely sixteen years old. He had a copper medal of George I around his neck, six cartridges in his matchcoat pocket, and a small whisky flask nearly empty. Maybe that was why the boy had been so careless, Salathiel thought. He took the medal for good luck—and the scalp.

He dragged both the bodies back into the underbrush and covered them over in a hollow with leaves. The wolves would attend to them promptly. No one would ever know who they were if they did find them. There was no use starting a blood feud with the Delawares, he reflected. He obliterated the traces of where they had been lying, picked his way carefully down a rocky spine where he left no tracks, and threw the young Indian's musket, and the rest of the useless articles, into a deep hole in the stream.

A noise of hoofs on the road startled him and he looked up to see the mare coming trotting around a bend in the road as though she were going somewhere. She stopped at the ford and whinnied at him. One of the cheek straps of her bridle was broken and the bit hung loose. Probably she had broken free when she heard the firing.

Here was a sorry complication. He might not be able to catch her, and he didn't want to have to wade the ice-covered stream. It was too swift to have frozen over hard.

He stood up, let her catch the scent of him in the wind, and then moved off up the road calling and holding his hat out like an oats bag. She dashed about for a while doubtfully. Once she started back. Then she thought better of it and came dashing right through the ford, whickering and blowing her nose after him. Yet she was shy and would start away when he came near.

It took him a good quarter of an hour to catch her in a kind of exasperating game. He finally got near enough to vault into the saddle. He sat on her while he mended the cheek strap with a thong from his moccasin. Then it struck him that it was the fresh blood on the scalps that must have made her so shy of him.

A few minutes more and he was galloping after Japson as hard as the mare could go. He left the Indian rifle hidden by the ford. He was irritated with his horse and made her go hard. Japson would now be from five to seven miles ahead, he supposed. If he had heard the firing, he might be making a run for it. But he thought he hadn't. Musket shots didn't carry far in hilly wooded country, and there would be the clatter of Japson's four horses on the stones.

The way was stony enough; jagged, conglomerate boulders with frozen gravel over them. Here and there mica glittered in them like a streak of silver. He had never seen stones like that. He let the horse pick her way here. She was beautifully sure-footed and sharp-shod. After a while he came to a long stretch of corduroy covered by clay. The engineers had laboured sorely here. It was the approach across a mile of high-lying swamp to the main ridge beyond. There was a bridge near the end. He galloped over that and just at the edge of the rise, where the road soared upward in a series of scored zigzags on the mountain, he overtook Japson.

The meeting was quite casual. Japson had dismounted and was tightening the girths and lashings on his pack horses in order to make the climb.

"You don't need to worry about that now," said Salathiel.

"Good morning," said Mr. Japson, glancing up from an obstinate buckle that had detained him. "Ah, my young friend with the ragged ear." Then he saw the scalps at Salathiel's belt. "Well," he added, "thou art a determined young man!"

"Back to the fort, Mr. Japson," insisted Salathiel, pointing towards Ligonier with his thumb. "I'll trouble you for your pistol—and your knife."

"Thou may'st have the knife," said the Quaker, drawing out a smooth, long-handled table knife from a case that held, besides, a pewter fork and spoon. "I have no pistol. I never go armed."

"Keep your table gear," said Salathiel. "Ain't you afraid of wolves, or bars at least, that you carry no firearms?"

"I'm afraid of nothing," said the Quaker quite simply. And Salathiel saw that it was true.

"In that case I shall have to tie you on your horse," he said, and prepared to do so. Obviously there was no use pointing his rifle at such a man.

"No, no," said Mr. Japson. "I won't resist thee. I'll go."

"Git then," said Salathiel, "and remember, I kill. That may at least be of interest to you."

Mr. Japson turned his pack horses back the way they had just come, started them off, and rode quietly behind them. Salathiel followed him a few yards farther back, silent and watchful of both his prisoner and the road. They continued without speaking back to the ford, where he stopped and retrieved the Delaware's rifle. Mr. Japson recognized it. It was one he had traded for a mass of magnificent beaver pelts four years before at Harris's stockade. The rifle was a fine one, a German gun. Japson said nothing. They rode on again slowly. The horses were beginning to tire.

"Art thou a king's man, Salathiel Albine?" asked the Quaker suddenly without turning his head.

"No," answered Salathiel, instantly suspicious and more watchful. Yet somehow the use of his name had mollified him.

"No," he repeated. "I serve Captain Ecuyer. And I try to serve him well. But I have no oath to the king."

"Swear not at all: neither by the earth, for 'tis his footstool; nor by heaven, for 'tis God's throne," said Japson, smacking his lips appreciatively at the taste of words.

"You are mistaken, Mr. Japson," said Salathiel. "The two verses go this way in the fifth of Matthew"—and he quoted them correctly.

Mr. Japson now turned around to look at Mr. Albine.

"Keep going," said Salathiel. "Here's some Scripture to go on: 'And their laws are diverse from all people; neither keep they the king's laws: therefore it is not for the king's profit to suffer them.'"

The Quaker bowed his head thoughtfully and smiled. "Certainly not for the king's profit," he said. "Thou art learned in the Word. And thou wast born in this country, and west of the mountains?" he asked.

"Aye," said Salathiel—and the words of the Seneca chief came pat to his mouth, "the water of these rivers is the blood of my veins."

"Well said, my friend," answered the Quaker. "I also was born in this country, by the banks of the Delaware. It is *our* native land." There was a pride in the Quaker's voice which Salathiel had never heard there before. He found himself responsive to it.

"It is a good land," he muttered, "good!" He almost added "mine".

"There is none other like it on the face of the earth," insisted Mr. Japson. He paused for a moment. "Does it not strike thee, friend Salathiel, thou may'st be serving Captain Ecuyer too well?"

"What do you mean?" demanded Salathiel, surprised and indignant, but mostly surprised.

"The captain is a sworn servant of the king of England," said Mr. Japson. "England is not here. This is God's country. It and the people of it lie in the fold of His hand. Dost thou think these hills and forests are the king's?"

"No," said Salathiel, "I do not. They belong to no man. I have heard say they were here before even the Injuns came."

"Yet the king has said we must not come here. And that those who have come must go back over the mountains. He has said we must not trade here. People like thee and me who were born here are not allowed to come into this land. It is the king's—and the Injuns'. Dost thou believe that?"

"It is a hard thing to believe, if you come to consider it," replied Salathiel. "I had never thought of it that way before."

"Thou shouldst begin to ask thyself who this king of England is," continued the Quaker. "What wilt thou do for thyself, Salathiel Albine, who art not permitted to stay in the land in which thou wast born?"

"I'll go east to the settlements. I want to see the wide sea water and the world."

Mr. Japson grunted like an Indian and said no more.

As for Salathiel, he rode along thoughtfully. He began to have a secret respect for the Quaker. There was much to be said for such men. Kaysinata had always admired the Pennsylvanians. Presently they came in sight of the fort again and rode for the gate.

"When thou dost get to Philadelphia," said Mr. Japson while they were waiting for the gate to be opened, "thou hadst best come to see me. We might have some more talks, and we might find each other helpful. I live on Fourth Street betwixt Chestnut and Mistress Nicholls's racing stables. Fourth Street. Fourth Street, the house farthest in. Canst thou remember that?"

"I'll write it down," answered Salathiel. "What does 'Fourth Street' mean?"

Mr. Japson gaped at him.

Just then the gate swung open.

32. In Which Soft Bargains Make Hard Feelings

THE INTERIOR of the fort was a busy spectacle. The Highlanders were assembled in full equipment and at rigid attention before their barracks. Sergeant McLaughlin was walking up and down before them looking exceedingly grim. Facing the Highlanders was the company of Pennsylvania militia with their noncommissioned officers in charge. They were laughing and carrying on.

From time to time some of them, who were evidently on detail, came from the storehouse or from the direction of the huts and laid down articles of various kinds—clothes, arms, blankets, and equipment—on a large pile immediately in front of the company. For some reason not apparent to Salathiel the appearance of many of these articles was greeted with bursts of laughter, catcalls, or ribald remarks. It was that which seemed to be annoying Sergeant McLaughlin.

This undisciplined confusion was bad enough, but it was many times magnified and twice as noisy in front of the stone steps that led up to the headquarters blockhouse.

Before the door of that building was assembled a crowd of women, some of them so ragged as to be half-naked, several with babies, and all clamouring aloud for admission. One old woman prowled about the blockhouse like an ancient mangy lioness, looking as though she would spring on the roof and tear the shingles away.

"God damn the lobsterbacks" and "Ecuyer is a bastard thief from hell" were among the more delicate of their screamed assertions. Around the edge of this crowd of loose-haired furies stood some of their men, looking sullen, but for the most part silent.

"It's the owld English game," shouted one vixen with fiery red hair, "drive us from the land and starve our childer. Divil a sop have I had for me tiny darlint these two days." She held up a baby in a filthy shawl and fairly waved it at the crowd. It howled obligingly. Moved by this appeal, the women gathered apparently to storm the steps en masse, when the baby began to vomit copiously a spray of sour pap that scattered the forming cohorts. Some wry laughter mixed with restraining remarks from the men served to calm matters down. The two Highlanders standing with fixed bayonets by the door now managed to make themselves heard.

"Bide a wee, haud yer hoorses. You'll be heard when your toorn coomes."

As if to confirm this, Mr. Erskine appeared and called from a list, "Mr. and Mrs. Turner." The woman and her husband pushed in through the door eagerly.

What this was all about, Salathiel had no idea. It looked like the mutiny of the washerwomen of Fort Pitt all over again, he thought. Suddenly he became intensely aware that several hundred eyes were turned on him and Japson while they sat their horses with the gate being closed behind them. A curiously boastful and savage instinct overpowered him when he found himself the centre of so much attention. He snatched the scalps from his belt, held them up dangling for all to see, and gave the death helloo twice.

A roar of appreciation came from the colonials. Many of them now began to make sport of Japson for having been caught and brought back. Then Mr. Erskine came out again to see what was the cause of the new uproar.

As soon as his eyes lighted on Albine and his prisoner, he smiled delightedly and beckoned for them both to come in. After turning over the pack horses to McLaughlin, Salathiel took Japson over to headquarters. The Quaker sat down in a corner, keeping his hat on and seemingly quite at ease.

Captain Ecuyer was seated near a table behind which Mr. Yates was ensconced with plume pens, an inkpot, and several long lists both of persons and of things neatly written and laid out before him. Ensign Erskine stood near the captain with his stocking dirk drawn, and there seemed good reason for this, since the captain's face was scratched and bleeding and his wig still lay before him in a badly trampled condition on the floor.

Despite that, the captain was patiently explaining something to the couple that stood before him, while from time to time he daubed his face with his handkerchief.

"Whatever has been taken from you will be returned, Mrs. Turner," he was saying. "It is only the articles which belong to the king that will be kept by the quartermaster. What is it in this case, Mr. Yates?" asked the captain. "Turner's the name."

"One musket and a forage cap, sir," said Mr. Yates, checking his papers.

"All the rest will be *returned*, Mrs. Turner," repeated the captain, "and before the day's over."

"Ike here, that's my man, bought thot shooten iron from St. Clair's store and guv good Portygee joes for it," said the woman. "Hit's ourn!"

The man nodded emphatically. "Thot's truth," he said.

"I've no doubt of it," said the captain, "but you see, Mr. Turner, the musket was stolen. It has the crown mark on it. We know the soldier who sold it to the store."

A torrent of abuse broke from the woman's lips.

"Hold your horrid tongue, Rachel," cried her husband. "Can't you see the captain's a gentleman and will deal honourably wid ye?"

"How will ye be gitten' any meat in the woods withouten your gun, ye fool?" his wife spat back at him.

With one hand Mr. Turner made a motion of respect and despair towards the captain and led his wife out with the other. She was still cursing.

There was a pause for a moment as the door swung open on the yelling mob of women outside and then banged to again. The captain ran his hand over his wigless pate and looked at the Quaker smugly sitting in the corner with his hat on.

"Friend Japson," said he, "blast me, if I'm not much obleeged to you for your work here! You can see," he added, pointing to his bleeding face, "that I am not the only one who feels deeply about it. Perhaps you can explain how so much of his Majesty's property seems to have passed over the counter of your store into the hands of these miserable inhabitants."

"It's quite simple," replied Mr. Japson. "It happened in honest trade. The garrison has never been paid since they came here. They need things desperately. The soldiers traded what they did have for what I had to offer them at the store. In some cases the people friend St. Clair has brought to settle here had certain coins. They in turn bought what the store had to sell them."

"Which seems to have been, as near as Mr. Yates and I can make out, about half the equipment of the garrison," replied Ecuyer. "While you were taking your early ride this morning, I took the liberty of temporarily impounding all the property in the fort. We are now in the midst of sorting out the king's and returning what is legally theirs to your late customers. Since you think this is 'so simple' I suggest you take my place here and oversee this process yourself. Your wig is a natural one and will not be pulled off quite so easily as mine. And you will find an able and accurate assistant in Mr. Yates. All you will have to do is to reverse the process that went on over the counter of your shop; to wit, purchase back the king's property. Mr. Erskine will see that it is returned to the members of the garrison to whom it belongs, item by item. Quite simple, friend Japson, does thee see?"

"Thou *canst not* mean it, Captain Ecuyer!" cried the trader, for once jarred out of his habitual pious calm. "Why, it will cost me two hundred pounds sterling at the least!"

"What do you think it would have cost if this fort had been lost, Mr. Japson?" enquired the captain. "Let me remind you: all the treasure the crown has lavished to extend and defend these frontiers for years past, the lives of soldiers, and houses ablaze from here to Carlisle. Women and children in the flames . . ." Ecuyer halted, trying to control himself.

"I know nothing of all that," replied Japson. "Such things belong to the princes and powers of this world to decide. All I know is I have to make my living. And I am a man of peace."

"Who buys and sells the muskets out of the hands of his Majesty's troops," interrupted Ecuyer. Salathiel had never seen him so angry.

"Swap for swap," interrupted Japson, not a whit daunted.

The captain rose from his chair and picked up his wig from the floor. He dusted it off and looked at the Quaker in complete amazement. For the first time it came to him fully that the man really believed in and meant what he said. Christ deliver me, he thought, and it is for this kind of a swine-louse that Bouquet and I have poured out the blood within us and the talents of our souls.

"Mr. Japson," he said, "I owe you an explanation. I did you the honour to think you were a villain. I see now that you are only a dangerous fool. Now come and sit down here and take the consequences."

The Quaker paled, shifted his hat onto his knee, and hesitated.

"See to it that he goes through with it, Mr. Yates," said the captain, walking over into the corner by his bunk and sitting down weakly. "Albine, come here and do what you can for me. I'll need all your skill. That woman nearly tore me apart. Hang a blanket over a string, will you. Demme, if I want any more of these viragos to gaze on my battered charms."

Salathiel strung the blanket across the room behind the captain's chair and went to work on him. He was shocked to find Ecuyer dangerously exhausted, and for the moment unmanned. He was about to have a chill. The experience of the morning, which had culminated in an assault upon his person by an hysterical woman, had shaken him more than all the difficulties of the journey and the hardships of the day before. It was at this juncture that it was borne in on Salathiel that Captain Ecuyer was not getting better; that he was slowly dying of his wounds and exhaustion.

"I must see it through until next spring. I must. I can't disappoint Bouquet," Ecuyer kept muttering.

Brandy, hot applications, and a rest lying down brought him back to a semblance of himself in an hour or two.

He then insisted upon sitting up in his chair and being refurbished from head to foot. A fresh wig and some black patches on his pale face gave him a peculiarly rakish and dissipated look like that of an old courtier who had quarrelled with his mistress. He looked at himself in his pocket glass and laughed. Salathiel's account of the capture of Mr. Japson and the taking of the two scalps was then listened to intently and with approval.

"But you must give up these savage customs," said the captain. "I was particularly shocked to hear you give the death helloo. It seemed to me you forgot yourself there."

"I'm afraid I remembered my old self—and didn't know it," replied Salathiel.

"That is even more serious," replied the captain. "You must try to remove such impulses from your soul. Now—my boots. I think I can bear them again."

From behind the blanket curtain Mr Japson's difficulties could be heard going on. It was only when he realized that Mr. Yates would turn him loose into the mob assembled about the door that the Quaker had finally consented to "take the chair". The news of what had happened had gone around outside. It was regarded as an excellent joke and poetic justice for the trader, and every individual or couple admitted to see him made the most of it.

As the day lapsed towards evening, however, all this came to an end. The last of the inhabitants were finally appeased, if not wholly satisfied. Mr. Japson, pale and haggard, had paid up. What belonged to the garrison was returned to them by Ensign Erskine and Sergeant McLaughlin. The property of the inhabitants which had been seized for inspection was given back, and the last check made against the final articles by Mr. Yates.

All were now inclined to put an end to what had been a laborious and nerve-racking day. Nevertheless, at five o'clock Captain Ecuyer had the garrison assembled, the quartermaster's store shack opened and every missing item of equipment down to the last button inspected, and when missing, replaced.

For that purpose the prisoners of the night before were released, paraded, and after a short reprimand returned to ranks without further punishment. One of them, the Irishman O'Neal, was not to be found. But McLaughlin informed the captain that he was undoubtedly in the stockade and probably hidden in one of the huts.

The release of the militia gave considerable satisfaction to the Pennsylvanians and all hands were pleased at having their outfits and equipment renewed. For that reason both the militia and the Highlanders stood without a sign of impatience for three mortal hours in the bitter cold, while Ecuyer's Prussianlike inspection and re-equipment went on.

By nine o'clock a new garrison seemed to have taken over the post. The late ragamuffin militia had disappeared and a formidable company of completely armed and quite soldierly-looking men stood in their place. The Highlanders once more resembled themselves in every particular, except a broken bagpipe which was beyond repair. Sergeant McLaughlin was ready to weep with joy.

Ecuyer then took them over, put them through some movements ending in a hollow square, and made a brief appeal, quite unexpected, in a strong, soldierly voice. He ended by remarking that the pay chests were expected at Bedford by December at latest, and that it was his and Colonel Bouquet's intention to have every man on the frontier paid before Christmas.

"Men," said he, "return to your quarters, cleanse your persons, your habitations, and your arms like soldiers and Christians. What infractions of discipline have occurred here I shall overlook. But from now on I shall punish relentlessly. Cut your hands off rather than part with your rifle guns. Your lives and the defence of this province depend upon them. In a short time you will be relieved here"—he paused as a rustle went through the ranks—"and you will be sent forward to Fort Pitt to go down the Ohio next spring with Colonel Bouquet. With the help of God it is his intention to force the savages to return their captives. Prepare yourselves to liberate your countrymen and restore them to the arms of their families, prepare to meet a cruel enemy that you already know so well. God save the king. Dismissed."

Ecuyer turned and staggered up the steps, with the help of Mr. Erskine, who now regarded him with veneration. The men scattered to their barracks, supper, and an extra tot of grog. A new kind of rational and disciplined noise filled the stockade. Only in the direction of the huts the quarrelsome grunting of hogs or an occasional human altercation broke out.

"There must be liquor loose over there, Mr. Erskine," said the captain, pausing to catch his breath at the top of the steps. "If we have any more trouble tonight I shall make an example that will long be remembered. Perhaps I have already been too lax. There comes a time when mercy to one may be cruelty to all. I dislike such moments."

They went into the blockhouse together, where a leaping fire and a smoking supper promised both cheer and surcease. The table was set—with four places again.

"Mr. St. Clair seems to be perpetually expected and always absent," remarked the captain as he sat down and drained a glass of wine to the dregs.

33. Another Side to the Same Question

THE MEAL BEGAN. A few minutes later St. Clair and the two militia officers rode into the fort, half-frozen and hungry as wolves. St. Clair was greatly worried at not having met Mr. Japson at an appointed rendezvous at the old Shawnee Cabins east of the Allegheny Mountain. He had waited for him there until a shot fired from ambush had ripped up the back of Lieutenant Neville's saddle and caused them all to take cover. Altogether, it had taken them nearly three days to ride over from Bedford, about fifty miles away. St. Clair cursed the Highland sentry heartily for his delay in opening the gate and the precision of his challenge in receiving him.

"By God, you ought to know us by this time," said one of the militia officers. "What's all this hifalutin nonsense about?"

"Strict orders, sir," replied the sentry.

"Ensign Erskine's?" St. Clair snorted.

"Aye," said the sentry, "his verra ain, sir."

"I'll soon take the feathers out of *that* young coxcomb's bonnet," grumbled St. Clair to the militia officers, as they dismounted.

"Let that arrogant bastard find out how things are for himself," remarked the sentry under his breath. "I'd give a month's pay, if I had it, to see his face when he walks into yon room."

The three officers began to bellow for someone to come and take their horses.

Captain Ecuyer laid down his pewter soup spoon and listened.

"His Highness has undoubtedly arrived," said Mr. Yates. "He and his tactful myrmidons."

"Do not rise or pay any attention to them when they come in, gentlemen," said Ecuyer to Yates and Erskine. "I'll do all the necessary honours. Albine, put another bowl of soup on the table for Mr. St. Clair. See that the two colonial officers are fed in the corner with Mr. Japson. They're close friends of his, I understand; or should I say customers?"

"Thou wouldst make the distinction," replied the Quaker, and went on eating his supper, of which Salathiel had served him a generous portion. He had already resumed his complacence, and the fact that he was a prisoner scarcely seemed to annoy him at all.

St. Clair and the two militia officers now came storming up the steps with a loud scraping of boots. Considerable hard swearing marked their appearance, for Lieutenant Neville, having had his saddle practically shot from under him, had consoled himself with enough rum to restore his nerves and partially paralyze his legs. He had to be dragged along, and the whole party now precipitated themselves through the door with a crash. St. Clair was about to call angrily for assistance in getting the lieutenant to a bunk, when the words were stricken from his lips by the sight that met him.

Captain Ecuyer, wig, scarlet jacket, epaulets, and all, sat at the head of the table, facing the door with the fire burning behind him. Yates and Erskine sat on each side of him, and a vacant chair with a bowl of soup smoking at the empty place was awaiting someone. Mr. Japson was in the near corner of the room, where Salathiel, towering six feet four, stood beside him. His head was near the rafters and his hatchet face and cold grey eyes appraised the newcomers quietly item by item.

St. Clair and Ensign Aiken stood stock-still, while Lieutenant Neville slumped casually to the floor and sat there. The two who remained upright seemed to be standing at bay.

"Good evening, *Mr.* St. Clair," said Captain Ecuyer at last. "We have been expecting you for some time. In fact, a place at the table has been reserved for you at the request of your friend Mr. Yates." Here he indicated the vacant chair. "Won't you sit down?"

"I'm certainly greatly obleeged to my friend Mr. Yates," drawled St. Clair.

"You are more in his debt than you know," countered the captain. "Pray join us. Your soup will soon be cold."

St. Clair removed his greatcoat, gloves, and muffler. "And these—er—other officers here?" he asked, waving his hand loftily towards the colonials.

"I'm afraid we shall have to forgo their fascinating company this evening," said Ecuyer, "inasmuch as they are both under arrest. Mr. Erskine, suppose you take his hanger from the officer who is still able to stand. Albine, put the gentleman on the floor into a bunk. Or, if he be able, he can join friend Japson in arrest in the corner. All of you will remain here until further orders, of course."

"Am I to consider myself under arrest, too?" demanded St. Clair, his face turning scarlet.

"Not unless you insist upon it, sir. Since you are no longer in the army, I should prefer to settle what mutual business we have here as man to man. You can, of course, join Mr. Japson if you desire."

"Oh, the devil take it all!" exclaimed St. Clair, flinging himself into the vacant chair at the table. "I might as well acquiesce, I suppose. No doubt I'm indebted to Mr. Yates for more than a place saved at the table. Mr. Yates is an extremely old friend of mine," said he bitterly. "It takes one Scot to ruin another."

"You do Mr. Yates an injustice, St. Clair," said the captain. "Recollect please, I'm not a schoolmaster who goes about gathering tales in order to inflict punishment. It is what you and your agent there in the corner have been doing here at Ligonier, and elsewhere, that has forced me to take certain measures. And what you have been doing here is notorious. It has disrupted the discipline of this fort and threatens to interfere with Colonel Bouquet's expedition. I refer to the supplying of the savages with arms and ammunition, besides other things, and the consequent encouraging of them. To further that and your profits, you, sir, tried to impose yourself on this young officer, your countryman, as the commander of this fort. And you have stirred up strife in the miserable militia here, and at Bedford, I am told, by involving them in your trade and interest. Now, this is all true. Deny it if you can. I can see it with my own eyes. It is not a mere jealous tale by Mr. Yates or anybody else, I can assure you. It is a fact. And at this time with the frontiers hanging by the thread of one road, and this place like a bead upon it, your conduct is tantamount to treason. My own duty is clear and I propose to see it done."

"And just what do you consider your duty to be, Monsieur Ecuyer?" demanded St. Clair.

"Your attempt to settle people here at Ligonier must cease, St. Clair. Your people must go back to Fort Bedford with me. And I will permit

no trade to go on west of the Allegheny Mountain for any reason whatever. You have probably heard of the royal proclamations about trading
with the savages, Mr. St. Clair?"

"Yes," said St. Clair. "I've heard of 'em."

"I trust I have answered your question plainly, then," added the
captain.

"You have made yourself painfully clear. But man cannot live by proclamations alone, you know, captain."

"Mr. St. Clair," said Ecuyer, "I have answered your question. Now
I wish you would answer one of mine. How is it that a certain British
officer I saw only a few years ago in Canada leading his men gallantly
against Montcalm is now engaged in trading enterprises that amount to
giving aid and comfort to the enemies of his king? Certainly they are
seriously interfering with the desperate efforts of Colonel Bouquet and
myself to defend this harried frontier. At least I thought I might expect
a certain *sympathy* for those humble efforts from a former comrade. But
I find the opposite. Frankly, I am perplexed. It is this contradiction in
your conduct which astonishes me. Is there an explanation, and what
can it be?" Ecuyer leaned back, putting the tips of his fingers together
while he sat gazing at his guest interrogatively.

St. Clair stirred uneasily. He poured a glass of rum and water, drank
half of it, and still hesitated. Then he began in a low voice, without a
trace of his usual pomposity or easy arrogance. For a while he managed
to be simply and naturally impressive.

"Candour is the most costly of all virtues," said he. "Yet I shall be
frank with you, Captain Ecuyer. You are known to be a man of honour,
one with clean hands." He raised his glass, looking at the captain, and
drank it off. "Your very good health, sir. I confess that under other circumstances I might envy you. But other climates other customs. If I
make you my conscience now, it is because I think you will not abuse
the confidence." He paused.

"Proceed, sir," exclaimed Ecuyer. "You are advancing your works by
slow stages. I demand only the honours of war."

St. Clair laughed.

"With me it is like this," he said. "I am a Scot. I came to America to
make my fortune, and for nothing else. When I found I could not do it
in the army, I resigned. I married me a wife born in the colonies, and
my children are and will be natives of this country. I shall remain here
the rest of my life, and hence the interests and advantages of this place
are hereafter and forever my own. Against all other interests, captain,
even against the crown and its officers—when they conflict."

He paused, and Captain Ecuyer leaned forward. In the corner Japson
gave Salathiel a dig in the ribs, as much as to say, "Listen, young man."

"Now what you and Colonel Bouquet, and a great many other Europeans and Englishmen, do not realize," continued St. Clair, "is that the

interests of the crown and of us Americans are not always the same. They are frequently at variance, and I venture to say that they may become increasingly so if the crown continues its present policy towards the western lands. For instance, you and Buckey—pardon me—wish to defend the frontier for the king. But the best defence of the frontier is to permit the people to settle here and exterminate the Injuns. In the end it would be better to let me settle the poor people I have brought to Ligonier, at great personal outlay, than to maintain a garrison here at greater public expense. And for how long? For forever, if you had your way. No, sir, it is to my advantage, to Mr. Japson's and his kind, to the advantage of everybody except the king and his ministers and his officers, to open up this country across the mountains to settlement, trade, and a vast continental prosperity that surpasses and overleaps the island imagination of all at home. In this adventure for profit, but also for better and for worse, I have cast my lot and set my compass, lead where it may. I have not sold out, as you may think. I have simply transported my vital interests to this place and against all others they are now my own." St. Clair brought his fist down on the table.

"Land?" said Ecuyer, drumming his fingers on the chair arm. "Land, Mr. St. Clair?"

"That is one way of saying it. Yes, if you will, land, in America!"

The captain nodded and smiled. He looked tired and said, "I've heard that before. But not quite so well put. Well, you have been candid and eloquent in your own cause, St. Clair. You will go your own way, I mine. But since you have so declared yourself, there is one thing it is my plain duty to demand of you. That is the paper given you by General Stanwix, reviving under certain conditions the lieutenant's commission you have resigned. It was yours on only one supposition, of course; that you would use it to further the interests of the king as a loyal officer. And you have been using it not for that, but for your own purposes. I must, therefore, demand the surrender of that paper, sir. And I shall return it to the present commanding general with your own explanation as given to me tonight. Do you have the paper on your person?"

"Perhaps, and perhaps not. At any rate, you will not commit highway robbery to get it, I take it?"

"No," admitted Ecuyer, "you are going to give it to me."

"Yes, but only under certain conditions."

"Mon Dieu!" cried Ecuyer. "Is there nothing you won't bargain about?"

"Between a Scot and a Frenchman, what can be exempt?" laughed St. Clair. "I will give the paper to you—it is at Fort Bedford—if you will let the people I have brought here remain. Even Mr. Yates will tell you there is a good legal argument for that, and . . ."

The captain held up his hand.

"Agreed," he said unexpectedly, "provided you and Mr. Japson will return with me to Bedford without making any further trouble."

It was now St. Clair's turn to hesitate. He did so for a minute or two, looking over at Japson, who finally nodded.

"Very well," said he. "I agree. My word upon it. Well, you *did* get your honours of war, captain."

"But that is about all," said Ecuyer.

He rose and bade them good night. The three Scots made their excuses and went over to the Highland barracks for draughts. In that pastime all rank was forgotten in a commonwealth of skill. Japson and the two militia officers finally retired to their bunks.

"Now help me to bed, too," said Ecuyer to Salathiel. "I've done all I can today—and a little more. Bedford tomorrow! Tell Burent to be ready. I wonder how long it will take? The mountains will go up and down and, O Lord, so will I!" He sat down with his hand to his forehead. Salathiel started to help him to bed.

"I have a plan for you, Albine," he said later, as he crawled under the covers. "I've been thinking something over, and we'll discuss it with you at Bedford. No, don't press me about it now. Tomorrow I want you to take full charge of the trip. There will be quite a company, not all as friendly and helpful as they might be. I'll not be able to do much more myself, until I see a surgeon. So you'll be in charge. I'll depend upon you. You did well with Japson today." He extended his hand out of his bunk.

"And so, good night."

34. Fire

BUT THEY were not able to get off next day as the captain had hoped and planned. Captain Ecuyer was not able to move. He lay in his bunk and slept from pure exhaustion. Salathiel made it easier for him by explaining to everybody that a wheel had come loose from the wagon; that Burent's back was still too stiff to drive, etc., etc. The captain was grateful for this—and so were all the others, for a damp snow began to fall early that morning. In the mountains it would be miserable. The Monk came in and built up a huge and comfortable fire, ate a flooring breakfast, and sat down like a tailor to watch Salathiel pamper his gun.

At the table Yates sat with St. Clair and went over the survey and the papers for the grant of land. For a while there was a hot dispute. To St. Clair the boundaries as described by Mr. Yates seemed, as he put it, to have "attenuated his parcels".

"And look," he cried, "look how the Loyalhannon sweeps around on me and cuts all the meadows out."

"You can hardly expect me to alter the course of the river just to suit you, Arthur," suggested Mr. Yates.

"Arthur me no Arthurs," exclaimed St. Clair, his face blazing. "B'Gad, I'll have to be made surveyor here myself to get my rights. You haven't taken in either the pond or the spring west of the fort. I must have them for the site for the manor house."

"We can probably manage the pond by altering this west boundary angle just a little."

"But the spring, the spring!" insisted St. Clair.

Mr. Yates leaned back in his chair and looked across at his companion with a smile in his eyes.

"Do you remember a dappled pony that broke its leg—and you shot, Mr. St. Clair?" demanded Yates, leaning forward suddenly and looking his companion in the eyes.

"Why, that was years ago, years ago, at home in Thurso! I'd forgotten it. I swear I had."

"But I haven't," said Yates.

"And so I am to pay for it now, Mr. Attorney?"

"You should at least have offered to do so years agone."

"How much will the spring cost me—Edward?" said Arthur.

Mr. Yates held up the fingers of both hands. "Guineas," said he.

"I thank God you're not like that bairn o' the widow by the owld toll gate at Thurso. Do you mind it? A sax-fingered freak," chuckled St. Clair. "I'll pay."

Not without a certain thought of admiration for his boyhood friend's being a true Scot, St. Clair counted out ten gold pieces and returned his lightened purse with a sigh.

"You might consider coomin' oot with me here and managin' things aboot this settlement, Edward."

"I might," said Yates. "I might. I've been thinking of seating myself in the wilderness sometime."

"*Arr,*" said St. Clair, "you'd do weel! Think it over. And you a surveyor, too." He chuckled again.

Yates nodded. He now began to alter the plats and the descriptions in the deeds and grants to take in the spring and the pond. St. Clair sat smoking before the fire, his feet high on the back of another chair.

While this was going on Salathiel had been marching silently up and down the room, going through motions with his rifle. He unslung it, rammed home a make-believe cartridge, primed, and presented it a hundred times. The ceiling was just high enough not to interfere with these exercises. The captain's silver watch by which he was timing himself ticked in the hands of the Monk, who called off the seconds as he had been told.

"You could handle it faster standing still, couldn't you?" asked St. Clair, who was watching the performance with interest.

"Yes, but I want to learn to reload it on the run," said Salathiel.

"Sort of a running fire," grinned Yates.

"Exactly," said Salathiel.

St. Clair took the rifle and examined it with great interest. A double barrel was new to him. He made some valuable suggestions as to firing and inspected the set of the flints. "One would do," he said; "a double lock seems unnecessary. If you get to Lancaster, take it to Jacob Ebey, the old clockmaker near Manheim. He's ingenious. He'd be able to fix it."

Salathiel stored this address away in his memory, along with Mr. Japson's on "Fourth Street".

Ecuyer was awake now. He felt greatly refreshed and insisted upon getting up and going out, despite their united protests.

"The king's business and invalidism are enemies," he said and smiled. "There's that fellow O'Neal. He's loose yet. Or did they find him, I wonder?"

He and Salathiel went out into the snow. There had not been enough of it to close the roads. It was a bright day, but it was getting colder again. Ecuyer gasped in the cold as they walked over to the barracks.

O'Neal had not been found. Mr. Erskine was now red-faced about it. He and Sergeant McLaughlin had hunted the fort through like two terriers after a rat that morning—but no O'Neal. Yet he had been seen only a few hours before at one of the huts owned by a McClanahan, one with a grievance.

"Let him alone," said Ecuyer. "He'll give himself away shortly. The McClanahans all smelled of whisky. Did you notice it, sergeant?"

"I did. They're a family with braw breeths," said McLaughlin.

A good deal of the breath-sweetening beverage was loose in the village, evidenced by a gradually growing delirious noise about the huts. They were celebrating the return of Mr. St. Clair in some of Mr. Japson's whisky.

The captain all but exhausted himself by putting the garrison through a mock Indian combat. He enlarged on the new drill and tactics for fighting the savages that he and Bouquet had devised. He was most careful in instructing the leaders in this native mode of warfare, which most of the men took to naturally.

The rest of the afternoon was taken up in an enquiry he conducted into the conduct of the two militia officers. They were both so sullen, and the testimony against them was so grave, that he suspended them from active duty and ordered them to return to Fort Bedford for a general court-martial. Mr. Pollexfen was confirmed in command of the militia and appointed his own officers.

How the fire started no one ever found out. Probably O'Neal started it out of pure drunken mischief. Increased pandemonium at the huts and a terrible fuguelike squealing of swine provided the first alarm.

Smoke was rolling from the east end of the stables and the litter in the pigpen was seething in flames almost before the startled sentries on the platforms could announce it. Burent rushed down to the stables to rescue the horses, and it was he who first reported the presence there of O'Neal.

"He's standing on the roof now," he gasped. "He threw a knife at me through the hole from under the rafters. And he's pitching pieces of burning bark from the slabs into the straw pile. It's the pigs what's spreading the fire," insisted the excited little Englishman, "the pigs!"

This sounded unlikely, but those who rushed out of the blockhouse soon saw what he meant.

The walls of the stable and the pigpen, where the unfortunate animals had been carefully confined, had become crackling sheets of flame. The swine were fat, and between two blazing walls they were literally cooked alive. In the intolerable heat they became living torches of roaring flame, screaming like a thousand organs played by maniacs and rushing about at furious speed.

It was at this juncture that someone, either out of mistaken mercy or quite deliberately, opened the gate of the pen. Flaming and shrieking confusion started galloping about the fort, rushing under the miserable huts and driving forth their shouting and fear-stricken inhabitants. One of the huts took fire and another column of flame began to crackle and roar at one end of the village. Half-crazed dogs fell upon one another. People began to shoot at the pigs and a child was wounded.

Meanwhile, O'Neal pranced up and down along the stable roof, overlooking his success and spouting a drunken ode of blasphemous triumph. In the lurid light of the flames now beginning to take hold on the Saxon roofs, he saw reflected the refulgent glory of the O'Neals and ten thousand other thatch-firing ancestors. Poteen, a keg of which he had dumped on the pigpen and set fire to, was also seething through his veins and brain and loosed in his mouth the tongues of bards and devils. It seemed to him he had turned the world into a volcano, and that it would run off in molten lava, leaving him godlike and alone—on a burning stable roof.

The long roll of the drum at headquarters put an end to a period of delirium which had lasted exactly seventeen minutes, but which secretly pleased everybody, except the little boy who had been shot in the hip, the burning pigs, and a few officers. It was a relief from the dreadful monotony and menacing silence of the forest that for years now had encompassed them all. That natural siege had temporarily been lifted. For five minutes everybody screamed his head off or roared. And then— the drum.

The garrison fell in; order resumed. From the top of the steps Captain Ecuyer gave his directions and in half an hour the flames were washed out with water, wet bags, mud, and snow. Half the stables were burned, one hut—the McClanahans', and the stockade wall was scorched. O'Neal had been rescued, overpowered, and put in irons.

Seated at supper an hour later, Ecuyer looked about him and at the grimy and soot-smirched company in the blockhouse. All of them had a certain chagrin and surprise fixed on their faces that seemed to peer through their grimy masks in a kind of dumb, ineffectual protest against the anarchy of unexpected events.

"Did you ever chance to reflect, Mr. Erskine, upon a convenient place about this stockade for hanging a man?" asked Ecuyer.

There was a moment's abysmal silence.

"Yes, sir, as a matter of fact I have thought about that several times," said Mr. Erskine more cheerfully. "There are three beams which stretch out from under the gatehouse floor just as you go out of the gate, for instance."

"One will do, Mr. Erskine."

"The middle one, sir?"

"Why go in for symmetry at a time like this?" said the captain, looking annoyed. "See that the rope is stout and have the decency to inform the man. O'Neal, of course."

35. Rope

SO THEY HANGED O'Neal next morning at sunrise.

The entire garrison was out, drawn up in the little square between the barracks. And every other man, woman, and child in the fort was looking over the backs of the soldiers at the one man standing on the cart under the gatehouse.

"Summary" was hardly a swift enough term to describe the briefness of the court-martial which had been accorded the Irishman in the dark of the early morning. He had been allowed his say, which consisted of a defiant statement that he was mortal sorry he hadn't been able to burn the fort to the ground, and a demand for a priest. There being no priest nearer than Maryland, he was sentenced, driven standing up in a cart under the beam projecting above the gatehouse, and the noose fitted about his neck.

There was a curious convention about hangings in all English-speaking lands. A hanging was at once a spectacle, a moment of moral edification, and legal vindication. Indeed, it was one of the few ways in which a common man might hope to transcend the common oblivion of commoners, and his fitness for having done so was judged largely by the eloquence of his own statement at his final taking off. It was considered to be the right, even the duty, of the condemned and the privilege of the spectators to participate mutually in a moving and admonitory farewell.

But the poor Irishman, when he was driven out under the gate and the rope put around his neck, could at first say nothing at all. He could only stand in the cart, weep, and look towards the officers, who were standing in a group at the top of the stone steps leading up to the blockhouse.

"Speak up, Shamus, now gie us a word, mon! The sun will soon be oop, and it will be all over wid ye," called one of the men from the crowd.

"Oi," said O'Neal, "it will be all over wid me. Oil go down into darkness. Oil not be seein' the sun!" He kept muttering.

"Captain Ecuyer," he called suddenly, "*must* I wait till the sun rises?"

" 'Twas the sentence of the court," said the captain.

In the growing light the figure of the man in his shirt with the collar turned down, and his hands tied behind him, shivered while his teeth chattered. The captain could hear his watch ticking in his own hand. In another minute the sun would be over the mountain, he figured.

"It's the cold makes me teeth to click, good paple. Not me heart. I'd have you remember thot. Me heart is a ragin' lion," cried O'Neal at last.

"I'll have a mass said for you, O'Neal, when I get home," called the captain, touched by his courage.

The sun seemed to be deliberately delaying.

"You're a gintleman, captain. I'm sorry I cursed you, I am. Do you forgive me for it?"

"I do," said Ecuyer.

"Give me bundle of plunder to Mrs. McClanahan. Do ye be hearing me, Maggie?" Somewhere in the crowd a woman sobbed. "You're the only charitable hoor in the stockade. It's me all I'm lavin' you."

A golden radiance beat on the man's face, suddenly transfiguring it. The glistering edge of the sun's rim looked over the Laurel Mountain and filled the valley of Ligonier with light. The sunrise gun crashed. The drum rolled, beaten frantically by the Monk with tears streaming down his face. The gate swung open and the cart drove out—leaving the body of O'Neal swinging darkly like a pendulum in and out of the shadow of the gatehouse.

He raised his feet, which were tied together, once or twice, flexed his legs frantically at the knees, and then was still, except that he slowly spun around. A woman screamed. Then the drum stopped. Its echoes died, rolling away up the valley of the Loyalhanna into ghostly silence. No one moved. The troops blinked in the sunlight . . .

"Mr. Erskine," called the voice of Captain Ecuyer very clearly, "cut the body of that man down in half an hour after I leave this fort and give it decent burial. Raise the flag after the body is down. I'll be back here in two weeks' time, and I shall expect to find a strict watch kept and good discipline." He raised his voice slightly so all could hear. "And I leave *you*, sir, in command of this fort."

With that the captain walked down the steps and climbed into the wagon, which had been ready and waiting for him for an hour past.

"Gentlemen," said he, turning about on the little ladder to address a small group of horsemen, some of whom were already mounting, "you have your instructions. Be good enough to follow them to the letter. Move off, Albine."

Salathiel rode ahead on the mare. He had to lean aside to avoid the hanging body as he rode through the gate. The garrison came to present arms as the wagon rumbled out of the stockade. O'Neal's heels dragged along its roof, scraping the canvas gently. The captain looked up until the shadow of the dead man passed. "I'll remember the mass," he said aloud. There were others who more richly deserved hanging, he thought. He went on tying himself in the swinging seat with his long, silk kerchief. It was over fifty miles to Bedford and two ranges of mountains to cross between.

36. Owls at Ray's Dudgeon

ST. CLAIR on a raw-looking gelding, the two sullen militia officers, Mr. Japson with his string of pack horses, and three inveterate deserters from the militia being returned to Fort Bedford for discipline, rode about fifty yards behind the wagon. They were all armed but had no powder. If there was an Indian attack the captain would serve it out to them then and let them defend themselves. Otherwise he was not taking any chances. This arrangement had been made at Salathiel's suggestion.

Another fifty yards to the rear rode a party of four of the Pennsylvanian riflemen under the temporary command of Mr. Yates. These men were frontiersmen from the vicinity of Bedford and Will's Mountain, excellent shots, and were to be trusted, according to Captain Pollexfen. Their cabins had been burned out by the Indians the summer before, and they therefore had a natural dislike for redskins and for all traders who supplied "the varmints".

Mr. Yates was the best mounted of anyone in the little procession. He rode a fine grey "loaned" him from the governor's stable and the Penns' own stud in Philadelphia, and he rode well. He had no rifle, but two immense horse pistols in holsters, and a short sword. He was a cheerful companion, joked a great deal, and the four Pennsylvanians had soon accepted him as their leader in fact as well as at the captain's command, when they found he was neither a soldier nor an Englishman. A rumour had gone about that he was a cousin of the Penns who had come out to settle.

"You had oughten to seat yourself in this ya kyounty, Maister Yates," suggested young Tom Pendergass, whose family had long been settled near Bedford. "My dad did mortal well with carn, whisky, and tradin' fer pelts before the Injun troubles begun. He has a big store and tavern at the fort now. All of us boys has been driv off our land. But we'll be back, and the axes ringin', soon as Buckey burns the redskins out on the Muskingum. He's got the knack of whippin' them at their own game. Him and the little rooster up ahead in the wagon air the boys for we'uns, even if they do be king's men. Thar's no shenanigan about 'em. Now I'll pint out some right desirable bottoms to ya while we ride along."

"Girls' or farm lands?" demanded Mr. Yates, a repartee so much appreciated that he was forced to remind them that loud whoops must be subdued to chuckles in the enemy's country.

This merriment of the rear guard was in stark contrast to the silence and occasional remarks exchanged in a bleak undertone amongst the party nearer the wagon, headed by St. Clair. He himself was for making a bolt for it. But he could get no encouragement from Japson, who would not abandon his pack horses, nor from the deserters, whose spirits, never too high, had been entirely cowed by "having been rid under a hanged corpse". This, they contended, was a portent of imminent disaster.

"Be damned to you," said St. Clair, "for a parcel o' yellow dogs!"— and confined the rest of his growls and invective to the ear of Japson. These were none the less effectively interrupted when Ecuyer occasionally looked out the rear of the wagon.

Meanwhile, and so far, they were making pretty good time.

To Salathiel riding forward, and ranging ahead sometimes as much as a quarter of a mile, the country unfolding before him was a continual delight, and his minute examination of it for possible lurking foes a positive pleasure.

The damp snow of the morning had now frozen into a fairly solid surface crust, giving the horses good footing and just permitting the wheels to break through and roll without bogging down.

They were soon up and out of the rolling hills and crossing a comparatively bare plateau of mountain meadows in which lay the little stream and valley where Salathiel had taken the scalps only the day before. He rode back here and brought up two of the Pennsylvanians from the rear to help him in scouting ahead. They knew the country intimately. And, if anyplace, it would be on some of the dense reaches of the mountain wall ahead that they might be ambushed.

A surprise of a different kind did, in fact, lie right ahead of them, for Salathiel at least. It was the abrupt end of the plateau and a sudden drop into a great wooded valley a good thousand feet below, beyond which the Laurel Hill rose towering. To a man from the low river lands the unusual sensation of height was overpowering. He stopped for a moment in his tracks, and the two Pennsylvanians, realizing the reason, laughed.

"Hit hain't nothin' to what's beyont," said young Pendergass. "But this here *is* good bar country. Thar's caves in the bottom o' the branch." They stopped the procession to examine the road and the country ahead with extreme care. Some miles away a slight mist rising from the valley attracted Salathiel's attention.

"I was wonderin' ef you seen it," remarked Pendergass. "Hit hain't Injuns. Hit's a warm spring. Leastways hit's warmer than this hyer winter air, and she fumes. Me and par spent a hul day sneaking up to surprise 'Injuns' thar some years ago. Par was right mad when we found what it was. Thar's a salt lick near by."

Indeed, after some minutes they could see a movement of something making that way through the woods.

"Elk or buffalo cattle," grunted Murray, the other Pennsylvanian, after watching for some time. "And I can see another passel on 'em goin' south 'long the mountain."

"The wind's from the ridge," said Salathiel, holding up a wet finger.

"You're right, friend," agreed Pendergass, "and them critters is handy shy and spry these days. Looks like if thar be any Injuns, thar way down on t'other side o' the mountain."

"Liken they be," said Murray.

So they agreed to move forward—and their troubles began.

The road down into the abyss ahead was icy in stretches where springs had burst out across it. They had to let the wagon down inch by inch with the pack horses toggled on behind and holding back desperately step by step over such places. One of the beasts slipped, rolled; was cut loose by St. Clair with splendid agility; crashed with a scream into the forest below. He was hung there, transfixed on a giant dead oak tree.

"You'll be paid for that one, Friend Japson," said the captain. "He was lost in the king's service."

"But not for the others?" asked the Quaker.

"Not for the others," said Ecuyer.

"I will sue thee in the provincial courts," called the outraged trader. "Thou shalt see!"

"There is a Scripture against going to law one with the other. Shall I quote it?" asked Ecuyer.

Mr. Japson turned purple, and St. Clair laughed—but at that moment the caisson skidded and threatened to pull the whole outfit over the edge after the lost horse. The Scriptural banter ended in a chorus of profanity and frantic "whoas" apparently addressed to various divine persons.

It took them over two hours to reach the branch near the bottom of the Laurel Hill. From there the road soared up over that mountain in a series of zigzags and banked curves directly into the sky. And the mountain was a wall of solid maple forest.

They stopped here and broke fast in the valley in a thicket of ancient but huge and hollow sycamores. Two or three of these trees gave the whole party shelter, while the horses were tied to the wagon and overlooked by two men with rifles, sitting high in the branches. A wolf loped off among the big trees.

"No one here," said Salathiel. Young Pendergass nodded. "Wolves here is a comfortin' sign," he admitted.

Ecuyer laughed to himself at the horrid comfort of the wilderness. He asked St. Clair to eat with him, and that ex-officer and up-and-coming gentleman looked pleased in spite of himself. They built no fires. The horses were rested, watered, and fed. Shortly after midday they forded the creek that lapped the foot of the mountain and began to climb.

It was desperate work.

"Only a Switzer like Ecuyer would try to take so heavy a wagon over the mountains in winter," remarked St. Clair. Japson agreed. But they all threw themselves into the task. As many horses as possible were made to draw. All minor differences were forgotten in the little party, for if they were attacked now it might be a close thing. It might go hard with them. No rescue would be coming. The captain issued a charge or two of powder to those without it. The Pennsylvanians ranged the woods ahead on both sides of the road as best they could. They were certain no one would try to desert here.

The wagon came up and up. At the worst places Ecuyer got out and hobbled along. He was obviously in great pain, yet his practical suggestions for making progress were constant and skilful. They stopped, breathed the winded beasts, and went on.

The afternoon passed away. Just before sunset they came out on the top of the ridge.

To Salathiel's surprise it was not like the top of a mountain at all, when he looked eastward. The valley was behind, but a broad tableland undulating easily and sprinkled with dense thickets and snowy open spaces lay before. The mountain was actually several miles broad at the top. Beyond in the sunset glimmer lay a welter of peaks seemingly incredibly distant, and wrapped in a glowing, translucent haze of fading scarlet lights and deepening blue shadows.

"Them's the Alleghenies and the peaks beyont," said Murray. "God send we're in the Shawnee Hunting Grounds tomorrow night. We kin take shelter in the valley. Hit's cold enough here to freeze a jug o' whisky. Push 'em on, friend Salathiel, the harses ul git the heaves standin' steamin' in this hyer thin, cold air o' the mountaintop." A blast like the intimate breath of winter roared across them.

So it took little persuasion on Albine's part to get them under way again. The horses fairly stampeded for shelter. The wagon rolled, bumping along the rocky road, rumbling, and striking fire from the stones and tires in the twilight.

Just as the stars began to come out and a new moon was sinking, they turned off the road into a clearing in the centre of which was a dark mass of low entrenchments and the sawtooth rim of a stockade lonely and dark as a castle left from other ages.

Now was the hardest time of the day for Salathiel. Everybody was exhausted and was for standing around near the warmth of the logs. There was no preventing such a fire being made. The men simply built it. As soon as it was going he had to drive them from it and to work. The powder issued to the deserters, to Japson, and to St. Clair was taken from them again.

They propped the big gate in place and wedged it. Salathiel asked Yates and two of the Pennsylvanians to watch on the galleries. The rest, even the "gentlemen", he insisted should cut wood, start the supper, and prepare generally for the night. Ecuyer came out and set an example, axe in hand.

Burent and Japson with two of the deserters put up the horses under a lean-to shed half collapsed with deep snow on the roof, as best they could. Blankets went on the wagon teams and mare after they were rubbed down and stones dislodged from their hoofs. The old sheds were many feet deep with rotten straw and leaves. Water was drawn from the garrison well after smashing in the head ice with a boulder.

Salathiel brought the remains of the pig out of the wagon and grilled and roasted them over the fire. Potatoes were baked in the coals, and hominy cakes fried in the dripping grease. Some of the men produced loaves of bread baked at the fort. A handful of brown maple sugar cast on the sizzling hog meat caused such an appetizing odour that the sentries on the galleries called out with impatience. Promises of special cuts scarcely bribed them to remain on duty. Captain Ecuyer emerged from the wagon with a small puncheon under his arm and served out a good glass of black, fiery Jamaica rum to all present in grace or disgrace.

"Lum, lum, him heap good," cried young Tom Pendergass, rubbing his stomach and doing a shuffle about the fire like an Indian. "What kind of country must it be that grows juice like this here?" he demanded after downing his share.

"Rum is a little essence of Paradise squeezed out of hell, young man," said Japson, who had once been to Jamaica.

"Attar of nigger sweat," suggested St. Clair, also inspired.

"Gentlemen, you libel my contribution," said the captain, driving the bung home in the puncheon with mock indignation. "Rum—'tis the courage of fighting Dutchmen and the main brace of the royal navee. Gentlemen, your health." He downed an entire glass at one gulp without a shudder, while St. Clair regarded him with admiration. A ragged cheer greeted the captain's noble defence of the white man's solace and his command to fall to on the victuals.

"Here, Murray," said he, heaping some pine slabs high with smoking cuts, hominy and potatoes, "carry these to the unfortunate sentries on the galleries and tell them to watch while they eat. Many an Englishman has lost his scalp for dessert at an American dinner. And see that the rum gets to them too!"

Laughter followed Murray, who obviously had his plans for an extra sip at the expense of those on watch. Mr. Yates was soon shouting down his thanks and reporting that the place was about to be taken by storm by owls. Nor was this entirely a joke.

The old stockade called "Ray's Dudgeon", built by Forbes in '58, swarmed with owls since its garrison had departed, and the birds kept swooping about until blinded by the great fire they would make a pass over its heart and fall snapping on the ground to lie on their backs with their claws drawn up threateningly. Callahan, one of the deserters, was badly bitten when he snatched one up to "take home to his lil gal". His thumb spouted blood and he threw the bird into the fire where it shrieked like a lost soul, roasting.

"That's *you* in hell, Callahan," said St. Clair, who thought he knew how to deal with what he called "frontier cattle". "You've walked under a hanged man, and now you've roasted an owl. I doubt you'll last till morning. It's bad, *bad* luck!"

Callahan was visibly shaken and went off to sulk.

"God damn a brute like that," continued St. Clair.

"You ben't used to roastin' yet, Maister St. Clair," remarked young Nat Murray. "Me grandad, an old white-haired man, was tied up by a passel o' Shawanees in 'fifty-seven and had his legs burnt off to the knees with me grandma watching. Then they—"

"None of that," said Ecuyer sternly. "Every man here knows what we're fighting, devils that live in these hills and haunt the forests."

A growl of assent went around the circle. Only Japson seemed silent.

"Give us a song, St. Clair," exclaimed the captain, "a good rousing one."

"*Lillibullero, bullen a la,*" sang St. Clair in an unexpectedly fine tenor.

The rest joined in, for among the Scotch-Irish Pennsylvanians there was scarce one that did not remember the good Protestant chorus of King William's days, the anthem of Orangemen.

Ecuyer gave out the watches for the night, and cautioned them with an earnestness that went home to be mortal careful and stay awake. "For one slumbering sentry is the death of us all." The men around the fire scattered to find what places they could to sleep in among the half-ruined cabins.

In the lean-to and among the horses Callahan sat sucking his bleeding thumb and cursing. He was from old Irish Baltimore, a good Catholic, and the Orangemen's songs made his heart turn black with hatred. He determined to make another break for home.

The night and time wore on.

It was soon Salathiel's turn to go on watch. He had the second, and later the last watch in the morning. He and Murray and Pendergass went up and relieved Yates, and the other two Pennsylvanians on the galleries.

Quiet settled down on Ray's Dudgeon, broken only by the gurgles of owls and the screams of a panther hunting in the ravines lower down beyond the crest of the mountain.

The three passed to and fro on the platforms, keeping themselves warm, awake. The stockade was built at the bottom of a saucerlike depression, and it now struck Albine why this was a good plan.

It was another exalting night. The high mountain air was a new sensation and experience for Salathiel. He was not tired, he was even glad he was up on the platform overlooking everything. Sleep could come later. The mountains were surpassing his expectation. He felt the rum in him and the good supper. He laughed quietly to himself.

Outside the stockade the wind swept through the bare branches of the forest and sang like a sorrowful squaw. Inside, all was still. The fire burned down to glowing embers. The oblong of canvas over the wagon shone dull yellow with candlelight from within. The captain, St. Clair, and Yates were having a round of loo. Occasionally their conversation and a laugh sounded distant and muffled. A light flickered here and there in the windows of the huts and went out.

The card game in the wagon broke up. Albine heard St. Clair and Yates saying good night and walking off into the darkness. Soon only the horses were stamping now and then. The noises of the forest prevailed. Over the stockade the stars slowly wheeled and marched to the westward, white shimmering clouds of them such as he had never seen before. A fox barked and sniffed along the gate. It would soon be time to change the watch. He saw the animal sneaking off through the trees. He watched it through a loophole—and then he saw something else.

It was a man gliding from tree to tree. Salathiel watched the line he was taking. Presently he would be on the rim of the "saucer". There was a patch of snow there. He would have to cross it. Salathiel could see the sights of his rifle only against that snow. He aimed there and waited. Suddenly the end sight was blurred by a shadow on the snow. The two sights came in line. He fired. He peered out again. Either the man was down, or he had missed his shot.

Then he saw a figure running across through the trees and against the stars. There was an agonized scream out in the darkness. Salathiel fired his other barrel, aiming at the same place he had fired at before. He had almost forgotten that he had another barrel!

The fact that Murray and Pendergass were good men was proved when they faced out and watched at the loopholes when Salathiel fired, instead of running to him with questions.

But there was plenty of questions from below. The captain was out, demanding what the firing was about, and St. Clair, too. Some of the others came tumbling out with their rifles.

"Who fired?" demanded Ecuyer.

"I did," Salathiel answered, still keeping an eye on the section of view through his loophole. "There were two of them, captain. I think I got the first one. Then an Injun came to scalp him. I don't know whether I got him too, or not. I think the first I fired at was a white man. Maybe one of our own people. He seemed to be leaving the stockade."

"Where's Callahan?" asked the voice of Japson suddenly.

Several voices began to call "Callahan" in vain.

"Guess he's made a break for it," remarked O'Toole, one of the deserters, "and that big renegade bastard on the platform's shot him. I ain't goin' to lave him out there to be scalped," he whined. "He's me nevvy. Me sister will go woild."

Considerable stir was going on down in the darkness.

"You men go back to your huts," said Ecuyer. "I'll shoot the first one of you that moves towards the gate, myself. You can see what happens to you outside."

The glint of a pistol in the firelight confirmed the captain's sincerity. The bereaved uncle of the late Callahan and his companions departed, cursing under their breaths.

The captain doubled the watch on the platforms. Everyone, including Japson, took a turn. But nothing more was seen or heard.

Towards morning Albine and the party first on watch got some sleep but not much, for soon after dawn they cooked food and prepared for an early start. It was the captain's intention to reach a place called the "Shawnee Cabins" on the other side of the Allegheny Ridge before evening.

He called Albine aside and cautioned him to push on without regard to the fatigue of those following. "And keep a good watch in advance, for I wouldn't be surprised if we meet a train of pack horses and drivers. I think Mr. St. Clair and Japson have long been expecting them. They have not been able to send back messengers to warn them not to set out. I rather think that's why Callahan was so anxious to escape last night. He could have deserted more easily when he got to Bedford. It is my intention to turn this caravan of traders back," said the captain significantly. "Ammunition to the savages now might be the ruin of Bouquet. If we can catch these people redhanded, it will put a stop to the trading business at least until the campaign's over, I feel sure."

There was only one incident that marked, and that with quiet chucklings on the part of several, the departure from the Laurel Hill stockade.

The men under charge of attempted desertion were put to drawing water that morning from the well for the horses. As Salathiel passed them, he recognized the voice that had called him a "renegade bastard" only the night before. It belonged to a large, loose-jointed fellow with red hair and bristles bursting from his ears. As the man was without weapons, Salathiel laid his own rifle and long knife aside and walked up to him. The man seemed inclined to dodge what was evidently coming his way. As he did so, Salathiel jammed the captain's little water bucket down over his head, not gently. It proved quite difficult to get off, and the sepulchral remarks of the man in the wooden hat were appreciated even by his friends. The two militia officers stood by laughing heartily.

The wagon and its attendant cavalcade got under way that morning to the tune of considerable laughter, despite the tragedy of the night before. Merriment, however, did not travel with them more than a rifle shot from the gate.

In the snow patch on a small rise where they turned off on the road, the body of Callahan was found half scalped and shot through the back. There was no sign of the Indian except a scalping knife dropped in the snow near the dead man, and a trail of blood as far as the road. It ceased there or it could be traced no farther. Just how the Indian had got away was not plain. It was a source of great satisfaction to Salathiel none the less that both his shots of the night before had evidently found their mark. He patted the butt of his rifle affectionately and saw that Murray and Pendergass and the others regarded him with increased respect.

They stopped long enough to tie the body of Callahan over the empty saddle of his horse and went on. A little farther along they buried it some distance off the road.

"Owls," said St. Clair to his small group of followers, "owls! What did I tell you last night?" He enjoyed their consternation and winked at Japson, who could not see the joke. O'Toole and his friend began discussing in an undertone what they were going to do to Salathiel.

It was now getting sensibly warmer. Captain Ecuyer made that his excuse for demanding extreme exertions from everybody to push forward. Halfway across the valley to the Allegheny, Salathiel and his advance guard found a letter stuck in a cleft stick by the side of the road. It was addressed to Mr. Samuel Japson in a sprawling hand:

Friend Japson—Me and Lt. St. Clairs nigger Jed come as far as this lookin out for you. Thought you and him was coomin back to gyde us over the hill west. Not finden you we stopped here half a day and then took back to Chowanee cabins where is the men and harses and goods waiten in the big grove tol you come. Seen no redskins nor sines on em. Came an express Fryday from Harriss on Susaquahannok sayin sum pay chists was on the way from Carlysl with starlin. Looks like brisk trade at Raystown soon promises. Prendergass in high hopes hez

tooken 5 kags offen you for his place and promises coin. Hope
you find this. Will wait at cabins while vittels holds out.

Your obgt. serv.
T. Maxwell.

So that was why Japson had been so anxious to get ahead of them,
and why the captain had been so determined to hold him. Now they
would know where to find the traders. And from what Maxwell said it
looked as though there were no Indians about.

Of course, he could not depend upon that, Salathiel pondered. There
was no date on the paper. And some of the Delawares who had been
following Japson might turn up. It was probably one of them who had
scalped Callahan last night. All at once Salathiel remembered the letter
he had found in the pouch of the Delaware he had scalped. How could
he have been so forgetful! Well, he would give both the letters to the
captain now. He folded it up in the letter found by the road and sent
both back by Murray after cautioning him not to be seen giving it to
Ecuyer. Also Murray was to tell Burent not to spare his horses. Then he
took up the march again and pushed on towards the mountain. Murray
overtook them only with some difficulty on his return.

"The captain says, 'that's good'—and he wants to see Albine at the
noon halt."

They had begun the ascent of the Allegheny Mountain and were a
quarter of the way up when the halt came. Salathiel found Captain
Ecuyer quite elated over the finding of the letter.

"It puts these gentlemen in our hands," he said, "if we play our cards
right. Now I've altered my plans a little. We'll camp tonight at the top
of the Allegheny in the entrenchment at the crest. After the camp is
asleep I want you to take the four Pennsylvanians, go down the mountain and make an attack about dawn on the traders camped in the
grove. *Panic* them back to Bedford. Don't kill anybody, if you don't have
to. Make them think you're Indians if you can, but see to it that all the
trade goods are left behind. They can take their horses, arms, and per-
sonals if they wish. Arrange it by making terms, or any other way.
Burent and I and Yates will keep Japson, St. Clair, and Company in
hand till morning. You can wait for us tomorrow till we get down the
mountain. Now I told you at Ligonier I had something in mind for you.
Well, this shall be your test for fitness for certain other things. Don't
tell your men anything of this until just before you leave. Be especially
careful of the two militia officers under arrest. They are St. Clair's
friends. Japson, too, is keen as a fox. Wait until they are all asleep
tonight. I leave the details to you. See to it!"

"See to it," Salathiel kept repeating to himself. It was the captain's
favourite phrase. Well, he would *see to it,* he promised himself.

They resumed the ascent of the mountain, but more slowly. The captain even managed to trump up some plausible delays. It was not difficult to find good reasons for stopping. The climb was a killing one. On the higher slopes the embankments of Forbes's engineers had in some places washed out. Burent was much admired for his skill in getting the wagon up at all. It was twilight when they arrived at the "Allegheny entrenchment", and the captain's decision to spend the night there almost met with applause. Watch was set, supper prepared, and the captain pleading his great fatigue as a reason for retiring early, all settled down for the night.

"No owls here," said St. Clair to Albine. "Not a one."

"I take that for a *good* sign, sir," Salathiel replied, and grinned in the dark as St. Clair went off to smoke a pipe and go to bed.

37. Panic as a Cathartic

IT WAS ABOUT eleven o'clock of an extraordinarily clear, moonless night when Salathiel gathered his four Pennsylvanians together and explained what was in view for the next morning.

They had managed to leave the camp in the little entrenchment without anyone but the captain being aware of their departure.

Salathiel brought with him a bag of shot, powder, some boiled meat, and hoecake sufficient for one meal, also several pieces of the captain's charcoal. Well beyond hearing of the camp, he now halted and made his plans known while everyone blacked both hands and face with charcoal.

The four Pennsylvanians entered into the scheme with grim enthusiasm. All of them had been driven from their clearings and forced to take refuge from Indians at Fort Bedford. Murray and Pendergass had both been born near Raystown. So they knew the country about Fort Bedford as only young hunters could, and it was understood they should act as guides.

It was finally agreed that they should attack about an hour before dawn and try to palm themselves off as Indians on a raid—"which won't be no hard stunt, neither," asserted one Harry Banner from the Juniata water gap—"'caise the mostest of these here pack-horse drivers and men is from the German settlements, and all them Dutchmen knows about Injuns is that they yells like hell fustest, and then scalps ya."

"Well, we'll yell like hell," said Salathiel, "and I'll jabber real Shawnee at them, and a few shots might help. Time to git on now. Watch we don't meet some of the real article layin' for us as we go down."

A growl of approval met this caution, and they swung off in single file with Murray leading at a good pace.

The road began to tend downward rapidly. It was suddenly much warmer on the eastern slope. The cold northwest wind which had

plagued them for days was suddenly cut off. The road swung unexpectedly outward around a great shoulder of shaly rocks. Towards the east
the mountain here fell almost sheerly to the broad floor of the mighty
valley below. There was the feeling of being high, and alone among the
stars. All felt this, and they stopped for a moment as if by common
consent.

"Come over here, Albine," said Murray. "I want to pint out the lay o'
the land to you."

Salathiel approached the unprotected outer edge of the road on cat's
feet. Just ahead of him it seemed that Murray was about to walk out
on invisible levels of atmosphere and swim among the stars. They
stopped, of course, at the brink.

"Wal," drawled Murray, "what do ye think of our country? God,
y'oughter to see hit by daylight!"

But the night was quite enough for Salathiel.

Immediately beneath him was the roof of a dark forest that undulated
over the swelling floor of the valley, ending eastward against a far-flung,
black mountain wall whose edge was hung like a great floating ribbon
along and across the stars. Beyond that, great masses of fleecy white
clouds staggered up into heaven with black windows through which appeared glittering, familiar constellations and the dim eyes of unknown
stars. And against the cloud curtain, lower down, was a jumble of dark
peaks, domes, and profiles of mountain crests, high, disconnected, and
lonely; the mysterious midnight country of a beautiful, terrifying dream.

"Ain't no Injuns goin' to drive us out o' this," commented Murray,
after respecting Salathiel's silence for a proper time.

"Nor no traders neither," he added. "Man! Ya oughten to see the
harvests hereabouts. The black loam's two or three feet deep even on the
hillsides, oncet ye git the trees down and let the light in; carn, punkins,
wheat, taters, and you kin grow tobacker ef'n yer want to. And thar's
sweet springs and the music of livin' streams. Hit's God's gift to them
that kin keep it."

"Looks like it's worth fightin' fer," admitted Albine, who could not
tell what his eyes saw and how he felt about it. "If we can once git
things settled, looks like thar's homes for all of us somewhar"—he flung
his hand out with a sweep as generous as the landscape itself.

"You're right, friend," agreed Murray. "Reckon we've come fer to stay.
But look," said he, lowering his voice. "Do you see that ring of little
lights twinklin' away north there? Thought they was stars myself at fust,
but they be too low down. They're on the valley floor, and that's the
fires o' the pedlars waitin' in the grove fer Japson. And thot's whar we
must be, come mornin'. And it's a many a mile away."

They returned to the trail to report to the others what they had seen.

"No more haltin' now," said Albine. "Keep going down, Murray.
When you git pretty nigh tell me and I'll give you my scheme for drivin'

these fellers back. Git your packs and your straps set now for a long swing down the mountain."

"It looks farther than it is," said Murray encouragingly, and struck off downhill in a steady hunter's stride.

When the night birds ceased towards morning they halted by a spring, ate hastily, and looked to the fresh priming of their pieces.

They had now reached the level of the valley floor.

"It's about two miles to the grove now," said Murray. "They must have let their fires die down, or we'd see the glow over yon hill. Shows they ain't keepin' much of a watch after all. Well, Mr. Albine, and what now?"

Salathiel was tickled. It was the first time anyone had "mistered" him as a superior.

"Here's the scheme me and the captain agreed on," he drawled. "Thar's five of us, and I hear thar's open space all around the grove which is kind o' set out and bare like on the top of a hill."

"Thot's right," agreed Pendergass. "Hit's the very picture."

"Well, we'll spread out all round it in a ring. You'll have to jedge your places pretty nice. Each man about the same distance from t'other. I'll give you half an hour fer that. Then, jes when the first grey shows in the sky, I'll hoot like an owl goin' home. Like this . . . You can all reply one by one a few minutes apart. When it gits round to me again I'll know we're all set, and I'll 'wha-hoo' twice. That'll be the signal fer all ready. I'll fire, and then we'll all begin to yell like Injuns and let the rifle fire go round and round the ring. Let 'em think thar's a hundred Injuns in the grass. And move about a bit so they can't fix on your gun flash. And mind you, keep firing one after t'other with about a minute between. That'll give you all about four minutes each to reload, and mind you keep it going. Make them keep their heads down, and if they fire back, fire at the place the flash came from. If they holler for terms, let me do the talking. And if they make a break for it, shoot 'em down when they gather. Each one of you will have to make enough noise fer a hul tribe. Now everything, firin', yellin', and talk will go round from left to right, sunwise turn. Kin you remember it?"

A chorus of reassuring growls from the darkness was the encouraging reply.

"Wet your whistles now at the spring and don't forgit to wipe your rifles agin, if ye crawl through the grass. I'll allow fer that. Ready?"

"Let out," said Pendergass.

They swung off silently as animals, scarcely making a rustle with their moccasins. Another half hour and they came out under the stars into a wide-open meadow. In the middle of it was a moundlike hill with a dark grove on the top. Here and there a bed of ashes glowed faintly when a breeze blew, marking the place of the now-neglected fires. A dog began to bark up among the trees.

"Dang it!" whispered Murray.

"Won't make no difference," murmured Pendergass. "He maunt be barkin' at a coon."

Salathiel gave the signal to fan out. One by one they began to feed themselves out into the darkness and to surround the hill. Salathiel stood where he was. He would wait and then crawl forward himself. In half an hour all should be ready. The people on the hill apparently slept on undisturbed, although the dog came rushing down the hill barking violently. Then he turned tail and went back again. Nothing else happened. Three-quarters of an hour went by. Over Will's Mountain to the east near Bedford a grey pencil of dawn made a stroke in the sky.

An owl hooted.

Slowly, a few minutes apart, four other owls replied. They seemed to be nesting all about the hill. The "bird" to his right Salathiel judged to be about three hundred yards away. "More than a rifle shot."

The dog was becoming frantic. Someone at the grove got up to quiet him violently. For the first time Salathiel saw the figure of a man moving among the trees higher up. He could now begin to make out the white roofs of several wagons up there, and piles of bales spread about in a rough circular barricade. The man walked along the top of the bales evidently hurling things at the dog.

"*Du Gottverdammter Hund, du.*" The dog gave an agonized yelp. A rifle cracked. Salathiel had shot the man.

His scream rang a terrible reveille through the grove. Salathiel emitted a horrid, bloodcurdling, gurgling wail.

The man on his left took it up and passed it on. Around the hill rifles exploded. Little spurts of red-blue powder flame and wisps of cottony smoke dotted the grass. The wounded man kept on screaming. The dog was apparently going mad. Horrified roars and shouts arose among the horribly awakened traders. Bullets droned over their heads and smacked amongst the trees. Three horses tore up their pickets and galloped wildly away. A ghastly early dawn dissolved into infernal pandemonium.

"Injuns, Injuns!" shrieked the German pack drivers. "*Wir sind verloren. Herr Maxwell, wir sind verdammt.*"

Maxwell, Mr. Japson's trusted clerk, awakened with a spasmodic jerk out of a calm depth of winter slumber, where he lay wrapped in five trade blankets in the middle of a pile of soft bales. He sat up and looked about him in a shrieking inferno of terror.

He felt this terror before he could even begin to think of its cause. His body stiffened like a spring. Then a reflex of unlaxing began as he caught his breath. It hit the pit of his stomach and relaxed his bowels into his smallclothes as easily as though he had been an infant.

The Indians had come! Soon he would be roasting tied to a tree! A terrible groan escaped him. He tried to pray, but all he could see was a vision of his cubicle of an office in Philadelphia, the peaceful, high, three-legged stool he sat upon there with a quill behind his ear and the two big ledgers open before him. The company account of *Marvin & Drexel* was open before him with a mistake of subtraction in the third column—£1—2s.—6d. They must be completely surrounded. My God, what *was* a man to do?

He got up on his hands and knees and began to crawl towards the outer ring of bales. He peeped through between them. There were rifle flashes in the grass! Around and around the grove went the rifle fire. Whoops of cruel triumph and a wailing death dirge made him sick. A bullet passed him with a howl and dropped a horse. Someone fired a pistol from between two bales, the sole reply to the attack.

Then a complete silence ensued, except for the struggles and moans of the dying horse. Outside, and down the hill somewhere in the grass, Maxwell gradually became aware of a voice calling to him in Shawnee.

"Take your horses and your saddlebags and go. Go back to your own country, paleface," called the voice.

So it *was* a war party from beyond the mountains, thought Maxwell. Shawnees! He had traded with them often.

He replied. His voice quavered. "Friends here. Friends! We bring rum and powder. Blankets, bullets for you."

"What say, what say?" demanded the voice.

"Bring heap rum, heap bullets, much blankets for you."

"Leave um lum, leave um blanklet. Take um holses go, go," shouted the voice in English. "Us no shoot."

Maxwell explained this offer to his men. A babble of Plattdeutsch ensued from the terrified drivers. The rifles began to crack and bullets to smack against the trees again.

"We'll go, we'll go," shouted Maxwell in a lull of the firing, a glow of hope giving his voice some confidence again. "They'll let us go if we leave the goods," he shouted to his men.

"You go?" demanded the voice.

"Yes, yes," screamed Maxwell. "You no shoot?"

"No shoot," said the voice.

A rush took place for the horses. Two got upon the back of one and galloped off into the grey of dawn. The rest waited to see what would happen. The sound of hoofs died away up the Bedford road. Reassuringly not a shot followed.

There was a wild saddling and scramble. A couple of bales were tossed aside and a torrent of men and horses tore down the hill. As they scrambled up the road to the east a couple of bullets droned after them. It was five miles before they drew rein and waited for the stragglers to catch up. Mr. Maxwell was one of the last to arrive. He began to curse them for cowards and poltroons.

They took it quietly until someone suddenly shouted, "Who shit hi
breeches?"

A roar went up at that. It was true. Everyone now laid the blame on
Maxwell. They heaped curses on his head. Then someone shouted they
were being followed. A second but quieter panic overcame them and
they rode on towards the fort, drawing closer together as the sun rose
and revealed them to one another, haggard, for the most part unarmed,
and surrounded on all sides by the snowy wilderness. They were hungry
too. Someone had a bottle of schnapps and they drained that. There
would be nothing to eat till they got to the fort that evening.

Maxwell groaned as the liquor took hold of him. He began to think
of the goods he had abandoned. He began to think—that voice, had i
really been that of a Shawnee? Somehow, somewhere, he would ge
even with somebody for this.

Back at the grove sunlight was beating goldenly all along the eas
flank of the Allegheny Ridge, and Salathiel and his four Pennsylva
nians were enjoying a breakfast of unlimited rashers of bacon and pile
of johnnycake from a bag of meal that lay slashed open and streaming
out onto the grass.

Bales of loot lay piled all about them, at least a thousand pounds
worth of trade goods. This the Pennsylvanians hunted through with
more or less contempt, breaking into small chests with their tomahawk
and slashing open bales with their knives. Nor could Salathiel stop them
His insistence that no kegs of rum should be broached, and that one
good tot apiece must suffice, was as far as he cared to go—and that me
with some grumbling.

A somewhat tense situation was saved by the discovery by Murray o
St. Clair's Negro Jed hidden under a pile of bales.

He was hauled out praying. Fear had turned him a kind of grey
color. His surprise at finding his captors were "buckras" instead of In
juns was only equalled by his relief. He jabbered the lower Gold Coas
dialect of his youth, having been scared clean out of English for the time
being. He kept close to Salathiel, because he was the biggest man pres
ent, and he had assured himself he was white by rubbing some of the
charcoal off his cheeks. "Him buckra massa," he shouted. "Him no yan
niggah." And he began forthwith to cook piles of link sausages snatched
from one of the Pennsylvania Dutchmen's saddlebags, sprinkling them
with brown sugar as a peace offering.

All this, and the rounding up of several stray pack horses, consumed
considerable time. A huge fire was built before which everyone dried
himself out and several went to sleep. After some persuasion Salathie
finally prevailed on young Tom Pendergass to carry back a message o
their success to Captain Ecuyer.

"Reckon you'll meet him about halfway down the mountain," said
Salathiel, "and mind you don't shout out the news but just drop it quietly

n the captain's ear. The loss of these goods will be a sore blow to both
apson and St. Clair. You can't tell how they might take it."

"Who cares how they take it now!" exclaimed the young Pennsylvanian, and slinging his rifle, he set out at a trot.

Salathiel swarmed up one of the taller trees at the top of the grove-
crowned mound and took a look over the wide landscape that now lay
unrolled beneath him.

A wide undulating valley stretched endlessly north and south as far
as he could see, low hills covered with dark, bare forest interspersed with
patches of open snow-covered glades through which the road to Bedford cut a yellow scar. It could be traced eastward over the low crests
for many miles, twisting and turning. On it already some miles away
the frightened traders must be making for the fort. Westward the tremendous wall of the Allegheny Ridge marched down into Virginia, and
toward the east lay the parallel barrier of Will's Mountain. Over there
somewhere was the Juniata, and Fort Bedford.

He hoped the captain would be coming along soon, for the place
where they now were, the mounded grove called Shawnee Cabins, lay
in the midst of natural open fields with the forest enclosing it. And if
they were really attacked here by a wandering war party Salathiel felt
he could no more hold out than the traders had. Perhaps he should
also send a messenger on to Bedford? But the arrival of the traders there
with their story would probably bring a large party to rescue their goods.
No, on the whole, he had better not send another man away.

He wrapped his blanket around him and continued to sit in the
crotch of the tree, keeping a careful watch. In the camp below, the
remaining Pennsylvanians were now asleep in various soft nooks
amongst the bales. Jed was keeping up the fire under the pots and a
big lazy plume of smoke rose and drifted off bluely among the trees.
He could hear the darky humming a monotonous, contented song.
Besides Jed, there was nothing else to be seen moving or to be heard
in all that snowy, sunlit valley except some lonely flocks of crows and
the shifting cloud shadows on the roof of the forest.

Towards noon Salathiel's treetop speculations were put an end to
by the emergence of the wagon and its escort into a bare patch near the
foot of the mountain. In another hour they would be safe in camp. Captain Ecuyer must have got under way in the early watches of the night.
He had timed things nicely, Salathiel thought, and he would by now
have received the news from Pendergass.

Not a little numb from the cold, Salathiel climbed down and began
to urge Jed forward in the active preparation of the approaching midday meal.

38. In Which a Compromise Is Reached

BURENT'S SKILL in driving horses was not the only reason why the wagon had arrived safely at the foot of the mountain. It had also taken a combination of force and diplomacy on the captain's part, for both St. Clair and Japson had suspected the reason for the absence of Salathiel and the Pennsylvanians. But they also realized Albine and the others must have left the night before, and it was now much too late to warn the traders or to try to prevent what must already have taken place. Besides, St. Clair and Japson were once more minus their weapons, and the captain, Burent, and Yates were more than usually watchful.

The two deserters were trussed up in a way which precluded their offering resistance even if they could have been approached and persuaded to try to do so. Japson did try to speak to them just as they left the entrenchment at the top of the mountain, but he was warned off by Yates in a manner which caused St. Clair to describe that little attorney as a "truculent, young bantam" from whom nothing but trouble was to be had.

Mr. Japson agreed, but at that moment he was called to join the captain in the wagon. His string of pack horses, hitched on behind, were left to St. Clair, who rode his mount behind them in a rather dejected way, making an ineffectual signal now and then to the Quaker to *do something*. But the Quaker declined.

Their remaining hope was that Maxwell might have put up a successful resistance, or that he had either returned to or had never left Fort Bedford.

That the traders would be waiting for them somewhere along the route, they both felt fairly certain. Yet neither of them could be sure exactly where it would be. In fact, all was uncertainty and surmise. They scarcely knew what to do until the situation should unfold.

St. Clair therefore continued to exchange pleasantries with the captain through the back of the wagon, while Japson sulked inside. Mr. Yates brought up the rear of the procession with the two militia officers, the deserters trudging ahead, roped together effectively but in such a way as not to interfere with their marching along.

Burent exhausted his skill in preventing any untoward slips or slides down the mountain. He was successful. And it was in this order, and in this way, that the somewhat constrained company finally reached the spring over halfway down and stopped to water the horses.

Here they were met by young Pendergass, who brought news to the captain, which St. Clair and Japson would have paid sterling to overhear.

But Ecuyer was not able entirely to conceal his satisfaction at what he had heard. He became more cheerful, even animated. And it was characteristic of him that he should make the most of the situation and strike while the iron was hot to shape his future plans.

"Mr. St. Clair," said he, poking his head out through the end curtain. "Be good enough to join me and friend Japson here for a moment. I have some news for you. Perhaps we had best discuss it now and arrive at an understanding."

Digesting this as well as he could, St. Clair turned his horse over to young Pendergass and climbed into the wagon, which he overtook only with some difficulty through the mud.

They proceeded for quite a distance before the captain saw fit to enlighten him further. Ecuyer sat strapped into his swinging seat. He and the two lanthorns swung together with the motion of the road. Mr. Japson sat on a chest, looking grim, with his hat drawn over his eyes. The broad back of Burent loomed through the canvas ahead. After some consideration the captain began.

"In my situation," he said, "and in these heathen parts, it is not always possible to enforce the letter of the law. I must make arrangements to carry out my instructions as best I can. I am even inclined to make a bargain if possible, when, under happier circumstances, I might be bound to make no concessions whatever." He paused and looked at St. Clair and Japson.

"A sensible conclusion, I am sure, captain," interjected St. Clair. "I was certain when you encountered our—er—trading caravan on the road you would be willing to concede the point that business and trade must go on; since all that is necessary to do is to wink at the proclamations as you pass by. Now, I confess I have considerable interest in friend Japson's venture, but . . ."

The captain held up his hand.

"I thought as much," he said, "and I also thought that, since your traders have seen fit to abandon your goods and retreat to Bedford, this might be an auspicious moment, from my standpoint, to talk things over." He paused for a moment to let the full import of the news and the situation sink in.

Mr. Japson stirred uneasily. St. Clair's cheeks flushed with a sudden choler that gradually ebbed away to leave him paler than before.

"There's a thousand pounds sterling laid out in those goods, thou must know," said Japson, smoothing his coat thoughtfully. Whether he spoke to Ecuyer or to St. Clair or was just thinking aloud was not plain.

"A staggering loss for our Quaker friend here," said St. Clair. "I think you should consider carefully before you ruin a man for a mere point of duty, captain."

"Doubtless the title to the goods *is* in Japson's name," continued

Ecuyer. "No doubt *you* would see to that, St. Clair. But I also imagine the man who is backing him did not wish to lose so large an amount even of his wife's money, at one stroke. Am I right?"

St. Clair winced.

"What is it you propose?" he demanded. "All that I ask is that you don't call in that infernal little stickler Yates to drive your bargain with me."

"You may well be thankful you are not called upon to deal with one of your own countrymen, St. Clair," said the captain. "As for me, I am not inclined to be so hard as you may think. I wish to ruin no man. I am not likely to be among men much longer and, although they do not understand it, I really wish them well." He paused for a moment. "Yet I still have my duty to do."

His two listeners sat looking at him with astonishment. Somehow they both felt humble and quite suddenly and curiously in sympathy with the man in the swaying seat.

By God, I believe he *is* in a bad way! thought St. Clair.

"Thou wilt be merciful, then?" said Japson. "If so, I will no longer oppose thee."

"You can put it that way if you like, Friend Japson," said the captain. "It is rather the way I wanted it. What I propose is that, if I return these goods to you and Mr. St. Clair after we reach the fort, you will undertake not to trade in any manner with the savages until Colonel Bouquet returns from the frontiers with his men. What I cannot abide is that you, or any other white man, should be the cause of his undoing or the death of any of his men. Nay, I confess that I cannot even understand how you can do anything to hinder him."

"And you would let me furnish forth my settlers at Ligonier, then captain?" asked St. Clair in frank amazement.

"Certainly, but with nothing to supply trade to the Injuns."

"And thou wilt ask no bond of me?" demanded Japson.

The captain shook his head. "I will take either your goods or your word, Japson. I can keep your goods. But you can also keep your word. Which shall it be?"

There was a moment's complete pause in the negotiations. Both St. Clair and Japson were trying to think where the trick lay, or whether the captain was baiting a trap. But they could find neither. And it gradually dawned upon them and then burst into their minds with the full light of day that an honourable spirit proposed to treat them as equals. The captain understood this and said nothing more. He was even amused by their momentary silence. At last Japson motioned his acceptance to St. Clair.

"You have my word of honour, captain," said St. Clair. "I understand and accept your proposition."

Ecuyer touched his finger to his hat in acknowledgement and looked at Japson.

"It will cost me a pretty penny," Japson sighed, "but thou hast my promise not to trade with the savages till Bouquet return."

"Good!" exclaimed Ecuyer, assuming an easier and friendly attitude. "That will save us all a world of trouble. From now on we understand one another. We are all free to act now. The goods are at the Shawnee Cabins. I suggest we do all we can to press on there. I sincerely trust not too much mischief has been done."

Both Japson and St. Clair left the wagon with a feeling of release rather than chagrin. St. Clair was given his weapons again without comment. The Quaker took his pack horses in hand, and with the united urging of all hands it was only an hour past noon when the wagon and its escort reached the grove, where all sat down together to devour the stew prepared by Jed.

That individual gave a curious manifestation of joy at finding his master again. Every now and then he flipped off his feet and walked in a circle about St. Clair on his hands. Even the two deserters who sat roped together on a log had to laugh. A general feeling of relief and good nature took possession of them all. The sun was pleasantly warm and the stew comforting.

"It is at times like this," said the captain to Salathiel, whom he had called into his wagon, "that the enemy falls upon one and the massacre is complete. Beware of being at ease and comfortable."

It was a timely remark. There was not a single sentry posted and, for the time being, not even the captain did anything about it. He sat and listened to Salathiel's account of the "spoiling of the caravan".

"You have done well," he said finally. "When I get to Bedford, I shall go ahead with the plan for you that I had in mind. It will engage what I believe are your more important talents. That is, you will not be curling wigs much longer, I fear. But let that go for the time being. I mean to camp here for the night, or until help comes from Bedford. No doubt Captain Stewart, the commandant, will be sending out a party to reconnoitre this scene of carnage at least. It will be a strong party, if even half the story of the fugitive traders is believed."

"That is what I figured," said Salathiel. "But I'll post a sentry or two while we wait."

"Do so by all means," laughed Ecuyer. "I am glad you remember my hint. Remember it in the future too. And, by the way, I might mention that you no longer need to keep an eye on either St. Clair or Japson. We have arrived at a certain understanding."

Salathiel could make nothing of that, but he had long learned now not to worry about what was satisfactory to Ecuyer. He went out and posted his sentry in a tall tree and kept an eye on the deserters himself. Then he sat down with Murray and had a good smoke.

Japson was wandering about bemoaning the condition of his burst bales. Jed was shaving St. Clair. The horses ate eagerly and lay down to sleep or to roll in the leaves.

The afternoon passed slowly. The sun dropped behind the western wall of the Allegheny. Cold and the earth shadow swooped. The wide, cheerful valley was suddenly chilly and lonesome. Everyone hastened to gather closer to the fire. Mr. Yates, who was by this time regarded as the greatest wit in the world, by the Pennsylvanians at least, sensed the occasion and the opportunity to relate an anecdote.

There was something curiously magnetic about the little lawyer when he began to speak on his feet. He had the broad brow and the mobile mouth of an orator. Nature had compensated for skimping his bulk by giving him an outline at once dapper, swift, and effective. And he had also received a gift of gesture that was like a second tongue of accompaniment to what he said. He now stood before the fire with his coat drooping about him like a gown of precision. His voice reached out and arrested attention. Even St. Clair, who had always been annoyed by his existence, was forced to listen and reluctantly admire.

"Did you ever hear about the cross-eyed judge and the three cross-eyed prisoners?" began Yates, as the silence cleared the stage for his voice, and he looked about him entirely seriously.

"Ain't never heared on them, never," said Murray obligingly.

"My friend Murray reminds me of the description of Paradise in the Saxon poem," said Yates. "It was a place where 'not any lions never ate no lambs'—but let me go on with my story. It is a famous one. It was like this:

"The three cross-eyed prisoners were lined up before the cross-eyed judge, right to left as usual. And the judge looked on the prisoners, and the prisoners looked at the judge—and their mutual confusion was considerable. In fact, his lordship couldn't quite tell which prisoner was which, or just where they began or left off. So he said to the one that looked to him like the first prisoner, 'What's your name?' And the second prisoner answered and said, 'John Hobbs. But I'm not guilty.' And the judge looked at him and said, 'I wasn't speaking to you.' And the third prisoner said, 'I knew you weren't. I didn't say anything at all.' At this point the judge declared a mistrial."

Mr. Yates stood entirely still, quietly looking at his audience. Their appreciation spread slowly from one person to another. But both the deserters seemed to get it at once. Perhaps because they were still tied together and seated on the same log.

Salathiel let the gentlemen continue their conversation around the big fire, where he was glad to see the captain had felt able to emerge from the wagon and take part. With the more than willing assistance of Japson, he put the rest of the men onto repairing the damage of the morning and getting the bales and chests ready to go back to Bedford

By evening they were ready to move again as soon as horses could be obtained.

Shortly after nightfall three scouts from Fort Bedford rode in with the news that a troop of mounted rangers was on the way. Murray was sent to hurry them along, and about eleven o'clock they came threshing into camp. It was now too late to move, however. But Ecuyer gave instructions to have all in readiness for leaving as soon as it should be light enough to see.

Yet in spite of an early start before him next morning, and the long, strenuous hours immediately past, Salathiel did not fall asleep easily that night. Tomorrow, he knew, would take him across the threshold of the wilderness into the more complicated surroundings of a large town. For Bedford was to him a "big town". Counting troops and transport, the usual inhabitants, and refugee families, there must now be several thousand people at Bedford, all told. That *would* be something to see. And he was eager to see it—but he was also aware of possible pitfalls in unknown ground.

Turning over in his mind the past and future, he lay on a pile of the captured trade blankets, looking into the clear, white heart of a dying ash-wood fire.

He shifted uneasily as the fire fell.

Shucks! A man could see anything in a fire—the past, for instance. Nymwha said *he* could foresee the future there.

He smiled dreamfully to himself. Poor Uncle Nymwha!

How those old days in the forest, and the boy he had been there, how they had all passed away suddenly—gone like a hunter's dream when he wakes from some half-enchanted nightmare to the wild, cheerful sound of horns in the morning.

That was it! That was what had happened.

Somehow with good luck, and despite the bad, he had been wakened from that long, green sleep of the forest, the forest that was alive, but didn't know it was there. He knew *now*! Not that he knew all about himself yet. But he was going to find out, to measure himself against other men and things. That was what it meant to be looking into the fire as a white man instead of an Indian. You knew what you saw there was a piece of your own mind. Only when you were half asleep could you think it was real.

He laughed, half doubtfully, half in triumph, and settled down under his blanket for the night. The new rangers from the fort had the watch to keep. Tonight he would not be responsible for everybody's safety, not even to Ecuyer.

Now there was a man it was hard to serve! Your best, even when it *was* the best, was only just good enough for him. But who could equal Ecuyer? There would never be another man like the little captain; no one else would ever be able to say to Salathiel, "Albine, *do it*"—and the thing would be done. Why, that was almost like the centurion in the Bible! But he would never be able to trust another man so as to serve him like that. He would not want to find another master, even if he could. Once, and once only, a young man found his perfect warrior. Even among the Indians that was so.

And then—Ecuyer was passing on. He, Albine, knew that. There was a way you could tell. A certain farewell look that came into a man's eyes. Malycal, the white witch, had told him.

And so Albine would be on his own soon!

That was a sobering thought—and yet he faced it with certain eager anticipations. A free man, a young man, might leave some sorrows behind him—and go on. Why, that was inevitable! Time would tell. And meanwhile a man must sleep.

He closed his eyes against the glare of the fire that was somehow just bright enough to have drawn moisture from them.

A sunny section of the familiar forest road winding through a country of comfortable hills with bright patches of new snow on them stretched far into the distance. The wagon was ahead of him just going over a crest. Oh, yes, he remembered now. They were going somewhere, he and all the others, on a long journey. There was a town, a wonderful village just over the hill, they said. He couldn't see it yet. He must press forward eagerly—tomorrow—

Tomorrow he would be riding over the old Shawnee Hunting Grounds, that lost country he had heard the squaws sing about in sad, homesick dirges, around the Shawnee fires. He could hear Mawakis chanting.

Yes, Mawakis would be there—tomorrow—lingering about the site of the village, where she had played as a little girl. The marks of her tired feet were in the forest. She would run after him, but the wind would fill her footsteps with sand. Only the leaves would whisper where she passed. And he would ride by. He would see and understand like the Little Turtle. But nevertheless he would pass by now.

There was a town just over the hill where the wagon was going, and he was no longer the Little Turtle. He was—He listened, while the green light of the forest seemed to close about him. He listened. Someone was calling him.

"Salathiel—*Salathiel Albine,* you come out of those woods!"

Why, it was his own mother, his mother calling him! Of course, he knew his name. Sal Albine—*that's who he was!* And his mother had never died, after all. She was not going to scream—not this time. No, no, she was just calling to him to come out of the woods.

Suddenly he was a little child again. He dashed forward out of the trees and flung himself into her arms. How comforting, how smooth, warm, and beautiful she was! She was leaning over him. She was going to tell him now that . . .

"Sal, Sal"—he could hear her voice. Oh, if he could only hear what she was going to tell him. The words. Then everything would be . . . would . . . be . . . all —

Darkness ensued, complete, lasting, and deep . . .

. . . and what was that now? Sound again? Noise obstinate and disturbing. Something must be wrong . . .

Danger!

He sprang to his feet in one motion, grasping his rifle instinctively, ready for anything, completely and fully awake

The fire was out, fallen into grey ashes. At the top of the mound, standing tiptoe on a bale, a young trumpeter of the rangers was sounding over and over again the piercingly clear notes of the English reveille. It was like a hunting horn. Behind his small figure the eastern stars hung burning like clear lamps in the first grey of morning.

The camp began to stir. Horses neighed, and were saddled. Cooks blew impatiently on dull embers to kindle their breakfast fires. Ecuyer emerged from the wagon, calling out crisp, brisk orders. His breath smoked in the frosty air.

Albine stood for a moment, looking into the swiftly growing day over the mountains toward Bedford.

"Lord," he said aloud, "what trouble a man's mind can get him into at night! The only way to see the future is to march into it and find out."

He tossed his hair out of his eyes, and ran forward to help Burent harness the teams to the wagon.

Bedford Village

1. Horizons Old and New

BEHIND towered the Allegheny and before them the long wall of Will's Mountain, with a riot of peaks farther northward where the blue Juniata rushed through its water gap. Between lay the broad valley known as the Shawnee Hunting Grounds. This they would have to cross before reaching Fort Bedford on the river.

After the mountains the road seemed easy, rising and falling over the gentle swales of the valley floor, sweeping around great bends of the streams.

In the wagon Captain Ecuyer devoted himself to holding on—with his teeth to a cigar, and with his hands to the seat.

Outside, Salathiel ranged about on the mare pretty much as he pleased. She was stepping high and whinnied to her old teammates of the wagon and the troop horses ahead. Cornet Appleboy was responsible for the command, and there was small chance, in such force, of being ambushed now. With much of the responsibility that had accompanied him all the way from Fort Pitt thus shifted from his shoulders, Salathiel felt like a free man once more. He looked about him eagerly for the first signs of settlement.

He had often heard of this beautiful valley from the Indians who had adopted him. In the old days it had been the father of Kaysinata who had built his village at the grove on the mound and so given the name of Shawnee Cabins to the place. Only a few fire-scarred stones of the Indian hearths remained now.

Then the valley had been a paradise of game. Every stream was alive with beaver and fish. The brown bears had battened on wild honey and chestnuts. Buffalo and elk drifted undisturbed through the succulent glades. Not a smoke showed on the mountains. There had been blessed years of this for the Shawnees; a treaty which said solemnly that it should always remain so.

Then the white man came. Chimneys smoked at Raystown, as Bedford was then called. Rifles cracked. Axes rang. Indians were found murdered. White men did not return home. The game grew shy and scarcer. Again the red man flitted westward.

In the tales told by the Shawnees in their cabins of exile down the Ohio, on the Beaver and the Muskingum, this high, heavenly, mountain valley had been spoken of as their happy hunting ground, as the perfect homeland of their fathers. The Big Turtle had told Salathiel where the grandfathers were buried. He had spoken of the signs of the hills and of the stars by which one could find them sleeping in the quiet places by the streams.

So Salathiel looked about him now as they rode across the valley as though he half remembered having been here before; as if the whispers of a voice lost, but still familiar, had something to say to him which he could not quite overhear.

The three mounds shaded by the three great sycamores—they were no surprise to him. Or the level by the stream where the village of Mawakis must once have stood. Without thinking, he expected these landmarks. He was not surprised to find them there.

More consciously, he was looking for signs of white settlement. For every mile of the road eastward brought him nearer to those towns and cities, and pleasant, long-settled farmsteads about which he had heard and read so much.

So far he had been disappointed, for the country through which they had passed seemed as wild, untouched, and primeval as that along the Ohio. Leave out the road, and there would have been scarcely any difference, except the mountains. He had heard of many settlers in this place. Yet he was to be disappointed again, for there were none of them left in the valley. They had all fled, the spring before, back to the fort at Bedford. Or they had given up and gone even farther eastward. For if anything, the frontier was more dangerous now than it had been for some years. It was haunted by small raiding bands of Indians. They came and went capriciously. And they came to exterminate rather than to plunder. So the valley of the Shawnee Hunting Grounds lay desolate and desolated.

Towards noon they stopped at a clearing and prepared a meal on the wide, stone hearth. Then they were off again, rapidly. About two o'clock they came down suddenly into the vale of the winding Juniata and crossed it on a stout bridge of logs. Here there was an outpost, not often occupied. A couple of miles beyond, at the crest of a brisk rise, they were suddenly rewarded and cheered by their first glimpse of Bedford.

Murray, who was riding ahead, gave a shout and beckoned to Salathiel to ride forward. He did so eagerly, and this time he was not altogether disappointed.

The fort and the settlement about it seemed to Salathiel's eyes a surprisingly large town. The first thing he noticed was an astonishing number of chimneys all belching smoke. The whole place, indeed, was overhung by the blue haze from its own wood fires.

They were standing here at the top of a considerable hill that overlooked the town. The river made a wide loop at their feet. Here the road swung north to follow the east bank of the river, and about two miles away on a high bank of the Juniata, so steep that it almost amounted to a cliff, stood Fort Bedford and the jumble of roofs and chimneys clustered about it that was Raystown.

In the clear, quiet mountain afternoon the wood smoke hung over it like a hazy umbrella. A few windows flashed in the sun. But that was all. For encompassing the village in every direction, over a vast area of valley and hills, stretched the illimitable forest.

The only prominent building was the fort itself. It had five bastions and a peculiar gallery like a big ice chute, but roofed in and loopholed. It led down the cliff from the north gate to the river, so the garrison could draw water directly from the stream or make a sortie in that direction if besieged. This log gallery was the outstanding feature of the place, a genuine military curiosity.

For the rest, the view of the fort reminded Salathiel not a little of his first glimpse of Fort Pitt. The roof of the barracks shrouded with busy chimneys studded the interior of its five-pointed star. But the ditches around the place were smooth and grassy. And just across from the fort was a cluster of long shingled roofs of quite considerable proportions.

"Them's the hospitals," said Murray, pointing out the features of the place, "and they're mostly alers full; smallpox or the like."

"That's my pa's place," announced young Tom Pendergass, riding up. "Ye see the two big houses with a bridge between 'em t'other side of the fort? One's his store and taproom, and the far un—that's home! All of us Pendergasses is gathered thar sence the troubles. But we do have big nights round the fire in the bar. Hit's the biggest chimley west of Carlisle. You'll see some good times there, or I'm a liar." He clapped Salathiel on the back. "Will yer be stayin' on with us agin, Mr. Yates?" he asked as the young lawyer joined them. " 'Speck ma's saved yer the river room whar you left your things. Cap'n Ourry's adjutant wanted to hire it off her, but ma's a woman of her word."

"I hope she *has* kept it for me," said Yates. "It's the nicest room in town."

"It is!" Pendergass agreed enthusiastically. "It was my pa found the springs. 'Course the Injuns knew 'em fustest. They're over the hill there in the valley beyont. Gawd, but one of them stinks! And t'other will turn a man into a shitepoke in a jiffy. You ought to hev saw the place when Gineral Forbes was here with nigh eight thousand men. The surgeons put a guard on the water then . . ."

"But the Pendergasses have even stronger water than that," said Murray, laughing. "Comes in barrels."

"You bet," agreed Tom, "and we have a worm, too. Pa cooks his corn juice in it. It's fine spring water comes out. Ever taste it?" He smacked his lips.

Just then the wagon drove up and halted. Captain Ecuyer slowly got out and took a look at the place. He gave a grunt of satisfaction like an Indian, much to the astonishment of the rangers, and climbing painfully back, shouted to Burent to get on.

The whole cavalcade finally tore down into the place, Burent putting his horses through their best paces.

They came down the little street past the sutlers' houses where officers stood smoking in the doorways, and women and children hung out the windows. A gust of surprise and curiosity ran through the place at the sight of the wagon. People came shouting, more people than Salathiel had ever seen. Some of the houses were built of stone and had painted doors and shutters. There were flat river stones to walk on beside them. A few dooryards had strange tended shrubs in them. It was amazing. The houses seemed riddled with windows and openings.

They thundered across a bridge over a gully and drove along by the walls of the fort. The gate opened over a dry moat and onto the street. The bridge was down, and they swept in, leaving the sentries challenging foolishly behind them. There was no time for the guard to assemble.

Captain Ecuyer climbed down in front of the large officers' quarters and looked about him. It was the most luxurious building Salathiel had ever seen. It might have been in a European town. An officer buckling on his sword came running out the door.

"Where's Captain Ourry?" demanded Ecuyer.

"He's gone to Carlisle to fetch the pay chests," said the lieutenant, saluting.

"I thought so," said Ecuyer, "and I see ye keep the gate open so he'll be welcome any time with the cash!"

"Not after sundown, I assure you, sir," replied the lieutenant. "The gate's always closed then."

"B'God, I'm surprised you go to all that trouble," blurted the captain. "Albine, get my things into the house here, and be smart about it. Put some men on them to help Burent. And come in and tend me, for I'm mortal ill." He limped up the steps, threw the door open into headquarters, and staggered in.

The adjutant and the quartermaster's clerk were working over some papers together at a desk. The room stank of whisky and old candles. The clerk stood up and blinked at the captain. "Whadja wan?" he said.

"Congratulations to the second battalion," shouted Ecuyer in a fury. "Your gate's wide open, lieutenant, and I've been received with all the honours of a sutler. We *do* manage it better in the first—at times."

Captain Stewart's adjutant, Lieutenant Spenser, made no attempt to reply. Stewart, the commandant, had gone east to meet Ourry. Spenser was familiar by long correspondence with Captain Ecuyer's official opinion of the discipline maintained by the second battalion of the Royal American Regiment. The men hadn't been paid for over a year and the new recruits sent from Philadelphia were the dregs of society. In his opinion at least, the garrison at Bedford was on the point of mutiny. He hoped to God Captain Ourry would arrive with the pay chests soon. Ecuyer was obviously a very ill man with no patience left.

Maybe he could get him into bed—quick!

Without further ado he led the way to Ourry's quarters, had a fire built there, and sent for the surgeon. While they waited, Salathiel set about making the captain as comfortable as possible during the interval the things from the wagon were being brought in. Mr. Yates came in to offer his services.

Even in his pain, Ecuyer was "much obleeged". He thanked Yates, and he finally thanked Spenser handsomely.

"You're an adjutant I'd like to see in my own battalion, lieutenant," he said. "But for God's sake *do* see that the gate is closed, or we'll all be scalped in our beds some night. And hurry the surgeon, for the anguish of this wound is inexpressible."

It was Yates who finally found Dr. Boyd at Pendergasses' and returned with him. Salathiel spent an afternoon of sympathetic agony while the captain's wound was lanced and a probe thrust into his groin. A small piece of iron shell which had lodged there since the fight on the Plains of Abraham was extracted.

"You'll get better now—or you'll die," said the surgeon, sniffing the fragment doubtfully.

"That's the universal prognosis for all mankind, Dr. Boyd," grinned Ecuyer. "You're a good prober, but be damned to ye! I must sleep. Can't you give me a powder?"

The doctor complied.

The captain slept, but with a mounting fever and laboured breathing. Salathiel sat by him until late in the evening, when the surgeon called again and Burent came to relieve him as "nurse".

Dr. Boyd stooped over the captain, listened and shook his head.

"Sounds like inflammation of the lungs," he said.

"I 'opes not, sir," said Burent, rearranging the pillows so as to raise the captain's head. "Me old mother died o' that."

"I suppose you know what to do then," said the surgeon. "Call me if he starts gasping." He turned to Salathiel. "A bite of supper would do *you* no harm, I imagine," he remarked with a kindly smile. "Mr. Yates tells me you and Burent are devoted fellows. I like that. There's not a better officer in the service than Captain Ecuyer. But come, some of your friends have been waiting outside for news. We'll be at Pendergasses' if you want me, Burent."

They went out, to find Yates, Murray, and young Tom Pendergass waiting anxiously in the hall. A door opened. Captain Stewart, the commandant, who had just ridden in from Fort Loudon and was still mud-splashed, came out to enquire about Ecuyer.

"He's sleeping, and I'll not know much till tomorrow," replied the surgeon. "Any eastern news, captain?"

"General Amherst's resigned, and the pay chests are on the way," said Stewart, grinning.

"Good! 'Twill cheer even a sick man," said the surgeon. "As for me, I'm penniless. I've been living on your father's bounty, Mr. Pendergass, for three months past."

"Oh, pa's used to thot," laughed Tom.

They walked out through the sally port talking.

"Good God! so Cunctator Amherst's resigned," exclaimed Yates.

"And a damned good riddance," said the doctor.

There was not much to be seen of Bedford except locked doors, dark streets, and stars overhead. Every house was barred. The Reverend Joseph Jenkins and his family had been murdered that afternoon only two miles east of the fort, and their scalps taken.

"Pa told 'em," said Murray, "but they would light out for Big Cove. And now they've lost their har. Delawares, I hear. I 'low them rascals air still hangin' round. We was pretty durned lucky gettin' through from Ligonier ourselves."

To this all agreed with prophecies of more trouble to come.

2. Pendergasses'

CENTRE and glowing heart of the neighbourhood and of the new world in which Salathiel now found himself, the point of vital radiance for all Bedford and its vicinity was the tavern taproom with its huge, warm hearth, kegs of genial and fiery liquors, and equally inspiring friendly encounters and talk known as "Pendergasses' ".

Garrett Pendergass, "Prendergas, Pendergast or even Pendergaster", you could take your choice, for everyone knew him, was the host and patriarch of the establishment that overlooked the banks of the river just beyond and eastward of the fort.

While the formal sovereignty and nominal rule of the country round-about still remained with the king's commandant at the fort, the actual governance, control, and influence of the entire neighbourhood for a day's journey on all sides resided, at least in normal times, in the mind

and hands of Garrett Pendergass himself, a hale and hearty, still powerful, and white-bearded man of seventy.

Time and experience had stored up and kept for him the rarest of all
commodities, wisdom and happiness. Somehow in himself he did personify the achievement of what so many had come into the wilderness
to get: freedom, ease, and abundance.

To look at Garrett as he stood just a bit bowlegged before his own vast
chimney was to realize what time, patience, and genial zeal could wring
barehanded from the reluctant but exuberant forest.

Garrett teemed. He teemed with children, grandchildren, and things.
And his excess ran over and solidified in hospitality.

Whatever one might think of Bedford, whether one was a European
or an American, there was only one single opinion about Pendergasses':
it was a good place to be in, in this or in any other kind of world. Even
Indians liked to come there, when allowed.

It would be hard to describe the establishment exactly. For Pendergasses' was its own peculiar self, and no such set terms as tavern, inn,
trading post, ordinary, public house, mill, or general store could precisely
apply. And it was all of them at once, and so proclaimed itself by the
songs that emanated from the taproom, the hum of business about the
store, the clink of iron from the blacksmith shop at one end near the
road, and the intricate voices of the men, women, and children that came
from the hive—for it was that, too—and perhaps best described by Murray
in a simple homely term as a "goin' consarn".

Its houses, for there were two of them, faced the road on one side and
the river on the other. And the level riverbank between was covered
with a medley of small buildings devoted to various domestic, business,
and farm uses.

From the midst of these shacks and outhouses the two main buildings
towered up like two swans leading a flock of cygnets to the water. But
that is not to say there was anything fragile or graceful about them. On
the contrary, they were massive and substantial, built of the materials at
hand provided by the original clearing of the land.

The lower stories were of large river stones set in lime-puddled clay,
and the upper of walnut logs, vast fellows, the remains of a grove cleared
from the ground on which the houses stood.

"Such trees will never grow here again," said Garrett, when he and
his sons cut them down. "They are the kind the Lord makes when he
works all alone"—and he had refused to have them burned as the general
custom was when making a clearing.

Instead, he had made the frames of the houses out of the mightiest of
these trees and used the comparatively smaller ones to cabin him in.
Nothing but adzes, axes; nothing but wooden pegs had been used in
building. But they had been used skilfully, and both the massiveness and

the neatness of the place were the pride, envy, and model for the whole neighbourhood and its inhabitants.

Not that many other settlers could profit by the example set by the Pendergasses. Garrett had seven sons and four daughters. His wife was a little woman. But great and small they had all laboured together upon the place. And a great deal can be accomplished when something is done every day by thirteeen skilful and devoted people for twelve years.

Prime and vital nucleus of the establishment was the long room on the ground floor of the store building nearest the fort, known to the Pendergasses themselves and to all the older settlers as the "hearth room", and to others as the "taproom" or "general store". Combine the three, and a complete description, indeed a history of the place, could be had, except for the fact that before the fort was built the main dwelling had also served on several occasions as the blockhouse or rallying point of the whole Raystown neighbourhood for defence against the Indians. A few louvres and loopholes in the stone walls of its lower story and the heavy log section above, now all carefully stoned in or blocked up, was all that remained to tell of a time of private conflict with the savages, which had already passed.

Pendergass and his sons had built the hearth room for the ample living quarters and kitchen of an equally ample family, to which Garrett had prophetically seen fit to provide the largest and widest proportions that the hugest specimens of his giant walnut trees would permit.

Hence, the beams supporting the ceiling were twice the thickness of a man's body. The floors were of mighty planks ground smooth by the passing of time, innumerable feet, and the action of clean, white river sand. The windows were not numerous, but enclosed by shutters, iron bars, and glass, the first to be brought into the community. If anything, the apartment suffered from a certain lack of light. But this was at least partially offset by the fact that the long walls were plastered and white-washed, and that at one end of the place burned continuously and for-ever a fire that was never less than twelve feet long and might be nine feet high.

Indeed, the actual dimensions of the fireplace were even larger. A whole ox, a stag, or an elk could be roasted there, or a bear upon occasion. There were several stone ovens provided with separate flues in the body of the towering chimney, and the hearth itself, made of the whitest, smoothest, largest of boulders, rose a good two feet like a stage at one end of the apartment above the level of the rest of the floor.

To enter the hearth room, therefore, was to become immediately, although perhaps unconsciously, a spectator of a comforting drama of life. And the spectacle at Pendergasses' seldom failed to be interesting, since not the eye and mind alone were engaged, but food, drink, appe-tizing odours, and lively company also made their appeal.

As time went on, and the community had grown, the hearth room had gradually become a general store. Garrett had first begun as a trader in peltry, and he had imported goods to exchange for skins, both with the Indians and with the settlers, liquor being not the least of items. He had formed connections with merchants at Harris's ferry and later at Philadelphia, and he had prospered.

In due course of time a counter had been run along one side of the big room. Barrels and kegs with spigots, shelves heaped high with cloth, notions, and sundries lined the wall behind the counter. An abacus for doing sums, and several smooth, painted shutters covered with chalked names and amounts constituted the immediate bookkeeping of the establishment. And the counter itself, now stained and worn, had long performed in the dual capacity of a merchandising table and a drinkers' bar.

Only one important change had marked the coming of the garrison: the installation of a large grille made of hickory bars that could be let down from the ceiling, and behind which those who tended the store and served out liquor appeared to be so many felons or wild beasts pacing the length of their cage.

Transactions for drink at least were now always in coin. Money, both metallic and paper, had appeared with the coming of armies and the presence of important personages and officers. A cashbox, into which a large part of the contents of the paymasters' chests was eventually transferred, was installed. Trading in kind gradually became rarer, except with hunters and pioneers. Fights and disorders occasionally troubled the room. Truculent and notorious characters dropped in. The precaution of the grille was necessary.

The transition of the place from a dwelling house and store into a general inn and tavern had been gradual. Travellers had sought and obtained shelter at Pendergasses'. Newcomers, magistrates, and itinerant preachers came frequently. With the cutting through of the road westward, with the establishment of the fort and the passing of regiments, "everybody" who had business in the Western Parts, and quite frequently Somebody and his servant, stopped there.

The family had for long inhabited the log story above the hearth room. It was divided into a large number of small but comfortable chambers. Here at first they had tried to accommodate guests by the simple process of doubling up. But the constant crowding and disturbance had at last become intolerable, and Garrett had finally erected a second dwelling house next door, thus doubling his living space and filling the old tavern building to capacity, while his family privacy and domestic intimacies were preserved.

The marriages of his sons and daughters and the arrival in due course of many grandchildren had at last filled even the second building—and had also provided the hands to continue the establishment.

In addition, there were several Negroes owned outright and two In-

dian families, Cherokees fooled long years before by a governor of Maryland into leaving their native parts and now forever stranded in Pennsylvania. Their status was dim but their dependence and services plain.
They and the Negroes had cabins in the yard amid the cattle, poultry,
wagons, horses, and dogs.

From time to time the pressure of numbers had been relieved by the
departure of one son or daughter, with children, to settle on outlying
lands. Thus Pendergass cabins and clearings dotted the hills around. But
Indian forays and troubles drove them back again.

Queen bee of the hive, and, as her days went on, more and more
inclined to stay hidden in her cell, was the mother of the place, Mrs.
Rose Pendergass, an apple-cheeked, brown, little Englishwoman from
Devon. Someone must pay for so much exuberance, and it was Mrs.
Pendergass who did so. As the din, vigour, and complexities of life were
increased about her, she resigned quietly, enjoyed the seclusion of her
room whenever she could, talked comforting nonsense to the babies,
wiped their mothers' jealous tears away, and cultivated her garden. If
she sometimes sighed for the quiet and simplicity of her pioneer beginning, when her cabin first stood by the Juniata and the Juniata sang to
the stars, or for the earlier and more solitary devotion of her husband,
she said nothing. Deafness had at last come to her rescue and she now
moved in a silence and with an inner peace and patience which the
fullness of life had brought her.

As for old Garrett, he was completely devoted to his Rose. As she grew
a little feebler he had built a kind of covered way on trestles between the
store building and the house to save her steps, especially in winter, and
to ensure the ease and privacy of her passing to and fro. This bridge
was also appreciated by all the other women on the place, who could
thus do their chores about the upstairs rooms in the inn without descending to the bar below.

To Garrett and his wife the bridge was the visible symbol and link
between the two parts of their lives, the domestic and the public, and a
reminder that each was dependent and inextricably linked with the
other. It was a tie that bound. To the very last Mrs. Pendergass continued to use it and to appear upon occasions even in the tavern by her
old hearth. Her presence about the place lent an intangible touch of
natural refinement and an indestructible respectability. She was adored
by her sons and grandsons and their wives and daughters. Her matriarchal prestige, indeed, was already legendary. In her presence even the
boldest and rudest spirits were prone to remember whatever manners
they might be said to have forgot.

Such was Pendergasses' at Bedford, when on the night of November
4, 1763, Salathiel Albine accompanied by Edward Yates, Dr. Boyd the
surgeon, Murray, and young Tom Pendergass approached its main entrance from the riverside, saw a hint of young moonlight on its silver

shingles, heard the near-by rolling of waters—pushed open a heavy double door, and entered in.

3. In Which a Threshold Is Crossed

AND THIS TIME Salathiel was not disappointed. He had found what he had been looking for; something that was not of the wilderness. Certainly that night the hearth room at Pendergasses' was as far set apart from the forest, the winter, and the loneliness outside as anything manmade could be.

Old Mrs. Pendergass sat at one end of the long room with a spinning wheel, her chair on the raised hearth, with her back to the glowing embers of the great fire. The white yarn was coming off the wheel steadily to a low humming sound and the clack of the treadle, and being wound in a hank about the white, extended arms of her golden-haired granddaughter, Phoebe Davison. The girl, about sixteen years old, had a laugh like clear water poured from a silver urn. An old Negro woman with a corncob pipe in her gums sat dozing on a stool near the chimney. Garrett and two of his men were taking stock and rearranging the goods on the shelves in anticipation of the arrival of the pay chests when trade might be expected to reach a copious pitch.

"Stack the playin' cyards high fer all to see," old Garrett was saying as the door opened; "even the English parsons will be wantin' 'em. Thar's not a pack left up at the fort that ain't marked or worn thin." The cold draught from the open door struck him. "Come in, come in, gentlemen, I've been expectin' you these two hours and keepin' the coffee soup hot. How's the little captain, doctor? Pina, stir your stumps. What'll it be now, gentlemen, what'll it be?"

"Hot rum and butter," said Yates. There were no vetoes. Salathiel stood looking about him while the old coloured woman brought the rum and mugs.

The main area of the room, provided with one huge oak table and three smaller ones, had a floor scattered with gleaming white sand laid in patterns and evidently freshly put down. Several dip candles set in homemade sconces cast a yellow glow which, mixed with the firelight, was reflected softly but cheerfully from the white floor and the long whitewashed walls.

In one corner, at a small table of his own, sat an Herculean figure of a man dressed in fringed buckskins. He was playing checkers with a small boy whose resemblance to his sister by the spinning wheel was so striking as to be unmistakable.

"Crown me, Cap'n Jack. I'm in your king row again," piped the youngster. "Oh, goody!"

"Pizen me ef you hain't," rumbled the big man through a wealth of grey-streaked beard. "Here, Garrett, send this grandson of yours to his bunk. He's beat me again worse nor the French did Braddock."

"Go to bed, Arthur, it's dreadful late," said his grandfather. "And you too, Phoebe. Kiss your granfer."

The young girl tied her yarn carefully, and ducking under the counter stood on tiptoe to kiss her grandfather good night. As she did so she caught Salathiel's eye upon her and blushed violently.

He had no eyes for anything or anybody else. He had never seen anyone like Phoebe. His breath came quicker. She turned as she left the room and looked back at him with eyes as calm and innocent as blue mountain lakes.

"She's gone!" he exclaimed tragically and aloud, before he was aware of speaking.

"Like a doe in the woods at twilight," said Captain Jack, laughing, "but cheer up, young feller, mornin'll come again."

Old Mrs. Pendergass laughed musically. She could hear little, but she saw everything that went on.

"You boys from the forest," she said, "you be like zailors home from the zea."

Mr. Yates appeared delighted at Salathiel's being the centre of curiosity and attention, and slapped his large friend encouragingly on the back.

"You're coming along, Sal," he cried. "Demme, you're coming along!"

Salathiel was intensely aware of but somewhat overcome by all this. For him it was a confused and crowded moment, one forever memorable. He was conscious of having finally stepped over the threshold of the wilderness into the world of his own people that he had so longed to see. He was amazed and moved by the vision of Phoebe. He was confused by so many people; embarrassed by having spoken his feelings about Phoebe aloud; pleased and surprised that Yates should care that he was "coming along". He was also bowled over by the incredible "wealth" in goods and comfort of the room in which he stood. He felt his mind swimming triumphantly in the surprising comfort and solid ease of the place. And all this had come upon him and was to be digested at once and at one time. The net result was a feeling of rising exhilaration.

His people had done all this—and he was one of them! They were accepting him.

He felt an all but overpowering impulse to give the triumphant scalp helloo of the returning successful warrior. The impulse rose in his chest like a solid thing trying to escape through his mouth. He put his hand to his throat and stopped it just in time. Then he stood for a moment with his eyes closed.

Captain Jack was the only one who understood what was happening to Salathiel.

"Come over here, young feller, and set down with the rest of us," he said. "Murray and Tom Pendergass has been tellin' me about you. Garrett, hev you met Tom's friend, Sal Albine, him they was talking over this evenin'?"

Garrett Pendergass came dodging under the counter and across the room to shake hands.

"I hear ye turned a smart trick on the traders," he remarked. "Yer little captain's a clever man. Liken it will hit friend Japson hard, though. By the way, I was sayin' to the old woman I kin only recollect hearin' your name once before. 'Twas a young couple, a smith and his wife, stopped off with us when we were living out at Path Valley. They were tarnal bent on goin' clar to the Ohio. And that was long before the road was opened over to the forks of the Yough. From Connecticut, I think they were. It's 'bout a score of years. But I remember we wanted 'em to stay on with us. The missus was in a family way. Liken you're the baby?" laughed Garrett, looking Salathiel's six feet four up and down.

"I'd hardly know, sir," replied Salathiel. "You see, I was taken by the Injuns when I was a young'un. Why, it's only kind of by luck I remember my name."

"Wal, I jes thought it maunt be," said old Garrett.

"So you was kerried off by the varmints," said Captain Jack excitedly. "Wal, now, that's curious! Now, so was I. We'll have to talk some together, young feller. Tell the truth, I got suthin' in view. Suthin' might interest ya, and . . ."

"Gentlemen, gentlemen," called Yates. "Come over and sit down with the company or you'll miss the grog," at which the three, who had been standing in the middle of the floor talking, adjourned their meeting and joined the rest at the big table near the fire.

It stretched halfway across the room, a massive piece of oak furniture with two heavy wrought-iron sconces bolted into it at either end. The candles in these were now halfway burnt down, but shone none the less brightly on the red English phiz of Dr. Boyd, the tanned, lean faces of Murray and young Pendergass, and the engaging countenance of Mr. Yates. Salathiel, Captain Jack, and old Garrett now settled themselves at the same board with their feet stretched out under the table towards the warmth of the fire.

Mrs. Pendergass bade her husband good night and excused herself, after seeing that the old coloured woman had the hominy, venison, and bacon smoking on the table; hot water, butter, rum, and a spice pannikin going around. A large chicken pie as yet uncut smoked near the fire for further reference. Dr. Boyd filled the only glass tumbler in the place with rum and water, eying the proportions with the nice eye of an apothecary—and tossed it off.

"Two-thirds to one," said he, "is a proper night potation—hot."

Advised thus by the doctor, the meal began. Mr. Yates produced some dice from his vest pocket and began to throw.

"'Pon my word, Edward," said old Garrett, "I was in hopes you'd lost 'em at Ligonier. They cost me half your board last time you came to stay here. Wal, what is it now?"

"Low cast takes care of the company." Yates passed the dice along in a cup and prepared to keep score.

The surgeon cast extreme high throw with a sigh of relief. Murray won from young Pendergass, and Tom from his father. Old Garrett then rolled with Yates.

"What did I tell you!" said Yates. "These things are as good as a legacy to me."

Old Garrett grumbled and then lost to Captain Jack—and the last throw remained between Salathiel and Garrett.

Salathiel lost.

"Maybe he ain't got no money, pa," said Tom. "Liken you got some pelts, ain't you, Sal?"

So it was money they wanted. Why, then he had some. He began to fumble in his bullet bag. Some cartridges, some tobacco, one of five louis d'ors he had taken from the Delawares near Ligonier, the medal, and the two newly dried scalps came out on the table.

An appreciative roar went up from the company.

"Go on, go on. Ye can't tell what ye might dig up out o' that yit," said Captain Jack.

Old Garrett reached forward, touched the gold piece, and then began to fondle the two scalps with his stubby fingers. "They're worth a king's pound apiece in Philadelphy," he said. "That's the provincial bounty. I'll give ye two pounds Pennsylvania for 'em or your change in credit. That'll be enough to keep you goin' here for some time, ef you don't cast dice with Yates."

Yates nodded to Albine. Salathiel shoved the two scalps over to old Garrett. "It's a bargain," he said. He also extended the gold piece doubtfully. He had no idea what the supper would cost.

"Best keep it," said Garrett, after hesitating a moment visibly. "Reckon you're not paid yet, eh? I know the captain ain't."

"We'll all be paid when Ourry gets here with the chests," grumbled the surgeon. "I've three quarters due myself. It's a scandal, I say! Amherst wouldn't certify the paymaster's account. The least a general can do is to sign his name. Well, I hear Ourry's due at Loudon with the chests and train tomorrow at latest. That puts him only two days away. They say he has nearly fifty wagons in the convoy and they can't make haste."

"And Captain Stewart told me the roads were strewn with desarters all the way back to Lancaster," remarked Yates. "The commandant expects half of the recruits will be gone 'fore they get here."

"Speck so," agreed Captain Jack. "Them 'umble fellers from the east counties never would fight. It's riflemen, the Macs and Bucktails, the Presbyterian psalm-singin' stronghearts, not a passel o' pressed Dutchmen and pacification Quakers they want. Some o' those fellers looses their bowels when they hear a papoose howl for a squaw." He spat and looked up. The door had opened.

"Were you referring to me, sir?" demanded an angry voice unexpectedly. They all looked up now to see Maxwell and two militia officers coming in through the door. It was Neville and Aiken.

"Why, no, I can't say I was," drawled Captain Jack, " 'cause ye weren't here to refer to."

This being manifest, Mr. Maxwell swallowed his hurt pride with a jumbled explanation, and sat down with the two Pennsylvania officers at the far end of the room. Young Tom went over to serve them.

"I'm not payin' fer *them*, Mr. Pendergass," said Salathiel firmly.

"No, no," replied Garrett. "Of course not."

Mr. Yates looked pleased. He was exchanging horrid glare for glare with Lieutenant Neville.

"Still under arrest?" the little lawyer asked mock-sympathetically.

"Yes, Mr. Attorney, but we'll not be retaining you," said Aiken.

"Innocence needs no advocate, I suppose," countered Yates—and turned his back on them.

A certain constrained atmosphere had now fallen on the room. The two tables ate their respective suppers separately with a gulf between. After some prodding, Salathiel consented to tell the story of the trip from Fort Pitt to Bedford. He was not sparing of facts and drew forth considerable laughter. Mr. Yates joined in with his own version of things from time to time. The gentlemen at the other table soon had faces like thunder clouds, although their names were never mentioned. Maxwell's chagrin was only equalled by his brooding desire for revenge on having his suspicion confirmed as to who the "Indians" were who had stampeded him and his men.

"Ef'n that Irish gal from Frazier's ever shows up here, I'll be on the lookout for her," said Murray to Salathiel when he had ended.

"Yer might find her handy round the place, pa," suggested Tom.

"I know the place ye'd be handlin'," replied his father.

A shout went up.

"It hain't the joke ye think," joined in Captain Jack. "I've knowed Frazier and his old woman off en on from ever since Braddock's time. And I alers says murder is jes settin' on the ridgepole of his cabin, waitin' for ter climb down the chimney." He spat into the fire for emphasis. "I'm plumb sorry fer that colleen. And I doubt the pistol you left her, Sal, will do her much good. Wal, good night to yer all."

He rose and took his rifle and pouch down from some pegs on the wall. "I got some miles ter ride before I kin hole up," he remarked, and came over to shake hands with Salathiel. "Thanks for the supper, young feller, and don't forgit you and me has a powwow comin'."

"I'll not," said Salathiel. The rifle butt, he noticed, was decorated with a series of notches. Sometimes these occurred in groups of three or four, and there were several lines of them cut into the wood. Noting his eyes upon them, Captain Jack smiled.

"Kind of a hard time to be riding many miles alone around these parts tonight, ain't it?" suggested Salathiel as the door closed.

"Not for him, son," said old Pendergass. "He's jes hopin' he'll be follered. The only thing worries him is thar's not much more room left on his gunstock fer notches."

"Don't yer know who he is?" asked Murray, looking astonished. "Hit's the famousest story—"

"Excuse me for interruptin'," said the surgeon, "but I think I'll just step up to the fort and have a last look at my patient before turnin' in."

"I'll be goin' with you, doctor. The captain might need me before mornin'," said Albine.

"Good," replied the doctor. "Your friend Burent must know more about horses than sick men."

They bade the company good night regretfully.

"That's him, that's him," Salathiel heard Maxwell saying as they closed the door behind them and stepped out into the keen, star-flashing night.

The low, rushing sound of the river filled their ears. Somewhere in the town a dog barked. They climbed the steep path to the postern gate and answered a surly challenge.

"Advance friends and give the God-damned countersign," said the sentry.

"Cumberland."

"Cumberland, it is," muttered the sentry inside, and the chains rattled. The dim rays of a filthy lanthorn were flashed into the surgeon's face.

"Why, it's only Bones—and a scalp," said the corporal.

With some difficulty the surgeon restrained his impulse to knock the man down. He wiped his forehead as they walked across to headquarters.

"This detachment of grenadiers," the surgeon burst out, "are the damnedest, most mutinous, pox-riddled . . ." His feelings choked him. "By God," he added, "I hope Ecuyer *does* get better! What we need is a man that's death-bane for impudent rascals around here."

They entered the sickroom.

Burent and the captain were both sleeping soundly. In the thin shine of one low-burning candle Ecuyer's face on the pillow was like a wax cameo. He was breathing easily and a dream had laid a smile across his lips.

The surgeon again swore—softly. This time with relief.

4. Fort Bedford

BEDFORD was the first place in which Salathiel ever felt thoroughly at home. And the memory of it remained with him permanently and significantly, etched deeply on the fresh tablets of young memory by the hand of time. If there was something deep-bitten and indelible about the picture, that was due both to the beautiful lay of the hills and to the scalding acid of events which fixed them forever on his mind.

For a while, too, it had seemed as though Ecuyer might recover. For Dr. Boyd had not been altogether mistaken that evening when he had sworn with relief at finding Ecuyer apparently better, and his fever subsiding. The removal of the shell fragment from his old wound had at first done wonders for him. And even the wound from the stone arrowhead "sympathetically", as the surgeon said, had subsided during the week or ten days in which the captain lay abed after his first arrival at the fort. In fact, Ecuyer had seemed in a fair way then to get on his feet again.

"Rest and quiet is the prescription," said the doctor; "exhaustion and threatened blood poisoning, the diagnosis." After which Dr. Boyd bled his patient profusely. That at least did keep him quiet for a while. He was left quite too weak to get up. The trouble was that both the driving will of the captain and events were wholly against the patient's being able to take the surgeon's advice.

Ecuyer felt himself personally responsible for the organizing and forwarding of men and supplies to Colonel Bouquet at Fort Pitt. He knew that even the possibility of the expedition down the Ohio largely depended upon him. He had been given full authority and in using it mercilessly he was not one to spare himself. Nor was he being merely fanatical about it.

Authority was largely personal on the frontier. Those who could apply it and get results were rare. Few things were done for government out of patriotism, much for a man.

Now it was already apparent to Ecuyer, even in November, '63, that Colonel Bouquet's expedition against the Indians in the Ohio country, then scheduled for the following spring, would have to be delayed, might indeed never leave Fort Pitt at all, unless he, Simeon Ecuyer, greatly bestirred himself at Bedford.

He, and Salathiel, and Burent had arrived at Fort Bedford on the 4th of November. Luckily for the captain, it rained, snowed, and froze again the following week. Nothing much could be done. Everyone, friend and enemy alike, was stopped. Ecuyer had stayed in his bed in Captain Ourry's quarters. He lay there while his wound closed and the fever left him. He dozed and recuperated. From time to time he would come to himself and work feverishly. For, while he lay abed, that is not to say he got nothing done.

Captain Ourry had also been delayed by the weather with the pay chests, supplies, and recruits at Fort Loudon, some miles to the east of Bedford, and on the other side of the mountains. The roads and weather being what they were, it was impossible even to try to get through. But it was not impossible for Ecuyer to send Burent on to Fort Loudon to help get the wagons repaired and under way as soon as the weather should break.

So, two days after they arrived at Bedford, Burent had said good-bye, and departed in the midst of a blinding snowstorm, reluctant to leave the captain, but convinced that it was his duty to do so.

As a consequence, for the first few days at Bedford the entire care of the captain and his now multifarious affairs fell upon Salathiel. He was kept busy all day, and he got little sleep at night. Although Ecuyer was ill in bed, he was able to drive those about him at the fort, and Salathiel in particular, to the limit. And what weather it was! Raw, arctic cold; then rain and snow; then an ice storm to top it off.

It was in this welter of affairs, weather, hardships that Yates stepped in to lend a hand. He had come to the fort from Pendergasses' every morning to enquire after the captain's health. He would sit for a quarter of an hour or so and talk. Ecuyer was now looking about him for anyone he could get to help speed affairs along. He rapidly came to depend on Yates for a trustworthy account of what was happening from day to day. With a keen ear for talk and rumour, Yates seemed to have the state of the community and what everyone thought and said at his tongue tip. He was honest and straightforward. He liked the captain. They had come to trust each other at Ligonier. Salathiel learned a good deal by just listening to what was said.

It was during one of these morning conversations that Ecuyer reminded the young lawyer that he had never told him what the favour was Yates had said he was going to ask him at Ligonier.

Yates laughed.

"To tell the truth it was a trivial one I more or less made up at the time. I was making talk that night, you may remember, and I just wanted a point to bargain on."

"Nevertheless, out with it, man," insisted Ecuyer.

"Ahem," said Yates, considering. "Oh, yes, I do recollect now. You promised to let me have the receipt for the soup Albine served us that night St. Clair and the two militia officers came storming in. It was the best soup I ever tasted, and I rather fancy getting such things into my notes and diary as I go about."

"Ah, you keep a diary, do you?" smiled the captain. "I rather thought as much. Well, the favour is granted," he said.

"Albine," he called, "give Mr. Yates that receipt of Johnson's for the famous Queen of Scots soup."

Salathiel sat down and copied out the long receipt from the captain's memorandum book. He handed it to Yates, who looked at it, whistled, and expressed his thanks.

"Perhaps you have done me more of a favour than you know," said he. "By the way, I hear that Burent has arrived at Loudon and has already put the smiths to work forging snow runners for the pay-chest wagon. Captain Jack brought in the word only this morning. He's been east for a week."

"Good!" exclaimed the captain. The news cheered him greatly. "I knew I could depend on Burent," he added. "Now if we can only get these surly rascals at the fort paid, how *that* would help! The grenadiers are much the worst, I hear."

Yates agreed. "They do need a curb," he said. "But pardon me, I am not so rash as to try to advise you there. I am not of the military."

"To some extent we must *all* be of the military in these times," replied Ecuyer. "I was wondering if *you* would undertake to help Albine here with the correspondence, and give me your assistance in some other matters while I am laid up. Also, frankly, as matters now stand here at the fort, I do not wish to call in a new officer from a battalion that is not my own, or a raw military clerk. Certain matters of policy and promotions are involved. There might be leaks, I am afraid." He plucked the covers nervously.

"Let me advise you," Yates said, laughing, "in matters concerning the civil and militia laws of Pennsylvania. In that capacity I could be more or less at your service, sir. And most happy to be so."

Ecuyer looked grateful and relieved.

"Very well, I shall consult you," he said. "On detached service I am entitled to certify fees for 'necessary and unavoidable' civil aid. I take it this is both."

"I, too, can be ingenious," laughed Yates.

"Ask Captain Jack to come up to see me about this time tomorrow, if he is still about," the captain suggested as Yates rose to leave. "Tell him it's important."

"He'll be here, I warrant you," replied Yates.

The captain looked doubtful, however. "I am not so sure," he said. "That may require all our ingenuity."

"Thanks for the receipt for the Scotch soup," replied Yates. He grinned at Albine, and went out whistling loudly, much to the disgust of Captain Stewart at work down the hall.

That officer was not feeling so mortal cheerful. He thought he had a fine, young mutiny on his hands and was dandling it nervously. Good God, would the pay chests never come!

Thereafter, for many nights, and for some time to come, Salathiel had the able assistance of Edward Hamilton Yates, Esq., in the difficult drudgery over the captain's letters, records, and correspondence. Or rather, to be exact, Mr. Albine became the assistant and pupil of Yates, for the astute little lawyer took over wholeheartedly, although with great wisdom and restraint, and became in effect, though unofficially, a kind of civilian adjutant to Captain Ecuyer, and a careful and modest adviser in his affairs.

It was a purely personal arrangement and relationship amongst the three, Ecuyer, Yates, and Albine. It was rather typical of Ecuyer, who had a way of getting things done by the people who could do them and be trusted, whether they were official or not.

So the light burned late at Captain Ourry's quarters, where Ecuyer lay those first days at Bedford, and the letters and orders, the messengers and orderlies went in and out, and back and forth, while the garrison seethed with discontent.

For an invalid, Ecuyer did astonishingly well. Only Bouquet commented. "I see that you write letters with both your right and left hands now," he once remarked in a postscript. "But your new, third hand does puzzle me, though it's a right professional scrawl." This provided a much-enjoyed private laugh for the three conspirators in Captain Ourry's quarters. Outside, the sleet and snow still beat at the window. It was a mercy the last messengers from Fort Pitt had come through. Trouble was reported again on the road between Bedford and Ligonier. A party of Delawares, it was said, perhaps some of Japson's old friends.

Now all of these apparently minor arrangements and small affairs were actually of prime importance and consequence to Salathiel. The presence and help of Yates in the captain's quarters helped to ripen and solidify the friendship between him and the young lawyer. It might easily have had the opposite result, but the good nature and invariable tact of Yates carried the day.

From the first he seemed to understand instinctively what great store Albine set by his ability to help the captain as a clerk. It was the one thing that obviously raised Salathiel above the status of a personal servant. Johnson had never been able. But Albine from the first had been a help there. And in working with the records and correspondence Salathiel had been obliged to use and improve every jot and tittle of whatever skill in writing and what little practical education McArdle had been able to impart to him. That portion of his forest experience alone Albine regarded as his ladder to climb to the status of a civilized man.

As a consequence he had worked long and painfully, but accurately and laboriously, over the captain's accounts and at copying out his letters. He had often been slow and ponderous as a schoolboy. But he had always been faithful, and ever quick to learn and improve.

True, Ecuyer had often helped, pointed out or corrected mistakes when necessary, and he had frequently had to explain. Yet the captain

valued loyalty and faithful work more than facility, and he had been
secretly quite proud of, and always amazed at, young Albine's ability to
cope with the correspondence at all.

But at Bedford more and more of the captain's affairs had now to be
conducted by correspondence. He was in touch with officers and officials
from Philadelphia to Fort Pitt. At Bedford he was threatened with being
swamped. Only the slowness of communication for the time being saved
him. It was imperative, none the less, for him to have assistance. So it
was no dissatisfaction with Salathiel that had prompted him to turn to
Yates for help.

Yates, however, fully realized a delicate situation. He did not step in
and try to supplant Albine, or relegate him to the duties of nurse and
valet. He came to help. He had nothing but compliments, sincere ones,
for the neat and accurate way in which he found the captain's papers
had been kept. He shared the work and responsibility. He acted as an
equal and brought a welcome sense of companionship and a relief in
difficulty in doing so.

Yates and Albine got on. If Yates finally took the lead, it was only
natural and seemed fair in a field where he excelled professionally. And
when Salathiel finally left the captain he felt that no one except his
forest mentor, McArdle, had helped him more with pen, book, and
candle.

There were two other consequences of this time vastly important to
Albine. One was his move from the fort to bed and board at Pendergasses', the second was the beginning of his association and work with
Captain Jack. The first came about quite naturally, and of itself. Captain
Ecuyer had carefully planned the second. It was in fact part of a scheme
long cherished between the captain and Colonel Bouquet, nothing less
than the formation of a corps of woodsmen and rangers. In that enterprise Captain Jack's help was vital. Ecuyer therefore awaited his coming
with vivid anxiety. For Captain Jack might simply disappear into the
woods as he had done before.

But Captain Jack eventually presented himself at the fort one morning, although diffidently and with a certain amount of indignant bravado,
the result of a combination of conflicting impulses.

It was impossible for Captain Jack to enter a fort where the English
flag flew, and his Majesty's troops and officers strolled about in their
scarlet or green, without a tightening of the throat, a flood of sorrowful
and poignantly tragic memories that lay buried deep in his own and his
family history.

Because Ecuyer was a Swiss, and therefore turned out of a different
mould, Captain Jack had finally swallowed his hesitations and prejudices. In short, he was making a personal exception in Ecuyer's case,
because he liked and trusted him. But he disliked the surroundings and
atmosphere of the fort none the less. Nor was the old ranger being

merely eccentric in all this. He had ponderable and powerful reasons peculiarly his own for feeling as he did. Only those who knew who and what he was could fully understand him. And there were few who ever really knew his secret. Many stories were told about him.

5. The Secret Story of Captain Jack

CAPTAIN JACK'S last name was Fenwick. He was either a grandson or a grandnephew of that Sir John Fenwick who, in the reign of good King William, had lost his head on the block for his fanatical loyalty to the banished James. Sir John had headed a dangerous conspiracy in England and taken a leading part in a bitter affair. He had grievously insulted the queen, and that most dreadful and potent of all legal devices for punishment and destruction, an act of attainder working corruption of blood in his heirs and descendants, had, along with the axe, descended upon his devoted head.

Because the situation is so unusual, few can realize the predicament of those of the Fenwick blood who survived Sir John. They were physically alive in a world in which they did not legally exist.

In this condition of social no-men, the Fenwicks, if such they still were, had fled to the North American colonies with what apparel and small personal belongings they could collect by the combined mercy of their friends and the indifference of the authorities. There they had forthwith lost themselves in the kindly oblivion of the forests amid the Alleghenies. So successful were they in this that most of them disappeared; and reappeared, if ever, only under different names. They were literally forgotten and forgot.

Under these circumstances it is, therefore, not possible to say whether it was a son or a nephew of Sir John Fenwick who first built a cabin on what, in later times, became known as "Jack's Mountain", about a day's journey east from Bedford. Only Captain Jack, the cabin builder's son, knew. And he was not likely to tell. Above all, he would not set anything down or confirm any rumours. Indeed, he went down in local history and legend without a surname, known as "Captain Jack" alone.

And very much alone he was. His father had died a hopeless and embittered widower, leaving his son John a cabin, some pre-empted land, a sockful of old hoarded guineas, and a little corn meal. There were also the memories and secret pride for an ancient vanished name, which, to Captain Jack at least, had almost the force of an infernal legend in shaping his character.

"Alone" was indeed the word which always best described him. His giant size lent itself to setting him apart from the rest of mankind. In a roomful of people he towered above them, singled out and remarkable.

His iron-grey beard, his steely-blue eyes, the peculiar axelike feel of his profile and contour, outlined and made cruelly soft by the faded blood-red fringes of his buckskin hunting shirt and trousers, all contributed both to distinguish and to isolate him.

His voice was deep, suggesting a capacity to roar, while it remained disconcertingly soft and pliable. His few words came memorably from a red mouth ruled like a straight line under his thin nostrils, and finally, and perhaps most unconveyable in its meaning, except to those who actually saw it, he carried his rifle in his left arm like the proud father of a murderous child.

Yates said that Captain Jack looked as though he knew where the trap door of hell was hidden; that he had been there, come back, and wouldn't tell. And in this, as in several other matters, Mr. Yates was only being quite precise.

For Captain Jack (Fenwick) *had* been in hell. He had returned with difficulty, and he had devoted the rest of his time on earth to hunting down the devils who, he conceived, should be sent back to the infernal regions to which they essentially belonged.

It was quite simple if you knew why. It was this way:

When his father died, Captain Jack, then a lad of about seventeen, had buried his gloomy parent under a neighbouring oak, where it seemed likely to the boy that he might attract thunder even when dead. Jack had then taken the hoarded guineas and the corn meal on hand, arranged the meagre contents of the cabin for a long absence, sealed the latchstring with clay and resin, and scrawled on the door with charcoal, "This is Jack his place. Beware."

After taking a final look about at the wild scenery of the place which had detained his boyhood, and reading again the message to the world that he had left on the door of his home, he departed eastward accompanied by a fierce old hound, an axe, a musket, and the family Bible with some pages torn out, both of which latter articles harked back to Cromwellian times. He paddled down the Conodoguinet branch to the Susquehanna and stopped at Harris's, where he traded his musket and one good guinea for a horse whose youth had been spent, not idly, but in an extremely remote antiquity.

Thus mounted on a four-legged myth, he took the old trace to Lancaster, remarking casually before leaving that his old man was dead; that he himself expected to come back someday, and that he would certainly kill anyone who might happen to be occupying his cabin when he returned. To lend emphasis to this amiable thought he twinkled his axe in the air, easily, twenty feet up—and caught it by the handle when it obediently returned. At which all present bade him Godspeed with relief and alacrity, and he rode off without looking back.

At a small settlement called Paxtang a pack of curs ate his dog after a memorable fray, fragmentary in character towards its close, owing to the

intervention of the axe. Without waiting to ascertain the probably unfavourable opinion of the villagers in regard to the matter, he wiped his
axe off on some moss, and continued on to Lancaster. There his horse
died.

Noting that death seemed to dog his steps, he also concealed his uneasiness at that fact and the increasing evidence of civilization which
now began to surround him. He looked about him, and took measures
to cope with his new surroundings. He had his hair cut and done into a
neat queue. He bought himself the discarded wardrobe of a gentleman
and a pair of new boots from a Jew peddler. He paid him with the worst
guinea he had, and pushed on to Philadelphia.

Fate is lured by small bait. It was the clothes that caused a sober
Philadelphia merchant to direct Jack to the respectable London Coffee
House near the market. He took lodging there, and before long was able
to become the assistant to a surgeon-barber and dispenser of nostrums
for a small down payment and a note of hand. Mr. Williams, the surgeon-barber, had taken Jack for the son of a plantation owner of means.

This impression Jack was at no pains to correct. He had a few guineas
left, and fortune in the form of death still followed him. An outbreak of
ship's fever added suddenly to both reputation and income. His own
services and the nostrums of his partner were in constant demand.

As a consequence, both his fame and his fees were enhanced. And
before his note came due the second time, the fevers had claimed his
partner.

Thus within the short space of two years "John Morton" found himself in possession of a small cottage on the outskirts of town, a business
that throve on calamity, and a reputation for the cure of all those who
survived his semi-medical attentions.

Nor was John Morton a mere charlatan. He diligently observed, read,
and experimented in the field of his art. He finally made one innovation
of medical moment. He kept in his service for a trifling regular stipend,
and at his beck and call, several respectable and experienced widows
who had nursed, buried, and survived. These women he let out as
nurses. It was something no one seemed to have thought of before, even
in Philadelphia, and it was profitable.

In short, Dr. Morton was genuinely successful. He aided his patients
as much as any man then could—and was well paid for his trouble.

Not long after his partner died, John Morton had married a successful tradesman's daughter, one Mary Caldwell. And it so happened that
soon after they were married, Mr. Caldwell chanced to die in great pain
and internal discomfort—but unfortunately, not until after he had been
treated and well dosed by his son-in-law.

The medicine used had been a harmless concoction of slippery elm
bark, alum water, and aloes, a soothing and astringent affair at worst.
But Mr. Caldwell, who had a nice little property, had died *after* taking

the medicine, and apparently quite suddenly. The property went to his only daughter Mary, he being a widower, and it was Dr. Morton's "widows", the nurses, who began to talk.

In a few weeks the pearl of Dr. Morton's reputation vanished in vinegar. He was ruined by specious gossip.

In this crisis all comfort forsook him, save the consciousness of his own innocence and the constancy of his wife. Desperate, he finally consulted one Maria Carfax, who lived with an Indian at Conshohocken and had often sold him herbs for his medicines. She told him that because he had cheated Death of many upon whom the Black Shadow had already laid his hand, he had been called to personal account by the Grim Reaper and his own life was undoubtedly in danger. Death, Maria Carfax said, would not be denied, and if Dr. Morton avoided paying his forfeit now, it would be required of him thrice over in the future. The grounds for her assertions were those in the bottom of a teacup, but Dr. Morton was nevertheless impressed.

Remembering that death *had* dogged his steps, he returned to his house thoroughly frightened for the first and only time in his life. He lost weight. He brooded. He recollected now that he was a Fenwick with a legal curse on his head. He descended into the valleys of melancholy.

In this hopeless state of affairs his wife came loyally to the rescue. She disposed of their property and of the small inheritance from her father, quietly and at a loss. From the proceeds she bought a stout German wagon and a sound team. Into this she persuaded her husband to load their household goods during the hours of darkness, and to leave Philadelphia. The early dawn of a spring day found them rolling southward for Maryland.

Lord Baltimore's province proved to be another and a hospitable country. On the western borders of it, at a small but growing settlement called McCullough's Town, they eventually found peace, plenty, and happiness. Indeed, the ensuing five years lay afterward in the perspective of Captain Jack's experience like a shaft of sunlight across a long corridor of gloom.

The return to the familiar life of the forest and fields revivified and made a new man out of him. He changed his name again merely as a sensible precaution, but he continued his practice much as before. He was now known as "Dr. Caldwell", and he seemed in fact to have achieved a new personality.

He farmed, he rode about the country with his simples, and dispensed his herb medicines. He became much respected in the growing Scotch-Irish community. He and his good wife eventually became beloved. They did good and prospered. And in the course of time they had two children, a son and a daughter.

The Caldwells lived in a small valley that ran down to the Susque-

hanna, where the doctor had built a snug log house with his own hands.
There were flowers in Mrs. Caldwell's dooryard and a carefully tended
herb garden for her husband's practice. A stream sang its way past their
door, expressing, along with the voices of the children, their quiet happiness in married solitude. A new rifle bought from a Pennsylvanian
constantly enriched the larder. The Caldwells and the community in
which they lived prospered.

Then a certain Indian summer came. The French and English across
the ocean were going to war. No one at McCullough's Town remembered exactly what the quarrel was about. That it was an ancient one,
they knew from what their fathers from the old country had said. But
few in America cared any longer about it. In the spring there was fight-
ng somewhere west of the mountains, but that, too, was far, far away.
Then Death with a painted face came out of the forest.

Dr. Caldwell had been away on a two weeks' trip to Baltimore for
supplies. He was bringing home, in addition to a fine chest of carpenter
tools, which he had long scrimped and saved to obtain, some English
taffeta for his wife's gown and presents for the children. There was a
rag doll for the baby girl, a painted toy trumpet for the little boy. There
was white flour, household sundries, and a year's supply of powder, a
roll of lead, and a new bullet mould.

He had heard rumours of trouble on the way up, but the war was
young as yet and there had always been rumours of Indian trouble. He
took the usual short cut over a woods road to his farm on the river, and
thereby missed what would otherwise undoubtedly have attracted his
attention; the fact that McCullough's Town had ceased to exist.

It had been burned two days before and every soul driven away or
massacred. The dogs had been shot and eaten, the cattle killed, and the
horses stolen. That was the reason the doctor had not met a soul on the
road on the last lap of his journey.

The massive silence of the forest along the high banks of the Susquehanna was all that met the doctor on the drive down his own valley.
He did not hear any cowbells, and he thought that strange. He
blew on the painted toy horn at the stream crossing as he had promised
his little son to do. But there was only a brief echo and the complaint of
the stream which here ran under a log bridge. No dogs barked. There
was no running figure in a sunbonnet with the two children toddling
along behind her.

Suddenly he saw that his house was roofless and the logs seared by
fire. The being of Dr. Caldwell seethed within him like a volcano. Some
things he found out later, some he saw for himself at the time.

His was the last cabin that had been taken in the raid. The valley was
lonely. The party of drunken Hurons and five half-breed Frenchmen
had stopped in security to celebrate and be ingenious before moving on.
The record of their brief visit is not conveyable in letters. It can best be

understood by holding some member of the body in a flame—and no
withdrawing it. Mrs. Caldwell had finally been hanged. She was stil
there, scorched. What had been a little boy was shaped like an egg.

As darkness came on, the person that had achieved being Dr. Morto
and Dr. Caldwell dissolved, or sublimed, in a kindly oblivion of mad
ness. An insane man presented the rag doll to the remains of his bab
girl suspended over the telltale ashes in the fireplace.

Then the little girl came out on the hearth and danced for him in th
grilled streaks of moonlight streaming between the burnt-out intervals o
the logs.

The hallucination was final and complete. He was never able entirel
to shake it off. He thought he gathered his child up in his arms an
drove away. He felt her weight and he saw and heard her. She remaine
in the wagon with him for some days. He must have fed the horses some
times, and existed mechanically. Some weeks later, exactly how long h
never knew, he lost the little girl. She vanished. Occasionally she calle
to him. He began to realize he was wandering both mentally and physi
cally. What had happened? Somehow he had crossed the Susquehanna
God alone knows where.

Eventually he found himself with a team of emaciated horses covere
with sores, wandering northward through the woods on a packers' trace
The outlines of the mountains were the first thing he began to becom
fully sensible of and to remember. The hills where he now found him
self were vaguely familiar. He was also conscious now of an incredibl
fatigue.

He rested, fed the horses and himself, and then went to sleep in th
wagon. His sleep was like a dip into death. When he awoke he wa
more sensible. Part of his memory came back. He first remembere
things that had happened some time ago. He came to a familiar sprin
and crossing of wood paths. He knew he was on the way to Harris's from
the south. The man he remembered best was Jack Fenwick. He coul
see that was who he was when he looked in the spring when he stoope
down to drink. His face had much altered. He looked drawn bu
younger, despite his beard. He had returned to his original self again-
alone.

But eventually Jack Fenwick remembered in every detail what ha
happened to Dr. Caldwell.

Shortly after this the stories began to gather about his name that late
turned him, even during his lifetime, into a legendary character.

Most people are diffuse or diverse in their interests, fortunately. Wha
in the end attracts permanent attention and fixes a reputation in mem
ory is a man with a single end in view, one which he pursues relent
lessly. That a certain insane tenseness frequently accompanies the ma
of one purpose seems only to cast a more focused and strange light upo
his doings. It accentuates him by contrast. And if, as frequently hap

pens, the man with one idea has no fear of consequences in the attainment of his object, a "hero" is in the making. Such a man can be completely rational about one thing alone. But he can often be superrational about that, and to be superrational is a characteristic of genius.

Captain Jack was a prime, although an obscure, example of the type described. From the time he recovered his memory after the massacre of his family until the cooling hand of old age fell benignly upon him, he pursued one object, was possessed of only one mastering desire, to accomplish which all else, both people and things, were merely means. The end, of course, was the extermination of Indians. In that line he became both a hero and a genius.

Nothing could have caused more astonishment at Harris's, for instance, than his arriving there at the time he did. The place had been turned into a fort, a stronghold for the whole region. Only a few miles westward the frontiers had been swept clean in the first triumphant raids of the war on the hapless inhabitants. The cabins along the Conococheague had vanished in flames, and all those who had not fled in time perished or were dragged into captivity. Garrett Pendergass and his numerous family had taken warning and abandoned their homes. They now made part of the garrison at Harris's. Watch was being kept at the crossing with regular discipline and anxious care—when out of the forest, and on the dangerous southern bank of the river, one summer day emerged a loaded wagon and a lone driver. It was pure chance that Jack had come through from Maryland without being scalped, literally a crazy chance. It looked like fate.

Jack did not stay at Harris's. After a rest and a brief period for reflection and cogitation he set out for his cabin that he had left years before with "Beware" scrawled on the door. On a certain Sunday morning before dawn he had himself and his wagon ferried across the river and disappeared up the now-abandoned road into the western fastnesses.

It was now that the incredible-in-reality began. The second day out he was taken prisoner by a war party of fourteen Indians. Apparently he let himself be taken prisoner. He either was demented or he appeared to be so to the Delawares who took him captive. They deferred his fate to confer later about it. Exactly what happened is not clear. But about a week later Jack Fenwick arrived in his wagon at the cabin his father had built, with the scalps of fourteen Indians. A string of the more usable Indian horses was attached to the wagon. That was the beginning.

The Fenwick cabin was still standing. It had long been taken over and inhabited by a family of Christian Indians who had been converted by the Moravians. They had planted considerable corn and cleared the fields about. Raids had passed them by. The word "Beware" was no longer visible on the cabin door, but it might well have been, for the returning owner killed them all with his hand axe and buried them in the adjacent cornfield. One old woman, out berrying in the woods, alone escaped to bring the news to Harris's.

At the cabin Captain Jack set up a base for his lethal one-man forays. The terror of him gradually spread until his reputation became little short of supernatural. His principal strategy was to attack, always at a remote distance from his place of abode, an Indian village or a war or hunting party. He approached unseen, struck and fled. He outran, out-shot, and outdid his enemies in all things and particulars. Chiefs died, shot at the council fire. Young warriors, women, and children vanished. His name became a synonym for fatal misfortune. War parties were scattered in long and vain pursuits and were cut off individually as they turned back. In the end any who returned unscathed were counted lucky.

Finally Captain Jack took to wholesale methods of harassment. In dry seasons and high winds he set the forest afire. He burned out hunting grounds, cornfields, and whole villages. He ranged from Virginia to the New York borders, and at times and for intervals he disappeared en-tirely. Only occasionally was he known to act in concert with other white men. Here and there were a few lonely characters who knew him, whom he trusted, and who followed him when he called.

It took some time for his reputation to spread among the whites. He did not care whether they knew about him or not. He worked for his own satisfaction. He desired a reputation among the Indians alone. But the cabin of many a white settler was warned in the middle of the night by a voice from the darkness in time for its inmates to take flight or to put themselves in a posture of defence. And all the frontier forts of the Blue Mountains saw him from time to time.

Eventually the mountain where his cabin stood came to be known by his name. It will remain as an everlasting monument of his personal war long after his legend fades. The legend is dim now, but at the time those most intelligently interested in the defence of the province of Pennsyl-vania knew and understood the fiery lustre of his name. "That bloody man", as certain Quakers called him, was regarded by the more knowing authorities along the frontiers as the equivalent of a regiment. Among those who understood his worth best were Washington and Franklin.

In the year 1755, in the early summer when the British army ad-vancing against Fort Duquesne was only a few miles west of Frederick, Maryland, but already tangled in the wilderness, a sinister figure emerged from the forests at twilight and demanded to be taken to the commanding general. He would tell neither his name nor his mission. It was Captain Jack, his face blackened for murder at midnight, his belt fringed with dangling scalps, and his already legendary rifle nursed in his left arm with a composite epitaph of nicks upon its stock. In the company of a sergeant he passed between the campfires of evening towards the tent of the general, which stood on a small knoll.

Captain Jack bore a letter from Benjamin Franklin, and he was presented by Colonel Washington to General Edward Braddock about the time the general and his staff were sitting down to mess. The staff, dressed in scarlet and gold lace, looked at this apparition from the woods with astonishment and horror. Even the younger officers, usually inclined to laugh, found nothing funny in the grim frontiersman.

"This is the man whose reputation I have enlarged to you, sir," said Colonel Washington. "Far west of the mountains, which we soon hope to cross, the cries of Indian children are stilled by the syllables of his name." Colonel Washington then withdrew, leaving Captain Jack alone with the general.

The general shook the hand of the savage figure presented to him, not wholeheartedly. He could not conceal his astonishment and reluctance. In any event, he regarded handshaking as barbarous. And the mien of Captain Jack was anything but cordial, neither was it subservient or respectful. The general felt repulsed. He was angry before a word passed between them. He was not in a good mood anyway as he had been forced to give up his coach that very afternoon and to send it back to the governor at Annapolis. Captain Jack seemed gloomily to personify the grim and barbarous hardships ahead. The general glowered at him.

He then read the letter in which Franklin urged him strongly to retain Captain Jack as the leader of advance rangers. Before he reached the end his indignation rose. He had not thought of having any advance rangers at all. The terror of the name of English regulars would clear the way for the army. "You are overconfident, I opine," read the general. His gorge rose.

"Humph, humph," said he, "pshaw!"

He put the letter under a candlestick, and looked up at Captain Jack. "So you wish to serve his Majesty?" he asked.

"You have read Mr. Franklin's letter, general?" replied Captain Jack, restraining another reply with difficulty.

"I have, sir!" shouted the general, turning scarlet above his collar. He snatched it up again, rose, and led the way out of the tent, followed by Captain Jack.

"And my reply," shouted he at Captain Jack, "is that his Majesty's troops can do without your eminent services, and still conquer for a' that"—he rustled Franklin's letter angrily. There was a pause while for a moment the general and the woodsman glowered at each other.

"Farewell, sir," said Captain Jack prophetically.

"By God, Halket, you'd think I'd been dismissed," complained Braddock to one of his majors as he sat down at the mess. "I'll have to instruct Colonel Washington not to bring low characters like that to headquarters."

"A portent, a grisly portent from the woods," said Sir Peter Halket, and shivered uncomfortably.

"Nonsense, damned impudence!" snorted the general, crumpling up Franklin's letter. He tossed it into the fire kindled before his tent, and began to eat heartily . . .

In the years that followed Braddock's defeat Captain Jack continued to fight his enemies as relentlessly as ever. Later Forbes endeavoured to enlist him as a leader of rangers, but in vain. The experience with Braddock appeared permanently to have alienated him from the royal authorities. Only as time went on did Captain Jack come to acknowledge the advantage of a few trusted assistants.

Gradually, without there being any formality about it, a group of young hunters and woodsmen became his followers, and at times, and in special instances, assisted him in his forays.

These young hunters were all sons of old settlers and tried frontiersmen whom Captain Jack knew. There was a decided element of secrecy about this "forest brotherhood" of young men who had gradually gathered about him as their acknowledged leader.

All its members were Masons, or "sons of the widow". All came of families who had been harassed by the savages. All of them spent a time of probation in training with Captain Jack. Many of them lived with him on the trail or at his cabin at various times. The membership seems to have varied from year to year. But it was an honour to be associated with Captain Jack and it was regarded as a kind of accolade in woods skill and forest fighting, a warrant of dependable character to be asked to join.

Whether there was a password among them is doubtful. That rumour seems to have arisen from the fact that most of them were Masons. The wisdom of keeping their plans and their deeds secret, and the reputation and personal authority of Captain Jack, were all that was necessary

Yet some kind of organization there must have been. Colonel Bouquet contributed arms, powder, and rations at least once. He knew about the "Mountain Foxes", and so did Ecuyer. In Pontiac's war Captain Jack came to stay at Bedford, probably to be near his friend Garrett Pendergass. For many years they had been associated in one scheme or another. Jack finally built himself a cabin not far from Bedford. There he gathered his young Foxes about him from time to time. Part of this activity may have been for Masonic reasons. Masonry was then spreading along the frontier and both Captain Jack and Garrett Pendergass were furthering it.

At any rate, the old fighter now spent much of his time at his new cabin and about Garrett's place at Bedford, where he was much less alone than ever before. Indeed, the hearth room at Pendergasses' had served to soften even his embittered heart. Perhaps, too, the memories of many years before were growing less poignant and unbearable. Captain Jack was fond of the children at Pendergasses'. He was seen to whittle things out for them in the evenings, play games, and even to smile. Garrett considered this his greatest triumph in hospitality. Undoubtedly, too, a great many schemes were arranged before the fire at Pendergasses'.

It was Garrett, for instance, who had brought Captain Jack and Colonel Bouquet to speaking terms. In the colonel Captain Jack saw the nemesis of the Indians.

In this pact of mutual respect Ecuyer had also gradually come to be included as the colonel's man, as a Swiss and not an Englishman. It was in the summer of '63 that Captain Jack had finally received arms and assistance from Bouquet. That at least was a beginning of co-operation with the authorities. And the king's powder had not been wasted.

It was now Captain Ecuyer's plan to enlist the aid of Captain Jack and his young men in a closer collaboration with the military. The test of the whole matter was whether or not Captain Jack would come to the fort to talk with him.

Few important things are ever arranged simply. Ecuyer had asked Yates to speak to Captain Jack. But Yates was forced to work upon the old hunter through his friend Garrett. Captain Jack had at last consented to listen to Garrett's appeal.

What to say to him, in case he did come, was something Ecuyer had long and carefully considered. He knew most of the tragic story and Captain Jack's prejudices. He realized he would have to tread warily and make a powerful personal appeal. It was, therefore, with no small satisfaction, but also with some anxiety, that he finally heard the old hunter arguing with the sentry outside.

"Here comes the old devil now!" exclaimed Ecuyer as the heavy boots came stamping down the corridor.

"No, no," he exclaimed to Yates, who rose hurriedly, prepared to leave. "Pray stay, I may need you! And you, Albine, this talk will certainly concern you. Have the goodness to listen carefully."

With which preliminary remarks the captain settled back in the pillows and managed to look even a bit sicker than he actually was.

Captain Jack knocked sturdily at the door.

6. Captain Jack Associates Himself

SYMPATHY is always an excellent opener. When Captain Jack entered Ecuyer's room he immediately forgot his own hesitations and prejudices in a generous solicitude for his friend.

The expression on Ecuyer's face, his deadly pallor, the very position of his body under the bedclothes managed wordlessly to convey the extreme helplessness and sad predicament to which a brave and indefatigable man had at last been reduced. Captain Jack understood exhaustion when he saw it. Here was a silent and personal cry for help, not for a cause, but for a man.

Albine was surprised that to some extent the captain was obviously arranging this effect. But Yates was fascinated. He admired greatly the strategy of employing a state of helplessness to provide an opening for placing the first blow. And Captain Jack's guard was certainly down.

"Man, man!" exclaimed the old hunter in consternation, "I'd not dreamt they'd reduced ye to *this!*" He shook his head ruefully, and then tried to smile.

Ecuyer extended his hand and smiled back at him patiently.

"I do *much* appreciate your coming to see me," he said. "Albine, a chair for my guest! By the way, do you know each other? This should be a young fellow after your own heart, Captain Jack. Mr. Yates will bear me out in that, I know."

"That I will, and gladly," chimed in Yates. "But I know that Captain Jack and Sal have already met."

"Good!" said Ecuyer.

"Oh, aye, that we have!" exclaimed Captain Jack. "I had a good talk with him only the other night. Old Garrett thinks he knew his par and mar. However that may be, happen I could put him to better work than you can, captain."

"I've no doubt of it," agreed Ecuyer. "Prop me up, Albine, Captain Jack and I are going to make big medicine together to snare some of your red friends, and I never heard it could be done lying down."

"Only Quakers, pacificators, and suchlike try to make medicine in wartime by lying down," drawled the woodsman.

"It's a good position to place the feet of your enemy on the back of your neck, and not good for much else, as far as I can see," laughed Ecuyer, who was now sitting up and looking brighter.

"It is, it is," cried Captain Jack, smiting his knee. "Plague take 'em!"

"Colonel Bouquet and I are bothered by a good deal of half-hearted medicine making," continued Ecuyer. "The sad truth is we get no willing help, only forced aid, grudgingly given. None of the country people volunteered last spring when the colonel advanced here from Carlisle. Not one!" he exclaimed. "The terror of the Indians lay too heavily upon them. And to some extent they were right. For if Bouquet had been defeated at Bushy Run, the savages might well have descended upon Philadelphia or Baltimore. The people of Pennsylvania are only too willing to let others do their fighting for them—and to trade behind the backs of their defenders with the enemy." The captain smacked his fist into his hand weakly, but with emphasis, and flushed spots appeared on his cheeks. "You, yourself, they call a man of blood, sir," he said to Captain Jack. "I hear they have even been niggardly about paying you the bounty on enemy scalps you have taken," he added.

It was now Captain Jack's turn to flush angrily.

" 'Tis true," he said. "As for what they call me along the Delaware, I care not. The eastern counties have ever been indifferent to the sufferings of the frontier. As long as their own precious scalps were well glued on all was well, as far as Philadelphia was concerned. Mr. Franklin and his friends have been a noble exception to such base slavery. And the instinct of the Scotch-Irish on the borders has always been to strike back at the redskins and to stop the Quaker caravans loaded with whisky and scalping knives for the varmints. But what do the authorities do? They license the traders! And they regard the riflemen as mere provincials, as unfit to associate with the noble British regulars." Captain Jack's voice had gained in volume. "Now in Braddock's time," he began, "I . . ."

"I know all about that," said Ecuyer, reaching out and laying a restraining hand on the old frontiersman's arm. "But much blood and tears have rolled under the bridges since Braddock's time. Defeat is your great corrector of abuse, Captain Jack. So it's different now. Come, admit it. Don't you find it so?"

"I do, I do," admitted the old fighter—after a pause. "For instance, you have received me here like a man, like a gentleman. We talk face to face, and on the same floor. But you are a Switzer, Ecuyer. An Englishman would not be able to see me. Many a whippersnapper, whose fathers were less in England than mine, looks at me like a blind man."

"Now, there I can sympathize with you," interrupted the captain. "Both Colonel Bouquet and myself have felt the blue blindness of English eyes, of which you speak, and so has Mr. Yates here, I warrant you. Why, he is *only* a Scot!"

At this they all laughed together.

"Yes, it *is* difficult to bear," Ecuyer continued. "What you speak of is the curse of empire. The Frenchman born in France, the Spaniard in Spain, the Englishman in England—all feel themselves superior to the provincial on his native ground. Such is the pride of paternity combined with the air of the metropolis, and I suppose it will always be true—to the end. After all, it's natural. Few fathers ever come to regard their children as equals, much less take advice from them. But let us try to forget that here. We at least can agree on one thing. The common enemy must be defeated. The people of these frontiers must be harassed no more. And, sir, there is now an opportunity to strike back at the enemy in his own country. Bouquet would strike home at the Indians down the Ohio, release the captives, dictate a lasting peace. He has learned to conquer by using the savages' own method of warfare. That I think is what you have been doing, too. Colonel Bouquet is a great man, Captain Jack. But he will fail if we can't keep the road to Fort Pitt open. I am responsible to him for that. It was my thought that you might see fit to aid me. You could be of invaluable help. As for me, I am all but spent in the service of the king. And time flies, flies away for a lame man." Ecuyer sank back into the pillows, keeping his eyes fixed on the face of the man before him. It was some time before the frontiersman replied. His reluctance was still evident.

"What is it you would have me do?" he finally asked.

"Why, range the road from here to Ligonier," replied Ecuyer. "Prevent ambuscades, and bring us news of the savages."

"I could not do that alone," said Captain Jack. "It's a large territory, and a difficult one to cover."

"I did not suppose you could, although the terror of your name is great," said Ecuyer. "But you have a great influence with some of the best young riflemen and woodsmen in these unhappy parts. You could enlist the aid of such young fellows as Albine here, and put them to valuable work. Come, come, Captain Jack, you know that. No one could do more. In fact, no one but yourself *can* do it."

But the old frontiersman still hesitated.

"Pray consider what the captain says, sir," put in Yates at this opportunity. "Murray, the Pendergass boys, my friend here would all esteem it a privilege to follow you. I, myself, would wish to volunteer if you would let me."

Captain Jack was now undoubtedly moved. He cut some tobacco from a twist and cogitated it.

"Wal," said he, lapsing into the country jargon as he turned to Albine, "an' how do you take to the proposition, young feller? You know more about the Injuns than most, I guess. Say your say."

"I say *do* it, Captain Jack," exclaimed Salathiel. "As for me, I have an account to settle with the redskins. Mr. Pendergass was telling me the other night he thinks they shot my pa in the back on Christmas Day when I was little. But I'd follow you anyway. And I do know something of the Injuns' ways." He smiled. "Do it, sir, I say. Ever since I came to serve Captain Ecuyer he's always been right."

"That's the talk," cried Captain Jack, again smacking his knee. "Young man, I like your style, and, captain, I'm inclined to jine ye. But I'll do so only on my own terms."

"I never thought you would do anything else," laughed Ecuyer. "Well, sir, what are your terms?"

Captain Jack sat pondering. His face darkened for a moment; seemed to cloud over with a rush of blood. Memory was strong.

At this juncture a curious thing happened. Ecuyer made a gesture with one hand. It seemed a natural one. Salathiel could not be sure, but it looked to him like a certain motion of secret sign language that had been taught him as a finishing touch to his lore by Nymwha, the Shawnee medicine man. It was the plea of one warrior to another when stricken upon the field of battle. Only some warriors in some tribes would know it, Nymwha had said. For it was an ancient, a much-cherished and powerful sign. It was a motion not lightly to be made. Had the captain made it? If so, how did he know? Perhaps, after all, it was a mere coincidence. But at that moment Captain Jack replied. There could scarcely be any doubt of it now. How extremely curious! And these were white men.

Just then Captain Jack found the weed in his mouth more of an impediment than a help. He rose, went to a window, hoisted it deliberately, and spat out the wad.

He paused now with his back to the room, seeming still to be considering. The wintry, mountain air swept in, reminding Ecuyer of the difficulties still ahead of him outside. He shivered and drew the bedclothes about him resignedly. He had done all he could. At last Captain Jack closed the window and returned. He was more at ease now, almost affable, as he resumed his chair by the captain's bed.

"This is how I see it, captain," he said. "Young Jimmy Smith over at Conococheague valley is raising a company of rifles by subscription. They'll enlist, and take the oath to the king probably. He'll be commissioned, and he'll desarve it. But I won't do that. If you can manage to supply me with powder and shot, arms if I want them, and rations for, we'll say, ten, I'll undertake to associate some likely young fellers like your man Albine here, and I'll promise to patrol the road from here to Ligonier, and make it hard for the redskins in the adjacent parts. And I'll stick to it until Colonel Bouquet returns. And if he doesn't return, I will stick to it just the same for a year. As for pay—that would help. We'll be giving our time, maybe our lives. Manage something with the paymaster if you can. But I must make this plain, pay or no pay, I'm to do the drivin' of my own wagon. Just tell the Britishers we're fighting Quakers and it's agin our conscience to take an oath. Also, all the scalps, booty, and bounty belongs to us, and I take instructions from you or Colonel Bouquet, but from no one else. And, sir, you will listen to no complaints about my cruelty to the savages. We won't be cruel, we'll be quick—and they'll be dead. The best way of all to manage this affair would be for nobody to know anything about us except the 'savages', as you call them. Talk that advertises surprises is a scalping knife in the enemies' hand. That's my say, and I never thought I'd say it!" He looked at Ecuyer and smiled with a frown.

"But it's fair enough," replied the captain. "And I think it can be managed, even the pay. I'll write to Colonel Bouquet tonight for his consent. All shall be confidential. Do you think you can find me a volunteer to carry the letter to Pittsburgh? Meanwhile, will you go ahead with your plans on my word alone? I'll begin by releasing Albine to you as soon as you want him. That is a real earnest on my part that I am interested, for I value his services greatly. And now, sir, my best wishes and profound thanks. I trust you will soon be able to strike some shrewd blows for your country. I doubt not you will." Captain Ecuyer extended his hand from the bed.

Captain Jack pumped Ecuyer's arm cordially, with considerable emotion. He also shook hands with Albine and Yates as though he considered them part of the pact.

"Now that this powwow's over," he said, "I feel better. I'd like to see you both at Pendergasses' tonight, if the captain can spare you," he added. "We can start right away making our plans."

Mr. Yates and Mr. Albine were delighted and showed it. Captain Ecuyer smiled with relief, and Captain Jack clumped off down the corridor, this time without a trace of hesitation in his tread.

"Sir, I never can thank you enough," said Albine to Captain Ecuyer as the old woodsman left the room.

"Every dog has his day, or should have," laughed Ecuyer. "But never mind wagging your tail now, Albine. Wait—and see how it goes."

"But I'll never stop wagging my tail," exclaimed Salathiel. "I'm a lucky dog, and I know it, thanks to you."

Mr. Yates leaned back and laughed.

And so, pleasantly enough, that was how Captain Jack's "Mountain Foxes", or the "Fighting Quakers", began.

That also was why Salathiel came to live at Pendergasses'. For while the Fighting Quakers were not wholly a Pendergass organization, they were predominantly so.

It must be remembered that old Garrett Pendergass had seven sons and four daughters. There was Charles, the oldest, already grey, and married to an invalid; there was Tom, a few years older than Salathiel; then there were two sets of twins, Matthew and Mark, Luke and John. There was only a year between the two sets of twins, and they were all strapping young cubs. Tobias, or Toby, the youngest child, had been born halt in the left leg. He was bright as a whip, however.

As for the daughters, Polly was the oldest girl, a little younger than Charles. She had married one Murray, who had been caught out and scalped near their cabin in the Juniata water gap. Young Nat Murray was her son. Bella was next in age, but she had never married. She was her mother's favourite and had remained constantly in the house to help her. Rachel, the third daughter, was now Mrs. William Davison, the mother of Phoebe and young Arthur. She lived at Fort Loudon, where her husband was a prosperous tanner, but her children spent half their time in their grandparents' house. Sue, the youngest girl, was a bright, upstanding young woman, much given to fancy clothes and the vapours, as she was in doubt as to who was the best chance among many who came sparking. As Garrett would not put up with any bundling in his house, she found her choice difficult, and was sometimes inclined to pout or even to weep a bit over the strictness of her lot. Really, she was not able to make up her mind to leave her father's house and was inclined to keep on consulting her Bible or a pack of cards about her swains and her future.

Owing to the dangers of the times, most of the Pendergasses were again living with the old man at Bedford. It was not regarded as a hardship to come back to the establishment where plenty and peace reigned. The boys, who had taken up land and built cabins, all but Toby, had returned till times should be better. They all worked hard for their father. But Captain Jack's proposal that some of them should now become regular members of his gang of "Mountain Foxes" was not unattractive to old Garrett, despite the danger involved. He admired Captain Jack and thought well of the discipline and training both in character and as woodsmen that his sons would get. In addition, he was public spirited and felt that his family should do something for their friends and neighbors.

As a consequence, that evening in the big hearth room Garrett, his son Charles, and Captain Jack sat long over their supper, discussing in low tones the ways and means of putting Captain Jack's proposals into effect. They were joined about eight o'clock by Salathiel, who had been released by the captain for the occasion. But he had left Yates toiling over the correspondence, in particular over the letter to Colonel Bouquet, which was to go out that night.

It was arranged that Charles, who had no children to care for, should set out for Fort Pitt with the letter as soon as it was finished, and bring back the reply. He was an expert woodsman and knew the route to Pittsburgh well. Of the other Pendergass boys, Tom and Matthew and Mark were to join Captain Jack, along with Nat Murray and Salathiel, at the cabin which Captain Jack had recently erected near Bedford. This was more like a blockhouse than a cabin, which the old hunter had built for himself some miles down the range of Lookout Mountain, close by a limestone spring. The boys were to act as a "garrison" of this place, and be ready for any duty Captain Jack might call them out upon, day or night. Also, they were to practise and undergo certain trials and tests he insisted upon before taking the trail with him.

"For," said he, "I don't look forward to accidents. And even you bright young fellers might make just one mistake. I make a pint of never making—none. *None*," said he, smiting his knee, "not one! As for the several boys who'll be coming over from the Big Cove pretty soon, they're old hands, and they know my ways. But I'll not send for them till we hear from the colonel at Pittsburgh. Not that I don't trust Ecuyer," he added, looking at Salathiel, "but we'd best wait to hear from Bouquet."

It was at this point that old Garrett stepped into the breach with a kindly offer.

"Don't wait," said he. "No matter what the authorities do, I believe this is an excellent plan for ridding ourselves of the red varmints. And we might also stop any trading that pops up." He lowered his voice here almost to a whisper and looked knowingly at the table across the room, where Lieutenant Neville and some of his friends had just come in for a round of hot grog. "I hear that some of your friends over there, Albine, are pretty mad. You and Yates had better keep a sharp eye on them. Now, my idea is not to wait till you hear from Fort Pitt, but for you young fellers to go out to Captain Jack's tomorrow. I'll furnish ye with all that's necessary for livin' and shootin' out there, and I'll guarantee it, even if Bouquet won't carry out Ecuyer's plan. He will, though, if I know him. But anyway the road must be kept open, and the good people of this town have their neighbourhood freed of varmints so they can go to church and plough their fields without being scalped. There's an army at the fort trying to prevent that, but you boys can do better for our people by yourselves than all of the soldiers put together. So, I say, don't wait! And I'll back ye. Back ye to the limit." He brought his fist down on the big table so that the dishes crashed and the candles guttered in their iron holders.

Everyone in the room jumped.

For some reason or other the party at Lieutenant Neville's table, which had recently been joined by several other officers, was considerably disturbed and apparently annoyed. Their mutterings, subdued laughter, and conversational oaths were suddenly cut off. It was tacitly understood by everybody that the conversation thus interrupted was one that somehow concerned those gathered about Garrett at his table. All this was quite suddenly, but quite plainly, in the air.

"Blast me!" said Lieutenant Guy, a young officer with an impudent face, red from too much drinking. "Let's go back to my quarters, gentlemen. I'll guarantee at least y' won't be interrupted by havin' your host crash the dishes."

"I'll warrant ye won't," put in Captain Jack, "because, gentlemen, at Lieutenant Guy's quarters there aren't any dishes to crash."

"Nor any chairs to sit in, gentlemen," added Charles Pendergass.

"Nor any cups to pour liquor into," mourned Nat Murray.

"Nor any liquor to pour," added Garrett.

Now, this was quite true, since Guy had lost everything but his clothes at cards, and a general laugh at his expense went around.

"I see you're all against me," said the red-faced young officer, hiccupping sadly. "What—what can I do?"

"Well, you might pay for the suppers you ordered," suggested Garrett.

"Ah, so you might, since you ordered them," agreed Neville in spite of himself. He rose hastily. They all rose, leaving the red-faced lieutenant alone to face the music.

"All right! Post me for it. Put it on your damned charges, Garrett," said Guy, with a reckless gesture. "I'll pay you—when the pay chests come." He laughed loudly and stumbled out.

"*Gentlemen*," cried Garrett suddenly, just as they reached the door. He brought his fist down again hard.

They all stopped and gawked at him.

"The pay chests will be here tomorrow, and I shall expect every one of you to settle with me as soon as you're paid. Whatever you may have had to complain about tonight," he added ironically, "I've fed you, warmed you, and set good liquor before you for months past, and I've never dunned you, but I remind you of that now. Captain Ourry is camped just east of the water gap tonight. He'll be in tomorrow morning. Good evenin'."

This was news indeed. It would change the whole face of affairs at the fort. Salathiel was anxious to take the tidings to the captain.

"He knows about it already," Garrett assured him. "I sent young Toby up with the message to Yates some time ago. Burent brought the news this afternoon. He's upstairs in bed now, clean tuckered out. They had a hard trip, but they've got the chests and about fifty other wagons, too."

Just then the door opened and Yates came in with Toby. Evidently he had stayed only long enough to finish the letter to Bouquet.

"What's the trouble with that crowd outside?" asked Yates as he sat before the fire warming himself. "I met that mob of Neville's on my way down from the fort. They were all gathered at Baker's corner arguing, but they dried up like hardtack when I passed. A conspiracy, I'll be bound," he said contemptuously.

"I don't think so," said Garrett. "I told them about the pay chests."

"I wouldn't have," said Yates.

"I want to collect what's due me tomorrow, Ned," said old Garrett, "so I thought I'd just let that news get about, too."

"I've got some news for you," said Yates. "And most astonishing it is. I think it will interest Sal, here, more than most. When you left the fort this afternoon Ecuyer was in Ourry's quarters, wasn't he? Well, he's not there any more. When Toby came in with the news just before supper that Ourry and the wagons would be here tomorrow, what do you think the captain did? Why, he got up out of bed. Then he sent for Captain Stewart and had himself moved over into that tent next to the hospital. It's the grenadiers' row. And there he is now—and no one to look after him but Captain Forbes's orderly, who is an impudent rascal if I ever saw one."

"Why, in God's name, didn't Ecuyer come here!" exclaimed Garrett. "He could have had the big river room on our side of the house till he got well, and young Phoebe to nurse him."

"That's what I told him," said Yates, "but he says he won't put Ourry out of his quarters, even if he does rank him, and that too many of the company officers have neglected the troops and taken lodgings in town. There'll be trouble when the men are paid, he insists, and he wants to be among 'em till he starts back for Pittsburgh. And he says he thinks he will be well enough for that in about a week."

"I suppose he'll leave anyway," said Captain Jack. "It's just like him. And to think of Lieutenants Guy and Neville, and suchlike, boozing about and toasting their shins at every hearth in the town that'll let them!"

"Captain Jack," said Salathiel, "I'm going to stick by the captain till he leaves for Fort Pitt. It's the least I can do. Do you think you could get along at the cabin without me for a few days?"

"Wal, now, I've managed without ye for about fifty years," drawled Captain Jack, and then changed his tone: "We certainly kin, and you ought to be with Ecuyer now. He'll need ye. And you'll only be doin' what's right to stand by him for a while."

Garrett agreed. "As far as that goes," he said, "I think all of you boys had better put off goin' out to Jack's cabin for a day or two. You'd better stick at the store and help your old pa. Charley can go with the letter, but I'll need the rest of you for tendin' store and keepin' an eye on things. Maybe Captain Jack would just kind o' set in the room here till the worst of it's over."

"Happen he would," said Captain Jack.

"Now, Charley, you make ready to leave at daylight, before Ourry and his men get in," continued Garrett. "That letter's important! And mind your hair west of Ligonier."

"I'll go by way of the Turkey Foot instead of Ligonier," said Charley. "The old trace ain't like to be so frequented by lurkers."

"No, it hain't," agreed Captain Jack; "you'd better come back that way, too."

While this discussion was going on, Salathiel had borrowed a couple of blankets from the shelves, and rolled up a small parcel of cooked food.

"I don't know how the captain will be fixed," he said to Garrett. "You might ask Burent to come up first thing in the morning."

"I'll see that he does," said Yates.

Old Garrett followed Salathiel to the door.

"Get your own things together and bring them down here first opportunity," he said. "You can have that little room nigh the corner across from Yates. Tell the truth, I want ye in the house as much as ye can be when you're not off with Captain Jack. Ye can help out and it kind o' seems like old times with one of your name about." Old Garrett paused. "Well, well, now, be off with you. The captain will be needin' you, too. Did you ever see a garrison payday, Albine? No! In that case you've got a surprise comin', and likely it won't be a pleasant one. I expect trouble here for the next few days. Keep an eye on your friends. They don't love ye too much. I'll tell Dr. Boyd about the captain's leaving his bed. He won't like it, I guess. I'll give your compliments to Phoebe, too."

With that old Garrett laughed and let Salathiel go, closing the door behind him. Salathiel heard the bar fall in place and for a moment felt alone out in the cold. It would be good to have a room in that house.

He'd certainly move his stuff down tomorrow. Now that the captain had left the fort there would be no place for him except the tent, or one of the huts. Well, he'd see how the captain was.

The silence of midnight had fallen on the fort and little town as he breasted the rise towards the hospital. It was only after an argument with a grenadier sentry that he got past the barricade and into the captain's tent. Ecuyer was still awake and a candle burning. He made no attempt to conceal his satisfaction at seeing Salathiel.

"Did you expect me, sir?" he asked afterwhile.

"Not exactly," replied the captain, "but I did think you might come. It's good of you. You're your own man, you know."

This reply affected Salathiel greatly. He put the tent to rights and made Ecuyer as comfortable as he could. The blankets and cooked food came in splendidly.

"Ourry will undoubtedly be here tomorrow, and the next few days will just be the devil," said Ecuyer. "Mark my words. As for me, a man never knows how strong he is till he gets up out of a sickbed and walks. And now, good night."

Salathiel went and slept in the ark. The roll of drums awakened him at reveille. For a moment he thought he was back at Fort Pitt with Bustle beside him in the casemate. Then he thought of Phoebe. Maybe he would be seeing her before the day was over. But for the next few days there was small time for dreams or running after maidens.

7. Pandora's Pay Chests

MEDICINE is not the only field in which the cure prescribed frequently produces complications. Half the easements of life only introduce aggravations, and so it proved with Captain Ourry's pay chests.

Ask any subaltern hanging about the bar at Pendergasses' what the trouble was with the garrison at the fort, and he would probably tell you all they needed was to be paid. That explanation seemed reasonable, for the Royal Americans and the grenadiers had not been paid for over a year. Some of the militia companies had never been paid at all.

But to assert that all would be well as soon as government settled its accounts with its armed servants would be quite another matter. Ourry, Stewart, Ecuyer, who had all been through paydays before, had no such easy view of the matter. They knew that the most serious trouble often came afterward.

For every one of the good, round gold and silver pieces with the dull, but honest faces of Hanoverian kings minted upon them acted like so many imps of Pandora, once they had left the paymaster's chests, and

seemed to multiply and fructify trouble, disputes, and even violence as
they flew nimbly from hand to hand. The paper notes of the province
of Pennsylvania let loose amongst the militia were even worse.

Still, who would have thought that the mere paying of the garrison
would result in a few days' time in having two men shot and twelve
flogged; a barracks gutted by fire, a riot at Pendergasses', twenty-two de-
sertions, and a mutiny of the grenadiers. Not even Dr. Boyd, who was
something of a cynic, would have prognosticated that—although Captain Ourry, for one, and the commandant, Captain Stewart, for another,
might have. Ecuyer wasn't exactly surprised. He had long had his own
opinions about the state of discipline in the second battalion of the
Royal Americans. And he was treated by the grenadiers only the morning before Ourry got in with a kind of dress rehearsal in advance of
what might be in store.

Rumour, of course, was exceptionally busy. Everyone knew even
before the line-up for reveille roll call came that Captain Ourry's column
was coming through the water gap with the pay chests that very morning. "The pay chests are coming. They'll be here today." Everybody kept
repeating it. Pendergass and his boys had worked all night. The solid
grille by the counter was firmly in place. They were ready.

So was nearly everybody else. For the government was not the only
debtor in the community. Every officer, every soldier owed. They owed
one another, they owed the townsmen. They all owed to Pendergass.
They had all lived on hope, on credit, by borrowing, by begging—finally,
in some cases, by stealing. And now coin was coming; money minted
and printed. And money is one of the principal excitements and irritants
of life. Also, for once, it was a beautiful day. Ourry would undoubtedly get through safely with the wagons. Still, nerves were taut.

Despite the good weather, the day got off to a bad start. Several small
war parties had been hovering around Ourry's column from the time it
left Fort Loudon. But Ourry was wary, and the column proved too
strong to attack. The Indians had reluctantly given him up at the water
gap. Yet it would never do for them to return without any scalps. Consequently, on their way towards the mountains they had stopped to make
a combined surprise attack on an outpost at the Juniata crossing, two
miles west of the fort.

There was a detachment of grenadiers on watch at the ford, and they
had been caught napping. Four of them were scalped and murdered, a
fifth was scalped, but revived to stagger in with the news. It set everybody's nerves on edge. Indeed, the cries and groans of the unfortunate
man could be heard coming from the hospital just as reveille sounded.
Dr. Boyd was trying to prevent him from bleeding to death by sewing
his head skin across with catgut. The muscles clear down the neck would
retract.

Salathiel provided Ecuyer with an extremely early breakfast that

morning. He helped dress him as usual, and reloaded the pistols carefully at Ecuyer's particular behest. He also provided himself with one
of the pair of hand guns of which Frances, the Irish girl at Frazier's,
must still have had the twin. He then cut the captain a stout hickory
stick for a cane. Just as an afterthought he returned Kaysinata's tomahawk to his belt and kept it there.

"Now," said the captain, "stay close by me and do use your eyes in
a circle. Trouble often comes from behind."

With that, Ecuyer hobbled out of the tent onto the muddy grass
street before the huts, where two companies of the grenadiers were
assembling. It was from these men, if from any, that trouble might first
be expected, and it was Ecuyer's intention to nip the flower of anarchy
in the bud.

The scene was a somewhat disorderly one. A red-haired Scotch sergeant was in charge, but seemed not to be very serious about it. The
man in the hospital kept screaming at Dr. Boyd. The sergeant bellowed
perfunctorily at his men. The assembly ceased to beat. But the formation was slow and the men indifferent and surly. Some of them had to
be dragged from the huts. A good many appeared to be absent. Lieutenant Guy, who was supposed to take the report, was in bed in town. A
cheerful light of dawn glowed from the mountains, but everybody felt
ugly. Into this centre of sleepy and surly difficulty Ecuyer, followed by
Albine, came hobbling from his tent.

For a moment the silence of surprise fell heavily. The sergeant was
now busy arguing about something with five or six grouped around him.
He didn't see or hear Ecuyer, nor did those near him. The altercation
was too absorbing. But all the rest saw him.

"By God, it's an officer!" someone shouted.

"He must have been up all night then," yelled another.

A laugh went up.

> "They stay abed in the mornin';
> They won't get up in the mornin' . . ."

a fresh-faced young soldier began to chant. Several others took up the
refrain.

"Collar that lad for me, Albine," said Ecuyer, pointing with his cane.

Albine took the young soldier with a rush. A hearty bully with a horribly scarred face came to his rescue. With his hands on the young
soldier Albine was forced to use his feet. He lashed out and kicked the
newcomer in the stomach and laid him flat and gasping. The sound of
chanting ceased. The young soldier who had begun it now faced Ecuyer
and began to whimper.

There was another moment of ominous silence broken only by the
loud dispute around the sergeant, which was getting hot and hotter.

Some of the men looked ugly and seemed about to close in on Ecuyer, to release the prisoner.

But it was not yet time to draw his pistols, Ecuyer decided. It might precipitate matters. He intended to save the pistols for the general rush, if and when it came. That was the way every mutiny began, a rush usually followed by a murder. Officers are always in the minority. Sometimes they are a nervous temptation.

What prevented the rush from getting under way automatically was probably the clanging argument being carried on by the sergeant and his friends. It seemed to be just about to reach the state of violence. Most of the men stopped to listen.

Sergeant McIntosh, it appeared, had loaned money to his friends. According to him, all loans were to be paid back in full that day. But they were *not* all to be paid back, according to the debtors who surrounded him. The sergeant was no longer red; he was purple. As yet he had not noticed Ecuyer. He now flatly demanded his rights, cursed, and squared off for blood and money.

"Fight!" screamed a young drummer.

"*Sergeant!*" roared Ecuyer.

It was then, for the first and last time, that Albine heard what the little captain was mysteriously famous for—the furious voice of a lion. It was mysterious, because his small body seemed incapable of producing such a sound.

The sergeant staggered under the shock of the captain's voice.

"*Sir?*" said he, brought up standing, and hopelessly astonished.

"Get your damned yeomanry into line," thundered Ecuyer.

The furious bellows of the sergeant were now added to the angry roars of Ecuyer. Everybody was suddenly reminded terribly of authority. The two voices seemed to beat the men into line as waves form sand on a beach. The companies began to assemble.

" '*Shun!*" bellowed the sergeant.

"Call the roll," roared Ecuyer.

The loud, nasal clang of names, mostly Macs, began. Apparently, there were eight deserters. No one would be simply and casually absent on payday.

Ecuyer realized that these deserters must have been absent for some time, and that they had not been reported. The men saw that he knew. Just what the captain would have done under the circumstances, Salathiel wondered many a time afterward. But to a certain extent immediate decision was now taken out of Ecuyer's hands. Events intervened.

The sergeant faced about to report, and in doing so, of course, turned his back on the men. That simple action was the deciding factor. At any rate, Ecuyer sensed that a crisis was at hand.

"Tie that man's arms with your belt, instantly," he said out of the side of his mouth to Salathiel, who still held his man.

Almost at the same instant three men left the ranks and made for the sergeant. They were three from the group with whom the sergeant had just been arguing. One of them drew a knife.

"Jump!" roared Ecuyer to the sergeant, and pulled out his pistols.

The sergeant turned just in time to tackle the man with the knife and throw him violently.

Salathiel slipped in and felled another. The third now hesitated. He began jumping about in a circle with his knuckles touching the ground.

Meanwhile, Ecuyer was left facing the two companies alone, with drawn pistols. It was plain that he would shoot the first who now attempted to leave ranks.

No one broke.

The third man, who had at last made in and tackled the sergeant, now broke loose and came at the captain. Salathiel caught him by the foot and broke his leg. He lay writhing and cursing on the ground directly in front of Ecuyer. The captain, however, did not move.

Every eye was on his pistols and if he had shifted them even for an instant the rush would have followed.

There was one of those moments of crisis and tension which seemed to be suspended in the air on nothing, but like a palpable thing. It lasted possibly ten or even fifteen seconds, then—

Captain Stewart, the adjutant, Captain Forbes of the grenadiers, and three sergeants of the Royal Americans came from between the huts and ranged themselves beside Ecuyer. A company of infantry with fixed bayonets soon followed and stood at the ready.

Ecuyer put up his pistols. He poked a moment in the ground for a firm stance with his cane and leaned on it.

"A remarkably fine winter morning, gentlemen," he said. "How did you hear about it?"

"Corporal McCallum brought the news," replied Captain Stewart, wiping the sweat off his face despite the frosty air.

"Promote him," said Ecuyer. "March these mutinous rascals to the brick barracks in the fort and confine 'em there, Captain Stewart. Have you called the rest of the garrison to arms?"

"Yes, sir, they're standing to now," answered the adjutant.

"Send out and round up any stragglers or loiterers in the town," continued Ecuyer. "Now take these rascals who tried to attack us, Captain Forbes, put irons on them and clap them in the guardhouse. I'll attend to them personally, and promptly." Ecuyer pointed to the soldier who was groaning on the ground with a broken leg. "Send for a surgeon and have him set this man's bones. In his case a splint will do even better than irons."

While these arrangements were being made, the two companies of sullen grenadiers had been marched off. The officers now stood alone.

Captain Ecuyer stepped back and faced them. He took off his hat and bowed from the waist. "My obligations, gentlemen, for saving my life," he said quite simply. At the same time he looked at Salathiel and smiled.

Captain Stewart wondered. Not a word of reproach!

They all walked over to the fort and into headquarters together. Outside on the parade the battalion of Royal Americans and the company of grenadiers, which had not been concerned in the incident of the morning, stood to arms and at attention. The other two grenadier companies were already confined and howling in their barracks, where the smashing of benches was going on. Several officers came in from the town hurriedly, sweating at reporting late. The commandant, Captain Ecuyer, Forbes, and the adjutant consulted earnestly over a big table at one end of the room. Something was suddenly decided. All but Ecuyer rose and hurried out.

Ecuyer came over to Salathiel, where he stood waiting by the orderly table next the door.

"You have done well, Albine," he said. "Come to me after the pay is over and you shall receive your reward. Two pennies a day was the arrangement, if I remember correctly." The captain smiled. "But that is not *quite* all, is it? No, in this case there is something more. This is it." He reached out and shook Salathiel by the hand. "Good-bye," he said quietly. "I shall not require your services again. Remember me sometimes in the years to come as a friend."

Salathiel could not reply. Tears came to his eyes. He wrung the captain's hand and dashed out the door.

So it was over.

But he and the captain were friends. The savage boy from the forest had achieved that. In how many days? The pennies would tell exactly. He had forgotten how long it was. He was a man now. Ecuyer had made him that. And he was free! There would never be another Ecuyer. One gave one's self that way once only. Now once more he was alone. But not alone in the forest. The inhabited world eastward lay before him.

While these things passed like lightning though his thoughts he strode mightily across the square where the troops were lined up.

At the gate he realized that people from the town were pouring eagerly into the fort. He thrust them aside almost rudely. A punishment had been ordered. Word of that, or of a hanging, always flew about like wildfire.

Several people shouted at Salathiel that he was missing a good thing as they passed him. He kept on his way. He felt he was glad to miss whatever he might be missing. He was glad he was through with all of it and free to go where he liked.

He went directly down to Pendergasses' and pushed open the heavy door impatiently. The contrast of the interior of the tavern with the scenes he had just left was a pleasant surprise. The big hearth room seemed lapped in undisturbed peace. At first glance it looked to be almost deserted. A fire flickered and smouldered on the hearth. Phoebe and two of the Pendergass girls were seated knitting in a far corner. Captain Jack was dozing on a bench. At the big table Yates had his cards laid out, studying some intricate combination. Behind the grille at the counter, old Garrett and three of his boys were making a final check of the goods ready on the shelves. Except for some giggling from the girls and the ticking of a big clock, the place was silent. His private drama and the elation of the moment of his release vanished as he stepped over the threshold.

Phoebe looked up at him and smiled. For a moment he forgot everything he had been thinking. He stopped. Yates looked keenly at him as if he sensed something unusual. He shuffled his cards quite easily, and laughed.

"*Well*," said he, running the cards through the air from one hand to the other fluidly, "so you've come to stay, Mr. Albine!"

"Why, yes," admitted Salathiel astonished. "But how did you know?"

"Oh, just by this and that," replied Yates.

"Eh, what's that?" exclaimed Captain Jack, coming out of his doze on the bench, and sitting up.

"Why, Sal's one of us now," explained Yates.

"Why, of course he is. Sartin! I knew that all along," cried Captain Jack, smiting his knee. "How about a little toddy before the crowd comes roarin' in? Money and thirst will turn this place into a bear garden before the afternoon's over."

" 'Spect you're about right, Jack," said old Garrett. Leaning on the counter, he addressed the girls. "Now, the very first stranger that comes in here I want you young women to go upstairs right away and look after your mamma. And don't you pay any attention no matter how much noise you hear. There's like to be plenty!"

8. The Lids Come Off

CAPTAIN JACK proved an accurate prophet. Ourry's column poured rumbling, splashing, and clattering into Bedford about eleven o'clock in the morning. By one o'clock Pendergasses' was doing a roaring business with the new officers and men who came with it. They had been paid before leaving Fort Loudon; money burned their pockets. Once again solid coins rang on Garrett's tables and counter; bounced into his till. Fifty-four wagons with their crews and drivers were in the convoy, besides the reinforcements for Bouquet, of both regulars and militia, who had acted as escort for the paymaster's chests.

Everyone in town, and anyone from the fort who could get away, including wounded and sick from the hospital just able to hobble, lined up along the level stretch of highway before Pendergasses' to see the column come in along the road from the water gap.

Smith's Associators, a company of volunteer, militia riflemen, dressed in breechclouts, coloured headcloths, and long, fringed, leather leggings, were in the van. They strode nonchalantly but in good order, led by the vigorous, half-savage figure of Captain James Smith himself, a youthful replica of Captain Jack, looking more like an Indian than a white man. These riflemen were all frontiersmen raised from the vicinity of the Conococheague and Path Valley. They had many friends and relatives in Bedford with whom to exchange greetings and profane repartee as they passed by.

Captain Ourry, Mr. Fagg, the paymaster, and several officers of the staff of the incoming troops came next in a body, mounted on rather sorry-looking nags.

Ourry himself looked tired and harassed. He was a tall, cadaverous man. He rode gallantly, but with the exasperated embarrassment of a man with very long legs on too short a horse. The boisterous half cheers, half jeers of the crowd were visibly hard for him to bear. In reality, most of the inhabitants meant only to be roughly complimentary. But Ourry replied to no one except Burent, who, upon hailing him, received a cordial word and a smile with, "Well, sir, you see we're arrived. And we didn't have to use your sled runners after all."

Following him came the main attraction: three heavy, iron-barred, and mud-splashed coaches, each with a triple-padlocked pay chest firmly lashed behind. They were closely guarded and surrounded by a troop of mounted rangers in leather helmets. From the windows of these ponderous vehicles peered the smooth, pink, and well-fed countenances of the English clerks of the paymaster. They, in particular, received an uproarious but good-natured ribbing from the crowd.

Some people were unable to resist the apparently magnetic attraction of the metal in the chests. They followed the coaches to the very gates of the fort. But most of the crowd remained to watch the rest of the procession pass by, and these on the whole were the better rewarded.

For immediately after the coaches came a battalion of grenadiers in sparkling new equipment. These men were going forward to reinforce Bouquet at Fort Pitt. They marched with a verve and with so much vigour and obvious good discipline as to suggest that victory was already in their grasp. No such troops had been seen on the frontier for many a day. Their leader, Major Moncreith, rode by erect with the keen look of a sparkling but dangerous blade. An indomitable dandy, he brought forth the admiring huzzas of the crowd.

"By godson!" exclaimed old Garrett to Burent, "I've seen many a detachment pass to the frontiers since Johnny Forbes's time, but never more proper soldiers than these. And to think they belong to the same regiment as the present grenadier battalion at the fort! It only goes to show what idling in garrison will do. I hope the example of these new fellows will spread. But here come the wagons! Why, it's the finest convoy and the best loaded I ever did see. Burent, your hand shows here. And all newly painted, every one of 'em!"

Garrett was only voicing what many another thought. This was the most considerable and hopeful-looking effort government had made for years. It boded well for Colonel Bouquet. Here were men, arms, rations, pay, and ammunition.

For over a mile down the road the big white-topped and canvas-draped Pennsylvania wagons stretched off into the distance. Whips cracked, and the relieved wagoners shouted and sang. Indeed, a company of no ordinary voices brought up the rear with a volume of true harmony. It was a detachment of the Royal Americans, Welshmen, recruited exclusively from the Welsh settlements along the Delaware and in the Welsh Hills about the sources of the Brandywine in eastern Pennsylvania. They looked fit. They even looked glad at returning to active service. And they made the valley ring.

"Ecuyer will be glad to see these lads back again," mused Burent. "And look, Mr. Pendergass, there's a special nod of Fortune for you!"

"What do I see, what *do* I see?" shouted old Garrett. "Burent, I'll not forget this. B'God if I do!"—three wagons at the tail of the procession were just then detaching themselves from the column on the road and driving down into the innyard. Garrett fairly galloped off on his old feet to meet them.

They proved to be, as Burent well knew, three loads of goods and supplies from Harris's and Philadelphia, the arrival of which Garrett had long despaired of. At Loudon Burent had "pressed" them for the convoy and passed them on through. Now they came in the precise nick of time to replenish Garrett's storehouse and shelves. The old man could not do enough to show his gratitude to Burent or his appreciation to one Jobe Stottelmyer, the chief wagoner, who had rounded up his recalcitrant drivers, taken advantage of opportunity, and brought home the bacon.

So now the big wagons and their teams stood steaming in the yard by the river, with their loads high upon them. Garrett roared for hands to come and help unload, stopping only now and then during the process to knit his fingers together with satisfaction. Even the women joined in, carrying away the lighter articles.

Yet fast as the Pendergasses had worked, the news of the arrival of the three trade wagons spread faster. A number of local traders and small merchants came to stand about talking out of the sides of their mouths, plainly disgruntled and envious. Here was another proof to them that Pendergass and the authorities had a mutually profitable understanding.

In the troubles of the days which immediately followed, undoubtedly some of these men played their small troublesome parts. But so on the opposite side of the stage did Stottelmyer and his drivers, seven good men and true, who were now temporarily added to the house garrison at Pendergasses'.

Perhaps, both Albine and Yates contributed unthinkingly to a hidden resentment by their possibly too zealous assistance in helping to clear the yard of all idlers and strange lookers-on. But Captain Jack and his assistants were not in a delicate mood. They were even forcibly hasteful at times. There was small time to argue. In a few moments the first rush of Ourry's thirsty men might be expected to break like a wave against the bar.

Ourry's hungry, thirsty, but fresh and good-natured men were the first to appear. They hastened to make the most of their advantage over their comrades in the garrison, who could not all be paid until the next day at least, and from shortly after one o'clock until early evening they thronged the bar, drank steadily, ate heartily, and bought curiously of the most unexpected and useless articles, as soldiers do. In general, they possessed and overran the place.

Big as the huge hearth room was it could accommodate only a certain number. From Garrett's standpoint the art of coping with a garrison pay successfully therefore consisted in serving rapidly and keeping the crowd moving. Hence the man with the interminable narrative or the too lengthy and lugubrious song was always moved after a time, he scarcely knew how, out onto a stretch of greensward along the riverbank.

Some space there had been fenced off and provided with benches, a couple of fiddlers, a dancing bear, fighting cocks, and old Cloud Face, the Creek, as its master of ceremonies. That office—with a few drinks in him—the old Indian managed to fill expertly with an ironical dignity and a consciously comic air in the performance of it. His squaw and younger progeny brought pipes, tobacco, and liquor.

The officers and "gentry" were much harder to handle. The tables in the big room were reserved for them. Here in short was the weak point in Garrett's arrangements. Here had trouble—quarrels, disputes, duels, and even more serious disturbances—arisen in the past. Officers would linger over their cards and liquor. Traders, farmers, hunters, and wagoners gathered, drank, ate, talked, and disputed. Deals and bargains were made. Lawyers, even ministers were sometimes present. For all thronged to town on payday. And everybody found some occasion and excuse to drop in at Pendergasses'. Liquor flowed: wine, rum, and whisky. Of late, Garrett had also imported much Holland gin. Inevitably there was some trouble. And the hearth, or common, room was always the crux of the situation.

To cope with the various situations which might arise there required tact, firmness, good nature, and a knowledge of local character. Sometimes a swift and judicious use of force was in order.

Captain Jack, Yates, Salathiel, Nat Murray, and Mat Pendergass were told off by Garrett to have the big room in their special care. They began by weeding out certain idlers, old topers, penniless loafers, and borrowers who otherwise, on one excuse or another, would have infested and monopolized valuable space. This first unpleasantness having automatically been got over with, the establishment cleared its decks for more profitable action.

It was during the brief pause before Ourry's men arrived, when for a few minutes Salathiel had a short interval of leisure to look about him, that he first began fully to understand what a crisis in the affairs of Garrett and his establishment the occasion of a garrison pay provided. At such times the old man's friends, neighbours, and debtors rallied about him. But troublemakers also assembled. Hence, his dispositions and arrangements for meeting possible complications were both ingenious and of long standing.

The sheer convenience and wisdom of the two separate houses with the bridge between them now became more fully apparent. All the women and children were completely withdrawn and cut off from the tavern side of the establishment. The door giving access across the bridge was barred. The animals and poultry were brought into the barns and sheds and left there under the strict care of the younger Indian servants and of the watchdogs. The last by no means to be despised.

In the notable pay of '63, Garrett was enabled to put an extra guard on his horses and wagons and outside storehouses, owing to the presence of Stottelmyer and his drivers. Deserters were especially liable to become horse thieves, but the loss of a valuable draft horse and yokemate from the wagons was not to be tolerated. Garrett anticipated at least some attempts on his stables. In fact, this pay he looked forward to trouble in general, and was glad to be able to count upon Stottelmyer and his men.

The rest of the arrangements were simple, but effective enough. Like most good arrangements they seemed to have suggested themselves.

The Negro slaves, men, women, and youngsters, were assembled under the able tyranny of Agrippina, their grandmother, to cook, serve, and run errands for "de quality" in the hearth room. Pina sat on the raised hearth, switch in hand, watching the roasting meats, cooking, and overlooking the service of the tables. In the course of time Pina had reaped a small fortune from such occasions. All tips must be deposited in her apron, to be buried afterward beyond hope of resurrection under her cabin floor. Woe to the smart youngster who tried to hold back a penny from her.

Behind the counter and grille Garrett and his sons stood ready to supply drink or display the goods on hand. A small movable section of the bar permitted a sally onto the floor of the big room, in force, if necessary. And it was through this gate that the better customers at the tables also were served with the more select vintages while the crowd satisfied itself at the bar.

Captain Jack, Yates, Albine, and the others assigned to watching the progress of events and business in the big room sat at the gigantic table with the iron candlesticks at both ends, near the hearth. Or they moved about the room, mingling with various groups from time to time. To the casual eye at least they appeared to be only ordinary guests of the tavern. But they were always there, either in full force or in relays, and especially after dark when the frictions of the day often tended to burst into flame. Prevention of trouble was, of course, the ideal. Force was a last resort. For those who peacefully fell by the way, overcome by their own potations, the floor of a near-by shed had been covered deep with hay and softly set apart.

Such were Garrett's preparations for the moments of crisis in his life and business marked by paydays. And if his precautions and arrangements seemed to discover an undue apprehension, or to be fatuously elaborate, the answer is that they were not so. They arose out of necessity by experience.

To be sure, he might have obtained an armed guard for his premises from the commandant of the garrison. But to have done so would have been to confess that his liquor business was the cause of disorder with which he could not cope himself. The purveying of liquor Garrett regarded simply as a necessary, though a somewhat regrettable, function of his establishment. Its other activities were to his mind much more vital and important.

Between the Blue Mountains and Fort Pitt his was the only place where an exchange of civilized commodities went on on a large scale.

Take tobacco, for instance, or salt: he practically supplied them wholesale to the entire frontier. And then there were cloth, thread, small cutlery, and tools. Harris's, a hundred miles eastward, was the next place where a woman could get a thimble, or anything else feminine for herself. And the indwelling and social aspects of his establishment had long assumed an importance that was even political. In short, a bright light shone from Garrett's windows into the darkness of the surrounding wilderness.

All of this, the work of his mind, heart, and hands, the result of the patience, toil, and collaboration of his good wife and remarkable family, was not to be casually committed to the indifferent care of an "armed guard" at times of crisis. It required a diplomacy which only its proprietor could invent and supply, for Garrett's position was often a ticklish one.

Between the good-natured indifference or the toleration of the military authorities and the thinly veiled hostility of a certain portion of the community, Garrett hoed a difficult but expertly planted and cultivated row. Like all good husbandmen he had to garner his harvest when the season came. At such times he had the support and sympathy of all those who had sense enough to realize the importance of his establishment to the territory at large. But he also had would-be rivals who would ruin him if they could.

To Salathiel these events disclosed themselves with the curious quality of a continuous combination of inevitability and surprise. To the more sophisticated and lettered mind of Edward Hamilton Yates they seemed to occur like a naturally arranged but fiery little drama with its complications, violent climax, and final tragedy.

As remarked, the serving and entertainment of the new men who had come with Ourry went off well enough. They had begun trooping in about one o'clock and by four or thereabouts they were well satisfied. Many of them had then strolled off to loiter about the town and camp. A small group of officers lingered over their wine in the common room. But the excitement and novelty, the crowding and rush were over. Even the townsmen and wagoners who had gathered in felt this, and the bar was beginning to be quiet and comparatively deserted again.

"Well, you see how it goes, boys," said Captain Jack, putting his feet up on a chair, "just keep 'em happy and your eyes cocked, and it will all pass off all right." He looked unexpectedly relieved, however.

"Yep, looks like a quiet day after all," remarked John Nogle, the miller, whose mill lay only a half mile up the river from the fort. "Guess I'll go home now. Give me a tuppenny twist and a new clay pipe, Garrett. Beats all how the women kin smash 'em." Nogle nevertheless looked about him a bit disappointed. He had privately hoped for at least a *little* trouble.

Garrett smiled, knowing how well his hearty neighbour loved a fight. "If they don't begin to pay the rest of them today, belike it will pass off quiet enough," said he.

But they did begin to pay.

The first evidence of it was a continuous hubbub going on up at the fort, and a message from Ecuyer asking Burent to report to him immediately.

"I guess the captain has his hands full and the pay must be going forward. But that ain't exactly an easy and reassurin' noise up at the fort, is it?" remarked Garrett to Burent.

"No, it's not," agreed that neat, brown little Englishman, who obviously left reluctantly the shelter of the comfortable room he had been occupying upstairs. He bade Salathiel, who carried his leather hand trunk halfway up the hill for him, a regretful good-bye, and trudged on with the trunk on his shoulder.

Salathiel stood for a moment listening. Underneath the normal sounds of cheerful excitement rose a steady angry roar, a kind of threatening and continuous protest.

"What d'ya make of that, Albine?" demanded Captain Jack, who was standing before the door listening when Salathiel returned.

"I allow they've decided to pay the Royal Americans first, which means the grenadiers last. And the grenadiers confined to barracks are raising the roof," Salathiel replied.

This surmise was soon more or less painfully confirmed. A rush of customers from town. It was merchandise rather than drink that they wanted. Their accounts had suddenly been settled by the officers of the Royal Americans, they said, and they had hurried to Pendergasses' to be the first to replenish their supplies. They also reported considerable trouble at the fort. The battalion of Royal Americans was being held under arms, and there was a rumour that the mutinous grenadiers might not be paid at all. What the confined grenadiers thought of this was already patent to anyone within a mile of the barracks.

Doubtless it was this tense and disturbed state of affairs at the fort which accounted for the fact that the militia, which liked to be called the "Pennsylvania line", but for all that was usually paid last, nevertheless appeared next at Pendergasses', waving their paper bills and anxious to turn them into coin on almost any terms.

Garrett was considerably put out by this development. He must now be prepared to act as a banker on a considerable scale. Ordinarily he was willing to honour the paper currency of the province at a little over half its sterling exchange value at Philadelphia. Usually he made a good thing out of trading in paper money, despite the risk.

But the present case was different. The notes for the pay of the provincial militia in '63 were in the form of a special emergency issue authorized by the legislature for the purpose. No one as yet had had the opportunity to learn whether they would pass current or not. The privilege of first making this patriotic experiment was now to be Garrett's, and Yates thought it only right to inform the old man that the proprietors of Pennsylvania had not yet approved the issue, and that they might not do so.

Here was a quandary. If the notes proved valueless, Garrett would be in for a shocking loss. If he refused to take them, riot might ensue.

Around the big table Garrett, Yates, several officers of the militia, and one or two local Solomons gathered in conclave. Meanwhile, the militia and their numerous creditors, plus about fifty wagoners, became more and more impatient and importunate, damned the authorities as cheats; the legislature as Quaker bastards, and Garrett as a Shylock. Unless trade began soon, it was plain there would be pillage and violence. Only the trickle of a small quantity of liquor over the bar was serving to stave it off.

"We've been had," roared a big, moonfaced corporal in a bottle-green coat far too small for him. "It's just pretty paper with a promise on it. That's what it is. Here's what I think of 'em." And with that he twisted up a pound note and lit his pipe. "But there's no tobaccy in my pipe," he roared, pausing in the act. "No, I can choke on the smoke of liars, and damn well like it!"

A menacing growl of agreement went up. The crowd surged forward, and several laid hands on the grille and began to shake it.

"Just a moment, men," said a commanding voice. Major Cadwalader, a large florid man, impressive in his fine-fitting uniform, had mounted on the big table and stood aloft facing the crowd.

"Now listen. Mr. Pendergass and I have arrived at an agreement," he continued. "His house will take your notes up to half their face value in trade. I might say I've given my personal bond to him to cover the amount. So you can see *I* think the notes are good. Jennings, you can put *that* in your pipe and smoke it," he called to the big corporal.

A roar of laughter at the look of woebegone consternation on the corporal's face, and a cheer for the major shook the room.

At the same moment young Arthur Davison sprang onto the counter behind the grille and began to parade up and down it, shouting, "Well, well, what d'ya lack?" The crowd surged forward laughing, this time good-naturedly, and the trade began.

"You young devil, I'll have the hide off your behind for that," said old Garrett. "Didn't I tell you to keep in the house whar ye belong?" The boy fled upstairs laughing, for he knew Garrett was really pleased with his presence of mind.

Selling over the counter continued briskly, despite a lack of change and small coin. But the halt in affairs had nevertheless been unfortunate.

Cadwalader's patriotic offer had prevented a riot, but the major was known to have more political ambition than estate. So actually it was Garrett who took the risk on trading goods and hard liquor for soft money. And the resentment of the men had been focused temporarily upon Garrett and his people. Some of this resentment remained and certain people continued to cultivate it.

Captain Jack and his helpers, more especially Albine and Yates, began to be conscious of this as the afternoon wore on and the militia and their friends continued to monopolize the big room. Their officers, a number of traders, clerks, and the more prosperous wagoners and leaders of the teamsters occupied the tables which they could scarcely be asked to vacate before their betters and superiors, the ranking officers of the garrison and the more substantial citizens of the town, should arrive.

Among those present, obviously inclined to trouble, and being as unpleasant as they dared, were Lieutenant Neville and Ensign Aiken, Maxwell, Japson's disgruntled clerk, and several other characters whom Salathiel thought he remembered having seen not long before at Ligonier. Three or four of the teamsters from Japson's scattered caravan also were among the crowd, and they seemed bent on making things uncomfortable for Salathiel and Yates.

Yates, in particular, was hard put to it to keep his temper at times. Unfortunately, he had been overheard warning Pendergass about the doubtful nature of the notes, earlier in the afternoon. Neville and his friends were making the most of that. The word was even being passed along to newcomers. Both Salathiel and the young lawyer could plainly feel the atmosphere of gathering hostility that followed them and seemed to be closing in upon them.

Captain Jack was also soon aware that a train of powder was deliberately being laid. To his mind it led back plainly enough to Neville and Maxwell. But that would have been hard to prove. He nevertheless took measures to prevent some spark from setting it off, by calling Albine and Yates over to the big table and introducing them to Major Cadwalader. The major engaged them briskly in talk, which probably prevented the flash that was soon bound to come. At least he delayed it. Or perhaps the delay in the impending explosion was only accidental after all.

For a ferocious growling and scared shouts, the hoarse, agonized screams of a man in mortal trouble just then brought most of the people in the room to their feet and rapidly emptied the place of friends as well as enemies.

Jennings, the note-burning corporal, had, it appeared, undertaken an amicable wrestling match with the dancing bear. Corporal Jennings now lay on the ground, groaning hoarsely. Part of his face, most of his clothes, and a portion of that valuable part of the trunk which so conveniently covers the ribs had been clawed off him and lay about in bloody flecks and patches on the ground. The angry bear had departed across the river.

Into the midst of this excitement now descended the first companies of the Royal Americans who had been paid, given town leave, and dismissed. They fell upon the place like locusts. Whatever had been the plan of Neville and his friends was rapidly obliterated by the Royal Americans.

A number of the regular officers from the fort now appeared, settled their accounts with Garrett, and sat down at the big tables and to enjoy the finest vintages and fare which the house afforded.

Towards evening Captain Stewart, the commandant, accompanied by no one else than Ecuyer appeared. The latter was assisted by Burent. Ecuyer looked pale but more vigorous. He was welcomed by Dr. Boyd as the "best living example of my skill".

Room was eagerly made at the big table for the two ranking officers whose presence, with the expressions of obvious relief which they both unconsciously displayed, was a warrant that the affairs of the garrison must now be in a more satisfactory way.

Thus, with the rest of his customers either satisfied or in process of becoming so, Garrett himself now came over and joined his more distinguished guests at the big table. Conversation went on, and a feeling of greater ease gradually pervaded the place.

But the pay had not passed off entirely without incident. That was soon learned from both Stewart and Ecuyer. "After the lesson we gave those mutinous rogues this morning," said Stewart, "Ecuyer and I both hoped the day would go off quietly enough. But we underestimated the capacity for deviltry in the grenadiers confined to barracks. I admit I thought, when we told them they would be paid tomorrow the same as the rest of the regiment—all except those had up for court-martial—that it would quiet 'em down. And it did, until some of your men, Major Cadwalader, smuggled in liquor to the first company of grenadiers. As a result, someone set the barracks on fire from the inside. Half the roof was scorched before we could subdue those fellows and get the flames quenched. And it was some of your whisky, Mr. Pendergass, I am afraid. I hear you have two kinds; the fightin' kind, and the cryin' sort. *Do* try and see that the grenadiers get only the weeping variety hereafter. It's contrition and tears we want to encourage amongst 'em from now on."

"I'll take the worst of these rascals along with me over the mountains to Fort Pitt in the first convoy," said Ecuyer. "We can't try them en masse, and the severest punishment they can have will be to go forward to the seat of war, and to Colonel Bouquet, who has peculiar powers of persuasion."

"Fightin' for to keep on wearin' your own har is wonderful soberin'. I've known it to turn the pertest idjets plumb thoughtful," added Captain Jack.

"We'll see, we'll soon see," said Ecuyer dryly.

"I trust the pay of the grenadiers will pass off without further unfortunate incident," said Captain Frazier. Ecuyer respected Frazier, and now tried to turn the matter aside.

"I know at least one man who won't be led into much temptation by his pay," laughed Ecuyer. "Burent, give Mr. Albine his bag of pennies. I'll be bound, Albine, if you're not the most princely rewarded man, next to myself, that I know."

The captain then hastened to explain that Salathiel was receiving two pennies a day for his services, according to the agreement made between them when Salathiel had first been taken into Ecuyer's service at Fort Pitt. Everyone was amused and laughed at him.

Salathiel took it in good part. That Ecuyer seemed more like his old self, that he was able to come down to Pendergasses' and enjoy the company, would have made ten times the chaff that Salathiel received welcome to him.

". . . and I had a hard time convincing the paymaster I really needed so many pennies," concluded Ecuyer.

That there was something else in the bag besides pennies, Salathiel

soon discovered. He could feel a fairly large object wrapped up inside
He didn't care to open the bag before the company, but he nodded grate
fully to the captain, who looked pleased by his obvious gratitude. It re
mained for Neville to introduce the only deliberately sour note tha
marred the evening. He was sitting with the rest of the militia office
about Major Cadwalader at another table, and remarked as he watche
Salathiel heft his bag:

"A whole bagful of pennies, eh! Well, I guess in the end we all ge
paid just about as we deserve."

"Maybe that's what makes you look forward to your court-martial s
confidently, lieutenant," countered Salathiel.

Yates chuckled; it was an answer after his own heart. Neville turne
a fiery red and started to rise. Major Cadwalader laid a detaining han
on his arm.

"Now, now," said Garrett, "let's not spoil a nice quiet day. I wish yo
young cockerels would quit foining at each other. Do, do! You migh
find that bear and try to throw him, if you feel so ornery. Personally, I'
like just a little peace over my mug tonight."

Several others voicing their hearty approval of these sentiment
Neville was forced to sit down and contain himself.

"You might try some of your wit pleasant-like," chimed in Captai
Jack, supporting Garrett. "Now, they tell me *you're* quite a hand at
story, Mr. Yates."

Yates began . . .

"Gentlemen, it's closing time," said Garrett abruptly. "I hate to brea
up the company, but you can scarcely expect me to disregard regulation
when the commandant himself is here."

With that he and the boys began closing down the bar. The roor
gradually emptied.

Yates and Albine went upstairs to their rooms above the inn. Salathie
lay in the comfortable feather bed before blowing out his candle, turr
ing over the contents of the bag Burent had brought him from Ecuye.
and looking at the simple, but to him luxurious and remarkable furnish
ings of his little chamber. There was a white curtain in the window,
rough pine bureau, several jars and basins, and a rush-bottomed chai
In the bag were nineteen score pennies, tuppence, and two brigh
guineas wrapped in paper with the small dictionary he had used so ofte
in toiling over the captain's papers. This out of Ecuyer's stark povert
constituted a princely gift. How could he ever be grateful enough fo
the way things were turning out? He lay back, lost in gratitude, an
profoundly pleased at the comparative eminence and wealth to which h
had attained. He luxuriated in the enormous comfort of his surrounc
ings. What a bed! How well things were going!

Garrett paused to tap at Salathiel's door before retiring.

"Good night to ye, Albine," he said. "Don't ye go to sleep with you candle burning. Ye might set the place afire. Best get plenty o' sleep, too, young fellow. The hardest day's ahead of us tomorrow—and it's late now."

Salathiel took the hint. He reassured old Garrett by blowing out his light there and then.

If he had known how hard a day lay before him he would not have slept as soundly as he did. It was, as Garrett expected, "the hardest day", remembered for years afterward as the day of the big brawl at Pendergasses'.

9. The Big Brawl at Pendergasses'

THE REMAINDER OF THE GRENADIERS were paid next day. That provided difficulty enough in itself. The grenadiers were in a subdued but still an ugly mood. They threatened to take out their sense of indignation against the universe in general on helpless bystanders, since the authorities at the fort had made it plain that whip and gallows were on tap there as usual.

This feeling of disgruntled indignation had come to a head and the crisis had passed the day before, when Ecuyer had prevented its spreading into a general mutiny. Those who had become violently active in discontent, or too vocal, were now laid by the heels or had deserted. The chief grievance of not being paid had been removed. The suppressed resentment that remained was now forced into another path. It was now directed by the grenadiers against the other troops in garrison, more especially at the new arrivals. The result was a continuous series of personal and individual fights, grenadiers against the world.

From early morning, therefore, everybody at Pendergasses' had his hands full on the second day of the pay. Captain Jack and his helpers had a lively time. Once or twice it was necessary for Garrett and his sons to emerge from behind the counter and join in the skirmishes. Shortly before noon an attempt was made on the stables, probably by men intending to take horses in order to desert. But this was promptly squelched and put an end to by Jobe Stottelmyer and his drivers. Three grenadiers and two militiamen were turned over to Captain Stewart at the fort. He confined them.

After that it was "better". Most of those whose sense of grievance tended towards muscular outbreak had by noon been tired out, thrown out, subdued, thrashed, or overpowered. They now retired to tend to their abrasions or to sleep off the effects of their celebration. Milder and less indignant natures, even some grenadiers, remained to fraternize with the rest of the crowd; to eat and drink heavily, and to buy tobacco and small comforts while the rapidly diminishing stock held out.

About two o'clock trade rose to a crescendo. Most of the officers now came forward and settled their accounts with Garrett. Some of them even thanked him for his patience and generosity. By three o'clock it looked as if everything would end fortunately and the pay pass into local history as a strenuous but profitable interlude. Garrett was even seen once or twice to be rubbing his hands with satisfaction behind the bar. So far only one man had been seriously injured and a dancing bear lost. The bear might come back later. As the flood tide of custom began to ebb it became evident that a large sum in good hard cash had been washed in and would remain behind the bar—with little wreckage to mark it.

"So far so good!" confided Garrett to Captain Jack during a lull. "We must have grossed nigh six hundred pounds."

"So good so far," answered Captain Jack, "or that's the way I'd put it if you see it as I do."

Just then a large number of militia and wagoners came in, mostly for trade and small articles, and Garrett was recalled to his place behind the counter.

Captain Jack's remark, however, was not merely a cynical aside.

He had begun to notice that, as the officers and soldiers from the fort satisfied themselves and departed in time for the evening parade, their places were gradually being taken by customers less welcome and less profitable. And these customers, it seemed, had come to stay, for the brighter military colours faded out entirely at last into nothing but home-spun, the grimy deerskin shirts of some of the more bedraggled militia, or the soiled butternut of certain odd characters from town. Many of these were hangers-on of the garrison, doubtful and ugly-looking customers, for whom Garrett had little use.

Conversation gradually lagged, or was conducted by groups that appeared to know a dangerous secret withheld from the rest of mankind. Then there would be an occasional laugh, suddenly stifled. Tobacco fumes grew thicker as the silence grew more dense. Now and then someone else came into the room, bought a drink for himself and sat down preferably in a corner.

"I can't make head or tail of the way the trade's going," said Garrett. "Many of these gentry I never did see before. Probably they're drivers come with the convoy, or some of that scum that Japson left behind him. They buy by the hap'orth, and they act like they wanted to string it out.'

"Likely somethin's brewin'," suggested Captain Jack. "I kinda feel it 'cumulating like rheumatiz in the fall."

"It seems to me I see a remarkable number of our former friends and acquaintances," growled Salathiel to Yates. "Look, there are five or six of St. Clair's people from Ligonier bunched over in that corner around that Irishman O'Toole, the one whose nevvy got himself scalped top o' the mountain. Remember?"

"And shot, too, by one Albine, I believe," remarked Yates. "Didn't O'Toole swear he was going to get you for it?"

"He did," agreed Salathiel. "And two of these fellows from the militia we brought here to be tried for desertion seem to be in the room now. I'm not sure, though."

"Probably they've been turned loose by their officers after being lightly admonished," suggested Yates. "That's about the size of it."

"Quite a parcel o' the rest of this gang is traders and drivers from Japson's caravan, the ones we driv off," added Murray, who was standing near by. "And their friends from roundabouts, too."

"Doubtless," said Yates, "friends, and friends' friends. Well, our sins seem to be catching up with us."

"All we need is Japson and St. Clair sitting here to be sure of a fight," mused Salathiel.

"Japson and St. Clair are both in Philadelphia," answered Yates, "but I suppose their memory is still kept green. I'll bet you'll find Neville, and Maxwell, that hangdog clark of Japson's, droppin' in soon. And Lieutenant Guy and Ensign Aiken—with their friends. That's when the trouble will begin, I opine."

"Speck you're about right," drawled Captain Jack. "All this gatherin' needs is a leader to start mischief. Nice fix you young fellers got yourself into, if I do say it! Now all of you keep settin' behind the big table. Have Pina bring you a plate of victuals, and jes keep settin' and act natural like you was havin' supper. Don't *you* start the ball rolling. Leave that to them. I'm going over to speak to Garrett behind the grille, and I'll be back in a wink."

For some moments Captain Jack continued to talk earnestly with Garrett, who at first shook his head and then appeared to agree.

Meanwhile Yates, Albine, Nat Murray, and Tom Pendergass were served by old Pina. They all sat along one side of the big table next to the hearth, facing out, and keeping the table between themselves and the rest of the room. "Like a breastwork," said Murray, who had no trouble in giving a lively and convincing appearance of a man eating his supper naturally.

Presently Captain Jack came back and brought Stottelmyer with him, who also sat down and ate heartily. That made six of them together behind the long table.

Nothing had happened so far. It would have been hard to say just why the temperature seemed to be rising, but it was. They sat quiet, ready for any moves. The surly, muttered conversation in the room buzzed on. Finally Yates got out his cards and laid them before him for solitaire. He was inventing a new game.

None of them ever forgot that evening.

To anyone dropping in casually it would perhaps have seemed as though a half-fuddled company of fifty or more congenial topers were frowsting in the warmth and strong tobacco smoke through which the candles burned dimly and the lanthorns along the counter glared like dim but disapproving eyes. Draughts, chess, dice, and various card games were going on here and there. There was some conversation, but on the whole the company was a remarkably silent one. It was that which gave those on watch about the table and behind the bar a strong impression that they were on guard; that they, and everybody else in the room, were waiting for something to occur; that the tension was growing.

Once or twice a complete silence fell.

For some time now no one had even pretended to buy anything at the counter.

"What d'ye lack?" cried one of the Pendergass twins. "What d'ye lack?"

A laugh or chuckle here and there was the only reply.

But since everything so far was orderly enough, there was nothing to be done about it. Finally Captain Jack got up and suggested to Garrett that he might close the place for the night. But Garrett refused.

"I can't do that," he said. "It's fairly early yet. Word would go round we cater only to big spenders and close our doors on the poor ones. It's the worst thing they could say about us. Besides, if they are going to start anything, putting them out would only bring it to a head."

Captain Jack went back to the table and sat down. He had to acknowledge Garrett was right. But it seemed to him that everybody had been hanging on the result of his conversation, and that they had guessed what it was about.

There was now a complete silence in the place except for some snapping of new wood on the fire. Nat Murray leaned forward and mopped his brow.

At that moment the door opened, letting a great draught of fresh air in, and Lieutenants Neville and Guy, Ensign Aiken, Mr. Maxwell, and three tough-looking followers entered the room. A number of profane greetings were exchanged while the three strangers lost themselves in the crowd, and the officers and Maxwell came forward and sat down opposite Captain Jack and his company, whose plates had now long lain empty before them.

"Howdy, gentlemen," said Captain Jack, "we've kind o' been waitin' for ye."

"That's uncommon nice of you," replied Guy, seating himself about opposite Yates, and glancing down at his cards.

"Why, yes," put in Neville, "we hardly expected so much courtesy as that—and to find you all together! It's an unexpected pleasure." He ran his eye warily along the line across the table, but sat down unabashed across from Captain Jack.

Aiken faced Murray. And Maxwell, looking pale, sat down across from young Tom Pendergass.

"Don't believe I know *that* gentleman," said Aiken, indicating Stottelmyer.

"You wouldn't, he comes of a fine, old family," replied Captain Jack.

Everybody was pleased to laugh at this. Although Aiken turned brick red, he said nothing.

"Don't we get served?" cried Guy. "Let's have a round. Hot rum, Garrett."

Old Pina hastened to comply.

"Cap'n Jack, did you ever see a pure-white fox pelt, white as snow?" demanded Neville, as though to keep up the conversation.

"Can't say as I ever did," answered the old hunter. "I've heared half-breeds from the north say they cotched 'em in Canadee."

"Well, I've got a skin here. Like to see it?" said Neville. And without waiting for reply, "Gunther, bring that pelt over here and show it to the captain."

One of the men who had come in with Neville now emerged from the back of the room with a bundle in his hand.

Guy was attempting to talk to Yates. "Tellin' your own fortune?" he asked, indicating at the cards.

"Solitaire," said Yates.

"Always reminded me of mental masturbation," sniggered Guy.

"Can't say I have the same memories of boyhood," smiled Yates.

At that moment Gunther, the man with the pelt, reached the table and stood by Neville.

"It's as curious and pretty a fox pelt as you'll ever see," Neville was saying. "White as the driven snow! Show it to the captain, man! Unroll it!"

Everyone leaned forward.

A pure-white, albino fox pelt rippled down from the hands of Gunther as he undid the bundle. It hung dangling with its nose towards the floor.

Instantly everybody in the room rose as one man and crowded forward towards the big table.

"*Look out, look out!*" shouted Garrett.

Yates disappeared. His head cracked loudly on the floor.

Gunther had yanked him off his chair by his legs, drawn him under the table, and shot him out into the middle of the room. Three ruffians fell on him before he could get up.

Salathiel leaped on the table, picked Neville up by his sword belt, and hurled him like a log into the faces of the oncoming mob.

Captain Jack upset the table before him so that it now stood over breast high with its legs thrust back towards the hearth.

Salathiel leaped back behind it.

All this had been instantaneous. Salathiel only had time to hear Yates give an agonized scream, and then a wave of fist-fighting rabble came over the table and engulfed him.

His one idea was to get to Yates. He was sure they would kill him. For that reason he wasted no blows or small tricks for inflicting minor injuries on those who came at him. This was no time for tearing off ears. He picked men up and hurled them back where they came from. It was instinctive. For the first time his giant strength came into full play and being. For the moment it was effective. Few among the attackers had expected to be used as weapons against themselves. Luckily Captain Jack and Stottelmyer followed suit. At either end of the long table men had Murray and young Pendergass down and were worrying them. In the centre all those who crossed it had become ammunition to be shot back into the faces of their friends.

Heads cracked, shouts, curses, and animal yells filled the tavern. There was another concerted rush against the three giants behind the table. A splintering crash announced that Stottelmyer was using a bench on the heads of his enemies. He used it up. The strong oak was splintered on skulls. The war whoop rose in Albine's throat, and this time burst out. The sound of it seemed to madden Captain Jack. He wrenched a leg off the table and freed Murray of his tormentors. At that moment the grille came down with a sound like the wreck of a ship on a rocky coast and the Pendergass boys poured into the flank of the crowd.

Their rush cleared half the floor, and Salathiel was able to pick Yates up and half pitch, half carry him behind the bar, where he sank down either lifeless or unconscious, his face covered with blood.

For an instant as he sprang up on the bar again Salathiel was aware of the hideous clamour let loose in the place; of the groans, curses, and shrieks; of the roarings of Stottelmyer and the half-musical rhythmic moaning of old Pina and her family cowering back against the wall of the chimney; of the thud and smack of blows and the splintering crash of bottle glass all blent into one enormous devil's symphony. This he saw and heard in the bat of an eye, standing on the bar. But there he did have a second or two in which to think, and he could oversee the whole room.

The sortie of the Pendergasses from behind the counter had been enough of a diversion and surprise to drive the crowd back halfway down the room. But the Pendergasses could get no farther, no matter how desperately they fought. The sheer numbers of the crowd stopped them. Only those near the front could be reached, and those behind kept coming on. The Pendergasses were being pushed back towards the hearth, fighting like mad angels, but giving way. In a minute or two it would all be over. A howl of triumph burst from the crowd. Salathiel was just about to leap back into the forlorn hope, when, like the ground knocks of an earthquake in a furious storm, he became aware of a series of house-shaking blows at the back door.

Could it be . . . ?

He raced along the top of the counter and leaped off into the rear corridor that led by way of the back door into the yard.

The back door was bolted—bolted!

He threw the door open, and Stottelmyer's drivers, who had been trying to smash it in with a log, almost crushed him as they rushed into the corridor.

He managed to lead them back into the big room, leaping ahead.

Even in the few seconds that he had been away things had gone from bad to worse. The Pendergasses and their friends had been pressed back and behind the table. They were making a last stand there before the hearth. Blood flowed down old Garrett's face from a nasty gash. Captain Jack staggered and reeled. Even Stottelmyer was gasping now. He and three of the Pendergass boys alone delayed the end.

So evident was this that towards the rear of the room some of the crowd had turned aside to loot the bar and goods counter. Bottles and merchandise were crashing down from the shelves. Bales of cloth were flapping. All this could be seen at a glance.

It was the glimpse of empty space at the far end of the room that gave Salathiel the idea. The sight and impulse seemed one—the impulse to pick up the huge oak table and rush forward with it into the crowd. Stottelmyer saw the plan in a flash. He bellowed hoarsely to his men to help. Out of long habit they obeyed his roars instinctively. Someone slogged Stottelmyer over the head with a bottle and he went down. But his men had heard him. Five of them stooped and laid hold of the table. Salathiel had one end; Captain Jack the other. The massive planks rose slowly from the floor, a barrier and shield for those behind them; started forward; gained speed; came down the room like a moving wall with the iron pronged candlesticks sticking out before like stags' horns.

Old Pina jumped from her chair by the hearth, sobbing with excitement. The thing was totally unexpected. Men went down before the table like ninepins; were swept under it; trampled upon. With the impetus of an avalanche, their feet going like mad, the seven powerful men behind it slammed a half ton of sixteen-foot oak planks into the bunched bodies of the crowd caught at the far end of the room—rammed and jammed it home.

Puffs, oaths, hoarse breathings, a sound like falling grain bags, the frantic howls of a man pinned against the wall by the iron prongs of the candlesticks—bone crackings marked its sudden halt. Its weight fell with a padded thud on arms, on feet and legs trying to wriggle from under it.

"S—t, f—k, goddam . . . oh, Christ, I'm kilt . . . let me up, you ornery bastards. Jesus! God! I'm done . . . varmints . . . sons of bitches . . ."

There was no end to it. But words were no defence.

The determined men behind the table turned back and began knocking down every man who now tried to get up. The Pendergass boys rallied again, joined Stottelmyer's drivers, and continued the fight. They trampled on those who lay prone, while for a few seconds the battle swayed furiously up and down the room. The odds were now about even. Stottelmyer's six drivers were fresh, new, and terrible. They were enjoying themselves.

Someone wriggled out from the crushed mass of humanity behind the table, opened the door, yelling murder, and fled out into the night. More followed. Panic spread. Those who had been looting the shelves now cowered behind the counter. At the rear of the room the wide-open door suggested at once the end of the fight and the only possible exit, to marauders and defenders alike.

At the last there was a kind of gantlet running. Boots now came into full play. The Pendergass boys chivied those who remained caught in the room like rats around and round; routed out the skulkers from their hiding places. They knocked them silly, and sent them spinning down the line of Stottelmyer's waiting men, who booted them out through the open door with roars of delight.

Suddenly, except for those lying quiet on the floor, the room was clear of strangers. The defenders burst into a breathless shout of relief and triumph. On her knees by the hearth old Pina "bres' Gohd-a-mighty," fervently, and without end. She was also heard later on asking His forgiveness for having locked the back door as usual, and for forgetting to say anything about it.

According to the clock, about six minutes had passed since the nose of the white fox had pointed at the floor.

The big brawl at Pendergasses' was over.

". . . all except for the helpless and injured," said Captain Jack, looking about him and licking his bruised lips. "Now let's get rid of 'em. Let those poor bastards under the table up first."

It was remarkable how difficult it was to lift the table now. What they had done with it only a few moments ago now seemed impossible. It was already a legendary feat even to themselves.

Those who were caught behind or under the table begged for mercy and were allowed to leave the room unmolested. Some walked and some crawled through the open door. The man caught by the candlestick was helpless. He could only moan a little and curse. They carried him out and laid him down by the riverbank to be looked after by his friends, if any.

"We've got one or two of our own to nurse," said Garrett bitterly, mopping the blood from his own face. "Yates has lost an eye. It was that big, gouging lout of a Gunther that Neville set on him. He got away, too! Cleared out airly, the scum!"

"So did Neville and Aiken, along with Guy and Maxwell. They'll swear they had nothing to do with this; that they left as soon as the fight began," said Murray, feeling his bruises and loosened teeth.

"That'll all be true enough," said Garrett. "I thought I saw that red-headed Irishman O'Toole sneak out with them, too."

"Did I ever see a white fox?" mumbled Captain Jack dreamfully. "Well, I'll know one now. I'll get that white fox pelt yet!"

And curiously enough, although it was not quite what he meant, Captain Jack did get the pelt. It was picked up by Mark Pendergass in the yard only a few minutes later and brought in to him.

In the little corner room upstairs over the inn, Yates lay stretched out on his bed, where he had been carried by Albine. Phoebe Davison and two of the Pendergass girls were hovering over him. He had come to once, but luckily was unconscious again. He was terribly beaten up. He had a frightful blow on the back of his head and his left eye was irretrievably injured. In fact, it was gone out of its socket.

Salathiel stood looking down on his friend, filled with wild fury and regret. He was half out of his head with anger and chagrin. Only Phoebe and old Mrs. Pendergass, who came in to see what she could do, were able at last to prevent Salathiel's running out to do murder in the town. Captain Jack also helped to restrain him.

"It won't do you no good, son," said the old hunter, who had come upstairs with a strange surgeon. "You'll have to let things take their course now. Captain Frazier with a provost guard is downstairs, and they've taken things over. Now you go down, too, and get your own gashes and cuts fixed up. Dr. Boyd's looking after his friends in the big room. I'll be down myself in a jiffy. I've got a bad arm I want him to look after."

Thus cajoled, Salathiel left Yates to the care of the girls and the hot compresses ordered by the surgeon, and descended into the big room again. A provost guard from the new grenadier battalion was in charge with Captain Frazier. Bayonets glittered and lanthorns flashed on much scarlet and gold lace.

Captain Frazier, a precise little Scot with a sandy moustache, was making notes in his pocket memorandum of what was being told him by several people at once. He regarded Mr. Pendergass as a much-abused and outraged man. Arrests were being made in the town of anyone connected with the military suspected of having been in the fight. That was the best Captain Frazier could do. Warrants would have to be sworn out for any of the others.

But everybody knew that would never be done. Who and where were the miscreants? Where was a magistrate to be found? How could the warrants be served if once obtained, and who would serve them? On the harassed frontier the civil government of the province was not even a convenient fiction. Except for taking out land warrants, no one ever thought of the civil law seriously.

Garrett and Captain Jack looked at each other and smiled through their injuries. They knew they would have to protect themselves, and what measures they must take. The big brawl would only serve to hasten their plans. It would make the necessity of a secret combination of good citizens against rascals more patently evident. In the end, it would be a help for what Captain Jack and Garrett intended to do.

Dr. Boyd was kept busy for some time. There were a couple of arms to be set, a case of broken ribs, cuts and bad contusions to look after. Black eyes, swollen faces, and loose teeth could be left to cure themselves. Salathiel had a knife slash from his shoulder to his wrist. But it was a scratch.

"I wonder there weren't more lethal weapons used instead of fists," remarked Dr. Boyd.

"I think I know the reason for that, doctor," said old Garrett. "I'll tell you later. It fits in with what was behind the whole thing."

"Well, it's lucky for you people, that's all I can say," answered the doctor, as he finished bandaging Garrett's forehead. "The gash will heal without a stitch. You and Captain Jack got off light. He's bruised but not dangerously. Damned bad business, this brawling. I'm mortal sorry about Yates."

It was typical, however, that Captain Frazier scarcely seemed to notice that several people in the room had been rather severely injured. His indignation and worry seemed to be totally concentrated on the loss of goods and damage to property. The partially looted shelves were to him so many gaping wounds.

"Now what do you think your total loss might be, Mr. Pendergass?" he kept asking.

Driven at last to answer, Garrett finally replied, "Offhand, I should say about thirty pounds."

"Thirty puns, thir-r-r-ty puns! Mon, think of it!" the captain kept exclaiming.

Captain Jack and Garrett, followed eventually by the others, went upstairs to bed.

"'Mon, *think* of it!'" said Captain Jack, smiling ruefully, and laying his hand on Garrett's arm affectionately as they said good night.

"Why, we'll do that, old friend. We'll think of it considerable, won't we?" said Garrett, and laughed painfully. "Good night."

Salathiel looked in again at Yates. Phoebe sat by his bed with one candle burning. He wondered if there was anything he could do. But Phoebe looked up at him and shook her head, her finger on her lips. He whispered good night to her. For the first time in his life he felt thoroughly exhausted, not only in body but in mind.

Under the official care of Captain Frazier's sentries Pendergasses' at last lapsed into the silence of a hard-earned peace. But even in the sleep of nervous shock and exhaustion great green, yellow, and red sun-

flowers bloomed and burst and spun through seething darkness inside
the skull of Edward Hamilton Yates.

10. Conversations Overheard

AFTER THE BIG BRAWL, things rapidly settled down at Pendergasses'. Those most concerned either left town by a return convoy of
empty wagons to Fort Loudon or so comported themselves as to be monstrous inconspicuous. In short, it was remarkable how difficult it was to
find anyone who would admit that he had even been near Garrett's
place the evening of the big brawl, especially if he bore a black eye or a
ripped ear. Some of the more seriously injured claimed they had been
hurt in accidents on the road. And they were prepared to produce witnesses, if necessary. But it was not necessary.

For all this diffidence suited Garrett well enough. Maxwell and his
friends had received so notable a check that it was not likely they would
be looking for more trouble for some time to come. Besides, both Garrett
and Captain Jack were planning to protect themselves and the town
from the repetition of any similar outbursts in the future in a manner
much more far-reaching and fundamental than the punishment of this
or that individual could provide.

At the fort, Ecuyer had Neville and Guy well in hand. Ecuyer was
taking them west to Pittsburgh and Colonel Bouquet. Discipline was
now being enforced amongst the Bedford garrison by the exasperated
commandant with an iron hand. Court-martials were functioning with
a reassuring precision.

To show that peace had returned, the damage in the hearth room at
Pendergasses' was repaired and the grille hung even more securely than
before. Trade with the garrison resumed shortly and went on quietly
and profitably again. Garrett and his whole household celebrated Christmas '63 before a roaring fire with old English custom and cheer: roast
beef, plum pudding, fiddlers, and all. Thirty-eight people great and
small, including some of the officers from the fort, sat down about the
great table in the hearth room.

It was hard to believe that so secure and happy a festival could be
held on that troubled frontier even under the protecting ramparts of the
fort. But held it was, with reels and dancing afterward; with toasts to
everybody from the king to Phoebe Davison, not forgetting poor Yates,
who was still unable to leave his room.

To Salathiel these days spent at Pendergasses' as the year '63 grew to
its close were the happiest he had ever known. He was in the house, and
as a member of the family. For ever since the night of the great fight in
the hearth room he had been accepted as such without further reserva-

tion. He saw Phoebe every day. The Pendergass boys regarded him as a welcome and giant accession of strength to their tribe.

The slaughter of the Philistines lost nothing in the telling. And, to tell the truth, neither Captain Jack nor Salathiel did anything to belittle it. In fact, they enjoyed the reputation they had painfully earned. The younger children of the establishment climbed over them and swarmed about them whenever they sat down, until old Mrs. Pendergass herself interfered in behalf of their peace. The women of the place were admiring and grateful. Old Pina was forever frying, stewing, or simmering "suthin' tasty" to tempt them. It was almost embarrassing, but it was also exceedingly pleasant.

How much of his swift and cordial acceptance into the ordinarily jealous and closely drawn circle of the Pendergass tribe was due to old Garrett's affectionate remembrance of his father and mother, Salathiel at first had no idea.

Like many young men Mr. Albine tended to regard his own desirability as rather inevitable. But Garrett's frequent and close questioning of him in regard to his early memories soon brought about two results: it convinced Garrett that Salathiel was certainly Lemuel's child, and it informed Salathiel himself of many things which he might otherwise never have learned about his parents.

He could never hear enough about them. He was particularly curious about his mother, and both Garrett and old Rose were frequently called upon to repeat in minutest detail the story of the sojourn of the giant blacksmith and his pretty Irish wife with the Pendergasses in what now already seemed even to them an era in the remote past.

Mrs. Pendergass from the first had entertained no doubts as to Salathiel's being the child of the young couple she had once so happily known. There was the name. And there were certain resemblances, traits of gesture and expression in Salathiel, which recalled both Lemuel and his wife to her mind. Salathiel seemed to have come back to her like bread cast upon the waters. His physical presence was a vigorous denial of any futility in the kindness and affection which Mrs. Pendergass had lavished upon his mother in the past.

Mrs. Pendergass's long-repressed grief over the disappearance of the Albines had never ceased to be a real sorrow. Secretly, she had continued to hope against hope that they might be heard from. She had even argued against Garrett's common-sense "I told you so", when the news of Lemuel's murder by the Shawnees on Christmas Day of 1748 had later been brought in by a Mingo hunter. Finally, it had all grown dim, a far-off painful music in memory like dreaming of long-dead children.

And then Salathiel had walked in out of the forest, a surprising, a comforting and satisfactory fulfilment for nearly vanished and vainly cherished hopes.

His welcome, therefore, was really not quite so mysterious as it might seem. He was welcome even in Mrs. Pendergass's own room, to be admitted to which was a kind of accolade of family approval. He came there often to hear about his mother and father and brought the "old lady", as she was affectionately known, seeds for her birds that languished in the winter, a new cage whittled out for them by his own hands, and special billets of hard wood for her chimney fire.

Phoebe and Arthur Davison, her favourite grandchildren, frequently came and sat in the room to hear their grandmother's stories. And if Phoebe sat a little closer to Salathiel on the big oak bench in the corner than she did to her brother Arthur, Mrs. Pendergass had no comment to make. Her eyes were better than her ears, however.

A pair of fur-lined moccasins made by Salathiel and embroidered by Phoebe confirmed her tacit approval of so natural a situation by being accepted and worn. When Salathiel repaired and reshaped an old wig of Garrett's, one which his wife had seldom been able to get him to wear, Mr. Albine's star approached its zenith. Garrett grumbled a little, but he too was amused and confounded by the domestic skill of a "wild man". In the end, Mrs. Pendergass did what she had never permitted herself to do before any of her own boys: she took out a small clay pipe from her reticule and smoked it while she talked to Salathiel.

Thus, after a long, active, and useful life, Mrs. Rose Pendergass's now passive role as a female spectator and mentor of existence in her own ample family was an interesting one. Yet it was interesting not only to herself but to others. Her deafness, she thought, was a positive advantage, for it enabled her to watch things happen without the prejudice of overhearing emotional sounds about them, and to arrange her conclusions on the already ample basis of her own experience, nicely and to the point.

Of course, all this interest which she kept up about her was quite satisfactory to Mrs. Pendergass herself. She had in fact solved the chief problem of women: How not to become superfluous after their children grow up and age leaves their husbands free to comparatively undisturbed sleep and self-consecrated days. She had unconsciously at first, and later deliberately, placated fate against her being left lonely, discounted, and neglected in deaf desuetude. And she did so by the deft and copious use of the two best agents for preventing so natural and likely an end to any decent woman's life: children and property.

Mrs. Rose Pendergass was an exceedingly womanly woman, the outer shell of her protective common-sense and right self-satisfactions was inhabited by "a wondrous tender, involute, and astute creature" that knew by instinct when to open and when to close its shell against the world.

She remained, therefore, secure in her key position. And her character and peculiarities were consequently the subject of constant interest and frequent review, not only in her own family, but in the neighbourhood at large and about town.

Officers from the fort, guests at the tavern, strangers who came out of a lonely wilderness to warm their feet or their hearts before the Pendergasses' fire, felt and noticed the pervasive, timeless quality in Mrs. Pendergass. They sometimes wrote home about her, or discussed her quietly, while Garrett was absent, over pipes and tall glasses. Something so eternally feminine in the forest, something so permanently human was both intriguing and refreshing, a balm to lost or homesick men. Nor did it seem to make much difference that Mrs. Pendergass was no longer young.

Surgeon Boyd, for instance, who had seen a great deal of life, both men and women, from the Punjab to Pennsylvania, including a surprising number of countries scattered between, speculated about Mrs. Pendergass considerably by both mouth and pen—as, indeed, he speculated about nearly everything else from stars to gallstones with ingenious and even whimsical comparisons and analogies.

It was he who maintained he had never seen anything to compare with Mrs. Pendergass, except in some Hindu households, where all the family, sons, new wives and their offspring, retainers and animals lived in one vast compound where the oldest couple ruled them all. And how curious to find something similar, although much more matriarchal, on the banks of the obscure Juniata. An accident, of course, something unusual in the colonies, Indian troubles had kept the family together. But how would it be, the doctor wondered, if more English settlers lived like the Pendergasses, instead of wandering off couple by couple into lonely cabins lost amid the hills?

Few really understood just what the doctor was talking about. But this problem of lonely families in America, and women in general, Dr. Boyd discussed frequently with Yates in the lawyer's small room just across the hall from Salathiel's, where the surgeon came every afternoon to bathe and dress his injured eye. Sometimes he brought an old newspaper or an interesting book and read from them. Or he read from what Yates found to be even more interesting; from **his** own *Notes & Queries*. The door of Yates's room was usually left open into the hall.

Lying on his bed, Salathiel could thus overhear the doctor. And Salathiel frequently lay on his bed then even in the afternoon. For it was now dark and snowy outside. There was little to do at that time of year, and he had never quite lost the habit of sleeping or dozing, when time served, like a savage or an animal. He would come up to his room, curl up like a wolf making his nest in the leaves, and settle himself down on the deep mattress, listening to the tags and snatches of talk as the women went up and down stairs. He could tell people by their footsteps. How strange and pleasant to be in a house like this, and with women. And Dr. Boyd was nearly always interesting. He talked and read to distract Yates, of course. But it was good talk and good reading, for all that. One learned things from it.

It was that way in fact that Salathiel first heard about "the wondrous tender, involute, and astute creature" that inwardly inhabited the outward shell of Mrs. Pendergass. It was Dr. Boyd talking to Yates. And Salathiel, as he listened, chuckled quietly.

". . . and this creature—" explained Dr. Boyd, who as a scientific philosopher took all his analogies from nature, and tried them upon Yates, whom he considered an understanding patient—"this creature is nothing less than the spirit of human mercy, the ultimate female sanity from which all animal affection and decency originally proceeded, and upon which, in the final analysis, society still rests."

Dr. Boyd elaborated on Mrs. Pendergass, and on women in general. Yates lay tense but still. He was aware that Dr. Boyd was expert in using conversation to keep his patients' minds off themselves, yet he had been interested in spite of himself. For some days he had not felt much pain. The hole in his head had become numb, stiff rather than sensitive. It was the use of the other eye alone which now most troubled him. The doctor continued his ablutions carefully. Something tinkled in the basin metallically.

"Not the tweezers again!" exclaimed Yates apprehensively.

"No, no, the necessity for that has long passed," said Boyd reassuringly. "You're doing remarkably well. The principal difficulty in these cases is to pack the cavity. It is important, too, for other reasons than appearance. A proper filling of the empty cavity enables you to use the muscles of your other eye with less strain. Now I have something here which might do at least temporarily. At any rate, I want you to try it. See if you can learn to tolerate it." With that he dropped something cool, round, smooth, and heavy between the eyelids and brought them down over it.

"That *looks* better," said the doctor doubtfully. "How does it feel?"

"It's cool, rather soothing, in fact," admitted Yates. "What is it?"

"A stone," said the doctor.

Yates lay quiet with both his eyes closed. The coolness slowly died away. He could feel nothing now but stiffness and weight and the gradual sensation of nothingness as the laudanum water in which the doctor had bathed the stone began to take effect.

"It's lucky for you I'm a bit of a geologizer," said Dr. Boyd presently, while observing the expression on his patient's face. "Were we in London or Edinburgh or Paris now, I could get you a fine glass eye. But I doubt they're to be met with anywhere in the colonies. I was going over some of the specimens in my natural collection the other day and just happened on this stone. It was curiously eye-like in some respects, except for one protuberance which I ground off with the gunsmith's rasp. Further alterations could be made if necessary. How does it feel?"

"Not at all," said Yates. "The strange thing is that it seems to put my other eye at ease."

"Excellent!" exclaimed the doctor. "Better than I'd hoped for. Take it out if it troubles you, but do try to get used to it. I'd keep it smooth and clean. It's a kind of volcanic stone, lava-glass. Oh, the Lord knows what it is! I picked it up in Sicily once when the transports lay at Palermo."

"A very *costly* specimen?" inquired Yates, grinning.

"No, my Scotch friend," said the doctor. "You can say I came to treat you with charity, and gave you a stone.

"And now I must leave you," he added. "Ecuyer is anxious to get off to Pittsburgh and I want to put some sense in his head and get his wounds closed before he goes."

So saying, the surgeon poured the water out the window and gathered up his things.

"Give the little captain my best," said Yates, "and by the way, doctor, apropos of Mrs. Pendergass, don't you think all her family ought to be great mathematicians?"

"Now," said Boyd, "now why so?"

"Well, their father must have had an eye for a figure," said Yates, "since their mother is so distinguished for multiplication."

"Tush!" said Boyd, and ran downstairs, laughing to himself.

He climbed the ascent to the fort thoughtfully, however, considering what he should say to Ecuyer. "If he doesn't take some rest and give himself a chance to recuperate while his wounds close, he'll die of exhaustion," muttered Boyd. "But I might as well talk Greek to a grenadier, I suppose. No, he's bound to be off with the next convoy. Duty!" sniffed the doctor. "Duty!"

The sentinel at the postern saluted, this time respectfully, but later on passed the word that Surgeon Boyd was cracked and could be heard talking nonsense to himself.

"Of course, I talk nonsense," said Boyd, when the rumour finally got around to him, "but it's the prerogative of every learned profession to talk nonsense. And after all, compared to what the clergy proclaim from the pulpits every Sunday, my nonsense is like an exercise in logic by the Spirit of Clarity."

11. Mr. Gladwin Comes Over into Macedonia

AFTER THE SURGEON left him that afternoon Yates lay quietly preoccupied with the new problem of the geological specimen in his head, trying to open and shut both his eyes together to get used to the stone. Somehow he felt that he ought to be able to see through it as if

the stone were a part of a pair of spectacles. It seemed at times as though
he could.

This effect, or illusion, was probably due to a compound of his great
desire to see and the fact that when he did open both eyes together he
could see with one—and then quite clearly. Finding the inward problem of his own sight thus solved to some degree, he now began to wonder how he might look to other people. Afterwhile he called to Salathiel
across the hall.

"Are you awake or asleep, Sal?"

"Awake. I've been listening most of the time."

"I thought you might be," said Yates. "I heard you come in an hour
or so ago. Come over a minute or two, won't you? I want you to see
something."

Presently the form of his tall friend Albine filled the frame of the
door.

"A great little talker is Surgeon Boyd," Yates went on. "Like most
widowers, he is philosophical about women. And he's a medical widower
to boot. We young fellows can't afford to be so philosophical yet. At
least not until we get what we want. But look here—throw that shutter
around, please. Now, what do you think my chances are?"

The cold winter light reflected from the snow outside fell on Yates's
face where he sat against the white pillows. He opened both his eyes,
looking at Salathiel.

It was impossible for Albine not to be startled, and not to show it.

Yates was pale and sallow from his ordeal. His broad forehead, sunken
cheeks, and pointed chin gave his face the effect of a triangle. And from
the top of it, from under arched and brown silken eyebrows, gazed a
pair of eyes whose combined effect was astonishingly disconcerting. The
grey of the living eye seemed to blend with the smooth ashen grey of
the stone.

"Fascinatin', eh?" prompted Yates, watching his friend's face.

"You're a devil," exclaimed Albine. "Why, you're like a rattlesnake
with the face of a doe!"

"Dear, dear," groaned Yates dramatically, "good Lord! Suppose you
hand me my shaving glass over here."

Into that he gazed long and carefully, turning it to various angles.

"I opine you're more truthful than comfortin', Sal," he said at last.
"I'm afraid I'll have to do my wooing either after nightfall or with gold.
But I do see professional advantages in this. Now suppose you were a
judge, or the jury, and I looked at you like this—and this?" He closed
one eye, and then the other. The effect was truly astonishing. He
seemed to be two different people.

"Well," said Salathiel, after considering, "I'd be willing to do about
anything you wanted. I'd almost be afraid not to."

"Precisely," said Yates. "The evil and the good eye put off or on. Now, of course, I can't see how I look with only the stone one open, but I must be a regular remora, or a Medusa." He laughed uneasily—and then went on to explain to Salathiel just what a Medusa was, in a jocular way. During the process two tears escaped him and ran down his cheeks.

"It—it don't seem to make any difference with the gals," said Salathiel awkwardly, trying to comfort his friend. "Sue Pendergass is always talking about you and telling your jokes over. She likes to be in your room as much as she can. And as for Phoebe, why, she's so devoted she stays watching you even when you're asleep."

"Ah, I'm afraid you won't need to be jealous about Phoebe any more," sighed Yates. "It must be your bulk she likes, Salathiel. There's so much of you it makes an undying impression. It can't be just that hatchet-faced, mangle-eared, grey-haired young man I can see even with one eye. There, there now," he hastened to add, "you *have* got a nice smile, an honest, level gaze. A bit piercing. But two eyes, both of 'em! And your hair tied behind in a queue with a neat bow, and that smooth deerskin shirt with the red muffler! All that's an improvement. Yes, it's effective. By the way, how are you coming on with Phoebe?"

Salathiel coloured violently and stirred uneasily. "To tell the truth, a little too well," he said.

"*Too* well!" exclaimed Yates. "Why, that's monstrous. She must have been flattering you worse than even I did just now."

"No, no, not that," replied Albine, "but happen I just remembered something this morning. Burent brought me a letter from a man at Pittsburgh. It came in the bag with the last express. You see . . . Well, the truth is I'm a married man!"

Yates put the mirror down on its face before him, lay back, and laughed.

"You get a letter from a man in Pittsburgh—and so you're a married man," he chortled.

"It was a letter from the Reverend James McArdle, the man who married me," explained Salathiel indignantly. Then he told Yates the whole story of the forest wedding on the island with a kind of hangdog air, ending with, "So you see, Jane's safe in Virginny, hired out, I s'pose, in the settlements there. And McArdle says he'll be coming east with the first captives Colonel Bouquet rescues and sends back home. But I wonder if he really *will* come."

"I'm rather certain he will," said Yates after a bit. He was no longer inclined to laugh, seeing his friend was in a real predicament.

"I'm afraid McArdle will come east and find Jane for you. You seem to have been a youthful sacrifice to respectability on a forest altar down the Ohio. It's too bad you couldn't have bedded down under the leaves a few minutes without having to marry the girl."

"I liked her, it went very well when we were together, and it was really the first time," said Salathiel.

"It's surprising what trouble a few moments' pleasure can get you into," mused Yates. "I wouldn't be surprised if it quite ruined your life. It might, you know."

"But I really didn't know exactly what I was doing," explained Salathiel. "It was McArdle and that fox-faced woman who insisted we must be married. It seemed an easy way out. It is curious to think that was only about a year ago. I was only a wild boy then. I'm a man now. You know, I haven't thought of Jane for months. I seem to be a different person now. It must have happened to someone else. Or maybe when I saw Phoebe she made me forget."

"Are you going to tell Phoebe?" asked Yates.

"Well, I'll think it over for a while," replied Salathiel, taking a deep breath or two and looking terribly troubled. "I'll have to sooner or later, I guess."

Yates nodded. "I wonder," said he; "it depends on how you love her."

"I love her *right!*" answered Salathiel.

Yates looked relieved.

"Do you think that marriage is good in law?" asked Salathiel.

Yates pondered a moment. "I'm afraid so," he replied. "Your wife has that writing on a piece of elm bark with the witnesses' names on it, and her ring. And there's the Reverend James McArdle. It's not likely yours is the only marriage he ever performed. Too bad, too bad! I once had a devil of a narrow squeak myself at Edinburgh. Nice little split-tail with a soul, or a heart, or whatever it is Dr. Boyd says is inside 'em. She had it. I felt sorry for her. But that's my story. I ought not to tell it to you now.

"Cheer up!" he insisted, seeing how depressed Albine looked. "Let's change the subject. Now, what's going on downstairs these days? B'Gad, it will be a relief when that strained muscle in my back lets me up again! I can see pretty well, as far as that goes. Well, has anybody new and interestin' turned up lately?"

"Six Creek Injuns sent by the governor of North Carolina. They have a blood feud with the Delawares and say they want to join Bouquet. They tried to pitch in the yard-garden, but Garrett wouldn't let them and sent them back to the fort. He's afraid Cap'n Jack or some of Smith's Black Boys might do away with, well, with six Creeks, accidental. They had a new blanket apiece from Garrett and a drag of Jamaica, and just stood around stinkin' by the fire."

"Must be a pungent addition to our fireside circle," yawned Yates. "Do they belch or grunt when formally addressed?"

"Both," laughed Salathiel.

"Princes of repartee, eh! Anybody else?"

"A man by the name of Gladwin from Philadelphy, who seems thick as thieves with Garrett and Cap'n Jack. You know, one of *those* fellows."

"How do you mean?" demanded Yates.

"Oh, you know," said Salathiel, and he made a certain gesture in sign language.

"Now where the devil did you learn *that?*" exclaimed Yates, sitting up again suddenly, despite his bad back.

"From my Shawnee uncle Nymwha in a medicine lodge on the Ohio long ago," answered Salathiel. "But I didn't know the white men had it till I saw Ecuyer and Cap'n Jack talking together that day in the captain's room at the fort."

"A medicine lodge!" said Yates. "Well, I'll be damned! Now that *is* a new one. Either you are a very observin' man, my friend, or—"

"Or what?" demanded Salathiel.

"Oh—maybe the Injuns *are* the lost tribes of Israel," ended Yates cryptically.

"The Reverend James McArdle thought so," replied Salathiel, to whom by pure accident the theme of the lost tribes of Israel happened to be an enormously familiar one.

"Did McArdle know the signs? This one?" asked Yates.

"Comin' to think of it, I guess he did," said Salathiel. "Now it never struck me before, but maybe that's why the medicine men let him alone to preach and to go around pretty much as he liked. Now that's curious, isn't it?"

"My friend," asked Yates very seriously, "did you ever hear of the Masons?"

"Masons? You mean stoneworkers, builders, the kind King Solomon borrowed from Hiram of Tyre to build the Temple—in the Bible, you know?"

Now it so happened that Salathiel could not have made a better answer by asking a question if he had tried a thousand years.

"I think," said Yates, "that we'll certainly have to talk this over together, and the sooner the better. Suppose you go downstairs now and ask Garrett and Captain Jack to come up here after dinner to sit with us in my room. Bring up my dinner yourself, Sal, if you don't mind. We don't want any women pokin' in. And you might ask Mr. Gladwin, too. Hurry now! Try to get them all before anybody steps out for the evening. Tell them it's important. It *is* important, Mr. Albine, for you."

And so it proved to be.

For when Salathiel went to bed that night, or rather early the next morning, he knew that all the masons were not the subjects of Hiram King of Tyre.

Captain Jack's delay in gathering his chosen young men about him and going out to his cabin to begin raids on the redskins was by no means accidental. There were several controlling reasons why he continued to linger on at Pendergasses' well into the winter. The winter itself was a powerful deterrent to action of any kind. Through January and February the snow lay in neck-high drifts in the mountains and communication westward was temporarily severed.

Toward the end of November, 1763, the indomitable Ecuyer had attempted to get through with supplies and reinforcements to Colonel Bouquet. But he had been attacked at the top of the Allegheny ridge, forced back to Bedford, and compelled by the condition of the roads, the insistence of Surgeon Boyd, and his own infirmities to delay and to rest himself. That, and the weather, had held him at the fort well into the beginning of '64. But, exasperating as this delay was, it undoubtedly prolonged the captain's existence. For even if he had been able to get through to Ligonier, he would have been stopped there by the snow-drifts, and he must certainly have perished at that bleak outpost away from all medical help.

Salathiel, however, saw very little of either Ecuyer or Burent that winter. They were at the fort and he was at Pendergasses'. As time went on, Captain Jack began to prepare for his coming raids westward, and in the early mornings at least, kept his "Fighting Quakers" busy in advance preparations. The various supplies which Garrett had agreed to contribute were secretly carried out to the cabin.

In this unobtrusive manner flour, corn meal, lead, powder, and salt pork, with a considerable quantity of other necessaries, including plenty of new flints, were quietly transferred to the cabin.

An ell with bunks for eight was added to the original small building and a small but secure storehouse built. This labour in the deep snow and mountain frosts was no small task, especially since everything had to be done with the greatest secrecy amongst an observing population. Yet no one so far had been seen either going or coming, and the stocking of the place was nearly accomplished.

"These mountains have big ears," said Captain Jack. "The best way to fool the enemy is to let him think nothing at all is going on until the blow falls. The hatchet is always its own best advertisement. That kind of no news is a good way to keep on growin' your own har. If a rumour of what we are about gits round, even among the Black Boys, we'll find ourselves ambushed as soon as we step over the river. The Boys have friends amongst the traders. And the traders have friends amongst their customers. So remember, when we start protecting the road, we're also going to stop a lot of trade in furs. I saw six pelts only yesterday in the hands of a man from Philadelphia, and I know where they came from. So mum's the word, and don't be seen goin' to the cabin. At any rate, don't any two of you go there together at any one time."

Salathiel, Nat Murray, Tom, Mat and Mark Pendergass were chosen for the work in hand. Two older men, Calvin and Sid McClanahan, had come over from the vicinity of Loudon to take part. But they remained constantly at the cabin from the very first and never came to town. It was known they had been on raids with Captain Jack before. They were strangers at Bedford, and their presence in town would immediately have given an inkling of what was up.

Perhaps the best guarantee against anyone's suspecting what Captain Jack and his boys were up to was the constant presence of Captain Jack himself, talking and smoking with his old friend Garrett sitting in the big hearth room at Pendergasses', and apparently taking his winter ease there before the fire.

That this ease was not quite so easy as it looked, Salathiel now understood. And he was also able to see what both Captain Jack and Garrett were doing, not only to prepare supplies at the cabin but to put the affairs of the whole community in better order.

Mr. Gladwin frequently sat with them. He was boarding at the inn, "snowbound," he said, from returning to Philadelphia. What his mission was gradually became evident. But only to those who were properly informed. The mystery was finally imparted to Salathiel by Yates, who had been designated to prepare his friend for taking the first degrees in Masonry when opportunity should serve and a lodge could be held.

Mr. Gladwin, it appeared, had come from the Grand Lodge at Philadelphia to organize the loose "Blue Lodge" Masonry, prevalent along the frontier and in the back country, into what was then called the "Ancient Arch", where ties were more binding, selection more particular, and higher degrees could be conferred. He was to be assisted in this work by certain of the officers at the fort, who had a military or travelling lodge charter under a grant to the 17th Infantry. And he was, of course, being helped by Garrett and Captain Jack, who were both Masons of high degree.

Now all this stir about Masonry was not a mere matter of love of ritual. Nor was it due simply to a boyish fascination for secrecy and a longing to be mysteriously distinguished in a society where conditions had levelled most men to a common plane of existence. Those allurements were there, as they always have been in Masonry from the beginning, but there was infinitely more than that to the movement which was then going on. In North America Masonry in sundry and various ways filled vital and long-felt wants.

No more apt and carefully devised scheme for bringing about a modicum of social cohesion in what was then virtually a state of anarchy on the frontiers could have been devised. It was admirably suited for the time and place.

In the terrible years of 1763 and 1764, when Pontiac's Indian raids had brought hideous confusion into lives that were only beginning to achieve some traces of human order in the savage scene of the wilderness, something heroic was needed to preserve the root ideas of civilization then in the precarious process of being transplanted. The frontiers needed to be replanted. It was itinerant preachers of religion and of Masonry who eventually supplied the seed. They did so at fearful personal risk, hardship and sacrifice. But the messengers came and the message was delivered. Mr. Gladwin, for instance, was an apostle of Masonry.

The effect of its propagation was to bring a sense of order and to give a point and direction to the existence of many who had heretofore been without either, unable to see anything in the universe but the chaos of nature in the wilderness that surrounded them.

But it did more than that. It raised many a poor lonely individual from a purely physical to a moral and social plane of existence. Like the ancient mysteries, it pointed to the spiritual and the divine at the apex of the pyramid. It was always personal and personified, latent and living in the individuals who devoted themselves to the task. Missionaries, whether lay, Masonic, or clerical, were therefore revered, valued, and respected by all who were not already lost in barbarism, fools, or too insensate to understand. Indeed, it was at this time that the almost superstitious respect for teachers and learning, an immoderate expectation of their fruits were first engendered in the land.

It is not to be thought strange, then, that even though Mr. James Callowhill Gladwin, a Philadelphia merchant, was only a benign-looking, grey-haired old man—it was not to be thought strange that as he sat talking with Garrett and his older friends, Mr. Albine and *his* younger friends should see something heroic in him and feel that he was to be revered.

They knew, for instance, that at the fraternal behest of Garrett and Captain Jack, Mr. Gladwin had mounted his horse at Philadelphia and had ridden by Indian-haunted roads through deserted country to the extreme border settlement of Bedford in order to spread and establish the message of his brotherhood. They knew he had left a comfortable home and a profitable business to do so, and that the success of his mission could be his only possible reward. Therefore, to them, there was something "worshipful" about him.

Salathiel also saw that all the older men who came to consult with Garrett and Mr. Gladwin—who so casually dropped in—but who sometimes lingered overnight at the inn at the express invitation and solicitation of Garrett, were of the stanchest and most trustworthy, altogether the pillars of the community. And this in a similar way was true also of the officers from the fort, who in one way or another seemed involved in the stir of what was going on. There was Captain Lewis Ourry and Dr. Boyd. There was Major Cadwalader from the militia, and several officers from Captain James Smith's Black Boys, lieutenants and subalterns of whom Salathiel knew little. To his great surprise, some of the noncommissioned officers and soldiers seemed also to be included.

But it was not only the older generation or officers from the fort who were involved. Quite a number of young men his own age, the friends of the Pendergass boys were evidently like himself going to be initiated.

They, too, were talked to by the older men and received with that good-fellowship and equality that was so heartening to their age.

That he was not alone but belonged to this class of young men, the sons of the respected citizens of the town and trustworthy farmers of the neighbourhood, was gradually borne in on Salathiel and served to encourage him and to give him a feeling of having an honourable place and a part to play in the community. Less and less he now felt himself to be a lone wolf, a wild product of the woods. More and more he was becoming a citizen.

Pendergasses' was, of course, the ideal place and common meeting ground for organizing any movement in the neighbourhood. There everybody male, who was not too young and who behaved himself reasonably, came and went with no questions asked. In furthering his favourite project, Garrett was thus only taking advantage of the fine opportunity which his own establishment provided. And in the bitter winter of '64 the opportunity both for broadening the base and "erecting upon it some of the higher structures of Masonry", as Mr. Gladwin put it, was unusually favourable.

Everyone who had not fled the frontiers at the earliest alarms had been forced by the terrible series of Indian attacks of the year before to gather in or about the town of Bedford close by the fort. The passing to and fro and the gathering of considerable reinforcements, both militia and the royal regiments, had brought not only the soldiers themselves but various supernumeraries and followers to the camp, barracks, and dwellings of the town of Bedford. The long pack trains required many horses and drivers. There were now more wagons in town than were seen there again for years to come, more refugees and strangers.

Much of this gathering array, men and animals, was to move westward to Colonel Bouquet as soon as the roads should be open in the spring. In the meanwhile it gathered behind the mountains at Bedford. In fact, that place had once again become what it had been only a few years before in General Forbes's time, a quite considerable military base. And it was now doubly crowded with the entire civil and refugee farm population of the Juniata district, together with a large number of traders from the East, attracted to what Captain Ourry impatiently called "This, our beautiful, accidental, mountain metropolis".

Both farmers and traders were only biding their time. The farmers to return to their lonely cabins and fields, the traders to repair to the fur-bartering Indian villages as soon as the state of affairs on the frontiers should permit.

But that time had not come yet. Despite Colonel Bouquet's victory at Bushy Run of the previous summer, the crisis still persisted. Indian raids and rumours of raids were frequent. Scalps were frequently taken within a few miles of the fort by wandering war parties. As yet only the hardiest and bravest of the settlers dared to venture anywhere alone. No family or individual exodus had begun. On the contrary, there was still a constant accretion of population. From as far south as the Virginia border and north to the Susquehanna all who had not fled eastward had taken shelter about the fort.

In March '64 the news came of the murder of the helpless Conestoga Indians at Paxtang, and of the later assault of the mob and massacre of the Indian survivors in Lancaster jail. The rioters threatened to march on Philadelphia. The alarm and excitement over these affairs were great and had repercussions even in the western hills.

Hatred and contempt for the puerile Quaker government of the province was stirring into restless revolt. The legislature at Philadelphia, mulishly disregarding the frantic pleas of the governor and the royal army officers to vote supplies for defense, had at last been compelled to look at a wagonload of scalped and mangled corpses riotously drawn through the streets of Philadelphia past the doors of the State House. Still remaining obdurate, they were at last forced by armed risings on the outraged frontiers to take cognizance of a universe where it had pleased God to release force.

The Quaker utopia by the Delaware, which had firmly closed its eyes upon the outer world in order to follow nothing but the inner light, blinked—and found itself in North America with a horrible glow of burning cabins on the frontiers. A "gift" was made to his Majesty in order that the legislature might shift the guilt of military expenditure from their own to a crowned head. The combined prayers, curses, and beseechings of Governor Penn, General Gage, and Benjamin Franklin, together with the petitions of angry city gentlemen and the shouts of gathering mobs, finally prevailed.

But not notably.

Hearing that Colonel Bouquet had "borrowed" two hundred Virginia riflemen from that province anyway, "Friends abstained from voting", and a thousand militia were authorized to assemble at Carlisle in the spring of '64.

It was in this condition of external war and internal confusion that Garrett and Captain Jack had determined to revive and strengthen the Masonic bonds which held many men of orderly and moderate opinions together, so that they could co-operate in mutual good will and common sense.

It was not that Garrett expected his fellow Masons to take direct action in this or that affair or instance. The lodges seldom did so. Their meetings provided rather a means and opportunity for the discussion of problems and the formation of influential opinion, a solemn free discussion under the protection of an oath of secrecy.

If Captain Jack, Garrett Pendergass, and others whose stake in the welfare of their community was more than usually considerable found their own interests best served by promoting peace, order, and good un-

derstanding amongst the more solid and thinking men of their neighbourhood—and if the lodges they cherished and organized tended to
make property safer and the way of the transgressor hard, that is only to
say that they marshalled public opinion effectively on *their* side, but also
to the general benefit of everybody except rascals and rioters.

As a matter of fact that is precisely what they were engaged in with
the able assistance of Mr. James Gladwin, who had had long experience
in planting and propagating Masonry along the frontiers and throughout the western settlements of the old Pennsylvania border. Like other
missionaries, he was devoted to the gospel he preached and propagated.
He had answered the call of his brethren to come over into Macedonia
and help. And he was quick to grasp the idea that, while the temporary
concentration of population at Bedford brought difficulties, it also provided an unusually ripe field from which to garner grain. That prospect
had in fact been the most telling argument in Garrett's letter to the
brethren of the Grand Lodge at Philadelphia, asking for help.

After Mr. Gladwin arrived and had discussed the situation thoroughly, things began to move rapidly. His plan was to reorganize
and straighten the Blue Lodges, or the "Hill Lodges", as they were called
at the time, because they usually met in the woods under open heaven,
by starting meetings, by bringing scattered or detached Masons together
again, and by initiating a large number of new and younger men as far
as the first three degrees. After the first work should be accomplished,
Mr. Gladwin had in mind taking some of the more promising brethren
farther along the path that led under the Ancient Arch.

Thus it was that in the garret at Pendergasses' the first meetings began.

12. Garrett's Garret

GARRETT'S garret was a long, low room extending under the roof of
the main building of the inn for its entire length. But everything else
about it was unexpected. Even to call it "low" is to be comparative. It was
"low" only in perspective when the eye ranged along its surprising length
and breadth. Without a single break or obstruction, it comprehended in
its dimensions the entire foundation space of the building below. Actually, the rooftree was a good fourteen feet above the garret floor. And
the house was hip-roofed. The giant walnut beams of the lower spill
rose therefore at an easy angle from the floor, providing ample space to
walk underneath them.

It was the dust-moted twilight of this loft that at first glance perhaps
made it seem mysteriously larger than it was. There was only one window, that in the south gable, since the chimney effectually blanketed

the entire north end of the house. But a warmth from the flues was thus pleasantly diffused through the place, a fact which winter travellers who had occasionally been given beds there had been delighted to note. Indeed, in General Forbes's time some twenty-odd officers of the Virginia Line had used it quite comfortably as a dormitory, until their stock of gentlemen's candles gave out.

The garret was approached from below by a steeply pitched stair resembling a ship's ladder. To ascend this through a trap door into the long, dimly lit room above was always a surprising and an unexpected experience. For the eye first took in an astonishing area of clear floor space as it came to that level, and then, as one shouldered one's self into the apartment above, and stood by the window, the entire untrammelled area of the place gradually became apparent like the arched reaches of a Gothic hall. It was a family joke of long standing with the Pendergasses that no gentleman had ever been brought there who had failed to exclaim as he first looked about him, "Well, I'll be damned!"

However, such exclamations were natural enough, for the very existence of the garret itself came as a surprise. From the outside of the house there was nothing to suggest it. There was only a bare, windowless expanse of shingled roof, a sight scarcely calculated to arouse speculation. A roof, of course, was taken for granted. And the garret beneath it therefore provided more genuine privacy and aloofness, more space for convenient secrecy, than any other place in town.

Hence, it was in Garrett's garret, and not in one of the barracks at the fort, as Captain Ourry had at first suggested, that the lodge meetings in Bedford village began sometime in February, 1764. But careful preparations and alterations were made beforehand to put the garret in order.

After midnight, when the bar was closed and the last patrons had departed from the big room below, the sound of the saw and a muffled hammering in the heavenly regions disturbed the women and children asleep in the dwelling house next door. Nothing was said about this, however, because the women were cautioned by Mrs. Pendergass to keep quiet about what they heard.

Under the superintendence of Mr. Gladwin and the critical eyes of Garrett and Captain Jack, the Pendergass boys, Murray, and Salathiel pitched in during the small hours of several nights and ran a panelled bench clear around three sides of the room. A low stage or platform was raised at the north end across the chimney, and on this dais was placed a wooden altar made to a design furnished by Mr. Gladwin. There were two smaller altars, or lecterns, situated opposite each other halfway down the room with a special chair behind them let into the bench. And there was also a simple but more massive chair set behind the altar on the platform.

Mrs. Pendergass, not without a sigh, lent one of her most long-cherished domestic treasures, a small width of Turkey carpet, to cover the platform. And Mr. Gladwin produced from his kit several rolls of canvas, which proved to be oil paintings of mystical import. These, an all-seeing eye, apparently enraged by what it saw, a divine hand coming out of a cloud, grasping a compass, with a beam of light and a bolt of lightning, were hung above the platform and against the chimney face at the end of the room.

But what was even more admired were three small pewter chandeliers, each containing a half dozen candles that, with due precaution against fire, Garrett had suspended on short chains from the rooftree, with tin reflectors above. The resulting illumination was truly astonishing and could only have been contrived in Philadelphia, whence the chandeliers had come.

In addition to three lights about the altar, there was a seven-branch candlestick set on a special stand by the worshipful master's chair, but this Luke Pendergass had to make himself out of bar iron under Mr. Gladwin's direction. Luke was the blacksmith of the family, while Mark was the carpenter. All the Pendergass brothers, even lame Toby, were skilful with their hands, but Mark excelled.

Mark owned a great chestful of carpenter's tools, including a remarkable variety and selection of planes provided with infinite chisel blades and gouges. Salathiel had seen axes, adzes, draw-knives and saws before, and had upon occasion used them. But he had never seen mitre boxes, squares, angles, small-saws and such a bewildering array of augers, bits, chisels, and gimlets. Mark Pendergass's carpenter's chest fascinated him. He made himself its owner's constant assistant, and during the renovation of the garret learned all he could from Mark, who was much flattered by the admiration which his skill evoked.

Between them, Mark and Salathiel not only made the intricate mouldings for the altars but also the panels for the seat that extended about the three walls. They sawed out in the old saw pit by the river enough pine boards to sheath-in the ceiling, standing up to their waists in snow in the pit, and sweating at that, to do it.

Luke forged what bolts and iron nails were essential. Still, iron was both scarce and expensive, and the sheathing for the ceiling of the lodge room was not only planed on one side and tongued and grooved, but finally set in place by white oak pegs driven home into the beams. And for every peg a hole had to be made.

All this took many nights of long, hard labour and afternoons in the saw pit. Yet the improvement was great. The rough underside of the roof shingles was entirely concealed and the room given a smooth finished appearance, even an elegance, which completely bowled over all those who first thrust their heads up through the trap door and looked about them. Finally, the floor was painted with triangles for a border surrounding the main design, an expanse of black and white checkerboard squares.

Mr. Gladwin had been present and presided at over a hundred initiations, and he regarded the first impressions of a neophyte as crucial. The instant when the lodge-assembled first burst on the view of the new initiate he called the "moment of great awakening". It was for him the supreme moment of existence. He remembered vividly the strange "memory" that had been aroused in him on the occasion of his own initiation, and he watched the face of every newcomer eagerly, when the light first burst upon it, in order to renew and to reassure himself vicariously of his own profound, initial sensations.

To many a simple frontier youth, in particular, the experience of initiation was frequently overwhelming, and in the back-country districts at least, Mr. Gladwin was not often disappointed, unless young faces lied. That the room at Pendergasses' was now peculiarly well fitted to produce the impressions he so much desired, Mr. Gladwin felt sure. And he had good reasons for thinking so.

For, instead of arriving in some rude loft, the new initiates would now seem to have been translated into the finished cavernlike abode of some powerful magician or spiritual personage, a being superior to and aloof from the wild nature without, and yet one who was always close by, lurking and immanent—for merely by ascending a garret stairs and coming through a trap door had they not found him and his worshippers at home? Only a missing password had been needed—and they had at last gained entrance to his very house.

So they would be duly astonished as they came through the trap door into the smooth, unexpected light; astonished at the seven candles burning in the many-branched tree near the altar, at the all-seeing eye looking at them, and at the double row of the familiar feet and faces of the worshippers. They would be astonished. But that was not what would astonish them most. It was this:

Each would suddenly feel that he had been alive for ages. He would instantly "remember" that he had often and often seen this familiar place before.

Whether the conferring of such high moments of mystical hindsight on initiates was a fact actually experienced by them or only a hope that it might be so, cherished by Mr. Gladwin, it would be hard to tell. He had faith. He was ambitious. And the effects he produced even by simple arrangements and in quite humble surroundings were seemingly always out of proportion to the poor means at hand. Those who first received their degrees under his presidence remained forever inspired by them. For it was the curious effect of Mr. Gladwin's personality to deepen and bring to life a mysterious presence in the ritual, until even literal-minded brethren were at times made aware of a soundless passing of unseen wings. Somewhere behind the bland, though rather rigid, face of this old Philadelphia merchant was a mind masterful in a priestly art. Men remembered him. And it made no difference that after a meeting it was only a simple old man on a homely horse who was seen to be riding away. Somehow he had conveyed part of his secret. And he managed to leave it behind him, operating.

At Bedford, at first, Mr. Gladwin had made no particular impression at all. He was pleasant and tactful, but essentially a quiet and an unassuming man. If it had not been for Garrett and Captain Jack's obvious reverence for him, Salathiel would scarcely have remarked his presence, beyond accepting him for what he actually was in this world, a merchant draper, one who had come to sell Garrett a bill of goods in a moment of great demand.

It was only natural that Mr. Gladwin's departure should seem to be delayed by the bad weather. And no one who was not otherwise informed thought anything more about him. But to those who did know, it was quite different. It was remarkable how in a short while Mr. Gladwin's quiet presence seemed to pervade and hold possession of the place; how easily and without attracting notice he became the vital centre of a far-reaching influence.

Within a short time after his arrival all the recognized Masons of the neighbourhood had been seen by him and interviewed. They simply dropped in and talked with him by the fire. Once or twice at night Mr. Gladwin paid a visit to the fort, or he went out for a few moments to see an "old friend" in the village. That was all.

And then the meetings of the newly organized lodge began.

They began before the alterations in the lodge room were entirely finished, and the only reason Salathiel was sure of it was that he had been asked to help carry up some paint to the garret and help spread it on the floor.

That evening a more than usually large number of "customers" gathered in the hearth room. Some even came early and had supper. Others dropped in after dark and had a glass. Perhaps the company was more distinguished than usual. But there was nothing especially noticeable about it. Individuals just happened to be there. Quite a few kept coming in and out. Mr. Yates was said to be giving a party upstairs. The hearth room gradually thinned out, leaving the usual wagoners, members of the garrison, and late town customers leaning over the bar or counter.

The two Pendergass boys who remained to serve seemed extremely affable and kept everybody well supplied and happy. Four Creek Indians who came for warmth and tobacco had three free drinks apiece by the fire. They stank quite normally. Members of the militia thumbed noses at them behind their backs, and departed. The bar closed a little earlier than usual. At eleven o'clock Mark clamped the grille down and locked the big door, after getting the Indians to leave. Then he and his brothers went up to join the lodge meeting in the garret, which had now been going on for some hours.

Salathiel went up and lay on his bed. The whole place seemed wrapped in sleep. Yates's room was empty, although his candle was left burning. At two o'clock in the morning Salathiel heard the muffled shuffling of feet on the planks overhead as the meeting broke up. People came quietly down the stairs and along the corridor past his room. Yates looked in on him, and they had a nightcap together. "It's good to think that you will soon be with us now," Yates said, as he nodded good night.

Apparently nothing had happened.

But in the course of that winter and early spring there were upwards of fifty young men about Bedford village who thought differently. They were the new material upon which Mr. Gladwin and Garrett and Captain Jack counted so greatly to broaden the foundations of their order. It might be, and as it turned out it was, many years before so many people were so conveniently gathered together again on the frontier. Mr. Gladwin could now see his prospective flock as a whole, black sheep and white. He and Garrett could pick those who promised to be leaders and men of influence.

The group of scattered brethren who had first been assembled and organized into a lodge in Garrett's garret rapidly turned in effect into a school of missionary Masons. Here and there about town, at the fort, and at Pendergasses', young fellows and a few older men were constantly being prepared for the first three degrees.

There was no general or active solicitation. News of what was afoot was most carefully passed on from one responsible person to another. Fathers brought their sons, uncles their nephews. Youths applied to Garrett or Captain Jack, and brought in their friends. The Pendergass boys alone accounted for a round dozen. Not everyone was accepted. And the distinction and honour of being chosen for initiation had a telling effect.

After some preparation, the candidates were finally passed on to Mr. Gladwin, to Garrett, Captain Jack, Dr. Boyd, or some other brother of high degree. These final interviews were quite solemn, but they were also impressive. And the older men seldom failed to make friends and admirers of those who came to sit at their feet.

Salathiel, for example, was first prepared by Yates. Yates was able to get up and move around now, although he had not yet left the house. For the most part he and Salathiel sat together in his room, while the young attorney explained to his friend the meaning and implications of the step he was about to take. He also helped him become letter perfect in those things which Salathiel must memorize, going over the words again and again. But they did not remain mere words. Yates opened up and extended the meaning of ancient texts and lessons like an intellectual fan.

Here again the early groundwork laid by McArdle proved invaluable. But Salathiel was able to appreciate that he was now enjoying the bene-

fit of instruction by a much broader and clearer mind. Yates's flashes o
humour and original insight were both helpful and startling. His wel
informed but lightly cynical wisdom was convincing. Yates was neve
pious, but he could still be reverent. So these talks turned out to be
good time well spent.

In fact, it was in these intimate talks together at Pendergasses' tha
the friendship between Salathiel and Yates was finally cemented and th
broad basis for its long enduring firmly laid. Yates was always amuse
by the natural simplicity of his friend Albine, but he was also impresse
by it in its complete honesty of purpose and directness of understanding
Here was a genuine naturalism, but here also was a wary simplicity tha
was instantly on guard, and seemed to be intuitively aware if it wa
being abused.

Much that was old in the world was pristine to Salathiel. That in
trigued Yates. But if Salathiel was curious and avid, eager to know an
even broad-minded, and though he was completely lacking in most o
the prejudices of conventional thinking—he was also alert and enor
mously careful about being fooled or taken in. He looked at thing
directly and saw them in their natural, unclouded reality. But he ap
proached them first with an all but savage circumspection.

Now it was this circumspect quality which Yates admired above a
in Albine—above every other quality save one. Neither of them wa
afraid of anything. They could decide on something together, and carr
it out against time, fortune, and the devil. And they both sensed tha
as a good basis for successful partnership.

"It's curious," said Yates one evening as he and Dr. Boyd, Mr. Glad
win, and Garrett sat together before the fire in the hearth room. It wa
the first time that Yates had come downstairs into the big room again—
"It's curious, but now take Albine. Sometimes I think his lack of wha
we would call education and my loss of an eye make us just about ever
in common sense. You see, by sheer accident we'll both always be force
to take a remarkably single-minded view of any proposition."

"I wouldn't worry so much about that lost eye of yours," interrupte
Dr. Boyd. "You can still see a good deal with one. It's not going to be—

"I'm not worrying," interrupted Yates. "As a matter of fact, I wa
thinking of certain compensations"—and he favoured the doctor humour
ously with a stony glare. But Garrett was anxious to hear what Yate
had to say about Salathiel.

"How much did your friend Albine really learn from his Shawne
uncle in the medicine lodge?" asked Garrett. "I've often wondered abou
that. You hear all kinds of tales about what the Injuns know and don'
know."

"Oh, not much," replied Yates. "I went into that carefully, too. Yo
remember we were all a bit startled by finding he knew the greeting sign
Well, the Injuns know that, and they know this sign, and this. Only

ittle different from ours. They give them like this, Albine says. And they have various grips. The redskins are particular on ways of shaking hands, anyway. Sal showed me one grip by which all the Turtles would know one another if they met up crawlin' about. Are you a Turtle, sir?" he asked Mr. Gladwin suddenly, leaning forward and shaking him by the hand with an arrangement of three fingers and a thumb.

"I'm afraid not—but I might be something else," replied Mr. Gladwin, looking surprised, for he had recognized the grip.

"Well, that's it exactly," continued Yates. "It's all a bit similar but never the same. There is only one thing we should all recognize as something in common. All the Injuns acknowledge the Great Spirit, and Sal thinks there are certain men in every tribe who could know each other by their Great Sign and be bound to acknowledge it. Such men are called 'The Children', he thinks—now that's funny, ain't it? But there's only a few of them. And Nymwha, Sal said, would never show it to him or talk much about it. It's the great secret of great chiefs and medicine men. And no one has ever known it who would not be too proud to abuse it. They make sure of that by some pretty severe ordeals, I opine."

Captain Jack sat listening somewhat gloomily during this talk about the Indians, but Mr. Gladwin nodded in agreement. "I'll tell you something about that," he said, after some cogitation. "I think their Great Sign is our Mercy Sign. An old Injun who was begging on the streets of Philadelphia once gave it to me. How he knew I might recognize it, I can't say. He was a Moravian convert, but he never learned it from them. I took him into my house, warmed him and fed him, and he died there. I was much condemned, of course, by some people for helping an Injun. There was trouble about a place for him in the cemetery. A certain vestry thought the potter's field would do. The Friends finally gave him decent burial. I never said anything about this before, naturally."

"I've heard it's like that, too," said Garrett. "As I remember, it was Nymwha or his brother who once gave me the greeting sign. I entertained them, too. It was in 'fifty-eight, I think, and I didn't know then—"

"I'm glad you didn't," exclaimed Captain Jack impatiently, "for it was that same Shawnee Nymwha and his brother Kaysinata who murdered this Albine boy's father in cold blood." Captain Jack paused to mutter something into his beard. "I heard about that from Chris Gist and he wasn't ever a liar. It happened nigh the Turkey Track crossing away back about Christmas, 'forty-eight. What's the difference what signs such varmints know?"

No one cared to argue with Captain Jack about that. Indeed, the conversation appeared to be about to bog down in sudden gloom. In the unexpected pause all of them noticed the tortured howling of a winter gale outside. It was no common storm. Mr. Gladwin looked at Yates and smiled.

"Send that boy to me before he's initiated," he said. "I'd like to talk with him. Send him tomorrow afternoon. He goes through with six others tomorrow night, I believe. Is he ready?"

"Ready," said Yates.

"I'm sure of it," said Garrett. "I've spent some time with him myself. He's a fine boy, and I think Yates here has done an honest job preparing him."

Dr. Boyd took a pinch of snuff.

"Tomorrow will make twenty-seven new ones so far," he said. "A remarkable record for a lodge in a howling wilderness. Now I was telling this Albine lad only yesterday that I've no doubt the Injuns would think that they could *make* their Great Spirit listen by carrying on high hocus-pocus in a medicine lodge. And I said a white man's lodge doesn't think that. I thought Albine might still hold some savage notions. But I found he hadn't. So I went on further to tell him that the chief difference between a white man's lodge and a church is that in a lodge we fear God but stand up before him and serve him by helping our fellow men; while in a church we are afraid of God, grovel before him, and try to save our own dirty souls."

Old Garrett laughed heartily. "It's a bold distinction, doctor; you'd better not try to make it with the chaplain."

"The trouble with you scientific men," said Mr. Gladwin, "is that you're always going about corrupting the youth."

"*Must* it be hemlock?" asked Dr. Boyd, waving his empty mug enquiringly.

"Make it hot buttered rum this time," suggested Yates, shivering. "It's a damned cold night and a wolfish wind goes prowling around."

"Why, a drop of rum makes a good period to any discussion," agreed Mr. Gladwin. "Garrett, can you manage it?"

"I know Pina can," said Garrett, leaning back in his chair and looking at his old slave where she sat by the chimney.

"Pina, Pina," he called. "Stir your old stumps! Hot buttered rum double all round."

The mutter of the old woman and the fumbling of the winter wind in the chimney seemed now to be making a conversation of their own. The long roll of the tattoo beating at the fort came only fitfully through the winter blasts like interrupted thunder.

"Wonder how long this fur-thickenin' weather's goin' to hold?" mused Captain Jack. "Somethin' we just talked about reminds me I've got a work to do. And it's well-nigh the first of March."

Remembering what the work was, the rest of the company drank silently, and with brief good nights retired.

"So the blood fit has come over you again, Jack," said Garrett as they climbed the stairs together.

"Aye, that it has!" answered the old hunter huskily. "Did you hear those voices in the storm tonight?" He stood in the hall, shading his candle and listening.

"Hark to that, would you?" His eyes glittered.

Garrett left him standing alone and went across the bridge to the other house to bed. Captain Jack's "fits" depressed him. He was glad to climb in beside his wife and be warm. Outside the snow drifted clear up to the lower window sills.

Captain Jack sat smoking alone in his room wrapped in a blanket. In his mind's eye he saw a place beyond the mountains called the Salt Kettles. There was a river and a high cliff. A wisp of smoke rose through the trees that were in misty spring foliage. Several canoes were drawn up along the riverbank. It was a peculiarly peaceful scene. Captain Jack pondered it carefully for several hours.

"Yep," said he to himself, "we kin! The whole kit and passel of 'em."

He knocked his cold pipe out thoughtfully and turned in. . . .

Salathiel had his little talk the next afternoon with Mr. Gladwin. He came away with the firm resolution to try to lead a better life. He saw now why that was desirable. No one had ever talked to him quite like Mr. Gladwin. He felt prepared now for the ordeal of the evening.

On account of the deep snow the lodge members were slow in assembling that night. The drifts lay belt-deep in places but the wind had died away at noon. There was a hard frosty stillness abroad in which the bells of a pack train rang like chimes. The half-frozen drivers crowded the bar and left before evening, well warmed. After that few except lodge members came in.

The seven candidates for the initiation that night took supper together in a corner by themselves. Besides Salathiel, there was his friend Nat Murray, Cornet Appleboy from the fort, John Nogle, the miller's son, William Smith and John Banner, farmers, and one Jonathan Dickson.

In view of the ordeal ahead, they were all somewhat silent and subdued. But after a jug was passed around by John Banner their spirits improved, and full justice was done to Pina's hoecakes, ham, and potatoes. Garrett came after supper and sat with them. He told them he had been initiated when he was only eighteen at Colchester in England, according to the old York rite.

"It is the most ancient rite of all, they say," he continued. "Some people think there has been a lodge at York ever since Constantine's time. Dr. Brandsford was a very learned man at Colchester in my day. He it was who wrote a book about old King Cole and Queen Helena, and he was also a very high Mason. I once heard him tell my father he had seen Masonic carvings on old stones along the Tyne River, that went back into heathen times. I don't know. But what you are going to learn and see tonight is not new. It has held men together in brotherhood for ages past. All of them were not fools," smiled Garrett. "It is important we should keep on remembering in this new country what they knew at home."

All of them sat listening attentively. They were surprised to hear old Garrett talk this way. He seemed to have grown younger as he spoke of his youth in England. Something happened to his tongue and voice, and he spoke for a moment with an earlier accent. Meanwhile, the lodge was assembling upstairs.

Presently the sponsors came for their candidates and drew straws for the order in which they should appear. Yates drew the shortest for Salathiel, and that meant he would be last.

"Come on upstairs," he said to Salathiel. "It will be some hours yet before our turn comes, and my eye pains me in the light."

So they went upstairs and sat in Yates's room with one candle burning dimly on the floor. From time to time the footfalls of the other candidates passed them, going along the corridor and ascending the stairs. They heard the knocks, and the trap door open. A shuffling of feet went on in the floor overhead. There were voices, and the door closed again.

It was nearly midnight when Salathiel was finally summoned and followed Yates up the ladder into the stifling room. The lodge rose to meet him, and he stood looking down the entire length of the place to the worshipful master in his collar and apron, on the platform.

It made no difference that he had lately helped to fashion this room with his own hands. The golden light of the candles, the presence of many people, the rows of aprons seemed all to have united into one thing that was something else. The ladder and the comfortable house beneath it had disappeared. He was translated into another world. Its walls seemed suddenly completely to surround him and to make him a part of it. And even as he stood there, its strangeness died away. He began vaguely to remember a forgotten acquaintance with this chamber like something he had seen before in childhood, like a familiar apartment recognized in a dream. He had come back here. How? It seemed to him that he had come down into this place, that he was now deep underground.

Yates vouched for him.

Through the yellow fire of the candles on the altar the master was now saying something to him.

He remembered how to reply.

The questions and the responses began.

What was happening seemed to be taking place outside of time . . .

An hour later he took his assigned seat among his brethren, a Free and Accepted Mason.

Afterward, when they went downstairs, Mr. Gladwin looked pleased. They were all pleased. They made him welcome among them. Old Garrett and Yates were positively happy about it. It was like a final homecoming. And about the fire in the hearth room, where they gathered that night before leaving, it was still the same. He belonged. He would always belong now, he felt.

For about the initiation of Salathiel Albine into the lodge at Bedford there was something which even its worshipful master and Garrett never suspected; could not, indeed, be expected to understand. But Captain Jack did.

"My boy," he said, "you are a free white man now. Never forget it." Then he passed his pipe across the table to Salathiel, who took a great puff and blew the smoke out through both nostrils ceremoniously. Captain Jack did likewise, and they sat watching the wreaths of smoke curling together into one cloud over their heads.

Captain Jack laughed cannily. "You damned Injun!" he said, "now *we've* got you," and he slapped Salathiel on the back.

13. The Women Underneath

AROUND, and underneath the business and doings of the men at Pendergasses', through the village of Bedford—and for that matter, everywhere else—flowed the activity of the women.

The frontier war, as all wars do, had greatly disturbed and harassed the women. It had uprooted them from their lonely cabins, where a wife could be busy all day, and half the night too, making and keeping children alive. Now for the time being many of them were concentrated about the fort and village at Bedford, while the white man settled his bloody accounts with the red, while colonels disappeared westward with regiments intent upon the business of killing.

But the aim of the women had not been changed. Their problem remained the same. Only the scene of their labours had been shifted. Theirs was not a business, it was not a job. It was not a game or a symbolic something that engaged them. It was nature and the thing itself; the thing that must go on. And the women were part and parcel of it.

To a lonely woman and her brood, who had fled suddenly from a dark forest cabin with a patter of moccasins close behind, despair and terror had been turned into hope and confidence by the mere sight of the Union Jack flying above the fort and over the roofs of the town. And, once having arrived—then, quite instantly, these family hermits were in the midst of many, many people and the cheering noise of life.

It had been quite bewildering to them at first. The newcomers were often shy, silent, and suspicious. Also there were many hardships to be endured. There was scant food at first, and it was difficult to find shelter. But then an amazing thing happened. They were not simply left to perish by themselves, while the woods brooded over their fate. They were helped to continue to exist by other people, by "strangers".

Colonel Bouquet, some other officers at the fort, and Garrett were the helpful "strangers". It was due to the colonel alone that an authorized ration for the inhabitants had first been forthcoming from the commissary stores. He had first seized upon the Indian goods and supplies to distribute them the year before. Then the army had been prevailed upon to help. And finally, the provincial legislature, having authorized some militia, now undertook both to arm and to send provisions to the starving frontiers.

"They think they've lost their souls anyway by voting for soldiers," said Garrett. "And I know they're good and scairt. But if Buckey wins down the Ohio, they'll all turn calm and holy and careless again."

"That they will!" agreed Captain Smith of the militia. "It's only the fear of death and God A'mighty brings Pharisees to their reason. And there's more Pharisees at Philadelphy than in hell and Jeerusalem together. No decent man would go there even for to be hanged now—and . . ."

But then Captain Smith began to roar. For the very thought of Philadelphia made him rage like a lion, and he foamed madly about Indian traders.

Yet actually the news from Philadelphia, Garrett knew, was not quite so bad as all that. And Garrett really knew. For he it was who had co-operated with Bouquet and Ecuyer in organizing supply, in hiring wagons, and bringing all the influence he could find in Philadelphia to get help for the frontier, and for his part of the country in particular.

Mr. Gladwin had helped. The merchants had assisted. They consigned goods to Garrett with the prospect of payment extremely remote. The Friends meetings made gifts. Some of the traders even "lent" their horses and drivers for mere wages and subsistence. City churches took up collections. From Arthur St. Clair came a gift of ten pounds sterling. The Penn family remitted certain rents, and the Quakers in England eventually bestirred themselves. Alarmed authorities bought supplies. A depot was formed at Carlisle where the militia was to rally, and where it was hoped eventually to bring the Indian captives, if Bouquet were successful.

All this had taken time and untold correspondence; demands, and arguments by Colonel Bouquet. Ecuyer even went east once, instead of west, to start the wagon trains and pack horses moving. He returned, and then disappeared westward again, leaving Burent to further transport at Bedford under Captain Ourry.

But even before the break of weather in 1764, wheels had begun to roll and pack horses to slither and slip westward. Herds of beef cattle and hogs were driven through as far as Bedford. There they were killed and salted down for hauling to Fort Pitt, for the road from Bedford to

Pittsburgh was still a tremendous hazard. Now and then a convoy got through as far as Ligonier. Ecuyer wore himself out accomplishing even that. But from Ligonier only a trickle of recruits and provisions went through to Bouquet.

It would take open weather and summer to move the mass of men and material for the Ohio expedition over the mountains to Fort Pitt. Yet for that very reason things tended to concentrate temporarily at Bedford. If one had any doubt of it, the lively noise of the place all through the day, and half the night too, was convincing.

It was a more hopeful noise now as spring came on. People were beginning to regain confidence. To the women particularly, the cheerful din of the village was constantly reassuring. The eternal, depressing silence of the woods had disappeared. Women no longer lay at night with straining ears and nerves. They could sit by a fire now, knitting, and talking to other women. The children slept and were safe. The worst to be expected was that mister might come home drunk. There was a lot of liquor about. But a man couldn't do just what he liked to his family in a town. People came and asked what in God's name was agoin' on. Besides, a woman could have a comforting nip by the fire herself—and pass her jug along.

Also there was plenty of food in town by the turn of the year. More than most people had ever seen before. There were potatoes, salt hog fixin's, and white flour.

Some complained about the white flour. They wanted samp and good yellow meal. Presently there was mother-of-yeast in fifty crocks about town, and then the white bread went better. If you had money you could get a bit of molasses or loaf sugar at Pendergasses'. That was *mighty* fine. It was rumoured that Mrs. Pendergass herself drank real tea. But some people exaggerated.

Still, it was an elegant house she had. If you were lucky enough to be invited upstairs, you saw wonders. It was like a house down east or old Virginny way. There were niggers and Injuns for help. You certainly learned things at Mrs. Pendergass's. Only a few attained the height of upstairs, however. Most people got no farther than the spinning room. But every respectable female went there. It was now the general meeting place for all the decent women in town.

The spinning room was a lean-to shed that stood against the dwelling house. There was a good puncheon floor in it, a rough chimney with a hewn-log mantel, and three windows that looked out up and down the river. They were the first windows with glass lights some people had seen. The wonder of the place, though, was a painted German clock with a silver bell that struck every half hour.

This "hall of the fine arts of spinning and weaving" was now thrown open to every housewife in town. And if the men congregated at the bar of the inn, the women gathered day after day, and gradually in increasing numbers, in the spinning room, where a fire burned, the clock struck cheerfully, the looms clicked and clattered, and the spin ning wheels whirred. On cold afternoons the spinning room was gen erally crowded.

Now, although this gathering at the spinning room was all quite natural and inevitable, it was also unexpected and enormously appreci ated by the women. Old Mrs. Pendergass had been eminently successful in thus providing herself company. She and her daughters really under stood how people should be managed. They had conducted life in a crowd in their own family for a long time.

It was Bella Pendergass who had learned most from her mother in this regard. The experience of many Indian alarms, when the family and all their neighbours had again and again been driven in to live near the fort, had given Bella much practice. She was completely devoted to her mother and not interested in mating. She was not cold. She had simply not been awakened to male necessity as yet, and all her energy was employed and found satisfaction in a purely female marshalling of domestic events.

In the spinning room during the crowded spring of "the '64", Bella arched the fine neck of a virgin palfrey, covered with a chestnut mane, and whinnied in the dust of a storm of work and gossip. Too frail to come downstairs frequently any more, her mother participated vicari ously in all that was agog in the town by means of her daughter's mouth. But Mrs. Pendergass was not too feeble to advise. She was still a one woman steering committee for the suddenly swarming neighbourhood And to be just, most of her suggestions were benign and wise. Law, of course, to Bella.

From the first there had been a certain prestige about going to the Pendergass spinning room. One primped. And invariably one looked one's self over for fleas. Carefully, for the town swarmed with them And when one was to be seen by other people in company it was nice to be appreciated for one's self alone.

Besides, the Pendergasses were known to be elegant. Elegant—and clean. Bella Pendergass actually smelled like a lady. Lilac-water, it was rumoured, was the cause of this. Only one faint whiff of virtuous fashion from the metropolis, it set the female world at Bedford on fire and the spinning room circle on a pinnacle of ladylike grace and sanc tity.

And, good Lord, how interesting it all was!

Even the men soon found that out. For, of course, certain overtones of the spinning room were confided to them by their wives—and others Nor was there anything idle about this talk. On the contrary.

It was Bella and several Mrs. Macs, for instance, who, finding out how many babies were soon going to be born, proposed to do something about it. They arranged to have the women who best understood sur

vival of arrival present at the moment. They even got Dr. Boyd to help
at difficult births—and for an army surgeon he learned a great deal.

Also it was Bella and two Mrs. MacPhersons, along with dark Mary
Sheean, the Irish papist, who practically constituted themselves a committee to find quarters for the forlorn refugee families in town. They
put the men to work building cook sheds and family shelters near the
hospital lot. They begged the use of cellars, lean-tos and haylofts. Animals were crowded to one side in barns to make room for human families, until temporary shelters could be built.

Mark Pendergass and his chest of tools was thus in constant requisi-
tion. Harried by Bella, and followed by Salathiel as an amused assistant,
Mark dashed from one place to another notching logs, fitting doors,
patching cracks against the weather, and framing roofs over crazy
shanties—even showing some people how to split their own shingles,
until it seemed to him he had built half the town himself. And for all
his trouble he got no pay.

"It's all for the love of God alone," explained Mary Sheean, whose
own red-headed brood of ragged young Celts had found shelter from
the weather in a wagon shed. It had a slab front added to it provided
with a window, which the boys stole from the fort. This nondescript
shebang became Irish headquarters, where potatoes were forever roasting
in a mud-and-stick chimney that frequently caught fire. There were a
good many Irish in the village, Catholics, much despised by the Presbyterian Macs, although everybody's children played happily together. The
Irish at least were grateful to Mark and his charitable gang of axe and
adzemen for helping build them in. But Bella was simply inveterate.
She drove her brother, until Mark complained that his sister was worse
than his wife in always finding something to be fixed up. Garrett only
laughed.

"Keep at it, Mark," said he. "Your sister's dead right. Get some more
of these idle, wenching lads to help you. The babies can't be born in
the snow. That's plain, ain't it?"

So Mark cursed, spat on his hands, and kept at it.

By early spring no more families were arriving and everybody had
some kind of shelter, even if it was only an old tent "borrowed" from
the commandant, and boarded in with slabs.

To tell the truth Captain Ourry had been most helpful to the inhabitants whenever he could. Bella and her women frequently appealed to
him. He soon had every confidence in Miss Pendergass, "a most respectable female". Some others weren't. Some of the bound servant girls, the
runaways especially, plied an ancient trade with the garrison. The Welsh
girls were the worst. They sang a great deal, and cheerfully spread the
pox.

"Garrison life in the winter," said Dr. Boyd philosophically.

Boyd more than any other man was of "some use", insisted Bella. She even told her mother she thought Dr. Boyd "understood". He had once been asked secretly to meet the assembled sisterhood in the spinning room. Babies. The subject was delicate but visibly pressing. Dr. Boyd's suggestions were masterpieces of practical innuendo. Of course, no one could mention the subject directly. He called babies "recruits". By pure indirection a kind of surreptitious midwifery was organized. Dr. Boyd told how it was done in Edinburgh, adding some observations of his own. In March there were fourteen "recruits" in the village, who arrived successfully. Only one of the mothers died. In cold weather there was not so much birth fever, Dr. Boyd noticed. Not so much as usual.

But the young children, boys and girls, were even a more pressing problem. Lonely youngsters from the cabins had soon discovered each other in town. They abandoned their families, except for food and sleep, and ran wild. The fort and village, long prepared to defy Pontiac and his warriors, was now taken by mass assault from the rear by small boys.

A host of fierce urchins dressed in coonskin caps and sheepskin nether garments defied the cold weather, chilblains, and the sentries at the fort, who, not being able to shoot them, fraternized. Boys swarmed at parades and guard mounts, begged food, stole. They rode slab sleds down the glacis and the steep village street. They played soldiers and Injuns. They fought furious snow battles and snowballed everybody and his Majesty's officers. They haunted the stables and picket lines. They slept in wagons, and crawled under the pest hospital. They slid on the ice of the river. They broke through it, and had to be rescued by long ladders and half-frozen dragoons, who crawled out after them.

A shinny game that kept perpetually breaking out on the parade directly in front of headquarters finally drove Captain Stewart, the adjutant, to take violent measures.

An official "bull" breathing anathema on boys and dogs appeared in the form of general orders. It proclaimed a curfew and imposed fines on parents and owners whose offspring and dogs remained visible, or even audible, after retreat had sounded.

But Captain Stewart's indignation tripped him into a too enthusiastic official prose. In a general order that soon became famous he had directed his sentries to arrest any dog caught in the fort, on sight—any dog which appeared to be "about to bark". It was that phrase which proved the captain's undoing.

Seventeen howling curs held prisoner at guard mount next day, and Ecuyer's undisguised chuckles of delight as the tall Highlanders solemnly explained to the frantic Captain Stewart that, "Ivery tike under arrrest undootidly appeared aboot t'bark, sir"—for a time forced the adjutant to take to messing alone in order to avoid a storm of ironical congratulations. Chaff, eventually from official quarters, descended not lightly upon his head. The shinny game removed itself to the moat, but it was cheered on from the battlements. And Captain Stewart felt distinctly that he was losing what everybody now called "Captain Stewart's War".

The curfew gave him surcease by night, but his days were long and filled with an agony of ingenious juvenile acrimony. The honest and sensitive young officer was soon the butt of his best friends at the fort and the object of general hostility in town, even though the seventeen dogs had all been reprieved. He was popularly supposed to be longing for the massacre of young males, preferably in the cradle. For it seemed only natural that a man who threatened to shoot dogs might also wish to murder children, and the Irish women clinched the rumour by calling him Herod. So "Herod" he became—to the unholy joy of the whole garrison. The name proved apt, for Captain Stewart was a nervous-looking, refined aristocrat with a thin mouth.

It was really not so salubrious for Captain Stewart.

Just before retreat—and curfew—large gangs of boys accompanied by loping, leaping, and frantic mop-eared hounds appeared before the south bastion of the fort, where there was a splendid echo from the high ramparts. There they shouted horrid things in unison. What the echo repeated about Captain Stewart was inevitably overheard by the garrison, and caused even strong sergeants to simper at attention.

The echo from the south bastion soon proved to be a powerful one. In a rude manner it repeated public opinion, and reverberations of it were eventually heard rolling back and forth even in official correspondence:

> Tell Captain Ourry at Bedford to put an end to the troops
> of arch [*sic*] young rebels who so plague the garrison there.
> The petty pilfering of the public stores by pets of the soldiers
> must stop. His Excellency is annoyed and thinks Ourry too
> complacent with the inhabitants. He instructs you . . .

wrote headquarters to Colonel Bouquet, and Bouquet wrote back to Ourry at Bedford.

"Pets!" exclaimed Stewart bitterly, "pets, sir? While I'm called 'Herod' by every mother in town and forced to drink alone at Pendergasses' in Coventry, sir, I'm now censured by headquarters for being complaisant! What are your orders, captain? I shall be only too happy to enforce them. Perhaps if a few boys were hanged in chains? Shall we erect a tall gallows and inform his Excellency that . . . that . . ." Captain Stewart choked.

"Now, now, captain," replied Captain Ourry in a mollifying tone, "*I* am not censuring you. I was merely calling the situation to your attention. I have no orders. I have every confidence in your own ingenuity."

Captain Stewart snorted, saluted, and withdrew.

Over a tall drink of brandy he confided his troubles some hours later to Surgeon Boyd in a quiet corner of the hearth room at Pendergasses'.

"He wished merely to call the situation to my attention," drawled Stewart. "As if *I* didn't know, as if *I* didn't have the situation called and bellowed out at me everywhere I go. It's that damn echo, you know. We can't fire on children from the south bastion just to prove we aren't complaisant. What!"

Boyd laughed.

"For God's sake don't laugh," cried Stewart despondently.

"I'll tell you what, Stewart," said the doctor after a bit. "You're not going about this as a widower like myself would. You're a bachelor. And so it hasn't occurred to you that the thing to do is to get the women on *your* side."

"Really! What do you want me to do? Marry that echo?"

"Oh, no, I'm really being practical. You have a revolt of boydom on your hands. Now why don't you go and talk with the Queen Bee of the hive here? I mean my old and much valued friend and fireside companion, Mrs. Rose Pendergass."

"Why, I'd talk with the devil in horns and tail, if it would do any good," growled Stewart. "But look here, Boyd, ain't this just another of your damned Jacobite plots to put a hoax on one of the king's men? Frankly I'm not in a mood just now to be had just for tickling your funny bone."

"On my honour it ain't a plot," replied Boyd. "But you are in a delicate condition, captain. You admit that. And so I suggest you talk it over with Mrs. Pendergass. All that you'll find is a wise old woman with a Devon accent thick as cream."

"I once hunted on Exmoor," said Stewart. "Well, lead on. But if word of this ever gets about, by God, doctor, I'll call you out."

"Never a word from me," laughed Boyd, as he rose to show the way to the dwelling house.

Taking his hat and his reputation in his hands, Captain Stewart reluctantly followed the surgeon over the Bridge of Sighs into what he called the "women's quarters" next door. Mrs. Pendergass was at home. In fact she was drinking real tea.

And that was why it finally came about that a school was started in the official precincts of the fort itself in one of the vacant barrack rooms. "Captain Stewart's Academy," Boyd insisted upon calling it, thus putting the credit for its foundation where he wanted it to lie. It was ably presided over by one Malcolm Hume, lately discharged from the grenadiers as an invalid, because both his feet had been frozen and one had finally dropped off at the hospital.

The school flourished under Mr. Hume. Roughly at first, and then steadily. Mr. Hume proved hard as flint, but he struck sparks that kindled a light in darkness. Long after the Indian troubles were over, when even the fort was gone, Mr. Hume continued to provide a copperplate hand for succeeding generations of youths to copy from the best schoolmaster in all the valley. Thus "Captain Stewart's War" ended unexpectedly in planting the first seeds of learning at Bedford—but for boys only.

The girls as usual were left to their own educational devices. And, as usual, out of sheer circumstances and the varying incidents of existence they provided themselves with a preparation sufficient to continue life successfully. Theirs was an informal and instinctive method of acquiring the ways and means of existing with all the reasons for doing so taken for granted. It was an education by imitation of doing rather than by word of mouth. It was self-generated, and the practice began with dolls and ended in grandchildren.

At least that was the way it seemed to Surgeon Boyd one bright, snowy afternoon as he sauntered down from the military hospital on the hill to Pendergasses' in the valley. He was badly in need of a hot dram to pull himself together. On occasions, particularly after screaming amputations, the circle of Dr. Boyd's awareness became hugely wide, intolerably vast.

He seemed to be able to think of everything at once; to see and to hear petty details of what was going on everywhere. And in this vicious circle, while his mind vivisected the world into its various organic functions, and yet kept telling him and explaining to him how beautifully one part fitted into another—he was walking down from the hospital to get a drink at Pendergasses'.

By God, he needed one!

There were only a few ways he could stop himself talking to himself. He could talk to someone else, like Yates, and let *him* reply. Or at night he could write in his commonplace book; get a whole section of himself out of him and into the book and locked up. Jail for Chatterbox! It was a nice big book with a brass lock on it. But it was nearly full now of explanations of the relations of this thing to that, medical notes, geological and botanical data, philosophical arguments—downright, barefaced metaphysics.

His secrets.

Since it was a very clear winter day with the sunlight glaring on the snow, all the small details of everything that was going on were projected upon the dark retina of his mind with a clear-cut brightness and an automatic memorability that forced him both to notice them and to try to put them each in place. Particularly, he noticed what the girls and women were doing in the village. He needed women. He missed his wife bitterly—and the little girl. Cholera. Bombay.

Most of the small girls in this village seemed to be nursing dolls, too. Anything would do for a doll. A log with a whittled head—the carving was not important. A corncob with beady eyes did as well, or a double-pronged root. Anything! Anything wrapped in a bright rag. But these objects upon which to lavish affection had other clothes; delicate, gossamer-spangled robes in which the tender fancies of tiny women swaddled their imaginary offspring. Anybody with half an eye could see that rags were really elfin splendours.

How any cocksure philosopher might be struck dumb with astonishment, thought the doctor, to be able to observe what he was now suddenly aware of—that underneath the grown-up human life of the village was a sub-race of gnomes, babies' babies, misshapenly beautiful, with starlight streaming from their eyes; with bright berry mouths kissed passionately by little mothers; hushed, whispered to, put to sleep, wakened, dressed, spanked, and sung to until they came to life in queer corners where female children played at keeping house in empty barrels or held pavilioned courts under the royal drapery of their mothers' lousy, moth-eaten shawls.

And, if our strolling philosopher were not of an entirely mechanic or logic-chopping turn of mind, mused the doctor, then he might reflect that out of extreme delicacy emerges ruthless strength; that most little white girls remember all by themselves, even when alone, a dim green country where their as yet unborn children walk. A land of dolls, trolls, and fays, bright with magic morning. The original, northern, elfin homeland of the race.

Cool and mysterious it is lying far in the secret past. Delicate, but yet immortal and natively recollected. Out of it mighty commonwealths of men eventually erect themselves and walk into the sunset, making the land to flourish, and then to smoke and vanish behind them.

"For," said Boyd aloud to himself, "the fierce son of woman arises out of his mother's green country and marches forward into the flaming destruction of the future years."

Having said it, the doctor suddenly recollected himself, looked around to be sure he had not again been overheard muttering nonsense, and made hastily for the door of the big hearth room at Pendergasses', and a chair by the fire. All that old Garrett saw when he came in was Dr. Boyd as usual: a rather sturdy, red-faced Englishman in a worn surgeon's uniform with rusty spots of old blood on his faded scarlet sleeves, a man with troubled blue eyes. What he wanted was a long drink, quick.

Garrett gave it to him and excused himself for a moment, remarking that he would have to step out and put an end to the infernal racket that was always going on next door.

"You're not liable to put an end to *that*," mused the surgeon. "It's not infernal, it's human. And I'd like to bet it's going to go on here for the next thousand years or so—at least."

The contents of his stone mug now put an end both to Dr. Boyd's muttered remarks and to his thoughts. He looked relieved, and the wrinkles about his eyes relaxed. The noise next door at the dwelling house increased. Dr. Boyd laughed confidently. For whatever he might think of his more recondite cogitations, he felt quite sure that his last observation that afternoon was quite right. The din next door might well make even a philosopher curious as to what was going on there.

Rightly considered, the din next door might even be said to be memorable. The noise there certainly promised to go on for many years at least. In the Pendergass dwelling house was concentrated more life, vigour, and various promises for the future than under any other roof in town. In that respect it was unusual, in all others typical of the intense domestic life of the neighbourhood when driven in on itself for mutual safety and shelter from Indian raids. Only at Pendergasses' there were more people in one house than usual, and it was a bigger house.

Altogether, there were eighteen people who had found shelter under the dwelling house roof, including Garrett, who always slept there at night in the big family bed with old Rose. Only death finally parted them. But Garrett was the only man who did sleep in the house regularly.

Besides the old couple, there were now only women and children in the dwelling house. All of them were members of the Pendergass tribe, except Diamond, the slave girl, who nursed everybody's babies, and little Liza Shockoe, a blond orphan child of three winters, taken in to be mothered by everybody during the troubles of '64.

Bella and Susan Pendergass, Garrett's two unmarried daughters, had the room next to their mother's on the upper floor. Their sister, Mrs. Polly Murray, a widow, the mother of Salathiel's friend Nat, occupied the hall with her young son, Martin. In a small room at the end of the same hallway slept Phoebe and Arthur Davison, also Garrett's grandchildren. The two Davisons were only "avisitin' over from Fort Loudon," where their mother Rachel lived, father William being a prosperous tanner of that place. Thus most of Garrett's more immediate family were on the same floor close to old Mrs. Rose.

On the floor underneath in four rooms and a large entry slept and dwelt the "in-laws": Charles's wife, Chloe, a sick and childless woman; Emma and Clara, Matthew and Mark's wives with their children, five in all. There were Emma's "little Garrett", Jane, and Edward, ranging from four years to eighteen months; and Clara's twins, Frank and Thomas, aged two, the envy and pride of the whole family. Little Liza Shockoe was just tucked in. Mat and Mark Pendergass were thus by force of circumstances temporarily separated from their wives and slept downstairs at the inn.

"But that is just as well, for the time bein'," said Garrett. "I don't need to tell you why. You're just across the bridge away, and you'll not be in a constant *ding-dong* of babies. Till ye *kin* git back to your own cabins, it'll kinda be more decent and restful all round."

One peep into the "women's quarters" was sufficient to make even an ardent husband agree. There were plenty of beds and trundle beds there, packed close, but no place for dalliance. In fact the dwelling house was almost entirely given over to the children.

Up and down the wide stairs in the lower entry, and all day long, crept, played, and scrambled the babies and young children of the house. They also invariably had infant friends in from the village, whose mothers were only too glad to leave them there whenever they could. Then, too, there were pups and kittens; occasionally a miserable chicken or a duck or two to make Roman holiday for the infant populace, and to add to the squawks and screams, the pounding and racing of feet, the wails and clatter.

At the top of the stairs sat the black Diamond picking tow or sewing, quelling quarrels that became too violent, and snatching up youngsters who fell down stairs bump by bump or required liquid or solid attention, comfort or reproof.

Diamond did well with an Ethiopian tact and a soft, soothing voice which seemed made to comfort and reassure infancy. Casualties were mostly minor. But the entry for all that was a frantic place, a mad mêlée of small children, where a modest kitten could hardly get its business done in a corner before it was snatched back by the tail into the maelstrom of never-ceasing play.

Sometimes Phoebe came to take charge. She would tell stories and say rhymes, aided by young Arthur, with all the pack perched below her on the shadowy stairs. Or sometimes it was one of the Pendergass sisters, Clara or Emma, who relieved Diamond. All the women passed through the entry at some time during the day, even Bella and Sue. It was the main viaduct of the household, and the incidents of its traffic, and what could be glimpsed through the door when it swung open into the wagonyard, were news and wonder to the children. On good days they played in the wagonyard itself with the papooses and pickaninnies; with the entire animal population of the place.

Cooking went on in the outside kitchen and the yard; washing, candle, and soap making. Beyond the big gate wagons with chimes of ringing horse bells went by on the road. Somebody was always cutting firewood with an axe or sawing planks in the pit. The only flock of tame geese in that part of the world hissed, and chased everybody. There were horses, cows, pigs, and poultry. There were the cabins of the Negro slaves and the Injuns to wander in and out of—and friends there. There was a blacksmith shop, and a small tanning pit and shed. An elk or a bear brought in by Captain Jack or Salathiel usually hung nose downward from the slaughter bar. There were dogs, pet coons, and rabbits. Altogether it was not a bad place to commence life in—the yard.

There you could watch the women coming to the spinning room in the afternoon. At times, if you were both big and good, you could help with the work in there. And just before sunset Grandpa Garrett called everybody into the house by the fire downstairs to read from the Good

Book. Then there was hot corn-meal mush, milk, a strip of bacon, Now-I-Lay-Me, and bed. The best of it was you never had to sleep alone. You were not afraid when you were at Grandpap Pendergass's—and there was a war. No Injuns could git ya, and there was company. Lots of little cousins, and uncles and aunts. There was plenty to do always.

Certainly there was plenty for the women to do—always. But they, too, like the children, tended not only to make the best of things, but to enjoy and profit by the experience of being at Grandpa Pendergass's. There was also company for them. There was the warm security of the tribe, and the solid comforts of the establishment. There was really less work to do than when they were alone on new clearings with their husbands. For the women parcelled out the work among themselves. And the whole place functioned as one family under the able direction of Bella and the experienced advice of old Mrs. Pendergass.

Above all, there was a certain abundance, even a wealthy feeling about being at Grandpap's, for the trade and ample supplies at the store brought to hand many things and materials which were not available or only the rarest of luxuries at a combination home and blockhouse in the mountains.

Perhaps that was why there was a fine air of security and hearty happiness about the place that in future times made stories of it a golden legend in the family memory of the tribe. Undoubtedly in "the '64", when everybody was at Grandpap's, there was a note of confidence, a cheerful excitement, a higher pitch to the women's voices at the dwelling house than usual. And the men weren't always around, either. They had the inn and the store, the war, and jobs about town to keep them busy. The women could get their heads together and hatch something out. As for Grandpa Garrett, he could be counted upon to sympathize. It was all right to have him sleeping in the house. He was a wise old man, and he helped.

Bella was responsible to a great extent for the smooth way in which life went. No one was jealous or puzzled about her. It was instinctively understood that Aunt Bella was not going to marry. The whole family were in a way her children, and what she did was for them and not for herself. She had tact. Her orders were phrased as personal requests. She consulted you, and then you had to do what you yourself had advised. That was Bella's way.

Everything, as it were, marched. Hers was a triumph of tribal house-keeping. If matters became difficult there was always Grandma Rose, who presided over the whole house afar off, but as a court of final appeal when disputes threatened, and as the dispenser of nostrums and rewards to young and old alike. You knew when you came to Grandma's room and sat down by her chair that she would understand—that the trouble whatever it was would be settled. She could giggle a difficulty into a joke. She was old, but she was still amused.

Her cheerful joking was sometimes a bit hard to understand. But you accepted it, for Grandpap and Grandma were both Old Country people. They had known and they were still in touch with the far world beyond the mountains, with Philadelphia, and with "home"—England. Everything you couldn't make yourself came from there—in a wagon. So you listened to old Garrett and Rose, because they knew. And they had read books, too. Grandpap got letters!

How it would be when the old folks died, many people wondered. Aunt Bella, it was understood, would probably get the dwelling house, and Uncle Charles would certainly be left in charge of the inn. Bella was the only one who could run the house, since Aunt Chloe was sick, and Charles was only a good trader and storekeeper. Most people were content to think of Bella as remaining in charge of the old place. It would seem natural. Only Aunt Sue still remained to be taken care of. Everybody wished she would finally make up her mind and marry. She was the darkest and handsomest of all the Pendergass girls. Everybody, even Grandma, wished Sue could get her cards and her Bible to agree about picking a man. It was said a number of young fellows had asked her. Yet she never said yes.

There was always something a bit mysterious about Sue. Even her sisters didn't really know her. And there was young Phoebe Davison. She and her brother Arthur were Grandma's favourites. It might be just as well if Phoebe would take it in her head to marry. She might be managed into the idea. That big Albine boy looked hopeful. But he seemed to be holding off. Or maybe Phoebe was just too shy and young yet. She could wait, but Sue was getting along.

As for Uncle Charles, nothing was to be feared from him. He could be counted upon to run the store well and look after Aunt Chloe. They would never have any children. Aunt Chloe was in a bad way. She had a lump growing under her arm that didn't get better. And she was often so queer now. She sat cross-legged like an Injun squaw and moped, her hands in her lap.

All these things were talked over between the women at the dwelling house. The plans for the coming year were pretty well understood. Before summer came and everybody went back to their cabins, if the troubles were over, both Sue and Phoebe ought to be married off and set up for themselves. Aunt Chloe could be taken care of by one of the Injun women at the big house easily enough. She made no lively trouble. As for little Liza Shockoe, she could be farmed around among the family until she was old enough to be bound out. It was Sue especially, and perhaps Phoebe, who must be put in a way of settling down. The younger Pendergass boys would, of course, find girls for themselves. So all of them agreed.

Sue had her own view of things which she succeeded in keeping absolutely to herself. And that was the wonder of it in a big house like her father's full of other women and prying children. But she was a woman of great ingenuity, of careful, physical slyness. She was like two people, she told herself. But to everybody, to everybody but Nat Murray, who was a nice boy and kept his mouth shut for his own reasons, she was just open-hearted, temperamental but biddable Sue Pendergass. The other person was sulky. Sue, nervous and tightly-drawn, liable-to-snap-at-you-Sue just before the regular crisis—when "she had to have her stomach let down".

She absolutely had to have herself attended to or she couldn't stand it, the tension and breathlessness, the feeling of crawl. Her hands shook then, and she was no good. She couldn't get along with herself or anybody else unless she had her stomach let down regularly, and Nat Murray did that for her neatly and pleasantly. There was no comment or nonsense about it. He just knew the signs when he was needed.

They had a wordless understanding about it. After he was through, everything was fine, clear as a whistle for Sue. If Bella had been married she might have suspected something. And ever since Nat's father had been captured, and the Murray cabin at the water gap burned, Nat had always been about the house a good deal of the time. Besides, it had all started a long time ago with Sue. She and Nat hadn't exactly been little, but they were young when they started to fool around. That was the way Sue had discovered what was the matter with her—and the cure.

But Sue wasn't in love with Nat. It was just helpful to have him around, because she quite understood it would never do to have any somebody let her stomach down for her. A man outside the family might get excited about it and talk. And Nat was always so kind.

"I'll bet you don't know what's agoin' on, Nat," she whispered.

"Oh, yes, I do. I can feel it very plain," he said.

And that was the way it had been for a long time. But lately—lately it had been different with Nat. She heard he had been running after some Irish girls in the town. Maybe that was it?

Anyway, last time, only two months ago, he wasn't her quiet Nephew Nat any more. He had used her. He had even been rough about it, and held her down when she, when she . . . and now for a long time she hadn't needed him. She wouldn't even speak to him, in fact. But there seemed to be something there, growing.

It was characteristic of Sue that she said nothing about that either. She felt well, even triumphant. And as soon as she became sure of what had happened she determined to make it all right. Bella and Mother need never know. And she would even fool Nat so he would never be able to laugh at her or say a word to anybody. She intended to get married, and to get married quick. All she had to do was to play right into Bella's hands. She could say yes to some man, and then let Bella hurry the wedding.

Everybody would be mighty glad of a wedding while they were all in

the same house together. And there were now plenty of beaux hanging
around for Sue to choose from. In a way she was a catch. After that last
time with Nat, Sue understood now why the boys were so interested.
She pondered carefully and picked the best candidate.

About the end of February both her cards and her Bible kept telling
Sue every day to marry young William Tredwell, the farrier's son. He
certainly had been bothering her a lot lately, and in other ways than one
it was a relief to say, "Yes." William was delighted with his sudden good
luck. Bella and Garrett were downright happy when Sue told them. The
news ran through the household, and everybody started sewing baby
clothes for Sue.

Nat never batted an eye. Anyway, he would not be around much
longer. He and Salathiel and the twins would soon be off with Captain
Jack stalking the Injuns as soon as the weather turned. That might be
any day now, and that suited Sue well enough. The sooner the better.
She even had time to think about helping Phoebe in her affair. It was
about time young Albine declared himself, all the women thought. But
Phoebe, the silly, only blushed when Sue talked to her and would do
nothing about it herself. She had spent a good deal of time nursing
Yates. Maybe she liked him better? You couldn't be sure. But it was
something for Sue to talk over with all the other women while her wedding clothes were being made and fitted. Mighty elegant stuff her pap
gave her, and in these times! But Garrett was very pleased that Sue was
getting married.

"Sue, I believe you're getting fatter," said Bella one day while she was
fitting her.

"Fat and sassy," said Sue. "I'm that contented!"

And when she came to think it over, she was. William Tredwell was
strong, a dark, and a tall youth. It might be different with him. Anyway,
he wouldn't wait long after they were married. She could be sure of that.
So he need never know, since he was marching west with the militia.
No, they could be married before the roads over the mountains were
open, in the big hearth room, early in March. There would be a big
crowd, all the family, fiddles and a jamboree. She went about the house
singing.

As for Phoebe, she found in the absorbing preparations for Sue's wedding a profound satisfaction and comfort. She felt she was only re-
hearsing a prophetic drama of her own wedding with Salathiel, that
would come afterward—someday. In a short while Sue's approaching
wedding seemed to Phoebe almost like her own. She didn't stop to consider. She simply dreamed of a wedding. It became the favourite scene
in the starry pageant of her constantly recurring reverie, a trance of
springtime happiness by day, and of April longings and tender hopes
that flushed her young cheeks and breasts at night, as she lay thinking
of her wedding—and Salathiel. But it was in this vivid mental picture of

her wedding that all her longings centred. And in Sue's nuptial preparations Phoebe tasted it all in reality and lived it in advance. You could have told that by the way she smoothed Sue's wedding skirt down and draped her bride's shawl. Sue's skirt was of velvet, the gift of her mother. And someday there would be such a wedding skirt for Phoebe. Who could doubt it? The very thought of it made Phoebe shy and happy.

It was really a question whether at first Phoebe Davison was not more in love with love, and a wedding, than with Salathiel. He, of course, had started it all. And it *was* pleasant to have him about the house, and so near her just across the bridge in the inn at night. She had often watched the light in his window. Coming and going from nursing Yates she had frequently met Salathiel in the hallway at the inn. She had even learned to manage that a little. Afterwhile, they had come to stop and talk with each other. In her grandmother's room when Salathiel came to visit she had even sat close to him, quite close. But these meetings, the actual tall and overpowering presence of Salathiel, were almost too real, too disturbing.

In Phoebe's dream of their wedding Salathiel was just quietly "there". It was her bright bridal dress that stood out against the misty, imaginary greenery where the pageant went on. Phoebe was not so disturbed as the others that Salathiel had not spoken yet. She knew that he loved her. And time seemed to halt and to hover waiting for *her* occasion.

Meanwhile, Sue was being married sure enough, and the whole family at the dwelling house were absorbed by that. So busy and so preoccupied were all the women over Sue's fast approaching wedding that Phoebe's affair scarcely entered into their thoughts at all. Even she scarcely noticed how little she actually saw Salathiel. He was out hunting or he was busy about the place. They smiled at each other when they met, and that was enough. Besides, Salathiel and Captain Jack and the twins had something mysterious under way. Salathiel told her they might all be gone hunting for a while when the weather broke. So in Phoebe's mind both weddings, Sue's and her own, went on to the exclusion of much else that she might otherwise have felt going on about her. She baked cakes and sewed. And her eyes shone large and happily, looking into the future.

And then one day the weather changed. It was only a week before the wedding.

The first soft, melting breeze of the year came lazing up the valley from the south. The ice broke. The sound of the river began to lap and gurgle again past the Pendergass door. As the snowbanks in the valley went out, the rushing Juniata began to sing and to hiss over the big stones in its bed. Higher in the mountains the snow still lay deep, but the country would soon be open again to those who cared to follow the lower game trails along the streams and valley. The spring wind curled in Captain Jack's nostrils like smoke, and a great impatience overpowered his mind. Yet he was dark, stern, and gloomy. The blood fit was on him. The forest called.

"Git your packs ready," said he to those who were to follow him to the cabin. "Thar's a deed to do, and you to be made ready for it. Happen we'll be gone two months. And say no word of it. I'll not be tarrying for any girl's wedding. Keep your mouths shut."

He looked at Nat Murray significantly. Nat wondered if the old man knew. Well, it would suit him all right to go. It seemed to suit Sue. She hadn't even a kind word for him any more.

Past the middle of one night about the beginning of March, Phoebe awoke suddenly. There was no wind, but the river seemed to be louder than ever. Something was going on. She could hear the men stirring about in the house next door. Once the tones of Yates and Salathiel's voices talking quietly came to her ears. Now and then a candle passed his window. She got up and looked out. Mat and Mark, and Nat Murray were in the yard below talking together in low tones. Captain Jack came out and joined them. They seemed to be waiting. She could hear Garrett saying something from the back door in a cautious tone. Suddenly she knew what it meant. The men were going! Captain Jack was on the war path again.

She moved swiftly and without thinking. She covered up Arthur warmly to keep him quiet, and slipping on a wool cloak and a pair of old moccasins, she made her way across the bridge and opened the door into the upper hallway of the inn.

For a moment she thought Salathiel had gone. The only light came from under Yates's door. Then she heard them both talking.

"Good luck, Sal," said Yates. "*I'll* be all right. You bring yourself back with the spring. It will be a long time. Demme, I'll miss ye! You don't want me to say anything to Phoebe, then?"

"No," said Salathiel emphatically.

They were talking about her!

She put her hands over her breast standing there in the dark of the hall. Now the door was opening.

He came striding down the corridor. At first she thought he would pass her without seeing her. Then he saw her and stopped short just at the top of the stairs.

They stood looking at each other in the dull-red firelight from the room below that was just reflected from the ceiling. In the faint rosy glow, which seemed to flow from her clothes and face, Salathiel saw his angel waiting for him. Her long golden hair fell over her shoulders shimmering, and her eyes were tender with sleepy love. She was his. He could take her. He knew that. This was the great opportunity. Yet he mustn't touch her. It was forbidden.

He swayed towards her, driven . . . held back. He *couldn't* tell her. Not now!

"Are you goin' away, Sal?" she whispered in the half-dark.

"Yes."

"You'll not be here for the wedding?"

"No . . . but I'll bring *you* back something, Phoebe."

"Oh!" she gasped. "Oh, that will be beautiful, beautiful!"

"Like you!" he exclaimed, and drew her to him.

"Oh, Sal," she said after a while, "oh, Sal, I only meant to say good-bye to ye."

"Ain't I asayin' it?" he blurted.

Then he kissed her frantically again, and blundered downstairs, dashing a mist of tears from his eyes. He met Garrett in the hall below and almost passed him without speaking. The old man paused in surprise. Then, just in time, Salathiel turned and came back holding his hand out awkwardly.

"Oh, Mr. Pendergass! Sir, I want to thank ye for taking me in here like you have." He gulped. "And thar's something I must tell ye. I guess maybe I ought to tell Miss Phoebe first . . ."

"Now, now," said Garrett, laughing and looking up at him as he stood in an agony of embarrassment in the firelight, "I guess what you have to say can wait a bit, son. Can't it? Bring yourself back here. Be tarnal keerful. Your pap, you know . . ."

The old man's face worked.

"Now git along with you, git along, or you'll keep Cap'n Jack waitin'. And he ain't in a mood for that!"

Salathiel darted out, slinging his pack and gun.

And then, instantly, all the warm world of the house behind him vanished.

In the wagonyard Captain Jack, Nat Murray, and the Pendergass boys stood waiting. The cold sheen of moonlight glittered from the long barrels of their rifles and the hatchets at their belts.

They moved out silently on moccasined feet.

Only Phoebe, her white face pressed against the window, saw them go. For a moment a sudden premonition of terror changed the happy beat of her heart.

She went back to bed, and clasping her sleeping brother close, lay and shivered. The patches of moonlight on her crazy quilt slowly turned to darkness. Somewhere on the distant slopes of Will's Mountain a panther screamed.

Salathiel was there.

14. Death at the Salt Kettles

THE SCREAM of a panther—

What is that to most people—to those who have never heard it? But to Salathiel Albine it recalled always and forever "Death at the Salt Kettles", the grim and stealthy doings of a certain wintry spring. Part of what it was like to be a white man from then on found voice for him in the merciless lion of the mountain, flashed in the moonlight from the bared fangs of the wolf.

Salathiel had come to learn many things at Captain Jack's cabin, to be a pupil in a stern school. As they flitted up the valley that night from Pendergasses' the panther screamed and the harsh echoes replied from Poorhouse Mountain. There seemed to be several panthers hunting that night.

Phoebe Davison was not the only one who heard them.

There were seven in the brotherhood of arms at the cabin. There was a vacant bunk for someone who never joined. But in that empty bed, as though such things were equivalent to another companion, they kept the tow, the patches, the ramrods, lead, and bullet moulds for readying their rifle-guns.

From the first it was a decidedly silent brotherhood. The moody blood fit lay heavily on Captain Jack. It rolled out from him like a dark cloud, enveloped them all, and settled down like a pall. No one questioned why that should be. It seemed natural. Just as the panther's scream had set the key, Captain Jack's moodiness seemed to provide the atmosphere for what they were preparing to do.

The first thing Captain Jack did was to strip them of every last unnecessary article. The Pendergass boys especially had brought along certain small luxuries, even a small bag of tea and a pot. These, and some fancies contributed by the women, were now made into one small bundle and returned the next morning by Mark, without comment. Salathiel sent back the silver watch Captain Ecuyer had given him, for Phoebe to keep for him. Sid and Cal McClanahan, who had kept lone guard at the cabin for six weeks past, looked on at these proceedings and laughed. They sympathized with the "old man's" Spartan rule. Indeed, Captain Jack's discipline was more than Spartan; it was North American.

For Captain Jack now relapsed completely into the life of the forest, and of the forest as he had known it forty years before. No one could have surmised from the life they led at the cabin that there was a strong military post and a thriving settlement only a few miles away at Bedford. For the seven at the cabin, the town, the fort, Pendergasses' had for the time being ceased to exist. The log hut, hidden in a small cuplike vale on the east side of Lookout Mountain, might have been lost in the Ohio wilderness a month's travel westward, so far as occupants went.

The place was lapped about by folds of hoary forest. There was a never-failing spring, a few sink holes in the limestone full of snakes, sumacs, and young sycamores. Some lonely open glades like green lanes led through the forest, under a spread of mighty walnuts in the direction of the "Stinking Springs".

Down these "lanes" the deer fed even in the winter. There no one had come yet. There was not even a path or a trail, except that worn by dainty cloven hoofs, for the new human tenants had taken good care to wear no telltale trace to their door. Only a light blue mist shimmering hazily over the top of the chimney when they cooked marked their occupancy of the cabin.

"Looks like a house that the yellow varmints forgot to burn," said Captain Jack, "but ef they do come now they'll sure find seven kinds of trouble at home. Wisht they might!"

But that was too good-wishing to come true. The kind of trouble those at the cabin were looking for would not come to them now. They would have to find it. The Indian war parties that traversed the country were no longer searching for lonely cabins to burn. They were now all intent upon waylaying small convoys, or ambushing wagons, expresses, and working parties along the road. And in this work they were only too frequently and dreadfully successful.

It was characteristically Captain Jack's plan to meet them and then outreach them at their own game. When the open spring weather should come, he intended to bring retributory sorrow to many an Indian village, and to lay lethal ambush along the trails and forest traces that led back towards the Allegheny valley.

Meanwhile, until the snow melted, he would practise and repractise those at the cabin until they were letter perfect in every detail of their work. And above all he would teach them to hunt as a pack.

"Makum all one hatchet," said Cal McClanahan, grinning.

"And that's the idee, and don't ye forget it," replied the old man. Captain Jack was beginning to feel his age at times. The days of his lone raids were over. But those who came with him now he still wished to control like younger limbs of his own body and mind.

After nightfall they kept watch two by two. It was no mere plodding sentry-go. It was an art in itself of scouting in every direction through the darkness around, and waking the relief when the time came, noiselessly. It was constant vigilance by every sense.

"Trouble comes by night, and death at early morning," said the old hunter. "Many white men perish in their sleep. While the deer browse and the moon whispers to her dead, that is the time for surprises. Yet to be surprised is the greatest disaster of all."

It was only now and then that Captain Jack talked. For the most part he was silent. When he did speak he expected his words to be remembered. The rest of the time he appeared to be intently listening rather than to be simply negatively quiet. Every night before they turned in he told them a brief story out of his own experience.

"Only one thing the Injun can do better than the paleface. He hath a far keener nose," Captain Jack would say. "For the rest, don't forget ye be far smarter." He generally ended on that note.

Salathiel compared all that the old man said with his own forest upbringing, and saw that Captain Jack was right; that he was wiser than Nymwha and keener than Kaysinata. And in thus thinking over the past he remembered again, as he lay in the darkness looking up at the top of his bunk, the dead child he had buried near Pittsburgh; how his father and mother and the baby had been murdered. He even dreamed one night of the lost days in his father's cabin when he was a small boy. The brindled ox came and smelled him. He heard his mother scream far off, "underground". But this time when he wakened he was a white man and not an Indian again.

In the mornings, after they had eaten and rid up, Captain Jack always read a fine, bloody incident from the Old Testament. He would open his worn copy of the Good Book on his knee. But Salathiel saw that he opened it anywhere; that he knew what he "read" by heart.

Then they would get to work with the rifle-guns. That was where the two McClanahans came in.

Rifle shooting with the brothers McClanahan was the art of a lifetime. Their astonishing perfection surpassed that of merely good shots in the same way and to the same degree that the performance of a musician of genuine genius outsoars and distances the skill of merely talented and hard-practising professionals. Sid and Cal McClanahan were brothers not only in blood but in craft.

They saw to it that each rifle of the newcomers was carefully fitted to the firing habits of the man who shot it. But not until those habits had been carefully corrected and re-formed. Everyone spent hours, entire mornings, in aiming practice from all positions. They drew beads on things near, far, and in the middle distance.

Then they shot at marks.

Next the sights were subtly filed, shifted, blacked, or brightened. The balance of a piece was carefully changed. The habits of each man and the peculiarities of his rifle-gun were almost piously discussed. And of grease, powder charges, patches, and flinting there was no end of experiment and proof by trial. Every man had his own bullet mould, and each learned to cast and pare his own bullets to suit best the barrel of his piece. Of nice readjustment of trigger pulls there was no end. And then one day there *was* an end.

"For either we've larned ye, or we hain't," said Sid.

"The rest of shootin' is all shootin'," insisted Cal.

So they shot.

They shot in the morning. They shot most of the afternoons away. And towards the last they began to shoot in the twilight, and even after darkness, at dim blazes on the trees.

This shooting practice was Salathiel's great opportunity for perfecting himself in the use of his curious gun. The McClanahans were doubtful at first of a double-barrelled rifle, but they became respectful after trying it out. They put on a new double rear sight so that each barrel could be aimed singly, and they corrected the left barrel, which shot low, by changing the grip of the piece. Albine they found a more than decent marksman. Sid especially spent much time and effort on him. And it was now, too, that Salathiel practised for hours at a time his trick of loading while running and turning to fire. He always used cartridges for this stunt and thus reduced to a final minimum his motions in loading. He cocked, bit off the cartridge, rammed it home, primed, whirled, and fired the piece.

"I might be as good as four guns in one for a while, if I keep on," he said hopefully.

"Liken you mighten," admitted Captain Jack, who was impressed by Salathiel's perseverance and improvement. He and the two McClanahans had at last been converted to what they called "Albine's stunt".

"Try makin' a ca'tridge for primin'," suggested Mark Pendergass one day. "Make a kind o' powder pill to fit the fire pan. It's your powder horn that takes up most of the time loadin'."

After some trouble they succeeded in making a small paper pellet of powder that crumbled in the pan under pressure of the thumb. That cut down the time for loading almost a third. They all felt elated by this invention. Some of the others began to use the pellets, too. Albine persisted in his practice. Eventually his skill seemed uncanny and he was enormously proud of it. It was the one thing he boasted about like an Indian.

"Lieutenant Francis said this gun would bring down Fortune, when he gave it to me," Salathiel was fond of repeating, while patting the stock. "She's a good-luck piece, I do aver."

"Good luck and straight shootin' generally go together," admitted Captain Jack. "But it won't do to depend on your gun alone. Sometimes powder gits damp. Keep your hand in by throwin' your hatchet and knife, too. Don't forget 'em."

So at a peeled post set up near the spring, hatchet and knife throwing went on as a kind of game whenever there wasn't anything else to do. Nat Murray excelled. He won most of the tobacco in camp and sold it back at monopoly prices. Even Captain Jack was driven to gathering sumac leaves for his pipe, until Nat relented.

Two weeks of this kind of work and they had all taken full measure of one another and were now impatient to "have it out with the varmints". But Captain Jack delayed. He was well enough satisfied with their individual progress, but he was not quite so sure how well they could act together. He spent the last blustery days of March in expeditions through the hills to the eastward, hunting, and living in the forest as though entirely surrounded by enemies.

There was enough real danger to lend a vivid reality to this practice of swift night moves, of sudden feigned attacks, of swift assault and retreat, and of scatterment and rendezvous. Above all they learned to move forward or to retire, to close in and to scatter out according to a careful system of signals of animal and bird voices perfectly memorized, with one set for use by day and another by night. The last deep, wet snow of the season fell, and the supplies they carried began to run out. But they ended by tracking down the "painter" on Will's Mountain.

It was an all-day and all-night chase. The big cat eventually took refuge in a high tree in a swamp. They could easily have shot it, but it had been agreed that there was to be no firing, and Salathiel brought the beast down by a beautiful throw with Kaysinata's war axe. The razor-keen tomahawk buried itself in the animal's brain.

"Good for you, Sal," said Nat Murray generously. He had tried first and missed.

Even Captain Jack was satisfied with this performance. Even in his opinion they were all now "one hatchet", and he led the way back to the cabin.

"Rest up and git ready," he said. "We'll be leavin' as soon as the snow melts off, and it's set to turn warm now. I'll be leavin' you for a little. I'll be away until tomorrow evenin' at the fort. Sid McClanahan's in charge."

They spent that evening and the next morning patching moccasins, casting bullets, furbishing rifles, and making up their packs.

They dressed now in nothing but deerskins and blankets. They wore leather stockings, breechclouts, skin shirts with deep pouches, and a tied, thong belt from which hung knife, tomahawk, and tobacco pouch. They slung their powder horns and bullet bags across their shoulders by baldricks, and they carried their rifle-guns with a greased leather cover over lock and breech.

The blanket pack was made square rather than long or oblong. It was a mere bundle lashed with rawhide thongs. It contained a tinder box with flint and steel, an awl, a packet of needles and thread, a small sack of corn meal, salt, a slab of bacon, and a thin iron plate, bowl, and horn spoon. These latter articles had all been supplied from Garrett's store and were quite unusual. The whole bundle was slung over the left shoulder. Extra powder horns were carried by some, and a few flints and small gun parts. Everyone had a pipe and a fine-tooth comb. The last evening they anointed themselves with bear grease, hair and all, before the fire.

Then they ate heavily, slept, kept on sleeping all day—until after darkness Captain Jack returned with news.

They had now been away from the town for nearly a month and he had quite a number of items to tell them. They sat, listening eagerly, while he furbished his rifle and made up his pack in the same careful and deliberate way that he talked.

"Wal, men," said he, "I slipped into the village last evenin' like a fox raidin' a hen coop. And nobody saw me, and not a dog barked till I was plumb thar. Only in this case some people was right glad to see the old fox. Garrett and Mr. Gladwin, Yates, and Dr. Boyd was havin' a noggin by the fire. So I said, 'Make it the same, Pina,' and they all like to have slopped their swipes, for I'd come in powerful soft.

" 'How are ye, ye old murderer,' said Garrett.

" 'I'm gloomy fine,' says I. 'Happen, if yer don't keep that door barred, ye might all lose your har some night.'

" 'We maunt,' said Garrett. 'How's your den o' mountain foxes?'

" 'Tolerable for cubs,' I told him. 'What's the news in this hole in the woods and stronghold of the cra-own?'

" 'You tell him, Yates. You're a lawyer. You're used to talkin', and Dr. Boyd ain't,' said Garrett, and went over to bar the door, laughin'. So this is what I gathered up out o' sundry quips and quiddities from Mr. Yates. Pendergasses' news firstly:

"Nat, Sue's married after a big feast and fiddlin'. She went west to Pittsburgh with her husband in the last big convoy over the mountains, three weeks gone. So you can rest easy, Nat.

"Mat and Mark, your wives and children and the twins are flourishin'. Your brother Charles ain't so healthy. When he came back from Pitt four days ago, his wife Chloe was so tarnal glad to see him she up and drew a knife acrost his throat. They've got her tied up in old Pina's cabin, and Dr. Boyd sewed up Charles pretty neat. I'll tell you about the letter Charley brought back from Buckey at Fort Pitt in a minute. Meanwhile, Albine, here's some news special for you:

"Yates said to tell you he's doin' all right. He's got special orders to do land and boundary surveyin' in these parts for the Proprietors. Him and St. Clair is in it together, I hear. They're out runnin' lines in the village now every day with Mr. Lukens, the province's surveyor, and some of the royal engineers. He said to be sure to tell you your old friend, the Reverend Jim McArdle's come to town to preach . . .

"What's that, Albine?

"No, I didn't see Miss Phoebe. I didn't see any of the women that evenin'. And I went up to the fort airly next mornin', 'cause Captain Ecuyer's come over the mountain from Ligonier and I wanted to talk with him. It ain't likely he'll ever cross the mountains agin. But I did git to talk with him.

"Captain Ecuyer showed me Buckey's letter to him that Charley brought back from Fort Pitt. The colonel has authorized us to act as independent rangers and scouts, but not more than ten at a time. We're to be able to draw rations and ammunition, and we're to git the same pay as labourers on the military road. That's two shillins starlin' a day. We're not to be carried on any militia roll or as part of any command. Thar's no oath required, but we're to take advice and directions from Captain Ecuyer, and to sarve for six months if he wants us. I'm to be responsible for ye, and ye are to abide by what I say. Now do ye understand, and do the articles suit? I'll take silence for consent. Anybody kin quit now and nothin' will ever be said by any of us. Remember, you're puttin' your lives in peril. Now I'll wait for a moment to hear."

Captain Jack stopped lashing his pack and stood waiting expectantly. A sombre silence filled the room.

He waited a full minute and then began tying his pack again.

"That's *good!*" he said. "That's a fine Pennsylvania, silent Quaker oath."

"*Fightin'* Quakers," insisted Mat Pendergass.

"Yes, *fightin'!*" agreed Captain Jack, taking his rifle down from its pegs on the wall. "And seein' that's the case, let's start now!"

A suppressed hum of approval met this sudden suggestion, while they tumbled into their equipment eagerly and slung packs.

"Put out the fire, Albine. And, Murray, you wedge the door. Reckon the par*fume* o' that painter's hide will help keep most four-footed varmints away. He-cats stink powerful."

A few minutes later they swung up the hill in single file. Captain Jack led, while the McClanahans brought up the rear. The night was moonless, but a frosty clear one. From the head of Lookout Mountain they gazed out over the town and valley below. Only a few lights winked fitfully in the village below. Captain Jack halted and stood looking at the distant mountains for a moment.

"That country is still demon-hanted over yonder," he said—"and I'm growin' old!" Then he muttered a favourite saying under his breath:

> "All the King's horses, and all the King's men
> Kin never grow har on a scalped head again."

"Promise me," he cried, turning on them suddenly in the starlight—"promise me you'll never spare a *single one* o' the yellow varmints that falls to your hands!"

Going down the line in the darkness, he made them promise him this solemnly man by man.

They struck off on an old trace that led south of the village, and then straight towards the mountains and the setting stars.

Two nights later found them camped in a deep stream fissure on the western slope of Chestnut Ridge, nearly twenty miles north of the military road west of Ligonier.

To recite the bare chronicle of the weeks in the forest that followed would be eventful, but tedious. Although it was a time full of incident, danger, and surprise, it was the same kind of incident frequently repeated: the waylaying and cutting off of small war parties of Indians making their way eastward from the Ohio valley to harass the Western Road, or to raid far eastward over the mountains among the more unsuspecting and securer settlements.

There were many such raids and many small war parties that fateful spring of '64. The Indians were both bold and desperate. They badly needed horses, powder, and lead. Under these sporadic onslaughts the frontier writhed and shuddered, waiting until Colonel Bouquet could move down the Ohio and carry the war to the very capitals of trouble. Then only there might be peace. Meanwhile there was a constant petty, but merciless warfare.

It was not in Captain Jack's tactics merely to patrol and protect the Western Road. His strategy comprehended a much larger plan which included forays and attack, surprise, and terror, the ambushing of a large number of the enemies' war parties over as far-flung a spread of territory as possible.

That was why Captain Jack had kept his party down to seven expert, carefully trained assistants. Add only a few more, and he would have had to carry or to cache supplies and move much more slowly. He preferred to multiply his force by time rather than by men.

And the event proved him to be right. In six weeks' time his "Fighting Quakers", or "Mountain Foxes", as they were more usually called, stopped four war parties on their way eastward, and three more plunder-and scalp-laden bands coming back from the settlements. One party was twelve strong, the others ranged from five to nine. From none of them did a single brave escape to carry the tale of their undoing. Their horses were sent to Ligonier, and their scalps went into Captain Jack's "bounty box", with the date and whereabouts of their taking off.

To be sure, it would take some time for the effect of these lonely forest disasters to reach down the Ohio. But Captain Jack counted upon that, for he did not wish to make his enemies too wary too soon. Yet nothing travels so fast and so far as the rumour of mysterious catastrophes, and before a new moon had gone through all her phases, squaws were wailing in many a village in the Ohio valley, and puzzled chiefs sat exchanging views over their pipes and the ominous fact that so many notable braves neither returned nor sent messages explaining their whereabouts.

Nor was the discovery, towards the beginning of May, of six scalped Hurons, all lying in a single grave along the bluffs of the Allegheny, notably reassuring. Their trail ended there and none seemed to lead away. But no one, not even the Mingoes who found them, maintained

that Hurons buried themselves. Suspicion was thus sown between th
tribes as to possible treachery amongst themselves.

As a late spring burgeoned quickly and gloriously into a warm Ma
raiding suddenly ceased. Convoys between Ligonier and Fort Pitt bega
to roll freely and unattacked. Captain Ecuyer, completely worn out b
the harassments and fatigues of the preceding winter, finally collapse
at Fort Bedford and was carried to the corner room at Pendergasses
where he afterwards died.

As Captain Jack sat on a rock at the top of the Allegheny Mountain
thinking of this and reading Ecuyer's letter, he determined to give th
secret, bloody work of that memorable spring his own indubitable signa
ture. He preferred to be remembered other than by sunsets. At least, h
admired the blood in them more than the gold.

As he looked about him at the exceedingly tender spring foliage o
the mountaintop, his inner eye was reminded of something and rove
backward to that idyllic scene of a river, a high cliff, canoes drawn u
peacefully beneath it, while smoke ascended lazily into a smiling, blu
sky—all of which had once flashed so powerfully into his imagination a
Pendergasses'. His thin nostrils distended slightly while he pondered.

Finally he called his fellow workers about him by a low whistle.

"Men," said he, "we'll be returning to Ligonier for a day or two t
refit and sleep. There's a powerful big work to do. It's at a place calle
the Salt Kittles, nigh a hundred miles from here. We make tracks now.

On the sunny afternoon of May the seventeenth, 1764, as grim an
savage looking a band as ever emerged from the sombre gloom of th
forest appeared before the now carefully barred and watched gate at Fo
Ligonier. Evidently Ecuyer's memorable enforcement of discipline in th
winter of '63 had been effectual, for it was only after considerable parle
that Captain Jack and his men were finally admitted carefully one b
one.

Certainly, there was nothing in their appearance that was reassurin
to anxious sentries. Only their dense beards still proclaimed they wer
white men. The rest of their faces, even their hands, were blackene
with charcoal. They were lean. Their deerskin clothes were patche
grimy, and rain soaked. They had now been living in and on the fores
for nearly two months, engaged in a man hunt day and night, in whic
while they were hunters they might easily become the prey. They ha
covered on foot hundreds of miles of country. There was a mass of scalp
in Captain Jack's "bounty box", and only a couple of charges left in h
powder horn.

The garrison and the miserable inhabitants of Ligonier gathered abou
them and looked at them silently and with cold chills. A child started t
cry. It was the only, and a proper, comment on their appearance. Wit
the best will in the world, no one could regard these bearded stranger

as ordinary friends and kindly neighbours. A couple of crow feathers, which Salathiel had stuck in his hair, were like an unpleasant surprise. They made horror seem jaunty. Even the militia was squeamish about welcoming them into barracks.

But into barracks they went, while Captain Jack conferred with Lieutenant Blane, who had been sent back to take command of the post at Ligonier, where he had done so well only the year before.

Salathiel found that he had now little interest or curiosity left for Ligonier. All his friends of a few months before had been moved west to Fort Pitt. Only in what remained of the settlers' village were there still some familiar faces. But there were no attractive ones.

After an hour's talk with Lieutenant Blane, Captain Jack emerged from headquarters to tell his men to "git what sleep ye kin. Spend the rest o' the time refittin', and git generally rested up. Because," said he— and he all but sang the phrase—"thar's a great work to do!"

So they slept like tired hunting dogs, they ate, went to swim under the walls of the fort in the Loyalhanna Creek, and then sat about on their beds in one corner of the barracks, repatching their sorry clothes and moccasins to make them last longer.

Albine had come up out of the creek new washed, and a shining young giant. His yellow beard and hair threatened to become one gleaming halo. "An awful temptin' scalp," said Sid McClanahan. So Salathiel soon took special care to tone himself down. He braided his now quite long hair closely into a club queue. He shaved, blackened his face and locks to look like midnight; blackened himself from the waist up. For in the warm weather he now went about again like an Indian in breechclout and moccasins, except when actually on the trail. The red turtle still sprawled on his breast, and he put back the black crow feathers in his hair. His hatchet-shaped face and relic of an ear, his long rifle and the hatchet and knives at his belt left nothing in grimness to be imagined. Captain Jack was proud of his "young giant", but none of the rest resented it, for in their recent raids Albine's skill in the ways of the forest and the Indian had been scarcely less than that of his leader. Only a sure ripeness of judgment, a certain inveterate determination were lacking. But Captain Jack supplied all the determination any of them needed.

Indeed, in this brief interlude at Ligonier Captain Jack seemed little less than exalted and under the compulsion of a fanatical zeal for smiting the heathen in which even he surpassed himself. He took little sleep; seemed to need none. Most of the time he spent with Lieutenant Blane, explaining and perfecting arrangements for the projected attack. He at first repulsed, but at length succeeded in imbuing that somewhat phlegmatic officer with his own fiery intensity of purpose and confidence. Nor was this at all mysterious.

For in the surprise attack on the Salt Kettles Captain Jack saw the crowning effort of his career. He was not unaware that old age was stealing rapidly upon him. The last two strenuous months especially had confirmed his reluctant admission of the fact. And he intended to finish the long chronicle of his bitter wars against the savages by a final memorable incident.

In fact, the thoroughness and scope of the coup he had in mind called for a larger force than he could muster in his own band. And for that reason, more than any other, he had resorted to Ligonier to obtain the assistance of Lieutenant Blane and his garrison. The lieutenant had received strong instructions to co-operate. The plan finally agreed upon for the operation was simplicity itself.

At a point about a day's journey north of Ligonier, near the old Venango trace, where the Loyalhanna Creek emptied into the Kiskiminitas, there was a notable salt lick and saline springs, or wells, to which from time out of mind the Indians had resorted in the late spring to boil down salt in their largest kettles. So ancient was this custom, and so important the salt, that even before the white man had arrived, tribal warfare had been suspended to admit families from many tribes and regions to encamp peacefully at the Salt Kettles for the brief operations of the season.

But it was not only its peaceful tradition but the lay of the land about it, which made the place so liable to hostile surprise. And upon both factors Captain Jack counted heavily.

The salt springs were situated on a low-lying, open flat on the north bank of the Kiskiminitas River. There, naturally, the Indians camped while making salt. But the opposite bank for several miles up and down was nothing but a perpendicular, rocky cliff, nearly a hundred feet high. The top of this escarpment completely commanded the encampment on the flats below. And the Indians always clustered about the wells in a spot only a convenient, although a long, rifle shot across the river from the top of the cliff.

"Too far for a musket, but ranged for a rifle-gun. Liken they won't hev thought that over," pondered Captain Jack aloud.

It was his plan to occupy the top of the cliff opposite the salt wells, under cover of darkness, to murder the Indian watchers found there, if any—and then at high noonday, and with complete impudence, to open rifle fire on the unsuspecting saltmakers below.

In his mind's eye, and out of long experience, Captain Jack was sure he could foresee just how the Indians would act when the surprise rifle fire first burst upon them from the top of the cliff. The squaws and youngsters would vanish instantly to take shelter and hide. The warriors would rush to their canoes and make off, either up or down the stream. Probably the latter, in order to go with the current. Whether they would try to gain the top of the cliff at some point and attack would depend on how many of them there were and how strong they thought their enemies to be. They might simply try to get away. It was to prevent this that Captain Jack had appealed to Lieutenant Blane.

The Mountain Foxes, reinforced by six of the best riflemen from the post, were to open the attack from the top of the cliff. But two detachments from the fort, consisting of the more experienced woodsmen amongst the militia, were to occupy both riverbanks along convenient flats, one party some miles above, and the other at the first swampy meadow below the Salt Kettles. The militia was to be in considerable force, about fifty in all, and if the Indians offered to stand ground and shoot it out at the Salt Kettles, they were to close in on them from all sides.

The details of this scheme were thoroughly explained to the officers and men carefully chosen to take part. Every possible eventuality was faced and openly discussed with the men by Captain Jack. Each item of equipment and arms was thoughtfully checked.

"For ye can't just give orders in a case like this. Not if you reckon to have 'em carried out," explained Captain Jack. "Every soul has to make it his peculiar business."

And the old hunter of men succeeded in making it just that for everybody. His savage glee over the favourable prospect of the impending massacre was curiously infectious.

Meanwhile, the McClanahans returned from a scout to the Salt Kettles and reported that five pots were already boiling there.

"That means thirty or more savages, a number of families, and maybe more to come," they said. "Man, they're careless these days! You'd think Venango might have taught 'em a lesson. Thar's Injuns at the Kittles from several tribes."

"But all Injuns," replied Captain Jack significantly.

"All on 'em," said the McClanahans, grinning.

They waited till the 23rd of the month to make ready, and then started north on the old Venango trace, after nightfall to avoid any possible observation. Halfway to the Kiskiminitas, and about dawn, the force divided into three parties, a dozen rifles under Captain Jack making for the cliff above the Salt Kettles, while the other two detachments of about twenty-five men each branched off to the right and left to take up their positions on the river.

Captain Jack and his men plunged directly into the forest and made their way slowly towards the cliffs, skirting the Loyalhanna Creek most of the way. The old hunter took his time and moved forward with infinite precaution. It would take many hours for the two flanking parties to reach the river. Their positions there would have to be taken up under cover of darkness. Even the slightest alarm would be fatal to the enterprise. Consequently, it was about an hour before midnight when Captain Jack cautiously reached the vicinity of the cliffs.

He sent Albine and the two McClanahans ahead to deal with any

Indian watchers. But after a careful scout they found no one, and the entire party was soon disposed along the top of the cliff, in excellent wooded cover, and looking directly down and across the river at the Indian encampment at the Salt Kettles, precisely opposite. The dim glow of nine fires could now be counted, but all was quiet.

"They're just makin' salt," whispered Nat Murray contemptuously. "They're not thinking of fightin'. Injuns generally do one thing at a time."

"Stop mutterin'," said Captain Jack. "Keep watch by turns, and between times git what sleep ye kin. No snorin'."

The morning of the 25th of May, 1764, dawned.

It was one of those balmy mornings that in a belated spring swell the eager buds into a sudden burgeoning glory throughout the Pennsylvania mountains. From the valley below, the haze of the nine fires ascended easily into heaven; grew in volume as the Indians arose in their encampment and began innocently to boil salt.

Salathiel remarked it was one of the most beautiful days he had ever seen. From the top of the cliff the thirteen riflemen peered down at the leisurely activities of the Indian encampment below. In a murmuring talk the two McClanahans and Captain Jack, his eyes fixed on the blank page of revenge flung wide open before him, conducted a discussion as to the range of sundry objects on the other side of the stream.

Looking across the river at the encampment below was to young Albine like gazing down a clear vista of time into his own forest past. Now that the range had been agreed upon, he lay gazing through a notch he had made in a rotten log for a rifle rest at the familiar activities of the Indians on the flat below. He could identify himself with most of what was going on down there. He finally became lost in a reverie over the scene and the memories it recalled.

As the day advanced, the smoke from the kettles rolled thicker and higher. Yellow flames flowered under the pots. Now and then the shrill voice of a child broke the silence of the forest. The river rippled while the stock doves moaned—and Salathiel was back in the forest again, playing happily without thought, his daydream like an interplay of sun and shadows. At noon Captain Jack woke them all to attention by a low, tense command.

"R-r-ready!" he growled.

The line of rifles poked through the bushes. Everything was artfully disposed for rapid firing. In the heat of the day the Indians in their camp below had ceased to move about and sat quiet in the shade. They were so many still marks, unconsciously arranged. Each rifleman picked his separate target and drew a bead. Ten seconds passed, slow as a minute. The line of prone figures stiffened.

Captain Jack's rifle cracked.

Twelve others crashed in unison.

Flocks of startled birds rose swirling and crying along the cliff.

There was a brief interval of silence, punctuated only by the bark of Salathiel and Murray's rifles. They alone were concentrating on puncturing canoes. Their bullets seemed to drone slowly across the river. Then there was one terrific yell from the Indian camp.

The surprise had been paralyzing and complete.

It was for this particular moment that Captain Jack had waited and planned. Eleven rifles had apparently found many human marks, to judge by the scurry of the survivors. But only two rifles had continued to talk, while Albine and Murray were putting holes in the bottoms of canoes. Meanwhile, the rest had reloaded and waited. That brief delay had given the Indians a comparatively quiet moment in which to recover and rally. They had underestimated the attack. They swallowed the reassuring bait of silence. Screaming fierce war cries, they rushed for the canoes on the riverbank.

"By the eternal," exclaimed Captain Jack, "they're ourn!

"Hold your fire, hold your fire!" he kept repeating.

They waited until the survivors of the first volley were bunched about the canoes and had begun to launch them. Then the pitiless rifles began to bark again. Yells of anger and consternation arose as several warriors dropped, and when water spurted through the bullet holes in the bark as the canoes shot out into the river. There were six of them.

But Captain Jack was now cursing, and black in the face. It had not been his intention to open fire again until the canoes were well on their way. One of the riflemen borrowed from the fort had not been able to restrain himself, and had precipitated the volley.

As a consequence many rifles were empty when the canoes strung out and passed directly in front of the cliff. That was to have been their final moment of catastrophe, possibly of annihilation. The supreme opportunity had been lost by lack of discipline.

They tried to make up for it as best they could. They fired as rapidly as possible at the retreating canoes. But two of them had gone up the river, and four down. So the firing was divided. The range rapidly lengthened. Undoubtedly there were hits, perhaps several. Yet, despite the leaks, all the canoes that had been launched got away. They tried to follow them along the cliff, but the going there was difficult, and good aim impossible. In a few minutes they were all back again, and looking glum enough.

Captain Jack sat on a rock, nursing his still smoking rifle. The large blue veins on his forehead stood out, and throbbed as he looked at one Hawkins Poteet, who had fired too soon.

Albine thought for a moment that Captain Jack might strike him down. For a while the old hunter looked at Poteet, speechless. When finally he spoke he was hoarse with rage.

"Liken your pa didn't mean it when he got you, young man," said the

old man witheringly, "just nervous on the trigger, liken you. God blast
ye! Ye ought to be back home playin' pis-titty with the gals."

For the rest of his life Hawkins was known as "Pis-titty Poteet."

Captain Jack's disappointment was so great that a few moments actually passed while nothing was done. Perhaps for the first time in his
life he let his rifle fall forgotten to the ground. Then came a violent
outbreak of firing down the river. The four canoes were trying to run
the gantlet of the militia. It sounded like a brisk engagement. Captain
Jack sprang to his feet and was all action again.

"Albine," he said, "you and Murray and the McClanahans take keer
o' them hidin' out acrost the stream. Go over there and do like I told ye."

With that, he led the rest off downstream in the direction of the
firing, as fast as they could make their way through the thicket.

And so, by far the worst of it, the dirty work, was left for Salathiel
and the three others to finish up across the river. Not that there was
any opposition. In a way, that *was* the worst of it. What they did had to
be done deliberately and in cold blood.

They had to cross the river first. It was much too deep to wade, even
holding their rifles over their heads. And at first they were not sure what
might lie ahead of them on the other bank.

So they left Sid McClanahan to watch and cover them from the top
of the cliff, while they crossed. Then, to avoid climbing down the face
of the cliff itself, they cut back into the steep valley of the Loyalhanna
Creek and came out at its mouth, where it emptied into the river. The
gorge there was piled high with dead trees uprooted by old floods, and
it was the work of only a few moments to thrust the heads of some of
them together to improvise a brushwood raft.

Not a shot was fired. The opposite bank seemed silent and deserted.
As they came out on the surface of the river they heard the firing downstream still going on intermittently. Not a sound came from the party
above. Sid shouted from the cliff that all was clear. A few minutes later
they were across and the deserted encampment lay before them.

"They're all hidin' out," said McClanahan. "You two start routin' 'em
out. I'll begin here and wait for Sid to cross."

So saying, he began in a matter-of-fact way to scalp four dead Indians,
who had been felled by the fire from across the river as they rushed for
the canoes. He worked calmly, neatly, and fast. For a moment Salathiel
and Nat Murray lay watching him.

"That's two for you, pappy—and two for you, ma," said McClanahan,
while his knife flashed. "And one for sister Sue!" There was a sudden
scramble as he knocked over an empty canoe, and his axe flashed. A
young Indian fell without a groan—"and one for sister Sue!" repeated
McClanahan. "Now you boys had better get goin'. Here comes Sid now.
I'll wait for him. Best to hunt in couples." He laughed, and began to
string the scalps on his belt.

So Salathiel and Nat Murray went up into the camp, where five half-huts stood, near the salt kettles.

There were two Indian crones sitting together in one of the huts. They were very old. They must have been brought along only to tend fires. They sat and said nothing. You could see by their eyes that they already counted themselves as dead. Albine and Murray knocked them on the head. Murray scalped them.

"That's two for you, granfer," he said. "One for each foot you had burnt off." This, as a kind of explanation to Salathiel why he kept the scalps.

"Happen they'll most all be squaws here," he added, and spat.

"Come on," replied Salathiel.

They ranged out into the country behind the camp. It was a fairly open natural meadow in a great bend in the river, with small clumps of sumac thicket here and there. Trails in the thick, virgin grass of spring were not quite so plain as sentences on a page. But eyes could read them.

"Here we go," said Murray. "Two on 'em!"

The trail led, after a short distance, directly towards a remarkably huge specimen of a lone sycamore. They lay down in the grass, some distance away, in order to peer through the branches.

"Look out!" exclaimed Murray. An arrow had just buried itself in the ground some yards directly in front of him.

"Boys," said Salathiel. He could see them plainly enough now, dark and high up in the big branches, cowering close to the trunk. He remembered his days with the young Shadows.

"Jump!" he called in Delaware. "Jump and run!" One of them did. It was the boy with the bow.

Salathiel shot him.

The other youth set up a dismal calling and kept climbing about through the branches. Murray ran up and brought him down with his axe.

"Them's both yours," said Murray generously.

Salathiel took them. It was expected of him. He was surprised to find the two scalps gave him no satisfaction.

"One for your pa—and one for your ma?" said Murray inquiringly.

Salathiel nodded.

They went on to the next thicket. They flushed a young squaw there, who tried to run for it. Then she stopped and made pleading gestures. She even started to come back towards them. That was a little confusing, but Murray shot her. They didn't stop to take her scalp. There wasn't time.

At a distance of nearly a quarter of a mile the two McClanahans were now hellooing lustily. They had evidently found what Murray called the "main parcel". The flat *bang* of an ancient musket from a dense clump of hemlocks that stood like an island in the midst of the swampy meadow sounded more like defiance than a serious attempt at defence. It was the only shot fired at any of them that afternoon.

Sid McClanahan laughed as the slug bullet droned through the air overhead. "Nothin' but squaws and old men in there, I reckon. Maybe some childer, too."

"Damn hit, thar's more on 'em than we thought," observed Cal, wiping his rifle thoughtfully. "Even Cap'n Jack ought to be fed full when we git through with this. Pity they didn't all make tracks separate. Some on 'em might hev made it then, maybe." This was the sole sign of compunction anyone showed at the Salt Kettles.

The four of them were now standing together a good musket shot back from the clump of hemlocks, listening. But no further sounds came from the small island of trees. Downriver the firing had completely died away. They stood hesitant as though awaiting a signal. Then upriver a sudden fusillade broke the peace of the valley and the spell under which they seemed to be standing.

"They're gittin' 'em up there, too," said Salathiel.

"They'll git 'em all," said Murray.

"Come on!" exclaimed Cal McClanahan. "Let's git it over with here. The rest will soon be comin' back. Scatter out first, and then we'll run in on them from all sides at once. I'll whistle."

So they scattered out, surrounding the clump of hemlocks, and then stood for an instant, waiting. Cal gave a shrill hawk's whistle, and they rushed in from all sides.

There was a green twilight under the thick tent of the evergreens. Streaks of sunlight filtered through the low-hung branches. Cowering there in the wash of flooding shadows, like rabbits when a dog is near, the victims lay quiet. Some of the children whimpered. There were ten Indians in all in that dismal thicket.

On them the axe fell flashing, once. The only mercy shown was the swiftness of the deed. It was all over in a few minutes.

The four avengers walked away from the little island of trees. They walked away silently.

From the height of the bank several canoes with militia in them could now be seen coming around a bend down the river, nearly two miles away. The two parties caught sight of each other. The men in the canoes stopped paddling and waved their caps. Upstream all firing had now died away.

"Cap'n Jack will soon be here," grunted Cal McClanahan. "Hope he likes it."

"We've sure been right thorough," said Sid.

They were now walking down the riverbank to meet the oncoming canoes. Albine slowly fell behind the other three. It was his intention to have another look through the thicket where Murray had shot the young squaw. She had had a cradle bound on her back, he had noticed. And she had tried to come back for some reason.

Long afterward he came to regard his curiosity about this dead Indian woman as the cause of his greatest misfortune.

The dead squaw, still unscalped, lay only a few yards from the thicket, out of which she had at first broken in terror—and to which she had been trying to return when Murray shot her. When Salathiel came back to the place where she lay, he found, as he thought he would, why she had tried to return.

The child was a toddler, just able to get about on his own feet. He had evidently come out of the thick bushes and found his mother.

He was quite happy. He sat in a small patch of white river sand, in the sunlight, and played with a string of bright almond-shaped beads, yellow with a red center. Just a few feet away, but in the shade of the thicket, the dead woman lay on her side in the grass, her eyes half closed. She might have been dozing. But this was, momentarily at least, quite satisfactory to the baby.

Salathiel came upon all this suddenly, but stealthily, stepping through the grass on cat's feet like an Indian. The child looked up, paused, and held out the beads to him. The man didn't take them. He crouched down, watching. The child went on playing.

There was a curious suggestion about those beads. They showered like drops of blood from the child's hands in the sun. And at times they looked brown, hard, even jadelike, shaped like the eyes in the baby's smooth Indian head. That topknot! Here was the rattlesnake's egg hatching—hatched, and playing in the sun.

He squatted for a moment, watching. An ugly compulsion was on him. It grew. He was close to the ground, alone, looking around again at the tall grass and towering trees, the immense depth of shadows, the strange, high sky. A child's vision of things. It all rushed back upon him. He remembered. A cold terror gripped him, complete and paralyzing. He heard his mother scream. Something broke in his head. All the tenseness of his horror was suddenly expelled through his muscles, the muscles of a man now.

He struck the child in the nape of the neck a lightning blow with the hard side of his hand. It died instantly. It died still clutching the red, amber-coloured beads in one hand.

He got to his feet. He looked about him, surprised to find himself in a familiar world again. Why, it was over! No one need ever know. And that babe of his mother—that other child he had buried near Pittsburgh—himself—his own stolen self—all his pain and terror had been given back again. It lay still with eyes closed, asleep forever on the ground. He would return later and bury it; get it out of sight.

What had he to do with this? Nothing. There had been a motion of his right arm. It happened like being hit on the knee and kicking out. It had relieved him. Somehow it had done that.

He left both child and squaw lying there. The shadow of the thicket was creeping over them both. He walked down to the riverbank and said nothing. Nat Murray looked at him enquiringly.

The first of the captured canoes was coming in from downriver filled with jubilant militia. They gathered together and fired a joyful volley. The cliff re-echoed the crash of triumph. From both up the river and down the careless crackle of rifle fire answered back this *feu de joie*. All the fleeing canoes had been stopped. All the warriors in them had been taken. Their scalps dangled now from many belts.

Captain Jack sat in the bow of a canoe and the scalps were shown to him, one by one. Sid McClanahan told briefly of the clean sweep they had made in the encampment. The last of the flanking parties now came in. Three men had been wounded, and one killed. He had been in the party upriver. He had sunk in the stream when they had closed in on the last canoe. Who was he? No one seemed to know. It had been a small price to pay for so complete a victory.

Captain Jack's face shone with relief and satisfaction. His ruse had been perfect. Not a soul of all the Indians had escaped. It had been death at the Salt Kettles, death complete and final. The nine Indian fires still smoked peacefully in the face of the declining sun.

Such fires were slowly going out.

"Everywhere," growled Captain Jack. His desire was coming true. He had had a full taste of it. For the first time he felt avenged, his cup of hatred emptied. The men gathered about him on sudden impulse and cheered him. He thanked them calmly. His thanks were sincere. After him the good work would go on, safe in such hands as theirs. He, himself, might even go home now and wait in peace for the end. No voices would call to him from the shadows of the woods at twilight. No faces would mow at him from the flames on his own hearth. The end could be peace for Jack on Jack's Mountain.

He turned away from them and went down to stand by the river of clear water that ran by the bitter springs of salt. His throat was still raw with powder smoke. He laid his rifle in the grass and knelt down to drink from the river. He drank deep, and thanked his God in his heart. But when he rose and stooped to pick up his rifle again his hand hesitated. A tremor shook him. The long rifle-gun lay in the grass, shining, with many nicks on the stock. But there would soon be rust upon it. His work was over. He was of no use any more. The full realization numbed him. Finally he picked the rifle up and cradled it in his arm.

From that day Captain Jack aged rapidly. In a few months he looked and acted like an old man.

All of them crossed the river and camped that night at the top of the cliff. They made fires freely there, for they were in ample force, and victorious. They felt strong. The crackling flames leaped high, throwing a dark, orange glow through the woods. They ate the Indians' provisions gladly, bear's grease, and maple sugar from deer-head bags made by the squaws—their coarse, sweet corn pone. They devoured the small deer the Indian boys had skinned for them, and there was plenty of salt for that meat. They laughed in their beards, and boasted. Supper over, they sat about the clear fires and dried the scalps against the heat after they had spread them out on small willow hoops. There were thirty-eight scalps in all.

Nat Murray insisted that there should be thirty-nine. Twelve warriors had fled downstream, and eight upriver. They were all accounted for by the militia. According to Murray's arithmetic, he and Salathiel and the two McClanahans had accounted for nineteen about the Salt Kettles, and they were now one short. Murray argued vehemently about this. He finally narrowed it down by elimination to the squaw he had shot by the thicket, and neglected to scalp.

"But I thought you lingered behind to do that, Sal," he said reproachfully.

To placate him, Albine acknowledged that he had not taken the woman's scalp.

Murray seemed to feel he had been cheated. Finally, nothing would do but crossing the river again to make the work complete. Seeing that he was bound to go, Salathiel agreed to go with him. He had grown to like Murray, and he wanted to keep his respect. Nothing else would have made him cross the river again.

All was quiet at the Salt Kettles. The last embers of the fires were dying out by the empty huts. Murray and Albine went carefully, but they went swiftly. It was a matter of only a few minutes before they found the little thicket again. It loomed up plainly in the starlight in the middle of the flood meadows. Neither of them could be mistaken about the place. But the body of the squaw Murray had shot was gone.

"Maybe we overlooked some on 'em," said Murray.

"Maybe we did," replied Salathiel. He remembered he had forgotten to search through the thicket that afternoon.

And now the body of the child was gone, too.

But he said nothing about that to Murray. That was his own business, he reckoned. And he reckoned right. Even the beads had disappeared. He felt for them carefully in the grass. His fingers found where the child had lain. The beads were gone.

It was dark. Only the stars winked blindly. But for an instant he saw those beads flashing in the child's hands in bright sunlight.

He drew his sleeve across his confused eyes—and they went back over the river again.

"Reckon I was wrong," said Murray when they stood by the fires again. But he looked at Salathiel reproachfully.

They said nothing to Captain Jack, for neither of them wished to spoil for the old hunter a tale of death that, in his mind, was a perfect and complete affair.

Everyone always spoke of it that way. It was called "Death at the Salt Kettles".

15. Old Bonds Loosen

SEVEN grim individuals were returning across the mountains to the village of Bedford, in the spring of 1764. But even as they advanced through the forest their grimness seemed to drop away from them. They were in another, gayer mood. They suffered from no doubts or compunctions. The scene of death at the Salt Kettles lay behind them. They were happy to have proved themselves by so notable a slaughter. The scalps they were bringing back would be both profitable and acceptable. Their enemies had been warned and weakened. Vengeance had been full fed. So they felt appeased, relieved and satisfied, instead of guilty. They, themselves, were unscathed, and the rising tide of young summer seemed to bear them triumphantly on the crest of its green flood as it swept northward through the valleys and spilled over the mountaintops.

Captain Jack and his rangers did not return with the others to Ligonier. He had sent the militia back to the post with thanks and much praise to Lieutenant Blane, who, on his part, promptly seized the occasion for pouring encomiums on Captain Jack, and incidentally himself, in glowing official dispatches.

Colonel Bouquet at Fort Pitt was delighted. He sped the victorious news of the Salt Kettles to the troops still at Bedford, hoping it would also inspirit the new levies assembling at Carlisle. Ecuyer on his sick-bed at Pendergasses' was cheered by the glad tidings and the approval of his revered colonel. For a month all raids had ceased. Despondent settlers waiting at Bedford to return to their burnt cabins, and begin life over again, found hope renewed as the much-magnified rumour of the affair at the Salt Kettles spread around and about. Before Captain Jack returned to Bedford it was being talked of even in Philadelphia as a good omen, as the fortunate prelude for Bouquet's Ohio campaign. Captain Jack was a hero, his men paragons. They were blessed and called wonderful. Meanwhile, where were they?

Meanwhile they were lingering in the Garden of Eden, enjoying their chosen reward. It was hunting, always the preoccupation of heroes, the prime anodyne of care.

Captain Jack was one of the few people who then knew his way thoroughly through this tangled maze of hills and upland streams. He had sometimes taken refuge here from Indian pursuers in the past.

"We're poachin' on the presarves of the Long House," drawled Captain Jack, "and it's contrary to the king's proclamations, Gawd bless'm! But only the Lard will know. We'll leave no sign of ever bein' here. We'll vanish our way through."

This was the kind of life which some men were to keep moving westward and westward in order to find over and over again, until the Pacific beaches bared their teeth in foam and the hope escaped them. And there was not a man in all the seven of Captain Jack's band who was not conscious of his luck of living in a faultless springtime; of joy in the effortless bounty of an existence without regrets and forebodings; of wonder at the overflowing, exalted magnificence of the hills.

North of the Conemaugh it seemed as though no one had ever been there before them. The empty forest stretched park-like and endless, where there had been no underbrush for centuries. The rooted columns of its aisles and porches rose sheer and tremendous through the green, sun-streaked twilight, to a distant leafy ceiling. There were few fallen trees. Only the crowns of these forest sovereigns were doffed to winter. They scarcely bowed to storms, and only lightning or whirlwinds could finally bring them down. Even in their "cemeteries", where tornadoes had struck, they still stood upright, their bleached skeletons erect in death. But there were not many such places among those sheltered hills.

Now and then there were successions of open, sunny glades. It was between these grassy amphitheatres that the game trails led onward in every direction and eventually nowhere.

Through these glades, forests, and mountain thickets, through the pond-dotted natural meadows, and along the bottoms of beaver-dammed streams the seven Mountain Foxes moved circumspectly but choicely, selecting only what they called the "fancy places" to tarry and camp in. They made smokeless punkwood fires by springs of the coldest and clearest water in favoured spots. They slept under bowers of branches to keep off the night-gathering damps. They chose some small, perfect valley and loafed. They lived delicately, taking exactly what they wanted and no more. This restraint was due alone to the art of Captain Jack, who had long ago learned from his enemies to refrain from useless animal slaughter. They had only to stretch out their hands, and their legs a little, to find and take. So they were nice and particular.

They swam, slept, ate when they were hungry, enjoyed the warmth of sun-struck places, sat in the shade, groomed themselves with fine-toothed combs whittled out of hardwood. They discussed in drawling talk the advantages of the country, pointed out the best sites for thriving farms, wrapped themselves in their blankets nightly and went to sleep under a sailing moon.

For Salathiel this was living on as satisfactory terms as he could then imagine. Like all the others, he literally forgot everything but the day and hour at hand. Tired from the chase or by some solitary adventure with Mat Pendergass or Nat Murray, he slept dreamlessly. He even ceased thinking about Phoebe or longing for her at night. In fact, he forgot her and everyone else he had ever known, save his companions in those woods. No one else seemed to have existed. It was full-time, no-time, now.

Even Captain Jack was now able to forget the past, and he was not anxious to think of the future. Indeed, he kept putting it off. He had lingered in this wilderness for some weeks, deferring the hour of return when he knew things would go his way no more, when his work would be over and his leadership laid by. Only the gradual waning of ammunition forced him to move. He edged slowly and reluctantly in the direction of Bedford. But at last he admitted that their powder was getting dangerously low.

And so one morning quite suddenly, by common impulse rather than by command, they started definitely homeward. They crossed high, wind-swept ridges. They plunged downward at last into the dense thickets of a valley forest, followed a deer path along an ever-widening stream, and came out of the green gloom of the trees one early July afternoon on the wide, middle reaches of the shallow Juniata.

Instantly it seemed to them they had escaped out of the wilderness, so sudden was the change. The quiet talk of the wide river seemed domestic and familiar after the headlong rush of shouting mountain streams. And accident contrived to confirm their impressions of nearing home.

The road to Bedford skirted the opposite bank, and along it, even as they watched, white wagontops came gliding through the trees. Sunlight flashed on the weapons of the escort, the muffled yoke bells of a convoy dimly chimed.

"By God," exclaimed Mat Pendergass, unable to control his emotions at such a cheerful sight of so much company again—"by God, you can't get them fellers to still their bells, not for no orders! God bless'm! Stottelmyer!" he bellowed. "Ho there, Stott!"—until the echoes along the river yelled and stuttered back again.

"Ho—ho—Stot—Stot—myr."

The startled and flustered convoy came to an instant halt. Men came tumbling out of the wagons with guns in their hands. It was some moments before the bearded wanderers made themselves known and certain of a friendly welcome.

But what a welcome it was, as they crossed above a rapid, leaping from one giant stone to another and climbing up the opposite bank! The wagoners came swarming down to meet them and carried Captain Jack up out of the water on the shoulders of the crowd. None of them had any idea that the news of their exploits had preceded them. But it was soon quite evident from the hail of handshakes and backslapping that left their shoulders and paws sore. Even the young English lieutenant in charge of the escort actually came to congratulate Captain Jack, much to the latter's embarrassment. Indeed, they were all shy at first and could find little to say. The crowd seemed enormous. They had forgotten that there could be so many people. But a jug put an end to their embarrassment. The white whisky burned them—and they talked. They talked with relief and like a house afire.

Mat Pendergass had been right. It was Stottelmyer. He and his stout wagoners were in charge of the convoy: ten wagons, and thirty pack horses; twenty beeves for the fort.

"Do ye think I wouldn't know that yoke chime any place I heard it, when me and Mark made it!" Mat kept exclaiming. "It's sweet as silver bells!"

Someone produced a fiddle in the fourth wagon, and to the sound of its gay rasping and the cheerful *bur-r* of a jew's-harp the convoy resumed the march and plodded on up the valley of the Juniata towards Fort Bedford.

They camped that night at the water gap. The fires leaped high and the jugs passed around. Only Captain Jack, who would drink nothing, sat taciturn and moody again. In this wild scene in the river gorge, even in the unexpected triumph of his return after his most notable campaign, he felt a sense of ending. Forbes Road would be opened now. Prophetically he felt that not only his lifework but the reign of savage terror east of the mountains was past.

Someone was playing a bugle, a fiddle scraped, the flames wavered, and the men sang. Even the outlying sentries of the escort sat in pairs and smoked comfortably. Their path westward was open and beckoning them on. They could lay plans now for homes in the new lands, after the war. It was only Captain Jack who was thinking of the past. The mind of everybody else in the convoy was content with the present or ranged the future. Salathiel was thinking that night as he went to bed in Stottelmyer's wagon of the cities he had not seen that lay eastward, of the great world by the salt sea. He was still bent on going there. He had not forgotten. He would talk with Phoebe about it—tomorrow.

It seemed to Salathiel when he returned to Bedford that life would go on very much the same as it had the winter before. He had certain vague plans about how he was going to make it go. But nothing went as he had expected.

Young Albine was aware of a perverse direction of events almost as soon as he had swung off the wagon when the convoy came in and the thundering greeting of the crowd, which quickly assembled in the hearth room at Pendergasses', was over. The welcome home had been hearty and genuine enough. But despite a deal of backslapping, hand-shaking, treating, and even rough but well-meant flattery, it was impersonal. It was simply part of the general welcome and approval which the village and the garrison wished to show to all of Captain Jack's Mountain Foxes, Fightin' Quakers—or how-do-ye-call-ems? It was one thing to be a bit of a hero, and respected accordingly, and another to find old friends, especially the only friends he had, curiously changed, and changed they undoubtedly were.

"How be ye, young feller? You've done well, too, I hear," said old Garrett, as though performing a duty. Somehow Salathiel failed to meet his eye. How he envied the greeting Garrett gave to Murray, as though Nat had been one of his own sons. Salathiel felt that when he had left for the cabin that night back in March he had almost become one of Garrett's family. What had happened while he had been away—and where was Phoebe? She had not come to meet him. Why not? Where was she? Could it be that McArdle had talked with her, or with Garrett? Probably.

He sat at the big table after the crowd had left, almost paralyzed by the thought. How he wished now that he had faced the music before he left. But as he thought of Phoebe, her image banished everything else from his mind.

Phoebe! Phoebe!

It seemed impossible that even under the strong drug of war and the spell of the deep forest he had ever forgotten her, even for a moment. All the days and nights of hardship and absence, all his young, iron strength and longing for his golden-haired angel now flowed back upon him in an intolerable fire and tumult of longing to see her, to take her in his arms again and say he had come back.

Phoebe! Phoebe!

Every familiar angle of the house spoke of her. There was the place in the hall at the head of the stairs where they had said good-bye. He knew now that it was because of her that Pendergasses' had become like home to him. For that reason he had come to love the very curves of the hills about the village of Bedford. He knew he must find Phoebe now or suffocate. He must find her and live with her or something in him would die.

And all this tumult and dire necessity of emotion was a confounded surprise to him. Until now he had not really understood how hopelessly he was in love with Phoebe Davison. It had been a shy dream last winter, something too delicate to examine carefully and plan about practically. Somehow, somehow, their love would come out all right. Somehow he would get over or around that ugly difficulty about Jane; the threat that McArdle's coming to Bedford implied. He would explain how the marriage had happened. He would tell Phoebe now. He would appeal to Garrett. He would run off with Phoebe if he had to! Of course she would come with him. He had to have her. He understood that now.

His return, the sudden entry into the hearth room, where he had first seen her, brought it all back to him intolerably, insistently, overwhelmingly. He knew now that nothing else mattered. And yet, how *was* it to be accomplished? How? A premonition of unbearable tragedy turned him cold, then left him hot and restless. And this crisis seemed to have been forced suddenly and violently upon him by the very fact and simple act of his return.

After the welcoming crowd had come and gone, he still sat at the big table in the hearth room, pondering. He had gradually been left alone. Even the two McClanahans had relatives in town. Yates was away on a survey of the southern boundary eastward with Mr. Lukens, he had been told. Too bad! He needed Yates now. Over at the women's house next door he could hear the voices of all the Pendergass boys and Nat Murray.

He listened.

The voice he hoped most to hear was not there.

Surely she would have come to look for him. She might at least have done that. He looked around the empty room. No, she was *not* here. And so great was his longing for her that for a dizzy instant he thought he saw her standing on the hearthstone just as he had seen her that memorable night when he had first entered the room.

It was a genuine hallucination. It was the kind of vision which men who had lived lonely lives in the forest sometimes saw. The vision of her that was in him had come out. It now stood on the hearth where she had once been. It was the dream which unwittingly he loved more than Phoebe herself. His sheer intensity of emotion projected it into the room. It was his young, new, and clear love. And she was maddeningly beautiful. Thus he saw her as he had once seen her for the first time. And once again he heard the voice of old Mrs. Pendergass saying, "You boys from the forest, you be like zailors home from the zea."

And then all this was dissolved into a mist in his eyes and a buzzing in his ears, and he saw only his huge, helpless hands gripping the hard oak table before him till his knuckles turned white. That table! Why, he had killed men with it!

He rose now, seizing it; actually shifting it from its ponderous base. He wished to rush with it, racing and crashing down the room again. His emotion and perplexity culminated thus in a sudden access of anger and blind action. But the table was really too heavy to be moved even by a young giant in a passion. It was like events. Its sheer weight and resistance brought him to himself again. He sat down and remained quiet for a while, breathing heavily, but looking affairs in the face.

Well, he would go next door and find out what *had* become of Phoebe.

He walked quietly enough down the passageway and out into the yard. All the Pendergasses were upstairs in the women's house. He could hear that Captain Jack and Garrett were there, too—in old Mrs. Pendergass's room, no doubt. Captain Jack was drawling away, and now and then old Garrett and the others laughed. There was plenty to tell, he thought. The others would be listening avidly, all of them crowding to the door. Outside there was only the lonely music of the river. In the yard, basking in the hot, July sunlight the chickens made dust nests and crooned with satisfaction. He saw that he had been forgotten. Probably they had not meant to leave him out. They had simply overlooked him. He would go up and brave them anyway. He would see.

He started towards the door, but just as he entered he met Charles Pendergass coming out. Salathiel looked at him, startled, for there was a great red weal across his throat, and he looked like the ghost of the man of the winter before.

"Why, Charley!" he said, and held out his hand. "I'm terrible glad to see ye."

Charles took his proffered hand slowly and looked at him as though he scarcely seemed to be there.

"Oh, yes," he said at last. "Oh, I know you! It's young Albine. I'm kind of forgetful sometimes these days." He pressed Salathiel's fingers spasmodically, and dropped them.

Salathiel felt ashamed of himself. He had had no idea that Charles had suffered so much. He, too, looked forgotten. He stifled the eager question that was on his lips to ask another. "And how's Mrs. Pendergass?" he asked. "Your wife, I mean," he added doubtfully and awkwardly.

Charley stood for a moment on the upper step, looking out over Salathiel's head. Apparently he saw something across the river.

"Why, she ain't doin' so well," he answered at last in a faraway voice. Unconsciously, he put his hand to the scar on his throat. "No, she really ain't doin' so well," he repeated slowly. "They've got her chained up over there in old Pina's cabin. Ye ain't heard her screech, hev ye?"

"No," said Salathiel, "no, I haven't."

"That's good. I thought I did just now," said Charley. "That's why I come downstairs." He continued to stand on the step, feeling his throat helplessly.

"I'm downright sorry, Charley. 'Deed I am!" said Salathiel. "I did hear of your trouble, and I'm sorry. I'm really sorry," he kept repeating.

"I know ye be," said Charley, afterwhile. "I—I—thank you for it." He extended his hand again. Salathiel took it, and he also took the opportunity to ask his own question.

"Where's Phoebe, Charley?" he asked breathlessly.

He had to wait a moment for the reply. Charles Pendergass looked at him thoughtfully and seemed to be considering his answer.

"Who? You mean little Phoebe Davison?"

Salathiel nodded emphatically.

"She's gone away," said Charles. "She went out to Pittsburgh to visit sister Sue."

Salathiel still stood there.

"No use askin' for her," Charles added. "Maybe you'd better not." He pressed Salathiel's fingers again before dropping his hand.

"I see," said Salathiel. "I guess I understand."

Charles Pendergass again nodded solemnly. "Gone away. You can't never be sure about women," he said. A look of mutual sympathy passed between them. The plaintive voice of the river swept through both their minds, saying the same thing.

At that instant someone threw open a window in the inn building behind them and called out, "Albine! Salathiel Albine, come up here!" The tones of the voice were enormously familiar. Salathiel turned and looked at the upstairs window near the corner of the inn. Out of it protruded the well-remembered red face and half the sturdy body of the Reverend James McArdle, the mentor of his forest days. The wheel of time seemed to slip a cog backward, hesitate, and then go on again—now—with the voice. "Come up here, my boy. I want to see you, and so does Captain Ecuyer." Mr. McArdle appeared to gesture impatiently as he shut the window.

Salathiel turned away from Charley, and with a feeling of impending disaster tightening across his chest, walked back into the inn and mounted the stairs to Ecuyer's room.

He had to pass his own chamber and Yates's at the end of the hall. He glanced into the two familiar rooms as he went by. They were empty, just as they had been when he had left to go on the raid. Both Yates and himself seemed to be away. He braced himself for what was to come, and knocked at Ecuyer's door.

"Come in, sir," said the still firm voice of the captain, but in the flat tones of a sick man.

Salathiel pulled the latchstring and walked in.

Mr. McArdle rose from a chair where he had been sitting by Ecuyer's bedside and came over to meet him. He put both his hands on Salathiel's shoulders and said, "God bless you, my boy. I've never ceased to pray for you. Thank the Lord I find you safe!"

McArdle's warmth was so real and his pleasure at seeing his pupil again so obviously genuine that Salathiel could not help but respond. The minister might be the cause of his undoing with Phoebe, but he had also "saved him alive" from savagery. The memory of all they had been through together came back to Salathiel on seeing again the friend of his boyhood years. And so it was with great, although not without mixed, emotion that he took him again by the hand.

Possibly it was some awkwardness or hesitation that Ecuyer observed in Albine, or perhaps it was the sheer grotesqueness of the appearance of the two together, which now caused the captain to conceal a smile with a cough, and the cough with his hand. Albine was still dressed in the full panoply of a ranger, and McArdle, who also was no dwarf, in an old plum-coloured suit he had had conferred upon him somewhere, plus a clerical stock he had more recently borrowed from the Reverend Mr. Puffin, the Church of England chaplain at the fort. Ecuyer was both edified and amused.

"What a reunion it is!" he exclaimed from the bed. "You haven't grown any smaller, Albine," he said as Salathiel came over to greet him, "but you see I have. I'm withering." His thin fingers felt sensitively feeble in Salathiel's fist. "You can have no idea how a man entirely out of it like myself envies your strength."

Salathiel, of course, blurted out that he was sure the captain would soon be getting better. Ecuyer looked at him with eyes that now seemed to occupy most of his face, smiled, and made a quiet, little negative motion with his head.

"Hardly," he said.

There was an instant's silence.

"But let us not talk about *that* any more," the captain added. "Now that you have come back, Albine, perhaps you will look after my body again for a while. Mr. McArdle has been devoting himself to saving my soul. Between you I might pass out successfully." He laughed with a sudden surprising gaiety. All his energy now seemed to be in his head. His eyes twinkled with mischief.

"But sit down, gentlemen, sit down!" he insisted, seeing their embarrassment. "Let us hear what Albine has to say. I hear he has been abroad in the wicked world. What news from the devil's kingdom, my lad? I've been hearing a great deal about heaven lately." He motioned Salathiel to take the chair beside his bed.

Now, there was only one chair in the room, and one very small stool. Albine was quick to take the captain's hint and sit down in the chair, removing an open Bible from it, and laying the still open book carefully on the captain's bed beside him. McArdle did not take any too kindly to the stool. It was quite a low one.

"Possibly there is another chair in the next room," said the captain.

"No, no," said McArdle. "I'll leave you now, sir. I know you will be desirous of talking with Salathiel. I hope he'll consent to what you want. 'Tis a Christian service ye might well do, even for an infidel, Albine," he said, and then turned to the captain.

"Oh, sir, do you now ponder well on what I have laid before you. The way is plain. The only way. I have left it open for you there at the fifth chapter of St. John."

"I'll consider it, McArdle. Indeed, I will," said the captain. "I'll ponder it carefully. But suppose you ask Mr. Puffin not to come until the day after tomorrow. I'll need a little time to think over *your* exposition of the matter."

Mr. McArdle nodded. He took this as a compliment to his own powers of persuasion, which deserved ample consideration.

"I'll tell Mr. Puffin," he said. "But remember, your time is short."

Ecuyer grimaced slightly as the minister went out. McArdle turned suddenly at the door and said, "Come up to the fort and talk with me as soon as you can, Salathiel. I've got something that nearly consarns you to relate. Maybe you'll know what I'm driving at. But good news," he added encouragingly, "on the whole, *good* news." He smiled, and closed the door as he went out.

It was Salathiel's turn to look disgusted. He struck the arm of his chair impatiently.

The captain laughed wryly.

"What's the matter?" he asked. "Is he fishing for your soul, too?"

"I'll tell you what's the matter!" Salathiel burst out—"that is, if you're not too ill to hear me, captain. I've got to tell somebody."

"For the last two weeks," replied Ecuyer, "a blessed numbness has come to my relief. I am cold from the waist down, but I no longer feel pain." He put his hands behind his head, leaned back on the pillow, and stared out the window a minute. "No, once more I can be interested in the difficulties of other people. The trouble with pain is that it makes you think only of yourself. I've been *beside myself*, as they say in English. And there is nothing quite so boring as that. It will be better to die than to go on that way. So I really would like to hear what you have to say."

"Before I came to you at Fort Pitt," began Salathiel, searching out his words slowly, "I was married to a girl named Jane Sligo. Mr. McArdle married us on an island down the Ohio one fine day to save woman-talk. We were running away from some Shawanee lodges on the Beaver, him and me, carrying along with us some captivated women and children to try to slip them through the Injuns into the fort. But we soon found we couldn't. So McArdle hid with the women and children at Nymwha's camp near the sawmill, while I got into the fort myself with Sergeant Jobson. The other soldier with us was scalped. We barely made it. You may not remember all of this. It was just before I came to serve you at the beginning of the siege."

"But I do remember," said Ecuyer. "And I also recollect that you thought me unfeeling not to send across the river for the captives immediately—and thus ensure their massacre with the probable loss of the rescuing party as well. Also, you wouldn't be satisfied until I let you go over alone to try to fetch your wife. I couldn't refuse you that. But you came back without her, and minus an ear, too. Well, where is your wife?"

"I don't know," said Salathiel, with an obstinate look.

"But the Reverend James McArdle evidently does," said the captain.

"Has he said so here?" demanded Salathiel uncomfortably.

"Of course," replied the captain. "He has been asking for you, and telling your good news. Your wife, it seems, escaped back to the inhabitants, and so did all the others. McArdle himself took them through the woods to Redstone Old Fort, while we were being besieged. It was quite admirable of him, I think."

"Oh, McArdle, McArdle, what a man he is!" exclaimed Salathiel, beside himself with exasperation.

Ecuyer leaned back on his pillows again for a while and looked out at the distant mountains. "I know how such things are. I am truly sorry for you. To lose the one we love with all our soul is the worst of misfortunes. Nothing makes up for such a loss. All else that follows is dust or buffoonery, a play without a plot. It is not even much of a tragedy, for no one cares. At Geneva, when I was little, we used to pay a *denier* to look at a shadow play in a magician's tent. The most dreadful things frequently happened amongst the shadows. But they had no faces, so we children always laughed. Well, my little play will soon be over now," he added. "I have had my money's worth, and the magician will soon be asking me to abdicate my stool. The management continues; the actors and spectators change . . ."

Some of this seemed irrelevant to Salathiel. He was not thinking of Jane as the one he loved with his soul. And he was surprised at the feeling with which the captain had spoken. Towards the last he had been gesticulating, while he sat up. Albine had never expected Ecuyer to talk with him like this. Ecuyer seemed nothing now but a sick man talking to a fellow sufferer. And he was even more surprised when the captain concluded with "Yes, I am *truly* sorry for you. I am sorry, because I understand. You see, my life was changed by a minister, too. She married *him*."

Salathiel pondered this.

"And she loved you?" he asked.

"Oh, yes," replied Ecuyer. "But that doesn't prevent things from happening, does it? Your Mademoiselle Phoebe loved you, for example. Why, she as much as told me so when she left this packet with me the night before she married Burent. She was so completely miserable that she talked, and she had a good cry, poor girl—" Here the captain reached under his pillow and took out a small package wrapped in cloth. He held it out to Salathiel, who seemed too dazed to take it . . .

"Oh, you didn't know?" exclaimed Ecuyer. "I thought they'd have told you. I'm desolated to be the first with such news!"

"Married Burent! Married Burent!" Albine kept repeating, trying to make himself understand the news. He fumbled with the package while his fingers began to undo it automatically.

Once again Ecuyer lay back on his pillows and gazed out the window with a faraway look. "I'm afraid I may have said too much. But someone would have told you before long."

"That little, brown man," Salathiel was saying. "Why, who would ever have thought of him? Burent!"

"But an excellent man," said the captain, "one of the most loyal and honest I have ever known. And he was here, and you were away. And you had said nothing to Phoebe, had you? McArdle's news must have come to her as a terrible shock. Burent had Garrett's permission to ask her. He told me himself he had long had his eye on the girl. I knew nothing of your affair at first, nor did he. I think you should at least have spoken to Garrett Pendergass before you left. He came to me, after he had talked with McArdle, and he was much cut up. He had greatly admired your father, he said. And he had thought of you almost as a son. But Garrett also loved his granddaughter. I would still speak to him," said Ecuyer.

"And Phoebe?" asked Salathiel miserably. He did not tell Ecuyer that he had tried to tell Garrett that night before he left.

"Mistress Burent went west to Fort Pitt about the beginning of May. She had been married only about a week. Yes, it was McArdle who married them. Burent has at last received his commission, thanks to Colonel Bouquet. He will be in charge of completing the fleet of bateaux to take the troops down the Ohio this fall. They have married quarters in the environs of the fort, I hear. They are safe. That is something." He paused a moment and looked at Salathiel significantly. "Do not try to follow them, I beseech you," he said earnestly. "No good can possibly come of that now. It will be best to think of Phoebe as finding happiness with a good man, but . . ."

"Lost!" exclaimed Salathiel.

"Yes, lost," whispered the captain.

Salathiel's face worked, despite himself, and like a boy he buried it for a moment in the bedclothes. His forehead rested on McArdle's Bible.

Ecuyer felt an affectionate impulse to place his hand on Albine's head to comfort him—but the remnants of Salathiel's shorn ear showed through his hair. The captain instinctively withdrew his hand. His sympathy must remain understood, or not understood—as the case might be.

"Do not hate me for what I have told you, Albine," he said. "I have my own selfish reasons for asking you that, too. I wish you would come back to me for a few days. I need you. It will not be for very long."

Salathiel got up still grasping Phoebe's little packet. He would have liked to cut off his head, because his face had betrayed him. For a moment he could not answer the captain.

"But you *will* come back?" asked the captain plaintively. "We're both quite alone now, it seems." His voice trailed away.

"Of course, I'll come back!" exclaimed Albine. "God A'mighty, what did you think! I'll stay to the very end."

"That will be it," said Ecuyer, reaching up and clinging to his hand. "And *to the end* how we all keep thinking about our own precious selves. Now, take your love's bundle and see what's in it. Not hope, I'm afraid. It's only the silver watch I gave you, I imagine. I thought I heard it tick. If so, it passes between us again at a great moment. Now go, but come again in the morning, won't you?"

Salathiel promised and slipped off to his own room down the corridor to be alone, and to see what really was in Phoebe's bundle. He closed the door quietly behind him.

Left alone, Ecuyer looked at McArdle's Bible where it still lay open on the bed, at the fifth chapter of St. John. He smiled feebly. He knew that whole Gospel by heart. His grandfather had long ago made him learn it in Latin. He closed the book impatiently.

"*Bon Dieu*," said he to himself, "why is it these ministers think they can bait a trap for my soul with the stale cheese of everlasting life? What a lure! Sleep, my St. John, sleep is the lure for a tired soldier. Poppy-seed!"

He lay watching the sun setting behind the hills. He grew drowsy. But any sunset now might be his last. Dr. Boyd had said so just before he left Bedford for Fort Pitt. Now, there was a man for you, thought the captain. No whining. No prayer dust on his knees. He had a respect for a dying man. Ecuyer wished that Surgeon Boyd could have stayed with him till the end. "He might have kept those heavenly foxhounds off my trail just before I have to go to earth," he muttered. "He had a way with him."

"*Merde!*" he exclaimed aloud. "How they close in on one at the end, these ministers! They'd catch the faint steam of my last breath on a mirror to call it a confession of faith . . .

"O Lord," he prayed, "if it be possible, rid me of thy faithful servants, the Reverend James McArdle and Mr. Charles Puffin."

He waited as though for an answer. Outside the sibilant rush of the river became audible, the twilight deepened.

"Thanks, Holy Comforter," said Ecuyer, grinning into the darkness. "I know," he whispered to himself at last. "I'll get human help. I'll fight to the end. By God, I'll send for the village schoolmaster!"

He let the Bible slip off the bed to the floor.

The sun had by this time plunged far behind the hills. In the growing gloom of his lonely room Captain Ecuyer painfully composed himself for sleep as best he could.

Back in his room, Salathiel found everything just as he had left it nearly four months before. His small belongings and the few extra clothes he had were waiting for him. Then he became aware that they had all been carefully put away and nicely rearranged. There were also new white curtains tied in with gingham strips, and a box with withered violet plants in the window. Arthur, he knew, had painted that box for Phoebe. The plants were dead, the earth about them dried. He crumbled the dust through his fingers.

So she had come here while he was away. She had kept the room garnished against his return. And then one day she had stopped coming. It must have been weeks ago. He shoved the small, painted box full of dead leaves and black violet blossoms behind the curtain.

Doubtless, at Fort Pitt the quarters of Mistress Burent shone—and had living blossoms in them. Yet it still seemed incredible. It actually made all six feet of him feel weak. He sat down on the bed and slowly unwrapped Phoebe's packet. It was carefully done up in an India kerchief he had given her. It pained him now inexpressibly to remember that this kerchief had been his only gift to her. She might have kept it, he thought.

The silver watch Ecuyer had given him, and a carefully folded and sealed letter fell out on the bed. He broke the seal with his thumb and spread out the paper. His strong hands trembled. Traced in the round, clear hand of Phoebe, in her grandfather's best red ink, and written out fair like a school exercise, he read:

To Mister Salathiel Albine
Dearest Sir—
Please find enclosed in these soft Folds the Silver Watch you did send for me to keep for you until the Time might catch up with us again. But what did I hear today! Oh, my Heart is stopped and stilled like a small Bird frozen in his Nest. That I did love you, I confess. But now there will be no Time showed on this Dial for us to pass together. I am going to marry Mister Burent, the Cooper. Now all our children will be the little Brown Man his. Oh Lord, Mr. Albine. I can say no more. I *must* go away. Do not try to find me, Sir. Do not I pray You. And I will always think of You as a true Man if you let me alone, yet try to think of You no more, as do You of me.

Give this Kerchief to your Wife when you do find her, and say nothing to her either. I opine You did not mean to be so close mouthed with me always. For that Reason I do not give You back your Kisses. The Watch I leave with Captain Ecuyer, because your Friend Mr. Yates is gone off Surveying for a while. I was indeed left alone—but now have taken good company for Life, if no more. I would it might have been better, and bite my Tongue. So farewell—and no more 'till we do meet as Angels.

Yours once,
Phoebe Davison
Fort Bedford Village, at my Grand'f'ter Pendergass House.
Old May Day, A.D. 1764

And that was all.
But that was entirely too much for a hardened scalp-taking, child-

murdering, young woodsman like himself, who was not at all prepared for what violent feeling could do to him. He knew he had lost his mate—and so the rest would be as Captain Ecuyer had said. It was a moment of brilliant agony, and he sat there on the bed while the large muscles in his arms and legs twitched, and the sweat came out in cold beads on his face.

Finally, he began to struggle to repossess himself, for it was panic at the assault of what seemed to be an unknown person within him that brought him to his feet and started him walking up and down the short space of the room, until he went hot all over and then unaccountably weak and cold.

He sat down again, full of shame and astonishment at what had happened to the big body, which he had always thought was his. For a moment he forgot the cause of unease in pure preoccupation with the effects. That helped. And when he next glanced at Phoebe's letter he was able to take it up, fold it without reading it over, and quietly drop it in his old pouch along with other trinkets of the past.

A certain self-pity, defiance, and anger had now risen in him. Twilight was falling, and his room was fast turning dark. But he didn't mean to be left alone there, no matter what had happened! He guessed at the time, and seizing the silver watch, set it, and wound it with its little key and with a certain bravado. He shook it.

The watch suddenly began to go.

He could feel it in his big hands, ticking away against his pulse—he could feel a long, lonely lifetime beginning to flow steadily forward. And it was then, and only then, that tears came to his relief. His shoulders shook, and he sobbed like a child . . .

Afterwhile the worst was over, and he belonged to himself again.

He then made careful preparations. He put on the best clothes he had, and transformed himself from a Mountain Fox into a presentable frontier gentleman. He carefully removed every evidence of the late grimy and bloody business, from beard to clothes, and prepared himself to go downstairs into the hearth room as much another man as possible.

He intended to look everybody, including old Garrett, full in the face. He would have it out with the old man *now*, and with McArdle too! And he would stick by Ecuyer until the end. After all, Ecuyer was the only person alive he really cared about; loved, you might say,—and he was dying.

He was glad now that Yates was away. It made things much simpler. Yates would have had a great deal to say, probably. He closed the door to Yates's room, as well as his own, as he went out. Those closed rooms seemed to belong thoroughly to the past. He looked in on Ecuyer quietly before he went downstairs. The captain was asleep, breathing faintly. He closed that door also.

Without faltering, he passed the hall landing where he had said good-bye to Phoebe, and taking the turn on the stairs, found himself in the hearth room again.

There was no feeling that that cheerful room belonged to the past. Garrett and Captain Jack were having supper at the big table together. He stood for a moment quiet and tense, breathing in the familiar, homely atmosphere of the place.

Besides Garrett and Captain Jack, there was no one else in the room, except sleepy old Pina, who had been serving them. It was a warm summer evening. All the doors and windows stood wide open. Outside he could hear the subdued music of locusts and crickets. Far, shrill voices from the village came floating over the deep undertone of the river. Only a small cooking fire glowed redly in the chimney. A full moon dreamed on the stream outside.

Nothing could have been more peaceful and seemingly substantial than the long dark, quiet room at this hour of evening hush. And in the midst of it the two grey-haired old men were leaning back smoking their pipes, their dinner dishes pushed to one side. They sat there with an air of completion, with such a friendly understanding and venerable ease that Salathiel envied them from the depths of his homeless heart.

He had never seen Captain Jack looking so content. He seemed decidedly older, but his tenseness and grimness had relaxed like a strong trap that has been sprung. At that moment he actually reflected something of Garrett's serenity. They were talking quietly over their glowing pipes; smiling unconsciously at each other with candid eyes—and Salathiel would not have disturbed them then for the world.

No, he thought—as he paused again for a moment at the door of the back hall, such scenes were not for him. He had lost his place at that table of plenty and board of peace, fumbled his welcome there. It would be better if he found lodging in the village now—or wandered back alone into the forest. He could always do that, he remembered. Afterwhile, he could build a cabin in some remote cove of the mountains and live by hunting—after Ecuyer was gone. He turned to go silently before they saw him.

Outside in the wagonyard some moon-fooled cockerel broke into a ridiculous, gargling crowing, followed by a faint clapping of immature wings. It was a positively abortive, untimely, and useless defiance of the universe. Yet there was something comically gallant in the voice of that boy chicken—and both the old men removed their pipes from their lips simultaneously to laugh.

"False dawn, and a young cock dreaming," rumbled Captain Jack.

"Aye, moonlight! Do you remember?" replied old Garrett, looking up with a swift smile of recollection lighting his lips. "Do you remember how it was once? I jealoos I'm prejudiced to young roosters in the moonlight—" and he stopped short, startled by the apparition of Salathiel towering by the corridor door.

"Albine! Where in tarnation hev ye been?" Garrett shouted. "I've had young Arthur looking for ye all over town this afternoon—and not hide nor hair. Come over here and sit down! You been mopin'?" He looked at him closely. "All primped up, eh? What fer?"

"Oh, I've been visitin' with the captain," said Salathiel, trying not to show his vast relief at having been summoned to join them; at being invited back into life again. They must never know how he had doubted that they would care to speak to him again. "Ecuyer wants me to take care of him again—well, until the end," he explained. "And I've been with him most of the afternoon."

"So you got my poor Phoebe's letter then," said Garrett in a tone so low that it seemed almost an aside.

"Yes, I got it," acknowledged Salathiel, and his eyes twitched.

Garrett saw that and looked away, embarrassed. "I kinda thought ye might be up to somethin' foolish this afternoon, young feller," he said. "I've been worried about yer. Thought ye might have packed up your kit without sayin' nothing or seein' me, or . . ."

"No, no," exclaimed Salathiel. "But I didn't know how you might take it. Mr. Pendergass, I *did* try to tell you that night I left. I was sartin goin' to tell you I was married—and you—well, you stopped me."

"That's what I figured out afterwards," said Garrett. "But not until James McArdle came clangin' his tongue agin the roof of his mouth like the clapper of a church bell. What a convinced talker he is. He begets trouble—and then he wonders. I'm sure he has no idea what his tongue hath done now. But what could *I* do when you yourself managed so ill? You should have told Phoebe long ago. It was terrible hard on her. I do blame you much for that."

"I meant to tell her. I always meant to, and yet I couldn't bear to for fear of hurtin' her. And I wanted her. I needed her bad." He ended somewhat dismally and desperately.

Garrett nodded. "Now I'm right glad to hear ye come out flat-footed that way," he said. "My granddaughter, Phoebe Davison, is a lovely gal! I can't blame you. Tell the truth, I'd kinda hoped"—he checked himself—"well, well, I couldn't bear to tell her myself, and it took my old Rose to face it. She it was told Phoebe. And after that I couldn't forbid Burent. He's a good man, you know."

"Yes, he's a good man," acknowledged Salathiel. He wondered how often he would have to admit that. He wished Garrett would have done. Captain Jack was all ears.

"Course, the Burent business was a great surprise to me," Garrett rattled on. "I did remember afterwards that he'd been hangin' around. But it was the women finally fixed it, I guess. And Phoebe was a proud little soul. She wouldn't let her disappointment disappoint them. She'll soon be seventeen. Oh, well, it will be all right after her first baby comes, Rose says." But here Garrett paused and shook his head.

"Gal trouble, eh? Gal trouble!" remarked Captain Jack. "I didn't think you were in it quite so deep, Sal. But sooner or later it comes to us all. Now, my advice would be to find that young wife of yours and straightway go to bed with her. That's the cure, and that's what it all comes to in the end."

But Garrett shook his head again.

"Maybe so," he said. "But don't try to tell that to my Rose, Jack. She'd say there was a time when you knew better."

"Maybe I still do," admitted the old hunter. "Maybe I did—once." He shifted uneasily under some too poignant memory. They were all uneasy now, talking so much about women. It was old Pina who came to their rescue by plumping down a great dish of steaming stew before Salathiel.

"Lord! Here we've been talking nothin' but gals, gals to this young wolf, and I'll bet he's nigh belly-starved. Eat your dinner, man! It's a good one," insisted Garrett.

So Salathiel fell to without further urging, and found that even if he had lost his love he still had his appetite—and that it was *not* so difficult to return to life, after all.

Indeed, afterward he went out and sat on the door stoop overlooking the river, where Garrett and Captain Jack smoked and gossiped, as old men will, tilting their sturdy chairs back against the grateful coolness of the stone wall, while fireflies flashed up and down the valley and two lanthorns hung like fixed stars somewhere above the dark ramparts of the fort.

It was a noble July evening, warm and cool, with light airs drifting through the calm. Out of the placid reaches beyond its upper bend the river poured itself forever past Garrett's door, talking in low, liquid tones of some wild secret of the moonlight. It was a secret too lovely to keep, one which Phoebe had—and had carried away with her. And for that lost balm of love-in-quietude his heart yearned and grieved, and he listened. What he could never say for himself, the river that summer night was saying for him in the solitary moonlight. He heard it and listened understandingly. The shape of his thoughts he covered slowly with a pall of blue tobacco smoke.

Good-bye, Phoebe, vanished Phoebe Davison, farewell . . .

Afterwhile he began to hear another conversation that was going on. He turned to it for homely comfort.

It was Garrett's tongue retailing in easy bursts of liquid conversation, punctuated by half-stifled ironical laughter, the sprightly news of the neighbourhood along its banks. For old Garrett had not lived by the river and with his wife without being much affected by both. It was of news of the neighbourhood that he spoke that evening. He ran on.

With a deep undertone of wisdom and wise solemnity, for that matter, if you cared to listen. And it was in that way that Salathiel learned what had been happening at Bedford Village since he had been away:

How the faces and the character of the garrison at the fort continually changed now as reinforcements went forward to Bouquet; what that gallant colonel had said to Captain Ecuyer, when he had come east going to Carlisle; how reluctantly Surgeon Boyd had gone west when his turn came to take charge of the hospital at Fort Pitt. "Where the pest is ragin'," said Garrett. "Poor Boyd had a premonition he will never get back. Oh, well," sighed Garrett, while he knocked out his pipe, "some people do think too much to be happy."

Yates might be expected back at any time—Salathiel was now glad to hear. He and St. Clair were surveying land grants and engaged in some scheme for settlement after the troubles were over. "Even Buckey has took up five hundred acres somewhere in this valley, I hear." St. Clair, it appeared, had got himself appointed a surveyor too, and Yates would go to Philadelphia soon on some legal business connected with the project.

Albine pricked up his ears at that. So Yates was going to Philadelphia! He might want company.

The lodge had grown so that they were holding meetings now out in the hills. "It's not entirely safe yet," admitted Garrett.

"No, but it's summer," laughed Captain Jack.

They spent some time talking over the notable siege that McArdle and Mr. Puffin were conducting for the capture of Captain Ecuyer's soul. "Maybe we ought to come to his relief," drawled Captain Jack.

"He ain't asked for it," replied Garrett. "I think it helps pass the time for him, to tell the truth. Not much time left for him to pass, if Dr. Boyd was right. Thinnin' out of the blood. Gineral weakness and no hope. A slow passing for a great little man!"

"Aye," growled Captain Jack, "by far the best o' them all!"

They sat silent for a while.

"You can be a help there, Sal," said Garrett afterwhile, poking his thumb at Ecuyer's room. "I'm right glad you've agreed to stay on with him. He misses Phoebe. She was a fine little nurse."

"I'm stayin'!" said Salathiel.

"Will you be goin' after that wife of yours, do you think?" asked Garrett presently.

"I'll think a long while," said Salathiel.

"I know, but I kinda wish you would," persisted Garrett. "Tell the truth, Charley ain't doin' so well since his wife cut his throat acrost. And the other boys are all bound for to settle out. There might be a place for you here if you cared to linger. Years ago I tried to persuade your pa to stay with me. Now you're back, in spite of him and t'Injuns. Kinda looks like fate, doesn't it? Well, I'd like to see your children, too, tumblin' about my door here, even if they bean't Phoebe's. It would make me feel that things begun away back yonder are bound to go on.

That's a good feelin'." Garrett coughed a little, and cleared his throat.

Salathiel was so surprised he made no reply.

"Now thar's a proposition for you, young'un," said Captain Jack at last. He knocked out his pipe with an air of finality. He and Garrett rose and went in. Salathiel heard them laughing about something as they went upstairs. He sat on, alone with the river in the moonlight.

All that he could remember presently as he waited, dozing or spell-bound, on the cold doorstep, was two voices saying:

"It's not entirely safe yet."

"No, but it's summer . . ."

And what a summer it proved to be.

16. Summer

THOSE old men's voices Salathiel heard talking about summer in the moonlight plumbed deeper than he thought. His moonlight had been badly darkened, but summer went on.

And into the ripe, hot mood of it he drifted, unsettled as to the future by the loss of Phoebe, strangely at rest with his savage past by the killing of the Indian child. Between those happenings he was left footloose. Old ties had ceased to bind. Familiar scenes irked him.

Temporarily he was listless. Only the uncertain lingering of Ecuyer kept him at Bedford. He ceased now to make plans. While he waited for Ecuyer to die, he seemed ambitionless. It was even a relief to be able to devote himself to the captain. For the time being, there seemed little else to do. He did not care whether he found Jane or not. Somehow or other old Garrett and Captain Jack had stated his case for him. "It's not entirely safe yet." "No, but it's summer." That was it exactly. Nothing was certain, except the season.

It was not that he remembered their words precisely. But the mood they had evoked remained with the season that made it. Summer—summer in the mountains poised heavily, hot in the daytime, cool at night, at once fierce and delightful. It lay draped along the high ridges in a flame of eternal green, alive, brooding, and waiting. It seemed to be waiting for some change that must come soon, and come with a vengeance.

For that change Salathiel waited, too. It was one of those seasons of quiet crisis in a man's life, when, for reasons which he cannot entirely fathom, he knows he is temporarily stopped. He no longer tries to foresee or control events. Some depth of wisdom tells him to submit his case to fate. So the time went with Salathiel that summer, and so it was that events temporarily took hold of him.

Let us piece them together and make a chronicle of that summer as

nearly as we can. The journal which Salathiel had been keeping befor
he left to go raiding with Captain Jack he resumed again when he cam
back to Bedford in the summer of '64. But his entries are mere fragment
and asides about what went on. Piecing it all together it must have bee
about like this.

The seven in the brotherhood of Mountain Foxes did not hold to
gether very long, it appears. Ecuyer was in fact essential to them. H
was the only king's man with whom Captain Jack would deal person
ally—and everything with Captain Jack was personal. As Ecuyer lan
guished, then, so did the brotherhood and his plans for employing ther
as rangers. For a brief while they seemed to have been used only part o
the time in local scouting or as messengers in the vicinity of the for
For a week or two Murray and Salathiel kept watch on the road from
post established on the high, sphinx-like front of Lookout Mountair
They had a spyglass and a rough pole for signal flags up there. All tha
they did was to report the passing to and fro of convoys and arme
parties. It was nothing more than alert loafing. At times the Pendergas
boys came to relieve them. Then even that nominal duty ceased. Captai
Jack returned to his cabin at "Echovale" and resumed his lonely lif
there. Occasionally he returned to Bedford for a talk with Garrett or t
be present on the evening of a lodge meeting. Eventually, we find hir
receiving pay for himself and the "services of his gallant rangers", whe
Captain Ourry stopped at Bedford on his final trip to Fort Pitt with th
main force of the new militia levies for the Ohio campaign.

Meanwhile, besides tending the captain, there could not have been
great deal for Salathiel to do. Indeed, had it not been for Ecuyer's mi
erable plight he would probably have gone to live at the cabin wit
Captain Jack. As it was, he lingered on in his room at Pendergasses
alone, and moody enough in that hot July weather.

Off and on, Salathiel must have seen a good deal of the Reveren
James McArdle during that hot summer weather. Undoubtedly he sa
him when McArdle came to argue with Ecuyer, which was almos
every day. And the diary also notes several long talks with him at th
fort.

The Reverend James was living at the fort then with the Reveren
Mr. Puffin. Bouquet had found McArdle most helpful in explaining hi
lists of the numerous white captives, and for his minute knowledge c
the western tribes. The colonel had detained him to go with him into th
Ohio country as an interpreter. The lists, which Salathiel had saved
were proving invaluable, and McArdle was in official favour. In th
interim, while Bouquet was at Carlisle, the two ministers had set asid
their minor theological differences to plan a mutual recruiting campaig
for the kingdom of God. Between them, they were trying to organize
"woods preaching", for the conversion of the Bedford townspeople an
the garrison. The plans for that great preaching fell through at the time

though they held it the next summer at Carlisle. Salathiel, however, got a lick of the tongue now and then by way of a personal sermon from both clerical gentlemen. In their opinion he much needed it. McArdle, in particular, was indignant to find that Salathiel was not enthusiastic about going after Jane.

McArdle had in fact worked well and hard to save Jane Sligo and the other women and children the summer of the year before. He made this all quite plain now and in some detail.

After Salathiel had left him he had waited for nearly two weeks for some word of rescue from Fort Pitt. After that he was afraid to wait any longer. The Indians were closing in all along the river during the worst days of the siege, and at any moment the presence of himself and the women and children with him at Nymwha's camp might be discovered. Indeed, it was finally due to Nymwha's care and cunning that they were not discovered and massacred immediately. Three days after Salathiel had reached the fort Nymwha had guided them by night southward over the deserted plateau behind Pittsburgh and hidden them in a slate cave. The woman with the cancerous breast had died and was buried at night. Otherwise they were afraid to show themselves, or even to light a fire.

Nothing further having been heard from either Salathiel or the commandant, Nymwha had at last taken his own horses, and picking the refugees up one evening, had guided them on a long circuit as far south as the Great Meadows, where he left them in McArdle's charge to take them the rest of their way to Redstone Old Fort, on foot. Luckily the country was deserted. They finally arrived, starving but safe, about the end of May, and were kindly received by the garrison and the family of one Captain Cresap, a Marylander, who took Jane and the other women and children in.

All of this McArdle insisted was due to the "marcies of Providence" alone. Yet he was inclined to claim a considerable share in the divine credit for having invoked it by the power of prayer. And he was also surprised and even sorrowful that his "favourite pupil", as he now called Albine, seemed to show a lack of moral understanding in not immediately improving the occasion.

For there was no doubt that Salathiel could easily find Jane, the minister insisted. She was probably still with the Cresaps at Redstone, only a few days' journey through the forests from Bedford. Even if Jane had gone back to the inhabitants, even if she were in Virginny, Salathiel could still follow her up.

Now all this business with McArdle that summer was quite complicated for Salathiel. He admired his old friend greatly for his bravery, his zeal, and his determination. He had an old-time affection for him. He knew that he owed him much for his education, and he was grateful. For these reasons he did not refuse to go after Jane. But at Bedford that summer Salathiel saw another side of McArdle; his blind and persistent pursuit of the soul of Simeon Ecuyer to the very brink of the grave.

It was at once a ludicrous and a merciless exhibition of theological zeal. Salathiel had grown wise enough to understand that. It was now a year and some months since he had left the lodges of Kaysinata and the bodily simplicities of the forest. The time for him had been crucial. In that long year he had learned more than he might learn all the rest of his life. The field, which McArdle himself had harrowed and sown, had sprouted, had grown into tall grain. It was not ripe grain yet, but it was no longer green. More had happened to Salathiel in that year than McArdle could imagine. Much of Ecuyer and Johnson, something of Yates, Garrett, Dr. Boyd, Captain Jack, and many others had been transferred to Albine. He had listened avidly and learned well. He had been married, and profoundly in love, and he had lost both his wife and his sweetheart. He had seen much fighting in a cruel war, and dipped his hands deeply in blood. Initiation into the lodge had aroused him both morally and mystically. He thought clearly and arrived at his own decisions. Physically, he had grown and hardened into a graceful giant of a man. And all this was a blank page to McArdle, who continued to address his "favourite pupil" as though he were still the Little Turtle.

This was unfortunate, critical for Salathiel, to say the least—for in the forest of life he had now reached a place where there was a weblike meeting of many trails. He could not see far down any of them. There was no guide to be consulted. To the questions he shouted at the silence he received no answer, save an echo that seemed to question him back. Yates was away. Garrett and Captain Jack had spoken. It was summer. After a springtime of sudden and violent growth, he was tired. That summer at Bedford he paused for a while in a kind of limbo of doubt and inner inertia. A push down any trail might start him rolling like a stone in the direction given.

Here was the great opportunity for the teacher who had done most to guide him thus far. If McArdle had only been a bigger man—if he had been only a little wiser! But he was not. Zeal had made him blind; official recognition, pompous; authority, harsh.

And so it was by the humane example of an "infidel", rather than from the eloquence of a divine, that Salathiel learned that summer; that he had some questions answered.

In the corner room above the bar at Pendergasses' Simeon Ecuyer lay dying.

Ecuyer died about sunset on the evening of July the twenty-ninth, 1764.

In an age which can scarcely paint an oil portrait without resorting either to sly or to bestial caricature, whose all-absorbing occupation is to dishonour and destroy life, men despise themselves and hate others for

being beasts of prey. To them the death, the mere manner of the demise
of an individual may seem, if anything at all, puerile. But they are not
honourable men who thus dishonour themselves, and it was not so in
July, 1764.

As his hour approached, Ecuyer was afraid of one thing only. He was
afraid that the processes of dissolution at work in his carcass might make
it appear at the last that his body was the abode of something less than
a man. He feared that pain might pull his strings like those of a mario-
nette and force him to make his exit jerking and dancing to a scurvy
tune that Death often whistles through his teeth. He feared that. He
knew that when the automatic obtrudes on the rational it is always horribly absurd. And horror frequently demands the relief of laughter.

It was, therefore, with a feeling of relief that some days before he died
he found the agony which had threatened to control him was turning
numb, as nothingness advanced upon the citadels of life from his feet
upwards. His worst sensation was soon that of slowly turning cold. And
this he could not help from regarding as an improvement in his condition. In fact, the constancy, even a certain serenity, which Salathiel
always remembered as having accompanied the captain towards the end,
was probably due to this small, but important alleviation.

The western window stood wide open in the summer weather, and
Ecuyer looked out calmly at the distant mountains. He could still enjoy
the view. It even reminded him of home. He could still think clearly,
lying in bodily peace. Surely this was a mercy. He counted the red ball
of the setting sun each evening like a last bead on the rosary of existence. He hailed another morning with surprise and joy. In its last brevity
life was again made childishly wonderful. Especially in the late mornings, as the heat of the day mounted, it seemed as if the energy which
had been withdrawn from his extremities was being re-concentrated in
his head.

That at least was the way it appeared to those who came to see him.
To himself it seemed as though his mind floated alone in his head. Free
will freed at last, he thought. To the very end he saw and heard well.
Feeling went first. The thing that Salathiel remembered most about this
time was that, day by day as the summer grew hotter, Ecuyer turned
cold.

That final time with Ecuyer lingered always with a strange quality of
its own in Albine's mind. Possibly because he had just returned from the
forest, it affected him more vividly than it might have otherwise. But
even so it would have been intense and memorable. For either the captain was awake and his mind keen and almost feverishly active, or he
was asleep and exhausted; towards the last, unconscious perhaps. So it
was a time of poignant waiting, and there was not a great deal for him
to do, except to be there when Ecuyer awoke. Yet that meant most of the
time.

"Good!" the captain would say. "Now, I do not wish any more to be left alone. It is extremely kind of you to stay with me."

Altogether, from the time he returned until the captain died, Salathiel was with him ten days and nights. On some mornings Bella Pendergass came to relieve him, but Ecuyer was not so pleased to see her as she expected him to be. His eyes would follow her about the room full of a solemn mischief, and then he would ask her like a Frenchman why she had never married.

"You will be lonely," he would say, and shake his head warningly at her.

After that she came only briefly to dust the room. Some of the settlers' children occasionally brought in wildflowers and stood shyly while he thanked them. Then they would run like young deer.

Captain Jack came over once from the cabin. He talked for a while about old times before many whites had come into the country, and how it went in the forest when he was a boy.

"I have been thinking much of the days when I was a lad, too," said the captain, and then went on to speak of Switzerland with the wistful eloquence of an exile. The old hunter listened raptly, until Ecuyer finally grew silent, overcome by regret.

"Oh, it's best to be young," said Captain Jack, shaking his head knowingly. "An old man grows tired of himself."

"So I am lucky, then, you think?" smiled Ecuyer.

"Probably," replied Captain Jack, "unless those ministers be right." He grinned at Ecuyer, and then his expression suddenly changed. "Captain, you are the only man in a red coat I ever knew that's bound to be saved, if there's justice on high," he burst out. "You've been a terror to the enemy and a comfort to the poor, harried people of these hills. Brother, we'll miss you sorely." He shook Ecuyer's cold hand with emotion, and departed.

"There goes an honest old fanatic," said the captain, "and a brave and valuable one. I feel I have been promoted."

There was also a letter from Colonel Bouquet which Ecuyer would often ask for. He read and re-read it several times. He would laugh as he conned it over, and once there were tears in his eyes. Finally, he burned it over a candle.

"My compatriot is a great man," he said to Salathiel, while the paper curled in the flame. "Bouquet is by far the best general officer they ever sent to these colonies. If he should ask you to serve him, I would advise you to consider it carefully. He would remember you for having brought in the lists of the western captives. And Bouquet never forgets any service rendered, no matter how small. That is a trait rarely found in a man of the world."

He paused for a moment to crumble the ashes of the letter thoroughly.

"I also shall remember you," he said significantly, "for not leaving a

roken man to die alone in a strange land. May there be someone to do
s much for you, if you die without property. Even the corpse of a rich
1an draws crowds—but flies arrive for the same reason. You have no
1ea, at your age, how rare it is for anyone to do anything out of simple
indness of heart."

Salathiel was surprised by this outburst, which may have had some-
hing to do with the burnt letter, but was unexpected.

"I have nothing else to do with my time, sir," he answered.

"But time is the best gift of all," asserted the captain. "It's the ultimate
ommodity. If anyone takes it away from you, you have lost your life
efore you die. I ought to know. I have been hired most of my time."

"But Captain Jack would call it 'well employed'," replied Salathiel.

"Perhaps," sighed the captain. "And yet . . . *work for yourself*," he
1apped suddenly, "or else die early! By the way, isn't Mr. Yates ex-
•ected back soon?"

"Not for a fortnight, I fear."

"Much, much too long for *me* to wait," mused Ecuyer. "Lawyers who
ravel far abet delay. And afterwhile with them is never soon. The fuse
•f my carcass will not sputter long. Bring me pen, ink, and foolscap now
-and some sealing wax. I must sleep first. But remind me, please, when
do wake, of the task for my pen. And let no one come up to see me this
fternoon."

This was about a week before Ecuyer died, the 21st of July, since the
urt, holographic will, which the captain drew that afternoon, is so
lated.

As the principal item in the captain's estate was his horse, no lawyers
ppeared to help him divide it equitably. But he was not left without
•enefit of clergy, so to speak. The two ministers came regularly every
1orning about eleven o'clock.

Ecuyer was at his best then. For a few days he seemed positively to
njoy disputing with them. They were both sincere in thinking he was
•ound for the fires, but that a deathbed repentance and a declaration of
aith might yet save him. They laboured hard to obtain both, sweating
n the molten summer weather, and at thought of the hot wrath to come.
McArdle did most of the talking. Mr. Puffin occasionally supported him,
•ut confined himself for the most part to urging Ecuyer to partake of the
acrament. That alone would be sufficient, he said.

McArdle's pleading was directly from the Scriptures. And in that
:cuyer met him text for text. It was over the interpretation of Holy Writ
hat they disagreed. That invariably took them into theology, and a
langing argument. And there McArdle was lost in realms he had never
:limpsed before. Assisted by the captain, his own logic led him into
•earful traps. Afterwhile, Ecuyer would stop, laugh, and explain to him
ome horrid dilemma.

"So you can see, Mr. McArdle," he would say, "it would scarcely be

advisable for me to submit myself entirely to your judgement in so delicate and eternal a matter, when you are quite hopelessly confused about
it yourself."

"I warn you, sir. I solemnly warn you," McArdle would trumpet indignantly through his nose. "Your time is short here—but how long
there!"—and he would then paint a fairly competent picture of hell.

"Repent before it's too late. Only *say* you believe, I beseech you,"
pleaded Mr. Puffin, who on one occasion went down on his knees.

"Surely, you would not have me lie my way into paradise," said
Ecuyer.

Scandalized, they would leave him at last—but only to return next
day, fortified with new arguments and texts. They were not going to let
Ecuyer be damned easily, for word of the battle they were waging had
got about. Not only the captain's soul, but their own reputations as
converters were now at stake. People watched their comings and goings
for nearly a week, dubiously. One day a small crowd of the Pendergass
boys and their friends gathered under the captain's window, after the
ministers went in. They listened, and heard Ecuyer laugh. Garrett put a
stop to such gatherings, calling them shameless. He thought the same of
the ministers, and said so. But it was not so easy to stop them. They had
the force of much pious opinion behind them, and he was only a tavern-
keeper. Besides, Ecuyer himself seemed to suffer them gladly.

The truth was, the captain had let himself in for more than he had
at first anticipated. He was now failing faster than he had supposed he
might. The time soon came when he could no longer argue, nor take
pleasure in doing so. The two ministers took this as a sign that he was
weakening, which he was, and redoubled their efforts. They prayed together at his bedside long and hard.

Lord! thought Salathiel, if Ned Yates would only come back! He'd
stop it!

It was not possible for Albine himself to do anything with McArdle,
who vehemently reproached him for remaining silent at such a crisis in
the captain's spiritual affairs.

It was only three days before he died that Ecuyer finally called in Mr.
Hume, the schoolmaster.

The last time Mr. Puffin and McArdle came down the corridor to
Ecuyer's room, they found Mr. Hume sitting by the window eating an
apple, and the captain propped up, waiting for them, too. Salathiel with
his arms folded sat near the head of the bed. Ecuyer's eyes snapped, and
he smiled at the ministers. Two empty chairs had been set in the middle
of the room, awaiting them.

Now, there was a certain air of formal preparation about these dispositions which was not lost on either of the men of God. They had hoped
for a formal repentance, before witnesses, and they sat down expectantly
in the chairs, facing Ecuyer.

"Gentlemen," began the captain, "this is a somewhat *eery* occasion. I have assembled here the kind of audience which I think you do most deserve." He paused.

"Ah," said Mr. Puffin, exhaling with relief.

"How d'ya mean?" demanded McArdle, inhaling suspiciously.

"Why, there are five here present, but amongst us there are only five ears," said the captain. "And from now on my own also will be closed to your appeals. That would leave only three ears for two of you to preach at. I do thank you for your efforts on my behalf," he added, "but don't you think from now on you can find more and other ears elsewhere? I beseech ye to do so."

In the silence that followed, Mr. Hume lifted his wig and began to laugh. Mr. Puffin, to do him justice, rose to depart, but McArdle was not to be daunted. Ears or no ears, he drew a Testament from his pocket and began to read it.

"This is my beloved son. Hear ye him," he shouted.

"This is my esteemed friend, the schoolmaster," roared Ecuyer, summoning the last of his strength. "Hear ye him."

McArdle paused with astonishment both at the voice and at its pronouncement.

"Mr. Hume is prepared to submit on my behalf an incontrovertible piece of human wisdom—if you persist, sir," said Ecuyer. And in fact Mr. Hume had laid down his apple.

McArdle still waited for a moment, looking about him. He was not sure yet what the captain intended. Then he flushed angrily and began to read again from his Testament.

"Mr. Hume," said Ecuyer.

"Two times one is two; two times two is four; two times three is six . . ." began Mr. Hume in the indestructible tones of a schoolmaster. McArdle flipped the leaves of his Bible with exasperated astonishment, and fixing on the fifth chapter of St. John, resumed desperately.

Under the low ceiling of the room the two men seemed to be intoning a liturgy in which the bald facts of the multiplication tables warped themselves through the woof of the rich prose of St. John, weaving a kind of Gregorian chant. Ecuyer closed his eyes and composed himself as though for a long nap.

At "seven times one is seven" McArdle closed his Bible with a clap and stalked out. Mr. Puffin awaited him somewhat sheepishly downstairs.

Mr. Hume completed the eighth table all alone—and stopped.

The captain opened his eyes and looked at the two empty chairs.

"The rest is silence," said Mr. Hume aptly.

"I hope so," said the captain.

"Albine, bring me my little leather purse out of the top drawer yonder; also brandy and three glasses." The captain filled the glasses himself.

"To the success of your future secular instruction," said Ecuyer. They

drank the toast together, after which Mr. Hume received a gold piec
gladly.

"To your very good health, sir," cried the schoolmaster, and draine
his glass. They all laughed. Even the captain. "Also, at your service,
said Mr. Hume, pocketing the piece.

"I hardly think I shall need you again. My health, as you may hav
heard, is really not so good." Ecuyer shook the man's hand. "Good-bye,
he said quietly.

Salathiel put the purse back in the bureau, and stood the empty chair
against the wall.

"Albine," said the captain thoughtfully, "when I die that purse wil
be yours. There is not much in it, only what's left of my last pay, but
want you to promise me this. Do you remember that Irishman w
hanged at Ligonier?"

"Of course."

"Do you remember his name?"

"Yes."

"Well, save a guinea for me out of that purse, and the first time yo
run across a Roman Catholic priest give it to him to say a mass for tha
Irishman's soul. Promise?"

"I promise," said Salathiel.

"*Finis!*" exclaimed Ecuyer, sinking back into the pillows contentedly
Almost instantly he fell into an exhausted sleep.

The ministers came no more. Salathiel was now prepared to deal witl
them if they appeared. But the last days of Ecuyer ran out swiftly anc
in peace. He received no more visitors, except Garrett and old Rose, wh
came to his room the day before he died and sat with him for a while

Salathiel left them together and went to his own room. He was in n
mood then to encounter Mrs. Pendergass. The gentle, friendly voice
sounded on for some time together on the other side of the wall. Wher
he returned after they had left, the captain was smiling, and there wa
a small spray of wild roses in a bottle on the window sill.

"And now," said Ecuyer, "no more! Not even the officers from the fort
Keep the door fast closed against the world and stay with me, my friend
Fetch me no food. That is all over now."

Salathiel locked the door and sat down to begin his vigil. He saw th
captain expected to die that night.

But he was still alive in the morning. Salathiel then settled him a
comfortably as he could in the bed. The captain seemed to have entirel
lost the use of his legs.

After that Salathiel did not leave him for an instant. The day wa
fearfully hot, but Ecuyer shivered, and signed once to pile the bed
clothes on him. In the afternoon he asked to have the bed drawn neare
to the window, so that he could look directly at the mountains withou
turning his head. He had himself propped up until the light fell full o

his face. He seemed to feel the sunlight, and put his fingers to his cheek. "That is better," he said. "Farewell, Albine."

As the afternoon advanced, the heat in the room became intolerable despite the wide-open window. But Salathiel did not dare open the door. It was probably Bella who came and knocked timidly once. He went softly to the door. "Wait," he whispered. He thought he heard her tip-toeing away. He squatted down close by the bed now. The captain began to speak softly in French. Salathiel sweated. The captain was not talking to him. His eyes glowed.

About sunset Ecuyer began to twitch with his hands. The signet ring he wore dropped off and rolled under the bed. He sighed ever so deeply. Salathiel rose from the floor and leaned over to look at him. At that moment the sun was setting behind the Alleghenies. The room suddenly went grey. Ecuyer's head fell to one side.

Salathiel stood in the gathering twilight and wept silently. He was utterly and painfully alone.

Long after dark he began to hear the river and the crickets again . . . outside . . .

Summer!

There was a song called "Past Caring and Past Faring", which the musicians used to play at the fort, and there was a wild, tuneful bub-bling of the flute that ran all through it with a devil-may-care Irish lilt to accompany the melancholy melody, like white gulls rising from dark waters. Salathiel never heard the song again or elsewhere. It passed westward into the forests with the grenadier musicians who played it. But through the hot summer of '64 all the garrison and village at Bed-ford hummed it, whistled it, and the Welsh girls trilled it by moonlight, sitting by the river, with their grenadiers, under the walls of the fort. It expressed perfectly the mood of the moment; the long waiting, the sor-row of past troubles, and a hope of venturesome, audacious escape in the flute notes. It was the first catch that sang itself into Salathiel's heart.

It was in the air.

The grenadiers had played it as they came back in quick time after they buried Ecuyer. The captain had had it all—the slow music to begin with, the horse with the empty reversed boots in the stirrups, the flag-swathed coffin, the three good volleys at the end, one for each Person of the Trinity. The white powder smoke from the gleaming muskets drifted across the face of Lookout Mountain like the flick of a handkerchief dis-posing of dust in hot weather—and time went on, while Ecuyer lay there in an unmarked grave, looking out over the old Shawnee Hunting Grounds into the sunsets.

There was no churchyard in the village then, and they had laid him high up under a cliff, safe from wolves, underneath the talus. The Masonic brethren in their aprons had turned out under Garrett; there had been a company from the Royal Americans; and the grenadier band.

Mr. Puffin, despite McArdle's strenuous protest, had read the burial service, mindful of the arrival, expected at any moment, of the courteous but lionlike Colonel Bouquet.

And so it was all over. All over for Ecuyer, that is. Salathiel was very much left behind that summer. Phoebe was gone, the captain had vanished, Yates was away.

To be sure, Ecuyer had left a little property, mostly personal belongings. And these, much to Salathiel's surprise, the captain had willed to him: a purse with about thirty pounds in it, the horse, the wagon; all his chests, books, firearms, and clothes went to "my young friend, S. Albine, as a token of my esteem for his devotion, and with an admonition that he take good care of my faithful mare, Enna". His sword, the land in Maryland, his gold signet ring, and a small box with a sealed letter directing the disposal of its contents, Ecuyer left to Colonel Bouquet.

There was much difficulty with the garrison quartermasters over gaining possession of the ark. But one night Salathiel borrowed a team from Stottelmyer and dragged the big wagon away from behind the hospital —and then the shoe was on the other foot.

Garrett let him put it under a shed in the river yard, where it stood like a big tent on wheels, safe, and ready to go—but as yet Salathiel had no idea whither. He put all his new-found possessions into the stout chests in the ark and locked them up. Quite a fortune for a young woodsman! That is, he now had something more than the clothes he wore and his rifle-gun. He hung about waiting for something to happen.

But nothing happened.

The weather grew hotter as August began to slip away. There was a lodge meeting in the hills, scantily attended. Mrs. Pendergass sent for him and wept about Phoebe. He was depressed. It was impossible to say how much he missed Captain Ecuyer. McArdle gradually became unpleasantly insistent that he should keep his promise to set off to find Jane. Garrett also thought it was the right thing to do. The Pendergass boys were all planning to return to their cabins before autumn, and were much absorbed by their preparations. Everything at Bedford now seemed quite the opposite of what it had been only the winter before. He took to swimming in the river a good deal at night, and grew morose and restive. Finally he saddled the mare, took the rifle-gun and his raiding kit, and set off to see Captain Jack at "Echovale".

At least they would let him alone there. He could range the woods with the old hunter until Yates returned, and then find out his plans for going to Philadelphia. Hunting in the forest, he might be at peace.

He started about dawnlight one morning, but when he got to the cabin Captain Jack was away. "Conococheague" was scrawled in charcoal on the door, and that meant the old ranger had left to go to his even more lonely cabin on Jack's Mountain. He might or he might not return soon. Salathiel seethed with disappointment. After a long run of luck, everything now seemed to be going wrong. Was a perverse fate dogging him now?—he wondered. He decided, if he decided anything, to find out; to surrender to events and see what would happen.

In fact, there was a moment standing before the closed door of Captain Jack's cabin when he ceased to will anything at all. Perhaps for a recent graduate from the woods too much had been forced upon him lately to digest. Anyway, he let the reins go slack and sat there looking at a closed door.

He sat on in the hot sunshine. The mare stamped. The flies bothered her. Finally she moved off.

He laughed, and let her have her head.

She took the trail up the side of Will's Mountain and let herself down gingerly into the Springs valley beyond. They struck Shober's run afterwhile, and the new wagon road through the forest to Fort Cumberland, which ran along it. It was good going there in stretches, and the mare began to trot.

Salathiel did nothing to check her. She was headed south for Fort Cumberland. She might have turned back to Bedford, but she hadn't. He laughed again. The road to Cumberland was one way of going to Redstone Old Fort.

That evening he made a small supper fire somewhere near the Cumberland valley and sat smoking contentedly. He had humorously made up his mind that, while McArdle might be wrong, the mare must be right, and he might as well press on to Redstone Old Fort and ask about Jane. He wanted a woman badly. And, after all, Jane was his wife.

He sat trying to recall to himself what she was like. He could hardly remember her face now. Yet he had only to look into the fire to see Phoebe's gazing at him from the embers like a clear picture. Well, he would make the best of it. He would find out at Redstone Old Fort who and what awaited him.

But he would take his time about it. He was alone in the woods again. Away—and his own master. He found he liked that. Why had he been so anxious to learn what other people wanted him to do? And who made the rules they were always pressing upon him? He hobbled the horse, put out the fire, and went to sleep looking up at the stars and clouds moving across the branches.

Now that he had killed that Indian child he could go to sleep peacefully enough. He need never fear hearing his mother scream again. That thought occurred to him the last thing, and very deep down, as he drifted off into the serenity of oblivion.

The next morning he knew he had found himself again. He wakened whole and keen. Not a single disturbing sound came to steal his attention. Not a leaf rustled. It seemed as though the weather had paused. The mare rolled in a patch of sweet fern and then lay contentedly looking at him. He yawned, and stretched happily in his blanket. Good Lord, how much freedom he had been missing! He sat up eagerly and caught intangibly, but none the less certainly, the first aloof freshness of autumn, a tang of unmistakable crispness in the air.

Summer was over. He had come through!

Somehow that summer had posed him a difficult crisis, had even threatened to stop him. But he felt he was over the crest now, free, and a man. As he breathed in the vigorous hint of autumn to come, he knew it. It had taken the loss of Phoebe, death at the Salt Kettles, the passing of the captain, all that and much more, to pour the molten metal of youth into a sterner and more enduring mould. And now the die was cast.

He would go on with what lay before him, no matter what. He could do it. He desired change, and a conviction of great change lay upon him. Suddenly he knew what it was, even if he could not tell yet how it might come to pass. It would happen.

Wilderness, farewell!

17. Wilderness Farewell

BY NOON NEXT DAY he was at Fort Cumberland, where he lingered only long enough to obtain some tobacco and to exchange news. Here for the first time, and from a Virginia storekeeper named Crump, he heard talk of the stamp tax and trade troubles with England. A red-headed young man by the name of Drew roundly denounced government and the Parliament, standing on a whisky keg in Crump's barrel room. He drank with the red-headed man. The whisky was fine, ripe juice, and he rode off westward along Braddock's Road in the afternoon sunshine feeling happy and free from care.

The Cresaps were still at Redstone, he had learned, among other things. Also he had told them at the store he was going after his wife—and afterwards that stood him in good stead. No one at Cumberland knew anything about Jane.

Braddock's Road was scarcely more than a track through the forest now, but it had been kept open by pack trains and a few salt and powder wagons that went to Redstone by way of the Great Meadows. There Braddock was said to be buried in the road, close by Colonel Washington's old entrenchments at Fort Necessity. Just west of that the road crossed over the Laurel Hill and pitched down into the valley to the cabin of Henry Beeson. He, together with his sturdy neighbours, Windle Brown and Frederick Waltzer, had occupied the valley since before Braddock's defeat.

Beeson was a devout Quaker. The Indians respected the Broad Hat for his peaceful honesty. They had long ago made a private treaty with him and scrupulously kept it. Alone of all the cabins in the district Beeson's chimney never ceased to smoke. His cabin lay only a little more than sixty miles west of Cumberland, but Albine took a good ten days to get there, taking time off in the woods to loaf, swim, hunt, and smoke his fine Virginia tobacco.

At the Great Meadows he camped for two days, well hidden from the road, and let the mare get her belly full of grass. Enna was a fine, young roan with two white socks on her forelegs, and Salathiel was now grown very fond of her. Both of them enjoyed themselves thoroughly at the Great Meadows. Early September had laid light fingers on the foliage, and in the early morning the mountains smoked. By midday there was a deep-blue haze in the distance. He went about now feeling like the king of the world. He even began to grow careless about concealing himself.

At Beeson's, however, he was brought up short by an encounter that changed his life.

It was after dark when he arrived, and supper was long over. Friend Beeson, however, welcomed him, helped him to put up the mare in the shed by herself, and remarked casually that it would be much better to leave her there than in the stable.

"For," said he, "there are three old Senecas have been camping near the farm for a fortnight past. They'll not harm me nor mine, but a stranger's horseflesh might tempt them, and they usually come at milking time to the barn. They're as fond of the warm, new milk as kittens be."

"I'm fond of it myself—with a little whisky in it," laughed Salathiel, who had already taken a notion to the obviously simple and kind-hearted Quaker, his broad hat and equally wide smile.

"Right thou art," said Beeson. "Come in and I'll see if I can't contrive something for thee. We'll at least warm a bowl of mush, even if it do be late. Liza, Liza, put a knot on the fire," he shouted, as he went into the house, leaving Salathiel to finish rubbing down the mare.

"Amy," Salathiel heard him call from inside the cabin. "Where'st gone to, woman?"

"I've gone to bed, Henry," replied a pleasant female voice, probably that of Mrs. Beeson. "I'm plumb dickered out. No use thy calling for Liza. She left this morning and took her bundle. Cleared out without so much as a thank-ye-kindly. I've been doin' her stint all afternoon while thou'st been down at the byre. Have we company?"

"Young feller from out Bedford way. I'll tend to him myself."

A few minutes later, when Salathiel came into the cabin, he found a bowl of hot mush and a jug of new milk on the table, with Mr. Beeson sitting by smoking his pipe.

"Thou'lt have to provide thine own liquor," said the Quaker, glancing at the milk a bit deprecatingly. "I never keep whisky here on account of the Injuns. They don't bother us so much when they know there's never none on the place."

"Do many of them come here these days?" asked Salathiel.

"Quite some, off and on. But they never did harm us, nor we them," said Beeson proudly. "It's been like that from old times now. They know Friend Beeson and his farm."

"It's a pity there aren't more like you, sir," said Salathiel. "I do aver there'd be less trouble if 'twere so."

"Aye," agreed Beeson, sighing. "We've always tried to do what we can. These last two years have been the worst of all. Many fleeing from the heathen wrath have passed through here. They go as they come, too," he added, a whit bitterly. " 'Twas a poor papist girl came only a fortnight ago come First Day, half naked. She ran off through the woods from somewhere nigh Fort Pitt. She'd been lost. She offered to work for Amy, and she was sartin in a bad way. Wouldn't say exactly what happened. I didn't press her. Injuns, I guess. It's best to let 'em forget, if they can. Wal, we fed her and guv her an old linsey-woolsey, and a mighty good bed—and now she's lit out without sayin' a word!"

"Maybe the Senecas you spoke of scared her off," suggested Salathiel, stifling a yawn.

"Maunt be. I hadn't thought of that. She was mighty scared about suthin' most of the time."

"I suppose you've seen a good many others like her," suggested Salathiel, with nothing particular in mind.

"Lots on 'em!" exclaimed the Quaker. "Why, 'tis only four months ago Captain Cresap and his good lady brought fifteen poor souls through here, takin' them downcountry to the settlements. They'd been gathered in at Redstone Old Fort for over a year, and victuals was gettin' scarce. Women and children all. Some on 'em had been captivated, I hear . . ."

"What!" cried Salathiel. "What's that?"

He was very much awake now. He began to talk and to question Beeson rapidly. In half an hour he had told his own story of his search for Jane, and obtained every last bit of information he could.

There was no doubt of it. Jane *had* left Redstone with the Cresaps, and gone downcountry with them. The old Quaker not only remembered her distinctly in the crowd of women and children, who had stayed with him overnight, but he also recollected her unusual name when it was recalled to him.

"Mrs. Albine! Yep, that was it! Some said she was a widow. And a nice, upstanding, yellow-haired, clean-faced gal she was."

As to where the Cresaps had taken her and the others, Beeson had no idea. Probably to Baltimore, he thought.

"For it's easier to git nurture for orphaned little ones in a town like that, and t'others kin bind out and git keep on some of the big planta-tions along Tidewater. At least so Captain Cresap says."

"Well, I'll ride over to Redstone tomorrow and find out from Captain Cresap himself," said Salathiel determinedly.

The Quaker laughed. "Thou'lt not do that," he said. "The captain and his lady passed through here agin, goin' back to Baltimore, only last afternoon. Why, I wonder thou didst not meet them on the road from Cumberland."

"I stopped to hunt at the Great Meadows," explained Albine angrily. "They must have passed me, and I never knew it. Damn it, I do have the worst luck with women!" Which remark brought a mild request from the Quaker to refrain from profane swearing.

So Salathiel went to bed in Beeson's loft. There was no use going on to Redstone Old Fort. No, he would have to turn about and follow Jane downcountry, clean back to the settlements—maybe to Tidewater or Bal-timore. He had a good horse and some of the captain's money along, luckily! He'd go. He wanted his woman now. He needed her. It was a long time now—and he didn't relish what Beeson had said about some people thinking Mrs. Albine was a widow.

The bunk in the loft had the fishy fragrance of a woman about it, and he realized that it was probably the one in which the girl who had run off that morning had slept only the night before. But it was a "good bed"—as Beeson had said. It had a deep feather mattress. Under the low roof, and in a dark loft, he slept late.

In fact, it was fully an hour after sunrise when he came down next morning, and both the Quaker and his wife were out at the barn milking.

He helped himself to some side meat and hominy, which stood warm-ing in a pan in the ashes, and then took a drag at his pipe. He felt calm and happy now that he had made up his mind to go downcountry after Jane. He would wait till his host came back into the house, settle with him for his lodging, give the horse a good feed of oats, and depart. Now he would be going to see the settlements, at last, and with an object. When he found Jane they would . . .

The shadow of a head crowned with a feathered turban fell across the doorway. Whoever was there had come noiselessly, and now stood quietly listening.

He shifted his rifle from the table before him and laid it across his knees without making a sound. He sat still, every nerve taut, his hand on the trigger and the two barrels covering the door. The shadow on the threshold remained . . .

"Go away, Little Turtle," said a familiar Indian voice afterwhile. "You heap bad man. I know you."

That roused him. In two strides he made the door, leaped past it, and whirled about.

Leaning against the wall of the cabin, unarmed, and with folded arms, stood old Ganstax, the Mingo, the Seneca chief whom he had last seen at Frazier's cabin near Pittsburgh. He looked at Salathiel and the double-barrelled rifle with utter contempt.

"Go away," he said imperiously.

"Thou art an old fool, Ganstax," said Salathiel to the chief in the Algonquin tongue. "It is time for thee to tremble—not to command." He touched his rifle significantly.

Ganstax smiled. "You no kill big man," he said in English, "you kill squaw; you kill baby!" He spat on the ground at Salathiel's feet.

So that was it! And so now he had a blood feud with the Senecas. That meant a private war with all the Six Fires of the Long House.

"My people have heard of the great Little Turtle and his brothers, the Mountain Foxes," continued Ganstax. "They have heard of their mighty deeds. Me show um dead baby!"

"Good!" replied Salathiel, burning with hate. "I will send them more, by and by." Then the devil prompted him. He drew out his purse. "Ganstax, Chief of the Senecas," he said. "Here is a New York shilling for you. Buy firewater for your brave people—and they will forget."

The old chief tensed himself against the wall.

"I'll not kill you here at Beeson's," he said in his own tongue. "This Broad Hat is a man of honour and of peace. I have smoked and shaken hands with him."

Salathiel laughed and patted his rifle. "Twin eyes, she never sleeps," he said significantly.

He turned on his heel in contempt and walked away, leaving the old chief standing against the cabin wall.

He saddled the mare swiftly, keeping a wary eye for any more shadows falling across the sunlight. For a moment he suspected Beeson of having given away his presence at the farm. But a little further reflection convinced him that he did the honest Quaker an injustice, and that Ganstax must have seen him when he rode in the evening before.

Had Ganstax been at the Salt Kettles?—he wondered. He might have been. There was that one thicket he had failed to search through. But what did it matter now? Ganstax knew, and so did the Iroquois. Well, it was not his intention to wage a war with them alone, not now at least. He had other ends in view. And continuing to live was not the least of them.

He rode out of the shed without attempting to conceal his departure. Ganstax still stood with folded arms by the cabin door. The other two Indians were down at the springhouse at the foot of the hill. Drinking milk! He laughed. Snakes liked it, too. He clapped heels to the mare and dashed off in the direction of Redstone Old Fort. At the end of the farm lane he saw the Quaker coming back and waved to him to wait.

"Mr. Beeson," he said, "here's what I owe you for my night's lodging.

You've earned it. Your good reputation, I think, has saved my life. My fame with Injuns is of another kind. Happen those Senecas are old friends of mine. Do you see?"

"Meanin' it ain't healthy to tarry, with them here?"

"Exactly. I'm going to Redstone Old Fort. Tell them that, will you?"

"I'll tell them what thou sayst," said the careful Quaker. "Stop by again when they ain't around."

"Maybe," he replied, and started off down the road westward.

Once in the woods, he urged the mare into a gallop. Some miles along the road to Redstone he came to a deep creek. He plunged in. But in the middle of the ford he turned the mare's head downstream and swam for some distance with the current, and around a bend.

Two days later found him back at the Great Meadows after making a long circuit eastward, far south of Beeson's, and over the Laurel Hill. He was heading east again for Fort Cumberland, and so far he had seen nothing of the three Senecas. He thought he might venture to light a fire tomorrow.

"Tomorrow, and tomorrow, and tomorrow" . . . What was that thing McArdle used to quote so much—something not from the Bible, but just as good? Ah, yes—"and all our yesterdays" . . .

Lately he had begun to think a good deal about the future. The death of Ecuyer had made it painfully clear how mortal a man is. And he was still young enough to think that life was tragically short. He might die early, too, with all the Iroquois so anxious to assist. It was fine autumn weather, a grand, clear, starry night. But, despite that, he felt uncomfortably lonely and friendless that evening at the Great Meadows—without a fire—and the unfortunate Braddock buried some place near. He had better be hastening to see all he could of the great world beyond the mountains, of places where there were people, cities, ships, and the sea. Otherwise, it might be too late. He was doubly satisfied that his search for Jane would take him there directly. And he would be right glad, tarnal happy, to find him a companion for all his tomorrows. Somebody, b'God, who wouldn't up and leave him! He and she, they'd go over the hills of the world together hand in hand, and *then* home. Oh, yes, he supposed so—home at last . . . When he awoke it was tomorrow again, tomorrow in the silent forest.

Enna rolled and snorted in the deep grass, kicking her white socks in the air.

He saddled her eagerly and rode back along the road to Cumberland, trotting, galloping when he could, hungry for a cooked meal. Even if they had followed him, he must have left Ganstax and the others behind now. They *might* have gone to look for him at Redstone. One more night in the woods alone . . .

He pulled up suddenly.

Along a muddy stretch in the sandy bottom where he was passing were the firm, graceful footprints of a woman going his way. She was no squaw, with that high arch and the narrow-pointed tracery of delicate toes. Like a lady, he thought. But a little lame, or worn out walking in bare feet.

"Liza!" he exclaimed—that girl who had run away from Beeson's.

She must be on the road not far ahead of him. He wondered if she would try to hide while he passed.

He set off more slowly, watching her footprints in the sand and dust. They led on. Once he saw a snag of her dress on some briers. Here she had rested by the road. She must be tired and hungry by now. He urged the mare forward. From the top of the next hill he saw her. She was sitting on a log with her bundle on a stick beside her. She rose hastily at the sound of hoofs.

"Liza!" he shouted. "Wait, gal, wait!"

For a moment he thought she would run into the woods. But seeing him so close, she evidently thought better of it and stood waiting. He galloped down on her and drew up . . .

Liza?—No, no, it was the Irish girl he had seen being whipped at Frazier's nearly two years before.

He sat staring at her in astonishment. She was gaunt, starved, and haggard. But she was still darkly beautiful.

"Frances! Frances!" he cried at last.

"Aye, meself it is. And maybe this time you'll be after givin' me a lift, Mr. Albine," she said quietly, looking him straight in the eyes and trembling—but not from fright, he thought. He leaned down and caught her hand and held it.

"Happen this time I will," he said humbly. "But you'll ride like a lady," he added proudly, while he dismounted.

"In that case you'll be actin' like a gintleman," she countered.

It was the only reservation she made, and in a weak voice. But he liked her all the more for it, and for not surrendering too abjectly even in desperation.

He began tying her pitiful bundle to his saddle rings, and laughed encouragingly.

"I'll make ye no false promises, proud woman," he said, "but I will cherish ye like a man. Climb up and see." He patted the saddle invitingly.

Without hesitating further, she put her hand on his shoulder and mounted. The mare looked around at her new rider in surprise.

"Where were you agoin' to, Frances?" he asked, half teasingly.

"Why, I was goin' to seek you out at Bedford," she said. Suddenly big tears ran down her face. "And now I've found you on the road," she sobbed.

"So you have," he said, overcome by sheer amazement, and began leading the mare up the stony hill just ahead, walking her.

He never doubted the girl's assertion nor thought it strange she had kept him in mind. He had never forgotten her either. He might have gone back after her to Frazier's if it hadn't been for Phoebe, and the war —and Jane!

At the thought of Mistress Jane, now, he frowned. The widow Albine, eh! Well, why not?

He looked again at the tall girl in her bedraggled linsey-woolsey sitting there in the saddle. For all her rags, she rode with dignity and grace. He remembered the lovely form those rags covered. Her lustrous black hair swept back into a loose coil from her pale forehead. Her wide, grey-blue eyes met his own frankly, but appealingly. Her eyes were wonderful. The cheekbones stood up high in her wan, oval face. She was quite peaked and worn, but still with an undaunted air about her. Her mouth was sad, but her lips were bright and smiled at him bravely.

"Frances," he kept repeating, "Frances, Frances," trying to realize her actual presence, and that he was not alone on the long road through the woods any more.

"Yes, what is it?" she asked.

He had not intended she should answer him.

"Lord, I'm glad I've found ye!" he suddenly blurted out. "I'd like to put a kiss on your mouth."

"I'll save it for you," she said. "I'm a tired woman for your kissin' now. Belike I'd not be able to give it back to ye."

He felt ashamed of his outburst after that. He saw her feet were puffed and bruised, and her long legs bleeding in several places from thorns. She needed to be taken care of. He strode on more impatiently, making Enna step out into her best walk. He was afraid to make the mare trot, for fear the girl might not be able to hold on. She needed sleep and food. He could plainly see that she would not have been able to walk much farther alone. She needed to rest and soak her swollen feet in a cold stream. It was a good forty miles to Fort Cumberland yet, and they would never be able to make it under two days—walking! In the far distance a storm was brewing. Thunder grumbled and groaned.

He stopped for a moment to ponder, trying hard to remember the local lie of the land ahead. He had hunted at a place near here on his way down. Frances looked at him apprehensively. The mare stomped.

"Maybe ye'd better reconsider, Mr. Albine. Might be ye don't know what you're after taking on," she said uneasily. "I'm no package wrapped in silk and ribbons to bring ye good fortune, even if ye did find me like lucky money in the road. I'm trouble—and it's the divil's own time I've been havin' in the hell of a world."

"Why, I don't doubt it," he said, looking at her. "But don't you misdoubt me. I'm only tryin' to make a plan for us."

"Oh!" she said. Her eyes widened, and she asked mischievously, "Goes thinkin' so hard?"

"No!" he said. "But good thinkin's always still."

She bit her lip, seeing she had scratched him deeper than she intended. Then she leaned forward in the saddle. "I only meant I've got to rest soon, and get somethin' to eat. It's a long time since I left Beeson's, and me walkin', and afraid of every shadow that flitted across the way." She swayed a little and caught herself.

He jumped up behind her, and holding her firmly in the saddle, they moved off at a more rapid walk. How unfeeling he had been. He must remember she was not a squaw. He gave her a drink from his flask and felt her grow warmer gradually. She sighed afterwhile and leaned back contentedly against him.

"The crature makes me head spin," she said—"and me heart beat hard. Feel it?"

"Yes—" he laughed encouragingly—"I think I do—not that I'm *sure* you have one," he whispered.

She looked up at him enquiringly. Then she turned about as far as she could and gave him a kiss.

Something went to Salathiel's head, too.

"That's right," he said gravely—and gave her kiss back to her. "And now, if ye can only hold on by yourself, I think I can find a roof to cover us even if it storms bad. Hear that thunder?"

"It's growlin' far away," she said.

"It's a big September storm comin'," he answered. "And in these hills ye can get an icy drenchin' on a hot day. It's best to take shelter when we can. But I'll have to lead the horse again."

She accepted his decision without demur. "I'll hold on."

"Good!"

They rode on, and he pressed the horse to a faster gait.

"This is it," he said, dismounting. "I thought we'd find it soon."

They had come to the place he had been looking for, where a lively stream came down out of the hills and crossed the road at the bottom of a steep dale.

He turned up the creek, leading the horse for some distance along the gravel bars and boulder bed of the stream itself. The thunder rolled much nearer now. But he knew where he was going, for he had sheltered comfortably here on the way down.

Presently the stream curved sharply back into the hills and they passed the site of an ancient beaver dam at the throat of a glen. The old ponds behind it had long been drained, and there the stream had filled in the level, making a smooth, wild meadow some acres in extent. Through this the creek still wandered from one deep pool to another. At the upper end was a fall over an outcrop of rock nearly ten feet high. The valley there was one mass of maidenhair fern. Short-stemmed grasses covered the floor of the place under tall buttonwood trees, with high feathery clumps bordering the stream. Even in her fatigue and hunger the Irish girl looked about her with visible pleasure.

He lifted her out of the saddle and carried her up the hillside well above the level of the meadow and the creek. The gaunt buttonwoods made an open grove there. Halfway to the crest, where the stream had once cut through the hill, a giant coal seam lay exposed between its double outcrop of slate. It was like a black cliff. But it had crumbled in places and spilled out its dark treasure fanlike over the slope below. There were hollows weathered in it, "rooms", with shiny walls of blue coal that ran back at places twenty feet or more into the hill.

" 'Twill be dark here," he said. "But at least it will not be cold comfort."

The leaves of many autumns had drifted in and covered the slate floor. He stood listening for the possible whirr of a rattler, but the place remained silent, and he laid her on his blanket in a leaf-packed ledge. He swept a space of floor clean down to the slate, and arranging a nest of stones swiftly, filled it with lumps of weathered coal, and kindled a flame. In its rocky basin the fire soon became incandescent and threw a bright light and a grateful warm glow against the damp walls and the low, black ceiling of the place. She watched him, revelling in the relief of being off her feet, and filled with a strange sense of security and protection.

"I'll find you a much better house later," he assured her quite seriously. "But this is safe, high shelter at least. And it's coming on to storm for sure. Sometimes there's sudden floods in these valleys."

"Sure and it's a roof, a hearth, and a fire you've found us already," she said in her musical Irish tones. "What more do ye want to thank God for?"

"Meat to put on the fire, for one thing," he answered. "Now I'll be leavin' you for a bit. Don't be scairt. I'll be back soon."

"I'll not be tremblin'," she replied. "Do ye know why?" She laughed, and drew from the bosom of her dress the small pistol he had given her at Frazier's nearly two years before. "Sure and it was a grand gift ye gave me. Better than ye knew. I'll tell ye about it—tonight."

"Good gal," he said, giving her a reassuring nod. Then he mounted Enna and rode off through the grove of buttonwoods. She lay quiet, waiting, a look of new peace and relief on her face.

The thunder rolled ever nearer, the lightning dazzled. Gusts full of the freshness of the oncoming storm tore by through the trees outside. She heard him fire both barrels in rapid succession somewhere down the valley. Then in a few minutes he was back again with two fat grey squirrels dangling from his saddle and a great bundle of long grass curved across the mare's neck. He tied Enna as far back in the cave as he could, and cast the fresh fodder down before her. He built up the fire again generously with large lumps of coal. It smoked densely and then began to flame and glow. Enna munched.

Frances lay watching eagerly the meal now in progress. Outside the first sheets of rain tore down the valley. There was a brief patter of hail, and then a violent deluge began. They heard the note of the waterfall rise gradually over the noises of the storm to a steady roar. Trees crashed. Somewhere on the mountainside above, the lightning fell with a stunning smack. The roof above began to dribble and drip here and there through the slate.

"Never mind," he laughed; "the only thing we have to worry about here is not the water, but setting the mountain on fire. Down the Ohio I know a hill that's been aburnin', the Injuns say, for nigh a hundred years. French trappers kindled it long ago."

"I'm not mindin'," she said. "Where do ye think I'd have been now, if ye hadn't happened along?"

"That's so," he said. "You might have been caught in a rush of waters." He looked at the little meadow below them in the valley already beginning to flood. An even more furious beat of rain began. "This storm looks like the end of the world!" he exclaimed.

"Only the beginnin' of it for me," she said.

"All right," he answered, without noticing her earnest gratitude; "now come over to the fire and eat."

They feasted on roast squirrel and hot johnnycake.

Afterward he gave her some soothing herbs he had gathered to bind on her feet. They sat quiet, close together in the glow of the fire. It was no ordinary thunderstorm that blustered and blundered on through the trees. It was the great tempest that harried all the southern mountains towards the end of September, 1764.

Darkness gradually closed in and the fire in the cavern peered out into the stormy night like a wild, red eye from a black socket. But no one was there to see it, except those who tended it. And for them it shed only a mellow and comforting light . . .

Over a hundred miles northwestward, at Pittsburgh, Colonel Bouquet also was congratulating himself that the new troops left Bedford in time to avoid the "summer tempest" and that he had all his men and munitions over the mountains at last. A few more days would see him ready to leave Fort Pitt. His helpful friend Ecuyer would be sadly absent, but Mr. Burent had the bateaux flotilla ready and the colonel could now move down the Ohio and into the Indian country beyond, secure in his line of supply. The Reverend James McArdle accompanied him to interpret strange tongues . . .

But in the coal cave west of Fort Cumberland McArdle's favourite pupil neither knew nor cared any longer how fared the Indian war. He had made a truce with life at last, even though he found it in strange places and along forbidden paths.

The great storm passed. The floods subsided. The sun came out again, and the forest glowed in a Joseph's coat of tattered autumn colors. Salathiel and Frances tarried on in the valley. The season turned into Indian summer—and for them into an Indian moon. They slept in each other's arms—for there was only one blanket, Salathiel explained, when the time came—and they slept well. If any Senecas or others followed them, the great storm had washed out the last vestiges of their trail in both stream and road. No matter how long the "truce" they had made between them might last, they would always remember their first days together in that valley with the eternal voice of the little waterfall. And in the frosty nights, about the great coal fire in the heart of the hill, Salathiel heard from the woman who lay beside him the complete story of her life, in Ireland and in America, up to the time she met him again.

It was a story full of tears and laughter, but an honest tale hot off the griddle of life. There was nothing smug about it—and she had told him all.

Into her past he had already tried to fit his own. As the days and nights had passed in the lonely valley, he told her everything about himself that he either knew or could remember. It was a comforting kind of lovers' confession in which they forgave each other, and resolved with the confidence of a mutual absolution to go on together, despite the world, evil, and bad luck. They would try actually to fit the future together as they had managed to accommodate each other's past. But their future would be mutual. They would share it, as they had already shared their bodies and minds and the days and weather in the dark cave by the fire.

He made her no promises. She expected and exacted none. They would go on, over the mountains, and downcountry to the settlements. They were agreed upon that, but not much more. The rest was understood and left nebulous.

The mountain nights were growing rapidly more frosty now. When the time to leave came he made her a pillion out of his blanket, and they rode out of the valley together on Enna; and took the road eastward.

Thus about the end of October Salathiel appeared once more at Fort Cumberland, with Frances riding sedately behind him. He dismounted before the rough log building that bore a sign in homemade letters saying, "Josh Crump—Gineral Store".

"Wal," said the proprietor, who was leaning against the doorjamb as usual, "wal, now, ain't that nice! I see ye've done found yer wife after all. Howdy, Mrs. Albine," he added, spitting out a large wad as a tribute to the lady. "How be ye?"

"Fine," replied Frances, and gave an ingratiating smile. "But I've been where there ain't much to be had. Have you got any boltin' for makin' clothes?"

"What d'ye lack?" cried Mr. Crump.

"Everything the Injuns didn't have," replied Salathiel, giving Frances a wink. "Step down, my dear, and have a look at Mr. Crump's merchandise."

"Aye, step right in, step right in!" cried Mr. Crump, removing his shoulders from the doorjamb at last. "Now don't you be blushin', mistress, I've seen gals lookin' much worse off than you do, comin' in from bein' captivated. You're lucky to have found your man."

"That so?" Salathiel asked Frances in a whisper as she dismounted.

"Oh, I'm a lucky woman now, I know that," she said, apparently to the storekeeper. She laughed, while her eye ran along Mr. Crump's meagerly stocked shelves.

And so it was that the first of Ecuyer's small legacy to Salathiel went to buy calico and some other vital things for Frances Melissa O'Toole. Mr. Crump whistled when he saw gold pieces, and everybody in the dark little store was suddenly quite happy, including Salathiel and Frances.

It was surprising what a guinea or two could do. For the first time it was thoroughly brought home to Salathiel that he could "git" with his purse as well as with his rifle. So he "brought things down" from Mr. Crump's shelves which Frances "aimed to git".

They stayed with the Crumps for several days at Fort Cumberland while Frances made new clothes. They could have done better buying at Pendergasses', Salathiel said. But Frances would not hear of riding into Bedford in a tattered linsey-woolsey and bare feet.

"I'm no naked blanket girl," she said. "I aim to be somebody." And in a surprisingly short time she appeared as somebody, and no denying it.

When Salathiel rode off to Bedford with Frances behind him again, Mr. Albine had learned something about what a needle and a woman can do for each other. He scarcely knew Frances when he looked at her now. But he was a proud young man.

"Look what I have, and be damned to you!" seemed to emanate like a challenge from his cocky manner; from the way he rode in his saddle, erect as a trooper; and from the way he let "Twin Eyes" sleep in the hollow of his left arm with a sparkle and a glint like Captain Jack's baby. Enna, under her double burden, stepped more gravely and sedately, as though aware of her new responsibility. Only there was nobody along the lonely valley road to Bedford to see them. Exactly what he would say when he got to Bedford with Frances instead of Jane, he wasn't sure. At least they would make a handsome entrance into town.

They laughed together over "Mrs. Albine" having been taken for granted at Cumberland. They had done nothing to confirm the impression, except not to deny it. They had simply accepted it.

"But what *will* you be sayin' at Pendergasses'?" demanded Frances, who, like a woman, wanted the future made clear.

"I'll wait to see what happens," replied Salathiel. "It depends"—whether McArdle is there or not, he added, but to himself alone. He'd see. He wouldn't try to deceive Garrett. No, he had made up his mind to that. The rest must turn out as might be. Besides, Yates might have returned. He hoped so.

So they rode on through the late autumn weather, bright with the hint of November frosts to come, and the last painted leaves falling. He began, humorously now, to whistle the tune of last summer, "Past Caring and Past Faring", while he kept his eyes keen for every shadow falling across the road. You could never tell. It wasn't entirely safe yet.

About six o'clock they rode into the village of Bedford.

All that the "triumphal entry" lacked to be triumphant was an audience. Enna stepped her highest and best, snorting at the familiar scents of the neighbourhood. The young couple on her back rode with more dignity than their years demanded. But there was no one to watch them pass. It was dark, and Salathiel had forgotten that it would be, having left Bedford in the long summer days. Only a few windows glowed dimly in the village. The rows of barracks lay silent at the fort. Even the hospital showed only a few lanthorns. Bedford seemed but the ghost of its former busy self. You could hear the river and the wind in the trees, it was so quiet.

Of course, he might have expected this. He knew what had happened even before he passed the first deserted sutlers' houses. The troops had marched west to Fort Pitt. The settlers had scattered to rebuild their cabins before snow fell. The life of the town had vanished. Instead, there was silence, and here and there a solitary candle burning behind a window. He was glad to find, almost surprised to see, a Highland sentry on duty at the gate of the fort as they rode past. Only the coloured servants and the Indian help were in the yard at Pendergasses'. The ark stood lonely, towering under its shed. The only light in the "women's house" came from Mrs. Pendergass's room. It was a calm welcome.

But once in the familiar wagonyard, he sprang down and helped Frances to dismount. By the feel of her hand, she was hot and nervous. While a young darky finally answered his calls and took Enna off to the stable, she stood smoothing her skirt and re-tying her bonnet. He put his arm around her encouragingly and gave her a kiss.

"That's better," she whispered. "Oh, Sal, I do hope they'll take me in! They're like your own folks, aren't they?"

"Don't worry," he said. And—quite worried himself—he pushed back the big door of the hearth room.

"Phoebe!" he thought—and then thought of her no more.

At the extreme end of the place near the hearth Ned Yates and Arthur St. Clair were having a bite and a bottle between them. There was no one else in the big room at all.

"Demme!" cried Yates, looking up at the sound of footsteps, and shading his eye against the candles. "Demme, if it isn't my old friend the Little Turtle—and? His lady turtle!"

He rose and came forward cordially, the curt dapperness of his small person was somehow set off and enhanced by the trim wig, and the black patch he now wore over his left eye. He contrived thus, inadvertently, to convey a hint of something deftly sinister in dark contrast to his good-natured grey eye and bright smile.

For a moment that evening, after a long absence, Salathiel saw his friend as a stranger again, and felt his enigmatic stare. He had recovered all his poise, but he was changed and matured by his tragedy. No use trying to deceive him.

"Yates," he said, "this is Frances."

She dropped him a curtsy, and gracefully. Only for an instant a smile puckered the corners of Yates's mouth as he bowed gravely.

"Congratulations!" he exclaimed—"to both of you!"

"You have a swift wit, sir, I perceive," said Frances.

"Oh—you perceive that," laughed Yates. "That *will* make it pleasant."

He took her by the hand and led her down the room to where St. Clair was still sitting at the table.

"Arthur, I want you to meet the young lady my friend Albine has had the good sense to bring back with him. Mr. St. Clair is our arbiter of elegance, fashion, and decorum in these parts, madam."

Always a bit pompous, St. Clair invariably rose to the bait of a compliment, no matter how broad the hook. He was wearing a small sword that evening—as he might have in Philadelphia. He rose now to confirm Yates's outrageous assertion, and bowed formally.

"Mistress Albine, 'tis indeed an honour to greet ye."

Yates kicked Salathiel a tap on the ankle. "Fast work," he whispered.

"Have ye supped, mistress?" St. Clair was asking.

"I'm hungry as a wolf's mother," confessed Frances. " 'Twas a long ride from Cumberland."

"Heavens on earth, sit down with us here then!" exclaimed St. Clair, pulling out a chair. "Albine, you've grown no smaller, I see. How's that double-barrelled gun of yours? Did you ever get it fitted with a single lock as I advised?"

"No," drawled Salathiel, "I've still got a trigger on both my barrels. You know, I rather like taking my choice in a double chance." He looked at Frances and laughed.

Yates nearly suffocated. He patted Frances' hand under the table. "Used the *right* barrel this time. Glad he got you?"

"Very!" she said, and blushed to the neck.

"Pina, Pina!" roared St. Clair impatiently. He was hungry himself.

The old woman came hurrying into the room—and all hopes of supper disappeared for the time being in her overwhelming excitement at seeing Salathiel and the girl he had brought with him.

"Do God, do God! Do bless 'em both! Miss Bella mus' be told. De bride mus' be welcome to de house." The old slave's voice trilled on with African fervour and excitement. Her first announcement was directed to the entire yard, where she went to spread the tidings. And in another moment the hearth room was invaded by all the servants of the place, staring, jabbering, and pressing as close to the table as they dared to see Marse Albine's new woman.

"Good Lord, we'll never, never get supper now," said St. Clair, looking annoyed at the hubbub he had precipitated.

"Where's Garrett?" asked Salathiel anxiously.

"He's gone to Fort Pitt on a contract—luckily," laughed Yates. "But Bella's at home, and ready for anything, I'll bet you."

At that instant Bella herself, with old Pina hobbling and jabbering behind her, came hastily through the corridor door.

Salathiel was forever grateful to Bella Pendergass for the welcome she gave to Frances that evening. Whether she understood that Frances was not Jane, he could never be sure. The two women obviously liked each other from the first. In fact, it was he who almost spoiled it by attempting to explain: "Of course, she's not a *bride*. I've been married a long time, you know. I've just found her, and . . ."

Yates kicked him again just in time.

"Of *course*," said Bella, taking Frances by the hand. "Pina's an old fool. But you must forgive her. We all want you to be welcome here. My father will be sorry not to have been here to greet you, when he hears about it. Nigh the whole family's away for once, workin' out on the clearin's. But Mother's at home, and she'll want you to come over and stay with us—for the first night at least. Guess you'll have to put up with your old room again, Mr. Albine. I hope you won't mind. Mother and I will look after your Frances. She must be tired ridin' the woods. Have you any things, mistress?"

"Only what I'm wearin', ma'am," said Frances.

"Where ever did you find that habit? I never saw a handsomer one," exclaimed Bella, with obvious envy, as she led Frances over the bridge to the women's house.

"It's all out of your hands now, Sal," grinned Yates. "Bella and Mrs. Pendergass have taken charge."

The three men sat down—looking disappointed and relieved.

"I make it a rule to ride a natural mistake as far as the first hurdle at least, Sal," remarked Yates, laying his hand on Albine's arm. "There's no reason you *have* to tell them everything at first."

Salathiel didn't know exactly what to say. He was both pleased and annoyed that Frances had been led off by Bella.

"Damn it! *Stop* that jabberin', Pina," he finally shouted. "Here! Give

your family and all the big Injuns a go at some grog. And for Lord's sake
bring us some supper. I'm starved." He slipped the old woman a yellow
coin.

"God bless ye, God bless ye, Marse Albine. De good Lord send yah a
hunder chillens, and all twins," cried Pina, bowing, wiping her hands
on her apron, and shooing her progeny and the Indians from the room.
"I'll dish yah up a hot mess in a little jiffy outside in de summah
kitchen."

So it was over—and Frances bedded next door.

The rest of the evening he and Yates sat listening to St. Clair unfold
his plans for a new settlement to be made at Ligonier.

Salathiel was greatly pleased to find that both St. Clair and Yates had
really been waiting for his return, and that they regarded his help in
the new settlement as important. How curious that, after all the trouble
of the year before with St. Clair and Japson, he was now to take part in
helping them bring people to Ligonier. There was no trace of resentment of the past in St. Clair's manner. He was now all affability and
business. He deferred constantly to Yates, and listened carefully to any
suggestions. How times had changed!

St. Clair was inclined to prolong the discussion indefinitely, since his
own interests were so heavily involved. But even though he was going to
bed alone, Salathiel wanted to stop before midnight.

"I'll put Frances in the wagon then, and we'll all go downcountry to
the settlements together," he said at last. "When do ye start?"

Yates hummed something about the animals going into the ark two by
two before answering. "Thursday," he said. "Day after tomorrow, if you
can get horses for the ark."

"Wonder what Ecuyer would say, if he could see Mistress Albine going downcountry in his precious *voiture?*" Certain memories of the past
twisted St. Clair's mouth momentarily into a wry smile.

"Oh, I don't think he'd mind," said Albine. "He'd not wish *any* of us
to be lonely, I'm sure." It was now Salathiel's turn to kick Yates on the
ankle. They broke up after a nightcap and went upstairs chatting.

Despite certain associations of his lonely old room, after the day's ride
Salathiel stretched out comfortably. After all, Frances was safe in the
next house. The move east had been settled. He'd get horses for the ark,
somehow. With his ranger's pay and the legacy he had nearly sixty
pounds in hard money. He had his rifle, Enna, the wagon, bright prospects, and Frances. Those last nights at Pendergasses' he slept well.

Salathiel and Frances busied themselves the next afternoon arranging
things and re-stowing the wagon. She was delighted with the ark, "a
rollin' shebang on wheels". Everything was in it; even Johnson's valet
kit and the wig-furbishing outfit. Bella came out to help, for she and
Frances had rapidly become friends.

"I do hate to see ye leavin' before Pap comes back," Bella kept saying.

"It's right lonely already with the house so empty; with even Charley away! Mom ain't been feelin' so well lately, either."

Bella sighed. She could see long lonely days ahead for her at Pendergasses'. Wartimes had their compensations after all, she thought.

Salathiel and Frances had only one serious ordeal to face before faring eastward. It was saying good-bye to old Mrs. Pendergass. On the last evening they went to the house together and Bella took them up to the old woman's room.

She was sitting in her chair before the fire, as usual, almost birdlike in her white cap and fragility, but still alert.

"Your cap's awry, mother," said Bella, putting it back into place.

"Let be, let be," said the old lady impatiently, while pinning her bright blue gaze on Salathiel and Frances.

"So you're goin' to leave us, Salathiel Albine, and take your girl downcountry to the old settlements," she said. "It's a fine lass you've found yourself. Did you know she looks like your mother? Ah, well do I remember her, a blue-eyed, dark-haired O'Moore." She patted Frances' hand affectionately.

"You're like your father Lemuel, Salathiel. You go with an Irishwoman, too. But you go east—this time?"

"Everything seems to point that way, ma'am," said Salathiel.

"Aye," said she under her breath, "tides ebb and flow." He thought she had said something in disapproval.

"But we'll be comin' back soon, and stop off to see ye," he explained hastily.

Mrs. Pendergass laughed.

"You Albines are all alike," she replied. "You'll be comin' back soon, will you? That's what your pap said when he set out for the west-running waters—and he never came back again. I thought maybe you'd listen to Garrett and stay on here. But it's town life you've set your heart on, I can see that. Well, go and see the towns, get the smoke and the sting of them in your eyes. You're both young yet . . .

"No, no," she went on, motioning to Salathiel not to interrupt her, "I'll *not* be seein' you again. I'm as sure of it as that the woods be green in zummer! And that's the reason I called you both here, to give you a little zumpthin' to remember me by before you go."

She fumbled in her sewing box and drew something out by two faded strings.

"It's a babe's cap your mother knitted for me when my Matthew was comin'. Or was it for you, Bella? I forget now which of the babies it was. It was in other days. But I thought you might like to have it, Salathiel, to give your Frances. It looks a bit like an Irish bonnet." She sighed, and handed it to Frances directly.

"I'll kiss you for that, mother," said Frances, and she flung her arms around her, with tears in her eyes.

"Good-bye, young woman," said the old woman. "The Lord be with ye!"

She shook hands with Salathiel.

They went out of the room together and turned at the end of the hallway to look back. She was still sitting in the firelight, smiling.

They went to bed together that night in the wagon. The start next morning was to be long before sunrise.

But faithful Bella was there to wave the ark and its crew out of the yard. She threw her apron over her head as she went into the house again. Yates drove for the time being, having left his lame horse at Loudon two weeks before.

It was a still, starlit autumn morning, Guy Fawkes Day of November, 1764. The road down the valley glimmered before them with silver patches of hoarfrost. St. Clair followed some distance behind the wagon on a sturdy gelding. Salathiel rode ahead, curbing Enna in to keep pace with the party. He kept whistling the refrain of "Past Caring and Past Faring", until Yates shouted to him to "desist".

He laughed and began singing to himself instead. He had seldom felt so carefree and deeply happy.

Dawn overtook them at the water gap, where the Juniata cuts like a bright sword through the mountains. By the time they came through the pass the sun was rising directly ahead of them out of the misty eastern hills. A wide and magnificent sweep of wild landscape opened up ahead. The day suddenly brightened. The hills blinked and stood outlined against the oncoming glory. His pulses quickened in the growing light.

Salathiel was some distance ahead of the wagon now. He drew up, waiting for it, and rose in his stirrups to look about him.

Behind, the long western ridges curled with the frosty smoke of November. The road led on over many a shining hill before. It dipped and disappeared, and appeared again.

The wagon came in sight.

Yates and Frances were sitting on the big seat together now. Frances had taken over the reins. Salathiel shouted to her exultantly, and she shook the four horses into a rapid run. Yates began laughing as the teams stretched out and came to a gallop.

Oh, what a morning!

Oh, to be free in this great natural world!

Salathiel knew they would know what he meant—

He rose in the stirrups again and thrust his rifle sparkling in the sunlight towards the western mountains. He threw his other hand up openpalmed, eastward, in a wide, wild, happy gesture. Good-bye, wilderness; good day, tomorrow and tomorrow and tomorrow—

Farewell, and hail.

Toward the Morning

1. A Mountain Approach

AS TO JUST EXACTLY what Melissa did see that morning, it would be hard to say. The trouble is there was nothing familiar with which she could compare her experience afterward. So she could never explain it to others. Indeed, she could never fully understand. It was something queer and lonely. A fit of seeing-everything-at-once, sometimes a peep ahead through the glimmering spokes of the wheel of time. Or so she thought.

That was particularly troublesome.

It was especially terrible to know afterward that certain things were bound to happen. To be sure of it, and yet not be able to get anyone to listen to her. But of course not! If things were going to happen, then no talk could turn them aside, no warning. Her warnings even made things happen. They became diabolically a part of the fated happenings themselves. The Father of Evil was in that.

"Sure the devil was in it somewhere," she would say.

She always remembered that morning on the wagon seat, when she first felt certain that she was with child, as the original of these spells. It began with a feeling of uncontainable triumph, of having overcome the universe and beaten down Death himself. She could not use all the life that kept welling up within her. It flooded, fountained, spurted, a prideful joy that rose and cascaded over the walls of her mind. And then she felt, she *saw* everything, all at once. Became part of it. Could look with the eyes of a hawk.

Afterward, long afterward, it became harder and harder to find her way back again out of such spells.

But this morning on the wagon seat was the first time the thing had happened to her completely. There had been only a few fiery glimpses of it before, when life had been especially full of terror, when things were very bad. This morning there was a great joy about her vision.

And she was honestly curious about it. Not frightened at first. She was flying high. The more she saw, the better it was, she thought. Perhaps she ventured too far. "Up there" she had seen everything going on at the same time.

But people travelling in a wagon along a road, for instance, came across things one at a time. They bumped into a series of unexpected events. And if she told them what she remembered having seen, beforehand, they laughed at her. Pretty soon, when they came across what was coming, they were annoyed at having been told about it. They made a joke of it to protect themselves. And she was it.

Ah, it was only too true that they laughed. At best they smiled. She found it so the very first morning that the thing happened to her. She tried to tell them a little, when she came back again to the wagon seat, just a few glimpses of what she had seen going on—of the rivers flowing away through the hills underneath the sun, of the harp, and the road—the road that lay across the mountains from east to west.

After all, there was nothing so strange about her seeing all that. The harp came with her out of Ireland, out of the past. And she had been over that road coming west with old man Frazier only a few years before. Now she would like to see what was going on along it.

It was easy, while she had been "up there". She had just leaned eastward on her wings into the sunrise and left the wagon behind.

The road below snaked-it along through the forest, climbed and fell, made a ribbon through the trees that tied the East and the West together.

She saw four grey wolves chasing some elk through the forest. Their pace was swift and ruthless. They must be hungry to hunt and howl so in daylight. The day had not stopped them. But it was lonely country. All the farms lay deserted, lonesome little burnt-out clearings as far as the last mountaintop.

She went over that final mountain range like a swimmer over a wave. Up! She was flung up again into the sky.

On one side of the Tuscarora the chimney pots of Fort Lyttleton smoked white in the morning shadow of the mountain; on the other, at Fort Loudon, the smoke floated upward like black wavering scarves in the yellow sunlight.

She could see clear up the valley to Aughwick, a hazy patch in the forest. She could see the Susquehanna glittering on the rim of the harp, with the blue horizon beyond. And the roads, the people, the small houses among the trees! This was as she expected it to be, as she had remembered it. In this valley the people were still there. They had not gone away, leaving their cabins to the wolves and stars. Hope in the dawnlight was still bright down there. There were ploughed fields. Frequently there was dust along the road. Travellers. A great dust, a

flashing of sunlight through a yellow cloud of morning haze lay along
the road leading down from Carlisle.

She leaned eastward again into the full daylight, easily, curiously.

But she was sinking now, falling rapidly. Her speed was intolerable.
Dizzy. She was flying nearer the ground, yet everything was swim-
mingly confused. A town she remembered vaguely—a night of trouble
there with Frazier. The millwheel in the flashing race. And she was
over it, skimming along the road into the dawn. Sickened, afraid, falling.
Ashamed of something, she remembered. Of something hidden in that
great dust cloud rolling slowly westward there.

That pillar of cloud by day!

What people were these on the march through the wilderness? Who
were coming west into the savage hills; into the Garden of Clouds, where
the rivers rise out of the earth to walk down to the sea? Who were more
terrible than the red devils that dwelt in the garden? Who feared neither
their cruel hatchets nor the wild wolves? Who laughed at kings? Who
would inherit the earth without meekness, to spoil it in days to come?
Who but the ancient enemy of her race? The Sassenachs. The harp
haters. The long-beards with the low Scotch accents. They who had
forever moved into the sunset, implacably armed. The old ocean plough-
ers, the hill and valley ravagers. It was they! They were on the march
down the long road from Carlisle in the morning sunlight, headed west
for the mountains, with the pillar of cloud by day rolling behind them.

A man of God, a grey-bearded prophet of Jehovah, was leading them,
going on before on a great piebald horse that stepped into the west, one
iron shoe after the other, possessing the road behind him slowly like
due notice. Her heart failed her at the sight of him.

Had she not read about that steed, and the other horsemen, in the
English Bible at Frazier's cabin, secretly at night and by firelight? It
was the forbidden Book that would wilder the minds of the laity, the
Book the good nuns had warned her about over their embroidery at
Cork. The Book was in the bag strapped over the saddle-bow of the
prophet, along with his axe and rifle. She knew it. She had read it.
And now her mortal sin was overtaking her. The remembered glow of
the firelight on the page now enveloped the crowding, seething images
of her vision.

The sun flashed through red clouds of dust smoking up from the road
below. There was a glimpse of white upturned faces, of moving white
wagontops. A dismal bellowing from the horned cattle driven along behind came like the braying of war horns through the smoke. There were
shouts, and the sound of cruel blows with sticks. The rifle barrel on the
saddle-bow of the prophet sparkled, caught fire, blazed. Ah, the terrible
face of him under his grim hat, the straight, firm lips! He spoke. Flames
came out of his mouth now, fire and brimstone.

She shrank back amazed, terrified into thought again. She was only a

hawk, a small helpless bird. They might bring her down. Only a bird—
was she? Who was she? Holy Mary, her mortal soul! Remember it?
Frances Melissa O'Toole. But where?

There.

As from a great height she caught sight of herself riding on the
wagon seat. Her head was sagging down towards her knees and her
hair hanging into her lap.

She came down out of the sky like a stone.

Smash . . .

The shock whipped her back against the seat-rest. Out of darkness the
road ahead gradually began to glimmer under her eyelids. Her heart beat
till it nearly burst the veins in her temples. Then her eyes cleared slowly
on familiar scenes. She was back. Thank God!

But was there no one to pity her?

She began to cry out bitterly. She began to call on the name of the
man who had brought all this trouble upon her. Why, she had nearly
died up there! Almost—she had not been able to come back again.

Yates turned towards her in blank amazement.

At that instant she clutched him violently by the arm.

"Sal, Sal!" she kept calling distractedly.

He pulled the horses up, dropped the reins, took hold of her and
shook her. She was rigid, as tense as iron.

"Melissa," he shouted. "Wake up! Look at me!"

Why, the girl was beside herself! The pupils in her eyes were dis-
tracted, wide, and full of strange lights in darkness. Weird! He shrank
from her. Not his girl, thank God! Salathiel's!

If he only had some cold water. Anything!

He rose and whistled shrilly through his teeth, beckoning for help
to the two riders ahead. They turned and looked at him inquiringly.

"Trouble!" he shouted. He waved his hat impatiently.

"Aye," whispered Melissa, "trouble, trouble it was!" She clutched the
hair back from her forehead, threw it behind her over her shoulders.
She looked at him through her fingers.

"Did you see me that way, Edward Yates?" she demanded of him
suddenly.

"I did," he admitted, still looking shocked.

"Never a word of it, then—not to him!" She clutched his arm again
anxiously.

"Very well," he muttered. "You tell him."

He gathered up the reins, still watching her thoughtfully. One of the
horses began to paw the stones.

From somewhere she produced a comb and began to use it with swift,
skilful strokes.

"I'm no hag now, am I?" she asked, and looked at him suspiciously.

"No, no," muttered Yates uneasily, "of course not!"

Damn the girl, he thought—the wild woman! She was actually smiling at him now. Her eyes had cleared and were a beautiful hazy grey again. Pretty! And yet only a minute ago . . .

The swift beat of hoofs and the creaking of saddle leather approached. Albine and St. Clair rode up, to dismount anxiously by the halted wagon. They looked puzzled. Yates had obviously been much excited.

"Better look after this girl of yours, Sal," he said. "She gave me a bad turn just now. Looked quite ill a piece back."

"You take the mare, then," replied Albine instantly.

"How d'ye feel now, my dear?" he asked, climbing up on the wagon seat and putting his arm about her. The long rifle-gun fell unnoticed between them.

"Better," she said, clutching two stray black locks, one in each hand, and looking up at him. " 'Twas a bad spell, Sal. Sure, I've got something I want to say to you."

"I'll be right here," he said, and gave her a reassuring squeeze.

"All right?" inquired St. Clair. He raised his hat deferentially to her as he spoke.

"It's all right I'd be, if aither of you two gintlemen on the fine harses would provide me a drink."

Yates looked at Salathiel sitting humbly on the wagon seat and laughed. "There's a keg in the wagon," he said. "Garrett's best, I believe. Now we *gentlemen* on horses . . ."

But Arthur St. Clair drew a long silver flask from a saddle pocket, unstoppered it, and offered it gallantly.

She applied her moist lips to the neck of the metal bottle and gulped. She leaned back in proportion as the angle of the flask tilted higher. Her throat rippled.

"That's brandy!" exclaimed St. Clair at last.

"Brandy it was," she replied, wiping her mouth, and finally tendering him the flask, which sloshed emptily.

"Thanks to you, Mr. Arthur St. Clair, maybe I'll be able to kape meself on the airth," she said. "Did ye ever fly off on the wings of a hawk?" The colour came back into her cheeks, and she laughed with relief.

St. Clair looked puzzled. It was Yates who replied.

"Horses, horses, my fine lady, are what we ride on, with four feet on the ground." He touched up the mare until she pranced about the wagon eager to be off. St. Clair strapped his flask back in place, mounted without comment, and the two rode off ahead up the road.

"Now, I never saw anybody in my life change so instantly," remarked Yates to St. Clair. "You know, I found myself all of a sudden riding along with a stranger. That girl looked like—" He choked back the word "hag", remembering his promise to Melissa just in time.

"Haggard," said St. Clair.

Yates nodded.

"And I know what that really means," insisted St. Clair. "There was an old nurse once took care of us at Thurso, came from the Islands. James Stuart would have had the boots tried on her in his day. Now, take this Irish wife of Albine's—" He grew reminiscent as they jogged on. Yates was glad of the change from the wagon to horseback. No one could be more interesting and absorbing when he wanted to be than Arthur St. Clair.

Back on the wagon seat Melissa sat contentedly and quietly finishing the braids in her hair. She sat there without looking at Salathiel or saying anything. There seemed to be nothing the matter with her whatever. He could not help feeling somewhat annoyed. Yates and St. Clair had already disappeared around a bend ahead.

"Well?" he said at last, looking at her inquiringly, and wrapping the reins around his arms.

"It's high time you took the reins into your own hands, Mr. Albine," she replied tartly and unexpectedly. "Maybe there's more in this wagon than you think."

"Everything in the world is in it for me, Melissa," he replied simply and gently.

She relented at that and laid her head against his shoulder.

"One thing is in it that isn't in the world yet. But it soon will be," she added. "It soon will be!"

He gazed at her thoughtfully and gave a low whistle.

"So it's that way with you already, Melissa?"

"It is," she said. "I know!"

To her delight he looked thoroughly pleased.

"A boy?" he demanded inevitably, and without thinking.

"Now, how would I know that, Mr. Albine? How would I be after knowing that yet? But get on wid ye, drive on, and belike I'll be telling you something else you'll meet on the road ahead."

"What more could you have to say?" he replied, and slapped the raw-hide reins triumphantly along the backs of all the horses at once.

The wagon rolled down into the woods with sudden speed. There was a straight stretch across the valley here passing north of Sidling Hill. The teams began to catch up with Yates and St. Clair. The wagon dogged them steadily now, until they remarked the new pace and pushed on more rapidly. Neither the four horses in the traces nor the girl on the seat had any doubt that a man who could have his own way with them was driving. She sat content with the local present now, warmed by a pint of brandy and the reassuring presence of her man. The horses stretched to it. Sixteen hoofs clattered and smacked a constant staccato tattoo. The heavy wheels trembled and rumbled. The little cart danced to see such sport—its wheels spinning.

Afterwhile, above the roar and clatter of the rocky way, Melissa began to try to relate, somewhat breathlessly as they rolled and pitched along, the more salient portions of her "dream". He could see that she had been frightened by it. But he put that down to her condition, always something mysterious to a man.

He listened and made his own silent comment. Doubtless, they might meet with wolves. Wolves were coming back into the deserted country desolated by Indian raids. And he had heard about the Scotch-Irish gathering at Carlisle. But it seemed unlikely they would be making west for the mountains so soon. As for the hawk and the harp, and flying over the hills—and her fall—why, he was quite used to her wild turns of speech and Irish twists of fancy by now. He liked them.

He put his arm around her and laughed encouragingly.

He wrapped her in a warm shawl, because she was still shuddering a little. Presently she stopped talking and lay back against him.

The forest road slipped past into the west with every turn of the wheels. It gradually began to slope upward, winding away amid the steep rolling foothills of the Tuscarora, towards the dark main ridge of the mountain itself. Somewhere up there, guarding the pass, Fort Lyttleton watched from a broad shoulder of the mountain. The pace became slower, a long, steady, wearing pull. But he kept the horses at it. He whistled and he clucked to them encouragingly.

This was the last barrier. On the other side of that high cloud-tossed ribbon lay the long-settled country that stretched to the sea; the people in the dawnlight, farms, towns, and the city. Ships! For how many years now had he longed to see them, to return to his own!

Somewhere on the steep road ahead sounded the mournful hunting howl of a grey wolf, replied to by his companions—and a whole pack of echoes. Let them hunt, let them go by. Enough of that! He glanced impatiently into the steep wild glens and forested ravines that now began to lie behind and far below him as the wagon slowly but determinedly mounted towards the clouds on the range above.

Think of it, tonight they would be at Lyttleton; tomorrow night over the mountain, and safe at Fort Loudon! And then . . .

He pondered earnestly the face of the woman leaning against him, curled up and asleep on the wagon seat, draped in a many-folded shawl.

She looked as though she really had fallen from the sky, and she had not awakened yet to the ways of earth. Undoubtedly, there was something disconcerting and mysterious in her expression. Her mouth trembled and was drawn in when she breathed. The helpless curves of her body concealed in the shawl appealed to him. He pitied her. He felt poignantly that she was being used without her knowing it. She stirred faintly. Suddenly he remembered the sensitive white creature he used to find in a river mussel shell. When its lid was torn off it withdrew slowly into itself. Too much light in the wide-open world. He leaned over and kissed her softly on the mouth.

Come what might, he meant to stand by her in the days ahead. He began to wonder about the house he would have to be making for her soon. What would it be like? Where would it be? Unconsciously, he began to drive more carefully.

2. A Warm Welcome

WINKING FIRELIGHT reflected from the mountain wall just beyond, many deep voices singing together, sudden glimpses of clustered lights and huddled buildings—all this roused them at last, after a steep haul up through owl-haunted ravines, to invest eagerly such welcome signs of human settlement with the hopeful anticipation of a comfortable night. Indeed, the forest seemed to fall away before them as the road emerged now onto the grassy flats and level clearings of a broad shoulder thrust out from the main ridge of the Tuscarora itself. Its final crest still towered black and forbidding just above and beyond.

Here, though, were wide open fields with calm constellations overhead. A stockade and a string of wayside cabins loomed up along the road before them. The singing grew louder. Owls and croaking night birds had been left behind in the wooded hills and thickets below. Song and comfortable firelight at least foreboded a companionable evening.

But just then the men's deep voices paused in their chorus. Dogs howled. Showers of sparks rose abruptly from fires behind the black wall of the stockade and drifted out slowly across the stars. The constant clatter of the wagon wheels and iron horseshoes was curtly hushed by an unexpected stretch of mossy turf. They drove on intently and more smoothly, but a certain furtive quiet now resumed. The two horsemen cautiously drew nearer the wagon. The road itself seemed to be conspiring to keep their close approach to the fort a solemn secret.

On the wagon seat, Salathiel fumbled in his waterproof pouch for his cherished silver watch and held its white-enameled dial over the faint glow of his stubby stone pipe. He puffed intently, studying the spidery Roman numerals. Rank forest tobacco and killikinick had so far had to comfort him for lack of supper during the unbroken journey up the mountain. Frances Melissa had slept comfortably most of the way, leaning against him, wrapped warmly in her shawl. Yet for him the steep stony drive had seemed a long and intricate climb, winding up through the winter darkness, and he was surprised to see that, actually, it was only a quarter past eight by the watch.

No, on the whole, he thought, they had made confoundedly good time on their first day's journey. Not even a horseshoe had been cast. And there was no snow to speak of in the mountains, as yet. Tomorrow they should be over that last cloudy mountain wall ahead. It was only a couple of miles away now! And after that . . .

He slipped the watch back into the pouch thoughtfully. It was keeping *his* time now, and with Frances Melissa beside him. He clasped her hand in the darkness and felt her fingers respond sleepily. Luck ought to hold for a while, he felt. Fair promise of good weather was in the air tonight. It was a clear, starlit mountain evening with moonrise coming on, frosty and deathly still. He gathered the reins firmly and brought the tired teams to a trot, and together—for the last stretch of road to the gate.

The wagon swerved sharply to the left with its escort. It finally pulled up at a walk along a level stretch of meadow under the pointed log walls of Fort Lyttleton. They watched the black edge of the log parapet slide like the teeth of a saw across the glare of firelight from within—and stop.

The fort was essentially nothing more than a large stockade set in heavy fieldstone foundations. It was a "burg", in the ancient and primary meaning of that term, a fortified farm in the forest. The provincial authorities and scared neighbours had erected it frantically eight years before, during the notable troubles following Braddock's defeat. They had hastily enclosed within its stockaded area the sturdy log farmhouse, barns, and outbuildings of one William Patton. His ample home, with its cold, unfailing spring in the cellar, thus served as military headquarters when there was a garrison in the fort, and always as the centre of news and hospitality for all that western side of the mountain and the road through the Tuscarora gap.

Locally, the place was usually called "Patton's"; or sometimes "Sugar Cabins", after an insignificant settlement of log huts in a maple grove situated a short distance eastward on the last flat before the final, steep zigzag of the road to the summit began. Fort Lyttleton, Patton's, or Sugar Cabins—by whatever name—everybody agreed the place smelled sweetly of fragrant maple sugar boilings in the early spring, of rare summer clover, and of the perfume of peach brandy from William Patton's copper still in the fall.

William, on his part, had consented with alacrity and a certain canny zeal to assist the authorities in turning his inheritance into a tower of refuge and an ordinary of entertainment for the not inconsiderable population of a long-settled neighbourhood. Patriotism and profit were thus for once honestly made one. His defensible farm was the logical place for the neighbours to "fort-up" in during Indian raids. In fact, the fencibles of the district always assembled there on militia days. And if, as Bill Patton observed, more peach brandy were consumed in the face of the enemy than when his back was peaceably turned, no one need be the loser thereby.

'Twas merely the dividends of time and of family foresight that he now so generously shared with others, he averred. Was it not his grandfather, Isaac Patton, who had so sensibly first built the old log house over the spring in such a fertile, sheltered, and convenient spot on the old Glades Path?

Perhaps, it was more in keeping with the convivial fame of Patton's than with its military reputation as Fort Lyttleton that the big gate facing the road was found to be standing invitingly wide open, when the wagon and its cavalcade finally drew up silently before it, long after nightfall on the evening of November the fifth, 1764.

Puzzled by the total lack of anyone at the gate, it was Arthur St. Clair who had held up his hand and given final signal to halt. Whether he was more upset by the dangerous failure of the garrison to post even a single sentinel or by the absence of appropriate ceremony to mark the occasion of his arrival, it would be hard to tell. At any rate, St. Clair was sorely disappointed after a hard day's journey by this anticlimax of no welcome whatever, and he now sat his horse, halfway through the neglected gate, gazing at the wide interior of the stockade with an expression of indignant chagrin.

The bright interior of the fort was awash with firelight from several bonfires: only the gate lay in dense shadow. And Guy Fawkes Day was being observed inside the stockade, not only by the Royal Highland garrison, but apparently by everybody else; by the neighbours from near-by Sugar Cabins, and by all the other Scotch-Irish settlers, farmers and hunters, gathered in from miles about.

Immediately across a much worn and rutted "parade ground", and before the long whitewashed log cabin of the Patton house, which boasted the unusual feature of a wide and neatly railed and roofed-in porch, stood a dense crowd of wild figures, men and boys, massed about a shallow pit, where some large animal was being roasted whole over a bed of intensely glowing hickory coals. A bank of their intent white faces with deep shadowy eye sockets under shaggy coonskin caps gazed raptly into the fire. But there were other and even more potent attractions.

Set to one side before the porch were four rum kegs and two whisky barrels, one with its head stove in, over which a transparent blue flame hovered and hesitated like a tremulous spirit of the night.

These also were the centre of constant attention, and much passing to and fro—especially from a company of about a dozen already lugubriously jovial souls who sat to one side, singing determinedly, about a select bonfire of their own. They had only to rise and kick a few curs out of their way in order to reach the kegs. Yelps, therefore, were fairly frequent.

However, these occasional howls from outraged dogs served to punctuate rather than to interrupt the more continuous lyric efforts of their masters' chorus. Before the choir stood its leader, a gaunt and rail-like personage, in a coat made exclusively of patches. His voice, a deep bass, seemed to be hiccuping from inside a bucket, and he kept waving a large empty toby in one hand to mark the funereal time of a ballad concerning a maiden's virtue undone.

To Mr. Yates, who had dismounted by the wagon, and was now impatiently holding his nag's nose to keep her from whinnying, there was something so incongruous and so unnecessarily fatuous about the peculiarly indigenous scene before him that he could scarcely restrain a great silent laugh in the back of his mind from being echoed aloud by his lips.

Shouts of self-appreciative laughter and catcalls followed. The gaunt leader began to make a mock speech, standing before the kegs.

The chorus came round the third time. The dogs howled.

"No, you don't, my fancy lassie," said Yates, squeezing his horse's nose like a sponge to prevent her whinnying. "I'll gie that horse-laugh mysel', when the time comes." He sensed that his companions were in sympathy with this; that they were watching, too. Their astonishment at so unexpected a scene and a certain creepy feeling of approaching crisis in the firelit drama before them had served so far to keep their attention fixed.

For, watched secretly even from a short distance, there *was* something naturally compelling and even sinister about the bright interior of the stockade set in a frame of starry darkness. And this was especially true of the centre of interest, the crowd of dark, fur-capped figures and lean, long-eared hounds clustered around the glowing pit with the liquid firelight washing over them. Above their heads, dimly visible against the moon-etched mountain beyond, towered a vague pyramid of piled combustibles crowned by a shadowy gallows! From that in turn dangled a long helpless figure whose feet alone could be plainly glimpsed, and then only when they swung listlessly and let the yellow firelight play on them from below. It was plain, however, that those feet were shod in a pair of fine, new, beribboned scarlet mules. Nothing could have been more extravagant, more unexpected—and fatuously real.

"Belike 'tis an image of the Howly Father they'd be after burnin', the foul Orange traitors!" exclaimed Frances indignantly. "And the new, red shoes—reft from a good Catholic, I'll wager!"

"Hush, for heaven's sake, ma'am," said St. Clair. "Let's stay oot of it all, and watch!"

Salathiel chuckled, remembering how dearly St. Clair's caution had been bought.

Frances subsided temporarily. For a while all in the wagon party were content to be unobserved and uninvited spectators. Albine jumped down from the outboard to hold the heads of his team. Frances Melissa stood up on the seat and craned her neck, delighted with the bright novelty of seeing a crowd of people again.

Two men in fringed shirts began to shift the carcass roasting on the fire. It was lifted up sizzling. Someone shouted loudly for "Leftenant Grant".

The door to the farmhouse opened and an ungainly redheaded officer in a Highland bonnet and flaming tartans came out and stood leaning over the railing. A tall impassive Indian wrapped in a dirty blanket followed him and leaned back against the whitewashed wall. Over two streaks of white paint on his cheekbones his eyes glittered. He had the face of an old hawk. Two women in linsey-woolsey, and a ragged little girl, several small boys, and a tall smooth-faced man with iron-grey hair appeared; then a couple of black women, a squaw, and some young Highland officers—the porch rapidly filled up.

"So Patton's enterteenin' the Grants," muttered St. Clair.

"Maybe he can't help himself," said Yates, "there's fully half a company of Highlanders here. They must have marched over from Loudon lately."

St. Clair grunted.

"We'll see," he said.

The big redheaded Scot on the porch held up his hand. The noise about the fires died down.

"Men," said he, "I've high hopes there's none amongst ye but will find the enterteement provided the nicht—gratifyin'!"

A reassuring shout with a ragged attempt at a grateful cheer followed.

"'Tis a braw bricht Protestant nicht the nicht," shouted a little man, evidently a Welshman, poking fun at Grant's Scotch accent. There was a good-natured laugh here and there.

"Aye, onyway it's a' that!" continued Lieutenant Grant, unconsciously banging the porch rail for emphasis with a large pewter mug. "An' I'll no deespute wid ony of ye the nicht aboot the hard feelin' goin' the rounds in these hills o'er some o' the late measures of goovernment. But I'm sure in these parts ye will no want ony new people crowding in on ye to make land trouble. I can promise ye the garrison'll see to that. And as for the Injun traders—"

"Aye, wot about 'em?" a tall hunter shouted.

"Why, as for them, it's only the traders licensed by goovernment, only the treaty goods goin' forward to Mr. Croghan, the king's Indian agent at Pittsburgh, that we'll let pass."

"No, no! No more hatchets for the damn yellowbellies. Leave that to us!"

A general growl of assent followed this reply from several in the crowd. Grant made a deprecatory gesture.

"Aweel," he said, "it greets me sair to hear o' them that would sow trouble between his Majesty's loyal subjects and his faithful troops. So we'll let a' that go by the noo. And noo," said he, drawing himself up to his full height, "noo I'll gie ye the toast for the nicht. Wha will no join me in it?"

He leaned over the rail suddenly and filled his mug with whisky from an open barrel. Then he stood up again.

"The king—the Protestant suc-ceesion, no popery!" he bawled.

Everyone, but a few of Mr. Croghan's Irish on their way to Fort Pitt, sitting sullenly apart about their own fire, roared a hearty reply and crowded forward to fill their mugs and leather botels at the barrels. A stream of people with brimming cans soon began to return to the pit fire, where two hunters with flashing tomahawks and knives were cutting up the smoking meat. Men snatched hot pieces of it and tossed it briskly from one hand to the other as they made off.

Yates, who was especially ravenous after the long supperless haul up the mountain, would have ridden forward at this juncture to claim a share in the feast. But he was restrained by St. Clair.

"Bide a wee, Edward," he said. "Tarry for the main event. If I know my cousin Wully Grant, yonder, we shall have a fiery spectacle worthy of Vauxhall Gardens, the nicht. 'Tis not for nothing Mr. Grant was known at home as 'Whuzz-Bang Wully'. Goonpowder is his forte, Indja rockets and Chinee crackers his delight. Him and Guy Fawkes, indeed! Aye, now, did I no tell ye! The pyrotechnic illumination begins!"

Yates laughed. His belly hunger was real, but not so overpowering that he could not pause to enjoy a bit of irony and humour at the expense of an eccentric relative of St. Clair's. And the illumination was already proving to be startling.

Somewhere behind the crowd a Catherine wheel began to sputter. A fiery glare from a row of bonfires, which a young coloured boy now ran about kindling with a torch, soon blent into a genial ivory glow, one in which the entire interior of the stockade suddenly stood out against the deep shadows in startling relief. A large tomb-shaped stone magazine and several other whitewashed buildings emerged starkly and rigidly from the darkness, providing instantly a bold background. Behind the crowd at the roasting pit, someone lit a tow cresset, and a sparkling and sputtering of powder fuses began.

"Hold your nags, Albine," cautioned St. Clair, anxiously. "Wully Grant is up to his old tricks wie goonpowder. We'll hae some braw fireworks—"

"And trouble," added Yates. "Look at Croghan's Irish over there by the forge shed. They've a keg of their own stuff, private. But they look sullen. Some Quakers amongst them. I think I see broad hats."

"Aye, they'll drink, but they'll no sing nor fight," replied St. Clair. "This is a Scotch-Irish cove in the hills, and the Presbyterians do swarm. Losh! What did I tell ye?"

A large rocket took off with a swish, soared over the parapet, missing it narrowly, and dropped into a field beyond, where it exploded. A sudden apprehensive silence gripped everybody.

Two Catherine wheels burst into a frantic whirl of glory. Another rocket followed.

Someone lit the pyre underneath the gallows. A sheet of flame leaped up, revealing the lank figure dangling from the crosstree. Draped in an old bedgown arranged in churchly folds, even though its paper triple crown was more like a fool's cap than the bishop of Rome's mitre, its meaning was plain enough.

An appreciative roar and din went up from all the Protestants in the crowd. The flames crackled and licked the red-shod feet of the "Pope".

From the porch a child's voice was heard crying out frantically, "My red shoes, they're burnin' up! My red shoes! Stop! Stop them, Aunt Tibby. You promised! Oh, oh, my red shoes, my dear red shoes . . ." The door opened and the child was hustled off the porch. Inside the cabin, she could still be heard shrieking hysterically in protest. The house dog began to howl.

From her point of vantage on the wagon seat, Frances spluttered indignantly. She climbed down from the wagon seat impulsively, her eyes shining and her face aglow.

Salathiel put a restraining arm about her as she passed him, where he was holding the heads of the lead team.

"Now, now, sweetheart," he said, "Mr. Croghan wants his Irish to keep the peace and watch the trade here. He'd sack them if they lifted a hand. It's peltries and not the Pope he most cares about."

"Ah, the black fuzzy heart of him! Croghan and his everlasting furs!" exclaimed Melissa. But with Salathiel's arm about her, she grew calmer and eventually stood quiet.

"Besides," chimed in St. Clair, anxious to compose matters, "all this foolin' over Guy Fawkes Day is only a joke now in the New World. Wha really cares? No, they forget. Maybe it's *not* the Pope dangling over the flames yonder. Maybe it's Guy Fawkes instead they mean to have sport with. Guy Fawkes! Dinna ye ken him? The mon that told King Jamie to his verra face the goonpowder was to blow all the Scots in England back to Scotland."

Melissa laughed. She was not taken in by St. Clair's well-meant fibbing.

"But there's not enough powder in the world to keep the Scots in Scotland, is there, Mr. St. Clair? You and Mr. Yates are both livin' ividence of thot!"

They all grinned into the darkness at her retort. Yates began to say something feelingly about supper, and to lead his horse through the gate. The rest prepared to follow him, when circumstances and gunpowder combined in a flash to stop them all in their tracks.

For it was just at that instant that something went horribly wrong with the elaborate pyrotechnic arrangements of Whuzz-Bang Wully Grant.

The only warning was a young coloured boy in a thin white shirt, who dodged through the legs of the crowd like a scared rabbit and streaked away into the night.

Before the faces of the crowd, and between them and the porch, there was a blinding arc-like flash, and a clap of thunder.

A cloud of pungent white powder smoke rose on a wispy stalk from a burning powder chest and collapsed like a rotten mushroom over the heads of the crowd. In the midst of this half-luminous mist, the spectral forms of men and hounds could be seen madly careening, milling about, shouting and howling as though in a bad dream. The chest glowed with renewed energy and began to vomit fire like a small volcano.

Rockets, whizzing Catherine wheels, squeegees, signal grenades, and partigoes banged, streaked, and sizzled through the scattering crowd. Something like a bomb hurtled into the heart of the fire under the gallows and blew the pyre and the figure over it to smithereens.

A rain of flaming wood embers and fizzing powder sparks showered the now madly deploying company with a fine catholic disregard for their Protestant sentiments. Coonskin caps blazed, racing across the night like meteors. The beards of patriarchs threatened to become burning bushes. Fiery-edged holes widened like wildfire through the folds of old blankets and greasy shirts. A tall Highland sergeant was briefly glimpsed racing for the well, emitting a column of smoke from under his kilts.

The crowd dissolved madly in all directions.

Left alone in the middle of the parade ground in a self-illuminated panic, a large shaggy dog, mysteriously on fire behind, chased his own tail with hideous clamour.

The air cleared slowly . . .

But against the clear yellow glow of the remaining bonfires, dark figures could still be seen rushing wildly about, beating their caps out on their knees, the sparks out of their clothes, and each other on the back with oaths, roars, stampings, and bursts of cursing.

All this finally swelled up into a single hilarious chorus of sheer relief and grim human triumph, when a tidal wave of dogs, evidently mistaking their hysterical tail-chasing comrade in the centre of the scene for the cause of all this calamity, fell upon him en masse, furiously, and then upon one another. Dogs took over the spectacle.

Leaning against the whitewashed wall of the cabin, the old Indian on the porch had undergone a bombardment of firebrands, flying embers and sparks, alone and with unchanged attitude. During the worst moments he had raised his blanket before his face, but his expression behind it probably remained the same. The flying sparks that fell on his blanket were quenched by its ammoniac reek. He had not deigned to brush them off, and he still stood there like a carved figure, impassive as ever, an unmoved spectator.

It seemed quite likely to Edward Yates that it was this old redskin who must make the final comment on the elaborate trouble and tumultuous catastrophe so artfully arranged by the white man. And Mr. Yates was not disappointed.

As the dog fight began to disintegrate into its component parts, its cause forgotten in its own agony, a modicum of decent silence resumed. Both the victors and the vanquished removed themselves painfully into the shadows to whimper in self-pity and lick their wounds. Finally, only the dead remained.

A pause in both sound and events ensued.

It was during this apparently normal interval that the hawk-faced old redskin on the porch wrapped the folds of his blanket about him with all the dignity of a Tully, stepped indifferently over some still-smouldering débris on the porch steps, and plunged his head and shoulders into an open whisky barrel. There he remained for some time, resting his hands on the rim, like a thirsty traveller drinking from a deep spring in the summer.

At this point Frances returned to the wagon, giggling.

St. Clair struck his hands together in ironic sorrow. "Ah, Wully, Wully," he said, "how sair thy subtle plans hae gone agley!"

Yates gave a low whistle to his friend Albine, and together they led the still-sweating and nervous horses into the stockade.

Even then no one seemed to see them. Except for the old Indian with his head still in the barrel, the place appeared suddenly deserted and devastated.

"Aweel," St. Clair said deprecatingly, "ye canna say we've no had a warm welcome, Edward."

"I *Will Grant* you that, Arthur," replied Yates, grinning. "Your cousin is a blithe original."

"Losh, mon, losh!" exclaimed St. Clair, instantly on the family defensive. "Is there naught human or divine you will no quip and make a poon aboot? The Grants are a perseestent race, bound to leave their mark wherever they go."

"Undoubtedly!" said Yates, pointing to the scorched circle in the grass, where the chest of fireworks had exploded.

The two ascended the steps to the Patton house together, still arguing. Salathiel was left holding the horses. The door to the house, he noticed, still remained discreetly closed.

Presently a barefooted little girl with tear-streaked face peeped out and let the gentlemen in. The door closed again.

Albine stamped impatiently. It was decidedly cold and he was very hungry. The day should come when he would not be left just to hold the horses. What in the world was going on in the house there? he wondered. Some people would rather talk than eat.

Inside the wagon Frances lit a candle and tied on her best bonnet carefully. She sat waiting for Salathiel to come for her. She was going to be respectable, and respected. He would have to remember they were a family now. Manners—manners were what counted most in the world, and they were in the world now, leaving the forest behind them. She sat peering into Ecuyer's little field mirror as though into a crystal, with a comb held in her hand.

Finally she peeped out. Salathiel was tying the two riderless horses to the porch rail. The moon had risen and was peering with a wry half-face over the mountain edge, pouring a grey light into the stockade. Curious people were closing in now on the wagon from all sides. There were surprised whistles, and excited voices calling. She gave a final touch to her hair. She tied the strings under her homemade bonnet even more primly, and sat waiting.

Outside, drawn up before the porch stoop, the long wagon faintly glimmering with candle shine stood ghostly and alone in the moonlight. It seemed suddenly to have materialized out of nowhere, along with the big man with the rifle who stood watching over it at the head of the double team.

The breath of the horses ascended regularly now. They were too tired to be impatient. The man with the rifle began to stride up and down.

My God, would they never get done talking in there!

He stopped suddenly.

The house door began to open, throwing a widening fan of cheerful light across the floor of the empty porch.

3. Levee by Firelight

WILLIAM PATTON, a plump smooth-faced man with iron-grey hair, followed by Edward Yates and a couple of Highlanders, came out on the porch. For an instant before the door closed behind them again, Salathiel caught a glimpse of a crowded tavern room with leaping flames running up the chimney, the glow of candles, and a flash of brass buckles and gold buttons winking through tobacco smoke, where shawled women moved about serving. The door banged, and Mr. Patton came forward hurriedly to greet his unexpected guests.

Yates nodded reassuringly to Salathiel, pointing out the two Highland soldiers who now came down the steps, one to watch and the other to lead the tired teams off to the stables. As soon as the horses were gone, Albine walked quickly to the rear of the wagon, where he was introduced to Patton, and was thus on hand to do the honours quite satisfactorily for Frances Melissa herself when she finally came tripping down the ladder out of her boudoir-on-wheels with a certain mincing air. She made a deep Dublin curtsy to Mr. Patton, one that summoned forth his best bow in reply and also produced an instant change in his attitude towards Salathiel, upon whose tall, gun-nursing, half-Indianlike presence he had been apt at first glance to cast a respectful, yet a decidedly quizzical eye.

The appearance of "Mistress Albine", for as such she had been presented by Yates, had, indeed, hastily forced Mr. Patton to revise his social estimate of his guests upward. Anyway, he thought, he never had been able to be sure about people coming downcountry. They might be anybody to whom anything had happened on the wild frontiers. Inevitably, they would bring back *some* bizarre impression of the savage wilderness upon them. He had even seen white men returning tricked out in feathers, earrings, and copper paint; staid commissioners at that! But Mistress Albine's bonnet, her neat shawl-draped bodice, and her black gloves, picked up by a stroke of feminine luck at Pendergasses', were not alone respectable but somehow fashionably genteel. At least she contrived to wear them that way. For Frances Melissa O'Toole had not only the charming Irish gift of being a natural actress but also the full sense of an occasion. She instinctively thought herself into her parts, and her native interpretation made them real.

Salathiel, Yates noted with satisfaction, was already learning to support her in her dramatic rendering of various little episodes of life, as a sensible partner should. He had handed her down from the wagon with a pride and tall proprietary affection that were impressive in a man of his size and obviously troublesome potentialities. Six feet four inches in flawless buckskin, with a double-barrelled rifle-gun—and an ancient tomahawk peeping with a curved smile from its smooth sheath at his belt—all that, and the implacable, impassive countenance of a Roman standard-bearer minus one ear, tended to provide Melissa with what might be termed a positively sombre impact of protection, yet one which overshadowed her gratefully like the loom of a giant sycamore falling across the white petals of a flowering dogwood tree.

Despite his initial confusion about the Albines, few implications in either the appearance or the manners of his guests were lost on William Patton. And he was far from being impervious to an arch smile and limpid grey eyes under a deep bonnet. Not many such came his way. Ladies travelling to or from the frontiers were novel and rare attractions, not only to him, but to everyone else. Indeed, by this time the scattered crowd was again beginning to gather full of eager curiosity about the distinguished newcomers, the fancy lady, and the big illuminated "ark".

So far as Lieutenant Wully Grant of the 42nd Highlanders was concerned, it was probably an exceedingly fortunate thing for him that the wagon had driven into the stockade at Patton's precisely when it did. The arrival of so sumptuous a vehicle, the emergence from it down a rear ladder of a neatly dressed and comely young woman served instantly to fix the whole curiosity of the crowd on the novelty and to pose a topic of conversation and speculation of more immediate and paramount interest than even the devastating failure of Mr. Grant's late fiery spectacle could provide. The fireworks were over; the wagon was standing before the porch, *now*. It seemed to have materialized mysteriously out of the moonlight. To learn that it came from the west, from Bedford, only lent a touch of the incredible to the mysterious. Most miracles on wheels, or otherwise, in that remote part of the country came from "the City".

It was only a few minutes, therefore, until the crowd was again packed more densely than before and in larger numbers before the porch at Patton's. Even the suspicious and timid who had betaken themselves to a more than safe distance during the fireworks now returned. Women and small children from the quarters now pressed in freely amongst the men. There were whites, blacks, and reds, including indentured servants, a few Negro slaves, and several families of permanently stranded Cherokee Indians.

Both St. Clair and Yates were familiar to a large number in the crowd. These old acquaintances now came forward eagerly, others crowded at their heels, and all desired to meet and to talk to the Albines.

Now, it was Mr. Patton's intention to take full advantage of this new twist in events to forestall, if possible, any complaints by aggrieved participants in the recent disastrous celebration. So it was that with much more than ordinary ceremony Mr. Patton placed Melissa's arm ostentatiously over his own and led her up the steps onto the broad whitewashed verandah. There he turned to face the crowd, and began to hold forthwith what might be termed a kind of firelight levee, with Melissa as the principal attraction, Salathiel the guest of honor, and Yates acting nimbly as the master of ceremonies.

The affair soon became an integral part of the evening's festivities, a social and a genteel success, in which the late rude fiasco of the fireworks was a triviality that good manners and refined local pride must be bound to overlook; only the rude and ignorant could still harbour resentment. Perhaps the final touch was the inclusion in the reception line of several of the embarrassed but delighted married women of the settlement. Thus the explosion in which both the "Pope" and his red shoes had so violently disappeared was gently passed over and conveniently overlooked. Yates bounced in to lead Mrs. Patton out on his arm in order to join the festivities on the porch.

"Lawks!" said she, throwing an India shawl about her. "What's agoin' on out there?"

"A sudden reception, ma'am, a levee, a veritable rout," replied Yates, gaily, "and Mr. Patton wants you with him *immedgit!*"

"Well, I never!" she exclaimed, catching sight of her husband with Frances already making her twentieth curtsy beside him. "Now, how long has *this* been agoin' on?"

Yet from the very first there developed an active sympathy between Frances Melissa and Matilda Patton. Mrs. Patton saw intuitively that night that Melissa was acting for the men, but in need of feminine comfort and understanding. From certain strained shadows about Melissa's eyes she even suspected her condition, and it was not long before she had made her excuses to the women neighbours and ushered Melissa off the porch and back into the warm room, leaving Mr. Patton, St. Clair, Yates, and Salathiel to hold the fort there with what cheer they might maintain, for men alone.

It was some time before Albine fully realized that he was the centre of much genuine interest and cordial curiosity. But when he did it was a helpful surprise. He had managed at least to snatch one mighty pull at one of Mr. Patton's barrels, that which the old Indian had lately been unable to empty, and it had warmed him through and through. Hunger, fatigue, and his usual passiveness vanished. In many who now came to shake hands he recognized brother Masons. Some of them had come over from Conococheague, and now wrung his hand and said "how". It went well. It was pleasant beyond expectation thus to find himself launched into the world, travelling in a far country, yet still among friends.

It was going to be all right with him, he concluded. He had really broken with the wilderness. He was coming over amongst his own people, and they had received him. They were even proud of him. His fame, it seemed, had spread clear over the mountains.

Men wanted to meet "the lieutenant of Captain Jack". They spoke of the affair at the Salt Kettles, of the big fight at Pendergasses'. They asked him questions about his double-barrelled rifle-gun. They even knew its name was "Twin Eyes". They were roughly congratulatory and humorous about Melissa. They looked at him towering there beside Patton, they tested his grip. They liked him!

Suddenly, he found himself talking with great ease, responding to so many so naturally that his Indian reserve and taciturnity vanished. He no longer felt inclined to be laconic or briefly ironical. He was not even ashamed of his size. For the moment, he felt its advantage. His handclasp became warm, even formidable. Several felt the pain in their knuckles and numb fingers for days afterward.

Perhaps Yates was the only one who did, or who could, understand how important this evening at Patton's was to his friend. Probably that was why he kept stirring it up quietly and making it go. It was, Yates knew, for Albine the step over the threshold of the mountains into the world beyond. For his own reasons, too, it was important to make it go. It was better to present the lion in Salathiel than the bear. Bears were sulky and people were inclined to bait them. On the contrary, lions . . . so Yates thought.

At any rate Salathiel never forgot that evening at Patton's. Long afterward he could recall with singular vividness Melissa standing there beside Mr. and Mrs. Patton, curtsying in the light of the bonfire and the winter moon. He remembered forever the long whitewashed front of the house with red firelight winking from the lower windows and a low still candle or two upstairs; the wagon and the trundler in the moonlight, surrounded by a crowd of curious men and boys, with the kilted sentry leaning silent against the big rear wheel, smoking a pipe. But above all there remained the warm sensation of welcome, of having been received as somebody in this world; himself standing on the porch, towering above the others—himself suddenly warm-hearted, "married", and Frances safe in the warm house behind. Here he was welcomed, believed in, blood kin!

4. An Empty Hand Is Extended

MORE THAN SATISFIED, indeed genuinely relieved by the general trend of events, Mr. Patton now saw fit to put an end to the gathering on the porch, and to invite those of his friends who still lingered there in close conversation to further entertainment within.

His little ruse of delay and distraction had worked well enough. The crowd as a whole was now engaged in hearty enjoyment of both the liquid and the solid refreshment so amply provided. To these Mr. Patton now reinvited his guests' undivided attention. He broached another keg of hard cider and left amid the cordial clamour of those who had lined up to drink his health.

Raucous-voiced demands for explanation from Wully Grant had long since died away. Those who still felt inclined to make trouble for dear distraction's sake itself looked at the tall man with a tomahawk in his belt, now standing alone on the porch, and refrained. They turned more easily to the immediate satisfactions so close at hand.

The scattered bonfires were built up again. Here and there convivial singing in a minor key was resumed. Croghan's Irish, it was to be observed, had retired during the late bombardment and were now assembled with their own whisky keg and some smoky lanthorns in the exclusive shelter of a wagon shed at the far end of the yard.

Albine had not gone into the house with the others. He was uneasy about the wagon. Everything he and Melissa had was in it. And there was still a considerable crowd of the curious gathered about. People peered inside and kept trying to peep and pry under the canvas. It would be just as well to have a word with the Highland sentry, who had shifted post and now sat like a wooden man with his arms folded on the lower step of the rear ladder. There was something familiar about him, Salathiel thought. Probably he was a veteran, but it would do no harm to rouse him tonight to a closer watch.

So thinking, he descended the steps in a few sudden strides, and lighting one of the old whale-oil lanthorns that had come from Fort Pitt in the side chest, he flashed it in the face of the half-stupefied sentry and motioned for him to accompany him inside.

Salathiel was proud as the devil of his wagon. In his own mind it

peculiarly marked his status as a white man. It was his rolling estate on
wheels that he had inherited from Ecuyer. It, and the sturdy trundle
behind, contained all his worldly goods and chattels, everything he had
accumulated since he had ceased to live like an Indian, except Enna, the
captain's mare, which Yates was riding to Carlisle for him. Thus the
wagon was a substantial and tangible measure of his personal progress
Possessions, he had soon found, were one of the things by which his
civilized friends measured him.

If only he owned the four wagon horses, too! Enna was too light for
anything but the saddle. He needed the two draught teams. But they
were not his—not yet. They had been lent him by Stottelmyer as a great
favour, and he was simply taking them over the mountains to be turned
over to that lusty wagoner at Carlisle. Perhaps he might be able to strike
a bargain with Stottelmyer himself when he came back from Fort Pitt
He must manage it somehow, for he had grown very fond of the big
capable greys. But what would bargaining with the "Dutch" at Carlisle
be like? he wondered. He had a few furs on hand, but only a handful
of coins.

Meanwhile, the wagon with Frances Melissa in it was house and
home. She had added what was now the most unexpected thing about it,
a touch of the daintily feminine. Her clothes and personal things exhaled a vague odour of orange water and lavender, parting gifts from
Mrs. Pendergass herself. Poor Captain Ecuyer's verbena was no more.
Lavender now vaguely pervaded the whole wagon. It was very much as
though a grim and mustachioed artillery sergeant had been found at
inspection wearing a fragrant lilac instead of a pompon on his hat . .

"Verra deeferent from the days o' the guid captain," said the Highland
sentry, grinning, while sniffing the air tentatively, and gingerly sitting
down on the edge of a padded chest to look about him.

Salathiel peered at the man more closely, as he notched up the small
lanthorn before Melissa's mirror.

"Dinna ye recollect me, Mr. Albine? I've watched this same chariot
for ye before. At Ligonier it was, the nicht o' the fire, before they hanged
the puir ree Irishman."

"Oh, so it was you, then," said Salathiel. "I thought I knew ye, Mac.
You're one of the several Alexanders in Ensign Erskine's company,
aren't ye?"

The man settled himself on the chest more easily now for having been
recognized.

"Sax we were, but sax we be no longer," he said dolefully. "Kenneth
and Donald niver marched back from the Muskingum. Nor the wee
wanthriven drummer wi' his sharny trews and duddy polony and no hair
on his pow. Do ye mind him? Puir laddie, he couldna surveve bein'
scalpéd twice."

"Bad, heap bad!" said Salathiel, assuming the Indian. He remembered

he little drummer with the head like a ghost mask, vividly. "But I do
ejice that ye're still here to be recognized, my friend."

"Noo, Mr. Albine, I take a walth o' satisfaction in thot masel'. I'm
ⵍlad I'm still here to take a wee nip wi' ye to the memory of puir Ken-
⵰eth and Donald, and the wee tonsured laddie—and to watch your
⵰onny auld hurley-hacket."

A flask passed silently between them, and the red spots came out over
he high cheekbones of the Highlander as the good Cumberland rye
⵰ok fiery hold.

They sat talking for some time about Bouquet's march into the Ohio
⵰ountry and old times. Half an hour passed—and so did the flask . . .

"An' so ye're a married mon, and a' thot," continued the Scot, as
⵰alathiel seemed inclined to linger and poured out a further ration into
⵰ mug. "Tell me noo, how *did* ye iver find yoursel' a bonny hempy lass
⵰ike yon pratty one in this green desert? Ye maun well be a mighty
⵰unter before the Lord to do thot."

"I found her lurking from Injuns in a coal mine," said Salathiel.

"Noo, did ye!" replied the Scot, genuinely intrigued. "Then you maun
⵰e a luckier mon than I am, for I've worked i' the coalheughs at New-
⵰astle as pit boy, and I didna fare nearly so weel. All I got was a skelpy-
⵰immer and a ripple-dose gudlin i' the dark."

"Bad, heap bad," grinned Salathiel. "Happen I'm more prick-me-
⵰ainty than you be, Alex. Or more chancy." He put the flask back in his
⵰hirt-flap this time.

"Aye," sighed Alexander, reminiscently, "but thot was no hum-
⵰udgeon, I'm tellin' ye."

"Well, at least keep your eyes open this time, won't you? I mean keep
⵰ close watch on the wagon," admonished Salathiel as he descended the
⵰rief ladder in the rear.

"Thot I will," answered the Scot, and then stuck his head out to
⵰hout, "You'll find the wagon safer wi' me than your lassy is wi' all the
⵰antin' officers in there, to say nothin' o' Whuzz-Bang Wully."

With this negative Scotch assurance ringing in his ears, Albine made
⵰or the porch—and it was then that in the moonlight a curious, and to
⵰im an unnecessarily memorable, thing happened.

As he started to mount the steps he found himself weirdly confronted,
⵰bout chin-high, with a grey-coloured hand held out like a cup at the
⵰nd of a long thin arm. Both the hand and the arm were withered as if
⵰hey had once been in the fire, and the fingers seemed at once to warn
⵰im away and yet to threaten and to beseech him to put something valu-
⵰ble immediately into the hollow of the shadowy palm. All this he saw
⵰nd felt as *one* thing, instantly, before he saw the man behind the arm.

Seated in the black shadow of the porch pillar, with a foot thrust out
⵰nto the moonlight on either side, was a dim bundle. Salathiel became
⵰ware of a head on it with bright eyes and flesh the same colour as the

moon shadow, of a vague mouth from which came a whispered whin

As he mounted the steps, the hand continued to mount with hin
until, as he stood on the porch level, it was finally thrust up at him o
of the darkness about waist-high, propped from its elbow set on an in
visible knee.

The voice continued in a strange accent to ask him for help. Th
fingers wriggled persuasively, desperately, with sharp nails clutchin
inward, asking, demanding like the voice.

The words were a travesty of English. But more shocking to Albin
than either the strange accent or the depressing tone was the smell tha
rose from the bundle. It was undoubtedly a white man's smell, "wo
stale in hickory smoke".

Now, Salathiel had always taken it for granted that begging wa
purely an Indian prerogative and convenience. But here was a whit
man and necessity in one stinking bundle. He stopped, half from su
prise and half from chagrin, detained by the hand. He could not get pa
it without thrusting it away.

"Who and what might ye be?" he exclaimed impatiently.

"Some call me 'Taffy', your honour," whined the voice from th
shadows. "I ply the western road. I take what little charity there may b
betwixt the mountains and the dape salt say." The figure wriggled lik
inky flames. "In Philadelphia I fell among Christians."

"Well, you've come to a good place here," said Salathiel. "They'r
givin' both meat and drink away down there around the fires tonight
He made as though to step forward. But the hand remained.

"What more do you want?"

"Money! Tomorrow will be another night. 'Tis coin alone will alway
do the trick."

Salathiel continued to stand, pondering this. He remembered he ha
some of Ecuyer's gold, some loose shillings and pence, a couple of scalp
he had traded for a bad beaverskin, a twist of killikinick, and a copp
medal of George I in his pouch. The watch, he now recalled with
twinge of uneasiness, he had left hidden in his bunk. But, after all, th
wagon was well watched.

"Look you, you are tall and mighty," whined the voice. "Give me
Portagee joe, a pine shilling, an old Bermudy hog piece, anything—any
thing round and hard. Look at me pore feet." He wriggled them in th
moonlight.

They were bad.

The moccasins were tied with strings and old rags woven into th
rotten openwork of what was no more now than mouldy leather lac
Through the holes peeped the chilblained bunions and calluses of on
David Ap Poer like white fungi growing on a rotting log.

Yes, the feet were bad. But the hand was worse. And that was all c
the man he could plainly see.

On a swift impulse that was not quite anger, he fumbled in his pouch and smacked something into the hand that snatched at it.

"There's a cud of comfort for ye," said he, and tried to pass on.

The fingers clutched the brown twist of tobacco, and crushed it.

"God damn ye," said the whine, now in a rising key, "God damn yer big carcass! May the fever get ye and wither yer prat into a long bony point like the arse of a frog."

The voice continued to come out of the shadow, but the hand had withdrawn into it.

Salathiel laughed, and strode across the porch towards the closed door. There had been something eerie and disconcerting about the incident—but he would give it no further thought. What was going on now in the big room? he wondered. Had he talked with the Highlander too long?

The door opened with a round brass knob, and that for an instant halted him, too. It was a new kind of latch, iron. He got the knack of it, entered, and closed the heavy panels quietly behind him. His first sensation was that the ceiling was so high that he need not take off his fur cap. He removed it, however, and leaned back against the door.

The big iron lock clicked.

Outside in the shadow of the log pillars, the unfortunate descendant of a long line of Cambrian bards and chieftains sat cogitating his sorry predicament. Ages of old European oppression and half a lifetime of new North American misery were concentrated in him personally. He had come too far west. After this Lancaster should be his western limit. Begging and petty thievery needed many people, excess and luxury to flourish on. A big, bad town. There was only one place like that in all the colonies. And, as a matter of fact, he did better along the waterfront at Philadelphia than anywhere else.

He must, he *must* get back out of the wilderness. In the hills near Wilmington he had some Welsh relatives. But how to get there—that was the question. Money, something to swap for food and rest at night must be had. The tall man with the pretty woman—he had watched them, peeked into the wagon at her. And what he *had* seen! A gift was in order. But nothing—a twist of tobacco!

How long before the Highlander in the wagon would doze? he wondered. He spat down the steps thoughtfully several times.

Finally, he gathered his ragged blanket-coat about him and slipped into the darkness around the shadowed corner of the house. The drinking might go on for a long time here and there. But not all night. Already the crowds about the various fires and empty barrels were beginning to break up. Nor was it likely that any hounds would bother him. He hated watchdogs like hell, all curs. Fleas were the only thing he and they had in common. But the dogs had met a mighty defeat tonight. They had literally devoured one another. He stopped to laugh silently at the remembrance. A cloud drifted across the moon slowly.

He'd wait awhile. It was cold outside in the corner of the big chimney under the loom of the wall. But cold quieted fleas. Even the lice in his hair might stop crawling. Yes, he would wait. No one but Croghan's men knew he was at Patton's, and they were going west tonight.

Well, he would not be with them.

5. A Pair of Moccasins and a Bowl of Duck Soup

THE LOCK CLICKED behind Salathiel, and he looked eagerly about him. The ceiling was high, and it was a big, long room. The red firelight winked through shadowy yellow candle-shine, itself suffused through a veritable fog of tobacco smoke, in which the candles shone here and there like fixed stars. To his right, and at the far end, a frame of double-tiered bunks filled with fresh straw ran clear across the chamber. Here was evidently the main sleeping accommodation for ordinary travellers. On them several young Highland officers had already spread their plaids and cloaks and lay sprawled out amid a dim blur of colour, dozing, or playing cards sleepily in the folds of their blankets; observing, hoping fervently that the rest of the company would soon retire.

Over in a corner a couple of Highland sergeants, with a platter of smoking venison collops on the side, were playing draughts and making moves between bites. "I'm in your king row, MacPhearson. Mon, dinna ye see? Croon me, croon me!" Sergeant MacPhearson swallowed a hunk of venison thoughtfully, and reluctantly complied.

Two bored young ensigns wrapped themselves in their tartans and crawled back into the recesses of the straw bunk. They lay down as far away as possible from a red-faced Highlander with a bagpipe tucked under his head. From time to time he emitted short squeaking snores, plaintive wheezes that might have come from his pillowed instrument, whose pipes rose out of the straw behind him and seemed to look down reproachfully into his face. All that end of the room was now a sombre blaze of colour with the plaids of the huddled sleepers smouldering in the firelight, their claymores and glittering harness hanging from pegs on the wall.

"A verra wild and warlike scene," Whuzz-Bang Wully Grant suddenly remarked in a loud voice to Yates, who with a calculating squint was leaning back in a chair near-by, watching him throw dice. Mr. Yates nodded.

"Like a huntin' lodge in the Heelands," suggested Lieutenant Grant.

"Precisely," said Mr. Yates, "all but for the trivial absence o' bonny Scotia herself."

"Ah, ye ken the blue lochs, then, the long shinin' firths, the bracken

he wild glens," sighed Lieutenant Grant, a boyish look of patriotic cun-
ing overcoming his habitual scowl.

"Loch Lomond's long been me ain dimpled favourite," replied Yates.

Lieutenant Grant pondered this as a possible basis for fellow feeling,
or some time. He was a man who always thought everything over care-
ully, and was usually wrong. "Hoo would ye like to pursue some sma'
ame wi' a fellow Scot to pass the nicht awa in this brutal wilderness?"
e asked tentatively. "Just twa homesick Heeland bairns oot togither wi'
handfu' o' siller for a peep at Fortune's twinklin' behind."

Mr. Yates pondered this alluring prospect, too. "After supper, sir," he
aid finally.

Wully Grant gave a deep disappointed grunt. He was not going to let
ass what he felt to be an unexpected opportunity for recouping himself
or the disappointments of the evening. "I'll cast wi' ye for the supper,"
e cried impulsively, rattling the dice box in his red fist as a challenge.

"Done!" shouted Yates, evidently quite unexpectedly to Lieutenant
Grant, and so saying, he shifted deftly into a chair opposite that gentle-
1an at the same table. "The best out of three wins, and I'm damned
ungry," he added.

Grant passed him the dice cup, wetting his large lips anxiously with
he tip of his tongue.

Salathiel, standing in the shadow by the door, grinned. He had seen
eople cast dice with Yates before. The tipple in the wagon had warmed
im and he was in a glowing mood, capable of enjoying the incidental
ramas in the room before him quite thoroughly. But even more ar-
esting was the domestic end of the establishment, where much cooking
vas going on and the Patton family and their favoured guests were
athered about the hearth. For several reasons the scene at that end of
he apartment seemed memorable.

The chimney was huge and the fireplace recessed into a cavernous
ngle-nook, where an old Negro woman in a flaring white turban and
littering eyes sat in the flame-wavering shadows like the Spirit of Dark-
ess herself. She held a lithe hickory switch poised in one hand. A
attery of spoons, ladles, forks, knives and skewers were disposed on an
ron rack before her. Pots on spiders, pots hung on adjustable hooks and
hains, kettles on swinging cranes, hooded roasting pans, gridirons,
inged baking moulds, and two spits driven by springs and weights,
ompleted the equipment of her culinary arsenal.

Pewter plates were stacked high on warming racks, and three sweating
lack youngsters tended the main blaze and the many little fires of
eaped coals underneath the pots and simmering dishes, where a hand
ellows was frequently applied. Their faces shone with sweat, soot, and
pprehension.

The crackle of the flames and of hot fat, the sibilant directions of the
ld woman, the hiss of frying, and the frequent swish of her switch all

blent into a kind of melodic whisper. That, together with the sighing of the chimney, the creak of the turning spits, and the hum of steam kettle provided an undertone and continuous accompaniment for the illumi nated drama in the smoky cavern, where the old black witch presided and her dark sprites tended the fires.

As for the rest, some fanciful comparison with the interior of a small theatre was inevitably suggested to all but the rude or stupid by the accidental design of the room itself. For the whole spacious hearth-space and the recess of the ingle-nook were panelled and framed-in by the oval sweep of a proscenium-like arch, the main feature of an ample wooden mantel intricately carved with acanthus leaves and supported by classic pilasters. This magnificent mantel was indeed the masterpiece of William Patton himself. On many a long winter evening he had worked over cherished pieces of seasoned wood, and from the best design book he could obtain from the City. In five years he had achieved the mantel and panelled-in half the room. And it was in this finished part of the room, garnished with some of Mrs. Patton's cherished Philadelphia fur niture, that the family now lived and the more genteel guests were entertained.

Over the high mantelshelf, and flanked on either side by shield-shaped silver sconces, hung an oil portrait of a florid-faced worthy in a periwig and the blue naval uniform of a captain in his late Majesty's service. In the painted prospect behind him was a ship careened on a tropical beach where brown natives under palm trees danced about a black cauldron. It was a good portrait of a powerful man, Richard Norris, Mrs. Patton's grandfather, who had been among the first English mariners to winter at Tinian with the hospitable Spaniards.

Quite accidentally and for practical purposes alone, but as though es pecially designed to lend depth to the foreground under the captain's ample red nose, two all but semicircular, high-backed oak settles ex tended ten feet out from the wall on each side of the broad chimney enclosing within their firm embrace a large oval space and a small round table. On this, set off by a snowy linen cloth, were displayed with obvi ous pride a pair of really impressive candelabra and Mrs. Patton's envi able silver tea service.

Here, with a bit of worn but spotless French carpet, and the chaste disposal of a few pieces of fine furniture, silver, and her even more precious china—by dint of feminine art-magic, Mrs. Patton had achieved to an astonishing degree an effect of comfortable elegance, good taste and settled ease in the midst of crude disorder.

It was this particular part of the room at which Salathiel was now gazing. This was the kind of thing he had come far out of the forest for to see. Beside it, his physical hunger for a more material supper was temporarily stilled. If there was still something of avid curiosity and of savage wonder in his examination of a scene, it now served only to lend

e bright magic of eternal novelty to his view. Everything seemed new
him, pristine as the candlelight reflected from the silver.

But there was no longer any fear, none of the awe of wary ignorance
his examination of his surroundings. It was not like that day when as
boy he had first peeked out over the cliff on the Monongahela and
oked down at Fort Pitt—a lifetime ago! He was no longer embarrassed
confused. Just a bit shy, conscious of the more than six feet of himself.

This evening, for instance, he still stood by the door doubtful of just
xactly how to introduce himself into the magic circle, where Melissa
as obviously already so much at home. A happy omen, he hoped, of
ings to come. Momentarily he was content merely to savour the at-
osphere, leaning back against the door. Something would happen;
meone would see him. Meanwhile, it was by far the most civilized bit
f human landscape he had ever glimpsed. The colour and the smell of
was grateful to his eyes and nostrils. He watched, and breathed it in,
ontent for the instant.

Behind the high backs of the settles the squaws passed to and fro,
arrying the food and drink to the tables at the far end of the room.
hey appeared and disappeared through the shadows on silent mocca-
ns, with only a faint shuffle. At one end of the left-hand settle Mr.
atton and Arthur St. Clair were having a glass and a hearty man's con-
ersation. Mr. Patton was slapping St. Clair's silver buckled knee in a
ery ecstasy of appreciation of a joke so subtle and so arrestingly humor-
us that they had both stopped drinking a moment just to laugh.

Suddenly Salathiel saw Arthur St. Clair in an entirely new light, that
f a good fellow out to enjoy the fruits of prosperity in ease and affability
-but always in a comely way. It seemed strange now that he had not
hought of St. Clair that way before. What if he was a bit pompous at
mes! How natural and happy, with what kindly blue eyes and fresh
oyish cheeks, he sat there tonight. And undoubtedly Mr. Patton knew
ow to tell a sly story.

Directly across the circle on the opposite settle two results of that
idiculous act—about some aspect of which Messrs. Patton and St. Clair
vere no doubt laughing—two babies only three or four years old slept
vith their arms about each other and a half-strangled puppy, ravished,
ut almost crushed by so much unconscious affection. Beautiful as young
ngels in a church window by moonlight when asleep, these two young
ons of Mr. Patton were little Saxon devils when awake. As yet neither
ime nor America had left any visible imprint upon them, although they
vere of the third generation born away from "home". They were still
tavistically blond, sweetly merciless, and English as hell.

Albine looked at them, and thought of himself. Had he once been
vhite and gold like that?

Sweat broke out on his forehead.

In the dark forest of dreams where his first memories began, and were

lost, he saw his mother's face leaning over him against the green light o
leaves; heard the soft tones of her Irish voice, talking to him, sayin
something vastly important . . .

He strained, listening inwardly. And then came the wait, the fierc
tension of fear, waiting, waiting for her to scream . . . not tonight . .
thank God!

Only he knew how the sight of sleeping children moved him, an
why. He remembered the dead child with yellow hair he had burie
near the burnt cabin nigh to Fort Pitt. Shades of himself and Captai
Jack! And the red baby playing with the bright beads in the sunligh
Ah—ha, young snake! His hand closed around the small neck . .
clutched . . . the smooth handle of his tomahawk . . . and brough
him back to himself in time to stifle the war-whoop rising in his throa
He seemed to be tumbled back into the room again, sweating.

By God, when he had his own house there would be no damne
Injuns sitting by his hearth!

Like the old chief there, for instance, the survivor of the recent bom
bardment and the hero of the barrel, who was now sitting precisely mic
way between the two settles with his back to the fire, wrapped in
frayed red blanket and frousting himself. A turkey feather hung dow
out of his hair into one eye. A jest? But there was no sign of life in th
furrowed and wrinkled bronze countenance behind it.

The chief heard and saw nothing. On the wings of firewater an
tobacco he had been transported back to the Great Smoky Mountains o
his fawnlike youth. Now and then out of the folds of his blanket on
hand crept tremblingly to his nose-haunted mouth. His writhing lip
sucked at a stub of a stone pipe, and throwing back his head until hi
eyes showed like two china moons, he slowly emitted a cloud of incense
The smoke curled easily about his head and then, descending fron
heaven in a back draught, eddied along the floor.

It drifted slowly towards the hearth.

At the same time the bristles on the neck of the largest dog Salathie
had ever seen would rise, and his black lips quiver, exposing a glimps
of white fangs as the big tawny English mastiff snarled silently at hi
unconscious tormentor, with whom, stretched out and relaxed in ever
fibre, he was reluctantly sharing fleas and the grateful warmth of the fire

Evidently he was an innkeeper's dog, for he alone had noticed whe
Salathiel had come in and was still aware of the stranger standing by th
door, but yet did nothing more than look at him warily from time t
time, his head between his paws. He watched.

The boys slept. Melissa and Mrs. Patton talked, fast, intimately. Any
body could see that already they liked each other; were deep in gossip-
much at home. Salathiel was delighted, but also somewhat astonished a
what he now discovered and overheard going on.

It was Frances Melissa, of course.

Melissa sat at the extreme near end of the right settle, Mrs. Patton in winged chair only half facing her. A low table with the remains of their recent supper and some untouched covered dishes had been pushed aside so that Mrs. Patton could draw up close. But that was only incidental to something else.

Seated in Melissa's lap was a small brown-eyed girl in a long woollen nightgown. She might have been anywhere from five to seven. Already she was "old", a mite of a woman. Her glossy brown pigtails fell gravely to her shoulders. There were traces of recent tears on her face, but she now leaned back against Melissa, pressing her head ecstatically against her bodice, and now and then bringing up her feet to gaze rapturously at a pair of pretty moccasins decidedly too large for her—moccasins which Salathiel recognized he had once made for Melissa at Cumberland. But there was no doubt to whom they belonged now.

In the candle and firelight the matronly Mrs. Patton in her white cap, Melissa calm now but still starry-eyed, both of them sat there basking in tide of warm comfort that seemed to flow from the little woman in Melissa's lap. Well!—Lord, he hoped it *was* prophetic! He had a sudden revelation: What women wanted was children! The moccasins twinkled again, and the little white legs gleamed.

"Laws-a-mercy," Mrs. Patton was saying, "you've won her body and soul with your nice pat gift. Says I to Mr. Patton when he come borrowin' those red slippers—'You don't know what you're doin', Wee-um!' And he didn't. 'Those mules are a gift from that nice Lieutenant Francis of the Sixtieth, him that brought the child in naked from the wilderness.' And then I showed him the letter that Mr. Francis writ Bridget from Philadelphia. The script of a scholar and a gentleman. Bridget, my love,' was the very words he writ, 'here's a pair o' red mules for milady's wardrobe, a little large, but you can skip in them until you grow up. And Mrs. Burd is sending you on some other nicknannies, drawers, and pettycoats, and a bib and tucker from Lancaster.' Now, wasn't that downright nice! Mrs. Colonel Burd's my own cousin, you know, she's a Shippen . . ." Mrs. Patton's voice made genuflection.

" 'Deed, I don't know how we'd ever have clothed the child if it hadn't been for Cousin Sarah and Lieutenant Francis. But don't think that stopped Mr. Patton and Wully Grant from borrowin' the shoes, and havin' their Guy Fawkes night chivaree, and nearly blowing up our stockade. Serves 'em right," said Mrs. Patton, jabbing her thumb in the direction of Lieutenant Grant's table. "He's daft over rockets and such fizzy truck, tetched, you might say. Politics it was, 'tryin' to rally the loyal sentiment,' they called it. *Ha-haw.* Men do beat all. It's cost Wee-um a pretty penny tonight. *He's* well burnt, I'll be bound."

"They burned my red shoes," cried the little girl, sitting up straight, her eyes brimming with tears.

"*Sh-sh*, mavourneen," said Frances, "now nivver ye mind that no more.

You've got new mules for your paddies, and Mr. Albine will be afte
making ye another pair that will fit your little fate, before he takes ye o
to your gran'ma."

The child still lingered on the verge of tears.

"Bridget," said Mrs. Patton, "you'll soon be ridin' to Carlisle like
lady in the great wagon with the fine grey horsies. And you'll be seein
your own grandma there. Now, what do you think o' that?"

"I'd rather stay with you," replied the child doubtfully, and hid he
face in sudden embarrassment against Melissa's shoulder.

"Sure, I'll be the one to take you along, nivver fear," replied Melissa
slipping her arm about her.

"My, but it's the soul of kindness of you," continued Mrs. Patton
"I've been that put to it to look after her. Not that she ain't the mos
helpful young creature alive, and a domestic little soul, but there's beer
no one I could trust her to on the road with so many wild and half
naked captives goin' downcountry to Carlisle. If her grandma hadn'
writ in and all, I'd keep her. Seems McCandliss was her pa's name
Virginians. All took by the Injuns. All of 'em . . ."

At this juncture Mrs. Patton was interrupted by the harsh voice o
Whuzz-Bang Wully, who began ordering supper for two in broades
Scotch. He wanted it served hot, lots of it, and instanter. There was
note of tipsy triumph and unnecessary urgency in his manner.

The impossible, it seemed, had happened. Yates had lost, and Lieuten
ant Grant was now insistent upon a glorious supper to celebrate hi
Scotch victory, a meal that should do both himself and his vanquished
countryman full justice. Mr. Yates was also buying the wine. No one in
the room was allowed to miss the point. Grant barked out his orders
Everybody stopped talking to look at him, and Mrs. Patton finally aros
indignantly to direct the flustered servants.

It was in that way that she first saw Salathiel standing by the door
Realizing that he must have been left there unnoticed for some time
her patience broke.

"I swan, Mr. Patton," she cried, "what's come over you? Here you b
gossiping and your guest leaning up against yon door until belike it wil
fall in with him." She approached her husband closer and said some
thing in a low tone that made his face burn.

Whatever it was, Mr. Patton made sudden excuses to St. Clair, and
betook himself rapidly to subdue the now vociferous gloating of Lieu
tenant Grant. Between him and Yates the redheaded Scot eventuall
subsided, and supper was decently served. A faint "Thank God" in
sepulchral tone coming from the straw bunk at the other end of the roon
caused Lieutenant Grant to stride in that direction viciously, and t
survey the row of his subalterns indignantly.

"Leave him to me, Patton," whispered Yates, while Wully stood with
his back turned. "Bring me your card-box directly after supper. I'll giv

you the nod when. And tell Arthur and Sal to be ready to join me in a brisk hand."

"Good," said Mr. Patton. "I'll tell 'em! And I might say I have one kag of powerful old peach brandy on hand. I'll contribute some of it. But watch it yourself," he warned, and winked.

"I'll watch it," grinned Yates.

Lieutenant Grant returned, having received no reply to his threats but snores and other unmilitary noises.

Meanwhile, Mrs. Patton had, with much clucking and tut-tutting, led Salathiel by the arm into the "family circle" and insisted upon seating him nowhere else but in her own wing chair. Nothing would do but he must sit in the place of honour and have his supper out of the covered dishes which she had been saving for him.

"What in the world delayed ye so long?" demanded Melissa.

"Oh, the wagon. And I was lookin' over the room," he answered sheepishly. "I hear I'm to make a small pair of new moccasins."

"Ah, so ye heard that," replied Melissa, tossing her head. "But will ye?"

The child also was regarding him gravely with her level eyes.

"It's a promise, isn't it? It's what *you* want?"

"It is," she said, and smiled tenderly at him. "Bridget, me love, say your manners to this gentleman, he's my—me man!"

With great dignity and complete self-possession the little girl climbed down out of Melissa's lap, placed her feet carefully in the right rehearsed position, took hold of her long flannel nightgown, and made him a deep curtsy.

"I hope ye find yourself in prime health, sir," she said, smiled, and swept a pigtail out of her eye.

Mr. Albine arose and bowed as Captain Ecuyer had once taught him, straight from the waist. He felt he could do no less.

"It's my great good fortune to be meetin' you, Miss Bridget Mc-Candliss," he said gravely, and took her small hand in his own. For a moment they looked at each other man to woman, steadily.

Then Bridget retreated with sudden embarrassment into Melissa's lap.

"He knowed my name!" she whispered.

"Sometimes he's highly intilligent, me love," said Melissa. The child nodded, still looking at Salathiel.

Mrs. Patton put her hand to her mouth, but was nevertheless seriously delighted at the proceedings.

At that moment Arthur St. Clair, who felt left out, came over to sit beside them. He was followed by the big mastiff, which lay down a few paces from Salathiel and regarded him doubtfully.

"Bran," said St. Clair, "this is the renowned Mr. Albine."

Bran growled.

Salathiel selected a bit of broken meat from one of the used supper plates and offered it carefully to the big dog. It was hard for him to realize that Bran was a member of the family and not a wild animal. He was big as a wolf.

The dog accepted the offering thoughtfully. Presently he swallowed it and wagged his tail. Everyone laughed, especially the child.

"Now that you've all met one another," said Mrs. Patton, "I hope you'll let Captain Albine have his supper. It's high time. He must be starved." Mrs. Patton conferred a military title as easily as she whisked the lid off the waiting platter. A mound of turkey, ham, roasted chestnuts, and yams still steamed fragrantly with a tang of sage. Mrs. Patton began to draw tea.

"Thank ye, ma'am. I *am* a bit hungry," admitted Salathiel.

The taste was new. This was high Pennsylvania cookery, he understood from the first bite. He minded his manners and used his knife carefully, but the mound on the platter disappeared like a haystack in a spring flood. St. Clair looked on with considerable amusement and not a little envy; Melissa, with some apprehension.

"Sukey," cried Mrs. Patton to a sloe-eyed squaw who came shuffling out of the shadows, "bring 'em heap soup."

"Well, my boy," remarked St. Clair—"*Captain*, I should say now, I suppose—I opine you must know you are almost over the mountains now. The Shawnees don't cook like that down the Ohio. In the City, Mrs. Patton's family sets a famous table."

"The Shippens," murmured Mrs. Patton, closing her eyes.

At this juncture Mr. Patton came and sat down, having left Lieutenant Grant and Mr. Yates in the midst of hired plenty.

"I was just saying you were a wise and lucky man to marry into a family of famous cooks, Patton," continued St. Clair.

"Now, I admire to hear ye, Mr. St. Clair," cried Mrs. Patton. "It's comfortin' now and then to be rightly esteemed." She glanced at her husband meaningfully. "Wee-um, I fum! I hope you won't ask me to put up with the vagaries of your bosom friend, Lieutenant Grant, any longer. I wish he and his hungry Scots would clear out and stay over at Fort Loudon. It's doin' our reputation no good in this neighbourhood to have them here. Some people will be wonderin' whether you're a Whig like your pa, or not."

"Wife," replied Mr. Patton, "you know right well Wully Grant's no bosom friend o' mine. I admit I was o'erpersuaded by Squire MacDowell and the commissioners to see that Croghan's Irish got through to Fort Pitt with the government trade goods. But you know there's been lawless doings in these parts lately with the Black Boys, a great stir amongst restless and feckless newcomers and burnt-out settlers. 'Twas Mac-Dowell's idea that by fetching a detachment of Highlanders here from Loudon we could give protection to Croghan's men this far, and then let em sneak off to Pittsburgh themselves. They have the whole season's supply o' treaty trade goods for the western frontier. It's no mere matter of merchandise. Croghan, you know, is the king's deputy agent to the far western tribes under Sir William Johnson. Well, what could I do but agree? They count me a loyal man, and the province has a legal claim to use this fort for havin' helped to build it. You know that."

Mrs. Patton sniffed. "That's no reason Wully Grant should be bellowin' at me like a bull o' Bashan in me own house, and you standin' by," she said. "He's a zany. And the fireworks—they blew up!"

"Aye," said Patton, "I *know* that! But it was his idea to improve on the occasion and rally the loyal Protestant sentiment of the countryside, being it was Guy Fawkes Day. And there was some sense to that. We figured by the time the liquor died out, Croghan's Irish could be quietly on their way without anybody bein' the wiser, or only maybe feelin' a little foolish the next mornin'. If it hadn't been for the damned fireworks!"

St. Clair laughed. "It's not the first time Wully Grant has burned his fingers with goonpowder," he said. "I could tell ye a tale of a fancy affair in Scotland soon after he came back from Inja. Him and the English Congreves and the Galts. 'Twas at 'Flowerbanks' on Creewater one night it happened. Rockets rocked and rocketed. But Wully's verra sensiteeve aboot it a'."

"No doubt he is—sensitive about himself, but no one else," cried Mrs. Patton. "That's the way with men like him. Now, I swan! What's happened to that lazy Sukey and poor Captain Albine's soup?"

She stepped briskly over to the hearth to hurry matters along.

"Listen," said Patton, leaning forward and speaking in a low tone, "the Irish will be leavin' in the early hours o' the morn. Tomorrow, please God, they'll be gone! Now I want to get Grant and his garrison men off the place, too, and safe back to Loudon. I don't want any more trouble here. There's enough hard feelin' in the countryside as it is, and I'm an innkeeper and no backwoods politician. Now, Ned Yates is goin' to take Wully on at cards tonight, and he wants you two to sit in on the game and take a hand. You know Yates can riffle the pasteboards cleverly. If Grant loses, he won't be able to pay, and he won't tarry long with us creditors."

"*If* he loses," laughed St. Clair. Salathiel grinned, too.

"I'll supply the brandy," said Patton. "Watch it though. It's powerful big medicine laid up in 'fifty-two by my pa. Are you as one on this?"

Both of them nodded happily.

"Good," said Patton, "good! We don't go in much for play in this house, but this will be a righteous exception. Only *after* the neighbours have gone, you know. Private!" Just then he happened to catch Yates's eye and winked, letting him know that all was arranged.

The growing intensity of an appetizing odour at this point caused
Bran to sit up and wag his tail hopefully again. Sukey arrived with a
large crock-tureen full of steaming black soup. "And hoe cakes are
comin'," said Mrs. Patton.

"Madam," said St. Clair, sniffing, "if that's the same delectable duck
soup I had a short while ago, I beg to be allowed to jine Mr. Albine in
another bowl—and to drink the health of the company. For it's nectar—
or is it ambrosia? Both! It's food and drink alike."

Mrs. Patton naturally enough flushed with girlish pleasure under her
matron's cap at so high-flown but earnest a compliment. She began to
ladle out the thick black soup to both Albine and St. Clair with the
ceremony it seemed suddenly to deserve. She tested it daintily with her
little finger and gave a nod. "Not scalding," she said.

St. Clair raised his bowl and looked at the two ladies across its rim.
"May the well-disarved plenty of this household be presarved, Madam
Patton"—he paused—"and continued into your own, Mistress Albine.'

To that both he and Salathiel drank.

The soup was so good that not even praise could spoil it. The tang of
an aromatic spicy odour married to a substantial rich meaty taste filled
Salathiel's throat and nostrils with a promise of belly satisfaction, one
which he found was instantly fulfilled. He drank the whole bowl and
saw that everybody was looking at him. Before he could have any more
he realized that he must say something. He winked at Mr. Patton.

"Melissa," said he, "it's this kind of soup that will keep a man from
ever wantin' to leave his bride."

"Belike in our house the trouble might lie the other way," she flashed
back at him. And they all laughed happily together.

"Good soup," said Mr. Patton, and patted his wife's hand, "good soup
Matilda, and for nigh twenty years past."

"Two and twenty," insisted his wife.

"My God, how *do* you make it, Mrs. Patton?" demanded Frances
Melissa, her eyes twinkling as she looked down into the face of the
child now asleep on her lap. "I'm after thinkin' I'd best have the
receipt of such a love potion to carry home with me, wheriver that's goin
to be."

Mrs. Patton, being practical, told Melissa—in detail . . .

"My goodness, whativer's the matter with that child?" she interrupted
herself.

"She's havin' a bad dream, a real bad one," said Melissa. "Wake up
me love, wake up, Bridget."

The child, who had been twisting and whimpering on her lap, sud
denly opened her eyes wide with terror and shivered. She looked at the
old Indian sitting by the fire. And, then, before Melissa could stop her
she dashed over to Salathiel and clung to him.

He lifted her up and held her close. "He'll not hurt you," he said

I'll never let him." Her arms went about his neck, and he felt her small heart beating violently against his own.

"Will you always stay close?" she whispered. "I'm afeared. You know what of. Please! Promise!"

"Always," he replied, "always."

He got up, and going over to the old Indian, took him by the shoulders and started him for the door. "Out," said he.

"Do you suppose she remembers . . ." began St. Clair.

"*Sh!*" said Mrs. Patton. "Now it's high time every one of these sleepy children was in bed. Sam! Rodney!" she cried, and went over to shake up the two boys.

"Yes, ma, yes, ma." They unwound themselves from each other and the puppy, yawning, while the pup barked. Bran growled.

"And you, too, you little tail-waggin' varmint," cried Mrs. Patton. "To bed with ye, off to bed with you all! Rodney, don't let that pup piddle the sheets. I'm tired changin' your trundle bed."

"No, ma," said Rodney, "but it ain't me."

"I think I'll retire myself," said Melissa, holding out her hand to Bridget, "if the gintlemen will koindly permit. And I hope you'll not mind sleepin' alone in the wagon for once, Mr. Albine. I'm to have a fine dape fither bed all to myself, says Mrs. Patton, and I find 'tis a superior timptation this evening."

"Aye, it's best so tonight," agreed Salathiel, "but I'll miss ye . . ."

"*Coo—coo,*" said St. Clair.

Melissa flashed them a brief bow. Bridget copied her, but with formal curtsy, as though her nightgown had a court train. She smiled at them through eyes still troubled with sleep and her bad dream.

The men and the mastiff watched the pageant of the women, the three sleepy children, and the scampering puppy disappear through the door in the corner. The soft swish of skirts and the patter of feet died away up the stairs. Bran put his head back on his paws.

"It's a funny thing," said Mr. Patton, as the pad-pad of small feet passed briefly overhead and then died away, "but *that* sound always seems to come runnin' out of the past and to be gallopin' away somewhere into the future. A house without it—well, you just keep listenin'."

" 'Faerie horses,' " remarked St. Clair, "was what mither called it back hame. I jealoos the old house at Thurso *is* pretty silent now." His expression grew thoughtful and remote with the far-off eyes of an exile. "*Hum-m,*" said he.

The good nights of Mrs. Patton and the children seemed also to be an understood signal of departure for the neighbours and friends of the family who had earlier been invited into the room. Squire MacDowell and his argumentative cronies adjourned their debate on the powers of Parliament, thanked Mr. Patton warmly, shook hands with his guests, and stamped out.

A general exodus of everybody who was not lodging in the house followed.

The two Highland sergeants left their draught pieces on the table and crawled into the straw next to the snoring piper.

As the door had opened from time to time to permit exits, Salathiel noticed that the yard outside had quieted down. The bonfires were burning low. Only a few figures still sat about them. The dark bulk of the Highland sentry could be seen silhouetted against the canvas of the wagon which glowed faintly from the pallid lanthorn light within. The moon rode high.

Probably Alexander was asleep, thought Albine. But he was *there*—and comfortable enough, no doubt. Well, let him wait. Afterwhile, when he was ready to go to bed himself, he would give him sixpence for his trouble—no, a shilling! Just for old sake's sake. One of the garrison at Ligonier and a veteran of Bouquet's expedition deserved a kindness. Probably it had been a mistake not to give that Welsh beggar a penny or two. He wondered if he had gone. Or was that hand still hanging in the air out there in the moonlight? No. He remembered now. When the door had opened the porch was empty and bright clear over to the steps. Pshaw! What of it? Tobacco was all right. Unconsciously, he began to rummage in his pouch in order to fill his pipe. He rose to get a coal from the fire—and found that Patton and Arthur St. Clair were filling their pipes, too.

"The weed goes well on a full belly in front of a fire at night," said Patton in low tones, as they lit up, passing the coal on small tongs amongst them. St. Clair relaxed, stretched out his sleek legs, crossed one fine boot over the other, and blew a cloud of fragrant smoke into the air contentedly.

Suddenly the big room seemed quite empty and silent. Even the servants had vanished. Only Yates and Lieutenant Grant still lingered happily over their wine. There were a couple of empty bellarmines before Wully and he was peeling the wax and wire off the neck of a third. Yates was talking in a confidential tone, but in the quiet room it was impossible not to follow what he was saying. An occasional snort or sigh from the sleepers at the far end of the apartment punctuated rather than interrupted his remarks. They sat listening contentedly. The three pipes glowed.

6. Conversation

YATES WAS TALKING about the difficulties of running the new southern boundary of the province of Pennsylvania:

". . . Jerry Dixon's thought to be better with his instruments than

Charley Mason, but they're both careful men, and if we don't get any-thing else, we'll get a true line east and west between the quarrels of the Penns and the Calverts. But the rub is that nobody knows just how far west to go before establishing a cornerstone to turn north. Probably, they'll compromise that—eventually."

"Thought they'd run the line clean west to Redstone or the Ohio," said Grant.

"The Ohio runs north from Pittsburgh, then west for a bit, and then south," grinned Yates. "They might have to go right on into the sunset. That would seriously annoy our friends, the Virginians, and cross their western claims. And then there are all of the Indian treaty tracts, the Iroquois presarves, and a' that. And did you ever read the strict words of the Penn grant? According to the amiable King Charles, the western boundary of Penn's province is supposed to wag its happy tail through the woods somewhere in the west, exactly as the Delaware River does on the east, curve for curve. Now, staking out that wriggle really would be a notable mathematical task. No, the best thing this present line will do is to settle the age-old quarrels between the Penns and the Baltimores. But soon there'll be new quarrels with Virginia about the western lands south and west of Pittsburgh." Yates laughed.

"You know," said he, putting his hands behind his head and leaning back confidentially, "now that the monsieurs have gone, this whole con-tinent would soon be hatching a snake's nest of petty wars between the colonies were it not for the home government, the regulars on the fron-tiers, and the king's ships."

"Noo, there ye spoke wi' a' the lair o' Solomon!" exclaimed Wully. "Take this verra mountain-i-ous neighbourhood, what's it but a mare's nest o' dawky Scotch independents and ramstam Irish snotters, dimo-cratic rascals that would play neevie-neevie-nicknack wi' the pearls i' God's croon. They make the life o' a royal officer tryin' to do his loyal juty a verra torment and crucifixion o' daft insults and petty mischiefs. Sometimes I do think it's more than I can abide."

"*Montani semper liberi,* you know," smiled Yates, "but I wouldn't suggest you'd get too much out of it for your trouble, Wully."

Lieutenant Grant snorted. His red hair seemed to rise and bristle. "A wee pittance, the pay of a puir subaltern, wi' the prospect o' Edinburgh garret lodgin's i' the Grassmarket on Scotch half pay for me old age. And the Grants are no well-heeled like the Hamiltons, I can tell you thot, Ed-ward *Hamilton* Yates. Most of them at hame are rejuced to mere bonnet lairds. It's lang syne a retired gentleman o' our ilk could live wi' honour in a tumbledoon castle on a loch in the west Heelands wi' a piper and a few gillies, on oats porridge and cold haggis. Mar's Year and the 'Forty-five put an end to a' thot. Puir auld Scotland!" sighed Wully, and tossed off a glass from the new bottle.

"I should think ye'd do much better to stay over here and seat your self on a new plantation, half pay and all," replied Yates.

"Aweel," sighed Wully, "noo thot's preceesely what I *do* plan for to do. Wi' the help of Cousin Jeemes Grant I micht find masel' a snug seat i' the wilderness, and some belly comforts, too. Cousin Jeemes has been verra forward-lookin', not to say canny, in takin' up land grants here and there. Hoosh! He's a wise mon, is Jeemes."

"Cousin James?" inquired Yates, raising his brown silky eyebrows. "You mean Major James Grant that was defeated on the hill nigh Pitts burgh in Forbes's time by bangin' the drums and playin' the bagpipes too early in the mornin'?"

"Aye, the verra same!" replied Lieutenant Grant proudly. "If there hadna been a wee bit too much whusky i' the camp the morn, maybe Jeemes would have taken Fort Duquesne from the salad-eaters before puir Johnny Forbes could get himsel' carried thot far west. And what a fine feather thot would have been in the war bonnet o' the Grants! But as the deil would hae it . . ."

"Oh, I see," said Yates, leaning forward with growing interest. "And so—now that Cousin James, according to the gazettes, has got himself appointed governor of East Florida by his gracious Majesty, I suppose all the more he's still the hope and mainstay of the Grants, and of the land grants likewise, eh?"

"Noo, Yedward, you put it *verra* preceesely, poon and all," admitted Wully, glad to talk about his family at any price. "You see, Cousin Jeemes and masel' started oot from Inveravon aboot the same time. In 'forty it was. He studied law and later on was commissioned i' the Royal Scots, while I went oot to Madras in 'forty-three as a gintleman-writer, a kind o' cadet-factor, ye ken, for the Honourable John Company. Sir Jeemes St. Clair was our guid patron. But he was a far better patron for Jeemes than for me, as it turned oot.

"I wint oot on the same ship wi' young Bobby Clive, and the gales drove us to Brazil, where we spent nine mortal months. Clive picked up the lingo, and I got something else equally native, but not so usefu', which, as God would have it, was the way me ain luck always seemed to rin, even after we both got to Madras. . . .

"Aweel, things nae went well—what wi' fireworks and a'—so I took the offer o' a guid Scotch ship's captain to transpoort me back to Lunnon, jist for handlin' his bills o' ladin' and company accoonts. And I was no nabob when I landed, I can tell ye, for I had only aboot eighty poonds starlin' more than when I went oot. Thot is, I had aboot eighty poonds.

"I was thinkin' o' walkin' back to Scotland and of settlin' doon to croftin' and to scones and oats, when one day I met Cousin Jeemes at the Cocoa Tree, whar mauny of us puir Lunnon Scots used to gather o' mornin's. Jeemes was havin' a cup o' chocolate and burnt sugar wi'

Sir William Congreve. And after I told me sorry adventure at Tanjore, what did Sir William do but invite me to come back hame wi' him and experiment wi' rockets! So I did, and afterwhile between us we burnt his auld coach-hoose doon.

"Noo, I'll no go into the ins and oots of a' we did and undid. But Cousin Jeemes suggested it micht be safer to hide me i' the colonies. They both said they would see what could be done. And aboot this time auld Aunty Jane Grant o' Inveravon died, leavin' me and Jeemes to share a wee legacy between us—and the resoolt of a' this was that I found masel' wi' a commission i' Montgomery's Heelanders."

"And now?" asked Yates.

"Ye can tell me a' the rest yoursel', Edward Yates. I was lucky, I suppose, to find masel' an officer amongst auld friends in a famous Heeland regiment. Then came the French war, and we were sent to America, and a'. But I've had only one promotion and been kept here in the backwoods most o' the time. Last nicht was the verra first chance I've had to take me talent oot o' a napkin. Losh, I'm like to rust away with it here."

"You haven't lost a battle yet like Cousin Jeemes. What do ye expect?" grinned Yates.

"Noo, I wauldna poot it thot way," replied Wully. "Jeemes Grant is a mon o' real pairts, for a' thot. He made a brilliant retreat in the Carolinas from Fort Loudon there, and greatly disteenguished himsel'. And he noo has more powerfu' friends in the War Department at hame, and in Parliament, and on the Board o' Trade. Ah, he's forward-lookin', as I said before, even in a retreat."

"Doubtless he'll look after you, then, since you're of his own ilk," suggested Yates.

"He will, he will thot," said Wully. "To tell the truth, there's always been a guid understandin' between us. And then Jeemes still has me wee legacy from auld Mrs. Grant in troost. Why, I've a letter from him only the noo, came by the last express rider, writ from St. Augustine hardly a month past, and his fine proclamation aboot East Florida enclosed. Have ye yet seen it? It's a' the talk."

Yates shook his head.

After some wrestling with his own bulky person, Lieutenant Grant produced a well-sweated piece of officially printed paper, and tendered it to Mr. Yates, with a light in his eye. Yates read it slowly, holding his hand over his black patch.

Yates finally looked up and nodded. "It reads uncommon well," he said.

"Hoots!" said Wully. "You'd better conseeder comin' doon under the palms to jine me in a planters' paradise on the St. Johns. You can make your fortune in indigo alone. Five hundred pounds bounty a year is bein' offered. And there's plenty o' neegars and contraband rum to be had cheap. It's a bonny new colony their Lordships are plannin'. It, and

West Florida. I hear of a Dr. Turnbull, a rich man in Lunnon, plannin' to transport immigrants from the Mediterranean by shiploads. You might better yoursel' conseederably, Edward Hamilton Yates. You maun try it."

"I might," said Yates, "later on, I really might."

Wully seemed more than usually pleased at Yates's serious consideration of his schemes. He grew confidential.

"Noo, I'll tell ye something," he said, "but in streectest confidence. If ye'll come and settle doon on the St. Johns, I can put ye in the way of gettin' some parcels o' the best seated land cheap. De Brahm, the government surveyor, is a guid friend o' mine." He looked as mysterious as he could, and leaned forward earnestly. "You see noo that Cousin Jeemes is a royal goovernor, it would never do for *him* to be holdin' great tracts a' in his ain name. So he's turned over some o' the land to me, in troost, and had the papers transferred to my name."

"All in the family," said Yates.

"Exactly," said Wully. "But not a' in Florida. There's aboot two thousand acres in New York on a lake in the Iroquois country. Jeemes, and George Croghan, and Hardenburgh went into it togither with the goovernor of that province and some ither canny folk some years ago. Since then Croghan's been livin' up there on his ain land in a cabin, with an Indian squaw. It's at the south'r'n foot o' a lang stretch o' shinin' water the savages call Ot-see-go—or how do you lay your tongue to it? But it's magic country, Croghan says, bonny as the Lochs o' Killarney in Ireland, or a broad blue Heeland domain, but untouched. You know Sir William Johnson's a squaw man. What a canny Christian tactic it is to prevail by marryin' the enemy and lovin' them like yersel'. It maun poot them a' at conseederable disadvantage."

"Not necessarily," said Yates. "It's always difficult to keep a savage peace, you know. And then, I confess, I'm delicate about unbelting. But, Wully, could you not dispose of some of this idle land for Cousin James, now?"

"Aye, a stock o' siller would come in handy the noo for the goovernor. He has ower much land, ye micht ken. And a sma' salary wi' prodigal expenses at St. Augustine. As for me, a fistfu' o' hard money for me ain sma' claims would no be a savage insult, richt noo." Wully licked his lips thoughtfully. "I'll no mind tellin' ye, Ned, if the wee cubes had gone agin me here the nicht, I'd have had to borrow to pay for the twa suppers. Me last pay's a' but gone, and there's no news of the paymaster at Fort Loudon yet."

"I'll think it over," said Yates, "and talk to ye tomorrow. But it's the northern land I do like most."

"Palms or maples, ye can hae your choice. A few poonds doon . . ."

"What are the papers like?" asked Yates.

"Direct grants from the royal goovernors or from the croon itself. You canna do better. All in order, all registered, surveyed, and the fees paid. I'll show 'em to you when we get back to Loudon."

"Agreed," said Yates. "Maybe St. Clair will be interested, too."

Wully's face brightened. "Noo, that's well thought of, Edward. You maun go into it togither."

"So we might," said Yates, "but *tomorrow*"—and leaning back again he managed to catch Mr. Patton's watchful eye.

"Well, let's join the others over on the settles there for a glass or two and a pipe before bed. I'll be glad to offer you some of Patton's best peach brandy. Seventeen-fifty-two he says."

"Noo, I'll no argle-bargle wi' ye aboot thot," said Wully. "And it's been a braw supper we've had togither, even if you . . ."

"Pshaw," replied Yates, "you never can tell how any man's luck will run."

"No, but I'm tellin' ye I'm a verra lucky mon at a' kinds o' games o' hazard, Mr. Yates. The luck o' the Grants, ye ken." Lieutenant Grant rose proudly, if a little unsteadily, from the table. "No doobt you can see that much wi' *one* eye," he added, and gave a great open-mouthed guffaw at this delicate bit of Grantian wit.

He followed Yates over to the fireside, like a lamb.

7. Cards

WHUZZ-BANG WULLY had no idea that his little joke, over which he was still chortling as he sat down confidently on the settle beside Arthur St. Clair, was a double-edged jest that might cut himself, his heirs and assigns, forever out of about three thousand acres of some of the most fertile land in North America. Yet such was the actual potential of his devastating wit. Everyone present had in fact been electrified by it, and the ways and means of his ambush from then on seemed genially to arrange themselves. Indeed, the whole affair that evening unfolded so good-naturedly, the drift of events seemed so spontaneous, that to his dying day Lieutenant Grant was never able to conclude whether—as in the case of rockets—he had been or had not been the innocent victim of irrational chance.

For as soon as he sat down on the settle by Mr. St. Clair that courteous gentleman rose and drew up a chair more comfortable for a Grant to sit in. By this means Wully found himself facing the small round table on which Mr. Albine's supper had so recently been served. And who should remove the remains of it now but Mr. Albine himself? Scarcely were the dishes gone when Mr. Patton, that excellent host, replaced them with two decanters of peach brandy, golden with the preserved summer of 1752, and four appropriate glasses.

Mr. Albine proffered Lieutenant Grant his tobacco, and Mr. Yates filled his pipe. Mr. St. Clair lighted it. All joined him in a toast to bonny Scotland—to the king—to her Majesty, that good woman! To the ladies upstairs—to ladies downstairs—to ladies everywhere. To Governor James Grant—to Sir James St. Clair—to the whole damned Penn family, widows, children and all. Mr. Yates knew all their names. And none of them were taken in vain.

The dry searing brandy went down more like liquid light than fire; and ascended, mixed with the fumes of previously imbibed potions, to enlarge, tickle, confuse and delight the otherwise sombre brain in Mr. Grant's thick skull so covered up by red bristles, until naked Good-Nature herself came out and swam in the cold melting pools of his wintry eyes.

Mr. Yates was on his feet, starting to say something, and with a brandy glass in his hand. He waved it. Another toast—a toast to Wully Grant? How extremely gratifying!

"To the lucky Lieutenant Grant. May his fortunes mount like a rocket, burst into heavenly glory, and scatter a few stars amongst us poor dwellers on earth."

Why, what a noble sentiment, how apt, how fitting!

With a Scotch mist before his eyes Lieutenant Grant tried to rise now to reply with adequate feeling. But he was not *quite* able to do so. His Scotch became too thick for his own tongue. His knees quivered under his kilt—and all the others as one man motioned him to sit down.

Mr. Patton was opening a brass-hinged wooden box, beautifully carved. Out of it came an oblong object wrapped in blue Bristol paper. Yates opened it, and a torrent of white seemed liquidly to pour through his hands. Suddenly it arranged itself in a neat rainbow before him, laid out on the table in an arc. A brand-new set of crisp, block-printed cards.

"What shall we play, gentlemen?" asked Yates, quite deferentially.

"Bezique," suggested Lieutenant Grant. "Loo," demanded Mr. St. Clair. "Irish loo," rumbled Salathiel.

"I never play in my own house. It's a rule of the tavern," announced Mr. Patton, gravely. "But I'll be glad to keep tally." Out of the convenient little box came a neat framed slate with pegs and holes down the sides.

"Agreed," said St. Clair.

"Irish loo has it," announced Yates with finality. "What's the loo?"

"Five shillin's a round," insisted Salathiel, "—and the same stake, with the fool left out. He retards the play."

All nodded their agreement. Lieutenant Grant was much relieved. He was afraid St. Clair might have suggested guineas for the stake. He knew St. Clair carried them.

At the last minute, looking a little sheepish, Mr. Patton decided to play a hand.

Might he?

"Of course . . . of course . . ."

"Gentlemen, the cards," said Mr. Yates, as was customary.

He fed them about him in a complete circle for all to see. Somehow they were all neatly arranged perfectly by suits. He withdrew the jester.

"Let's play," cried St. Clair, impatiently. "Mr. Grant with his active commission has the first deal, and leads."

Yates shuffled and handed Wully the cards. Lieutenant Grant reshuffled, cut twice, once with those on each side of him. He dealt swiftly and with an obviously practised hand that only trembled a little, throwing five cards face down around. He deposited the stack and turned up the top for trumps. Diamonds. Being Irish loo, no "miss" was dealt.

After five rounds with several passes and forfeits, mostly on the part of Yates and Salathiel, who were looed, there was a sizable sum at stake. It finally fell to St. Clair and Grant to play for it. St. Clair drew a five-card flush, and was already smiling at having looed the board, when it appeared that Wully had four cards of the same suit and "Pam", the knave of clubs. This was high and took everything. Grant had won. His face flushed and his eyes sparkled.

A really phenomenal run of luck now came the lieutenant's way. During the next five rounds when hearts were trumps, the knave of clubs seemed never to be out of his hands. Even when Yates laid a five-card flush with ace of trumps and the king, Wully was ready with "Pam be civil," and Yates had to pass the trick without revoking. Pam in the hands of Lieutenant Grant forced everybody to loo again and again. "Pam be civil" became a kind of war-cry on his lips, out-trumping everybody. Indeed, Wully seemed to be exemplifying the words of Mr. Yates's toast literally. His fortunes rose like a rocket, and burst into a shower of glory when at the final fifth round, again between him and St. Clair, he emerged with twenty-five pounds and fifteen shillings cold. Wully was triumphant. Everyone had had his five deals, and he demanded settlement.

Arthur St. Clair was not a little chagrined. He passed out five good guineas for the company, the extra shillings in which just covered his last loo, and prepared to retire with more dignity than profit. He felt that somehow Yates had managed to deal Pam to Wully an unconscionable number of times. Mr. Yates would, of course, have been the first to deny any such sleight of hand, and Mr. St. Clair knew it. But he still felt that he had been asked to subsidize a forlorn hope and to keep quiet about it, too. Well, it was now long past midnight of an expensive evening. He pressed his lips together firmly and began to bid the company a decent but rather curt good night.

At this, although it was still much too early in the morning to announce the dawn, Wully Grant began to crow. He really looked and acted like a red male chicken, wattles and all. His luck, he felt, presaged a better day. He had five red guineas in his fist and the brandy flooded the roots of his being with the very ichor of confidence. Seeing that St. Clair was definitely out of it, Wully began to rally Yates and ended by triumphantly chanting over him like a small boy:

> "I beat you at dice, sir,
> I beat you at loo;
> I lay I can beat you
> At baccarat-two."

The rhyme had occurred accidentally, and Wully was enchanted with it.

"I'll lay thirty pounds sterling to your five and twenty you cawnt," drawled Yates, and nervously twisted the patch on his blind eye, always a sign of tension and that he meant business.

Grant hesitated a moment. Despite the brandy, his Scotch caution reasserted itself. He cocked his head like a puzzled terrier considering. But it was irritating to have the potency of his family luck still doubted and—Yates had oiled the bait skilfully. The extra odd pounds in the hazard offered finally made Wully plunge again. He handed the cards to Yates as the challenged party, contemptuously bade him be banker, and impatiently signed for him to shuffle and deal.

St. Clair sat down again to watch the play. He now thought he began to see some strategy in Mr. Yates's tactics. Mr. Patton erased the tally for loo, set up the new bets, and ruled the lines for baccarat on his slate. He solemnly announced the wager, his voice cracking with excitement. He then gave Yates two more packs of new cards, and snuffed all the candles.

Yates "milked" the three packs together and began to deal. The evening entered upon its second and final phase, a trial by battle between champions.

The play between Lieutenant Grant and Edward Yates, Esquire, began. Both were playing for much more than either of them had, and both with great but traditionally different skills.

In a little less than half an hour the game of baccarat, which afterward affected so many people's lives, was over. Fortune swung back and forth. The pattern of betting repeated itself, and the stakes rose ever higher, with Yates acting as the imperturbable banker. From Yates's standpoint, the danger was that Grant would cry quits at some moment lucky for him and walk off with the bank. Yates's strategy as banker was therefore to make the prize so tempting that his opponent would always come back for one more deal. Twice Yates doubled, and lost. To cover that, and still to keep Grant hankering for more, was a heavy risk. Yet it was a certain swagger that Yates now developed which kept egging Wully on. Between avarice and caution, Lieutenant Grant was sweating. Probably, after a certain point, it was the brandy that really kept sustaining him. Or it may have been that there was so much at stake, it was win all, or ruin. The sum on Mr. Patton's slate soon registered one hundred and thirty-six pounds.

But a prime factor in the play now became progressively important. Memory. The winning of each hand now depended more and more on recollecting exactly what cards out of the three packs in use had already been played. Yates's meticulous memory now stood him in good stead. He could have called precisely all the hands that had been played that evening. Evidently Wully also could remember. But Yates felt that as the brandy began to die out Lieutenant Grant's memory might become dimmer. Yet so might his courage to stick. There was the rub. It was necessary, therefore, to seize the exact moment for the grand temptation, the instant when Grant would have only enough courage left to play one hand more. And Yates determined to strike when he thought the instant had come.

He had a brief run of luck, and then he deliberately lost. Wully grinned and placed his hands palms down on the table, resting, and looking quizzically and triumphantly at Yates. The three onlookers were transfixed. It looked as if the evening were over. Then Yates doubled the stakes. It was a comfortable little fortune, at least from a colonial standpoint, that he now offered. Everyone knew it must be the last hand that could be played. Grant hesitated and closed his eyes. Then he slowly raised his hands off the table and took up the cards.

They played through—and Lieutenant Grant lost. Four hundred and sixty-seven pounds sterling.

Wully shot his legs out under the table and sat stricken, breathing like a bull after the first stroke of the maul.

After a moment or two Yates took the patch off his blind eye and looked at Wully, stone pupil and all. This gave more satisfaction to him than having won. There was no doubt that even Wully got the point.

"Wh-o-o-o-o," he said, his breath whistling. "I might have known better than to play wi' a Hamilton. Losh! I'm ruint! Sell my commission? 'Twon't pay ye. Those queens, the jades! All the coort was there, when what I needed was jist twa pips. Aweel—" His arms slid out on the table slowly before him, and he laid his head down amid the welter of bright new cards.

All of them looked at one another and at Yates.

It was one thing to win, but another to have reduced a strong man and a fine brutal officer to tears. No one knew exactly what to do.

At last Salathiel got up and walked over to the table. He looked down at Wully and then shook him by the shoulders. There was no response. "He's not weeping," he said, "he's sleeping!"

"By God, so he is," cried St. Clair, much relieved.

And indeed it was not sounds of grief that came from between Wully

Grant's arms but the wheezing of a man asleep with his nose pressed close against the table.

Yates got up and snapped the black patch over his eye.

"I suggest we all make our little settlements with one another to-morrow," said he, and looked significantly at Grant.

"Good night, gentlemen," said Mr. Patton in a kind of awed whisper. "It's late indeed, but 'twas an eventful evening." He smiled deprecatingly. "I don't think I'll disturb our sleeping friend here, though 'tis truly a scene of ruin where he has laid his head." Mr. Patton handed St. Clair and Yates their night-lights. "First chamber on the right after the turn on the stairs," he said. "Try not to wake the pup." He and St. Clair disappeared into the cavelike darkness of the stairs. Salathiel and Yates looked at each other and grinned.

"What happened just at the last? I couldn't quite follow it," said Salathiel.

"Too many court cards, and then Wully forgot that it's better to make eight with two cards than nine with three," replied Yates.

Salathiel yawned. Only the steady glow from the great backlog now threw a dim radiance through the room. Yates and he stood a moment by the table, listening to the subdued chorus of the sleepers in the straw bunks at the far end of the room and to the steady wheeze of the gentleman with his face on the table.

"Will you ever get anything out of him?" queried Salathiel. "You know, Yates, if *you* had lost, he would have hounded you to the grave. And for a while it was a near thing."

"Close as a hound's ear to his head," said Yates. Just then the pad-pad of a child's feet passed suddenly overhead. Instinctively, they both looked up.

"Sounds like young Bridget," said Salathiel.

"Listen," said Yates, taking his friend by the arm as they walked towards the porch door, "I'll collect something out of this. Tomorrow I'll get his note of hand in acknowledgment for the total sum, with witnesses, before he leaves. And this fellow boasted to me that he is a landed gentleman and his relatives well-heeled. We'll follow him straight through to Fort Loudon. Leave the rest to me. I'll make him dig up his land-office papers there. And we'll see what we'll see.

"How would you like to join me, Sal, in bringing in settlers to the lake country in New York, or to the new colony in Florida? I rather fancy the northern lochs. Hamilton Manor, a Highland domain! And only the wild loons to laugh at us patroons. Why not? We could make a go of it there together. You won't always want to be working for St. Clair." Yates was so earnest and eager he went clear out on the porch with Salathiel. "It's a dream of mine, you know. And in this country such dreams often come true."

"I'll be with you, if you can get the land," answered Salathiel, after a little. "Iroquois country or not, you can count on me. What's a feud but a fillip? But I *must* see Philadelphia first. I want to do that, you know—and there's Melissa now."

"There'll be plenty of time for the City," said Yates. "But if the time ever comes I'll count on your promise—no matter what."

"Count on me, then," said Salathiel—"no matter what!"

Standing on the porch in the waning moonlight, they shook hands on it. Perhaps the summer of 1752 had been even more salubrious than they thought, its distilled cordiality overwhelming. Yates's candle blew out, and he teetered a little as he turned to go in.

"Damn it," said he. "Now I'll have to grope my way up the stairs in the dark." The door, however, closed quietly behind him.

Salathiel stood for a moment on the top step looking out over the interior of the stockade quite steadily. The moon was going down. A kind of grey half-light streaked with mist lent a false distance and mysterious perspective to everything. Except for the heavy breathing of Alexander, inside the wagon, an unearthly stillness and the biting chill of high mountain country in the earliest morning hours gripped the little fort. The bonfires had gone out and their ashes lay grey and still.

Evidently Croghan's Irish had departed. For some reason they had left behind them a lighted lanthorn in their shed. He could just make out its dim smoky glow. But they and their pack horses and wagons were gone.

Well, let them! he thought. To that extent Lieutenant Grant might be allowed to be successful. In another hour it would be dark as the hinges . . . he yawned at the sinking moon . . . a man did need some sleep.

He swung himself into the wagon, wakened Alexander, and gave him a drink and a shilling. Even in the middle of the night the Highlander appreciated both.

"I'll take over now," said Salathiel, "and mind, when you go in you don't bang the door. They're all asleep in there, even Wully Grant." Alexander departed quietly after the final nip.

Except for unbuckling himself and throwing his pouch and tomahawk on the floor beside him, Salathiel did not undress. He crawled into his blankets, moccasins and all, and dropped off instantly. He was tired.

But "they" were not "all asleep in there", as he had said.

Upstairs some minutes before young Bridget had suddenly trotted into Melissa's room and wakened her by crawling into bed.

"I want ye, Melissa, I want ye," she whispered. "There's something awfu' going on downstairs in the darkness. I know there is. I just know it. I don't want to leave you alone with it."

"Now, darlint," said Melissa sleepily, while moving over to make room for the frightened child, "just lay your head down here and come to sleep. It's too late for any pillow talk." She put her arms around the small shivering body and comforted her.

"But, you know," said Bridget, "I came to take care of *you*."

The last moon shadows lengthened eastward over Patton's. The place lay locked in deep slumber. All save one poor beggar, who was still miserably awake.

8. In Which Salathiel Takes Too Clever a Hand

THERE IS AN old saying that misery loves company. But this, like so many other popular and antique versions of the laws of average human conduct, is a general statement, and there have always been special and particular exceptions to it. Actually, only *some* misery loves company. And that misery which likes most to be alone is desperate and criminal misery. In every companion of its dangerous lot it suspects a potential Judas.

Mr. David Ap Poer, *alias* Taffy, was no exception to this last sad item in the sorry anatomy of misery and loneliness. There were times when for his own particular and peculiar reasons he found it not only expedient but essential to be alone.

If fate had been kinder, Taffy in his native Wales might have been entitled to be addressed as "mister", since his father was a respectable and learnéd man who drew rents. But since Fate had been a veritable bitch to Davy, the *alias* which had been humorously conferred upon him in America was seriously earned. Not the least fitting part of it was that no one who casually addressed him as "Taffy" had any idea how genuinely appropriate his nickname was.

For "Taffy was a Welshman, Taffy was a thief"—granted. But he was not only just that. He was a skilful, an inveterate—and an ecclesiastical thief into the bargain.

David Ap Poer's specialty was robbing churches of such hansable articles of communion paraphernalia as either their rich or their royal donors had seen fit to bestow upon a prosperous and faithful congregation. This consecrated swag he invariably deposited in the grave of some departed member of the flock in the churchyard near-by. Then he himself discreetly vanished from the neighbourhood until the confused hue and cry died fitfully away. And he stayed away until the mystery became as mossy as the stone under which the subject of it lay hidden.

Afterward, in due course of time and usually on a moonless night, Taffy returned with a bag. He then exhumed the reward of his dishonest labours, took it home, melted it down; and after adding a judicious amount of leaden alloy, cast it into passable counterfeits of sundry current coins.

Thus it was, first, in the judicious choice of the initial hiding place for his cache; and secondly, in his careful patience in deferring his immediate enjoyment of the proceeds that what must be conceded as, in a bad sense, the virtues of his professional methods lay.

But connected with the estimable rose of safety that the temporary deposit of his wages with the dead undoubtedly supplied, there were certain prickly disadvantages and thorny difficulties.

For he was often hard put to it to exist in the long intervals between his thoughtful denudation of churches, to say nothing of his delay in realizing on the proceeds afterward. Only the bitterness of past harsh experience and his fond expectation of those periods of affluence and respectability which followed his final coining of opportunity provided him with the necessary will power and patience to persist in invariably following out his all but foolproof plan. Frequently it was hard and bitter going. But not so hard as prison, whips, or the gallows.

Four times since his arrival in America, some ten years before, had David, for purposes of enlarging the circulation of the currency, levied upon the church. Three times Taffy returned successfully to Philadelphia. But his fourth church robbery had in some ways been an exception, and in several of its aspects a mistake. He knew that now.

Sitting cold and forlorn, with a greasy blanket wrapped about him, in a corner behind the chimney of the north wall at Patton's, David Ap Poer had had more than enough time to consider the quirks of fortune. He muttered a little as he chewed indignantly on the last of Salathiel's bitter shag. He spat and silently cursed. Probably it had been an error to show himself at all to that tall gentleman in buckskins. No one else besides Croghan's Irish wagoners knew he was at Patton's. He had seen to that. But he had managed to reconnoitre the Albines' wagon thoroughly and quite unobserved when it had first drawn up before the door, and the prospect he saw in it was alluring. Yet he had really hoped that the tall man might give him some money and thus save him further trouble. But no, no! Only a handful of tobacco! And he was hungry already.

The Irish took an unconscionable time to get quietly on the move. With a sentry in the wagon, however, that was just as well. Above all he feared being dragged to the frontiers by those mad Irishmen. It was lucky they had to sneak off. They would never dare look for him now. And afterwhile no doubt the Scotch sentry would go to sleep. Also there would be no dogs. So he waited and shivered, peering around the corner of the chimney from time to time to see if the light still burned in the big wagon. Lord, it was getting cold!

And that fourth robbery, what a fine botch he had made of it! But it had been a great temptation. It was the old Swedes' church at Wiccaco, a hamlet that was so near Philadelphia it was really in the City now, a part of Southwark. And thus so near home that he had not thought it

necessary to go through with the usual preliminaries. He had just walked
out one day and looked the place over.

It was a fine old brick church with plenty of lonely ground about
it. The new stone parsonage was near-by, and it was there that the pastor of the flock removed his church plate every Sunday evening—and
brought it back every Saturday night to prepare for the services next
day. Among the altar furnishings were some particularly fine chalices
and a gold cruse presented by Queen Christina herself to her subjects
in the New World, years before.

These and other particulars Taffy picked up from a garrulous ancient
named Nils Gestafson, who could remember when Philadelphia was a
forest, and almost everything which had happened there since. But he
was now blind, and so Taffy talked freely with him as he sat in the sun
at the corner of his farm lane.

The result of these conversations was that late one Saturday night
Taffy left his cellar with a large pedlar's bag over his shoulder. This
time he intended to bring the loot back with him directly. There would
be nothing to connect him with the robbery, nothing at all. All he did
was to walk over to Southwark, pry open a door, and fill the bag with
the altar furniture.

And then it happened. He was almost taken.

Someone was returning to the church. He saw the lights coming up
the lane just in time.

It would never do to be found with the loot on his back. He skipped
out, pried up the flat table-stone on the grave of the relict of one Sven
Schute, dropped the bag in the walled-in space, and let the stone fall
back in place. Then he lit out. But the pastor's damned little Pomera-
nian tike took after him, and he had to brain it. He heard them shouting
"Stop thief!" behind him.

And he heard more about it next day. The news was all over the City.
They hadn't found the stuff. But he was badly scared, and it would
never do to be seen around the Swedes' church now for months yet—
maybe never. So he would just have to let the stuff lie there, a treasure
without use.

In his desperation he hired himself as a waterer to Croghan's wagoners, who were just leaving town, and set out with them for the west.
He meant to give them the slip at Carlisle and pose there as a returned
refugee, but the Irish whisky got him. He was stone drunk at Chambersburg, and when he came to, the wagon was already halfway up the
mountain and being escorted by Highlanders.

The confusion of the celebration that night at Patton's was his last
chance to nip out. Without pay, of course. That was why he had risked
begging from the tall frontiersman, and why he was now sitting so dis-
consolate at the base of the big chimney, shivering, and waiting for the
light in the wagon to go out.

In a drawer in the chest at the head of the wagon there were some loose shillings. Taffy had seen them when Frances had been primping that evening just before she went into the house. She had opened the drawer to take out her comb and only partly closed it. He remembered that distinctly. He knew exactly where the money lay. Not much, only a handful, but in this God-forsaken spot it was his last, his only chance for any coin.

So he waited.

He was still waiting when Yates and Salathiel came out on the porch together. He watched Salathiel get into the wagon and saw Alexander leave. Then he waited for Salathiel to blow out the light. But there he was disappointed again, for the light was only dimmed. After a while, though, he was sure the tall man inside the wagon must be asleep.

He moved out from the loom of the chimney slowly, painfully, but soundlessly on his rag-wrapped feet.

It had been a long and active day, a momentous evening, and a night filled with anxiety and excitement. Even the iron frame of Salathiel had succumbed to the demands of nature. The big man in the wagon, where the small whale-oil night-lamp burned dimly, slept profoundly, undisturbed by its feeble rays.

Exactly what awakened him he never knew. He had had no dreams. But suddenly—it seemed to him instantly—he was wide awake, every muscle tense, and a quivering sense of threatening danger and of someone hostile near-by an unarguable conviction in his mind. With it came the instinct to keep still. He opened his eyes only slightly. He was lying on his stomach with his head pillowed on his left arm, on the left side of the wagon.

Nothing inside the wagon had been disturbed. He could see from one end of it to the other. The hind flaps were tightly closed just as he had left them. The canvas sides were intact. His belt, tomahawk, pouch, and leather harness lay beside him on the floor, where he had thrown them. His watch ticked under the blanket. The small dim light before the mirror at the head of the wagon cast a curious fan of gold rays on the canvas roof that seemed eternally motionless. Melissa's brush, comb, and poor little fineries lay waiting on the chest-top as though they had been left there by a woman who was dead. In the mirror the reversed interior of the wagon hung suspended in grey ghost-land. Peace, silence, soft light, stillness—and the presence of . . .

Now he could smell it. Wolf-stale and hickory smoke, salty, strong, nauseously aromatic. The man must be standing almost beside him just outside the canvas wall towards the head of the wagon. He smiled grimly and relaxed. He knew who it was. He waited . . .

At last a sound. The faintest of rasping on the left wall of the wagon. The drum-tight canvas trembled slightly. Immediately opposite Frances' chest and the small flame of the light, the blade of a small knife appeared through the canvas, sawing gently to and fro, cutting the fibre thread by thread. It was about three feet from Salathiel's head, where he lay watching it. He smiled again.

The brief tension of apprehension and fear of the unknown had completely left him. Curiosity, even a certain grim amusement, had taken their place. It was not yet plain to him exactly what the beggar was after. He did not know of the shillings Melissa had left in the chest drawer. Why was the fellow cutting a hole just opposite the light?

Surely it was not the small brass lanthorn he was after. What, then? At any rate, he would make him pay dearly for the rip in the canvas. Damn him for *that*, almost six inches of a vertical cut now.

The knife was suddenly withdrawn as it reached the wooden top strake of the wagon-bed. The pupil of a brown eye gleamed for several seconds at the hole, examining what lay before it. Salathiel lay quiet, breathing slowly as though in a deep sleep. The eye disappeared.

Swiftly and silently as a swallow, Salathiel's right hand dipped behind him into the deep shadow close to the floor and disengaged Kaysinata's tomahawk from its sheath. He held it firmly on the floor with the blade up, and with his whole arm extended straight behind him.

A hand—*the* hand, which only a few hours before had hung in the air so persistently before him, came through the flap in the canvas, and, as though it had a life and intelligence of its own, began to feel its way carefully across the top of the chest.

The arm that followed it was long, thin as and twisted like a leather rope.

The hand crept across the chest directly under the light. The fingers explored before it, they stopped to set Melissa's brush and then her comb aside. Once it picked up a ribbon, fingered it, and laid it down. Presently the fingers went over the chest edge, grasped the knob of the small top drawer and slid it forward. Then they groped for some time in the darkness. There was not a sound. But they were picking up, busy.

There was something entirely uncanny about this. Salathiel felt that he was looking at a disembodied hand. A thing acting of and by itself. He entirely forgot the man behind it. In the fierce concentration of the moment he thought and dealt directly with the hand alone.

It began to withdraw after a while, clutching something. It began to slide cautiously backward after the arm and across the streak of light. Now he understood. It was a hand full of shillings, several of which obtruded edgewise between the fingers and flashed briefly under the light. The hand was almost to the canvas now.

At the precise instant when the wrist was on the wooden rail of the wagon strake, he struck.

His arm and tomahawk flashed a complete arc from floor to rail, a blow of fearful force instinctively calculated. Steel bit through the bone and quivered in the wood. He let the hatchet stand there. It seemed to Salathiel as though the carved bone handle ought to hum.

But the astonishing thing was that, except for the single thud of the axe, outside for a long time there was not a sound, not a squeal or a whimper.

He was standing up now, ready for anything, listening . . .

Finally came a gasp. Then the swift pad-pad of muffled feet—and they were gone.

That was all. He reached forward and pulled Kaysinata's little axe out of the wood.

Then he went swiftly to the rear of the wagon, untied the flaps, and looked out.

Nothing but starlight and the white rime of a new frost on the grass. He bent down and examined the ground close by the wagon. The frost by the left side had been considerably disturbed. A trail of blurred patches in the grass led around the corner of the house. The man had been running, leaping apparently.

Strong enough for that, eh? he thought. Well, the fellow would have something to occupy him besides coming back to make more trouble. There was blood down the side of the wagon, but little or none he could find in the darkness on the grass. He wiped the side of the wagon off with some tinder rags. Tomorrow the trail in the frost would be gone. It would vanish in a few minutes, in fact. Nobody need ever know. Much better for Melissa not to be worried by this. He would just keep it to himself. But he would speak to her about keeping that chest drawer locked. Shillings were not so easily come by as all that! Hereafter . . .

A vixen yapped twice from a thicket down the road.

And so—that stinking white he-fox would have robbed the wagon, robbed Melissa of her little stocking-gift!

A rabbit shrieked—or was it a rabbit? He stood listening a moment, and yawned. Time for a little more sleep yet. The owls were still hunting.

He stepped back into the wagon—and saw the hand looking at him from the side by the rail, poised on the flat chest-top like a spider in the lamplight. The fingers had contracted. It was standing up now. It must have moved!

Damn that crab out of hell! Away with it.

He turned swiftly and dropped it into the salt box. Covered it up, out of sight.

Salt was expensive, but Melissa must never see a thing like that, not in her condition. He wiped off the top of the chest carefully, put the scattered shillings back in the drawer and looked about him. Ah, yes, one thing—one thing more.

He got out his darning kit and carefully and neatly stitched up the rent in the canvas.

Now, by God, that *was* all!

It was sleep now or sit up until morning all alone. It would be light soon enough now, he thought. He blew out the lamp and crawled in under his blankets gratefully. The last thing he heard was Captain Ecuyer's watch eating time under his blanket-roll.

It was a full hour later when some dogs far up the road at Sugar Cabins began to bay. He never heard them at all, nor the roosters crowing a little later for false dawn.

Sunrise comes late in November. The year is near its close.

9. Correspondence and Farewells

WHEN SALATHIEL looked out of the rear of the wagon next morning he realized that he had done what he had seldom done before, overslept himself. The sun was already over the top of the mountain, coming up out of smoking wreaths of mist, and even as he watched the whole place was a mad glitter of light.

"Never saw anything like it, did ye, young fellow?" said Mr. Patton, who was standing on the porch smoking his morning pipe, with one hand in his pocket and surveying the interior of the stockade with an air of proprietary pride.

"Thar's been a first-class dew-freeze. Hoarfrost, they still calls it, downcountry. Best one I ever see."

Salathiel whistled with polite surprise. Everything on the small plateau where Patton's stood looked as though it had been embossed in a glaze of silver and pearls by some mad magician during the darkness. The wagon, especially the wheels and hubs, was a thing of indescribable silver beauty. A small thicket half a mile down the road blinked and blazed with the flashing arcs of innumerable prisms. The buckets and barrels, every domestic article—no potentate had ever possessed their like. The pearly roads and paths winked.

"'Twon't last long," said Mr. Patton. "Must have been a cold wester crept down the ridge this mornin'. But it's going to be a wonderful day. And no snow yet! There hasn't been a season like this since 'fifty-eight. If it keeps up they're like to have St. Martin's summer in the vales below till pretty nigh Christmas. I've seen it that way before. Look, she's changin' already."

Even as he spoke the magic silver frosting began to fade. A cloudy blackness seemed to pass here and there over the grass, everything trickled and ran. The woods smoked. Only in the cold shadow of the house a small patch of the silversmith's handiwork remained. The wagon still glittered.

"It's a fine place you've got here, Mr. Patton," said Salathiel. "You must have been here a long spell for all the stumps to be outen the fields."

"Some of it was natural glades to begin with," replied Patton, "but we've been here nigh five and thirty years come next May Day. Grand-dad came in with the Chambers brothers to Falling Spring in the valley below. Yes, sir, 'tis a bit of Eden we have here through Path Valley, Amberson's, and the Coves. They were settled early by determined and discerning people. Your friend, Pendergass, came in a long time past, you'll recollect. But there was Marylanders with stone houses here long before him. If it hadn't been for the Injuns—" Mr. Patton sighed, and blew a cloud of smoke into the morning air.

"My folks came in with Garrett Pendergass," said Salathiel.

"Now, did they!" exclaimed Patton. "Oh, yes, I did hear you was carried off. By the Shawnees, wasn't it?"

Salathiel nodded.

"Well, Bouquet has settled accounts with them, I reckon," replied Patton. " 'Spect we won't have to have garrisons here much longer. Times are comin' when a man can really farm in peace, maybe." His clear blue eyes seemed to look far into the distance.

Salathiel looked about him again. It was amazing how different Patton's looked by daylight. Except for the stockade, the military features of the place now seemed to be nil.

It was quiet. The crowd had vanished. A few of the coloured servants and an old Indian or two stalked back and forth between the farm sheds, feeding the horses and stock. A squaw came out to the suck-pump to draw water. White smoke ascended from the chimney of the house into the calm morning air, until the sunlight struck it through and through high above the roof. It spoke of breakfast and all the comforts within-doors. The only reminder of the frontier was the big shed at the far west end of the enclosure, where the platoon of Highlanders were gathered about a large kettle getting their oatmeal porridge. Their tartans flamed bravely in the sunlight. How incongruous their presence here seemed. For the first time they looked foreign to him. This was a farm. Roosters crowed, and horses whinnied and stomped in the big stone barn. The lanthorn in the shed, where Croghan's Irish had left it, still burned behind a sooted glass.

"Yep," said Patton, "they've all gone. Must be pretty nigh to Bedford by now, or even past it. Well, that's a damn good riddance. And glory be, liken our friend, Wully, and his hungry Scots will be lightin' out for Fort Loudon sometime early today. They eat us out of house and home, and besides they're slow-payin' king's men," he shrugged his shoulders. "But come in, come in and have a bite yourself. I'm blattin' away like an old gaffer, as the missus would say, and you're young and hungry."

"I am that," admitted Salathiel. "I'll be with you directly."

He strolled over to the pump, pulling his shirt off, and began dowsing his head and bare shoulders in the stream of cold well-water that dashed from its spout. What a clever thing a pump was! He'd have one. He looked through the bright drops of water at the cheerful sunshine and the mountain rising steep and green before him up the road through the gate. The last short haul! That was all he had to make and he would be out of the woods. He paused a second. He thought he heard an echo of someone calling his name . . . pshaw! . . . God, he felt fine, glowing all over. Melissa must see the wagon before the sun struck it. The top was beginning to run off now.

He sprang to the door and opened it, "Lissa, Lissa," he called, "come out and see your silver chariot—hurry! And here's a posy for you all covered with pearls."

From where she was sitting sewing by the fire with Mrs. Patton, Frances rose smiling and, followed by young Bridget, ran lightly out onto the porch.

"Look," he said, "look," pointing to the wagon and trundler that still glittered like solid silver with the fast-fading frost. "And here, look at this!" He reached down and plucked a spread of clover that grew about the Pattons' porch.

"Fawncy now," said Melissa, her grey eyes veiling with pleasure as he slipped an arm about her waist and held her close—"fawncy, a set of shamrocks and all covered with pearls!" She fastened them in her belt and smiled up at him. "Fit for the Queen of Ireland," she whispered. "Fit for you," he said. For an instant a rainbow in the clover leaves winked as they looked down at them. Then suddenly the leaves turned black and the droplets of water ran down over her skirt like tears.

"Sure, 'tis a fairy fraud you've wished on me," cried Melissa, and laughed ruefully.

"Never mind . . ." he began.

"Hello, big man, hello," insisted Bridget, grasping him about the leg. "I'm here, too. And I'm agoin' to Carlisle with you, in the big wagon with the bells and the grey horsies."

"Are ye now, *are* ye?" asked Salathiel, a bit doubtfully, looking at Melissa.

"She certainly *is*," cried Melissa. "Come in and let Mrs. Patton talk to you about it. We're sewin' on her things and packin' 'em up."

"Kind o' seems to be settled, then," laughed Salathiel.

"I'm a lady, and I'm goin' to help ye," insisted Bridget. "I kin make the beds, I kin. All but the big bolsters. An' I know how to sew. I'm no poor squaw."

"I believe ye, little one," said Salathiel, picking her up. "You're a useful piece."

"That's what the McQuiston said when I was with Lieutenant Francis and her," said Bridget.

"*Uh, huh,*" said Salathiel, wondering at the familiar names.

They went in together, and Mrs. Patton looked up smiling from putting a hem in a small skirt.

Old Bijou, the coloured woman, was frying something in deep fat that crackled. The flames leaped and snapped cheerfully.

The lower part of the room was already hazy with morning tobacco smoke. The subalterns and sergeants were finishing their breakfasts. Yates and Wully Grant were laughing together over a table as if nothing at all had happened between them the night before. St. Clair sat leaning back, evidently with a full breakfast under his vest, upon which he jingled his watch fobs and little keys. Premonitory sobs and squeals from the bagpipe, which the piper was furbishing and adjusting, brought occasional answering low howls from Bran. Between-times his tail kept knocking a constant tattoo on the floor in a rhythm that somehow expressed the general air of satisfaction and good morning cordiality that now pervaded the place.

"Sit down and have your breakfast, 'Captain' Albine," said Mrs. Patton. "You've had a good sleep, I hope. Land, but you men were late last night, weren't you?" Her eyes twinkled, "But sit while I draw a dish of tay. You like it? I've got somewhat to talk to you about. It's the new member of your family. I mean"—she nodded towards Bridget—"at least she will be for a while. You'd best know all about her that I can tell you, so you can pick up her folks later when you get to Carlisle."

"Sukey," shouted Mrs. Patton, "some crumpets, hominy, pork chops and potatoes for the captain. Tell Bijou to look alive." The squaw shuffled off. "Here's your tay, sir. No, no, pour it in your saucer." She laughed, a little, embarrassed at correcting him. He drank the tea off gratefully. It was real Bohea.

"Just before you begin, Matilda," interrupted Mr. Patton, "I thought we might ask the Albines to stay over a few days with us. Over the Sabbath at least. You know the Reverend McArdle is holding a stump preaching up at Aughwick, him and his reverend helper—what's-his-name, the garrison clergyman from Fort Bedford. If they stay, that would give you and Mistress Albine a chance to catch up on the youngster's clothes here. And we'd like you to stay . . ."

"Thanks, thanks," said Salathiel somewhat hurriedly, putting down his saucer of smoking tea. "But we must be getting on. I once sat at the feet of Mr. McArdle somewhat extensive, you might say. He's a powerful preacher," he drawled. "I didn't know he'd been ridin' a woods circuit. Many people rally in to hear him?"

"Crowds from all over. Wagons when they kin or just horseback. The spirit sweeps 'em," replied Patton.

"Hm," said Salathiel, genuinely disturbed to hear that McArdle was so near. What would he say if he saw Melissa? No, no, that would never do!

"We'll be pushing on this morning, sir," he said finally. "Mrs. Albine is a Catholic, you know—and we'd best go down the mountain with the troops as far as Loudon, seein' they're goin' back that way. Thar's always a chance of a war party, and that when you least expect it. I won't feel cocksure till I get clean to Carlisle."

"Reckon that's good sense," said Patton. His wife evidently agreed. She was disconcerted at hearing that Frances was a Catholic. She might have thought of it, she told herself. Old Ireland!

"Bridget is a Presbyterian," she began quite unexpectedly, and then bit her lip with vexation.

"Madam, I'll *never* lift a finger to unsettle her faith," exclaimed Frances Melissa, her cheeks flaming.

A general embarrassment fell on the company. Bridget sat wide-eyed on Melissa's knee. She knew well enough she was being talked about. Yes, indeed she was a Presbyterian. Her ma had said . . .

"Darlin', run out with the boys and play on the porch, and take that pup along. He's a-badgering Bran," said Mrs. Patton. The child departed gravely, looking back once or twice.

"She's that biddable," continued Mrs. Patton, "but little pitchers, you know. Poor baby! About all we can make out about her is that her folks must have been gentle people, lived somewhere down in the valley, Shenandoah country, though what fork, of course, I don't know. Well, it's the old story. Her pa was ploughin' one day when the Indians burst out on him from the woods. 'Pears that he and some of the nigger boys put up a fight in an old tobacco shed, but they burned that over their heads. Mrs. McCandliss and young Bridget and a baby boy were dragged off west through the woods. Seems that all the poor woman could do was to snatch up the baby and a Bible from her burning house. Delawares, I hear they were. Anyway, they later put the little boy to the hatchet, and Mrs. McCandliss was terrible hurt trying to save him. She must have been dying, for she gave the Bible to young Bridget and told her to sneak off down the stream when they made camp that night. Bridget was to keep on wading in the branch as far as she could. Then she was to go through the woods in the direction where the sun came up the first morning, until she found white friends. She told the child she would certainly find friends on the third day.

"I reckon that's about as far as she thought the child would last, anyway. Or maybe she had second sight at the last moment and prophesied. The really wonderful thing is that a little girl so young as Bridget was then would understand and do exactly as she was told.

"It was just a little while after the fight at Bushy Run when it happened. And sure enough, it seems it was the third day after she ran away that Lieutenant Francis found her when he was bringing down-country some of the first of the freed captives from Fort Pitt. That McQuiston gal he carries on with was riding with him when she looks up and sees a wisp of dress caught in a blackberry patch on the side of a hill near the road. 'Twas no more than ten miles west of here. And there that baby was, half the clothes dragged off her by the brambles and her poor little body all scratched like she had been flogged, and her face smeared with blood and blackberry juice, but still clutching her little Bible.

"But do you think she'd forgot her manners? No, sir, when they washed her off in the stream and the McQuiston puts her shawl around her and pops a bit of biscuit dipped in wine into her mouth, the first thing Bridget says is, 'My ma said you'd come. She's Mrs. McCandliss, and she wishes to thank you.' And I'll swan, if she didn't make them a curtsy, and then fall down.

"All Bridget knows is she kept coming through the woods after she left the branch she waded down the first night, and she spent two more nights and climbed a little tree each time. She said she saw beasts with eyes that burned in the night. Well, I wouldn't doubt it.

"I will say, too, that the McQuiston was mad about her and wanted to take her on to Philadelphia. But Lieutenant Francis wouldn't hear of it. Not that he wasn't soft about the child, too. But he as much as said that the house he was setting up for the McQuiston in the City would be no place to nurture a young child in, and would I please keep her until he could find out who her people were. He said he felt sure they were gentle folk.

"And then there was that Bible with the family names in it. It's the smallest Bible I ever saw," remarked Mrs. Patton, rummaging in the basket of clothes and pulling it out. "Here you are, but you can't make out much about people just from their names."

"Oh, a good deal more than you might think, Matilda," said Mr. Patton. "It does take time, but Lieutenant Francis was pretty clever about it. He advertised Bridget in the list of captives being returned from the frontiers by Colonel Bouquet to Carlisle, and sure enough he found the child's grandmother. She seems to be a pious and decent woman and must have come all the way from Boston to Carlisle to search for the child. But judge for yourself. Here's her letter Lieutenant Francis sent on only a few weeks ago. I writ her, of course, and she must have mine by now. Jim Fergus carried it back."

Salathiel took the neatly folded double-paged letter in his hands with considerable curiosity and feeling. It amused him to think that Bustle McQuiston had taken a fancy to young Bridget first—and now Frances Melissa was eager to take her to Carlisle. It might be just as well if those two girls never met. He could sense trouble in that—over the little one, of course. He grinned.

But they were looking at him. They might think he couldn't read . . .

As he read, an astonishing thing happened to Salathiel. Tears flowed down out of his eyes. At the words "living death with the savages" he was touched to the quick, and he neither cared nor tried to conceal his ungovernable emotion. It now seemed a miracle to him that he also had escaped this living death, but how nearly! He would show his gratitude to his Maker by kindness to this child. He now recalled his light promises to her of the night before with a glow of satisfaction. "Always" was what he had said, and now he was glad and hoped it would be that way. Looking down into the basket of little clothes the women had been preparing so tentatively for the child's departure, he understood how much hung on his decision—and looking up again he saw how all of them were equally touched by his own emotion and respected him for it.

"Make ready," he said huskily. "I'll make her the new little shoes. We'll take Bridget to her grandma. And when I raise the new rooftree, we'll make a place at the hearth for her, too—won't we, Melissa?"

"Sure and I knew the great heart of you would find room for her," said Melissa, hugging his arm in happiness. "Maybe she'll be a playmate for our own soon," she whispered. So it was settled.

He rose from the bench suddenly very happy and with all the good feeling of doing right. Mr. Patton came over and shook him by the hand.

"No words can thank ye," he said. "We've had Bridget here for nigh two years now, until she's like one of our own. It'll be a sore loss for Matilda, but we have no right to keep Bridget from her own flesh and blood. Now you'll write and let us know, won't ye? Our hearts will follow after you downcountry."

"I'll let you hear, sir, you can rely on it. And you'll be seeing Bridget again, I opine."

"I have little doubt of it," said Patton. "We'll pay ye a visit when ye get well settled. Ye'll be findin' many of the brethren in the city, and I'll come down for the Grand Lodge when I can. I'll write the Worshipful Master." They gave each other a fraternal clasp. "Matilda," said Mr. Patton, "call the child in now. This company will soon be goin'. The time has come."

"Aye, Wee-um," she said, and went to the porch to bring the children in. They heard her calling from the porch, "Sam, Rodney, Bridg—et," and on the last name her voice broke.

Whatever was the nature of the conversation that had been going on over the breakfast fragments between Mr. Yates and Lieutenant Grant, the result seemed to be mutually satisfactory, for Wully Grant now rose up, his usual callosity of temperament restored to all its normal overconfident, red-cheeked vigour, to judge by the bull-voiced and overbearing tones in which he now began to bellow directions to his subalterns to get the damned detachment lined up and prepared to leave for Fort Loudon.

Yates passed a wink of amusement and reassurance to Salathiel as they went out together down to the barn.

"You would think," said Yates, "that it was the subalterns who had been delaying Wully. They would rather have marched hours ago. If the news of the Irish having slipped west with the trade goods gets about this neighbourhood before the troops leave, there may be trouble. They would be better off at Loudon."

"What conclusion did you and his Majesty's representative in these parts arrive at in the matter of the little affair at cards last night?" demanded Albine.

"Oh, Lieutenant Grant is quite willing to settle his gambling debts with his cousin James's land. He gave me his written acknowledgment. And I let him keep the guineas he won from St. Clair. It may result in broader acres for us later on. Hard coin is a' that matters wi' Wully."

"Did ye now!" said Salathiel, astonished. "You really want that land bad, don't you?"

"Yes," said Yates, "and I'll bear down hard when it comes to making the papers out at Loudon." He smacked one hand in the other. "Land grants are my specialty, you know."

"How will he arrange the matter with Cousin James?" inquired the curious Mr. Albine.

"I know not, nor do I care," said Yates. "That's strictly a Grant family affair. If Wully can transfer valid title, that's all I need to know."

They met Alexander and still another Alexander emerging from the big barn with the wagon horses all rubbed down, glistening and prancing in the bright sunshine and the brisk mountain air.

"Glad to do your Honour a sma' favour any time," said the big Highlander. "I hope I'll be watchin' the wagon for you again. I thought maybe you might hae a wee doch-an-dorris wi' me and Andrew before this severe march doon the mountain begins. The horses have had a bit more oats in their drench than the landlord himsel' might have measured ye. Fine grey beasties they be," said he, smacking the neck of the leader.

"There goes the pibroch the noo!" exclaimed Andrew. "Whuzz-Bang Wully will be awa at last."

The sound of the bagpipe skirling from the front porch for the assembly made the horses uneasy and inclined to rear. However, with the assistance of his two Highland friends, Salathiel soon had them harnessed to the wagon.

The reins coiled easily through Salathiel's hands as he drew them through the brass rings on collar and dashboard. So much early-morning solicitude on the part of the two Alexanders deserved to be rewarded. He coiled the four pairs of reins over the runnels to avoid untimely snarling, dashed a few buckets of water from the pump over the wheels and the sides of the wagon, thus obliterating the last possible traces of the affair of the night before, and after snaffling the bridle of the off leader to a ring on the front rail, invited the two Scots into the wagon for a parting drink.

The jug gurgled generously several times. They drank to luck. Then a silent one, standing, to the memory of "the little captain" (Ecuyer) and a final swallow to meeting again. Then with many a "good fortune to your honour, and guid faring wi' your bonny lassie" they leaped out of the back, their kilts flying, to run nimbly and take their places in the ranks, as the detachment formed-up facing the porch awaiting the final appearance of Lieutenant Grant and the word to march.

Salathiel looked at these Highlanders fondly. He had been through a bloody siege, frontier forays, and night and day life-and-death affairs with them. It seemed strange that, after all, he was not going to be marching off to Fort Loudon with them today. The life of garrisons had for a long time been tangled with his own. Nothing could ever erase the respect and affections of the past.

There they stood silent, impassive, a long row of kilts and bonnets, claymores and gorgets glittering, brown Besses grounded. The spontoons of the two young officers rose like silver fleur-de-lis above the heads of the rear rank. The piper stood two paces to the right on the flank. Grants, Campbells, MacDonalds, and Grahams blazed and glittered in the morning sunlight of the Alleghenies, *Caledonia invictrix*—a living sword of the British crown.

Given good leaders nothing would stop them. With them at Bushy Run, Bouquet had broken the ring of savages. And now they were using these soldiers to keep the people from settling the frontiers. What was wrong? he wondered. Didn't they know what they were doing, these men in London, trying to make a hunting preserve of all the huge country west of the mountains—a park for the fur trade with these soldiers as gamekeepers; when the people, when everybody in the colonies was hungry for land?

That was where real trouble might come, as he saw it. There might be a fight someday about that if they kept on. As for these stamps the lawyers were talking about, he'd have to inquire into that matter a little further. Lawyers and politicians always talked hotter than other people. And then, there was one thing that was certain. There was endless land. What a pity, then, to be using these fine fellows as bailiffs, and making them unpopular. He shook his head doubtfully at so perplexing a drift in events. No doubt, too, certain people had high and mighty attitudes that were irritating . . .

The door opened and the strident, overbearing tones of Lieutenant Grant, making life miserable for Sergeant MacPhearson, robbed the air of peace and the morning sunshine of its happy promise. Whatever the sergeant had done, it was probably not a crime, and no man should speak to another man like that.

In the end it simply proved to be Wully Grant's harassing way of giving an order to march. "Back to Loudon, awa wi' ye," he bawled, and came out on the porch red-faced, his claymore clanking—only to find the detachment already drawn up and waiting.

Most of the people on the Patton place had gathered to see the regulars depart. About twenty persons stood back a little distance from the porch and watched silently. The Pattons and their guests came out and stood along the porch rail.

Wully mounted his shaggy nag, lurching indignantly into the saddle. "I'll see ye at Loudon the morrow nicht," he said to Yates sullenly. He saluted Mr. Patton a mite morosely, and roared a command.

The line wheeled into column of four, the pipes skirled. Bran sat on his haunches and howled. The crowd watched without moving and without comment until the last file rounded the corner of the stockade gate. "Bluebells of Scotland" piped its way eastward up the road towards Sugar Cabins and the ridge. Now and then wild bursts of the shrill music came back more clearly, but always more softly and with the fading melancholy of lengthening distance.

A sudden cheerfulness and lack of tension seemed to flow back into the stockade. The king's men were gone! Everyone turned and went about his business. The children commenced to play. The work of the day began. After all, Patton's was a farm.

Two young Indian boys began to help load the wagon with Melissa's little horsehide bag, the willow basket containing Bridget's clothes, and sundry small packages wrapped in woven grass mats containing the offerings of Mrs. Patton and her family: brown eggs, clover honey, a loaf of maple sugar, hams, and a leaden canister of London tea.

"Way-gifts, way-gifts," said Mrs. Patton with tears in her eyes, refusing to be thanked for them.

Salathiel found her standing on the steps with Frances Melissa, who had pushed her bonnet back on her shoulders and was looking up earnestly with a clear sweetness of expression, listening to Mrs. Patton's last affectionate torrent of well wishes and good advice.

Bridget stood by, holding Melissa determinedly by the hand, her long heavy brown braids coming out of her fur hood. She was wide-eyed with suppressed excitement at leaving, but was also finding the parting with the Pattons an unexpected misery. In fact, up until now she had thought of it scarcely at all. Now she was leaving them—going away! Only her grey kitten would go with her, only the cat out of all the warmth and comfort that she had known and taken for granted for so long.

Even that young animal, wise in its own way, sensed the threat of imminent change in its surroundings, and the strength of fate. Thrusting its head out of the hole in the top of the small woven basket in which Bridget was carrying it, it mewed piteously, laid back its ears, and scratched.

Young Sam and Rodney, balanced precariously on the porch rail,

wriggled in nervous misery. "Sis is goin' away. Sis is goin' downcountry,"
blubbered Rodney. "Our sis is goin' away!"

"Shut up you—you little . . ." Seeing his father's eye upon him, Sam
didn't dare use the word *raca* to his brother, which the Scriptures for
bade. Instead, he fell off the rail onto the porch floor and lay there
crying miserably. Bridget stood shaking now, her brown eyes brilliant
with tears.

"Good-bye, Sammy, good-bye," she whispered. At that Sam took his
head off his arm and looked up at her and smiled.

"Good God," said St. Clair, "do they take to each other so young as
that? I'd forgotten."

Mrs. Patton gave Melissa a peck on the neck. The Irish girl suddenly
snatched Bridget up, kitten, basket and all, and turned her back on the
porch to let the child see the wagon.

"Look at the brave horses, me love," said she, "look at them standin'
there lookin' wise with their blinkers on them, all leanin' forward a bit
ready to go."

She whisked Bridget towards the rear of the wagon, glancing up at
Mrs. Patton with a swift tender smile as she passed under her. There
were tears in the older woman's eyes. Frances thrust Bridget into the
wagon, and once inside herself, pulled the rear curtains across. The two
sat together in the half-twilight under the canvas, listening.

"If that's money you're fumblin' in your pouch for, young man," said
the grave voice of Mr. Patton, "I'll have the hide offen ye, big as ye are
if ye even show it to me. What kind of people do ye think we be?"

"Oh, the best in the world," said Salathiel, dropping his louis d'or
back amid the scalps, and suddenly taking Mr. Patton's hand.

"Enough, enough!" cried Mr. Patton, wringing his fingers. "I'd not
be able to make change for ye now."

St. Clair and Yates laughed.

"We'll see you in Philadelphia come June, then," said Yates to Mr.
Patton, as he and St. Clair mounted.

"Yes, I think I'll come to the City with the missus when Bouquet
marches downcountry in the summer. Maybe he'll march earlier. Maybe
it'll be April or May, if the rumours hold true."

"Until then—" said St. Clair.

The two gentlemen rode forward to the rail and both took off their
hats together to Mrs. Patton.

"Madam," said St. Clair, "I'm mortal obleeged to ye for a more than
royal entertainment."

"In that sentiment," said Mr. Yates, "I wish to jine, but for a native
entertainment, for a Pennsylvanian—nay, for a Philadelphian welcome
It was worthy of the City itself."

The two gentlemen leaned forward slightly in their saddles, and re
placed their hats.

Mrs. Patton, her face shining with domestic pride justified, swept them a low curtsy from the porch as they galloped off.

Quite unexpectedly the wagon teams pulled loose and bolted after the two horsemen across the green parade.

Shouting a decidedly less ceremonious farewell, Salathiel leaped after the thundering wagon, and with considerable difficulty managed to vault into the seat and take over the reins. Luckily the turf was smooth and the curve to the road gradual. As it was, the trundler skidded and grazed the gate of the stockade. The big portal post cracked, and the splinters flew.

"Mercy, mercy me, Wee-um," cried Mrs. Patton. "I'm not sure you were right after all about those people. Look at that!"

"Time alone will tell, mother," said Patton, putting his arm about his wife as they turned to the door and went in. "You know, I'm never *plumb* sure about anything. But I still think we've done right."

"No, no, Mr. Patton," said his spouse, a little breathlessly, "you never was an obstinate man. I never did say that."

She sat down and wiped her eyes on her apron. Bridget was gone. She had always wanted a daughter, and her bowels yearned after the child.

Bran came and put his head in her lap. She wondered if he knew. Would they stop to see her cousin Burd at Lancaster? She hoped so. Colonel Burd had married a Shippen. She would like Bridget to see a great house like theirs. The Burds were so rich, and so very, very, very genteel.

10. In Which an Obstacle Is Surmounted

WHAT WITH ONE thing and another it had been nearly ten o'clock when Wully Grant had finally given the command for his Highlanders to march. It was half after ten when the wagon had so unexpectedly flashed out of the stockade gate—and a full five minutes later before Salathiel got the bits out of the teeth of the two lead horses, by dint of much jaw sawing, and the whole cavalcade settled down to a regular and decidedly chastened trot.

He had used the whip on the outside leader, the big gelding that was half a stallion yet, it seemed. He blamed him for bolting. That horse would still bear some watching, he thought.

What a start! And he had meant to be *so* careful. Luckily the road was all turf and moss here, and a steady upgrade straight through the brown-leafed woods so quiet now in the lee of the big ridge that loomed just beyond.

Already it was beginning to get unseasonably warm, a fine Indian summer day. Sugar Cabins should be just ahead, around the next shoulder. Probably St. Clair and Yates would wait for him there. How they did ride when they cut loose!

All this he kept telling himself just to put off looking around into the wagon behind. He wondered how Melissa and the child had come through the wild start. If anything had broken loose back there in the wagon—if one of the big chests had shifted . . .

And then he heard Bridget laughing, a steady, amused, giggling laugh, with long ripples of pure childish merriment in it like a small waterfall tumbling over pebbles.

"God bless her," he said, and turning about, raised up the canvas and looked behind.

Bridget was sitting in Ecuyer's swing-chair, kicking her heels. As she surged with the slow motion of the wagon, the cat, shut in its willow basket, emitted a series of growls punctuated by an occasional sharp feline explosion. It was such a miniature rage that somehow it was side-splitting. Melissa was laughing, too.

Just then he caught her eye. For an instant she frowned at him.

"So you let them get away from you at the very start, Mr. Albine," she said severely. "And wasn't I after tellin' ye only yesterday 'twas high time you took over the reins? And now listen to what you've done."

A fizzing yowl worthy of a small panther came shrieking out of the basket.

Young Bridget dissolved, the corners of her eyes turned upward like twin moons. Frances leaned back and joined in. He grinned at the sheer silly happiness of it, much relieved.

"You see what you have done," said Frances, swiftly moving up from the chest where she had been sitting and throwing her arms about his neck. She pressed so close to him that he was now forced to handle the reins blindly.

"Sal," she whispered, "I'm terrible, awful happy today! You did nearly spill us out, and you might have cracked the captain's mirror, if I hadn't caught it in the very wink of time. But it didn't crack—and I'm not alone in here any more. I'll be ridin' inside most of the time now. Just get us to Carlisle safe. That's all I ask now. But do keep the reins in your own hands. Maybe 'tis follerin' after the two gintlemen too close that makes trouble. Did ye ever think o' that? It's ourselves now—and her. Ourselves alone, if I'm to be like a wife to ye, Mr. Albine." Their lips met.

He turned to his outside view of things again and let the canvas fall behind him. But he pondered what she had said for the next half mile, letting the horses walk slowly up the ever-increasing ascent.

"Ourselves alone", eh? Well, that was a fine brave Irish thought. And he was going to make things right for Frances Melissa—and for young Bridget, too—and the little one when it came. Yes, they should have all that his strength and skill could bring them. He would do everything and anything. But "ourselves alone"?

So far what would he have done without friends and their advice, a man like himself raw from the forest? Where would he be now without them? Even McArdle had helped, had really saved him alive in the old days. He shook his head as though he had caught his hair in a thicket and would shake the leaves out of it. Could it be that Melissa was speaking of Yates—and St. Clair, and almost everybody else? Some white women, he noticed, wanted everything just for themselves—for themselves alone. And he had seen bitches that ate their young. They started to lick them all over as soon as they were born and just went right on through with it, and swallowed them, too.

But Melissa was not like that, he felt quite sure. She was just in the early mating stage, he decided, and didn't want anything, not even the shadow of something strange moving outside to fall across the entrance to the den where the young were. Also, evidently, she was afraid she might lose him. No, that wasn't it exactly. She seemed to be scared she might get lost herself! Sometimes she acted like a person who had been lost in the woods and then rescued, but wasn't sure of it yet. Take that spell yesterday, what was it she had seen, where had she been?

Bridget, he felt sure, would never grow up to be like that. Already she knew exactly who she was and what she wanted. She'd certainly make some wild leg-clutching boy into a good steady man someday and keep a warm fire burning on the hearth for him, too. But Frances Melissa? Well, he couldn't be sure.

In fact, you could never tell from one day to another just exactly who Frances Melissa was going to be. Sometimes she took the last ounce of strength out of him. Yet he could never tell just what it would be like next time. And then she always seemed to be asking him for help, trying to get him to hold her even closer; to find herself by being one with him. How curious! He had never thought mating could be like that. But maybe that was why he loved her so much.

Certainly he was tangling his hair in branches high over his head with all this thinking about women. He still had a sneaking feeling he never would have much luck with them. He had told Melissa about Jane Sligo, that lost girl-wife that a thoughtless boyish passion and McArdle's obstinate theology had wished on him. Melissa had laughed at him. Now, what could he say to that!

Where was Jane Sligo, he wondered, and what was she like? She was no girl any longer. If she ever turned up, if McArdle tried to be troublesome about her again! Well, he was no boy any longer, either! And he would protect himself and Frances against them both, and the whole world, too.

Hadn't he set out to find his wife again, and come back with Frances Melissa? It must have been meant that way or he would never have found Frances as he had. What McArdle had written on the piece of bark when he and Jane were married was only a boyish promise, something wrung from him by surprise. He had tried but he hadn't been able to keep that promise.

But the remembrance of the bark writing and the ring that Jane had kept often worried him. He hoped that she had lost it, and the ring, too. It was a bad-luck ring, the one which the sick woman had provided that afternoon when they were trying to sneak into Fort Pitt. Well, he was glad she had died. That was one witness gone. The whole forest marriage on the wild island down the Ohio came back to him vividly.

He hoped the other woman who had put her name on that piece of slippery elm bark would die, too. Nothing but trouble had come out of that affair with Jane. And how hard he had tried to find her! He rubbed his ragged ear thoughtfully. Sometimes it made his head ache, and it always itched. It reminded him of trouble—maybe of trouble to come.

At any rate he would take this much of Frances Melissa's advice. He certainly *would* handle the reins himself. And as for his friends and other acquaintances, and the various affairs he would have to undertake in the world on the other side of the mountains, he was going to be the judge of all that for himself. He would take Yates's advice, or St. Clair's, or that of anyone else who seemed to be a wise counsellor and a clever trader or hunter. There was something to be said for the way the redskins managed such matters. All the squaws did for the council fire was to bring wood for it. The men lit it, smoked their pipes there, and made big medicine.

Much comforted by this profound conclusion, he began to handle the reins more briskly and once more forced the horses into a lumbering trot.

Some of this cogitation had been unconsciously suggested to him by the sight of three steep zigzags in the road ahead. These and the pitch down over the rocks on the opposite slope were known to all unhappy wagoners as the "Stoney Batter". The Stoney Batter rose suddenly out of the forest and climbed up over the comparatively bare rocky ridge only about a mile away now. By sheer propinquity it was now forced upon his active attention, both as a physical fact and for what it signified in the life journey he had undertaken for himself and for those behind him in the wagon.

At the top of that ridge he would, so to speak, be looking down into his future. His past in the forest would lie behind him, hidden amid the mountains. The backbone of the main ridge of the Tuscarora, which the road just barely managed to negotiate on three steep boulder-piled inclines, was the final ridge of the Alleghenies eastward. Here was the actual physical frontier.

Below were the foothills, the valleys and plateaus of the long-settled country, the hard-won birthright of the English dwellers in the dawn-light, the domain of the paleface, where chimneys smoked, wheels rolled, and ploughs bit deep through open country conquered by the rifle and made good by the axe. There Europe had been brought over in ships and was flooding westward into America, dammed up for a while against the mountains.

To Salathiel the ridge of the Tuscarora was thus of much greater import and significance than would even a national frontier ordinarily be to a usual or casual traveller. For him, it was the barrier he had always dimly felt and often heard about, one he could now plainly see; a wall between him and all those things from which he so bitterly felt he had been cruelly disinherited. Now—now after years of hope deferred, struggles, and lonely yearning, he was about to surmount it and to go on down into the country beyond.

At the very top of the ridge the sun glittered on a mound of black wet rocks piled there either as a marker or as a point of survey by the first military engineers at the very top of things—mighty high! That would be his milepost, he thought, the marker between his youth and his manhood. Yes, he would make it so, a mark in time.

One more steep haul then, one more wild scramble. Those boulder-piled zigzags were narrow, stony, and steep. It would be close going with the big heavy wagon and the trundler. He might need help. He hoped Yates and St. Clair had not gone over the crest after the troops, ahead of him. He thought they ought to stand by to help with the two extra horses. Hadn't it been understood that they were going to wait at Sugar Cabins? By the way, what had become of that sweetly named place?

He came up out of a shallow swale where a small branch began trickling merrily westward through the forest, and halted to look about him in what had once been a considerable clearing. This was a place where people had evidently dwelt in peace "before the late troubles began". There were several empty cellars. A dozen or so hardy apple trees still survived. Some had a little, high red fruit that even the bears had not been able to get. Yes, a small settlement must have been begun here. Probably it was at the road's end then. He thought he could see the people leaving the day the news of Braddock's defeat came, the mad panic and the frantic flight. Or had the news come in the night, he wondered; struck silently with a painted face? That was ten years ago or more. Now the forest had come back. All but for a rosebush and a few red apples hanging highest on the scraggly bough. God, what a lot of trouble this country had seen!

He started the teams forward again, and following a curve that skirted a rocky shoulder, he found himself, almost before he knew it, in the midst of Sugar Cabins itself.

Its most notable feature just at that moment was a runny-nosed boy in a coonskin cap and shaggy fur trousers, who stood forlornly holding the heads of the noble steeds of Messrs. St. Clair and Yates. This youth scowled at the wagon and gave Salathiel a painful cross-eyed stare. His embarrassment at having to exist was patent, and he answered questions bashfully and slowly, blushing every time.

The two gentlemen were over yonder at Hank Laughlin's cabin, "jawin' with pa and ma"—it appeared. As to where "yonder" was, it was quite impossible from the double direction of the boy's eyes to guess with any accuracy. Salathiel, therefore, looked around for himself.

Four or five miserable log shebangs, evidently the remains of shacks once inhabited by Colonel Burd's road workers, lay scattered about through a fine open grove of sugar maples, containing some of the largest and oldest trees of the kind Salathiel had ever seen. There were many old holes and scores in the bark of their trunks, the sole evidence of industry that marked the settlement, unless a few pigs rooting listlessly in the autumn leaves here and there implied some modicum of care in their behalf. There were no windows in the cabins, and the slab doors were grimly shut.

Salathiel spat over the wheel in disappointment. What in time could St. Clair and Yates be stopping to jaw about here?

"Got a chawr?" asked the boy.

"Yes," said Salathiel, "hev you?"

"No," said the youth, "nothin' but sassafras." He spat some green juice.

At this brilliant turn in affairs, most of the horses blew their noses as a sign that they all recognized one another.

"The macaroni with one eye said ye was to tarry for him," said the boy suddenly, remembering Yates's message.

"We be," replied Salathiel.

The boy considered this for quite some time.

"I know ye be," he said.

"Good!" exclaimed Salathiel, and resumed silence. He heard Frances giggling again inside the wagon.

"While you're awaitin', big man, kin I come up and set there beside ye?" asked young Bridget, unexpectedly sticking her brown braids out from under the canvas.

He reached down and swept her up onto the seat beside him. She sat swinging her too-large moccasins and looking down at the youth holding the horses.

" 'Low, Hank," she said.

" 'Low, sis!" the boy managed. He blushed to the roots of his hair, and then gasped out, "Be ye goin' downcountry in that *thar* contraption, sissy?"

She nodded happily. "Yes, I'm agoin' to Carlisle for to find my old granny."

"Thought she was took off by the Injuns," said the boy, wiping his green mouth with the back of his hand.

"Not she," chirped Bridget, "she's from Bosting Town, and they don't have Injuns there no more. The Injuns give up and cleared out."

"Wal, we've still got 'em here," drawled the boy.

"I know," said sis. "At my house—at Patton's, I mean," she corrected herself, "I don't live there no more. But Mr. Patton's Injuns do be tame."

"Maybe," said the boy, doubtfully. "But arly this mornin' comes a little Welshman crawling up to Cousin Finney Laughlin's door with his hand cut clean off. And he says the Injuns done it to him just a piece up the road from here."

Salathiel looked about him quite unconcernedly. But he understood the silence and the complete lack of any sign of life at Sugar Cabins now. The houses themselves seemed to be listening for the war-whoop. He laughed a little at this unconscious tribute of respect to his former playmates.

"Did ye hear what that boy said, Sal?" cried Frances from inside the wagon, a piercing note of anxiety in her usually soft voice. "Belike some of your friends of the Long House are after followin' ye up. What are ye goin' to do about it?"

"I'm just agoin' to drive on over the mountain, Melissa, whar the people of the Long House won't care to follow. We're like to catch up to the troops before we get to Loudon, halfway down the hill. Besides, it doesn't sound a very likely tale to me. If they was Injuns, they'd hev taken this man's har instead of his hand. But here come St. Clair and Yates, and we'll hear the gist of it from them."

(The salt box, he thought, the salt box! He must get to it before Melissa prepared the next meal.)

Yates and St. Clair were coming from the nearest cabin, where a woman stood peering out the door after them apprehensively.

"Hank, you come right back in here," she screamed at the boy, who scarcely needed the warning. Hardly had St. Clair slipped a couple of pennies into his hands before he let go the horses' bridles and made a bolt for the house. The door slammed behind him.

"Injuns?" asked Salathiel.

"Oh, I don't think so," replied St. Clair. "Not a war party, anyway. It might have been a prowler or a renegade."

"Looks more like highway robbery to me," said Yates. "I can't make head or tail of it. There's a poor devil in there with his right hand cut off clean as a whistle just behind the wrist, nigh dead from loss of blood and terror. He's a stranger to all of them here. Crawled in last night, it seems, with a thong wrapped round his arm. The dogs found him first. He's clean out of his head now, talking in Welsh about a Swedish widow with a gold cup buried in her coffin. At least that's all I could make out of it. The Laughlin woman called us in to help rebind his arm as we rid by. Arthur and I have done the best we could. And I left a

little money with Mrs. Laughlin t' encourage her to take care of him, o
to bury him decent if he dies."

" 'Twas too much, Ned," said St. Clair. "They're not used to gold ir
these parts."

"It's all I have with me now," replied Yates.

"Aweel," sighed St. Clair, " 'twas a charitable impulse we both had."

Salathiel stood listening to this gossip somewhat impatiently. "It's nigh
noon," he said at last, "and I want t' get me to Chambers Mills before
nightfall. Wully said the road down the mountain has been new worked
lately and is in good shape. But I'd like to get on now. This talk of
Injuns has made the women anxious, and the sooner we're on t'other
side and away from it all, the better. But I guess I'll be needin' to borrow
both your nags for this last crawl to the summit. It does look like a bac
hazard."

"All right, Mr. Orator," said Yates, "as Wully Grant would say, 'Awa
wi' ye!'—and, of course, we'll see ye over the crest."

The reassembled cavalcade took off forthwith, with a clatter of hoof
and wheel rumblings that must, if anything, have been reassuring to the
scared inhabitants of Sugar Cabins, who viewed its departure cautiously
through their respective loopholes.

The deep-rutted road wound for a few hundred yards through the
temple-like sugar maple grove, dipped into a soggy stretch bordered by
scrub white oak, and then seemed to fling itself in one last level stretch
through a hemlock thicket straight at the face of the granite ridge. A
the very foot of this cliffy wall was a narrow rim of sleek green meadow
grass.

Rising sheer and swiftly above the tops of the hemlocks, the road
seemed to leap in what looked like a man-made stroke of lightning traced
in three zigzagged inclines to the crest of the mountain, about three
hundred feet above. It was by far the most ambitious and artificial piece
of construction on the whole of the "Glades Road". At the foot of the
first boulder-piled ramp the heavy wagon and the two horsemen accompanying it came to a halt for mutual consultation. Frances and young
Bridget emerged to look fearfully rather than hopefully at the goal so
high above, and no one had any doubt but that here was an obstacle
which it would take skill and determination rather than mere brute
strength and a merciless whip to surmount.

"Bejasus," exclaimed Frances, " 'tis a bit of the Giants' Causeway let
down out of the sky." At which, as if to confirm her comparison, the
front of a thin cloud began to drift across the top of the ridge, pouring
down over the summit a sinuous river of mist and veiling the cairn of
black rocks at the crest in a bright halo of sun-streaked fog. A light
pearly rain began to fall like dew on their upturned faces, and at that
instant Bridget gave a little gasping scream of joy. For the sun suddenly
threw an intense and complete circle of rainbow against the oncoming

mist above. In this the half-veiled dark stones seemed to mark the precise centre and to point like a hand.

The child was by no means the only one whose feelings were mysteriously touched. All of them stood gazing upward, their damp faces fixed in a quiet astonishment of delighted wonder. But the vision dissolved. The cloud fell in a shower of tinkling rain over the tops of the hemlocks behind them. Standing startlingly clear against the blue sky on the very crest of the ridge, they now saw the dark body of an elk with cloudy antlers staring down at them.

In the same instant Salathiel had covered it with his rifle. He fell down on his back behind the trundler and rested the muzzle of his long piece on the iron rim of the big artillery wheel. It was not a long shot, but it was upward, a high angle. He was just beginning to squeeze the trigger when Frances Melissa snatched the gun from his hands. It was so unexpected, it left him staring up at the sky, and into her face, blankly.

"Would ye be after bringin' Death into the middle of our good luck?" she panted. "Sure an' is the sign of the rainbow to be wasted on ye entirely?"

He rose slowly and stood looking at her, grim and white, shaking with anger. She gave him back the gun, which he slowly shifted to his left hand. The elk had gone. Salathiel stood there. She, and all of them, stood breathless, waiting for him to strike her . . .

In a curious and serious tone the voice of Yates reached out and seemed to take hold of the scene. "Brother," he said quietly, "it is time to turn your face towards the east, whence enlightenment comes."

Then, as the red mist cleared, Salathiel heard him, and remembered.

"Go back into the wagon, Melissa," he said hoarsely. "You've fouled the finest shot God ever sent me."

She took Bridget by the hand, and together they walked over to the wagon and got into it without looking back at him. Bridget was quietly weeping. She too had been badly scared. Melissa sat down and crossed herself. Her lips moved and her fingers flew. Bridget sat on the big harness chest, kicking her heels and watching. She did not approve of the way Melissa was saying her prayers. There was something strange and elaborate about it.

Outside, the three men turned earnestly to solving the problem of how best to drag the heavy wagon up the steep inclines and past the home of the clouds where the elk had vanished in the mist.

Yates and St. Clair unsaddled their mounts, which were temporarily fitted with two spare collars from the harness for an extra team carried in the trundler. That sturdy two-wheeled cart was unslung from the wagon and the two idle horses hitched to its shaft. Aside from sundry spare parts and harness and an extra wheel on the back of its caisson, the trundler was not heavily laden. Most of its freight consisted of peltry, beaverskins, fox, mink and others, which Salathiel had either shot, trapped, or traded in for a long time past. Actually, this "cargo" constituted most of his ready capital, since furs were always salable at some price. Their weight, however, on wheels, was comparatively light. Thus one team was able to haul the cart easily, and it was simply driven up the road to the summit and left there standing by the big cairn with its shaft in the air. St. Clair and Yates returned with the horses. The main difficulty, the wagon itself, of course, remained.

There were two sharp and short curves where the road reversed direction at violent angles, and it was a nice question whether the teams, as they swung around these, could keep the wagon moving. If it once halted it might indeed be difficult to start it again on so steep a slope. Most of the surface had worked off the road, exposing the heavy conglomerate rocks. Actually, the grade had here been constructed to pass the heavily laden wagons going westward *down*, rather than up, for most of the wagons going east were empty.

After some discussion, it was decided to hitch Yates and St. Clair's mounts in tandem before the lead team and to ride them at the same time to the top. Yates was to go first on Enna, the spirited little mare. Some drawing power would thus be sacrificed, but the gain would be in letting the two leading horsemen pick the way carefully and set the pace, thus permitting Salathiel to give all his attention to his double teams from the seat of the wagon.

It was nearly half an hour later before the change of harnessing could be completed. Nothing was left to chance. At this point Salathiel was especially glad that he had fitted his teams with blinkers at Bedford. He hoped that this would prevent any shying at the steep curves.

At length they stood ready to breast the first ramp, Yates and St. Clair mounted before, the two teams and the wagon stretching behind. They made a couple of wide circles over the grassy sward at the foot of the cliff to get the horses used to the new order, and then at a good fast walk, Yates headed for the first incline.

Each of the ridden horses snorted as it felt the unwonted drag come on its collar, but each was kept steady by its rider. The first team put their shoulders into it, feeling the urge of the reins, the second followed, straining together as one, the big wagon tilted skyward and was dragged upward slowly, rolling, bumping from rock to rock, its driver standing up, the reins like so many nerves in his hands, whip ready.

Twice one of the team horses stumbled and was almost lifted to its feet by the strong arm that pulled its bit and head upward by the reins. The thing to do was to keep them all pulling together steadily like one thing straining forward and upward without pause and without panic. The rippling necks of the big greys, the swing of their giant hip muscles, the line of backs all pointing forward was wonderful.

Yates swung around the first curve without mishap, and the climb for the second steep began. It was longer, but not so steep as the first.

Salathiel now began to talk to the horses, calling them by name, cheering them, and urging them onward. The second curve was so short that the two lead horses could do little hauling, and the whole brunt of the load came on the four beasts in the teams. They struggled here, straining fiercely, their hoofs clattering and slipping in loose stones. The ugly off leader, as the wagon almost came to a stop, humped himself for a kick. Salathiel saw the ripple of mutiny begin at his shoulders, but before the big back leg could slash out behind, the whiplash flicked his rump with fire, stung him into a surge forward that jerked the wagon around into its place facing the last slope. Once straightened out again, all six horses strove together.

Two hundred yards more, Salathiel judged. Yates shouted something about the road getting smoother now. He began to spur his mount. The last effort was necessary. The whip leaped out from the wagon seat. It cracked. Then it stung. At the lazy off leader it bit again and again. Laying their ears back and struggling forward frantically to escape the mysterious searing pain, the scrambling beasts seemed to pull the wagon loose from the force that was holding it back, and like a single many-legged monster writhed forward to the summit.

The iron of the wheels rang as the ark rolled out onto a wide flat space of bare table rock and came to a halt almost at the foot of the black cairn, where the trundler stood poised at the very edge of nothing.

Salathiel stood up on the seat and looked—eastward.

11. Pigtails and Horse-Chestnuts

EXPECTATION and Performance are difficult steeds to drive in a team as yoke mates, the former so easily outpaces the latter; and so Salathiel found.

He had fondly hoped to be in Chambersburg before nightfall, but it was well on towards nine o'clock of a clear valley evening when he pulled into that little settlement, better known locally as Chambers Mills. Here, only a generation before, Benjamin Chambers had established his plantation, a fine grant of four hundred acres, and his grist- and saw-mills, both at the mouth of the Falling Spring branch on the then clear and swiftly flowing Conococheague.

Travellers who then approached it from the westward were given a grateful welcome to the place by experiencing the first bit of consistently level, well-drained, and soft dirt road through open country east of the Alleghenies. In contrast with its former perpendicular performance, the highway now proceeded to ramble on gaily from one easily tilting crest of the eastward sloping piedmont to another.

The comparative silence of the wheels and the rapid rate of progress suddenly achieved seemed incredible. People breathed easily as the clutching fear of Indian ambush relaxed its hold. They spoke loudly, and, later on, they could even laugh again as their native good nature revived under a tonic of returning confidence. As Frances Melissa remarked, "Sure, their skins grew smoother."

So it was to come "downcountry" and to escape suddenly from the mountains. Everybody felt the relief and happiness. Even the horses pricked their ears forward expectantly and inhaled grateful breaths of fragrance from the clean mown pastures and good drying hay. And so it had been that November afternoon with Melissa and Bridget and Salathiel as they came "down into the province" and rolled along the level stretches of road leading towards Chambersburg. This, it seemed, was what a wagon must have been built for.

Once they had left the precipitous chute of the Stoney Batter behind them, and emerged by way of a rocky gorge from the cold shadow of the mountain wall itself, their journey seemed all at once to assume a more casual and habitually pleasant character. They were no longer oppressed by silence and their own loneliness. This was long-inhabited country. They passed the road fork to Black's Mills (now Mercersburg), where Captain James Smith lived, without stopping. From there on, cultivated country began. Crows cawed cheerfully across wide sunny fields. Now and then they met people along the road and exchanged cheerful greetings with them and neighbourly bits of news. Settlers who had been driven away by the raids of the summer before were already coming back. They heard about this and that family of farmers returning from Carlisle. Chimneys long left cold were smoking away again. Cattle were being driven home to familiar pastures. There were even a few enterprising pedlars about.

Only two miles west of the road that led briefly north to Fort Loudon they met one James Speer in a wagon piled high with goods, tools, and provisions, his decently kerchiefed young wife, Elizabeth, sitting demurely beside him.

St. Clair seemed to know Speer well. He was a sturdy, blue-eyed and broad-shouldered little Scot, who ran a small trading post in a wild and lonely side-glen halfway up the rocky gorge, just at the foot of the Stoney Batter. Two years before he had been driven away to Lancaster. Now he was coming back with a new wife and a full wagon to open up his small trading store in one of the two log cabins by the mountain spring in the glen. St. Clair, it appeared, was interested in the establishment. Either he had lent Speer some money or recommended him for credit to Philadelphia merchants. All brother Masons, probably. At any rate, cordiality and fraternity reigned as birds of local rumour and broad Scotch flew cheerfully about.

While Mrs. Speer sat blushing under her kerchief like the young bride that she was, listening to Yates's compliments and Melissa's soft accents, her husband displayed his new trading stock triumphantly to St. Clair, and from a small spigoted keg behind the wagon drew them a shallow pannikin each of as fiery a mountain beverage as ever started a slow Scotch heart beating under sturdy ribs.

"Thar's a whole bale o' prime beaver pelts in this sma' kag a' by itsel'," averred Jamie, patting the small fat barrel affectionately. "Say what ye will, mon, whusky's the ile o' frontier trade. And thar's no a painted savage beyond the tumblin' Tuscarora but would trade the har o' the best beaver i' the wilderness for one more panfu' o' this native heather-brew. And then how their askin' prices do tumble! I dinna ken how lang 'twill be before the wild hunters begin to slip back across the ranges again for a bit o' secret trade and a wee nip o' flamin' dew wi' honest Jamie, but 'twill no be so verra lang! And thar's a brisk commerce wi' the settlers aroond aboot coomin' into view. Times do be lookin' oop again, dinna ye think so?"

"I believe they be," replied St. Clair. "There's a new independent stir abroad in a' the colonies from Georgia to Massachusetts. Talk is a' o' growin' trade and commerce and o' more people comin' in. The frontiers will soon feel the pulse of life renewed, now that Bouquet has at last put the king's peace upon the western savages."

"Aye, thar's a braw grand fightin' mon!" exclaimed Speer. "I do hope the croon remimbers him."

"Perhaps," said St. Clair, "but 'tis more important just now that the Parliament should forget us. For a' thot though, Jamie mon, ye should do right well here even in your lonesome glen. Yon's a fine resting place for the thirsty gangin' o'er the pass westward, and the country this side is bound to fill oop wi' well-heeled farmin' folk. I hear Colonel Chambers has been layin' oot a bonny new town on his ain side o' the river this summer."

"And mauny a guid family from Antrim and the Land o' Cates, Campbells, Findleys, Wilsons, Langs, and MacAdams wi' their Eves expected shortly, all guid pious Presbyterian stock. 'MacThis and MacThat,' as they say," grinned Speer. "What I'll soon be needin' masel' is a couple o' brisk young Macs a' me ain to help tend the counter and till the farm. But ye ken leave that part to me, Arthur. The pleasure will be a' mine." And with that Mr. Speer chuckled and began to pat Mrs. Speer affectionately, instead of the keg.

A stick of barleycorn sugar for Bridget and a pair of red Carlisle stockings, which Salathiel bought for her on the spot without stopping to bargain for them, made perfect for all members of the company the bland air of the bright Indian summer afternoon for a spell of roadside gossip. They lingered for almost an hour, and it was nearly half after three when the two wagons finally reluctantly pulled away to resume their several journeys in opposite directions.

Bridget sat swinging her smooth scarlet legs and big moccasins from the wagon seat beside Salathiel. A look of dreamful satisfaction lingered in her wide brown eyes as though she had just glimpsed a vista of paradise, and the landscape of that country was still reproduced within. "Big man, will you make me some new red shoes, *too*?"

"I will that," said Salathiel emphatically, and then responded himself to the wriggle of complete satisfaction, one of happiness surfeited, which his brief and blithe answer produced in Bridget. The child sighed as if new shoes were almost *too* much to contemplate.

For that matter, Salathiel was feeling fairly well satisfied himself. Perhaps it was Jamie Speer's mountain cordial. But not altogether so, for while the others had been talking with the voluble little Scot, he had managed to slip back into the wagon and extract the severed hand from the salt box. It now reposed in his rifle pouch, but it was still not contained so surely in his mind. What should he do with it?

He intended to be honest with himself about this affair. He would act as he actually felt, and no shamming. Moreover, he would ask no one else's advice. When he got to Chambers Mills, he decided, he would smoke and cure the hand.

Having thus settled this manual question of morals satisfactorily with his own conscience, he dismissed the subject peremptorily, and whistled through his teeth to the horses and slapped the reins.

St. Clair and Yates had gained considerably upon him, riding ahead. Apparently they were still hopeful of catching up with the marching Highlanders. But there was little chance of that, he thought. They had lingered too long gossiping with James Speer. And Wully had been in a hurry with the troops. He would have marched fast. The sun was nearing the mountains already. He saw he would never make Chambersburg before dark now. But what of it! This was a pleasant road, and he was in the dawn country at last.

He called back to Melissa to come and join him and Bridget on the driver's seat. Already he had forgotten what it was like to be angry with her. But she hadn't. She came forward to sit with Bridget between them, secretly happy and relieved to find herself "forgiven", as she thought; actually, it was simply to take her usual place. The child hummed a wordless, happy little song, leaning up against her. The horses were going at a fast steady trot. Salathiel was smiling contentedly.

Suddenly confidence and the sunny calm of the Indian summer afternoon, as the shadows of the trees lengthened slowly across the fields, filled her with peace—while James Speer's sustaining drink still warmed her comfortably. Putting an arm across Salathiel's shoulders, she began to sing in a rich contralto a ballad, which, with her roguish Irish lilt and shaded irony of phrase, proved irresistible. After a couple of staves, they all sang it together over and over again.

And it was thus that Yates and St. Clair, who were waiting impatiently at the Loudon crossroads, saw and heard the big wagon, as it came trotting ponderously but gaily down the road. Salathiel drew up and looked at them inquiringly.

"We've missed catching up with Wully and his kilted retainers by nearly an hour," said Yates. "They're probably back in barracks by now. But it's only a mile or so from here to the fort. Now, Arthur and I have been talking things over, and—"

"Ned thinks it will be best if we follow up last night's little affair, and strike while the iron's still hot," interrupted St. Clair. "You see—"

"I'll garnish the papers off him now, and settle for what land we can get," continued Yates. "Either that, or probably we'll never get anything. Arthur and I think possibly we can manage the affair ourselves. But it might take a day or so. Wully will be fairly savage."

"That arrangement will suit me," said Salathiel, seeing he was not needed. "I can manage alone for a bit. We'll wait for you to overtake us at Chambers Mills. At the Davisons'—they've moved to the Mills, you know."

"You'll stay *there?*" said Yates. "All right, but . . ." and he looked significantly at Frances.

"Well, wherever we may be stayin', you'll soon hear of us, I warrant," said Salathiel.

"And if you'll be after needin' a lion to chase your unicorn, you can send down for this one," added Melissa, patting her man's arm.

"A lion? He's only a big bear," replied Yates, "but I think our unicorn will be a pretty tame one after tonight. Anyway, we'll try to bring back a piece of his golden horn, without asking for help."

"Here's to it, then!" exclaimed St. Clair, and drew out his long silver saddle-flask. "The only thing I got oot o' the game last nicht was a fill o' Patton's 'fifty-two peach brandy. You'll remember why *this* was empty, Mistress Albine." He looked at her, his blue eyes twinkling, as he shook the flask.

They all remembered, and laughed at her.

Nevertheless, as the flask went around, she tilted it up again at a high angle. After the first gulp, Salathiel snatched it out of her hand.

"Just like you did with the rifle-gun," he said, and grinning, handed the flask back to St. Clair.

She sat breathless for a minute, and then began to laugh. "Ye damned spalpeen, so ye'd snatch the drink out of me parched mouth, would ye? Sal, I guess we're even now," she whispered.

He patted her hand, and they drove off suddenly.

"We'll be stayin' at Nathan Patton's house, nigh the fort," shouted Yates. "Wait for us at the Mills until Monday, at least."

Salathiel waved a paw that he understood.

"So, we'll have to get along for a few days without the two noble gintlemen," said Frances, philosophically. He grinned and slipped an arm about her waist. "Yes, but *we* will miss them more than Wully ever will."

She tossed her head.

The way for the most part was now a gentle downgrade. He put his whole attention on tooling the horses along and maintaining a good steady clip. The big beasts seemed to know they were going home, perhaps the scents along the old road were familiar. The steady rhythm of their hoofs was seldom broken. But it was over twelve miles from Loudon crossroads to Chambersburg. He was determined to get there that night, and it would take about all that the horses had.

From a curve of the high road going over a long crest, they caught a glimpse of Fort Loudon looming up some miles away to the west near Parnell's Knob. Even at that distance they could make out the Union Jack flapping in the wind above the stockade. Then the slope of the land and a bit of woodland intervened.

Four miles farther, and just before sunset, they passed a long train of pack horses. It was a convoy of supplies going forward to Bouquet at Fort Pitt. Salathiel nodded to a young ensign of the Royal Americans, who headed the mud-splashed string with a lone corporal, but beyond that he made no acknowledgment to the storm of "howdies", shouts, rude questions, and ribald advice that greeted him and the wagon as he passed down the road. He saw no familiar faces among the riders, but many a loutish one. One little brown man with a beard did look vaguely familiar, but he had his hat pulled down over his eyes. A sergeant and two mounted men from the old 60th brought up the rear. Their familiar scarlet and buff-white gave him a homesick turn. But they were strangers all. He cracked his whip and drove on faster to get out of their rolling dust.

"Buckey" must be pretty confident of himself, he thought. Five men to escort fifty horses! Last year there would have been half a company at least. Too bad Ecuyer couldn't have lived to see this. He might be going home now to Geneva. Lord, how he missed Ecuyer, and blessed his name! He remembered his wholehearted admiration for Colonel Bouquet. "By far the best officer in the colonies" was what the little captain had said. "And if you are ever in difficulties, go to Bouquet. He's a man who remembers when you have once done him a service."

Well, he was in no difficulties now. But he would like to talk to the colonel. Where now was the list of Indian captives McArdle had given him to take to Fort Pitt? he wondered. It was just the kind of thing some ignorant clerk would mislay or destroy, because it was written on bark. But that list might be very helpful now to the colonel, since Bouquet was rounding up every one of the captivated from all the tribes at Carlisle. It would be mighty good medicine as a check on the chiefs' stories. How they would lie! The Injuns loved many of the adopted captives, and some captives would hate to leave them after years of wilderness life. Many would have gone permanently wild. It would not be easy to separate them. Then he remembered where one copy of the list was. It was in his own mind!

He began to say it over to himself, hearing his old singsong half-Indian, boyish voice recapitulating the names to McArdle, while he lay sprawled out on the floor of Kaysinata's lodge. Malycal used to join in. Yes, he could still "sing" them all. Lord, how well he remembered! And all the dim old ways of the forest, the deer browsing on leaves, all those beautiful wild islands down the Ohio—what a life it had once been! Unconsciously, he sighed.

Probably it was the oncoming of evening that had thus given a sombre cast and a retrospective twist to his thoughts. The twilight was beginning to deepen. Bridget and Melissa sat silent by his side. The horses trudged on monotonously. He was letting them walk part of the time now. He liked this time of evening—in a peaceful land!

They splashed into a broad but shallow ford, and in the middle of the stream he pulled up the teams to let them have a drink. Their long necks arched down towards the flowing water. Just around a curve in the thicket ahead, a liquid voice seemed to be talking with a continuous quiet excitement in an unknown tongue. It was telling a story he ought to remember, he felt.

"What's that?" he demanded suddenly. Instinctively, at a strange sound, his hand groped for his rifle-gun.

They listened. It kept coming closer.

"Sure it's the sound of cowbells," said Frances. "Cowbells! Someone's after bein' late drivin' the kine home this evenin'."

He had never heard cowbells before. There were three of them. Two that clanked, and one that tonked.

Presently at the other side of the stream the herd appeared with white mottled faces and stubby horns. They halted for a moment at the unexpected sight of the silent horses standing in the water, and then began slowly to cross. There were about thirty of them, cows, calves, and one small, shaggy brown bull with a broken horn. Salathiel fingered his whip. But they passed quietly on, stopping for a brief drink, and lowing softly. A dog of the long-haired Scotch breed burst out of the woods and began harrying his charges along. He paid no attention to the wagon whatsoever, but swam through the ford, and rounded up the stray calves and heifers on the far side of the little river like a competent thunderstorm herding small clouds before it. Bridget was delighted with this expert performance and clapped her hands. The herd took off down the road with the dog yapping behind, when an obviously excited boy on a newly broken-in colt showed up. His yellow curls flowed down from under his raccoon cap almost to his shoulders. Seeing the wagon, he drew rein on the riverbank, looking both startled and disappointed.

"Lost your chance to show off, didn't ye?" called Bridget.

The boy looked at her for a moment, horrified at having his thoughts read. Then he put his fingers to his nose and gave them a twirl. "You've got eyes like horse-chestnuts," he retorted. At that he began to cross over. "Pigtails!" he remarked, as he came opposite the wagon. Frances put her hand on Bridget's arm as the little girl began to bounce in the seat indignantly.

"Look here, young feller," said Salathiel, "didn't ye ever hear about loutin' your cap to the ladies?"

"Yes, sir," replied the boy sheepishly, measuring the distance between him and the whip with careful round blue eyes, "but this yere colt don't like fer to stand in cold water, and takes both hands."

"Hold him, then!" said Salathiel.

The boy did so and managed to remove his cap, too. A further cascade of curls drenched his shoulders.

"That's a handsome scalp ye got, sonny," remarked Mr. Albine. "If ye ain't right keerful somebody's liable to lift it for ye."

"I know," said the boy, "but I'm bound out, and the mistress won't let me nor her Jim cut our hair short. It marks us, she says."

"It does that. Who might ye be workin' for?"

"Mrs. Shaemus McKinney. Her old man was took off in the raids of 'fifty-six. But I'm none of hern. I'm Roy Davison."

"Kin of Arthur at Chambersburg?" he inquired.

"Cousin," replied the boy. "But my pa won't hev no more truck with hisn. They fit like bobcats when uncle moved his tannery to Chambers Mills. Liken you folks might tarry the night with us, maybe?" said Roy, looking at Bridget. He smiled at her archly. "Hit's a *big* stone house, and hit's half empty." Bridget wriggled. "And hit's nigh five miles from here to the Mills at the Falling Spring," he added, hopefully.

"Get on with ye, Mr. Albine," said Melissa. "There's no time to tarry here jist for these childer to fall in love."

Why not? he thought, remembering Phoebe. Somehow the boy had reminded him of her. Probably it was his name. But he looked at the sturdy youngster on the colt sympathetically.

"Good night, son. We'll have to be drivin' on," he said. He spat a disgruntled "giddap" at the horses. Just why he was irritated, he didn't quite know.

The boy sat watching the big wagon disappear down the road into the gathering twilight. He was late with the cows this evening. Mistress McKinney would wallop him well. But pigtails and horse-chestnuts for Mistress McKinney! He stuffed his gold scalp locks back under his cap and whistled softly, looking after the wagon disappearing down the road in the blue dusk. Suddenly a light shone out through the canvas behind.

Frances Melissa had taken Bridget off the seat and was putting the little girl to bed. Afterwhile she lay down herself on the long clothes chest. It was getting dark outside now, and it would be another hour, with the tired horses, until they got into Chambersburg.

Bridget lay looking up at the white canvas ceiling, her kitten beside her.

"Did ye like him, Mamma Lissa?" she whispered.

"Who?" answered Frances, teasingly.

"Roy—Roy Davison." She kept repeating the boy's name.

"Yes, of course, I fell in love with him, little silly. I niver saw sich hair, and the sunny smile of him. Oh moi!"

Whether it was Bridget or the kitten that did all the purring now, Frances couldn't tell.

Both she and Bridget were fast asleep when Salathiel finally rumbled over the timber bridge into Chambersburg a little before the late moon-rise and began to look for a place to stable the horses. He listened to the deep breathing of the sleepers with a curious mixture of apprehension and satisfaction.

Only the kitten came out to rub itself against his gaiters and demand supper in its own way. But where and how would he get supper even for a cat in a place as dark and lonely as Chambersburg seemed to be?

12. In Which the Little Turtle Laughs Like a Loon

SALATHIEL LOOKED about him as he stood in the starlight, and he could see very little. The overpowering impression of Chambersburg was a dark velvet silence poised against the continuous rushing of fall-ing water. Evidently the sound came from a dam and mill-race not far to his right, where Colonel Chambers's mills stood in a dark cluster, and the first beams of moonrise were beginning to shimmer on what ap-peared to be the metal roof of some large building. A little farther up the stream was a notably heavy clump of cypress, black against the starry sky. One dim light, and one only, showed feebly some distance to his left.

He left the wagon alone unwillingly and walked towards the light across a field full of muddy wheel ruts. As the moonlight brightened, he gradually made out that he was crossing a large public square, where four roads coming together traced a rough cross. Here and there in the lots around the edges of the common the roofs of houses now began to show above the trees. The light came glimmering from a long building with a platform before it like a low wharf or a roofless porch. Now and then the feeble radiance flickered and blinked. It seemed to be filtering through the panes of the largest window he had ever seen. Over a sliding door towards the far end of the platform was a store loft. There was also a swinging sign near the window. He could barely make it out:

Will Somerfield
Domestic Merchandise
&
Choice London Goods
Household Sundries
Victualler & Vintner
(Licensed Prov. Trader)

Will Somerfield, eh? Probably the merchant prince of Chambersburg. But where was he?

He turned to peer through the wavering squares of glass in the big boxed window. It was the first shop window he had ever seen. Inside, several bolts of fine figured cloth were unrolled for display, and there was a clutter of minor metal articles that appeared to be cutlery. The light was certainly dim. He pressed his forehead against one of the better panes and squinted beyond. Curiously distorted, the interior of a general store sprang dimly into view.

Somewhere around the corner of a long cavelike room, a log fire was flickering. He could not see the fireplace, but its reflected glow discovered numerous rows of shelves lined with shadowy merchandise. At the far end of the place on a broad wooden counter dangled the weighing pans of a pair of brass scales in the light of two thick candles stuck into jugs. Barrels and kegs were everywhere about. Seated on one of them before the counter was young Arthur Davison talking earnestly to a kindly looking old man in a leather apron.

Lord, how Arthur had grown! He was a tall youth now. He had his sister's regular features, her wide brow and her provocative mouth.

Inevitably, for a sick and tender moment, it was Phoebe and not Arthur that Salathiel's eyes beheld again. Phoebe, lost Phoebe Davison!

He weakened down to the soles of his feet again, just as he had that day at Bedford when he read her farewell letter. He closed his eyes. But he could hear her voice and her shy feet passing up and down the stairs by his door. Why, why had he so carefully hunted up this old agony for himself again?

Why? Because he meant to face the music; to bring his hopeless dream of her face to face with reality.

Yes, he must know about Phoebe. He would never see her again. But he could *hear* about her; find out, for instance, if she were still alive. And then, equally important now, he meant to take care that Frances Melissa should never learn about Phoebe. Instinctively he knew that it might be fatal; that it would be entirely different from Frances' knowing about Jane.

So he must carefully warn young Arthur. If necessary he would . . . Pshaw! That *was* an Indian thought. The boy had always liked him. He had taken him on his first deer hunt. Maybe he'd remember those days. He gave a certain shrill whistle they had once used as a signal at Pendergasses'.

Arthur looked up startled and with an incredulous expression of happy surprise. He listened . . .

Salathiel tapped on the glass, and whistled again.

An instant later the door by the shop window flew open while the small customers' bell tinkled violently, and Arthur stood there gazing into the night as though he couldn't believe what he saw.

"It's you, Sal! It's *really* you, ain't it?" the lad exclaimed.

"Heap much me it is," Salathiel replied, crushing the boy's fingers.

"*Owl*" cried Arthur. "It's you, all right! But, good God, Sal, that's the curiousest thing. I was talkin' to Mr. Somerfield about you when I heard your whistle. What do you think of that? Mr. Somerfield," he called to the man at the back of the store, "here's the very feller I was jes tellin' ye about, and he's got that rifle-gun, too!"

"Bring him in," said Mr. Somerfield, leaning forward with both hands pressed flat on the counter in frank curiosity. "Bring him in, son, and let's have a look at him."

"This is him, sir," said Arthur, "Sal Albine."

"Well, well, speak of the devil!" exclaimed Mr. Somerfield, shaking hands over the counter cordially. "Ever since Arthur's been clerkin' for me here, I've been hearin' a lot about ye. If there was as much goods went over this counter as gossip, I'd be a rich man. Happen ye didn't come downcountry to dispose of some peltry?"

"Wal, now, I have *some*, Mr. Somerfield," Albine replied. "Arthur and I might show it to ye tomorrow. I'll be right glad to. But I'm on my way to Carlisle with my lady and a little girl in the wagon. They're asleep out there in the common now. Happen ye might know where I could shelter the wagon and four tired horses for the night?"

Mr. Somerfield pondered. "You're right welcome to my sheds in the paddock behind the store," said he, still considering. "But then my back lot's full o' a sight o' poultry, and old lumber and plunder. Tell ye what ye do, Arthur. Wake up St. Clair's nigger. He's been eatin' his head off here jes doin' nothin' but waitin' for his master. Get him to watch Mr. Albine's wagon while ye walk him around to Colonel Chambers's. Liken the old man will open up the mill stockade for ye. Ye'll find *that* safe enough, and lots o' shelter for the horses in the big sheds. It's the building with the lead roof, the one where the whole neighbourhood usen fer to fort-up. Some folks call it 'the castle'. No one lives there now, but the colonel keeps the place in good repair."

"Sounds just elegant," said Salathiel, gratefully, "but I didn't expect a castle."

Mr. Somerfield looked embarrassed. "Now, sir, I'd take ye in here ifen I could," he said, "but Effie died nigh four years ago, and ever since I've been livin' all alone. I've got Arthur here in the store, and a couple of old niggers for gineral yard help. But there's not even a private decency with a sand box here fit for a lady, let alone comforts for a small child."

"Now, now, ye're bein' mighty kind as it is," drawled Salathiel. "I've no doubt Colonel Chambers will be able to put up one of Captain Jack's old band o' rangers for the night. We can all sleep in the wagon, anyway. It's only yard room I want."

Just then Arthur reappeared, followed by St. Clair's Negro servant, his eyes still heavy with sleep.

"Remember me, Jed?" asked Salathiel, shaking him awake good-naturedly. "Say, can ye still turn hand springs like ye did on the mound at Shawnee Cabins?"

"Do Gawd, sah," exclaimed the sturdy little Negro. "Yah ain't gwine fer fetch this fellah back ter de Injun country, be yah? Marster say stay hyah. Wait! Him come back soon."

"Yes, your master will be along in a couple of days, Jed. And he's aimin' to take ye back to the City with him then. So I've not been sent to get ye. All I want you to do now is to watch a wagon for about half an hour. Cheer up! No widow's son-of-a-gun would carry off a good boy like you to sell to the Injuns."

Jed looked greatly relieved by this news. But it was still with evident reluctance that he now accompanied Albine and young Davison out into the dark square, where the wagon loomed up impressively in the moonlight. Melissa and Bridget remained sleeping soundly. Salathiel determined he would not disturb them, and cautioned Jed to be quiet and not to discover himself on any account, as Melissa was nervous about black boys; he left him holding the horses' heads and returned to thank Mr. Somerfield.

"Why, it's nothin', brother," said the old man. "After you see Ben Chambers and git settled down, come over to the store and we'll have a snack over the counter out o' one of the fish barrels. I'll keep the fire goin'. By the way, Colonel Chambers is right active in the lodge here. Thought from somethin' ye just said that news might interest ye."

"Why, it certainly does, sir," Salathiel replied. "I'm obleeged for the information, and I'll try to drop around for a bite later on."

The old man looked pleased. "Don't forget, it's *Somerfield's* at the corner o' Front and Queens streets," said he, proud of his establishment and of the newly named streets in the new town. "But Arthur will guide ye. Now git along and try to see Ben before it's so late. Everybody ain't night-owls around here like me and young Arthur. Still, that was kind o' lucky for ye."

Salathiel agreed that it was. And taking Arthur by the arm, they started off to find Colonel Chambers.

"Old man Somerfield's begun preparin' me for the first degree," said the boy proudly. "I'll be old enough fer first questioning pretty soon."

"That's fine," said Salathiel. "You couldn't do better. Your grandpap Garrett would rejice to know it." He felt the boy glow under his approval, and came to a swift conclusion.

"Listen, Arthur," he said, "do you remember that buck we shot near Naugles' at Bedford a long time ago?"

"Why, it was my first! Of course, I remember."

"Wal, the Injuns, least ways the Shawanees, think that when an old hunter first bloods a younger one that way, the twain are kind o' bound to be a huntin' pair afterward, and to keep a tight lip about what they happen to know about any huntin' grounds shared between them. Now, would ye kind o' play Injun that way and buck me up?"

"Sal, ye know I would. Dang I wisht I had ye for a brother-in-law instead of . . . Oh, well, but that *was* the damnedest thing. Phoebe just cried her eyes out. We used to sleep in the same room, you know. She was more like my ma than a sister to me. But now I hear she'll soon have a young'un of her own. Say, didn't ye meet Mr. Burent in that pack train ye must have passed? Ye couldn't have missed him?"

Then Salathiel remembered. "Has he got a beard now?"

"Yep, and a gold watch with a big thick chain. But his beard's come out grey, for a wonder, instead of bein' brown."

"We must have passed each other. I guess he knew me," said Salathiel, "but I didn't know him. Happen I did kind o' think one of the riders looked familiar."

"Well, Mr. Burent's been here for a week past, stayin' with my folks down at our new tannery. Pa says they're doin' right well with the cooperage at Pittsburgh. And sis is expectin', come March. They didn't waste no time doin' it, did they? But you've got a youngster in the wagon yourself now, didn't ye say?"

"Her name's Bridget, and she's about seven years old," drawled Salathiel.

It took a second or two—

"She's *what!*" Arthur blurted out. He came to a halt from sheer surprise. "Now, how *did* ye ever manage that?" he demanded.

"That's what I want to talk to ye about," replied Salathiel.

He had determined to save himself as much anxiety as possible by taking the boy fully into his confidence. He felt he had lost Phoebe at Bedford by keeping his mouth shut too carefully, and he didn't want to lose Frances Melissa the same way.

Standing in the darkness at the entrance of a lane that ran down to the river, he told young Arthur Davison the whole sorry story.

"*So* that's how it was," said Arthur. "Oh, I'm glad ye told me, Sal.

Nobody likes to think they've jes been fooled, ye know. Do ye want me to tell sis sometime?"

"I'm goin' to leave that to you, Arthur. Yes, I'd like her to know sometime how it really was. But whatever ye do, don't make trouble for her. She's got her own family to think of now, and I've got mine. And we'll be miles and years apart. Maybe you'll understand it all a little better when you come to get married yourself."

"I can understand it now," the boy said firmly.

"I believe ye can," rumbled Salathiel. "Course the main thing is that not a word of this should ever get to Frances. Everybody thinks she's my wife. Naturally, I ain't goin' to be the first one to deny it—and it won't be healthy after this for anyone that tries to throw a spoke through the wheels of my wagon. We're havin' a baby early next summer."

"If it's a boy, name it after me, will ye, Sal? We'd both know why, and nobody need ever say a word. Lord, I'd like that."

"Now, that's mighty fine of you, youngster," Salathiel exclaimed, greatly relieved at this unexpected but happy turn of affairs. "Tell you what, ifen we're settled down by then, I'll write ye upcountry and let ye know. And ye can come down and visit with us."

"Suppose it's a gal?" said Arthur.

"Wal, then it will be one," replied Salathiel, laughing. "Still ye might like to come downcountry anyway, and I'd like to have ye for a while, just for old time's sake."

"Lordy, it'd be like bears' grease and tree sugar," chuckled Arthur, "seein' the City! Lord—ee! Don't ye forget now! Send to Mr. Somerfield at the store here."

"Oh, I'll let ye hear," Salathiel promised. "Now just where does our friend, Colonel Chambers, hang out?"

"Phew, I'd plumb forgot him," cried Arthur. "Come on!"

He led down a lane past a bare-boughed orchard. On an alley that ran between the mill-race and the river stood the small but comfortable log dwelling of Colonel Chambers just at the foot of his son's vegetable patch. From a shed in the rear came the rays of a lanthorn and the sound of chopping.

"Thought I'd lay in a bit of kindlin' for the night," said he, dusting off his hands, and giving Albine a keen glance and a nod. "Well, Arthur, what is it?"

"My friend, Sal, here, sir. Mr. Somerfield thought . . ."

"I'm Sal Albine, colonel," said Salathiel, stepping forward, "one of Captain Jack's men. Maybe you've heard of me from James Smith or some of his boys up the Connycajig."

"Heard of ye! Of course, I have, sir. Dang, if I didn't spot ye as soon as I laid eyes on that double-barrelled enjine of destruction you're fondlin'." They shook hands while Arthur looked on proudly.

"Come down to the house," said the colonel, carefully resuming his coat and wig, "and meet Ruhannah, my daughter. Mrs. Chambers is off visitin' at Shippensburg. But Ruhannah's here. She's married to Dr. Colhoun, but he's away tappin' fer dropsy and she's lookin' after her old pa agin for a while. Arthur, bring in that axe and the kindlin', will ye, son? But whar's your folks, Albine? Be ye alone? Where are ye stoppin'? Maybe ye'd like to look over some of the lots in the new town plot I'm layin' out here, eh?"

"I'd like to consider it," said Salathiel, "but just now I'm intendin' for Carlisle and the City. I've got my missus and a young one in the wagon—and four horses—all waitin' up on the square. Brother Somerfield thought you might let me hut-up for the night in your castle yard. I think that's what he called it."

"Somerfield's a good guesser," replied Chambers. "Of course, ye kin. Arthur, fetch a lanthorn, and the key to the stockade gate from the cabin. It's the big key behind the front door. You'd best show your friend the way over the mill-race. Mind the little trestle bridge, it's loose at the far end."

"I know, sir," said Arthur, delighted to be found so useful. "And I'll go and fetch the wagon for ye, Sal. Jed and I can bring it down here and pick ye up on the way. We'll lead the horses most careful."

"All right. I can have a word with the colonel, then. Try not to waken the women. And, Art, be sure to bring that kitten along. I'd get scalped if it gets lost."

Arthur hurried off after securing the key and the lanthorn.

"Spry youngster, that," remarked Colonel Chambers, holding the cabin door open for his guest. "He certainly spread your fame and glory in these parts. He's Burent's brother-in-law, the cooper at Fort Pitt. Know him? Mighty clever man, and the best cooper in the province, they all say."

"He's a mighty good man," agreed Salathiel, making a wry face inwardly. "Now, I wouldn't want to keep ye up, colonel. It's right late."

"Ye ain't keepin' me up, I'm doin' my accounts these winter evenings, but I do like a fire and warm hands and feet while I'm clerkin'. That's the reason we're stayin' in the cabin here. The big house's cold as a barn, unless you keep twenty fires goin'. I've a sight o' children used to do that, but they're all married and live out, every one of 'em! Ruhannah, who's just visitin' here, Jim, Ben, Bill, Jane, Adam, Joe, and Hetty. Scarcely seems natur'l, but really it's natur'l as time." Here the colonel produced a jug from under his desk and, slinging it back of his wrist over his forearm, poured a jet accurately into two noggins without spilling a drop.

"I suppose you got practice and learned to handle your jug liquor that way drinkin' birthday toasts to all the children," said Salathiel, admiringly. "You've got nigh as many as Garrett Pendergass, I reckon."

Colonel Chambers laughed. "No, that's only the old Connycajig twist on a jug. Speakin' o' childer, I was really just tryin' to tell ye why the big house is so empty now, and how it comes I can't take ye into the cabin here like I'd hope to. I built the stone house in 'fifty-six and put a lead roof on it later. Just to keep off Injun fire-arrows. Some wits laughed. But the old place contained their jests and kept the har on their heads through many a raid. Afterwhile, for all my follies, I was appointed justice of the peace and made a colonel of the line. So I mounted an old cohorn and a blunderbuss and made a kind of fort out of the house for the militia. My court and the blue lodge still meets there. I'm lettin' the house stand empty, but I'm keepin' it up. All the ginerals mightn't prove so clever as Bouquet, and we might have raids here again. Now, if you and Captain Jack would only settle down here, that'd be like a permanent regular garrison. Tell ye what, you and your missus come over to the cabin and have breakfast tomorrow mornin', and bring your little one. I'll tell Ruhannah and she'll set some extra batter for ye. Now, don't say no, it's all right, and I want to ask ye a lot of things about Captain Jack. He's an old friend o' mine. Well, 'here's powder in your horn, and good huntin'!' That'll warm ye! It's about ten years old."

"I feel that much younger already," said Salathiel. "It's powerful stuff."

The colonel looked up, listening.

"That must be your contraption comin' down the lane now, I guess," said he. "Sounds like artillery wheels. Have ye feed fer your nags?"

"Plenty, sir, and I do want to thank ye."

"Now, now," said the colonel, "you jes come over tomorrow mornin', and we'll really give ye somethin' to be thankful for." He followed Salathiel to the door and said good night to him.

Arthur was coming down the lane with a lanthorn, showing the way for Jed, who led the tired horses gingerly.

"They're still asleep in there," said Arthur. "And I found the kitten a fish head and put her in the seat-chest. It's only about a hundred yards or so to the castle. This here's the bridge now, the one the colonel said to be keerful about."

They were at the foot of the lane by this time, and the sound of running water filled their ears. After crossing the short bridge over the mill-race without mishap, they came out on a perfectly level piece of ground, with the mill-race on one side and the river on the other.

"The dam lies a bit farther down," said Arthur. "It's the spillway ye hear so loud. But here we be!"

A stockaded log wall lay directly across their path. It was at the gate of this that they now halted, while Jed held the lanthorn and Arthur worked the big key in a huge and rusty padlock. Finally it gave, a bar tumbled, and the double leaves of the gate swung inward.

Salathiel stood stock-still for a moment from sheer surprise. The space ahead of him seemed to end in nothing but a field of stars. It looked as though only a few hundred feet farther and they would fall off the edge of the world.

Arthur laughed. "It does kind of get ye at first by night," he said. "You see, this here's kind of an island we're on, and you're lookin' out over the dam at the lower end of it. The house is over this way."

"Guess I'll get it clearer tomorrow," said Salathiel, "but let's get the horses bedded down. They're near done in."

"Yas, sah, in a jiffy," replied Jed. "Dah's de sheds now."

They drew up in a deep-sodded stable yard surrounded on three sides by sheds and penthouses in solid array. The side of the yard next the riverbank was occupied by Colonel Chambers's stone house that stared stolidly in the moonlight. All its windows were tightly boarded with heavy oaken shutters pierced with loopholes. The lead roof, wet with heavy dew, seemed to be molten under the moon and to be dripping hot metal over the eaves. A flight of white stone steps led up to its massive but extremely narrow door. The effect was strangely unpleasant, even formidable. The house at night bore the expression of a merciless fanatic showing its bared teeth in a bad dream.

Something in the sound of the rushing and gurgling waters, the angry silence of the grim house guarding its dark island domain so implacably, convinced Jed that *this* was a place where it was not healthy for a young person of colour, only recently removed from Dahomey by slavers, to tarry in. Nor did the rugged profile and menacing outlines of the big white man tend to soothe his African spirits. It was all frightfully strange, and the moonlight in America was cold. Consequently, Jed shivered, but his fingers flew all the faster.

The horses were unharnessed in a trice. Arthur led them to the sheds, and Salathiel bedded them down. He gave them plenty of dry straw to lie on and a generous supper of corn with a dash of precious salt. Tomorrow they must have a rest and a good going-over by a farrier. No one could get horses over the Stoney Batter without casting a few shoes. And most of those remaining were worn or working loose. The harness was laid out for a careful going-over on the morrow, and then all hands turned to, to give the teams a good rub-down and currying.

Thus everything was suddenly done. Jed stood waiting hopefully, not daring to leave until Arthur should be ready to go.

"You won't have a snack up at the store, then, like Mr. Somerfield said?" inquired Arthur, who had visions of a night of talk and forest tales by Salathiel, before the fire.

"Not tonight, young'un," laughed his friend. "You forget I'm not alone like I used to be," and he motioned towards the wagon.

"Shucks," said Arthur, "I'd jes forgot. But kin I see you tomorrow?"

"Sure ye kin. I'll come over to the store, say about noon, with a bale of peltries I want fer to do a little hawse-tradin' over with old man Somerfield. You and him can paw them over first. And I guess any clever clark that brings in beaver to trade gets a bit of sugar on the side."

"Golly!" exclaimed Arthur. "Gol—*lee!*"

"Jed," said Salathiel, "you're a good man, and I'll tell your master as much. But listen—"

"Yas, sah, both ears am pintin' yuh way."

"I'll give you something right handsome when *you stop bein' scared of me.* Now, close the gate when you go out, and don't lock me in.'

"Yas, sah."

Salathiel stood watching them depart as long as he could see the lant-horn sliding along the mill-race among the willows. Suddenly it ceased to show at the corner of the lane.

Actually, *he* wasn't body-tired at all. Driving was wearing, but it gave him small exercise. Colonel Chambers's drink still made him glow. And it was luck to be alone again in a safe place like this, sequestered from all strangers. The moon was beginning to sail high, and there was a heartening touch of frost in the night air. He had no words to express his sense of triumph at having arrived thus in the dawn country. It was a feeling only, a sensation of satisfaction. Like a savage, he once more gave himself up to pure sensation and to being still and happy within. This place *was* good, a fine grassy level surrounded by a hedge of trees, washed on all sides by living water. It was like some of his islands of refuge down the Ohio. Only one thing troubled him. He still smelled of horses and the dust of the road.

Twitching a blanket off the wagon seat on sudden impulse, he slid out of his clothes and walked to the river's edge. He tingled. He stood looking out over the black pool, where the stream backed up into a deep lake behind the dam. Somewhere, farther up, he could hear the roar of the falls where the Falling Spring branch dived into the Conoco-cheague. Below, the dark roofs of the mill buildings rose vaguely above the dam. One seemed to be only half finished. But there was no one about.

Two or three night-feeding waterfowl were moving in the shadow of the opposite shore. The moony water flashed where they dived. Loons, probably. Winter could not be far behind. He gave the low chipping-cluck of their private night language, and watched them begin to edge over towards him cautiously. Then, suddenly, he sprang forward in a wide clean arc and flashed into the dark depths. As his head emerged, he gave the long weird laugh of the loon.

Two of the startled birds answered him, their wings thrashing violently as they took off into the night over the dam. The whole place rang with a raucous burst of wild demoniac laughter. In the face of the haggard moon, the Little Turtle pranced and capered on the riverbank, wringing the cold water out of his long hair, and dancing violently to dry himself off. He just felt fine.

Presently, he flung his blanket over his shoulders and ran back to the wagon. He crawled in stark naked, and squirmed under the covers on his bunk. He heard Frances stirring uneasily.

"So you're back again," she said.

He reached over in the dark and took her hand, pressing it to his lips and fondling her long soft fingers. Lord, it was good to find her here.

"Howly hiven," she whispered, "whir in God's beauteous world have ye taken us now? Hark to the rushin' of tireless waters! And what was that wild fleerin' laughter passed overhead jist now like a family rally o' banshees? Did ye meet up with them in yon empty house, in the quiverin' moonlight?" She sat up suddenly, badly scared by her own talk, and staring into the darkness.

"Lie down, sweetheart. Turn over on your easy side and sleep. I was jes talkin' with a flock of loons. You're safe on Colonel Chambers's isle, with the river and a fence all about ye. No one comes here but night fowl to feast on eel grass. And tomorrow . . ."

"Yis," she said, "tomorrow?"

"We're to take breakfast with Colonel Chambers himself and his new-married daughter, in their nice little cabin up a grassy lane."

"Ye do well by us, Mr. Albine. Ye're a right clever man."

"Handy to have about?" he chuckled.

"Yis," she whispered, and softly withdrew her hand. "I think I'll be wearing me new blue linsey-woolsey and the yellow snood ye got fer me at Cumberland, the morrow for breakfast."

"Wear somethin'," he said. "But I do like ye best with nothin' on at all!"

"Sal, you're a woild man tonight! I can feel it," she whispered. "Come over and let me soothe that little red tartle that's always gnawin' at your heart. Maybe it will lie quieter on mine."

The night and the sound of the flowing river surrounded them. They drifted as one down an ever faster moving current, until the music of the real river's thoughtless monotone was lost. Then they went over the dam together—but not the one Colonel Chambers had built to turn the wheels of his mills.

13. Morning Transformation

BRIDGET WAS UP with the dawn next morning. She had heard her kitten scratching and mewing in the chest under the wagon seat and got up to release it.

Under the fading stars the child felt herself entirely alone, but she

was pleased by this rather than frightened. She felt inherently able t
fend for herself, provided she was not helped too much. And she als
had a secret country that was hers only, one which she knew mucl
better than to try to share with anyone else. It was, in fact, too delica
and subtle a place of magic to suffer the slightest interference.

Bridget's private realm was always near-by, yet it could be found onl
by way of a kind of ghostly hide-and-seek that she played with hersel
Wild, lonely, and beautiful places, especially if they were mysteriousl
green, helped. Indeed, since they reminded her of her lucky escap
through forest solitudes, they usually suggested her play to her. It wa
a game she called "Finding Mrs. McCandliss".

As she stood listening to the river that morning, she heard familia
voices talking to her as though they were only a short distance awa
just around the corner in a recoverable past. All she had to do was "t
go back". Undoubtedly, then, this was a good time, and certainly her
was the kind of place in which to find Mrs. McCandliss.

Ga-trip, ga-trip, ga-trip, scuffed the loose moccasins on the small fee
tripping and scraping over the wet grass. Across the lonely front of th
grimly staring house the small figure passed rapidly, skipping, holdin
her skirts out, now this way, and now that.

She rounded the corner of the dooryard and came out onto the wid
open lawn that led over to the riverbank on the far side of the mansior

The light grew, the house shifted its grim shadows and slowly bega
to smile in the growing light. The small figure in the centre of the law
skipped faster and faster. Then she leapt nimbly out of her big mocca
sins, leaving them close together on the grass, and began to whirl on he
bare feet, her arms and her pigtails flying outward. All at once sh
stopped . . .

The rim of trees with their bare, black branches that grew thickly al
about the verge of the island, with the morning mist flowing throug|
them, kept whirling about her in a rapid circle. Gradually, the mist
ring slowed down. Suddenly it stopped, too. Her vision cleared. Sh
pressed both fists against her temples, hard. She stared . . . She knev
she would find her . . .

"Hello, Mrs. McCandliss," she whispered, "hello. Be'ent you kin
of cold in a wispy nightgown?"

The reply brought a confident smile to the child's lips.

While the sun rose small and redly-round out of the river mists dow
the distant valley, and then began to glitter like molten gold, Bridge
stood as though rooted, passive, with round, wide eyes, engaged in
long and mystical conversation.

It was not the kind of talk that can be overheard, listen as closely a
you will. It occurred neither in space nor in time. It went on in Bridget'
head. Her lips moved when she talked, and moved also to shape th
words of reply. She spoke and was spoken to. She remembered com

pletely again exactly who she was. But she couldn't tell where she was.

Wherever it was, she couldn't stay there long . . .

. . . afterwhile she found herself standing wide awake, looking out over the lawn and the roofs of the mills below the dam, into a patch of especially clear blue sky.

My, but it was going to be a pretty day! And it had been *so* reassuring to find Mrs. McCandliss. Of course she would mind what her mother told her to do, even if Mrs. McCandliss did have a hole in her head. She felt quite confident again.

Her kitten came to her through the damp grass, mewing piteously. She picked it up and let it snuggle against her. Talking nonsense to it softly, she walked back to see if her new folks were still asleep. As she neared the wagon, the cat jumped out of her arms.

Salathiel was up, stripped to the waist, and busy about the sheds, watering and feeding the horses. That was good, now there would be somebody lively to talk to!

"Here she is, Melissa. I told you so," shouted Salathiel, "and the kitten, too. They've just been out for an early morning traipse together."

Frances poked her head out of the back of the wagon, reassured to find Bridget had not wandered away—and just in time to see Salathiel toss her up on his shoulders and gallop off with her into the sheds, where with much noisy merriment the horses were roused and turned loose into a small pasture behind the sheds.

Nothing is more ponderously ridiculous than a full-grown horse rolling with four iron-shod feet pawing the air, while it looks at you skittishly from the corner of its eyes, its head upside down—nothing, except when it scrambles to its feet again and kicks out gaily behind like a colt, with heels dainty and trim as a watersogged mop. Bridget could scarcely laugh hard enough to suit the occasion, as the four horses squirmed and rolled about in the paddock.

And it *was* an occasion.

As soon as the horses had recovered from their astonishment at not being led out and hitched to the wagon for another day's desperate haul, it was as plain to Bridget, as it was to them, that on this particular sunny morning a holiday had been declared. It was going to be like a Sabbath day, only it was to be merry. To her, at least, it remained in memory as a wonderful day. For from the very beginning of it, from her standpoint, remarkable things continued to happen.

"Hurry, you two," called Frances from the wagon, "if that's Colonel Chambers's cabin where I see smoke rollin' out of the chimley, they're already up and gettin' breakfast. 'Tis with our best foot forward we'll stip over their honourable threshold this foin mornin'. Heat me a kettle of hot water, Sal. And come here, Bridget! I'm going to dress you fancy and do your hair."

Nor was fashion that morning to be confined to ladies only, as

Salathiel discovered when he sat down as usual to clean and polish his rifle-gun. While the small fire he had kindled to heat the water was doing its work, Melissa looked out at his languid activities and became unexpectedly emphatic.

"Sure, and it's yerself ye might be furbishing instead of pamperin' your rusty musket," she began pointedly. "Did it iver occur to ye that ye won't be needin' to nurse Twin-Eyes at your breast any more? With five mountain ranges and the king's royal armies betwixt you and your troublesome friends, you can wean your iron baby and lay her up in her cradle. Ye might even put on some dacent clothes, and do your lanky hair with a bit of a bow behind, and sweep the bristles off your craggy chin. What's the use of our haulin' a valet's kit over the high mountains if you won't use it in the lowlands? Do ye think I'd be after callin' it macaroni to visit Colonel Chambers with ye in a deerskin shirt and a turkey fither in your hair? How would ye like me to riprisint you in me ould butternut kersey, bare fate, and no shtays? 'Twould be a grand bow we'd be after makin' to your foin friends in that fattle. Look, the pot's boiling! So get out your razors and a bit of pomade."

"No wonder it's bilin'," said he. "All the time you've been droppin' hot coals onto it over my head. Liken I might bile over myself, if ye keep on."

"Go long wid ye," said she, "and make yourself into a gintleman. It ain't like ye didn't know how," she added.

"Oh, I know *how*," he replied.

"But the question is do ye know *when?*" she countered.

"Looks like it's goin' to be this mornin'," he admitted. He stoppered his rifle thoughtfully, and giving it a farewell polish, laid it away carefully in the slings under the ridgepole.

So all the time he had been heating the water for himself!

Secretly, he was delighted. How many times had he looked forward to what he was going to do this morning. He took the kettle off the fire, got out Ecuyer's case of razors, and for the first time in many a long day brought out Johnson's valet kit and looked it over. Afterwhile he unpacked his best blue serving suit from Fort Pitt and considered it carefully.

"What day is it, Melissa?" he asked.

"Sure and it's Saturday," she said. "I don't know what saint's day it might be. I've forgot. But why would ye be wantin' to know a mere trifle like the day o' the week?"

"Oh, I thought I might as well begin right, if I'm going to be shavin' regular from now on," he replied, and picking out the captain's razor marked "Saturday", he began to strop it vigorously.

Melissa was so pleased she had tears in her eyes.

She had a plan for getting on in the world and holding her head high. Now she felt she had a partner in the scheme, one who would not only act but was going to dress properly for his part. Sometimes she had wondered just how it would go in the City if he walked down the street, Twin-Eyes on one arm and she on the other. This was only going to be a rehearsal this morning, to be sure. But it might be an important first appearance, too. In all the country about, Chambers was regarded as the most respectable family.

Now if Bridget only had her new red shoes!

Indeed, if it hadn't been too much to ask, Frances would have liked to have had Salathiel get out the peruke-curling irons and heat them up to do a little primping on her own hair. *That*, she decided, however, had best come later. She sighed, but happily.

Nevertheless, it was a decidedly respectable and pristine, if not a fashionable trio which emerged from the old stockade gate about an hour later and took the path towards Colonel Chambers's cabin.

Melissa had not only put on her new blue linsey-woolsey and yellow silk snood, but had also seen fit to wear a broad wool shawl and a small straw beehive bonnet besides.

The shawl was deep blue, with a looped fringe knotted from heavy white linen cord, and had heavy scarlet flowers, roses probably, embroidered on it in concentric rings. Both the fringe and the roses Frances had contrived with her own skilful fingers. And Bridget, too, had profited by her ever-flitting needle and deft shears.

In the early morning hours before leaving Lyttleton, Frances had reshaped and stitched together a small butternut dress packed in Bridget's basket, one that the much-harassed Mrs. Patton had been working on for weeks. It was not hemmed yet, but if the bastings would hold, it would do, Frances told herself. She had only four pins to her name, and she had "borrowed" those from Bella Pendergass at Bedford.

This butternut dress, however, with a small white kerchief about her neck, pigtails tied with black bows, the new red stockings, and her brown rabbitskin hood gave Bridget a feeling of utter elegance.

She therefore tripped along, occasionally stubbing her toe, but otherwise daintily, carrying a large calfskin reticule with adult dignity. In this hairy maw reposed the badly battered and paint-blistered head and torso of an old wooden doll called Queen Alliquippa.

Alliquippa was Bridget's chief secret treasure and darling child. And her mother was now revolving maternally what might be done in town for improving the lot of her offspring. All that Alliquippa needed was everything. In fact, in the back of her mind, Bridget had already resolved that her Big Man could easily accomplish the desired rehabilitation. And why not? Look what wonders he had done for himself this morning! Indeed, except for his permanent size, his hawklike face and mangled ear, Bridget hardly knew him as she trotted along, looking up admiringly and holding his hand.

A white linen shirt, a leather stock, Johnson's carefully refurbished deep-cuffed Osnaburg blues with tails, a waistcoat, and small clothes to match; long black military gaiters and brass-buckled shoes, these, and a low-crowned beaver hat, which any macaroni in London would gladly have given ten pounds for, were the plain but none the less potent elements in a carefully pondered and long-anticipated transformation; one for which Frances Melissa, if she had only known it, had but to give a sign to bring about.

Actually, he had long waited for a proper opportunity to burst thus from his sombre forest cocoon. Not that he fancied a butterfly of fashion would emerge, but he had often dreamed of the day when some of the valeting skill he had so painfully learned at Fort Pitt to practise on others might be decently applied to himself.

Well, this was the morning! Melissa had certainly said "when".

Thus newly tricked out and fortified in his own opinion, he made his way along the mill-race path, despite the hisses of Colonel Chambers's flock of green geese, with Bridget clutching his left hand and Melissa leaning upon his right arm. The morning sun glistened, and the huge roses on Melissa's shawl bloomed. If they were a little enormous, they had been created thus hopefully for great occasions. And who, if he had met the three of them there that bright morning coming along the willow-lined mill-race, would have had the heart to stop Bridget skipping or Frances smiling, by saying so.

"Ow," exclaimed Bridget, "my toe!" and sighed a little breathlessly, for Salathiel now began to stride along more eagerly, as they crossed the small bridge over the mill-race and turned up into Colonel Chambers's lane. There the smoke still rolled quite reassuringly.

Mistress Ruhannah, no doubt, was busy making ready. From a large and hospitable door the leather latchstring could be seen hanging out.

They were only halfway up the front yard path, however, when the door was jerked violently inward and a shrill heart-stopping scream that died away into sobbing groans and agonized gurgles stopped them in their tracks. It was a woman shrieking, and she was in the house. The voice of pain continued, although more subdued.

"What the devil?" grumbled Salathiel, regretting his rifle.

"Jasus, sweet Howly Babe! Belike the colonel's married daughter has burnt the hoe cakes. And here we be all dressed up only for a family shindy." Frances began to turn away bitterly.

Salathiel put a restraining hand on her arm—but, indeed, as the crying in the cabin continued, the placid tenor of Colonel Chambers's domestic life did seem to be in question.

Then a tall ungainly woman, holding her face with one hand over her mouth, stalked out of the cabin, moaning. Blood oozed through her fingers. She gave the strangers a brief agonized glance, turned, and fled up the lane towards the town.

Bridget began to whimper.

At that Colonel Chambers came out on his stoop, and seeing his bidden guests standing at the gate huddled together, called out reassuringly. Plainly he was somewhat nonplused by their appearance.

"Rat-me, if I knew ye at first. Well, well, beaver hats, new bonnets and all! I'm delighted to know ye, madam. What a sorry welcome you've had! But you mustn't mind it. Poor Mrs. Flannery! It was a turrible wisdom tooth she had. If that tooth hadn't bealed as turrible as it did, I'd have had to use the horse pincers instead of the door. As it was, it popped out jist like a loosened bung. All it needed was a stout cord and a firm jerk. But I *do* wisht they wouldn't come around moanin' like Grief bewitched, before breakfast."

No one in the company was inclined to disagree with his emphatic comment—on the contrary. But the scene of dental carnage was soon forgotten as they looked about them at the genteel furnishings of the cabin parlour.

In one corner was the colonel's desk with the jug under it. In another stood a spinning wheel with a treadle, and a small tambour frame with some bright half-finished embroidery. A banjo clock clicked on the wall with a faint echoing hum from a loose bell spring each time the pendulum swung.

"Ruhannah," called the colonel, leaning through the door into the kitchen wing, "Mrs. Flannery's gone with all her pain, and here be our visitors. And mighty pretty they look," he added. "You'd best put off your check apron."

A merry-looking young blonde, dressed in stays with waist puffs and a wired skirt, came through the door, hastily rearranging her kerchief over her plump shoulders.

"My daughter, Mistress Colhoun," said the colonel, proudly. "Mr. and Mrs. Albine—and?"

"Miss Bridget McCandliss," murmured Frances.

Bridget's deep curtsy set a prim standard of manners. For a moment or two there was enough bowing, bobbing, scraping and murmuring of politenesses to make even Frances Melissa happy.

And certainly it was obvious that the Chambers were not only impressed but more than pleasantly surprised. For a while there was a certain formal tenseness in the air, something which Frances loved. It was the necessary prelude to respect, she felt, and squeezed her man's arm. She combined this signal with a little dig in his ribs, as they went into the kitchen together, to call his attention to the fact that her plan for getting on in this world was working.

He thought so, too.

They found their places naturally, the three females standing together at one side of the table. Colonel Chambers raised his grizzled leonine face and looked at the ceiling.

"O Lard," said he in a tone of reverent conversation, "bless these good victuals to our use. May we remember the labour of Thy servants in bringing them to our mouths, that health in humbleness, grace in plenty may be ours in serving Thee."

Whatever stiffness had once starched the atmosphere for a moment in the other room now limbered into good-natured ease and hearty enjoyment, as they all sat down to breakfast.

14. Breakfast

ALE IN THE MORNING is a positive social emollient, and the colonel's was of the best from his own brew-house.

Much to Salathiel's satisfaction, there was no "coffee soup", and so far Mrs. Colhoun had made no motion towards employing her mother's pewter tea set, the large urn of which smirked complacently from a table in the corner. There was small-beer for Bridget, however, and since the colonel laced the ale with a bit of brandy, tongues were soon loosened, while heavy feeding and light conversation flourished.

Mina and Tina Oister, mother and daughter, two coloured women with Nanticoke blood, who looked Moorish, with brass earrings, yellow head cloths and wadded gingham gowns, lent an almost buccaneer air to the broad, low kitchen room, padding back and forth in their rag slippers from the fire-in-the-wall at one end of the ell to the family table set at the other.

Fried hominy mush in quantities, cornpone fingers, tree-syrup, a platter of trout from the Falling Spring, sausages, scrambled eggs, and a cold venison ham were the principal topics discussed, along with local news, personal anecdotes by the colonel, politics and Masonic confidences; while the domestic chatter and gossip of the women, in which the two Oisters occasionally joined, encouraged by Bridget's appreciative giggles, overlapped the deeper voices of the men with recurring ripples of comment frequently breaking into laughter.

As the morning grew warmer, the colonel, without interrupting himself, threw open the doors and wedged up both the windows. Outside in the carpenter shed, Jed, who had developed the eye of a connoisseur for the quantity and quality of smoke rising from prosperous chimneys, sat on a wooden horse with his feet in the deep shavings, and from time to time received a platter from the kitchen.

Inside the cabin, talk flowed naturally onward. Like the river he had dammed, Colonel Chambers was inclined to monopolize and direct any loose stream of conversation into useful channels, those which might eventually turn the wheels of his grist-mills.

The colonel was conversing in a flat-toned Scotch-Irish idiom, one which almost amounted to a dialect, with certain local frontier peculiarities. But for all that, it was a very ancient form of plain English, and he was saying the kind of things that have always most concerned the folk who use the English tongue. He was talking about people, politics, and the land; how they could be brought together and best formed into a livable future. The colonel was much concerned with such matters, whimsically sometimes, but always consciously and carefully. For there was one thing peculiar to him and his kind in their time and place, they were fathering a commonwealth, and they knew it.

Colonel Chambers was anxious to have Albine and Captain Jack, and some of the others of his rangers, if possible, come to settle in Chambersburg. It was high time they were settling down, he indicated. And where better than here? For his old friend, Captain Jack, the colonel would do much—everything! As for Salathiel, he would give him a lot on the square in town with full five years to pay for it, and also advise him in choosing and help him to take up some of the best of the "slate-pine lands" along the base of the ridge. In a few years the land east of the mountains would be full of people. They were coming! He was certain of it.

Two congregations, nigh three hundred and fifty souls, mostly Marylanders but all Presbyterians, were on their way west from Carlisle even now. Rumour had it they were bound for more southern regions, however. Somewhere far south and west in the back country of Virginia lay their promised land. If so, they would turn south at Chambersburg on the old trace to Hagerstown, edging towards the sunset, to settle eventually about the sources of west-running rivers whose courses and ends only a few men knew.

"I swear," said the colonel, "if I was younger I might go with them." The thought of it evidently excited him. "Sometimes I wish I could live three lifetimes jist to find out what the tarnal place is like tother side of the big blue hills. But drat me, what am I sayin'! I'm gittin' along in years, and what I'm goin' to have to do is to try to argue some of these good Presbyterian folk into tarryin' on here. Maybe you'll jine me in that?" he suggested, smiling hopefully.

"That's what I'm doin' now, sir," replied Salathiel. "I'm to go and wait for a spell at Carlisle, until Arthur St. Clair can get a parcel of his new settlers together for me to lead over the mountains to Bedford and Ligonier. He's got land thereabouts, and permits for settlement. I'm promised to St. Clair for that service for a spell, and he's payin' me a bit, meanwhile."

"Only a bit, I'll bet," grinned the colonel. "But later you might like to bring people this way for my town, maybe?

"Now let me tell you somethin' about this country around here . . ." The colonel went on and on.

Finally, he seemed to be talking to himself. His pipe had gone out. The two Oisters were gossiping with Jed in the back yard. In the front room the voices of the women suddenly became audible again, as the colonel ceased. They were talking about needles and pins.

"You can get a whole paper of the best brass pins at Somerfield's store, and blue Bristol needles in beeswax, and fine linen thread," said Ruhannah Colhoun, evidently addressing Frances. "Somerfield's just brought up a couple o' stogies loaded with London goods from the City. I slipped over early this mornin', and my dear, he has some of the finest sheer paduasoy I ever took between my finger and thumb. Old Somerfield's stockin' up now that so many are usin' the Glades Road again. I'd buy now, if I was you. I'd buy before all those Macs camp here waitin' to go south. If you don't, you'll find everything high as a steeple when you git to Carlisle."

Here the colonel rapped his pipe out three times, and looking at Salathiel, smiled knowingly, nodding towards the front room.

"They've got half the secret," he said in a low tone, "but they don't know it. You'll see what I mean if some of those stump preachers come around and start to git the women excited. It takes men to remember God ain't love alone."

Salathiel nodded as if he knew and agreed. He was not so sure he understood the colonel fully. But he felt he was learning a lot. As for Frances Melissa and her pins and needles, he would certainly buy her some at old man Somerfield's, and maybe some paduasoy, too—whatever that was—if the colonel would only give him a chance. It was getting pretty late!

A burst of laughter came from the yard and the happy voices and exclamations of Jed and the two Oisters.

"That's that smart City nagur of St. Clair's out there," said the colonel, apprehensively. "If you don't keep your eye on the blacks, they drop work and talk the mornin' away. Now, what I was leadin' up to was a little politics.

"In Pennsylvania it's hard to tell where tradin' and religion begins and politics leaves off. Ofttimes they're the same. But as I see it just now there's three parties in this province: there's the Quakers and proprietary interest; there's them that would tax the Penns' holdin's and appropriate for the military but who want the crown to revoke the charter and send over a royal governor; and there's the Presbyterian independents on the frontiers.

"And then there's a whole world o' poor folks, runaway redemptioners, in these western woods that have jist gone on their own and really don't want no government at all. They want free land, free huntin', and wild livin' *ad lib*. They don't even want neighbours very nigh, and they're death on the redskins. As near as I kin tell, they want to kill the Injuns off and then live like 'em, and forgit everything else. They're native as rattlesnakes, and they're pisen to all but godly and orderly thinkin' and right-livin' folks. The truth is they're half heathen. Your friend,

James Smith, is one of 'em and kin always whistle up a gang o' Black
Boys for any slick mischief he has to do. He's a kind o' Robin Hood
around here. I guess that makes me a kind o' Sheriff of Nottingham,
only I ain't so easily fooled.

"The truth is there's a kind of civil war gettin' under way in these
parts. The Black Boys are makin' it hot for the regulars for tryin' to
enforce the proclamations, and they're out to stop all western trade. Of
course, this king's man, Wully Grant, up at the fort is a natural-born
damn fool. He's goin' around the country arresting folks without warrants and takin' their rifle-guns away from 'em. And that's agin' the law,
too. Liken he won't play the tyrant very long. I wouldn't give 'im more
than a few months at most before he'll be hee-hawin' for help to Colonel
Bouquet.

"The trouble is the proprietaries are helpless when it comes to quellin'
violence. The Quakers are no help to them there, and all the frontier
Presbyterian riflemen despise 'em. Last Christmas when the Paxtang
boys marched agin' Philadelphia to finish off murderin' the Moravian
Indians, it amounted to a regular uprisin' of the frontiers agin' the authorities. It took Ben Franklin to arouse enough spunk in the Philadel-
phians to put it down.

"I'll give Franklin credit for his common sense in preventin' blood-
shed and coolin' down the hotheads. But Ben's always led the fight in
the Assembly against the Penns and the Quakers. And now the legislature has sent him back to London at a good salary as agent for the
province, and to try to git the new Parliament to revoke the Penns'
charter and set up a royal government here like they have in Virginia.
I'm not for that," said the colonel, smiting the table. "No, sir, not by a
dang sight!

"I'd much rather have John Penn for governor, and the old charter
o' liberties and godly government, Quakers and all, than havin' some
hack o' the Ministry or a court favourite set o'er us for governor with a
Church of England council to throttle our lower house. Ben Franklin's
a smart and clever fellow, but maybe he's startin' somethin' that just
Poor Richard's common sense can never finish. Poor Richard always
sounds mighty Yankee to me. I wonder sometimes if it mightn't end up
here like William Penn said in his book, 'no cross, no crown', and with
Poor Richard talkin' in the State House at Philadelphia. Might be," said
the colonel, "might be!"

Thus it was that Salathiel first heard of Benjamin Franklin.

"Tarnation!" exclaimed the colonel, getting up indignantly. "Dang if
the nagurs haven't gossiped the mornin' away out there, and the breakfast mess still settin' on the table. Mina," he called, "send that pert city
boy out of the yard. Don't ye know better than to let a gentleman's town
jockey like that tickle your daughter?"

"Kunnel, suh," replied the older slave woman, "you is a mighty knowin' man. I listen to yuh about de Lawd, but ye can't tell old Mina nothin' much about men. Suh, I'se wintered 'em and I'se summered 'em, and when they ain't they is, and when they is they ain't. And that's de God's trufe about 'em."

At this bit of perky wisdom, the colonel laughed heartily, and led the way into the front room, where the ladies were discovered showing Bridget how to read the future in tea leaves: The women seemed to be quite content with the present, Salathiel thought. After a dish of tea and a few amenities were passed, he and the colonel departed to get the day's work under way. There was a lot to be done that day in Chambersburg.

15. Saturday Afternoon Amenities

CHAMBERSBURG—just to be in it was to be elegant, or so Frances Melissa thought. Mrs. Colhoun was that correct; so well dressed and agreeable; she was such a clever needlewoman!

The conversation that morning in the "clock parlour" of the colonel's cabin had been one of the most pleasant Frances Melissa could recollect. It was almost like being at a respectable wake, where dear Grandmother Past was lying in peace, with nothing but her virtues to be celebrated. Not that there was anything funereal in the atmosphere. Just the peace of complete decorum, and Frances' own secret sense of assistance in laying her own past to rest—all but the best of it. Bridget's being there was a visible and solid comfort. She gave a restful and assured family tone to everything, moving plumply about the room, helping competently with the tea things, and playing sedately in general at being grown up in miniature. Or was she playing?

Ruhannah's naïve yet wholehearted and sisterly courtesy was veritable balm of Gilead to Frances' much-bruised but still gallant soul. The bitter years and blows of slavery on the Hogendobler farm, the horrors of her escape from the madwoman, and much else were lulled to rest by the healing elegancies and amenities of the quiet feminine present.

Nor was this evidence of small-things-observable trivial or unimportant. Unwittingly, but none the less ardently, Melissa shared in the general urge of her age to become refined and elegantly artificial. But final success in this bore for her the peculiar stamp of personal necessity. Her individual salvation and integrity were now dependent upon what elements out of her past she might be able to mix as alloys in the running flux of events, in order totally to recast her future and renovate her personality.

That process was now under way in the little parlour of the log cabin at Chambersburg. Apparently Frances Melissa was simply sitting in a rocking chair, rocking and talking amiably with a friend. But invisibly both her past and her present were melting together in her mind into an elaborate amalgam. Instinctively that morning, she had sensed the passing over of an important threshold, and the necessity, as she had already pointed out to Salathiel, of putting her best foot forward.

In one thing, if not in many others, she had been fortunate. Her pasts had been many and various; and her experiences in them were not only wide but deep. In this she actually held an advantage over many of the more staid but purely provincial women with whom she saw she must now match herself, and she was beginning to suspect as much.

She looked up to see what Ruhannah Colhoun was taking out of her sewing basket.

Ruhannah was hemming baby napkins out of smooth old linen. "They have to stand constant bilin'," she said. Dr. Colhoun's baby was expected in April. It occurred to Frances that she might tell Ruhannah about her own. Then they could talk babies and baby clothes together. This passing inspiration proved to be most fortunate. Not only the Chambers and Colhoun households, but the rest of the town opened up like a lid on a linen chest.

Half the women in Chambersburg were having babies. Pregnant conversation thus, as always, was open-sesame to the town's ever gravid sisterhood of anxiety and hope. Before noon Frances Melissa had been in and out of five different neighbours' houses. She had had sympathetic bundles of dry herbs and green bottled embrocations forced upon her. She had whispered with Granny Boggs over the shocking shortcomings of midwives, while sipping elderberry wine. And she had been shown how to knit a small cap over a hoop with long fringes to keep the flies off a new baby's face in the summer, by Mrs. Lang. She and Ruhannah had both been warned against cats crawling into neglected cradles and sucking the baby's breath. As to when and how to wean a child, there were two parties in the village, and pretty firm about it, too. There were the two-year and the three-year advocates.

Dr. Colhoun himself rode into town about two o'clock, over from Fort Loudon, where he had tapped the old garrison storekeeper for dropsy for the third time. "It's near the end now," he said, cheerfully. He didn't believe in bleeding when the patient's blood turned to water in his veins. Otherwise, he bled heavily. St. Clair and Yates had sent messages. It seemed they would be coming through Chambersburg "not later than Sunday".

"*Sabbath* you mean, George, don't you?" suggested Ruhannah hopefully, as she presided with great dignity over the noon meal. Dr. Colhoun laughed. He was not only a surgeon but an Episcopalian. He was even known to play cards, when he could find anybody who wasn't afraid of losing his soul during the game. He and Yates, it developed, were by way of being cronies. Frances could see that the doctor was a wise young man and enjoyed a bit of gentlemanly wit. Archness with dignity was called for, she thought—and it sufficed during luncheon.

He took a fancy to Bridget, who brought him a coal for his pipe. Bridget asked his advice for Queen Alliquippa. The doctor diagnosed that played-out female at a glance. "Sutures," said he, "sutures are the only thing that will recompose her constitution," and he proceeded to sew on a loose leg with a catgut, and to bind a flapping arm back into place. For the Queen's appalling baldness he could do nothing. "That has gone too far," he said. "There's nothing but bare ivory on which to glue her crown. Surgeons are no good at that. You must apply to Mr. Yates."

Bridget pretended to understand, a little disappointed. Still Alliquippa was *so* much better, so much better composed than ever before! She was now all in one piece, poor thing.

After the meal, from which the colonel had been absent, they all took a brief nap, the doctor in his chair, with a handkerchief over his face. Later the women and Bridget went over to the store.

Their departure was well timed. Mrs. Colhoun heard from Jed that both her father and Salathiel were at Somerfield's and that a smart piece of trading had been accomplished that morning in some remarkable triangular deal. About the nature of this deal Jed was not clear, except that Salathiel had given him a half-joe.

"Come on, my dear, we will both soon be having children to clothe," said Ruhannah, laughing and giving the doctor a hopeful look. But, as usual, her husband seemed to be asleep when money was in question. "But there's faither," whispered Ruhannah. "Faither will remember how it is."

Frances hoped so. If there had been a deal, she thought she could count on her man. (And maybe old Somerfield might have a dash of the hot Jamaica black on hand. Just a dram.) Ale was so bitter in the afternoon. The doctor had not offered any wine.

"Alliquippa's naked," said Bridget, putting her favourite back in the cowhide bag. "She ain't got a single thing to wear."

"That's the way they come," remarked Dr. Colhoun under his handkerchief, but not until the women were well out the door.

There was quite a crowd hanging around outside Somerfield's. Much to Melissa's surprise, the wagon was standing before the loading ramp, but without the horses. A crowd of noisy little boys were pitching pennies around the platform, and the minister himself had just entered the store. Something was going on, something important. "Come on," said Ruhannah again. "Come on!"

The women raised their skirts with both hands and started to run.

Things happened a great deal faster in town than along the road through the forest, Salathiel discovered. He was reminded of those days at Fort Pitt when he was serving the captain and there were scarcely hours enough from dawn to dark to get his work done. He had liked that. It kept him from brooding. The experience now stood him in good stead. He had a lot of things to accomplish at Chambersburg that day, and to tell the truth, he had been not a little impatient with the colonel, who had talked the morning away from eight until half after nine o'clock, if Ecuyer's watch was right; and, of course, it couldn't be wrong.

Also, he reflected, this was Saturday when all work stopped at sundown. At sunset the Sabbath began. He was even surprised to learn from the colonel that there would be a lodge meeting that night. Something special, probably. He hoped Yates and St. Clair would ride over from Loudon in time to be there and pass in with him. He didn't care to visit alone. And then there would be the kirk tomorrow. A sermon, which, for some reason, the colonel was quite insistent he must hear. Dang! Melissa would have to be there, too. It wouldn't hurt her, he reflected. She might for once just keep quiet about being a papist, since she wanted to be so respectable. He hoped they hadn't noticed her crossing herself after grace at breakfast. He would speak to her about it.

All this ran through his head as he walked with the colonel back over the little path along the mill-race that morning. He brought Jed out of the carpenter's shed with a shrill whistle and bade him come along for a little light work. This pleased the colonel, who was meanwhile full of explanations as to the necessity of setting up two new English millstones Somerfield had packed in for him from Newcastle. Salathiel would have to come down and see them.

He promised to do so later, and then managed to leave the colonel at the stockade gate, where he and Jed now turned in on the morning's work. In the new mill below the dam, a continuous din of hammers could be heard above the roar of the falls and the crashing of planks. The open framework of the mill roof, rafter by rafter, was going up rapidly.

Jed was quite a different being by day. Merriment had taken the place of sleepy fear. And he was not only amazed but proud of the transformation in the appearance of the big white man.

"Sah," said he, "this fellah ain't gwine be skeered of yah no moh."

Salathiel remembered his promise and promptly gave him a half-joe. Rather too much, he thought, but then it was a poor coin and would not pass for full face value. Yet it accomplished his purpose that morning. Jed was ravished by sudden riches into sudden labour.

They fell to on the harness together. They cleaned out and made up the interior of the wagon, putting everything in place and locking all the chests and drawers, ready to go. Then they caught the reluctant horses, hitched them up, and drove over, trundler and all, to Somerfield's store. It was going on towards noon when they got there—but not too late for trade and for a delighted welcome from young Arthur. He looked at him in his new guise, but said nothing. If only sis could have been here, he thought.

The trundler gaped, and from it Salathiel took out what he considered to be his best bale of peltry. It was a motley collection, he knew. But there might be some good skins in the bundle, and it would be just as well to turn them into money now.

Arthur carried the bale in proudly, mentally calculating his promised reward, while the deerskin wrapping was removed and the thongs untied in the back room behind the counter. Here there was considerable floor space before the open chimney, a place Somerfield reserved for his widower's cooking, conviviality, and his more important transactions with fur-trading customers. Through the back door, two long, blue Conestoga wagons just in from Lancaster could be seen drawn up together like a couple of canvas-covered barges. These had been unloaded only that morning, which accounted for the overflowing stock of merchandise that now inundated the war-depleted store with barrels, crates, and bales; that crammed the shelves which had seemed so bare only the night before.

Mr. Somerfield was rubbing his hands. It had taken considerable finesse to get this fine bill of goods so far west with all the merchants clamouring for everything at Lancaster and Carlisle. There the troops would soon be paid off. There refugees, claimers, released captives and their families were gathering—and such a crowd of camp followers as had seldom been seen in the colonies. Trade was only waiting for Bouquet to march eastward; for the final winding up of affairs after a long Indian war. Yes, it was almost like finding treasure to have two wagonloads of choice imported goods sent through to Chambers Mills at such a time. But the Philadelphia merchant that Mr. Somerfield liked to refer to as "my city factor" kept his promises. Friend Japson's word was as good as his bond.

In view of his good fortune, therefore, it was with considerable complacency and with something less than his usual urge to clip the last penny that Mr. Somerfield now turned to view the skins of sundry small animals laid out by Arthur upon his kitchen floor. There were one hundred and twenty-nine pelts in all, and as various an assortment as he had ever seen.

"Looks like that naturalist's plunder, the man from Philadelphy—old Bill Bartram, that came through here in Forbes's time after lookin' things over around Fort Pitt—only ye ain't got no dried shrubs and birdskins in your pack," remarked Somerfield.

Salathiel grinned from the barrel where he sat. "Maybe so," said he. "I ain't a pelt hunter, ye know. This here is jist what I could fetch out of the woods at off times when I went out with Twin-Eyes, or whenever a stint of private trade came my way. But there's a right smart lot o' beaver there and a few otter and plenty o' black squirrel. Squirrels o' that kind be scerce south-away. I got 'em north of the Conemaugh, where most people have never been."

"But they all look like summer coats to me," objected the old trader.

"Spring, airly spring," said Salathiel, "when the coat's thin, but new and prime." He laughed at his own blarney.

Somerfield grunted. "Wisht there was more mink," said he.

"I never had the patience to trap the little varmints," replied Salathiel. "But there's a white fox pelt from Canady once started a riot at Bedford, and the big brown painter that stinks so persistent, I knocked down with a hatchet. He ain't so bad. Captain Jack never knew I skunned him."

Somerfield grunted again and sniffed. This was certainly a powerful bale, if nothing else.

"Tell ye what ye do, sir," suggested Salathiel. "Just figure it up and make me an offer for the lot."

"Reckon that's the only way," said the old man. He got his slate and, sitting down with Arthur, went through the assortment and jotted his decisions down with a constant squeaking of the stone pencil. He took nearly half an hour, and towards the end Mr. Somerfield seemed to be having trouble with his arithmetic.

"Thirty-six pounds, eighteen shillings, and four pence," said he, looking up at last. "And I don't say you mightn't git more for 'em in the City, but you'll have to allow me my cut for handlin' here."

"What kind of money?" asked Salathiel.

"Some coin, and the rest province script."

"Tell ye what. Call it forty pounds even, starlin' value; take out twenty-five pounds in trade goods, and give me the rest in coin. Maybe you kin make a bit for yourself on the goods that way. But the coin's got to be weighed, copper or silver, and no paper."

Mr. Somerfield scratched his ear with his slate pencil, considering. Then he went over to the till and unlocked it. "All right," he said, reluctantly, "but I do hesitate to part with the hard pieces. Even with tradin' it takes metal change."

However, he shook hands on it. And while the coins were being weighed and considered one by one, Arthur, who was in pocket five Spanish dollars, put the furs away to be pegged out on stretchers later and given a good going-over. Mr. Somerfield knew a trick or two when it came to slicking up pelts.

It was strange how the news of a deal going on got around town. Perhaps Jed had something to do with it. About two o'clock, the colonel himself had dropped in. By that time, exhilarated by a can of watered penny blackstrap, Jed was doing cartwheels before the wagon on the loading ramp.

A crowd of small boys gathered. Jed's half-joe had somehow turned into several smooth old coppers, and a noisy game of pitch penny was

soon under way, interrupted from time to time by the arrival of the boys'
parents, for it was Saturday afternoon, and the news of the new goods
at hand had been noised about. Then the women began to gather in
force, even those who could not buy came to stare through the window
and to finger the samples.

By three o'clock young Arthur had his hands full, measuring off cloth
on the brass nail markers on the counter, tearing it across or cutting to
the line, with one eye on Mr. Somerfield, who he knew would hold him
responsible for every inch.

But trying to be a grocer and calender all at once finally proved too
much even for the willing Arthur, and he was allowed to call in his
friends, the Culbertson twins, to help.

"Bless me, I'd no idea so many of the back-settlers had come home,"
said Mr. Somerfield. "Look at the farmers' nags tied up in the yard.
And half with pillions. Only last August the whole county was a desert
from here to Lancaster. I guess if you gave a war-whoop now they'd all
light out agin for Carlisle. But don't do it," laughed the old man, while
he and Salathiel worked on the ramp, loading part of the agreed-upon
goods into the wagon and trundler.

The game of pitch penny swarmed under, in, and about the loading
porch. It unrolled amid the wheels of the wagon with shrill shouts of
excitement and occasional fights and tears. The horses stamped and
switched impatiently, shaking their hides and the new yoke chimes.

"Dang, if that ain't a harsefly," exclaimed Somerfield. "It's the warm-
est November afternoon I can ever remember," he said, lifting up his
face to feel the grateful, unseasonable sunshine. "'Tain't like to last. I
heard loons late last night, and whenever ye hear 'em here, there's cold
close behind. Loons is the laugh of winter comin' on."

"Thought I heard one myself," smiled Salathiel. "Say, Mr. Somerfield,
have you got a good smith around here? Speaking of the horses, just take
a look at their shoddin'.'"

"Flannery's the only man can do it right since old McCormick was
scalped. But the question is, will he? He's a retired army farrier, and he
has all the tools and the skill, but his half pay is half too much for him.
Mostly he's skittled. Owes me a pretty penny on his store slate. Tell ye
what . . . But bedang, here comes his old woman now! Maybe you can
work on her, and if ye do, remember me."

Salathiel looked up to see a tall ungainly yet familiar figure with a
kerchief binding up her jaw approaching the store thoughtfully. He
raised his hat to her as she turned in at the door, and she stopped from
sheer astonishment.

"I do hope the misery has abated, Mrs. Flannery," said he. "You may
recall we met at Colonel Chambers's door this morning. He said he'd
seldom seen so large a wisdom tooth, one with three roots! I'm certain
you're much to be commiserated."

" 'Deed, it must have been turrible," said Mr. Somerfield, shaking his head.

The look of suspicion faded from Mrs. Flannery's tired blue eyes. Under her bandage and sunbonnet she tried to smirk with a kind of grimace that somehow reminded them both of a wrinkled cabbage.

"Now, it's sure uncommon kind of ye to remember my misery," she mumbled.

"Is Jim engaged today?" inquired Mr. Somerfield, innocently.

"*Him!*" she exclaimed. "He's got his bloody rope 'ammock out again with the warm weather. 'Twas a bad 'abit he brought back with him from the Havanner, along with the tertian fever. And there he lays swinging in the breeze, and the forge gone cold."

"Maybe between shakes he could be persuaded to make the sparks fly again—for a few Spanish dollars," suggested Mr. Somerfield. "Then you could git some of the things you want, mistress."

"I've four horses much need to be reshod, ma'am. And I'm willing to pay well for an honest stunt," urged Salathiel solicitously. The next smith would be at Shippensburg.

"It's poppy drops and a pair of new cloth slippers I need," muttered the woman. "Me old shoes are like a cheese drain."

Mr. Somerfield nodded. "Wal, ye kin have them, if you want."

"Happen ye have a nagur can tend the bellows?" she asked.

"Here's one," said Salathiel, reaching down and pulling Jed out by the heels from under the porch.

"Go 'long with this good woman and do what she tells you," he admonished the Negro sternly. "If you've lost any pennies, I'll make 'em up to ye." Shrill shouts of triumph and the sound of quarrelling over Jed's abandoned hoard came from under the platform.

"I'll follow with the nags in a few minutes, ma'am," said Salathiel— "and there may be two more horses," he added.

Yates, St. Clair and Roy Davison had ridden up and dismounted just as the affair of the barrel occurred.

"Anybody see that nigger of mine?" asked St. Clair. "How's he been behavin'?"

"I've jes sent him down to the farrier's to work the bellows," explained Salathiel, "and, by the way, if you two want your horses reshod, you'd best send 'em down now with the wagon teams. I've made workin' arrangements with Mrs. Flannery."

"With the old woman, eh? Then you're like to get results," said St. Clair. "Where's Flannery set up his smithy now?"

"I know, sir," exclaimed young Davison eagerly, "and I'll take the horses around for ye, all six of 'em, if this gentleman will let me talk to his little girl. I rode over this afternoon jes for to see her, hopin' you'd still be here," he added, addressing Salathiel. "Look, I brought this along!" He pulled a toy canoe out from under his jacket. "Hit's for her, for Pigtails! An old Injun made it. I thought maybe ye might let us swim it in the race together." At the thought of so much happiness, his voice died away and he appeared flushed and embarrassed at having disclosed his fondest dreams.

Salathiel looked at him gravely. "Take the horses around to Flannery," said he, "and then you kin come back and talk to Pigtails. Her name's Miss Bridget McCandliss, by the by. Ye'll have to find out yourself whether she'll go swimmin' canoes with ye. And don't forget your cap this time."

"No, sir," said the boy, removing his rakish ring-tailed headpiece there and then. A rush of golden hair inundated his shoulders. "Damn hit," said he, and bit his lip with vexation. "I allers forget about them long locks. Here, sir, please keep this for me while I take the horses around." He handed Salathiel the canoe as one man to another, and then began to cut the lead team out of the traces like a veteran.

Yates grinned at the droll sight of his large friend sitting on the platform with a toy canoe solemnly resting on his knees. "That's a sacred pledge you're holding there, Sal," said he. "I hope ye take it seriously. Your Pigtails has picked up a fiery young Romeo. He rid over from the ford with us and discoursed of love all the way. St. Clair was like to split, but promised his good offices. He's your Phoebe's cousin, ye know. By the way, are you stayin' at the Davisons'?"

Salathiel shook his head. "No, I managed not to," he said, and put the canoe upright in his pocket for safekeeping. "But I've had a good talk with young Arthur about certain matters."

"That's wise," replied Yates. "Melissa can be easily upset."

"She ain't goin' to be," said Salathiel. "But let's go in the store now. The colonel's in there and will be wantin' to see ye." As he rose, the surreptitious sound of pitch penny came through the platform.

"Gambling's a hard thing to stamp out," chuckled Mr. Somerfield. "Even in this godly village it goes on under the feet of the elders."

"What's that?" inquired Colonel Chambers, coming through a crowd from behind the counter, eating a sour pickle.

"I was just explainin' a curious fact," said Somerfield. "But here's Mr. St. Clair and lawyer Yates fresh rid in from Loudon."

"How's Wully and his fightin' gurls?" demanded the colonel. "Did Croghan's Irish get through all right? Any riders this way from Fort Pitt?" All five of them made their way to the rear of the store, where barrel chairs were pulled out before the hearth, and questions and answers and heavy repartee lightened by a touch of fiery blackstrap, which made St. Clair cough, went around.

Behind the counters out in the store, Arthur and the Culbertson twins flew about nimbly. Presently Mr. Somerfield left his guests in the back room and joined his clerks, slate and pencil in hand. He began to unroll some of the more flamboyant of his cloth for display.

Outside, the Reverend Mr. Muir Craighead had just ridden in from Rocky Spring, Old Church, to preach the morrow's sermon.

He was having a terrible grim battle trying to moor his obstinate and powerful jack mule to Somerfield's lamppost and to keep his remarkable clerical bag-wig on his pate. It was literally too much for one Presbyterian clergyman to do. So violent were his exertions that the white powder flew from his wig, and some Biblical language got mixed with the dust of what looked like defeat. Had any of the orthodox been listening, they might have been scandalized, for even a layman would have instantly gathered from Mr. Craighead's remarks that he now included mules in his views on the doctrine of predestination. The question was temporarily settled when the good man drew back for an apostolic blow and smote his mule on the side of its head with righteous indignation and a heavy black bag containing a big leather-bound Bible, two hymnals, a Westminster Confession, and a green ham. The jack staggered, sobbed like the brazen trumpet that shattered the walls of Jericho, and dazedly permitted itself to be bound to the lamppost.

"Ahaz, Ahaz!" exclaimed Mr. Craighead, while settling his wig, "bray on, unwilling bearer of the abused servants of God. Thou son of Jorham; Ahaz art thou rightly dubbed!"

It was precisely at this juncture that Ruhannah and Melissa, coming down the street with Bridget, had picked up their skirts and started to run.

They were, of course, in plenty of time. There was over an hour till sunset yet, and, in any event, the doctor's wife and her genteel visitor were not going to be neglected by a man who knew his custom as well as Mr. Somerfield. But despite that, owing to the pleasing excitement of a purchasing adventure, they were both in a hurry, and neither of them noticed that Bridget remained outside, where someone had something to say to her. They turned headlong into the store and made their way breathlessly to the rear counter.

" 'Tis some of your best new drygoods we want to look at, Mr. Somerfield," said Ruhannah, as the old man swept a place clear for them on the goods counter, and leaned forward to take their commands. "Imported goods," she whispered, looking about her apprehensively, but smiling, too. "Paduasoy!"

"There *is* that," said Mr. Somerfield, turning about and summoning Arthur. "And also there's Irish linen, silks from Lyons, English lawn, Bedford cloth, Scotch tweeds, and stout Osnaburgs, all recent imports by the good ship *Gilbert* of Lyme Regis, my city factor informs me. And the chiffons," he said, knowingly, "good lack, you never saw such chiffons!" As he spoke, he began to pick out choice bolts of cloth from the shelves and to assemble them.

"Arthur," said he, "show these two ladies everything they want, and git old Timba to come and hold a candle so they kin see the weave and the quality. And, mind you, no drippings git spattered on the cloth. This is Mrs. Albine, your friend's wife, you know, and, of course, Mrs. Colhoun." The lad looked at Frances so searchingly that she dropped her eyes. But that was only for an instant.

Soon neither of the women was conscious of the young clerk at all, except as a pair of hands that unrolled before them beautiful waterfalls of cloth. This they not only saw but heard. They heard the ripple and swish of it. But above all they felt it. Ruhannah was all sighs and envious hopeful little exclamations. Frances was silent. Young Arthur was disturbed by the far-off misty look in her grey eyes as she fingered the cloth.

She sighed deeply, running her hand down a bolt of crinkling crêpe. "Paduasoy," she heard Mr. Somerfield saying, "only one bolt of it. Smuggled! The finest weave out of Italy, and the first I've seen these many years. Times have been lean, you know."

Lean! Who should know that better than she?

"Twelve shillings a yard," said Mr. Somerfield.

Well, she would have it, yards of it! Enough to make up for the naked past; enough to make herself a dress and a bonnet—and a bodice for little Bridget, too. She would sweep through the streets of the City like a lady, a fine lady with a handsome child. If necessary, Sal could sell some of the horses. The best girls in Cork used to give themselves for less than a yard of this stuff cost. Why, it was worth it, worth it!

She heard Ruhannah calling, "Faither, faither." Of course, why not? She would call Salathiel.

The voices of the men in the rear room were suddenly stopped. Colonel Chambers and Salathiel came out to see what it was all about. They looked at the counter and the women and laughed.

"Yes," said the colonel, after listening to Ruhannah, "yes," a little doubtfully. "You know, I have other grandchildren, here and on the way." But he nodded and said something in a low tone to Somerfield. Ruhannah held her breath. Then it was all right. She could see that, and sighed. "Anything in reason" her father had said.

"Five pounds," said Salathiel to Frances briefly and to the point. He seemed in a hurry. "Your share out of this morning's trade. Git what you want for the family. Git plenty, git some needles and pins and skeins. I meant to git them for ye anyhow, and," he added in a low tone, "I'd git a little present for Mistress Colhoun, a ribbon or some falderal. You'll know what." He put his arm around her proudly, and drew her close to him. "Now I've got to git along to oversee the horses. It's been a good day, I opine. The colonel wants us down to supper this evenin'"—all this under the eyes of Arthur, who stood waiting, and kept looking out the door steadily.

"Five pounds!" was all she could murmur. "Oh, Sal—five pounds! But is it sterling?"

"Yes," he said, "five sterling!"—and strode out, calling to St. Clair and Yates to follow him and get their own nags at the farrier's.

Five pounds, that was more than she had got for a whole year's work when she was bound out at Frazier's. She turned to the counter proudly and began to buy.

It was getting dark now. It would soon be six o'clock, and the Sabbath. She must hurry. But old Timba still stood like a statue of carved mahogany holding the candles. Still there was light and time enough to buy paduasoy.

She and Ruhannah smiled at each other triumphantly.

16. Expressions on the Face of Time

DOWN AT THE SMITHY matters had progressed considerably faster than Salathiel had been given to expect. The smithy was an open shed with the inverted bodies of two old army wagons for a roof. There was an anvil, quite rusty now, a fine kit of farrier tools and a portable blow-forge all of which had accompanied Corporal Flannery out of his Majesty's service, when the corporal-farrier had been discharged as an invalid from the garrison at Fort Loudon several years before. Flannery's great pride was that he had once shod the charges of General Forbes and of Colonel Washington at Bedford. The Virginian had paid him, the general had died; but he remembered them both, with equal satisfaction.

Now, it was not by firmness of character alone or her two arms that Mrs. Flannery had prevailed on her veteran husband to resume his place at the forge that afternoon. His progress from the hammock to the anvil had been due to the moral force inherent in Colonel Chambers's remark to Mrs. Flannery earlier that morning, that afflictions are sometimes blessings in disguise. It had put an idea into her head. She determined to capitalize on her misery.

Looking up at his wife from the hammock that afternoon, Flannery had been shocked to see that her face was in a bandage and that she had lost a tooth. To the best of his recollection, she was entitled to nothing more than a black eye.

"Arragh now, mavourneen," said he, "sure and it was only a family tiff after a bit of poteen last evenin', and I niver did mean for to mar ye."

Instantly, she had him.

" 'Tis a poor frail woman I am," said she, "and no iron anvil for ye to lavish yer brutal blows upon, ye drunken harse-handler. Jasus! Am I always to be put upon and knocked about by a mere bog-trottin' Flannery like yerself? 'Tis not enough that ye should lie there, swingin' in your airy Injun pallet, denyin' me a crust for me famished mouth, but now ye must be after knockin' the most handsome teeth out of me jaw for fear I should ask ye for somethin' nourishin' to bite upon. Git up, ye miserable spalpeen," she screamed. "There's a gintleman like a giant out of Cornwall with four foin harses to be shod, a big iron stick under his arm, and milled Spanish dollars clashing in his pocket. Which would ye rather have rattlin' about yer impty pate? If ye've got a yard of Christian bowels left in your heathen guts, ye'll git up and strike a blow fer yer long-sufferin' wife—and she a proud Fitzgerald linked by the blessing of God, and as the divil would have it, to a poor fever-stricken farrier. *Ochone*," sobbed Mrs. Flannery, "*ochone!*"

Washed out of his hammock by this rising tide of domestic eloquence, the remorseful smith made no attempt to defend himself, but began to assemble his tools in a fit of low spirits humble enough to permit him to accept work as a penance for his sins. It was only when Mrs. Flannery led Jed up to the bellows by his left ear, and began to shout into the other one, that he saw fit to protest.

"'Tis a profound mistake you're after makin', Mrs. Flannery, to be handlin' another man's nagur boy that way. Ye should drive him to work by the power of words, instead of tryin' to guide him to it by his ear for a handle."

"As long as I have him by one ear and at arm's length, I know he'll never be out of my sight," countered his spouse.

"Only a man who was short-sighted enough to take the king's shilling when he was sober could refute ye," replied her husband, "and I'm that man."

Manhood, good-fellowship, and self-respect thus being caustically restored, Flannery began ringing his hammer on the iron of the cold anvil. It worked. And at about the same time young Roy brought around the first instalment of horses.

Later on, Roy brought Bridget around too, after the last team. The two youngsters sat together, watching the fascinating process of applying red-hot iron to the smoking feet of living horses. Other children soon appeared shyly from nowhere at the sound of the anvil. Surprised but pleased neighbours loitered by, and dogs came and went, waiting to snap up eagerly that greatest tidbit of dogdom, a reeking bit of hoof paring. Seeing himself the centre of so much approving attention, Flannery began to take an interest in his own work and gradually, as he warmed up, regained his form.

The unrelenting presence of Mrs. Flannery was also, no doubt, conducive to industry, for by half past five both the wagon teams were done, St. Clair's grey and Enna attended to, and without asking any questions, the smith proceeded to complete his task by shoeing Roy's colt, which had never been shod before.

"Mrs. McKinney will never pay for that," whispered Roy anxiously. "But I guess I can't stop it now." He and Jed helped finish up, after the smith had clipped the shaggy fetlocks, by polishing the hoofs of all the horses with beeswax, soot, and a hard brush.

It was almost dark when Salathiel finally came by to see what the farrier had accomplished. He was well enough pleased with the work, and agreed to pay for the colt's shoeing, too. The wagon horses were led off with instructions to Jed to bring the ark back to "the castle". Jed had a whole shilling this time, and young Roy got back his canoe and permission to go and play with Bridget. As Frances afterward said, "Sal ought to have known better than that." But all seemed in order and the day's work well sped, when something curiously disturbing, because it was so mysterious, began to overtake Salathiel.

It happened while the last shoe was being fitted on the colt. The song of the hammer, the red glow of the forge, the smell and loom of the smithy, began to feel vaguely familiar to him. For some reason or other, he suspected the presence of a big brindled ox near-by. Presently he began to fear that it would certainly appear and sniff at his face.

All this, to a matter-of-fact man like himself, was essentially disturbing. It was the same and yet the place was subtly changed. Things were not exactly as they used to be—*and ought to be now*. The man at the anvil should be bigger than Flannery. And he had golden hair, and mighty hands. Oh, yes, they were the hands that had made him his first bow. It was the smell of the hot iron that must be doing this; the small twinkling sparks on the white-hot shoe. He began to understand, he thought. And then the most disturbing thing of all occurred. It completely upset him.

A voice that was entirely familiar in its tones and emotional meaning began to speak. It seemed as though a door had swung open some place in the back of his mind—and he heard people talking.

"It is now past six of the clock, and the Sabbath has begun," said the Reverend Muir Craighead precisely with a slightly nasal and professional twang. "And it is the custom of the Christian people of this town to do no work after sundown, as the holy Commandment requires. I would advise ye to cease."

"To cease instantly," he was saying . . .

Who was this that had come out of the past and yet was speaking now, apparently to Flannery? The smith was gaping at him, his wife stood rigid in the corner. Jed paused at the bellows and looked up apprehensively. There was a tremendous tension in the air. What was wrong?

Now he knew.

Jed ought not to be there at all. No, it was a soldier in a red coat. There ought to be a soldier working the bellows! A soldier? Why . . . Why, this was crazy!

But he knew what to do now. It came upon him as though his muscles were doing their own thinking. He would pick up this canting minister and carry him out. By God, he would throw him . . . heave him through a window! The impulse was irresistible. Now!

He advanced on the Reverend Mr. Craighead with half-closed eyes, and then he remembered about the hands. They must be his father's hands!

Mr. Craighead gave an alarmed snort and retreated backward towards the Flannerys, into the revealing glow of the forge. His wig string, already badly strained in his bout with the mule, burst, and the wig slipped backward and down onto the back of his neck.

Salathiel found himself confronted by an unknown bald man, a total stranger, who was shivering. His hands fell helplessly by his sides, but they still twisted. *His* hands? Good Lord, whose hands *were* they?

Finally, he reached out and lifted Mr. Craighead's wig gently from around his ears and began to turn it about and examine it in the fire-light. He leaned over to do so, and by so doing managed to conceal his face until his great confusion passed . . .

"Let me mend this wig for you, sir," said he at last. "I have some skill in the craft, and a machine along with me in the wagon."

"By Jehosaphat, I thought ye were going to scalp me, young man," replied Mr. Craighead, relieved beyond measure. "You wild men from the frontiers, you're so unexpected and impetuous."

"Wal, in a way I have scalped ye," replied Salathiel, able to smile now. "But I'll return your hair to ye with a new drawstring, and all powdered, in time for tomorrow's sermon. You'll have to let me keep it for a while tonight."

Mr. Craighead thawed. His bag-wig was half his clerical presence, and he knew it. His head was stark naked and shone like a looking glass, but for all that he did not believe it could ever serve as a mirror of faith. He looked at his precious artificial locks dangling from Salathiel's big hands, doubtfully.

"You'll be *sure* to have it in dacent time for the morning sermon?" he quavered.

"You shall have it before breakfast," replied Salathiel. "Meanwhile, please, sir, accept the loan of my hat. I owe it to you, ye know, for the fright I just gave ye. I'm sorry. I find for some reason I wasn't myself. Mr. Somerfield's old blackstrap is mighty powerful—" But even as he said that he knew that he lied.

Mr. Craighead cleared his throat. "That does happen occasionally," said he. "I was just on my way down to the colonel's for supper when I saw ye standin' in here. I knew you're bidden to meat at the Chambers' this evening, too. As for the smith's work here, I was a bit hasty per-haps. We're strict old kirk in Chambersburg—but, pshaw, 'tis only the last shoe for the little colt. Flannery, you're a papist anyhow. Ye may work on."

So Roy's colt was shod, after all. Salathiel gave the Spanish dollars to

Mrs. Flannery as agreed upon, and he and the minister set off down the lane for the colonel's cabin together.

Mr. Craighead was quite curious about Salathiel. It seemed that he had heard something of his past.

"Ye were James McArdle's pupil, were ye not? I've heard him speak of ye with affection. He's a true servant of the spirit, a missionary to the lost and the heathen. He's a man of iron courage, dinna ye think?"

"I do, sir. But—he's lately given over, I've heard, to some peculiar and extreme views about matters I do not know much about."

Mr. Craighead chuckled. "I agree," he said. "Learnéd men have long tried to prove that the red Injuns are the lost tribes of Israel. But 'tis *not* Scripture, unless ye read it a bit cockeyed. As for myself," said he, "I think it enormous nonsense. 'Twill go hard with Mr. McArdle if he comes preaching his faith to those recently snatched from the cruel mercies of his 'Hebrews', at Carlisle."

"Does he plan to come there?" demanded Salathiel, by no means ravished by the news. "Colonel Bouquet will never permit it."

"Bouquet can do nothing about such matters after he returns from the woods to this province," replied the minister. "Every man, even every fool, moved by any spirit is free to propagate his views in Pennsylvania. 'Twas a provision especially made by William Penn in his first charter for the protection of zanies like old James Fox. Now the spirit bloweth as it listeth." Mr. Craighead chuckled.

"By the by, speaking of Bouquet," continued the minister, "your colonel is a colonel no longer. Have ye not heard that the last *Gazette* from London says the king's promoted him brigadier and put him in command of the southern department?"

"That's brave news! That's grand!" exclaimed Albine. "I rejice to hear it. Indeed I do."

"Aye, 'twill be a verra popular act on the part of the crown," commented Mr. Craighead. "I hear the Assembly is busy preparing a resolution of thanks, and well they may, for there can be no doubt but that Bouquet is the presarver of this province. If he were not a Switzer, they might have made him a baronet. No doubt he will go south now to complete the occupation of Louisiana into the west. You know, there's many a post up the great inland rivers where the lilies of France still wave. Either they haven't heard, or they're waiting for someone in a red coat to pull them down."

"That country seems far away," mused Salathiel. " 'Tis a pity we must lose Bouquet to it. But many speak now of those rich western prairies, and of the fair twin colonies in Florida."

"Not so far away," muttered the minister. "But ye can easily lose yourself there. It's a world unto itself. I hope you'll not be lured by it. Too many of our young men are wanderers now, and nothing more. And there's a mighty work to be done here."

"I admire to be this side o' the mountains," replied Salathiel. "I saw a sight of the back country yonder. I'll tarry downcountry for a while."

Thus chatting, they took the final turn in the lane to Colonel Chambers's. Somewhat to his surprise Salathiel found himself much at home with Mr. Craighead, and liking him. The minister was a quiet, unassuming little man, but with a touch of fire under his amiability. And there was no doubt he was a devoted servant of the Lord, with the divine sense of humour also vouchsafed him. Oh Lord, if McArdle could only have been more like Mr. Craighead!

"Mind ye now, young man, I'm depending upon you to cover my naked poll for the sermon. 'Tis a pious work ye may well engage in, even on the Sabbath," added Mr. Craighead, laughing and laying his hand appealingly on Salathiel's arm.

"I'll not fail ye, Mr. Craighead," replied Albine. "Ye shall have your wig returned tonight." And with that they went in to supper.

Salathiel was astonished when he went into the small clock parlour. There were about twenty people crowded into the low-ceilinged little room, while Ruhannah, Frances, the two Oisters, with several of the wives of neighbours were bustling about in the kitchen ell. All cooking was over, but the feast was to be laid, and, it appeared, constantly enlarged.

For it was lodge night. Friends of the colonel and Dr. Colhoun kept riding in. Salathiel caught the air of expectancy pending an important meeting. St. Clair and Yates were busy as usual talking with everybody. Mr. Craighead, with a small black cap, mercifully furnished by the colonel, was the centre of much respectful attention and some careful hilarity at his mishap. He seemed only half the man he was without his wig. Seeing that he was really and deeply embarrassed, Salathiel went out to the woodshed, and placing the wig over a small hard pumpkin, began some rapid repairs.

In a few minutes he called for Mr. Craighead and tied and fitted the wig over his head. The return of the minister redisguised as himself brought a shout of good-natured welcome from the crowd in the small front room.

But Salathiel also was welcomed, and unexpectedly.

The two Callahans were there, leaning against the wall in the corner, where their long rifles also reposed. There was a crowd pressing about them. At first Salathiel could not see why. Then they called out to him, and crossing the room, he saw an old man seated on a chair between them, a big man. His face was bland with the kind of smooth return to youth which senility sometimes ghostfully suggests. His mouth was straight and toothless. It was the voice that had changed most. His eyes were the same. It was Captain Jack.

"My son," said the old man over and over again, with his mouth quavering visibly. "Salathiel, it is good to see you yet again, Salathiel, my son."

And now for the first time Salathiel became fully conscious of having become the accepted heir of the admiration and gratitude for what Captain Jack and he and the Callahans, and other men like them, had done in those harassed days of darkness and massacre. They had stayed, fought, triumphed, and saved the province. Bouquet was the great hero, but he was a king's man. For the rangers, for the native sons and intrepid rifles of the frontier, was reserved the full measure of personal affection by the settlers.

Captain Jack was passing. It was plain to be seen. The change from only a year before was unbelievable. Curiously, he had returned down the ladder of life, and was now again an approximate ghost of the mild and once happy Dr. Caldwell. This, however, was more a physical than a mental reversal in time.

His memory was clear, but at most times not so active. He now tended to recall episodes in his more distant past. The feeling that his work was over, that like his rifle-gun he would slay no more but was laid up to rust away, had cancelled the importance to him of the future. Vengeance satisfied and the ruling passion of his life gone, as it had been since the great Indian slaying at the Salt Kettles, Captain Jack quietly awaited his end. Sometimes there were flashes of lightning in the old eyes and a far-off reminiscent roll of thunder in his voice and talk—and then Dr. Caldwell was sitting there smiling. Few remembered Dr. Caldwell, and none present had known of Dr. Morton, save Colonel Chambers.

Salathiel, of course, was not aware of all this instantly, and that evening it took him some time to realize it fully. But he was aware instantly that Captain Jack was not able to conceal his respect and affection for him, nor his belief that in Salathiel he saw himself renewed, and so looked to him as a son to carry his mission on.

Certainly, everyone else present that evening had felt the inner meaning of Captain Jack's greeting with the gestures and tones of voice that conferred upon Albine the old man's blessing.

The Callahans talked earnestly to Salathiel. They spoke of certain names already well known to him, and of others who were promising candidates for the small group of associators, riflemen, backwoodsmen and rangers, which, if he would agree to lead them when needed, they promised on their part to keep in touch with him and hold ready for his call. That he was going downcountry made very little difference, or even if later on he went to the City. They would pass the word along to him through the lodges and from time to time they would come to see him personally and confer.

This was the gist of the conversation at supper. And with Captain Jack sitting there between himself and the colonel, it was impossible for Salathiel not to promise to comply. And so he did—much to Frances Melissa's secret anxiety. She was not, in fact, able entirely to restrain herself.

Halfway through supper she suddenly demanded to know Bridget's whereabouts. He explained as best he could, and thus brought the laughter of the entire company down on himself. For Frances upbraided him angrily and brilliantly for letting the two youngsters wander off—and now, please God, what had become of them?

Soon no one present had any doubt but that Sal Albine was a very much married man, and that his wife had an able tongue. But that, fortunately, was the worst and the best of it, for before the last of a still-smoking remnant of venison pie and peach cobbler had been devoured, Roy and Bridget both appeared. They had been swimming the canoe in the mill-race together.

Roy, of course, had fallen in. Bridget hadn't, and had even taken off her new red stockings, which she extended towards Melissa as a kind of propitiatory offering and proof of her responsibility and foresight. Dr. Colhoun sent Roy up into the loft and told him to go to bed, as his lips were blue and he was shivering.

"We'll just keep him here till the morrow," said the colonel, "when no doubt Mistress McKinney will be in town inquiring for him, and wanting to warm him proper. The young rascal must have stolen off this afternoon."

"I'll speak to that cold-hearted woman myself," said Ruhannah, tossing her head. "She treats her bound help and the poor niggers she took over from the Marylanders like cattle. Her own flesh and blood, for that matter, is not exempt. And her prayin' louder and longer on Sabbath than anyone else!"

"The McKinneys be an obstinate clan," said the colonel, reminiscently. "They'd ruther be scalped than harkin' to another man.

"See that the boy upstairs has some supper, Ruhannah, and some comfort for the morrow," he added. "I mind me well going to sleep with the horror of taws in the mornin' hangin' over my young soul. Let the child say his prayers in this house in peace."

Ruhannah nodded. She loved her father for his strength, but above all for his never-failing "marcy", as she called it.

"Ma will be home for kirk the morrow," she said. "But I hope the lodge night supper was what ye liked, faither, especially with Captain Jack here."

"Ye treat us too well, Ruhannah," said the old hunter. "Ye tempt me to come back to live close by ye here in the town, as your father allers wants me to do. But I must go and settle up affairs of mine that I have neglected for half a lifetime and abide the coming of one more winter in my old cabin on the Blue Mountain. There I can smoke my pipe in peace, alone, and before the Lord. Yes, it was a good pie, my dear. Succulent! And venison's a dry meat mostly. An old-fashioned Sabbath baking it was."

Ruhannah blushed with pleasure, and looked at Mina and Tina in triumph that her own directions, rather than her mother's, had been carried out and were being praised.

The colonel rose, said a brief after-grace, and the company, leading their horses, followed him and Captain Jack down to the stockaded gate, where after a careful scrutinizing by some of the brethren, they were admitted one by one to the "island" that evening in 1764, talking quietly, and halting to pass through the stockaded gate, man by man. There were about sixty in all in the small procession.

Some wore the buckskins of the mountain wilderness frontier. Others not. Several rifle barrels borne on the shoulders of rangers moved slowly across the constellations, high above the heads of the crowd. There were many farmers in homespun, leading plough horses, two young officers from the fort in royal regimentals, and a distinguished visitor from the City in the fashionable garb of the town. But they were all one in inner tone and feeling.

The several accents of the different dialects they spoke had all merged in the quiet of the night into a subdued and murmurous tongue of common communication, the slightest intonations of which were significant and mutually intelligible. It was English that was thus being spoken, rude but ample. In it was hidden the reservoir of the past and the fountain of the future.

How different was this meeting from the atmosphere of suppressed excitement and missionary zeal that had marked the assembling of the lodge at Bedford in Garrett's garret. The ritual seemed to flow out of the past as a matter of old memory in which all were letter-perfect. The impression was that of piety and sustained order. The setting was less theatrical and less crowded. Except for a few officers of the lodge in aprons, regalia was at a minimum. The huge hall of the fortressed dwelling accommodated all comfortably and yet made a perfect theatre for intimate speaking. Log fires burned at either side in the massive chimneys, and candles at the cardinal points. The squares were chalked and would be erased later. Actually, this was the ruling assembly and moral nexus of the neighbourhood. As such, it was so understood and taken for granted. Opinions were openly discussed and policies settled here.

The meeting that evening was an important one. After some of the local and charitable problems of various brethren and their families were discussed, communications from the Grand Lodge and letters from several quarters were considered. Charles Humphreys of the "Mansion House", seven miles outside of Philadelphia, and a member of the Assembly of the province, discussed the understanding which the Assembly had arrived at with Brother Franklin on sending him as an agent for the province to England, and the possibilities of help to be derived from the brethren abroad.

Colonel Chambers made a plea for upholding the hands of the proprietaries in their old policy of toleration for all sects, and read some passages in support of his argument from a poem by Mr. Peter Folger, called "A Looking Glass for the Times, or the Former Spirit of New England Renewed," which had just been brought to him from Boston. It was a powerful plea for liberty of conscience written in old times, but only recently printed.

The Reverend Brother Craighead followed with a scheme concocted by some of the brethren to import and support a decent Protestant schoolmaster. He made an eloquent complaint of the tendency of the new generation to remain illiterate, and of the consequences to the community. Subscriptions for the bringing in of young Mr. William Thomas to start a school for boys at Chambersburg were pledged forthwith.

Captain Jack followed with an appeal that "his young mountain rangers" should continue to receive the tacit support of the frontier Masons as they always had in the past. All his rangers had always been sons of the widow. The promptness, secrecy, and freedom from government which they had enjoyed in the past, he asked to be continued. He made it plain that he was about to disappear from the scene. "My labours and my mission are o'er." And if anyone could have doubted this, the halting eloquence from the now toothless mouth, which made his valedictory sound like language already half blown away by the wind, was in itself the proof of his theme. He ended by pointing out Salathiel as the one best qualified to re-rally the "Fighting Quakers", when the time came. "And that time will surely be upon us in the nigh and onrushing future. Amen," said Captain Jack.

"The mantle of Elijah has fallen upon you, Brother Albine," said Arthur St. Clair.

There was nothing for it, but Salathiel must rise and accept. And he acquitted himself on this important occasion not only modestly but very well. It was a solemn promise he gave. How reluctant he was to give it, he was at some pains to conceal. The obvious pleasure and affectionate gratitude of his old leader were his immediate and only reward. It was arranged on the side that evening that Captain Jack should accompany him in the wagon as far as Carlisle.

The speech of the old partisan and patriot of the mountains was by far the most moving event of the evening, but not the most discussed. What was most immediately stirring and disturbing to the neighbourhood was the growing hostility of many of the younger men to the downcountry city merchants, and the trade with the Indians, which they roundly denounced. Colonel Chambers complained and warned of the growing lawlessness of the Black Boys. Captain James Smith, the Callahans, and others from Conococheague defended the "taking of necessary measures", short of taking scalps. A number of members spoke bitterly of having their arms seized and their houses searched by "Captain Grant up at the fort".

Nothing very definite came out of all this. It was quite plain that Injun traders were going to have to reckon with the Black Boys. Owing to the presence of Ensigns McNairn and Erskine from the fort, nothing more was said about dealing with Wully and the royal garrison, except perhaps elliptically by Magistrate McDowell, who spoke of the sins and the folly of rebellion against authority.

Two emissaries from the emigrating congregations then on the way from Carlisle were next heard from, and certain plans for seeing them on their way down through the Valley of Virginia and "cherishing" them through the winter were gone into. There were many Masons and their families amongst them. The lodge was adjourned as usual, except for a prayer by Mr. Craighead. It was after midnight, when quietly and with as little disturbance as possible the members dispersed themselves.

When Salathiel and Captain Jack finally emerged from the meeting, all this was evident to them and present in feeling, sensitive as they both were to every change and meaning in the weather of the wilderness and the hints in the atmosphere of any natural place. But it was so well understood, and so taken for granted, that neither of them saw fit to comment upon it. They were there; certain things were going on. The world as always, even when it seemed pleasant and contented, was secretly astir.

Captain Jack was to sleep that night in the wagon. Melissa and Bridget were tarrying with Ruhannah up at the colonel's cabin. Women were not expected to be near-by during a lodge meeting, and Ruhannah had especially asked them to stay.

So, except for Captain Jack, Salathiel shortly after midnight found himself alone.

Captain Jack went to bed gladly. He seemed greatly fatigued, indeed all but overcome by the effects of the meeting and the excitement of his farewell speech. After a few jocular comments on the luxurious headquarters bequeathed by the "little captain", and the follies of fighting Injuns from a palace on wheels, he lay back on Frances' pillow, swallowed a measure of old Cumberland rye gladly, and after only a few movements of his lips was asleep.

Salathiel sat watching him intently by the dim light of a single candle. There was the same large frame outlined by the blanket, but as his sleep became deeper the face of the old man relaxed and imperceptibly changed. It was possible now to look back through the mists of years and to surmise what Captain Jack must have looked like when a boy. It was a strange haunting of age by the lost ghost of youth. Nymwha had often spoke of this return. By the solemn and single light of the candle such things seemed possible, as he sat gazing at the old hunter's face in deep silence. The countenance was smooth and bland, only a little pitiful about the mouth.

Salathiel breathed deeply, which was as near as he ever came to sighing. He thought over the events of the long day. Finally, he rose and extinguished the candle. He had one thing to do yet, before the day could be called finished. It was the hand.

He walked down the row of Colonel Chambers's sheds until he came to the smoke-house. It was empty, all but for a small pile of hickory chips saved for kindling in a dry corner. A few of these he now arranged in the square pit in the middle of the floor, placing some dry rags amongst them from his tinder box. He struck a few sparks with flint and steel and blew on the glowing patch. In a few minutes the pile of chips began to smoke and smoulder. A blowpipe made from an old gun barrel extended under the sill of the door to the bottom of the fire in the pit. This pipe he now stopped with some clay to regulate the draught until the pile smoked, burning at a slow rate, and exactly satisfactorily.

Unwinding a moccasin thong, he suspended the hand by the wrist a few feet above, and directly over, the smoking pit. The hand spun slowly, barely visible in the faintly fire-tinged darkness. Clouds of pungent smoke ascended like incense about it.

Salathiel took a final look at it, and closed the door. Twenty-four hours of that steady heat and smoke, and the article would be "presarved".

He went back to the wagon, undressed, and lay down.

"Hickory smoke," muttered Captain Jack, turning over and sniffing. "Ye stink like a Shawanee."

But I'm not one, thought Salathiel, for all that. Tomorrow I'm going to the sermon with Frances and Bridget, in decent clothes, and like a Christian man. The smell of wood smoke shall not be upon me.

In the smoke-house the hand continued to point downward into the pit.

17. The Sermon

VERY EARLY that Sabbath morning Frances and Bridget were back at the wagon. While Captain Jack slept peacefully on, Salathiel slung an iron pot over a small fire and prepared a breakfast of corn mush, roasted potatoes, and sidemeat. This was quickly dispatched, and the two women turned in to primp themselves and each other for the great occasion of the morning sermon. Bridget, to be sure, was not much of a help to Frances, except as an ardent supporter and abetter of Melissa's desire to appear more elegant than anyone else.

Salathiel, however, was content for his own reasons to go along. He was pleased to find that not only was Frances not going to object to taking part in a Protestant preaching, but was apparently determined to make the most of it, at least from a worldy and visible standpoint. Of her motives for doing so, he could only surmise. As a matter of fact, they were rather complex, and she did not undertake to explain them.

Despite her small chance for indoctrination in the orthodox Roman faith, she remained in her own mind an ardent Catholic. Almost her first certain memory was that of being baptized in The Church at Cork. Her instruction by the nuns there, brief and rudimentary as it had been, had yet made a profound impression upon her. It was not easily, therefore, that she was to be persuaded to enter a Protestant place of worship. Above all, she feared listening to the reading of the King James version of the Scriptures.

To the English Bible Frances attributed a magic potency and capacity for ill. She regarded it as the wellspring of heresy and the prime cause of the downfall of the Irish. Besides the moral fascination of the Book, which she had experienced while cogitating by firelight in front of Frazier's hearth, there was the entrancing and convincing sound of its language. That wizardry remained indelibly in her memory, along with the conviction that she had committed a mortal sin in feeding upon forbidden poetry. To her starving and avid mind the Book had indeed proved a heady and confusing potion. But it was the only book in the cabin—and she had read it.

Now, this morning, she was actually dressing and preparing to go to a Protestant preaching! Well, she couldn't help it. She *must* get along in this world, even at the risk of trouble in the next. She must attain and maintain her respectability, or she was lost here and now. Also she must bring her fine husband along with her; keep him in his town clothes lest he go back to the woods again. And now there was Bridget! Bridget, that young limb and splinter of Presbyterian doctrine. She felt an inborn spiritual obstinacy in her already. She both sensed it and feared it. How would it be possible to explain to Bridget why she should not go with all the rest of the neighbours to listen to the Reverend Mr. Craighead this Sunday morning?

There was one great and consoling circumstance, nevertheless. As yet there was no chapel in Chambersburg. The service was to be held in Colonel Chambers's new mill, and the roof was not yet over it. Only the open framework of the beams was there. Therefore, strictly speaking, it could not be said that she was going *into* a Protestant chapel.

Thus, with apparent equanimity, Frances continued her own and Bridget's outer preparations to attend the preaching at the mill, while moving about quietly and whispering in order to avoid waking Captain Jack. And if her preparations of the morning before for Colonel Chambers's breakfast had been startling and effectual, the final results of her Sunday morning toiletring were little short of triumphant.

Defying the danger of being suspected of working after Saturday sundown, she and Ruhannah had locked the door of their bedroom the night before, and while the lodge met, they had revelled in the purchases

of the day and contrived between them to cover the bare bones of two
new bonnet frames with rich yellow paduasoy, and a small one for
Bridget with black silk. These, with the addition of blue-black ties and
hemstitched bows, were such pieces of worldly millinery as had seldom
swum before the eyes of the Lord in any congregation in Chambers
Mills—and Ruhannah knew it. Alas, there had been no time to make
new bodices. But the bonnets!—they would burst on the gaze of the
faithful unexpectedly as meteors.

Frances must still wear her dress of the day before, but there was a
new grey silk shawl and a neckerchief to match, both with long fringes.
And for Bridget, Melissa had borrowed a pair of small cloth slippers.
They were not red, but they fitted. This time she had out the hot curl-
ing irons, and everything else, for doing her own and Bridget's hair.
Bonnets required bangs curled in front, small ones, tight little ringlets.

So Salathiel had most of Johnson's kit in full blast that morning. And
it was his best blue woollen suit, good stockings, and no leather stock but
a tied cravat that he wore. Short of powdering his hair, he was now willing and even submissive "in going the whole hog" in the proceedings, as
he nicely phrased it.

One reason for this was that he had been told that the emigrants
were looking for a ranger to guide them south and west over the mountains, and that someone had recommended him to them. They were
offering one hundred pounds down and all found, Yates had said so,
and said it so that St. Clair could hear him. That was all right, but he,
Salathiel, was not going to turn west again, not now! Not even for one
hundred pounds and the lure of seeing new country. That he had to
admit did entice him. But since it *was* a temptation, he would rather
not have to meet it.

So the less he looked like his old self, the better for a day or two
at least. The emigrants would be looking for a tall man in fringed buckskins, nursing a long rifle. He would pass them by in a smooth blue coat
and silver buckles on his shoes. He finished by fastening on an old pair
that had once belonged to the captain, and giving his small-clogs a polish.
He also displayed the captain's silver watch and chain across his best
yellow serving waistcoat. But he was mighty glad Captain Jack slept like
a babe all through this dressing-up business. So far he hadn't even stirred.

It was half past nine almost exactly when Colonel Chambers, Mr.
Craighead, and Dr. and Mrs. Colhoun came down the mill path on their
way to the mill and the morning's preaching. Ruhannah's bonnet glowed
afar with a fine effulgence through the bare upper branches of the
willow trees. Colonel Chambers wore the regimentals of the Pennsylvania line but without his small sword. Mr. Craighead's wig was newly
powdered. From the black bag in which he carried his Bible, the ham
had been advisedly removed. Dr. Colhoun approached his Maker in a
modest grey surgeon's coat with cherry-coloured pantaloons, a black

three-cornered hat, and a little beaver muff that hung from his neck on an amber chain. In this he kept his empty purse, a full snuffbox, and both his hands on a cold day. It *was* turning a little cold this morning, he opined, and sermons were usually too long, especially in November in an open mill.

A small brass bell began ringing down at the mill. The colonel's party approached more rapidly. The Albines were waiting for them. They stood for a moment, regarding one another with mutual appreciation.

Colonel Chambers was especially well pleased. He would appear at preaching today with a most genteel and acceptable company. As the chief personage of the neighbourhood, and the landlord of many in the congregation, he felt properly complemented. It was an important occasion this morning. Mr. Craighead had come over from Old Church especially to preach the morning sermon. He was much beloved, and people always turned out in large numbers to hear him. And then there was a certain announcement the minister was to make, one which concerned the colonel deeply and the congregation at Chambersburg, too, for all time to come. The three new bonnets *were* a little gladsome. But then this was no Quaker meeting, and they were nothing to what even the Seceders were wearing in the City. Folks would just have to get used to a little style with a man of substance like himself as presiding elder. Sooner or later he would have in instruments for the psalm singing, too. "Trumpets and psalteries and harps before the Lord"—an organ!

"Good morning," said Mr. Craighead, cordially, touching his wig reminiscently and gratefully to Salathiel. His eyes twinkled as he looked over the women in their new shawls. "Some of us, I see, are making the fringes of our phylacteries long," he chuckled, and then led the way at a faster pace. For the bell had ceased clamouring, and he prided himself on being on time—whenever Ahaz would permit.

Under the fluctuating shadow and sunshine of a swiftly passing flock of clouds, the well-satisfied little company made its way towards the skeleton of the new mill. It would be a pity if it came on to rain, thought the doctor. But no, it would hardly do that. It might snow, if it kept getting much colder. Perhaps the raw weather would hold off until the afternoon? If so, it would still be comparatively comfortable in the sheltered valley below the dam. Indeed, there was a hush in the atmosphere of the place when they arrived there.

A larger congregation than even the colonel had anticipated was awaiting the minister. At the far end of the new mill the elders sat before a table reared on saw-horses on the raw plank floor. The open work of the rafters in the rough Gothic joinery of the gambrel seemed to sketch airily overhead only the bare reminder of a church roof. Beneath, the congregation sat on plank benches or were gathered in close about the new building, as close as they could press on either side and still see over the heads of the sitters from the rising ground about. The curious and continuous alternating of cloud-gloom and bright sunshine was startling and impressive; now everything was bathed in glory, then all was overcast and plunged in gloom.

It would be a hard thing to preach against, thought Mr. Craighead, as he walked up the narrow aisle between the benches and deposited his black bag on the big table. He took out his heavy Bible, leather-bound hymnal and psalter and arranged them carefully and somewhat dramatically, as was his wont. He then put on a large pair of square spectacles. Colonel Chambers sat down amongst the elders, facing his family and visitors, who were now seated honourably on the front bench. He noted with pleasure that Mrs. Chambers was there, just come in on time from Shippensburg. But ready to lead the singing as usual. He would like to have smiled at her if he could. But being presiding elder was no smiling matter.

Mr. Craighead turned, faced the congregation, and announced the opening psalm. They began in gloom, but a drench of sunshine suddenly poured down on them. And it seemed to the minister that it was not Madam Chambers, but the river itself with a certain hint of eternity in the hushed voice of its ever-rolling waters that set the pitch of the old tune. Two hundred voices filled the valley with song.

Back at the wagon, Captain Jack knew the 150th Psalm when he heard it. Indeed, he knew a great part of the Old Testament by heart, particularly the more sanguinary passages dealing with vengeance upon the heathen. He was up now, crouching over the remains of Salathiel's breakfast fire, and roasting a bit of sidemeat on a long fork. The singing of the congregation rose deep and clear, high over the roar of the distant falls upstream. The meat was turning brown. He hadn't meant to go to preaching this morning. He was glad the young folks had let him sleep. In the past he had heard a good many sermons. But the taste of the music was almost as strong in his mouth now as the taste of the meat—and he felt the better for both. This time he joined in with all his old-time vim. His voice echoed heartily against the face of the old mansion. He looked up to see Yates and St. Clair grinning at him through the yard gate.

"We wondered who was praising God all alone," said Yates. "We're bound for the preaching ourselves, but tardiness always likes company. Won't you come along, sir?"

"Wait till I finish my pork and taters," answered Captain Jack. "An old man needs his morning sustenance, Sabbath or no."

They came over respectfully and sat down by the fire to wait while he ate. Presently St. Clair produced his silver flask, and they all had a brief pull.

"That's better," said Captain Jack. "I don't git immedjit effect from my victuals any more." He raked a roasted potato from the ashes, broke it, and put salt on it.

"What surprised ye to hear a man praising the Lord all alone?" he asked out of the blue.

"Well, now," said St. Clair, "since you ask *me*. Praise by a congregation does sound more convincing. At least to me," he added.

"That's 'cause you're a politician, Arthur," said Captain Jack. "You think everything must be done by committees. That's the way ever since thar's so many settlers in these once lonely and decent parts. But if the chief end of man is to glorify God exceedingly, one God and one man is all it takes. Ain't it?" asked Captain Jack.

"Do you glorify him most by faith or by works?" inquired Yates.

"Oh, I won't quibble with ye, mister attorney," said the old man. "No doubt you're better at splitting hairs in a circle than I be. But kin ye tie a knot in them before ye lose both ends? And let me ask you this: as a man of reason, what did ye ask me to go down to hear the sermon this mornin' for?"

"For your company," said Yates.

Captain Jack dropped his potato, and grinned through his gums. "That's mighty well put, young man," said he. "Still I suspicion, as a lawyer *you're* lookin' for direct evidence. If so, testimony, indirect testimony is all you'll ever git."

"Then I'll be curious to hear what Brother Craighead may have to say this morning," replied Yates.

The *old devil*, he thought. Who would have guessed there was theology in him! To take for granted what he still had to prove! We might have been here all morning!

Captain Jack began brushing the ashes off his buckskins. He wiped his mouth off, too. "We'd better git goin'," he said. "That's the invocation now."

They set off for the mill together.

"Brother St. Clair will feel better where two or three are gathered together," said Captain Jack, a little too casually.

St. Clair turned pale and purple under his stock.

"But shucks," continued the old man, "it looks today like we'd do even better than that. It's no rump caucus down there."

There were, in fact, too many in the congregation that morning to hold the preaching in the mill. Everybody shifted to a hollow in the meadow near-by, a place that had frequently been used for field-preaching, weather permitting, long prior to the erection of Colonel Chambers's mill.

And there was good reason for this arrangement. For not only was the ground in the field of a convenient conformation, but there was a memorable pulpit naturally provided. It was the hollow shell of a huge poplar tree, which having once sustained a bolt from heaven a half century before, now contributed its convenient remains to echoing forth the divine thunders of the itinerant clergy.

Some rough-and-ready but ingenious axe work on its massive and heavily rooted lower trunk had cut into the solid wood a short semi-circular flight of steps leading to a floor within the tree itself. That in turn supported a rustic lectern. Above this the shell of bark still projected in a prolonged hollow oval and was tied together at the top with old rope and stoppered with tar. A few thin planks extending forward and upward had been inserted towards the roof as a sounding board and hung there by a rusty chain.

Crude as this rostrum accidentally furnished forth by nature might appear to the ecclesiastically sophisticated, it was curiously impressive and acoustically effective. For in it the minister stood ten feet above the crowd like a jack-in-the-pulpit; but in full sight of and within perfect hearing of all his congregation gathered in the hollow of the field before him. Furthermore, the pulpit itself served to confine those who used it to its own deeply rooted and earthy style. Any affected discourse echoed from its natural depths would inevitably have suffered the tragic fate of inadvertent comedy.

Yates, Captain Jack, and St. Clair arrived just when the congregation was shifting from the mill to the meadow, and in time to take their places amidst the others without arousing comment. A few open wagons were drawn up towards the side, where some of the farmers' wives and children sat overlooking the heads of the majority, who now seated themselves on the bare turf or on what fragments of logs, planks, and shingles they could secure.

After a short pause for all to get settled, Mr. Craighead, his black bag under his arm, and followed by all the elders, approached the wide-spreading roots of the old tree, and after giving the opening lines of a hymn, ascended the notched steps into the pulpit, while the congregation sang.

Had it not been that an air of wisdom and dignity, even a certain lugubrious solemnity, were the expected and habitual accompaniments of Presbyterian preaching, the droll appearance of Mr. Craighead in a wig, a square white stock, and a pair of large horn-rimmed spectacles peering from his bark pulpit would inevitably have reminded people of an owl discovered in a hollow tree by daylight. As it was, from long familiarity his neighbours took his appearance for granted and saved their comments for what he might have to say; and this in full confidence that it would not be as solemn as he looked.

For it was not Mr. Craighead's habit when preaching to

> "Draw a wrong copy of the Christian face,
> Without the smile, the sweetness, and the grace."

Nor did he, like so many of his contemporaries, preach by rote from manuscript with a flowing hourglass set before him. George Whitefield was his better original. He spoke by inspiration, timed himself by the mood of his listeners, and chose his text at the last minute by skilful intuition.

Quite often, indeed, he would open his big Bible haphazard and preach from the first text that happened to catch his eye and forefinger. And it was this method that he decided to follow that morning. He rolled his eyes upward—to take a glance at the now-threatening clouds —and prayed silently that he might be permitted to preach without interruption from heaven. Then he opened his Bible about the middle and found his text:

> "Thy people shall be willing in the day
> of thy power, in the beauties of holiness
> from the womb of the morning: thou hast
> the dew of thy youth . . .

Psalm One Hundred Ten, the third verse," said he, and paused impressively.

Mr. Craighead spoke with a clerical accent that had been acceptable some twenty years previously in certain Calvinistic circles in Aberdeen, where the Scots think that excellent English is spoken. His general utterance was both strong and clear. Nevertheless, it is not to be denied that on this particular Sabbath he *hemmed* a little, although without *hawing;* and hesitated, as it were, a trifle in his usual forensic stride. For the truth was that, as God would have it, the text he had blundered upon by divine guidance, taken out of its context, had no grammatical meaning at all.

Now this, as any kindly body who will stop to consider a moment can see, was a very serious predicament for Mr. Craighead. For, unless it rained, he was expected to detain, nay, to edify and inspire the minds and souls of his two hundred listeners for two mortal hours at least with an uplifting discourse on a subject without a theme. Not only that, but both his reputation and his living depended upon it.

Quite hastily, therefore, he rearranged mentally the phrases of his text, hopeful that a human meaning would emerge. But nothing of the kind happened. If possible, the result was even more impenetrable. And it was this which had given the good man to pause.

At the same time Mr. Yates looked up from the wagon wheel against which he was leaning, with an alert and fascinated stare. If he had answered Captain Jack's question candidly, instead of preventing it by courtesy, Yates would have had to admit that it was for such moments of intellectual crisis as this that he came to listen to sermons. Alone among those present he fully sympathized with and realized the minister's predicament, and it was his keen curiosity to see how Mr. Craighead might extricate himself that now caused him to gaze towards the pulpit with an all but burning intensity.

Nor was Mr. Yates's curiosity only an idle one. Between the practice of his own profession and that of Mr. Craighead he drew many valuable analogies. Both harked back in essence to custom and authority and were dependent for happy results upon persuasive oratory and the turning of awkward corners by neat rhetorical tricks. Hence, he was sorry to see that his good friend, the minister, was in difficulties, while at the same time he hoped to profit professionally by observing the method of his way out. That it would take considerable acumen he had small doubt. For the text had undoubtedly been recklessly chosen.

No wonder Mr. Craighead had paused. The question was, how in the world could he ever go on?

But go on he did.

After an hour of lofty eloquence, and without really making sense, Mr. Craighead lowered himself to take notice of the more notable spots of evil in the immediate neighbourhood and of the familiar failings of friends. These he dealt with forthrightly, and finally lit with an indignant flutter of wings upon the errors of the new generation. But it would not do to remain too long or permanently at so depressing a level. Then he launched forth again upon a rising whirlwind of prophecy.

The last of the patches of sunshine had passed some time ago. Mr. Craighead, in spite of the glowing predictions of his peroration, was ending in gloom. A brief spatter of rain passed down the valley, leaving a few glistening drops on the faces and clothes of the congregation. The minister looked up at heaven and smiled. His congregation, however, awaited his decision whether to go on with the sermon or not, apprehensively. Evidently the patience of the weather at least was about come to an end. But their anxiety was soon relieved.

"This will be the last preaching of the summer," said the minister— "a summer which has been out of all season graciously prolonged. For many years now we have met in the open, sung His praises and offered our prayers directly under the open roof of the sky. That time has come to an end. I have an announcement this morning that deeply concerns us all.

"Colonel Chambers has made an eternal gift to this congregation. It is the natural garden of cedars lying along the banks of the river in the town. A log church is to be erected there speedily. The labours of the coming winter will be consecrated to it. So, we shall meet no more together like the early Christians under the sky. Since time presses," said Mr. Craighead, peering anxiously upward again, "I shall read the terms of the gift only. Then we will omit the usual psalm singing at the end and depart immediately after the benediction."

He picked up a small piece of paper and peered at it. "The land has been left to you," he said, " 'in trust for the Presbyterian congregation of the Falling Spring, now professing and adhering to, and that shall hereafter adhere to and profess, the Westminster profession of faith, and the mode of church government therein contained, and to and for the use of a meeting house or Presbyterian church, session house, school-house, burying-place, graveyard, and such religious purposes.' May the Lord make us all duly thankful, and bring us at last to come to rest there in eternal peace. And now . . ."

The benediction followed.

Everyone left instantly. The wagons were hastily packed and driven off. In the grove on the hill near-by a hundred farmers' horses were hastily mounted, and with the women clinging on behind, clattered off in every direction into the countryside. It seemed as if the congregation of the Falling Spring were literally being scattered before the oncoming winter storm. Northward, the mountains were already dim with swirling patches of snow. In the valley, at Chambersburg itself, doors and windows were being hastily closed. Chimneys were beginning to smoke. Indian summer was over. The wind shifted eastward, and driving squalls of cold rain began to sweep from time to time across the vacant open square of the town.

"Ain't it curious," observed Captain Jack, while toasting his shins that afternoon before Colonel Chambers's fire after the midday meal, "how whenever thar's an east wind picks up in these parts along the Maryland border, everybody huts-up and has spiritual rheumatiz, even if their jints ain't begun to swell yet? There's somethin' kind o' lanky-danky and plaguey about an east wind. Hark to the rain beating on the windowpanes now, and only yesterday the weather was smilin' like your genial old aunt."

"Looks to me like we're in for a regular nor'easter," agreed the colonel, taking his jug from under the table. "I can spy winter marching down on us in battalions. Well, it's past time for frost now, and you always pay high for a too mild October. You'll have a foul journey to Carlisle, unless she freezes up."

"Reckon she'll do that," said Captain Jack, getting up to look out the window.

Salathiel was finishing loading the wagon in the rain at Somerfield's. He and Arthur were stowing it carefully for the last leg of the journey, in the yard behind the store. Meanwhile, Frances, Bridget, and Captain Jack were snugly ensconced at the Chambers'. Mrs. McKinney had been prevailed upon to leave Roy Davison, who had a sore throat and a fever, with the Chambers for a day or two.

At the store, Salathiel found he had considerable on his hands in the way of minor arrangements for departure before dawn next morning. Yates had picked up the lame horse he had left at Fort Loudon some months before. It was in fine fettle again. But Enna would now have to be taken care of, and there was Captain Jack's sturdy brown gelding, which the old man would not be able to ride back to Carlisle, if it continued to storm. Despite his protests, it was only common sense he should ride in the wagon.

Finally, a solution offered by St. Clair was found to be the best way out. Captain Jack's mount and Enna were to be driven as a third team for the wagon, and Jed was to ride postilion on Enna as far as Carlisle. Adequate harness and a drag pole for the new arrangement were put together that afternoon.

"Wisht I was goin' along," said Arthur several times. He looked wistful.

"Wait till the summer," said Salathiel. "I won't know where I'm goin' to be till then, or how long we'll be tarryin' at Carlisle. You'll be much better off here at Somerfield's."

"I suppose so," replied the lad doubtfully.

Suddenly Salathiel burst out, "Arthur, I jist can't take care of ye now. And you've got another year to serve with Somerfield, who's your good friend. Also, ye have no idea what it means to have so many mouths to feed. I'd be skeered to take on any more now. What with Jed wantin' me to buy him from Mr. St. Clair, you wantin' to come along, and your young cousin Roy beggin' me to buy his time out from Mrs. McKinney —why, thar's no end to it! And between you and me, maybe Captain Jack will take a little lookin' after, too."

"Roy!" said Arthur. "That young'un! Why, he's uncle Ed's brat."

"But a fine youngster, and our Bridget is much taken with him."

"Thought ye was jes takin' her to her granny," mumbled Arthur.

"So I am," snapped Salathiel, "but I ain't found her grandma yet, all I know about her is in a letter. And if I do find her, maybe she'll be sittin' at the hearth, too. You can't tell.

"But, there now," he continued, seeing the boy was much chagrined by his irritated tone, "I didn't mean to take my troubles out on you. It's jes that I've been gittin' a little worried lately about how the family does recruit itself. Tell ye what ye do. You patch up that old family fight with your young cousin. Have him down to the store now and then. Teach him to read and cipher a bit. Try to help him. And when I do git settled in the City, you kin both ride down. Never mind what your pa once said to your uncle Ed. You youngsters ought to stick together like cousins agin the world. All the Davisons be fine people! Don't forgit I'm mighty partial to 'em."

They finished the work in silence, but Salathiel could see that Arthur was turning it over in his mind.

Before dark all was in readiness. Only a trip to the smoke-house remained to complete the last item. But the longer it stayed there in the smoke and drying heat, the better.

He and Arthur went over to the colonel's and everybody was there for supper that night. Ruhannah was delighted to find that Arthur was so solicitous about his young cousin and insisted on helping out with him. As for Roy, he was noncommittal, surprised, and secretly pleased. Never mind what my pa said to Uncle Will, he thought.

"Sometime soon I'll ride downcountry and see ye, Bridget," the boy said as they prepared to leave the cabin that night. "Ye'd better git some clothes for Alliquippa, ifen she's goin' to go ridin' in that canoe," he called after her down the hall.

"Yes," said Bridget, and fled.

She and Frances and Captain Jack came over to sleep at the store that night to be on hand for the early start next morning. Yates and St. Clair would ride later, but promised to catch up with the wagon before Shippensburg. The good-byes were brief but heartfelt. " 'Pears like you've been here a month or more," said Colonel Chambers. "We'll be seein' you all again, I'm sure. Here's some muster rolls I want ye to take down to Colonel Burd at Lancaster," he said to Salathiel. "And I've writ him a line or two about ye, won't do ye no harm."

When they left the hospitable cabin that evening it was already starting to snow. There were eight degrees of frost on Colonel Chambers's London thermometer and it was getting colder. Salathiel went down to the mill sheds, put blankets on all the horses, and retrieved the hand.

That night the wind blew with an ever-rising crescendo. In the morning, it was shrieking through the bare branches of Somerfield's maples with the authentic howl of winter, and no doubt about it. Captain Jack was quite content, although he did not say so, to let them hitch his gelding in the lead team with Enna and ride himself in the wagon with Frances and Bridget.

Mr. Somerfield and Arthur saw them off by the light of two lanthorns. The six horses, with Jed hunching forward into the storm on Enna, jingled and jangled through the darkness along the icy road to Carlisle.

18. Swan Song on a Harpsichord

THE RUMBLE of turning wheels, the steely clatter of twenty-four hoofs on the hard-frozen road, billowing clouds rolling westward—that morning the whole countryside seemed on the move as they pressed on eastward in the direction of Carlisle. Weather gave the overpowering impression. The entire landscape appeared to be torn loose and flowing.

Stripped trees waved their bare arms in the blast. Long lines of brown leaves scuttled and swung sinuously before the storm, rising here and there into swirling fountains to be snatched upward and away. The day brightened slowly into universal silver gloom.

Along the road from time to time, moving with an all but military front and precision, battalions of sleet and snow advanced swiftly down upon the wagon—and struck. The icy needles of sleet pattered and slithered along the canvas, while dry flakes swirled. The horses neighed and snorted under the recurrent punishment; shook themselves until their new slip bells clanged and sang. Then the flurry would go by and the road open up before them again.

It was a grand nor'easter that was marching down.

Jed, with a battered three-cornered hat tied ludicrously over his fuzz by an old knitted scarf, which covered his ears and flapped behind him with ravelling ends loose in the breeze, sat hunched uncomfortably on Enna, a tattered blanket bound with twine swathed heavily about him. Still he was cold. Riding postilion for Marse Albine was not the fun he had anticipated.

Snowflakes caught and lay melting on his upper eyelids. He looked forward despondently into the advancing storm, squeezing his eyes tight shut as the grim blasts swept down. The mare's hard military saddle galled him. Between flurries he rode stolidly, half frozen, dreaming of the sun-stricken market square at Dahomey and its rustling palm trees.

Salathiel was rattling along in high fettle and the best of good nature. He was more than content to be on the way east again so close to the end of his journey. Carlisle wasn't Philadelphia, but it was *almost* there. No matter how St. Clair's scheme for settling Ligonier worked out, it would mean only a temporary wait for him and Melissa at Carlisle. He wasn't going to be balked of getting to the City now. At Carlisle he could lay plans for getting a toe-hold in Philadelphia. He might see Colonel Burd at Lancaster; deliver that letter personally. Why, he could even talk to Buckey himself when he came through. The colonel would certainly remember him as "Ecuyer's man". Buckey had been so amiable to everybody at Fort Pitt. Now, why hadn't he thought of *that* before?

Most of his serious troubles lay behind him, he felt. By comparison the future seemed positively simple. He was escaping into it, he thought. He couldn't help but feel fine about it. The future seemed so full of hope, of free movement, and of happy adventure. A little luck, a little *more* luck now, and . . . The whip cracked merrily.

It was something to have six horses and Jed outriding. How it did make the old wagon clatter along. They'd be in Carlisle that very night. He wouldn't tarry for more than time-out for the noon meal at Shippensburg.

The last flurry of thick weather rolled down the road behind him. The wind came keening and clear, out of the northeast. A high whirlwind of leaves and small twigs rose from the edge of the road down which the herd had just disappeared. It slanted forward in a cloud westward, seeming to be following them. Now and then a distant barking, a solemn bellowing, or an eerie note on a horn broke through. Then the sound of the wind swallowed all. The cloud rose higher, the sun looked through. God's people had passed.

He sat down and handled the reins again hopefully. Now that they *were* past, he was glad to be driving east again. He put his arm about

Bridget and drew her closer to him. Jed looked back and took courage from his smile.

A mile or so over the distant fields and scattered woodlands, the wood smoke from the chimneys of Shippensburg made a blue hazy patch in the winter air.

Out of the dark weather retreating into the distance behind them, St. Clair and Yates came posting down the road and overtook the wagon just as it was entering Shippensburg. St. Clair shouted something to Jed. Evidently the two riders were making a race for it. As far as Salathiel could see, they turned in at the same place precisely together.

He watched them dismount and tie their horses to the hitching bar before a stone building, where a cumbersome canvas-covered wagon, its teams lacking, was standing forlorn in the road. Leaning over a fire that had been kindled directly beside it, a man in a black cap was very busy about something. Except for him, there was no one in sight. A light, patchy snow covered the village, and had it not been for the smoke rolling from numerous chimneys, it would have seemed desolate. Certainly it was unkempt.

They were passing a rocky mound on the left of the street now, with the remains of a considerable stockade on it. Old Fort Franklin perhaps? He'd heard of it. But it had been abandoned not long after Braddock's time. Where, then, was Fort Morris? That must be Mr. Ed Shippen's mansion they were passing now! The finest house he had ever seen. He whistled and pointed it out to Bridget. "Shippen's," he said. She took it quite calmly.

"Marse St. Clair say pull in here," shouted Jed. He pointed to a low stone building with a parapet, and embrasures in the walls instead of windows, on the same side of the street as Shippen's. St. Clair's and Yates's mounts were hitched before it. He now saw that the wagon standing in the street had only two wheels. A lot of household stuff had lately been spewed out behind. Feathers had come out of a pillow and were still blowing about. The man in the black fur cap—and leather apron—was putting on a new axle. He had some thin iron rods heating in the coal fire near-by to bore rivet holes in the wood.

"They're watchin' fer ye in thar," said he, looking up and pointing with his hammer. "Tell 'em I'm nigh finished, will ee?"

Salathiel allowed he would. It was only as he was hitching the teams to the long log rail that he realized he was about to enter Fort Morris. The curious blind-walled stone building with nothing but one door in its long front was it.

"We're here!" he shouted.

Captain Jack and Melissa came down the rear ladder stiffly. The old man was carrying his hand-pack.

"Hope Rutherford has a right hearty blaze goin'," he remarked. "It really does be turnin' cold."

"What's the pack for?" asked Salathiel.

"I've got somethin' valuable in it I wouldn't trust ye with," grinned Captain Jack. "Let's go inside."

Bridget was already fumbling in vain with the massive wrought-iron handle of the fort door.

"That's a tough one for young customers," said the old man. "Better let your pappy snag on."

Salathiel leaned heavily on the lock before it gave. The left leaf of the loopholed oak door swung inward, and they felt the welcome warmth and smelled new whitewash. There was more warmth than light inside, however, and for a moment they stood in comparative darkness, trying to make out the puzzling features of the room.

The interior of Fort Morris was unique, almost cavelike. The floor, the groined ceiling, and its walls were all alike of dressed stone. Inside there was a single huge barrack room, with one tremendous open chimney for the garrison's cooking at its far end. Several ample stone platforms about three feet high rose at regular intervals along both walls. What windows the place had were deep embrasures let high in the walls like the ports of a ship. But these openings were now in process of either being carefully boarded over or smoothly bricked up.

The fire, the warm leaping heart of the room; a grey-haired woman in linsey-woolsey standing before it turning two fowls on a spit; another woman standing beside her helping, in a shimmering blue silk dress; the pointed ears and backs of two tabby cats solemnly watching the cooking. On one side, on the stone platform nearest the fire, sat St. Clair and Yates, a bowl of hot punch already steaming on the table before them. On another platform, immediately opposite, three tow-headed children leaned across a table staring fixedly at a cratelike object, as though they were mesmerized.

And so on down the apartment there were four platforms arranged along each wall. And the platforms were something to see. On them had been piled anything and everything that had once furnished the fort. Only one platform had turned entirely domestic.

On it was a dirty canopy bed, unmade, and with a tossed trundle-cot beneath. Several broken chairs, a small table, old clothes, a cradle, a boot-jack, a wardrobe, and two covered jordans seemed to be having a smug gossip together over what had transpired the night before. This "bedroom" without walls appeared indecent by naughty contrast, for all the rest of the place was swept, garnished, and whitewashed. Obviously the fort was but newly domestically occupied.

Just then, down the middle aisle between the piled platforms, they saw a tall lantern-jawed man in grimy butternut advancing towards them and about to speak.

"*Tut-tut, chuck—oooeee*" . . . an indescribably shrill whistle followed, echoed dully amidst the domes. For an instant they thought it must be the man was making fun of them. But he laughed at their natural confusion and held out his hand to Captain Jack.

"Well, old un, I 'spect ye had a big lodge night over to Chambers's," said he. "Glad to see ye ag'in. None the warse for the trip?"

"Nary a bit," replied the old hunter. "Here be some travellin' folks I brought ye. But jist for the noon snack. They're intendin' fer Carlisle."

"Wal, now, we'll dish them out some kind o' fixin's. Thar's possum stew and praties, if they kin take it. My name's Jim Rutherford, by the way," he added. He extended his hand to Albine carelessly—and winced. "Mr. St. Clair warned me ye were comin'. Some of the congregationers that jist passed through here was mighty anxious to have a talk with ye. They camped nigh us for four days, so we're et out like rats in a corn-crib. That's why thar's naught but possum stew. No, the fowls ain't any o' mine"—he nodded towards the woman in the silk gown. "Hern," he said. "That's right. Her and her man hev tarried behind 'cause o' wagon trouble. . . . Turkey-fither gentry!" he whispered, and beckoned them towards the fireplace.

That strange shivering whistle sounded again, and a raucous voice that seemed to be cursing itself swore like a sailor.

Bridget dashed forward and joined the children peering into the object on the table. For an instant she seemed to be enchanted, too. Then she screamed, "Look, M'lissa, look!"

The voice began to chuckle wickedly. Out of sheer curiosity, it was Salathiel who bent down over the table and looked.

Through the bars of a light iron cage with a brass ring on its top, a strange knowing bird sidled away from him on its wooden perch, flexing one glovelike claw in the air thoughtfully. It was green as the scum on a stagnant pool—and smelt like it. It gave a low chuckling whistle. But, of course, it couldn't . . .

"Poor Poll, poor poor Poll," it said. He *saw* it talk.

He all but fell down and knocked his head on the table out of sheer helpless astonishment. The bird talked!

All four children broke into screams of appreciation at finding a big man so obviously sharing their happy wonder.

"See!" said Bridget triumphantly.

"Come on over," whispered Yates to St. Clair, "this is bound to be rare. Our large friend is discovering something entirely new."

Everybody now gathered about the table with the cage on it.

The parrot, however, was not entirely pleased at being the centre of so much concentrated attention. He sidled back and forth on his perch, making deprecatory noises. He looked askance.

"He's a naughty, nautical old reprobate," remarked a clear, feminine voice, causing them all to look up.

It was the lady in the blue silk dress. She had come over from the fireplace and was standing close beside the table, holding fire tongs before her with something in them that glowed white hot. She was hardly more than a girl, with a grave mouth that threatened to smile at any moment. Her dark hair was a mass of ringlets and short curls. Her blue eyes shone with a tearful lustre, but the lids were red.

She stood very straight and slight. She was pathetically attractive. They all felt it, and gaped at her.

"Would you mind letting me give Poll what he needs?" she asked gently.

It was Yates who first guessed what she meant. He pulled two of the children away from the cage so she could approach it.

She reached forward with the tongs and dropped the heated half-brick into a small iron receptacle fixed in the bars of the cage under the perch. The parrot moved over and began to fluff its feathers and stretch out its wings in the grateful glow. It croaked happily.

"Well, I'll be double-damned," exclaimed Captain Jack.

"*Hush,*" said she in alarm. "You'll start him swearing, and he's just the profanest old—" She put a hand over her mouth. When it came away there was a smile there, and her eyes danced. "He's very very naughty, but I just love him."

"An extremely fortunate old bird, ma'am," replied Yates, bowing ever so slightly. He might have proceeded further, but the big door at the end of the room opened, and the girl's sensitive features froze.

A thin middle-aged man in the primmest of black suits came down the room. He had a determined face, and he kept his hat on. He glanced at the group around the parrot's table indignantly.

"It would be *much* better, madam, if you would give your undivided attention to hurrying the cookery, instead of gossiping idly with these doubtless—*ah*—very worthy persons," he added, running his eye over the company. "The smith informs me he has all but completed his repairs. As it is, the delay already . . ."

"Can we take the things with us?" she interrupted.

"*Impossible!*" he said icily.

She closed her eyes for a moment and stood perfectly still. Then she turned and went back to the fire. The fowls were done. Her husband stood looking after her for a moment. His mouth tensed.

"How do you do, Mr. Preston," said Yates.

"How do *you* do, sir?" replied the man, without looking at him. Then he dragged a small bench and table close to the fire, sat down with his back to the company, and awaited his wife's serving.

"Friend of yours?" inquired Captain Jack sardonically.

"Apparently not," replied Yates. "But I know him." He shrugged and led the way back to St. Clair's table, where Jed was hopefully helping set the board with wooden plates and spoons for all. After the potatoes and meat had been piled into one big earthen bowl, and the punch renewed, Mrs. Rutherford and her husband joined the company, while the children held a noisy revel all their own. Despite that, the parrot went to sleep. The meal began. . . .

Mr. Preston had risen from his chair, and he now announced in a voice that reverberated dismally, "Woman, if I've told you once, I've told you a score of times, we *canna* take the bed with us! It may be rosewood and cedar, or it may have been Grandma LeTort's bridal bower and death couch too. But 'tis too massive a piece for the axles of the wagon to bear." Mr. Preston wiped his mouth, and looked at his wife.

"But the spinet, my poor little harpsichord!" pleaded the girl, now openly tearful. "It's light, *it* will ride.

"See!" she continued, in one last attempt to mollify the marble. "Look! It's *very* light."

In her desperation, she went over to the wall and dragged a small spinet out from a pile of furniture, putting it in the firelight where all could see. Its wires sang faintly. They seemed to sigh.

"Hear?" she said. "How can you still listen to it, Andrew?"

"Felice," said her husband icily, "I'll have no sich godless instrument in the hoose. The meenisters will not permeet it. Your profane bird is the only conceesion to balladry I'll make."

"I'll have a last song then," she cried desperately. "And will ye stay to hear it, Andrew Preston? Durst ye listen to a swan song?"

"Aye, I'll hear ye oot," he replied, and folded his arms stoically.

"Candles, madam, candles, if *you please!*" the girl cried to Mrs. Rutherford. Meanwhile, she dragged the little harpsichord farther out across the stone floor with the fierce energy of anger. Two candles were brought her by the puzzled Mrs. Rutherford. These she took with shaking hands, lit them at the hearth, and placed them in two small sconces on either side of the instrument. A tense drama of protest informed every motion of her body. Unconsciously, she was making a ritual to express what she durst not fully say.

There was no one, not even her husband, who was not now intensely aware of this. The children stared and were suddenly quiet. Yates and St. Clair stood up the better to see.

She sat down at the instrument, with the firelight behind her and the twin stars of the candles gleaming beside her face. She tossed her curls back, opened the spinet, and looked at Mr. Preston fixedly.

To Salathiel the ivory keys grinned as though a horse had skinned its lips back from its teeth. The first chord that she struck swept him with a shock of overwhelming amazement. The quills striking on the little wires rang charmingly with small twanging echoes in the inverted cups of the stone ceiling. He sat there drowning in lovely sound. Music finally closed over his head . . .

She ranged slowly upward on the chords of an octave, her voice gaining smoothness and power as it rose. It was plain to St. Clair and Yates what she was doing. She had lost herself in memory and was practising on the keyboard as a child. Presently she hummed a brief nursery rhyme, accompanying herself. Then quickly, after the ripple of a merry prelude, came the full tide of a song.

It was something about a famous general who always rode a-cock-horse before going to sleep in his mother's lap. In the next stanzas he grew up, became a real soldier, and returned safe from the wars to his bride.

She soared now into the last verse, her voice ringing liquidly, with a little harplike banter on the upper keys.

The voice ceased; the music went on quietly, seeming to relate a wordless tale of ardent melancholy. In the candlelight the girl's face became languidly composed and grave. Her hands roved gradually down the keyboard into the sad minors of an ancient hymn.

She closed the harpsichord softly, as though she were saying amen with the covers, and then stood with her hand on it, patting it good-bye. Tears traced down her cheeks. She leaned over and kissed the dark wood. She blew out the candles.

He stood there waiting for her.

"Do you remember?" she asked in a low tone as she passed him. "Do you remember, Andrew, how it was when you first came to the old house at LeTort's Springs?"

"Yes," he said, "but why will ye 'mind me of those pretty times?"

"Because," she replied, "because . . ." She hesitated for a moment—and then, going over to the children's table, slipped a flannel cover over the iron cage and, taking it by its brass ring with two fingers, stood waiting for him resignedly.

"Come," she said. "Can't you see I'm ready?"

He came forward then and offered her his arm. "At least I'll have a bird to sing my profane songs for me," she added.

He let her have the last word.

She laid her hand over his arm, and they walked down the long room together, her shoulders beginning to droop.

"Poor Poll, Poll's a-cold," croaked the parrot, as the door swung open revealing the bleak street. Then it closed firmly behind them.

There was a moment's utter silence before they heard the rolling sound of iron wheels commence and then diminish down the street.

"The poor darlint, oh, that poor, poor darlint!" exclaimed Frances, springing up and going over to lay her own hands on the abandoned spinet. "And *him* like an old dry pipe stem. Oh, Mr. Rutherford, will ye not be takin' the best care of her pretty things?"

"For a year and a day, ma'am," replied Rutherford. "For that, I'm to be paid. Afterwards—who knows? Mr. Preston is a hard case, and no one can be nursing another man's plunder when he will not house it himself." The landlord of Fort Morris turned away to collect his reckoning for the meal.

Captain Jack said nothing, but continued to wait quietly at the table while the company broke up. Presently he beckoned to Frances and began to explain to her that she was to say nothing to Salathiel about his staying behind; and that his horse was to be driven on to Carlisle. He'd made arrangements for sending for it later. "No use of havin' a big set-to now," he said. "I ain't in a mood to take it."

All indeed was now in full bustle for the final departure for Carlisle. Jed was taking the nosebags off the horses and tightening the girth of his saddle. The women went to the jaques and the men to an intimate corner against the rear wall outside. Incidentally, the recent departure of Mr. and Mrs. Preston was casually discussed.

A general buttoning-up followed.

Just then someone passed at breakneck speed riding up the town street at a furious gallop. "Sounds like an express," remarked Rutherford. "They often go tearin' right through here for Carlisle. Say, did ye hear they say Buckey's started marchin' from Fort Pitt? Might be at Bedford now."

"'They say,'" quoted St. Clair scornfully. "What don't *they* say? The last I heard, Bouquet was due to march east by April at the earliest."

"Ye can't be sure," mused Albine; "now that he's been promoted, maybe he's in a hurry to wind everything up."

But none of them thought any more of the rumour. It seemed unlikely that Bouquet would march his rescued captives over the mountains in the winter. Besides, they had more immediate affairs of their own to consider.

While St. Clair stood in the street before Fort Morris, giving final instructions to Salathiel about waiting for the expected Ligonier emigrants at Carlisle, Frances and Bridget were inside, saying good-bye to Captain Jack.

The old hunter was going home to his cabin on Jack's Mountain. He would not be moved by any argument. He wished no fuss.

"It's jist come over me again," he said, "I must be alone. Tell yer young man I'll send fer him at Carlisle if I ever need him. Rutherford's bound boy here knows the trail to my old mountain shack. Now, git along without worryin' Sal any about me. Keep the horse till I send for it. Good-bye, and God be with ye, my dears."

Bridget threw her arms about his neck. It was only then that for an instant or two he showed any emotion. They left him sitting at the table filling his pipe.

When they hurried out, Salathiel was already in the seat, waiting, and the wagon drawn out into the street ready to move. St. Clair and Yates had ridden on ahead. They were going to the land office at Lancaster and were in a hurry. Jed was sitting on Enna, round-eyed, expounding something to Salathiel.

"Yas, sah, it was sure him, de pastor what preached at Chambers Mills yesterday. He done pass through hyah on his big jack mule like hot spit through a knot hole. And he hollers somethin' out to me real loud. Somethin' about a Marse John Gilpin. When I tell Marse Yates that, he jes larf like hell. He say he tink de reverend'll sure git to Carlisle fustest."

"All right, Jed," smiled Albine, "I guess Mr. Craighead's mule has decided to go back home. Now hold on tight yourself for the rest of the way, if you want to get to Carlisle, too."

"All right in the wagon?" he called back.

"All set and comfortable," replied Melissa's sweet voice. "*Please* drive easy, Sal. The horses be tired." He had no idea Captain Jack was not in there with the women.

He slapped the reins. The yoke bells chimed faintly, and they rumbled off up the long street of Shippensburg, bound for Carlisle.

It was the final stretch of the western military road that lay before them. The forest and the fort on the Ohio, where he had begun the journey "long ago" with Captain Ecuyer, lay actually only two hundred miles westward, and on the calendar not so far backward in time. And yet, measured in terms of fruitful experience and the span of his own lifetime, the country behind the mountains and all its ways of life slumbered in the eternal wilderness nothing less than æons behind him.

He had left old Kaysinata standing in the moonlight on the banks of Beaver Creek. Then he was a callow and savage boy. The Little Turtle had left the Big Turtle behind in the wilderness. He had been given an axe that evening and warned never to eat turtle meat.

This afternoon it was Salathiel Albine aware of himself and his shortcomings as a white man; aware of the past and the future; of God; of the world about him, and of heaven and hell. He could not help thinking of it that afternoon as he approached Carlisle, with surprise, and perhaps a certain justifiable satisfaction.

From Yellow Breeches Creek that rolled to the Susquehanna through the valleys only a few miles before him to the westward-flowing Ohio was scarcely fifty leagues measured on paper maps. But the mountains of a mighty frontier lay between. He had crossed them from boyhood into manhood, from darkness into the dawnlight. He would bury the hatchet of Kaysinata and enter into the inheritance before him. Almost he had been disinherited.

Carlisle, Carlisle, the yoke bells seemed to sing. After Carlisle he would not see the mountains any more at all. They were marching away from him now. They would soon be lost behind the horizon. He said a brief silent prayer of thanks and hope.

The road, badly rutted by transport, led away straight and steadily over low rolling hills of mixed woodlands and cleared farm lands. They passed no one coming west. They stopped only once. It was to retrieve a white object caught in the limbs of an old pear tree that leaned low across the road. It was a clerical bag-wig, hung there by its ribbons like a deserted oriole nest. This time it would take considerable repairing, and it was splashed with red mud. Salathiel laughed and passed it back to Bridget to lay away.

Then the patient teams began walking forward again.

As the early November twilight dimmed rapidly into the smooth darkness of a low cloud-hung night, a deep red glow burned brighter and ever more widely across the sky above the black outlines of tumbling forest. By eight o'clock they seemed to be approaching an immense conflagration. The clouds ran and slobbered with scarlet.

It was the reflection of a thousand campfires, the united glow from the greatest military base in the colonies and the rallying point of the western frontier. Carlisle.

At half past nine they pulled up in the broad open town square, drew water from the king's well, had a brief bite of supper, sent Jed with all the horses to Stottelmyer's stables, and turned in for the night.

The journey was over.

But Salathiel longed for morning. He was impatient to see what the dawnlight might have to reveal.

19. A Beautiful Whip Changes Hands

"SIX O'CLOCK of a clear winter's morning, and all's well. Fifteen wagons, fifteen to report."

Thus chanted the sentries of the garrison at Fort Lowther and the cracked voices of the two old codgers of the Carlisle town watch, seeming to mock one another in chorus. The watch rattled their staffs and passed on towards breakfast and their senile mendacities about Queen Anne's War, over small beer and scrapple.

It was still dark, but Salathiel bestirred himself. He slipped into his old buckskins more out of habit than design, and popping an iron saucepan on a spider over a charcoal fire, busied himself preparing a hot morning stew. The bag of charcoal in the side-chest with the smith's tools now came in unexpectedly handy.

While he stood, still a bit sleepy, watching the coals glowing under the pot in the morning darkness, he turned over in his mind the possible reasons for Captain Jack's unexpected decision to remain behind at Shippensburg. He had been not a little nettled and disconcerted last evening, when he first discovered that the old hunter was not along with them in the wagon. Frances ought to have told him. But as he listened to her explanations, he finally had to admit that she had probably acted for the best. It would have done no good to have had a painful parting yesterday at Fort Morris. And that was what it would have come to. For no one had ever been able to argue with the Half-Indian. His obstinate whims and moods were his law. Besides, Salathiel knew better than anyone else that when the necessity to be alone overtook Captain Jack, nothing could move him. It must have been a deep longing for the refuge of his lonely cabin that had suddenly seized upon the old man. Certainly Captain Jack must have wanted to get away awful bad, when he had just let them drive on, and told Melissa to keep his horse until he sent for it. Well, he would use the old gelding carefully. Later on he might pay the old man a visit in his mountain eyrie. Maybe the old hunter just wanted to die in peace. And a body was entitled to do his own dying, he supposed. But he didn't much relish *that* idea. He stared into the fire fixedly for a spell, while the grey light slowly dawned in the east. Finally, he shook himself clear of such doleful speculations and looked up.

Sunrise was late that November morning, and yet the dawn seemed to come swiftly. The details of the scene surrounding him emerged from a mist of wood smoke and fading stars into a firm, clear background of houses, people, roads, and streets.

He was in a wide-open town square, dotted here and there with wagons camping overnight like himself, and surrounded on three sides by dwelling houses; some of them of two or more stories, built of brick, stone, or logs, with ample yards and gardens between.

There were several large public buildings, the most notable of which were a log courthouse with a strong jail, an unfinished town hall already of promising proportions, and churches.

About these buildings there was already a considerable passing to and fro of people, a gradual assembling of horses and vehicles, as the business of the day got under way. An incessant barking of dogs and a rumbling of wagons, the lowing of cattle, and the spreading cry of crowing roosters, gave the impression of a far-flung and teeming neighbourhood rousing itself eagerly.

The atmosphere was clear. The storm had passed on. A light powdery snow lay in scattered patches on the roofs and ground. Ranks of brick chimneys curled forth blue smoke leisurely.

A convoy of white-topped wagons came down the Lancaster road and gathered waiting before the closed portal of Fort Lowther, their harness bells chiming faintly. Here and there a sow and her brood emerged speculatively into the open square. Somewhere an anvil began to clang. A woman called shrilly and banged a house door.

He stopped stirring the pot and stood up to look eagerly about him. His nose wrinkled. A faint underlying fetid odour and a smell of communal cooking and wood smoke both tainted and savoured the air. He smiled slowly. To him, at least, the general impression of Carlisle was overwhelmingly metropolitan. And yet, there was something uneasy and confusing about it. He felt that from the very first.

The east end of the square, however, was quite another matter. The public square was half pre-empted and solidly occupied by the broad front of Fort Lowther. Its stockaded log walls, over twelve feet high and two hundred feet long, extended across the eastern vista with squat-roofed rifle towers at each corner and a broad portal in the centre still blindly closed. The small postern beside it, however, already swarmed with a gathering crowd of workmen carrying their tools and awaiting admittance.

Officers of the Pennsylvania line in green and regulars in scarlet regimentals began to emerge from their various boarding-houses and ordinaries about the square and to stroll across it towards the fort. Behind the stockade itself a tentative humming of drums and a muffled tootling of fifes preluded the formation for morning roll call. As the sun rose suddenly out of the forest mists some miles away, a field piece boomed. The shrill music of the reveille squealed and rolled. A prolonged pulsing of drums shivered the air as the Union Jack unfurled into the sunlight. The lanthorns went out. The portals of the fort rolled backward, and the waiting crowd and wagons rushed in. All the town noises suddenly heightened and became more confident. The day at Carlisle had officially begun.

Salathiel called to them in the wagon to come out and eat. And while the music played "The World Turned Upside Down" and the hoarse shouting of many roll calls filled the air, they had breakfast together under the open sky in the public square.

It is a fair surmise that there were not many other people in the world that morning enjoying their breakfast so thoroughly as Salathiel. The tense apprehension of lurking danger had gone. Instead of the doubtful silence of the forest, on every hand now was the confident early cheerfulness of the town. Salathiel filled his pipe, took a long draw, and slowly exhaled through his nose. His eyelids drooped half over his pupils, and he sat looking down like an Indian lost entirely in the present. After a few minutes, he aroused slowly as the bell before the courthouse began with its insistent clamour to proclaim *all's well, all's well.* He smiled as Frances looked at him happily, her eyes wide and calm.

A few moments later Jed showed up, covered with stable straw, and looking serious and much cast down. The wagonmaster at Stottelmyer's had refused to release the horses to him when he had asked for them that morning. He had had an argument with the man, who had struck him painfully with a bull whip. He ate his mush and bacon slowly, with tears in his eyes. Marse Albine didn't seem to make much of it. Jed supposed he would just have to take it. Marse Albine even seemed pleased. He grinned at everything. Bridget was already demanding to be taken to her granny.

"Afterwhile," said Salathiel—"afterwhile. It may take a few hours to find your grandma."

To Frances' eager questioning as to where they were going to find shelter, he had the same laconic answer. They would find a house "afterwhile". His satisfaction in both appearance and expression was infractible. He ate heartily and was not to be hurried. They had come a long way. "Afterwhile," he kept saying—"afterwhile."

Afterwhile—he rose and entered the wagon.

So! They had begun by striking poor Jed with a whip! Well, he knew how to deal with people like that. Doubtless Stottelmyer had not yet returned. It *must* have been someone in temporary authority. But—he looked at Twin-Eyes in her sling, and considered. He decided finally to let her rest. Then he slipped Kaysinata's axe in his belt, set his coonskin cap at a truculent angle, and stepped out. When he got Enna again he would put on his town finery with all the fixins. Meanwhile, his present rig was more suitable. Just to make sure of it, he reached down into the ashes of the breakfast fire and smeared his face thoughtfully with a bit of charcoal.

Frances rose with anxiety and laid a hand on his arm. "You be careful, *Mister* Albine," she said. "This is no place for war paint." He nodded and laughed. "Just a bit of funnin', sweetheart, is all I hev in view. Now don't worry, I'll see you under a roof tonight, or I'm a son of a gun!"

"Big man," said Bridget, looking at him doubtfully, "Grandma Larned's a lady. I know she is. You might be mistook in a dirty face."

"I'll sure gentle her," he said. "Now help your ma to look after the wagon. I'll be back—afterwhile. Come on, Jed!"

He strode across the square towards the town hall, with Jed toiling after him, the burn of the whip stinging across his shoulders. The two women stood looking uncertainly after them.

"Now what the divil's got into him?" mused Melissa. "He looks like a Black Boy renegade."

The fifteen wagons that had been called for that morning, and a half score more, were crowded about the new town hall. Twenty-five competing drivers were trying to crowd into the bureau of the provincial commissary, a small room off the main hall. In there John Byers, Esquire, the wagon commissioner, was bargaining like mad for his king and country with eight Pennsylvania Dutchmen at once, and enjoying it. A convoy was making up to fetch barrelled beef from Baltimore by way of York. It was eight o'clock already, and so far *nobody* had been hired. Mr. Byers was masterfully roaring them down. Salathiel listened for a moment with amusement. Well, if anybody knew what was going on at Carlisle, it would be Mr. Byers, he judged. But the present thunderous moment was not entirely auspicious for questioning him. He would wait.

He then gave himself over to reading the innumerable notices, old proclamations, orders, and handbills pasted on the walls of the vestibule.

No wonder Mr. Byers had his troubles with wagoners. Just look at that—and an old notice, too, half torn off and fluttering in the wind. The order dated from Brigadier General Stanwix's time.

Underneath it was pinned an old certificate of the finding of a court-martial, signed—

SIMEON ECUYER, CAPT., R.A.R.

He stopped for a moment and bowed his head before that finger-smeared document. How was it that a mere piece of paper could continue to exist—while the captain . . . ? Oh, where, oh, where was he? Presently his vision cleared, and he resumed reading . . .

Salathiel read the second notice through twice and smiled to himself. The sad loss of Monsieur de Molyneaux seemed trivial in view of the contents of some of the other notices. This business of keeping slaves, too—there was something unchristian about it, a lazy fancy, he thought. At any rate, he would catch up with the bully who had lashed Jed. A fine lout, no doubt . . .

The rest of the wall was covered with rewards, and pathetic appeals in script, attempts to get news of or some word to those captured by the Indians. Hope, tragedy, and despair fluttered on the wainscoting, fading, being blown away and trampled underfoot.

And here was the latest printed list, evidently quite a recent one—

LIST of the Indian Captives Being Returned to Carlifle by Brigadier General Bouquet—

the unclaimed ones, the homeless, over two hundred.

He stood pondering this list of names long and carefully. He checked it against the roll that sang itself in his own mind. Yes, *most* of them were there, but *some* were absent. There might be several reasons for that. But it would do no harm to recite those lost names again to the brigadier. It might mean the salvation of some poor soul, some "adopted" victim. By God, he *would* see the general. And what had McArdle done about it? he wondered.

Just then a mass of wagoners rushed out of the commissary bureau, snapping their whips joyfully—hired! Jed cowered on the outside steps as they passed. The unchosen also departed, but sullenly. Silence resumed its reign unharassed by Mr. Byers.

Salathiel strolled into the commissioner's office and sat down. The gentleman was stuffing a lot of papers into a handle-box, evidently preparing to leave.

"Well, sir, what the devil can I do for you?" said Mr. Byers, looking up at last. He then saw fit to clear his throat respectfully. His visitor rubbed a bit of charcoal off his chin.

"Mr. Byers, can you remember names?" asked Salathiel.

"B'God, I'm ravished in my vargin sleep by 'em," rumbled the commissioner. "Come midnight, a fish-tailed St. Cecilia sits by my pillow and treacles my ears with the dulcet Dutch cognomens of half the blasted wagoners in German Pennsylvania. *Arbeleist, Bendendorp, Reinhold, Hogendorper, Weisenkrantz, Schimmelpfennig*—the damned burly ruffians, never a decent English syllable or native virtue in the lousy lot. God save the mark, his Majesty, and me!"

"Amen to all that," added Salathiel. "But did ye ever hear of one Campion Honeywell"—he drew Mrs. Larned's letter from his pouch and looked at it—"said to live in the square here at Carlisle?"

"On the *square*, and on the *level*, I never did," mused Mr. Byers, looking at his visitor meaningly. Salathiel gave him the sign.

Mr. Byers replied by producing a jug.

"Are ye one of Buckey's new Virginia rifles?" he inquired, after his turn at swallowing.

"Nope, I jist range the woods private with Captain Jack, doin' what good I kin in leafy places."

"Oh!" said Byers, looking a bit startled, "of *that* doughty brotherhood, eh? Maybe you carry a twin rifle-gun, brother?"

"Happen sometimes I do."

They both laughed.

"Now, that's curious odds," continued Byers. "The Reverend Mr. Craighead was talkin' about you and Captain Jack only last night. Better let me see that letter, I guess," he added.

Salathiel handed it to him.

Mr. Byers read Mrs. Larned's letter, grunting from time to time. "Seems maybe the old lady got some of her Boston names confused in this," he remarked finally. "I know of no Honeywells at Carlisle. But, tell ye what, the rider that carried that letter to Lyttleton will know. And he's here." Stepping to the door, Mr. Byers roared, "Fergus, Jim Fergus?" in the tones of an irritated lion.

"Presently, sir, presently," replied a pleasant voice.

In another moment a bow-legged little man in a semi-military riding rig came into the room, his spurs clanking. Salathiel recognized him instantly as one of the intrepid express riders who had carried letters between Bouquet and Ecuyer during the siege at Fort Pitt. The recognition was mutual. Fergus nodded pleasantly to Salathiel. "What do ye lack, Mr. Byers?" he said, his eyes twinkling. "Thought I heerd someone depriving a painter of his meat."

Mr. Byers relented. Express riders were privileged people; the survivors among them, few.

"Our big friend here wants to know if ye can recall a certain old widow woman, a Mistress Theodosia Larned from Boston town. Here's the letter she gave you for Patton's some time ago."

Fergus looked at it and the superscription briefly. "Why, sartain, sure," he said, "precious old Yankee grandma with nice bright silver hair. Neat as a new pin. Don't tell me you're bringing her little grand-daughter? She'll be transfigured into Glory at the sight of her. Couldn't talk about nothin' else, poor soul. When I gave her Mr. Patton's reply back from Lyttleton, I thought she'd melt in her own eye-water. Last I talked to her, she was fixin' to go to Manoah Glen's mill at Bilin' Springs in the mill wagon. It's silver to pewter buttons you'll still find her at Glen's mill. Ye know, I'd clean forgot. Thar's so dang many troubled ones hereabouts keep pesterin' me for letters." For a moment he looked troubled himself. "I'd try to find her today, ifen I was you. Ye kin, ye know, 'tain't far to Bilin' Springs."

"Just drive east past LeTort's old stockade, and take the south wending trace at the first forks," said Byers. "The Springs be about eight miles from there. Ye can't miss the big mill at the ford—and all."

So Mrs. Larned knew they were coming! Still Salathiel hesitated.

Then he decided to tell Mr. Byers about the predicament over having the horses detained, and the probability of Stottelmyer's still being away. He didn't want the stable-boys to raise a hue and cry when he came to take them. He explained at some length.

"Don't let that deter ye," said Byers. "The stable-boys don't own the nags. If they make any trouble out at the stables for ye, tell 'em *I* said the province has hired 'em. I'll put the two wagon teams on the special emergency roll. 'Tis an errand of marcy you're on."

"That's mighty damn civil of ye," replied Salathiel.

"'Tain't much," replied Byers. "Stottelmyer'll probably be back in town with Bouquet in a few days' time at most. Jim here just rid in with the dispatches. They've marched from Fort Pitt."

"Might be pulling out of Bedford now," added Fergus.

"You don't say!" exclaimed Albine. "Now, *that* is news!"

Mr. Byers looked embarrassed. "So it is," he said. "And it kind o' slipped out, you see. I'll have to ask you to put the seal on it. If it gets out too soon, the confusion here will be thrice confounded. There's nigh three hundred strangers waitin' to claim their kin. And crowds of other gentry, none so savoury. Do you see?"

"I'll button my gab tight, my word on it," Salathiel assured him. "Now thank ye ever so kindly, and give my regards to Mr. Craighead too. Tell him I'm nigh, and I'll be returnin' his wig directly. I found it hangin' on a pear tree."

"Now did ye?" guffawed Byers, slapping his breeches. "That'll pleasure him. His temper's as bald as his pate at losin' it. Come over and see us when ye kin. It's the small stone house, third down the west walk on the square—have another?"

"No, thanks," answered Salathiel. "I've got sober work to do. Happen ye hear war-whoops up at Stottelmyer's stable, don't turn out the garrison." He winked, and they shook hands cordially.

"Whoop away! I'll just hold my hand on my hair if I hear ye," said Mr. Byers. "All right, Jim. Thanks."

They went out together while Mr. Byers returned to packing up his papers.

"Here's a little somethin' I maunt tell ye," said Fergus. "Thar's an old Injun and his family sort of lurkin' fertive like on Yellow Breeches Creek nigh the Glens' mill. Doctor Scarlet they call him. He's an old yarb gatherer. Harmless. One of the convarted. Thought I'd jist mention him. The magistrates are all in a tither since the Lancaster jail massacre, you know. And poor old Doctor John was took off here not so long ago with horrid consequences. So I'd jist say 'how-how', ifen you meet Doctor Scarlet out diggin' 'sang, or buy a little rattlesnake ile off him for old sake's sake, like. It'll make smoother rubbin' fer ye here, ifen you do." Fergus looked quizzically at Salathiel.

"Makeum heap good medicine," promised Salathiel. "And if anything happens to Doctor Scarlet, don't blame me. I'm not warrin' on the Moravian convarts. All my scalps are lifted clean and honest, west of the proclamation line."

"Sure, sure," said Fergus, "I was jist talkin' in case. Say, do ye ever wrestle like ye used to at Fort Pitt? I seed ye there when ye was dandying the little captain. Guess ye miss him, like we all do, eh?"

"Mighty much, Jim," said Salathiel. "You might ride over and have a snack with us when we git to Glen's mill. Reckon I might stay there if I find the old lady, and the miller could put us up."

"Ye might do much warse," said Fergus. "Shelter's mortal scarce in Carlisle. And you kin be quiet at the mill. I know you woodsmen like to be private. I'll track ye down at the mill shortly. Jist now I've got some dispatches for Colonel Burd over at Lancaster."

"Now, have ye!" said Salathiel. "Maybe, then, you can take this letter from Colonel Chambers to Colonel Burd? When ye git back I'll look for ye at the mill." Jim took the letter, and they shook hands warmly. Salathiel had taken a positive shine to the man.

Now to the work at hand at Stottelmyer's stable. He meant to have the use of the horses. And the sooner he got to Boiling Springs that morning the better.

"Come on, Jed," he called. "We're goin' down to Stottelmyer's stable, and I want ye to pint out the bugger that lashed ye."

"Do gawd, Marse Albine, he's one big ornery Dutch *buckra*, dat feller!"

"No!" drawled Salathiel. "Well, I'm only goin' to play a little mumblty-peg with him. Boys will be boys, ye know."

He patted the axe at his belt. It felt smooth and cold.

Jed's eyes protruded. But he trotted along more confidently, the road leading out into the fields south of the town.

There was nearly a mile of stables and picket lines ahead of them before they would come to Stottelmyer's establishment, a place which Jed had found considerable trouble in reaching the previous night. A pack train was being loaded at a log warehouse. Stacks of fodder covered with dingy tarpaulins stretched out like a deserted city of dilapidated tents. For the first time it was brought home fully to Salathiel the extent of the English preparations at Carlisle.

And what were Pontiac's naked-arsed warriors compared to all this? thought he. Poor painted-faced animals, lurking amid the trees . . .

A staff officer in gold lace and scarlet flashed by on a black stallion. Salathiel felt proud. Bouquet had avenged Braddock. He was bringing back the English captives. Suddenly he felt like shouting, God save the king . . .

They trudged on for another half mile.

"Hyah we be," said Jed. "Dem's Marse Stottel's stables. I done crep' in an' slep' hyah all alone last night in de big log mow."

Stottelmyer's was the largest freighters' station on the western communications. There was a great log byre down one side; a stable-shed for fifty horses on the other. Log sleeping quarters for wagoners lay between them at one end. Idle wagons stood in the "off-pen" between the two main buildings. There was an armourers' shed; a saddlery and a small smithy, with a gate between.

Thus the internal square made by the establishment was nicely fenced off and even made defensible, if need be. Everything was whitewashed and the stables kept clean. A huge pile of manure was carefully thatched over.

The chimney of the bunk shed was smoking away lively enough as Salathiel and Jed pushed open the small hand-gate between the saddlery and the smithy and walked into the off-pen between the two main buildings. There a dozen or so wagons waited their turns to be called out. But at the moment there was no one in the yard.

"Likely him be dar," said Jed, pointing towards the byre.

Like most Pennsylvania barns, the big building on their left had a broad projection of the upper story on one side that jutted out along its entire length like a porch roof. Along the lower stone section under the "porch" ran a series of small windows and double doors. It was to one of these doors that Jed had pointed. Salathiel opened it very quietly and peered in.

He had never seen such a tremendous roofed-space before. It ran from one end of the huge barn to the other, with only a few posts here and there to hold up the fodder stored on the planks above. Ordinarily, it would have been a stable for cattle. But with no cows to keep, and ample horse sheds on the other side of the yard, this room was the storehouse for the wagon base, floored with slate flagstones, and clean.

At the far end of the place, a narrow glazed window ran clear across the end wall near the ceiling, and the lighted floor space under it had been kept relatively clear. There in fact was the office of the establishment, furnished with rude pine desks and tables and several bookkeepers' stools. These were vacant now.

But standing with his back to the light, and leaning over a table, with a quill pen in his hand, an open ledger and stacks of small coins before him, was an elephantine, moon-faced individual. Projecting downward near-by on a ladder from the ceiling were the legs of another man. He was evidently busy shifting something about on the floor of the loft.

Salathiel looked the prospect over carefully. The part of the room with the equipment piled in it was comparatively dark. Doubtless the man at the desk was Stottelmyer's wagonmaster, Hans Schmidt. Salathiel had heard rumours of him at Bedford. He bore a hard reputation even among wagoners. Salathiel beckoned to Jed to enter and pointed out to him the man at the desk.

"Dat's de man, dat's him!" whispered Jed, instinctively shrinking back against the wall. "Him got a bull whip two rods long!"

If so, Salathiel couldn't see it.

Perhaps Herr Schmidt had temporarily abandoned the whip for the pen? Nothing else about him, however, appeared to be clerical. He was pumpkin-shaped, with a broad rawhide belt for an equator, and colossal arms. He appeared to rest on a pediment and waddled powerfully. As he stood over the desk, now and then lowering his head and looking up again, it was hard to tell whether it was his moon-shaped visage or the fringed top of his bald head that comprised his countenance, so double-faced was the effect.

Obviously, here was a bearlike specimen, one with whom verbal remonstrance would be labour lost. Surprise, terror, and threats were called for; wrestling to be avoided. And it was along these lines that Salathiel decided to proceed.

"Jed," he said in a low tone, "will ye trust me?"

"Yas—yas, sah," mumbled Jed, backing a little closer to the wall.

"All right. Now take hold of yourself. I want ye to walk down there to the other end of the place, show yourself, and tell Schmidt your master sent you to git his horses. Be pert!"

"Gawd! He'll take after me sure t'ing, Marse Albine!"

"Sure he will. But don't let him collar ye."

"Jedu, no!"

"Run *this* way. Run back into the shadows. See? Ye kin dive in and hide amongst the plunder—and then I'll take care of Mr. Schmidt. Ye kin jist lead him on and leave him to me."

But still Jed hesitated. He was ashen-grey and sweating.

"De whip," he muttered. "Him cut dis feller clean in two."

"Not *this* time," said Salathiel. "Try it, Jed! Be a bold boy."

"Yas, sah, baas, I's gwine. I's gwine fer to go"—and with that Jed actually stepped out with a swagger, although his hands clutched convulsively in his sleeves. He threaded the piles of matériel on tiptoe, until he came out into the lighted space and stood before the terrible baldheaded white man. Twelve feet away he stopped. He stood there, but he was quite unable to say anything.

Hans Schmidt was finishing his payroll. He was deducting small fines and collecting his rake-offs. And it was a full minute before he looked up. His piggish eyes rested incredulously on the shivering blanket-draped figure before him, and finally focused to a gimlet point of rage. He rose slowly, one hand still on the table.

"Du kleiner schwarze Teufel du!" he shouted. "Vas! Haf I not tolt you I vil haf no black turds mixen mit mein good stable manure here? Raus!"

Jed cleared his throat tremulously, "Baas-man say he want dem same six hawses *now*. And wid new hawness," he added, with a certain impish twist of delight at his own inventive daring.

"Du lieber Himmel! Zo! Der vip haf nicht gelehrnet you. Vell, dis time I pop your gottam eyes out." Schmidt came ponderously from behind the table, his thumbs twisting in an anticipatory rotary motion over his fists.

Jed backed away slowly.

The man followed.

He seized a stool and dashed it at the Negro's head. Jed dodged, and darted back into the shadows, running zigzag like a rabbit between the piles of plunder.

He disappeared.

Herr Schmidt followed breathing heavily, waddling alertly on his square toes with ponderous stealth. He knew he had his victim cornered. He hated niggers with an insane animal animosity, such as a gorilla might feel for a chimpanzee. His lips worked and his eyes wrinkled his fat cheeks as he peered myopically into the shadowy gloom of the piled warehouse, trying to spot his dark fugitive . . .

There he was!—just behind that great pile of tarpaulins. Blut und Tod! Der verschreckende Hund. *Now*. His arms tensed, and he groped forward.

And then his hands fell back to his sides.

Something—something was curiously wrong, and yet vaguely and terrifyingly familiar.

Even in the shadows and twenty feet away, he could see that Jed had turned into something else. Was he being hexed? Nein—Ja! The figure crouching before him *was* an Indian. He was leaning forward with an axe in his hand.

Gott! It was even more terrible than that. It was the worst thing that could possibly happen. It was the wild man from Bedford, who had killed men with a table. He was here! Impossible—true!

The terrible man stood up; towered. Schmidt's breath sucked inward with the sound of an unprimed pump. The axe glinted.

"Murder!"

The man was after him.

"Wa-waw-wa . . . waw!" The shivering scalp helloo of the Shawanee rang in Schmidt's ears and unsocketed his soul.

He was lunging like a bogged elk now. The door, the office door! Lieber Jesu, the door! He tripped over the stool he had thrown at Jed, crashed, and blundered on.

Disemboweled? Nein. Castrated! He rolled with the pain, but he rolled towards the door. He was getting to his feet, still going, when the yell burst out just behind him again. He surged forward.

The man falling from the ceiling struck him down like a bag of grain. That fool had the advantage of him. He had started running while he was still in the air. The door opened. *Whiff*—the fellow was gone. The door closed. It banged in his very face. The bar fell down.

But he crawled, he still crawled for it. And he was just reaching up to . . . when something whizzed, smacked—and he saw the axe standing in the wood, holding the bar in place.

Trapped!

Life was all—and he was *so* young yet.

He caught his last breath, and puked a little.

"Get up, Schmidty," the voice said. "Get up, you big fat bow-wow, so I can tell yer face from yer behind."

Oh, no, he would never do that. He would just stay on his knees. If there was still any hope, he would make the most of it. He started to crawl slowly on all fours towards his tormentor. The man was standing there with a scalping knife in his hand.

So! He'd often wondered: to be bald and to be scalped. How would it be? Ach, Gott!

He put his head down on the floor, with one hand patting his bald spot, his pudgy fingers spread out over it protectively. "Gnädiger Herr," he murmured, "let your august eye-shine rest mercifully upon me, lieber gnädiger Herr."

"I'll knot yer hair fer ye, good and right, if ye don't get up," said Salathiel. "Get up!" he roared. The double-faced effect seriously annoyed him.

Schmidt got his hands on a table-top eventually, and managed with the assistance of his arms to rise and plant his fat fundament on a stool. He was still too shaken to feel even a twinge of shame or resentment. Never under any circumstances would he ever, ever annoy the terrible man who now sat before him with his arms on the table, grinning, with the big knife stuck upright in the wood still teetering back and forth a bit on its point.

"Look, Big Little-guts," the man was saying, "you struck Mr. Arthur

St. Clair's servant with a whip this morning. Do you know who Mr. St. Clair is? Do you want to spend the rest of your goddam life in the jailhouse?"

"Ja," gasped Schmidt. "Ja wohl!" Under the circumstances, so sheltered and permanent an existence as a whole lifetime in a safe prison was positively alluring.

But horrors! No—it had been the wrong answer. Himmel!

"And," continued the man, "when I sent the coloured boy to fetch the horses this morning, the horses Mr. Stottelmyer lent me, and my own mare, you were going to whip him and keep the teams. And to think that I'm still going to let you live!"

The wonder of this was too much for Herr Schmidt even to try to comment upon. He sat there in silent amazement. He trembled and he twitched, one great shaking jelly of abject gratitude.

Salathiel could stand it no longer. Some way or other he must return the quivering oaf before him to some semblance of a man. Already the whole place stank with the sour smell of his cowardice.

"Where's the whisky?" Salathiel demanded.

Unable to get the jug himself, Schmidt pointed it out. It was brought to him, and he drank. He gurgled. He set it down at last, and sat feeling the genial warmth course along his limbs. The pain in his groin was becoming bearable now. His hands stopped twitching of themselves. He could even think, a little . . .

He listened . . . ach, what kindness!

He would be permitted to ready the two teams that had been left with him. But *immediately*, and with new harness. He could groom and saddle the roan mare, tie a bag of oats on each wagon horse with three days' rations, and look after the extra little gelding like his own child, until it was called for.

Was *that* understood?

Ja, all of it, down to the last buckle, precisely. But wasn't there something he could do? Some special token of his everlasting personal regard?

Salathiel looked at him in amazement. Schmidt really meant it. He seemed scared into permanent gratitude for being left alive.

Well, then, yes, there *was* something. He could give the whip, which he had dared to use on Mr. St. Clair's servant, as a present. He could lay it very gently in the black boy's hands.

"Now, get up and get out, and give your orders. I'll write a letter to Mr. Stottelmyer here while I'm waiting, but I won't wait long."

Only the pain in Schmidt's groin prevented his bowing. He waddled stiffly to the door and shuffled through it. He looked up gratefully at the sun in heaven, and began with a note of chastened authority to give his orders to the stable-boys in the yard.

Only the whip, his marshal's baton as chief wagoner, stuck in his craw. It was such a *pee-u-tiful* vip. A monstrous black bull's pizzle with an elk-hide lash on it, a silver mounted handle and a wampum beaded thong. *Aber*, it would be best to deliver himself from temptation and give up the whip, for he, Hans Schmidt, was a terrible uncontrolled fellow, dangerous when he was enraged.

Inside, Salathiel finished his note to Stottelmyer rapidly and sanded it at Herr Schmidt's table. When he looked up Jed was standing before him, just where he had been standing a few moments before. They grinned at each other, man to man. Jed put his hand respectfully over his mouth. His smile *might* perhaps be too wide at the discomfiture of a white man.

"Now get out there," said Salathiel to him, "and when Schmidty hands ye that whip, don't be skeered. Crack it, and drive the four horses back to the wagon. I'm goin' to ride Enna this morning myself. And don't ye call me 'master' any more. See!"

"Yas, sah," replied Jed. He walked confidently to the door. Salathiel watched him.

"That's better," he said.

Lord, he was tired of all this slave business. It made cowards out of everybody, master and man. It was no good. If anybody was going to work for *him*, they'd have to do it the way he had worked for Ecuyer. By God, if they didn't, he'd murder them.

Outside, he heard the yoke bells of the teams begin to chime gaily. A whip cracked. The teams departed.

He walked out and mounted Enna. Schmidt was holding her. "Now keep on lookin' after Mr. Stottelmyer's wagons, and don't fail him no more liken ye did this morning," said Salathiel. Suddenly he reached down and crushed the man's hand in his own.

Herr Schmidt stood looking after him and gazing at his puffing fingers. Had he really meant what he said? He thought so. Anyway, next time he wouldn't be so afraid of him, and he'd sure let other people's niggers alone. No more jokes that made the world turn upside down. The *pee-u-tiful* vip was all—it was gone.

Salathiel passed Jed at a gallop on the way back. He noted that Jed was managing the tough horse with the yellow eye. Also he was cracking the new whip. Experimentally, to be sure, but with a rapt look.

As he cantered past the long sheds and loading yards of *Boynton, Wharton & Morgan*, Salathiel rose in his stirrups and let the mare go. It was elegant being back in the saddle again. It was a fine clear day, frosty, but not a cloud in the sky. A perfect morning for finding anybody's grandma. Now that he had the horses back again—five of them! And it was only ten miles to Boiling Springs.

20. The Mill on Yellow Breeches Creek

THE WAGON and the trundler, with the king's arrow on it, fading so rapidly now, passed through the east gate of Fort Lowther without question and took the road for Boiling Springs.

With good horses and Jed driving, a hard road, and only ten miles to go, Salathiel assumed that he might shortly arrive at Boiling Springs, following the directions given him by his friend, Jim Fergus, only a few hours before. At Boiling Springs he confidently expected to find Mr. Glen, the miller, and Bridget's grandma, to whom the miller had so kindly given shelter. And, since Mr. Glen seemed to be such a hospitable man, perhaps under the special circumstances it might also be possible to persuade him to give the rest of Bridget's "family" at least temporary shelter at the mill. Anyway, that was his plan and hope for the immediate future.

He now felt more than ever how important for many reasons it was to provide Frances with a decent and quiet place to settle down in, even if it were only for a short while. He'd promised St. Clair to wait for at least two months over the business of the Ligonier settlers, and St. Clair had retained him with hard money. He was bound to tarry until early spring.

But meanwhile, he and Frances must live somewhere in the vicinity of Carlisle. That was the rub. For only one night and a few daylight hours in Carlisle had convinced him that there was no lodging to be had in the town, and that camping in the wagon in the public square was not to be thought of. It would be an even greater hardship than any they had encountered on the journey. Besides, it was high time now to put an end to haphazard wayfaring.

What Frances Melissa needed now, with her child coming on, was the shining little house he had promised her. They needed only a modest roof, but a warm hearth, and privacy—some place in which to try the great experiment of living together. What forest wanderers and cave dwellers they had been! No, the next place would have to be home. Frances would inevitably consider it so, with a woman's sense of reality, and judge him as her provider accordingly.

That was why he was so anxious about settling down now. He remembered the many small household articles and the cloth she had bought at Somerfield's in anticipation, five pounds' worth! He recalled her longing for pretty things; how her hands were always busy over new clothes. It would not do to put off too long the hope that all this implied; it would be worse to disappoint it. It would be like . . . oh, it would be like stopping a young dog from burying a bone by taking it away from him. A pup seldom went back to bone-burying again, if he was balked.

It prevented the natural habit, he supposed. When a young dog was sagacious, he gave it up. Maybe young women were like that? Not squaws, of course. But Frances Melissa was no squaw just to do as she was told or to follow him about anywhere. He'd better not keep on disappointing her.

And so he was now fondly anticipating their arrival at Boiling Springs, and having Mr. Glen take them in. He could picture it all now. His and Frances' kindness to Bridget would receive its just reward for bringing her home. Mrs. Larned would be "in heaven", as Jim Fergus had said. Mr. Glen would be gratified at finding Bridget's family to be such respectable people—Frances in a new bonnet, and all. So they could all settle down for a while together. Anything, a room or two in the mill loft, an old shed—oh, he'd fix it up! He'd make himself invaluable to Mr. Glen . . . If not, he must go back to Shippensburg and hire Rutherford to take them in at old Fort Morris. That might do, but it would not be like Boiling Springs with Bridget's grandma. He couldn't bear to think of giving Bridget up. No, Boiling Springs was it! It just had to be.

"Get along, Enna!"

He touched the mare with his heels and beckoned to Jed confidently.

Certainly he couldn't expect Melissa to settle down in a hole in the ground like these refugees, the poor squatters, he now saw camped in the fields in lamentable huts and shebangs all about him. Their miserable "villages" seemed to line the road all the way down to LeTort's Spring. The wagon was a palace compared to such shacks. Any Injun could do much better with a few bent sticks and some bark. He was not prepared for such abject dirt and confusion; nor the, to him, intolerable stench. Was it possible white men could be reduced to this?

Yet, except for the main hold of the garrison within the stockade at Fort Lowther, where a reasonable degree of order and sightliness was visible, his overwhelming impression of Carlisle so far was that of a frantic welter of confusion, a pot boiling over into a seething fire. Once beyond the gate, he had expected to find the open country quiet and decent. But this! All the more reason, then, for pressing on rapidly to Boiling Springs.

Possibly Salathiel was contemplating his arrival at Boiling Springs a mite too rosily. To be sure, "the future blooms out of the past as a rose blossoms from its stem", but then there were some sharp thorns on the stems of the immediate past rooted about Carlisle and Boiling Springs that Salathiel knew nothing about. For the time being, the wagon went trotting into the rosy future confidently, while some of the thorny aspects of the past were not yet in view . . .

Outside the town, an animated and blowzy confusion, the effect of a disturbed past that lent at once a battered and devastated aspect to the immediate vicinity of Carlisle, was evident in all directions and for a considerable distance.

Since nearly a decade past Carlisle had been the much-abused military base, rallying point of forlorn hopes and scared militia, and scene of war-like preparations by the greatest military power in the world; but for its worst conducted, least successful, and most harassing wars. As a consequence, those itinerant sluts, Defeat, Confusion, and Despair—even Panic—had all picnicked in the pleasant meadows near-by and left their squalid refuse behind them.

It was the country around about rather than the town itself, however, that had most suffered.

The town lay in a gently undulating plateau in the very midst of a cleared circle in the dense forest which had gradually been pushed back on all sides to an average but irregular distance of some three or four miles. Hence, no matter in what direction you looked, the dark wall of the encircling trees was still visible at the end of every vista.

Into this open circle of half-cleared meadows, in many parts of which the stumps of forest trees still remained, the life-giving arteries of the place, the roads of the military frontier, converged from several directions, cut like the prisms of veritable land-canals through the all but invincible barrier of the primeval woods.

In the centre, then, of an open space in the forest, the village of Carlisle had grown about its well-planned and ever-hopeful public square, a common laid out by the colony's surveyors in the peaceful tradition of William Penn. But in '64 a large part of the square was temporarily intruded upon by the loopholed stockade of Fort Lowther, an ugly symbol of the grim troubles of the times.

But it was much more than a symbol. It was the prime frontier base for a military power, which, under the genius of Bouquet, was now at last manifesting itself abundantly, and for the nonce intelligently, from Carlisle to the DeTroit. And the fort, the town, and the extensive camps and "deposits" in the country around were vibrantly and hopefully alive.

It had not always been like that, however.

Again and again, Carlisle and its entire vicinity had swarmed and thronged with desperate military efforts and civil despair, during numerous expeditions and defeats. Now the place was in a preliminary spasm of readjustment and rejoicing, a hectic period of bitter regrets and fond anticipations that so often follows closely the end of a long and only finally successful war.

Bouquet's great and unexpected victory at Bushy Run of the year before and his final subduing of the tribes on the distant Muskingum were an inexpressible relief to the long-suffering inhabitants at the base. The intoxication of victory was, to them, something new.

For ten years past there had been few extremities of terror and misery which the patient but determined permanent settlers about Carlisle had not had to endure. Yet in the midst of continual flux and counterflux they had persisted admirably. The majority of honest folk and hard-working artisans of the place were sustained in their hope of a peaceful future by a prophetic quality of stillness in the countryside, one that needed only a brief piping time of peace to dance with fertility—we are assured—and "by those Monuments of Eternity itself, the Blue Mountains of the western distances," which, according to the local bard, "contemplated, over the shoulders of the horizon, with a constant equanimity, the modest navel in the belly of the forest that constituted Carlisle."

That, of course, is no way for respectable Monuments of Antiquity to carry on. Yet that, according to the rhymed and faintly amorous diary of Lieutenant Eustace Pomeroy of the Pennsylvania Light Infantry, was what *he* caught the mountains about Carlisle doing on the morning of November 8, 1764.

But conceding that Lieutenant Pomeroy of the Light Infantry must have had his contemporary moments, it is all the more the pity that he did not keep his eyes about him in regard to the conduct of the rivers near Carlisle. The rivers about Carlisle are as provocative as the mountains, and both the Yellow Breeches and the Conodoguinit are fast little streams. They play around with each other a good deal without ever quite deciding to come together, kept apart perhaps by a prudish lie of the land. And yet they take every opportunity to fall.

But not a whisper of all this got set down in our poet's couplets, not even an innocent aside in his commonplace-book. Perhaps the lieutenant was promoted, or he was evacuated too soon. At any rate, only the mountains, observed by the lieutenant on November the 8th, got told on.

Certain it is that the numerous rivers and creeks about Carlisle had long been the scene of much milling activity, and that along the course of the Conodoguinit and the Yellow Breeches many a snug enterprise had taken root and prospered, each in its own small hole-in-the-woods. And frequently a small settlement would begin to cluster about a grist-mill as the market centre of the adjacent wheat farms and the network of grass paths and hauling roads involved.

Boiling Springs, then, was a mill in the forest about ten miles south-eastward of Carlisle, situate only a furlong away from the spot where the Boiling Springs branch foamed into Yellow Breeches Creek. At this place there was a convenient ford over the creek, and a wagon track rather than a road crossed the little river at this point and ramified into certain forest trails and traces southward. In times of safety the "mill road" had been considerably used as a short cut to various places, and the ford was well known. As a site for a mill-dam, the Boiling Springs branch was little short of ideal.

The place had been picked out and settled sometime in the late 1740's by an educated and ingenious millwright, one Manoah Glen, said to have come from the valley of the Mohawk, a "Yankee-Yorker", who inherited the sterling characteristics and good sense necessary to charm success out of a waterfall and to improve upon his luck by marrying a "dame of French Protestant gentility full well endowed". This double heritage of gentle Huguenot blood and ingenious aptitude, he passed on to his two sons, John and Martin. Later on, they were pioneers in erecting some of the most successful iron furnaces of the vicinity, and both engaged largely in lumbering.

But in the autumn of 1764, the original miller, Manoah Glen, had been a widower for seven years. He was beginning to feel his age, and was much troubled at having to live and conduct his numerous affairs alone and in a deserted house. Both his sons were away from home: John, upon business at Conestoga, and Martin, in the Pennsylvania battalion with the redoubtable Bouquet. And, then, this particular autumn was the end of a long period of strain and anxiety for the aging miller.

For some years it had needed all the stamina that *Glen & Sons* possessed to hang on to the mill and keep the business alive at Boiling Springs through harassing rumours of Indian massacres, frequent defeats, and consequent hard times. Over and over again, the three Glens had been forced to see their little settlement by the ford deserted, when the entire village, except for themselves, fled to the convenient protection of the garrison at Carlisle. Finally the blacksmith shop, the ordinary by the ford, a couple of store-dwellings, and all the near-by farms were totally abandoned in the summer of '63, when the dire news of Pontiac's rebellion and the collapse of the frontier posts had been brought to Carlisle by Jim Fergus.

Only the Glens remained behind, clinging to their mill and the fine "mill house" connected with it, where all their mother's French furniture remained. But they clung to both their wheel and their hearth with a courage whose wisdom was hard to assess at the time. All they had was at stake, however, and there was a good deal of property. So they stuck it out, bored loopholes in the upper log story of the mill, kept the dam repaired, the race clear, and the wooden beams and gears of the "grist 'gin" slushed down—and last, and equally carefully, they kept their two young German redemptioners fast locked up at night in the mill.

Prophecies and bets as to their approaching end had not been spared them. But their reward for this "piece of foolhardy bravado" was to be given a contract to grind flour for the garrison by Colonel Bouquet, and to possess their house and mill in peace and quietude.

For they never saw any Indians whatever, except for poor old Doctor Scarlet and his sorry Delaware family, who settled down on the banks of Yellow Breeches Creek to gather ginseng, sing Moravian hymns at twilight, and beg a little corn meal from the mill every Sunday for "the love of God alone".

The wrinkled old "chief", the escort with a covered wagon from the camp, when a run of the mill was necessary for the garrison—these were all the people and only signs of human life the Glens saw for many a long day. It was only an hour's easy ride to Carlisle, but such was the stark terror of the countryside and the deathly silence that had fallen upon it, they might as well have been on a bayou of the lower Mississippi. Nevertheless, they made the best of it.

It was towards the end of this epoch of undeclared peace, during the early autumn of '64, when the news from the west was so reassuring and glorious, that John departed to have new iron-work fabricated at Conestoga, and to woo him a wife. Martin, the other son, was at that time on the banks of the Muskingum.

So, Manoah Glen was now left to his own devices and certain cherished memories of his once gay young wife.

She, in the perfect silence of the deserted village, broken only by occasional wild snatches of belated bird song, seemed to the aging widower to be invisibly present, like remembered music, in the lonely rooms of his long empty house. In the evening, especially, she simply seemed to be near him again. And from this feeling of her quiet presence he derived merely a familiar comfort and a sense of sweet companionship renewed. Only an unusually plangent note from the falling water of the mill-dam caused him to glance curiously, if not expectantly, into the corner at her dusty harp.

Otherwise, the pleasing monotony of his daily tasks engulfed him. His sons, of course, would come back shortly. That was the understanding. Their father was simply to hold the fort a while longer, until they and more prosperous times might return together.

And this he did quite contentedly with the help of his two young German redemptioners. They were not exactly good company, but they did help him about the mill. They also milked a few of the neighbours' abandoned cows that came wandering in, they cooked after a fashion, tended the two wagon horses, loafed, and grumbled together in guttural tones. That was the serene and quiet status of affairs for some time at Boiling Springs. For the mill had remained quiet so long that it finally fooled them. And birds began to build nests in the drying blades of its motionless wheel.

But as the days of Indian summer commenced to wane, and there was no harvest with new wheat to grind, Mr. Glen began to be weary of himself; of the constant sound of falling water, and the grave memories of his shadowy wife. He needed certain supplies, snuff in particular, and above all he longed for a word with his vanished neighbours and news of the doubtful progress of the war.

And that was why, one day at the very end of October, he hitched up the big blue mill wagon and, taking both the bound boys with him, set out for Carlisle.

21. Manoah Glen Drives Over to Carlisle

IT WAS A SCARLET and golden day. Mr. Glen drove leisurely. Karl and Johann, the two German boys, sat looking backward over the tail-gate behind, one of them playing a jew's-harp. Its monotonous melodic *thrumming* conveyed perfectly the sense of subdued contentment and mild lyric satisfaction that they all felt at going to town in such glorious fall weather.

At a ford over a small stream a couple of miles from the mill, Mr. Glen had Karl lead the team over the water. It was a nasty place. There was an abrupt gravel bank, and only recently a bolt of lightning had stripped the bark from a giant sycamore that stood on the south side of the ford. Horses reared up and carried on here. One of the flour wagons from the fort had been overturned and lay, wheels up, but bogged down in the water.

Mr. Glen didn't know it, but it was only when horses were coming *towards* the mill that they reared up and carried on. He took no chances, however. So he had Karl lead the team over the water, with a firm hand on the bridles.

Both Karl and his companion, Johann Krautze, agreed with Mr. Glen. They knew for certain the little ford in the forest was "hexed". Even the English knew that. Jenny Greentooth, the wrinkled old barmaid, who used to live at the ordinary at Boiling Springs, had told them so. The south bank of the stream was still covered for yards about with white lightning splinters from the thunder-smitten tree—and the smallest chip was an omen of bad luck that could sour cream or curdle a strong man's blood. The jew's-harp stopped twanging, and both boys shivered as they crossed the leaping water.

As they drove on down the road, Johann, looking out of the rear of the wagon, suddenly saw what it was that made horses go crazy. It was the great sprawling lightning blaze on the bark of the thunder-tree. It looked, in the shadows and sunlight shimmering through the trees—it looked like a ferocious white monster. Johann pointed it out to Karl, as they sat tight-lipped and silent together.

The devil had left the mark of evil at the ford.

Ten minutes later they abruptly emerged from the wall of the forest and looked out across a haze of yellow dust that covered the cleared meadows, to the distant jagged roof-line of Carlisle.

In the middle distance, at LeTort's Springs, was a large military camp. White-topped wagons crawled across the vista along the streaks of dusty roads. Smoke from many fires curled leisurely upward. Over the distant town hung a dusty haze of activity. Lord, it was good to be out of the woods and into the cleared fields again! The German boys started to sing shyly, the jew's-harp twanged away again, and Mr. Glen smiled.

It was between three and four miles from the place where they had emerged from the woods to the outskirts of Carlisle. As Mr. Glen drove along over the red-clay road, with the hovels and thatched "miseries" of refugees growing more numerous in the fields on either side, the miller congratulated himself that he had had both the bowels and the good sense to remain living at the mill.

He had not been to town for nearly a year now, and the sight of the squalor and slovenly confusion was shockingly unexpected and profoundly disturbing to his decent and sensitive mind. It was the kind of existence his father had left London to avoid!

As he drove on, his impression of unease gradually grew in intensity. After his undisturbed sojourn in the quiet mill house by the ford, rude noises, so many blatant people, and the numerous wagons converging on the town dazed him.

At LeTort's Springs, a mile or two outside of Carlisle, the first complete sample of what the town itself might be like burst upon him.

The muddy crossroads by the camp near the LeTort Springs bridge splashed and churned with noisy traffic. He and the wagon were both thoroughly spattered, and he got tangled with a convoy amid a maze of hucksters' wagons. As for LeTort's itself! Why, he remembered it when it was a serene old place; when the ruined stockade and blockhouse of James LeTort, the first Huguenot fur trader, was covered with coral-red trumpet vines and his friends, the LeTorts, lived next door in their fine new mansion close by the spring itself. But now?—Lord! The whole place was a hang-shutter tenement, a swarming hovel that literally stank. Nevertheless, he clambered down to scrape the mud from his person and, if possible, to buy a packet of snuff at one of the many booths.

Almost at once he was surrounded by a crowd of muddy urchins, and solicited, furtively but brazenly, by two young drabs in linsey-woolsey. Both of them, he felt sure, must be runaway redemptioners. He became helplessly indignant.

Their nubile and smutted charms left his widower's pulse unfluttered, but their misery and abject begging touched his heart. Finally, he consented to let them climb into the wagon with the two bound boys for a ride to Carlisle, where they claimed to have relatives.

What had become of the Le Tort family, he wondered, as he drove off. There was old Madam Anne and her musical daughter Felice. Gentle folk, gone where? He shook his head doubtfully. Of course there had been no snuff. Only rumours of the "gineral's" success and impending return were uncommon plentiful—and good. Well, that was one comfort.

Still, the rest of the way to Carlisle was for Mr. Glen a mile or two of nightmare. Folks from all over America seemed to be foregathering at Carlisle. And in that observation Mr. Glen was correct.

Not many of the frontier refugees had as yet ventured to return to their abandoned farms. Their exodus was just beginning. But the ranks of those who had departed were rapidly being replaced and augmented by other strangers of diverse kinds. They were now pouring into the town from all over the colonies.

Besides, captives rescued earlier had already been sent downcountry from Fort Pitt and were still encamped in the neighbourhood. The rest were confidently expected, especially those being released by the Shawanees. Nor was this all, for many others besides the captivated had been sent back to Carlisle in the summer of '64. All the matrons, laundresses, sutlers' wives, officers' servants, and various petty traders and camp followers had rigorously been returned to Carlisle from Pittsburgh and all the intermediate road stations. Bouquet would tolerate no needless mouths or "fancy persons" on his final advance down the Ohio. He had issued strict orders. He had swept them, one and all, back to the base.

These non-combatants in themselves, their hangers-on and dependents, constituted a small "multitude". But they were as nothing in either numbers or variety compared to the multiplicity of various other strangers, whom Mr. Glen noticed as he edged his team forward in a press of farm wagons, two-wheeled carts, and stray Conestogas, all indignantly jammed together at the narrow east entrance to the town. Just at that point a man with two young dancing bears was giving a performance on a bit of greensward under the southeast rifle tower. It was precisely where the road narrowed into High Street and passed on between the stockade wall and the opposite houses, in a narrow defile that led to the square. It was a strategic stance that had thus been chosen. And the bear-master, a bearded hulk of a fellow in filthy buckskins, knew it. He would not budge until a satisfactory toll was collected. Yet there were few German wagoners who cared to contribute, even to their own release.

Helpless for the moment, Mr. Glen looked about him, waiting with everybody for someone else to give the metallic password.

Before the east gate of the fort stretched a level tract of greensward hedged-in by extensive lines of abandoned grass-covered entrenchments dug in a time of panic ten years before. Through this pleasant green ran the old road to LeTort Springs, now used only for an exit. In the course of time the whole entrenched approach before the east face of the fort had gradually taken on the aspect of a small park. Here it was that the better and the more select, certainly the more pretentious people and personages of the town and garrison came to promenade and take the air—in the summer in the evening, after the heat of the day, and in the autumn in the morning, before the hour of the midday meal.

Now, it was about eleven o'clock that morning when Mr. Glen was held up by the bears. The entrance to High Street was along the lower boundary of the east gate plot, and he could look right over the crest of the old entrenchment into the artillery garden. Possibly two score couples, and half as many beaux and bachelors, were walking up and down. Several clergymen in decent black and even a few Joseph-coated macaronis were present.

The royal officers from the garrison with their wives; foreign officers from the Royal Americans with their housekeepers and mistresses; officers of the Pennsylvania line and their ladies of various degrees; rich and well-dressed merchants, a few trim-suited Quakers among them; some of the local landholders and gentry, three or four magistrates, and five or six well-known lawyers, all with their well-gowned ladies—strolled up and down, turned, stopped, bowed, curtsied, removed hats while white wigs shone, exchanged snuff, gossiped, and pleasantried with an air of gay decorum.

Someone, Mr. Glen could not see who, had brought a sedan chair from Philadelphia. It was carrried by four Negro lackeys dressed in blue livery, and reposed now by a neat pyramid of piled round-shot not far from the sallyport. There was a couple seated in it, possibly one of the governor's council, an Indian commissioner with his lady, or a great city merchant and his dame. The chair was the cynosure of genteel attention, and its occupants were holding court.

There was an obsequious crowd that continually changed about the sedan chair. Everyone who came out of the gate hastened to approach it, bowed, was introduced; bowed again, and passed on. The commandant and his wife stood next to it, talking.

It was this dainty group about the chair that especially attracted attention. It seemed wonderful that with the rough log stockade for a background it could dare to exist.

To Mr. Glen, at least, the fashionable agitation about the sedan chair, the chatter and goings-on of the several couples in the park, were of much greater interest and respectable concern than the rude shuffling of the two adolescent bears and the coarse shouts of their savage keeper. In fact, from where he sat, he could no longer see the bears over the tops of the other wagons now wedged in so hopelessly at the street corner. Also, he had no doubt but that exhaustion, indignation, or extorted generosity would eventually break the blockade.

Meanwhile, the human bear garden in the park was undoubtedly more instructive, even if somewhat disconcerting, for he found that he himself recognized many of the people who were putting on the select show on the green. To his old-fashioned and certainly conservative notions, there were quite a few promenading that morning who, to *his* mind, had small reason for being admitted to the walk at all—and this applied more specifically, he thought, to many of the females. Mr. Glen sniffed.

Other people in other wagons, however, were not confining themselves to quiet sniffs. The German wagoners, in particular, hooted, vented raucous laughter, shouted obscene observations, and insolently roared. These evidences of contempt and disapproval from beyond the slopes of Parnassus were at first disregarded by the nymphs and demigods of the Artillery Walk. But the din at last became so considerable, so pointed and prolonged, that the Olympians themselves about the sedan chair were finally touched to the quick.

The annoyed gestures of a gold-headed cane and a doeskin glove from the chair itself brought a sergeant of dragoons on the double from the gate.

Mr. Glen now watched the proceedings about the chair with renewed interest. One of the smallest of the gentlemen's extremely small hats was passed from hand to hand, the doeskin glove itself contributing. The sergeant then strode off in the direction of the man with the dancing bears. An expectant and grateful silence instantly accompanied him. The line of wagons stood quietly waiting. Evidently the gentry were going to be of some use after all.

" 'Ere," said the sergeant, looking down at the red-faced man and the tired tongue-lolling bears just beneath him, " 'ere's a 'ole bloody 'atful o' swag for you and your un'oly libours. A 'ole bleeding 'atful!" He held up the Lilliputian headpiece for all to see.

The bear-master put his thumb to his nose, but removed it immediately as the sergeant extracted a new shilling from the hat as a fine for the gesture. "An' if *hi* was you, me bahr-biten friend," he continued, "I'd tike them two 'airy pupils back to the kive of their hawncesters and crawl in arter 'em. For Gineral Buckey, ee'll be back hany di now, and 'e 'ites biby bahrs and halligitors and all sich pets like bloody 'ell. Now, be orf!" And with that the sergeant poured the remaining coins into the bear-master's eager hands.

What the sergeant had said—the news of Buckey's return—flashed down the line of waiting wagons like lightning. Men now handled their reins impatiently again. The bear-master dragged his cubs across the street into a bricked alley, and the pent-up flood of vehicles streamed headlong over the cobbles along the stockaded street amid a torrent of oaths, volleys of whip-cracking, and an infernal squalling of brakes that almost stopped Mr. Glen's old heart. From doorways and upper windows, women screamed frantically to their muddy brats to get out of the gutter, as the whole medley of clanking wagons and scared farmers on rickety high-wheeled carts hurtled forward, and gushed out into the open square.

Two minutes later the good miller, feeling faint and overcome, sat wiping the sweat of apprehension from his kindly old face, while he looked about him for a place of refuge in which to tie up his team. Every place seemed to be taken.

Finally, he snagged onto a hitching post near the west gate of the stockade which seemed to be providentially vacated, and after resting awhile to settle a bit of nauseous vertigo, he stood up in the wagon to look about him:

Godamighty!

What was the old town coming to? Whatever could the authorities be athinking of? The square seethed in blatant sound. Mr. Glen felt dizzy again, and had to sit down for a moment.

"London bridge is falling down—falling down," sang a shrill-voiced young slattern, tripping homeward, with a wooden pailful of beer that slopped over and foamed on her bare feet. She rolled her eyes up at the fat German boys in the wagon and gave the two girls an unpleasant wink. Mr. Glen she passed by with a twitch of one muscle in her eyelid. All the young people seemed to be in a conspiracy against him, he felt. Somehow or other the girl with the beer contrived to show a dirty chapped leg almost up to her—neck! Mr. Glen turned away feeling his nausea renewed.

It was *so* safe and private at Boiling Springs—oh, to be at home again!

He wished the two young hussies in the wagon would find their uncles. They still sat in the wagon buck-toothed and dirty-faced, simpering at his two bound boys. What could he do with them? He felt too faint to try to make them leave. And the boys, damn them! For a sad moment he wished that he had never come to town.

The weather was so much hotter than he had expected. It was hard at his age for a widower to put up with all this. But pshaw—he had errands to do. He could find shelter overnight with some of his friends. He stood up again, looking across the stir and confusion to see how he could pick his way, and what to do next.

Godamighty!

Over the familiar roofs of the houses on the opposite side of the square, far far away in the blue distance, the rounded tops of the leaping mountains seemed to be peeping down into the town. Mr. Glen's view of the scene, while not so exalted, was even more intimate, and the effect upon the quiet and orderly mind of the bucolic old widower was disturbing to the last degree. In fact, the surprising concatenation of sights and sounds threatened to overwhelm him. He stood upright again on the wagon seat, but his legs were trembling. Among other things, a perfect hell of a noise was going on. For a minute he could hardly think without closing his eyes.

Wheels rumbled like the sound of a constant ground swell before a storm; this ground-shaking thunder of heavy wagons ceaselessly rolling underlay all else. A welter and babble of talk, loud, offensive and insistent, reverberated from every part of the square. The square sounded delirious. It frolicked as though at the height of a carnival and seemed to be in love with its own novel disorder. It flopped and squawked in careless liberty and with a fearless, unrepentant, devil-may-care air.

From the open windows of boarding-houses and numerous ordinaries came the fused noise of revelry within; voices and the sound of various instruments blended. Liquor flowed. Outside the taverns, people danced and sang, while others wept and prayed. At the fort drums were beaten and bugles blew from time to time, speaking out clearly from another country beyond the stockade walls as though military order might suddenly debouch from the gate and impose itself forcibly. But so subtle a threat went unheeded. The square rollicked on, happy in its new-found sense of freedom.

Nothing quite like it, and on such a scale, had been seen in the colonies before. It was the aftermath of a long, savage, and continental war; a universal din of release and relief at emerging from the dangerous past. America was assembled, discovering itself, and enjoying it. Something new was being born, and was making a natal noise. The excuse for the occasion was morally satisfying and exciting. Everybody, in his own opinion, had come to Carlisle to help release the Indian captives and, incidentally, to celebrate the victorious return of Brigadier Bouquet.

All this, decidedly, was *not* the kind of world Mr. Glen had expected or hoped to live to see. The possibility of personal refuge and decent privacy seemed to have vanished from it. Rationally or not, he felt surprised, dispirited, cheated of his just expectations, and duly indignant. There were too many people here—too many kinds of people, and all free, unrestrained, absolutely on their own. What was going on? For the moment he was stopped. He could only stand and watch. His sons were away, and how was he going to deal with so many people, and so many people of different kinds?

"Godamighty, God-a-mighty," muttered Mr. Glen, as though only God were left to appeal to . . .

Well, he would have to leave the wagon where it was and pick his way across the square to Mr. Williams's house on the west walk. There he could at least sit on the porch and recollect himself. He had forgotten exactly what it was he had come to town to do. Lord, he hoped the Williamses would be at home. He climbed down slowly by the wheel spokes and told Johann to take charge of the wagon and to wait. He didn't have the energy to get rid of the two girls. He turned—and dizzy with a buzzing confusion, began to grope across the square towards the other side.

It was not easy. It was about the time when most people, not gentry, were going home for the midday meal. They made way for no one and had savage tongues.

Mr. Glen was aware now that something terrible had happened to him, that he was ill on the inside of his head. But he struggled on. The sky over the roof-line on the opposite side of the square had unaccountably turned inky black. Underneath, the houses grinned at him like a line of bared white teeth. And yet, there, infinitely remote now, was the sure refuge of Mr. Williams's porch. He could still see it. He blundered on, his feet unaccountably heavy, while he seemed to be burning up.

A grey mist seemed to be closing down on the line of houses just ahead. He walked forward blindly. Somehow, somehow or other, he found himself at last staggering up the three white steps onto the Williamses' front porch. He sat down, the flies dimly bothering him . . .

He was sitting in a big chair fanning himself with his hat, and Mrs. Williams was fussing over him and exclaiming. She gave him a good strong drink. *That* was a relief! He felt better almost immediately. The world cleared. He could fan himself and enjoy the cool breeze he made that way. It was splendid to be among friends—and the Williamses were always so kind. Old-time neighbours.

He mustn't move, Mrs. Williams said. He must just sit and make himself comfortable. No one had ever seen such hot weather, and November just around the corner. Good lack! It certainly was hard on old people, and he'd better sit still and cool off. Of course, he could stay overnight. Why, Mrs. Williams wouldn't hear of anything else. She sent a young coloured girl with her baby out to watch him, while she went in to air out the side bed-chamber herself.

Mr. Glen, the coloured girl, and the baby, who was sucking its thumb, all sat on the front porch and stared at one another. He did feel better now, strangely relaxed. He felt amiable once more . . .

Presently an old friend came up on the porch and sat with him. Campion Honeywell—he was down on a visit from Boston town, winding up the matter of a contract for army candles with the quartermaster at Carlisle. Campion Honeywell was as direct and incisive in his talk as he had always been. You would scarcely think that they hadn't seen each other for eight years. Why, Campion didn't even know that Mrs. Glen had died. And he'd known Marie so well. They exchanged reminiscences briefly. Honeywell did most of the talking; he managed to convey that he was pretty well off, and both his daughters had married well. Mr. Glen began to complain a little languidly of his widower's loneliness at the mill. The boys were away—and all that. But he didn't feel like talking very much.

But Mr. Honeywell's face lighted with sudden interest. Maybe he could help make things less lonely at the mill, he said. He'd brought a townswoman of his along with him from Boston. A competent old lady, poor, but she'd sold her house to get to Carlisle to try to find her captivated grand-daughter. Mr. Honeywell had provided her a passage down, and he'd found her a place in Carlisle for a few days. But he was going back to Boston tomorrow, and he was worried about Mrs. Larned—Mrs. Theodosia Larned. But where could she go, what would she do after he left? Could Mr. Glen take her in? Why wouldn't it be a good idea for him to take her back to the mill with him and let her be housekeeper there, while she was waiting for her grand-daughter—and the Glen boys were away. Mrs. Larned was respectable. She would like to earn her keep. Why not?

Mr. Glen thought it over. He could see no serious objections and several advantages. And Honeywell was quietly insistent. He had a brisk Yankee way with him when there was something he wanted to get done. Mr. Glen *was* still a bit faint. But, why not? Still, he would like to see Mrs. Larned and talk to her first. He couldn't introduce just anybody into his dead wife's cherished house.

Naturally, of course not!

But Mrs. Larned was staying only four houses away down the street. Mr. Honeywell would go and fetch her. It would be no trouble, no trouble at all.

Mr. Glen was left fanning himself again, while the baby sucked its thumb, seated on the floor before him. The coloured girl had been called in to help Mrs. Williams ready the bed-chamber. No one, least of all Mr. Honeywell, had any idea that the last pinch of sand in the bottle-neck of Mr. Glen's hourglass was running out.

Presently, Mr. Honeywell was back again with Mrs. Larned. He also brought Jim Fergus along. Fergus had just delivered Mrs. Larned a letter from Fort Lyttleton, and Mrs. Larned held it in her hand, trembling with joy. Her face shone with inward delight. It seemed providential that the old lady's grand-daughter had been preserved and that she might soon hold her in her arms.

Mr. Glen became now simply a third party to aid Providence. He liked the old lady. He was even touched by her justified faith and preter-natural neatness. While Jim Fergus sat on the steps, and despite Mr. Glen's feeling of exhaustion, he made the final arrangements with Honeywell and gave sensible directions for taking Mrs. Larned home to Boiling Springs.

It was all quite simple. He explained he had had a touch of heat and would have to stay the night at Carlisle. But if Jim would find the wagon, "hitched nigh to the fort gate across the square", the German boys could get Mrs. Larned's luggage and drive her back to the mill with them that evening. They would have to come back for him with the wagon next day. But after a night's rest, he would be feeling much better, he thought; and he could get all his errands done next morning. Meanwhile, Mrs. Larned could be making herself at home. The German boys would show her about the mill house and tell her where the house keys hung. She might keep a little eye on them. Would she? Mr. Glen smiled. The two old people nodded to each other. He liked the way she brushed her bright silver hair back from her forehead. Their understanding was peacefully complete.

Would Jim Fergus please find the German boys and tell them?

"Why, sartin," Jim smiled; and said he'd know now just where to direct the people who'd bring Mrs. Larned's grand-daughter to town. He'd sure remember.

Mr. Glen and Mrs. Larned shook hands. With a simple expression of deep gratitude, she departed to pack up the few belongings that she still cherished in this world—for Bridget. The wagon would doubtless call for her soon. Mr. Honeywell said he would see her off.

For a few minutes Mr. Glen was left alone again with the brown baby. The excitement and emotions of the past few moments had been intense. He had admitted a stranger to his house. Too easily perhaps—but he was *so* tired of being alone.

He sat pondering. The world seemed to be withdrawing to an indistinct distance. Alone! Why, he'd never felt so completely alone as he did now! It was hard to fill his lungs in this breathless silence. Lord, this was what he had worked all his life to prevent. To die all by himself, and not a soul to bend over him! Where was Marie? Where were the two boys? Where was he? Oh, the everlasting silence! All he could do was see now. The blood whispered in his ears. It made a noise like darkness coming on.

He looked out into the light to the very last.

The Negro baby squatted in a narrowing circle of sunshine before him. It was crying. He could see its face and mouth move. There were ants on its hands, and it was trying to lick them off. That was the way it was. Little things worrying a body. It was terrible, unbearable. Somebody must tell the baby. Why didn't its mother come? He would call for her, cry out . . . *M-o-t-h-e-r* . . . But he had no breath. He struggled for it. He tried hard. The ants were still crawling. Let me out of here! Let me go! Jesus! Enough . . .

Godamighty . . .

Mr. Glen's tired face fell forward and rested on his quiet breast.

22. The Sound of Flowing Water

THE BLUE MILL WAGON and the German boys called for Mrs. Larned and her luggage about the same time that Mr. Glen was making his final observations. The two redemptioners, although outwardly respectful, were both inwardly quite sullen. For Jim Fergus, on finding them sparking in the wagon with the two girls in the public square, spoke powerfully and directly. The girls decamped—and the wagon was at Mrs. Larned's door almost before she could get the hairy lid of her scuffed portmanteau closed.

Mr. Honeywell and Jim Fergus saw her off. Jim put an old rush-bottomed slat chair in the wagon for Mrs. Larned to sit on, with admonitions to the boys to return it promptly next morning when they called back for Mr. Glen. And after final instructions to Johann to stop upstreet at Mr. Williams's and get his master's last orders, they waved the old lady a cheerful good-bye and strolled across the square together for a pipe and a nip.

Johann did exactly as he was told. He stopped at the Williamses' door, and while Mrs. Larned and Karl sat waiting in the wagon, he went in to speak to his master, who appeared to be dozing on the front verandah.

The baby was now quietly sucking its thumb again. But on approaching his master more closely, Johann stopped in his tracks. Something in Mr. Glen's attitude told him that the good miller was not dozing, not dozing at all.

This was a shock even to the oxlike Johann. But he did not nervously betray himself. He stood stolidly pondering. He could not think quickly, but he was cunning. And it was quite plain that here was an opportunity which might save him two years' further service and cancel his articles profitably. He stood thinking over the situation carefully. Then he glanced at the wagon. They were just sitting there, waiting. Ja, py Gott, he would do it! But he would have to be careful; and what was even more difficult, be swift.

Just to make sure, he bent over and spoke his master's name.

But there was no reply.

He leaned down as if he were carefully and respectfully listening to instructions from Mr. Glen, and detached his tasselled ring-purse that was wound twice about his leather belt.

Then he backed away a few paces and said quite loudly, "Ja wohl, sir, ve vill do it—ve coom back *tomorrow*."

Mrs. Larned was looking at him as he walked back, but he managed a bit of a swagger as he climbed onto the wagon. Probably she had heard what he had said. He hoped so. He had never flinched, not even with the dead man behind him. He just climbed up on the seat with Karl and began talking to him softly in voluble German.

The wagon rattled off rapidly in the direction of Boiling Springs, and Mrs. Larned, seated comfortably in the kitchen chair, began to enjoy the late-afternoon ride. It would have been helpful if Mr. Glen had come out to speak to her again, she thought. But she knew he was tired, and there would be plenty of time to talk things over with him more fully *tomorrow*—wasn't that what he had said?

The bound boys on the driver's seat continued to converse in German. They seemed shortly to have arrived at a satisfactory conclusion about some important matter. Johann finally clapped Karl on the back. Once or twice they looked back at her. Perhaps they wondered how she was getting on? But she nodded reassuringly at them. And at that, they looked at each other and laughed.

A half mile or so beyond the fort gate, they stopped to pick up a

couple of barefoot girls picking their way along the road towards Le-
Tort's Springs. Evidently the boys knew them. There was some whispered conversation, giggles, a guffaw or two; and then Johann explained
in broken English that here were a couple of neighbours' daughters,
and he would like to give them a ride back home.

Mrs. Larned had no objections, of course. The girls did look unkempt,
slatterns, no doubt. But, then, this was Pennsylvania—and the manners
of the back-inhabitants were no doubt primitive.

Mrs. Larned rode the rest of the way to Boiling Springs with the
German boys on the seat before her and the two girls sitting together,
looking out behind. They never even glanced up at her. As twilight
came on, she gathered her precious bundles closer about her. The mill
must be farther out in the country than she had realized. The drive
did seem to be a long one. It was twilight by the time Johann led the
horses carefully over the water at the little ford, and black night fell as
they trotted on down the road through the forest. Mrs. Larned could
see nothing at all. At last they drew up in a starlit open space before
a dim building. Karl went in to fetch a lanthorn. They sat waiting.
No one spoke.

The first thing she was aware of was the sleepy noise of continually
falling water. Insistently, the quiet music of the place began from the
very first to sing itself into her ears. It was a peaceful sound, a constant
bubbling as though a great domestic kettle were forever boiling away,
singing a lullaby to itself of hearth and home. *Boiling Springs*—

Why, this must be Mr. Glen's mill! They were home!

Lights in the windows of the mill house began to shine. An approaching radiance poured out of its open door. Karl came with the lanthorn to
lead her in; Johann handled her luggage.

Afterward, when it was too late, she began to think that the behaviour of the two bound boys that evening *was* a bit strange. But at
the time it all seemed, as far as she could see, right enough. The only
thing that impressed her as being odd was that the boys seemed to be in
a terrible hurry about everything. Still, they took care to treat her
courteously. And who was she to complain or to give directions in Mr.
Glen's house? Yet how they did rush about!

Karl gave her the house keys. Johann with her luggage showed her
forthwith to what evidently must have been Mrs. Glen's own bedroom.
Karl had had to unlock the door for them. It seemed to have been locked
and closed for a long time. The key worked with difficulty and the
door complained. Had Mr. Glen really wanted her to sleep in his
wife's bed-chamber? she inquired.

"Ja, ja," replied Johann. Mr. Glen himself had told him to take her
there. Also to show her where everything was: the buttery, the store-
room, all the kitchen cupboards. She toiled after him.

He unlocked them rapidly for her. Sometimes he took an article out and gave it to Karl. They were loading the wagon out there in the dark. She could hear the girls chattering. "Hurry," one of them kept calling. "For God's sake, you Dutch fools, get a move on!" Yet the other girl came in and kindly built up the fire for her—between running in and out to the wagon, carrying various things.

Mrs. Larned offered to get supper, but the girl told her not to mind. This was the boys' evening off, she explained. They would take both the girls home and spend the evening together. It was bellsnickelin' time. They were in a hurry to get going.

Mrs. Larned pieced this together as best she could. Well, she would get her own supper, then, after they had gone. She didn't exactly relish being left alone in a strange house. But it was natural, she thought, for the hired help to spend their evening together at the neighbour's. She hoped they wouldn't bundle all night.

The boys continued to load the wagon, probably for going to town to-morrow, she thought. At the last, they put in several bags of flour and horse feed that they carried out of the mill. Ah, probably *that* was it! They were going to barter at early market tomorrow in town. Still, as moonrise came on, she stood in the doorway watching them doubtfully.

Finally, they all clambered into the wagon together and drove off rapidly, without even saying a civil good night to her. They left her standing there in the moonlight, alone and listening to . . . what was it? . . . oh, yes—the sound of flowing water . . .

My gracious though, what was that? Only some little owls? They made a melancholy liquid bubbling sound, too. She shivered, drew her shawl closer; and going in, closed the door behind her and locked it.

As she stood watching the slow play of firelight on the walls and low ceiling of the room, and the black shadow down the hall from the single candle left burning in the bed-chamber, she clutched her old hands to-gether in a sudden access of apprehension. The house was so deathly silent.

She stood listening, her heart pausing. In the breathless silence there was nothing but a faint windy stir from the fire and an occasional crackle from the burning sticks, like a wicked chuckle. And then, gradually, she became aware of it again. It seemed to saturate the log walls of the place, the mill house and the mill itself with an occasional dripping note from a subterranean harp and a low scarcely audible musical undertone; secret, confidential, soothing . . . the sleepy noise of ever-falling water . . .

She wakened slowly to hear the same music next morning. She scarcely knew where she was at first. She lay awhile like a child with her eyes closed, listening to the harp. It was a bit uncanny. Yet there were liquid runs on it that were positively cheerful. She smiled at her sleepy fancy that she was being welcomed home. She lay for a long while, resting. It had been a long journey. But she had slept *so* soundly, she felt re-newed and refreshed.

Also she had slept unconscionably late. It must be—why, to judge by the outside shadows, it must be well after ten o'clock!

She wondered if Mr. Glen had come back yet. That would put her in a pretty pickle. Her first day as housekeeper—and she a sluggard lie-abed like this. She hadn't slept like that for years. She sat up, listening. Except for some squirrels scampering over the roof, and the water, there wasn't another sound.

Yet it was cheerful in the daytime. The bedroom was cozy, dusty, to be sure, but the sun streamed in through a big window, reflected from the mill-pond. The light on the ceiling rippled. The house felt warm. She got out of bed, said her prayers in gratitude, prepared a bite of breakfast at the hearth, and went calmly to work.

The house was a positive delight. Outside, it was a substantial and ample log structure leaning up against the big stone mill; inside, it had been sealed with smooth chestnut boards, wall and ceiling, and it shone with a smooth grey silver light. Mrs. Glen's old French furniture lent a lightness and grace to the mill house, which was astonishing, almost immoral, yet pleasant. And there were hooked rugs on every floor, which at least displayed industry.

Despite some inevitable qualms, she was soon forced to admit to herself that here was a pretty tribute to the dead woman who must have made it. For as she first went about the house that morning, Mrs. Larned everywhere came across dainty posthumous traces of the miller's wife in every nook and cranny.

Yet it was equally apparent that no woman had been living in the mill house for a long while. Recent traces of the practical and somewhat ascetic life of the miller and his two sons concealed as with a useful disguise of contemporary masculine disorder the original more fragile and exotic character of the establishment as initially arranged by Madam Glen.

Here was a fertile field for Mrs. Larned's earnest New England housekeeping proclivities. She set herself determinedly to putting everything to rights.

Thus it was that the morning and the evening of the first day slipped away rapidly. Mr. Glen did not return. And then it was another day, and still another. The sound of falling water sang a soothing dirge for time. Mrs. Larned let the steeple-shaped clock on the mantel shelf stop.

In four days' time, if Mr. Glen had returned, he would have found his mill house shining, restored within to the comfortable and quaintly elegant state of the early days of his French marriage; but with a certain upright primness and sense of righteousness conferred upon it by a pair of precise, old Boston hands.

But Mr. Glen did not return, nor the German servant boys. Mrs. Larned remained completely and entirely alone. Not even a wagon rattled past the door. There was nothing all day long; nothing but two cows that came home every evening to be milked, and the interminable sound of flowing water. The cows were a welcome difficulty. Her old hands tired easily, but she managed to milk them.

As day succeeded day, and still no one came, it would be idle to say that Mrs. Larned was not concerned about it. She certainly was, but she was more puzzled than alarmed. Undoubtedly, Providence for its own reasons seemed to be playing a sorry trick on her. But the ways of the Lord were always mysterious, she reminded herself. And then, she was much too much a fellow-townswoman of both the Lord and Mr. Honeywell to suspect either of them of having collaborated in a joke. No, no, there was some entirely reasonable and serious explanation for her having been left alone that would eventually be vouchsafed her, probably by Mr. Glen himself. Patience rather than panic was called for.

Panic and loneliness indeed were neither of them likely to prevail against Theodosia Larned. She had inner springs of strength that sang to her like the everlasting waters that flowed by the mill. God's Word, which she read every night, was always of infinite comfort to her as the inspired confirmation of her unavoidable salvation. And this faith accounted for a certain simple complacency of contentment in Mrs. Larned, even when she was in great adversity. Sustained by it, her lonely hours at the mill became periods of grace in her own estimation, beads which she told, not without a certain penitential relish, on the stout thong of daily labour.

And then, almost equal to the comfort of the Holy Word itself, was Mr. Patton's letter from Fort Lyttleton, which she kept in her Bible and read every evening, too. Bridget, the grandchild whom she had never seen, was coming home to her arms. So the good Mr. Patton had written, and there was no reason to doubt him.

Indeed, Mrs. Larned was now as much convinced of Bridget's return as of her own divine election. The letter, too, was a confirmed article of her faith. She knew now that Bridget would undoubtedly come driving up to the mill-house door, and that she had been sent there to prepare a place for her. That was what sustained her as the days went on.

So—after the house in general was all rid-up—Mrs. Larned concentrated on getting ready for Bridget, and in particular on the bed-chamber where she knew the child would soon be sleeping. She cleaned it meticulously, wiping down the painted dado and the wooden walls. She disposed her own things there along with the presents she had long been preparing for Bridget, as favourably as possible.

On a small dresser, which she took the liberty of removing from another room, she laid out a set of hand-carved wooden combs, brushes, and toilet boxes before a small mirror not too much the worse for wear. There was also a neat sewing-case with needles, scissors, a child's silver thimble, and skeins of bright-coloured thread.

On a marbled French table in the middle of the room she placed one of Mrs. Glen's finest embroidered covers, a tall shining candlestick, and the Larned family Bible. She drew up a convenient rocking chair close by. The big bed in the corner she made up with double bolsters. From underneath the big bed she pulled out the trundler, mended its sagging cords, and pounded its long-unused child's mattress into shape. Bridget was to sleep there, next to the big bed, close beside her at night.

It was on the trundle bed that she laid out the doll that had once belonged to her own daughter, 'Dosia, and an outfit of tiny dresses she had made for it. There, too, reposed the new clothes for Bridget; dresses, knitted jackets, a red-ridinghood cloak, stockings, several petticoats, and small woollen underthings flounced with linen lace. All these she had made or restored herself with patient hands informed by love and the skill of seventy years. She arranged and rearranged them now, bedewing her handiwork with secret tears and the fond smiles of hope deferred.

For the window that looked out over the mill-pond she washed and re-hung Mrs. Glen's fine lace fensters and tied them in with broad smiling bows. On the window-sill she placed her only and cherished treasure of the painter's art, a small picture of a lamb done in tempera on olive-wood. The lamb, an eternal one, had been brought over from England by Mrs. Larned's great-grandmother, and had survived for three generations.

Yes, it was the Lamb of God, strayed innocently out of the catacombs by way of a vanished British monastery into America. It had come almost as far west as it could get. Only the cross had been lost during the journey, and its destination on the window-sill now looked final.

For the lamb was now the first thing that Mrs. Larned saw in the window when she came into the room. And she kept coming back through the doorway again and again just to admire him, and to be sure that everything was ready to the last item. What would Bridget do? Where would she pause to admire? What would she say? Mrs. Larned clasped her aged hands in youthful anticipation.

It did seem a long time that the Lord was requiring her to wait. After everything was ready, after she had explored and set to rights every part of the house, and even carried in some extra firewood, which gave her a lame back—still nobody came.

Perhaps, if it had not been for the misery in her back and her pain-fully stiff limbs when it came to walking, she might have tried to get back to Carlisle. For after a week, or was it a week, had gone by—she wasn't sure—her greatest worry was that she couldn't be certain when the Sabbath day would fall. But when *they* came, she could rectify it.

Certainly someone would come, sooner or later. Common sense in-sisted that the big mill and the mill house could not be left abandoned for too long. No, someone must come soon. And yet—how many days had she been there alone now, harkening to a dream-harp and the sad sound, the eternal whispering rush of ever-flowing water?

The evening before the weather changed and the storm came down, she ventured out of the house at last and hobbled painfully down the road. She couldn't even remember in what direction the town lay. It had been so dark that evening when they came from Carlisle. But she would try to see; she would try to trace the wagon by its wheel ruts and hoof marks. There were many of these old wheel marks in the road, however, and they told her a confused tale. Afterwhile, she came to a swift ford in a muddy river. It was not so far from the house, but it had taken her an hour to limp there. She now sat down to rest. To her terror, night began to fall.

How lacking in faith she had been to leave the house. Bridget might come while she was away! She sat on a log waiting, waiting for something, she didn't quite know what. She must have dozed. She came to herself again shivering and realized it was getting late. She was frightened now, frightened to the bone.

The moon rose and those little owls began. Down the muddy river around its first but distant bend, firelight was glinting redly, reflected across the yellow water. A faint high singing floated on the wind. It was some time before she recognized the garbled melody of a familiar hymn. The firelight on the water became wider. Around the bend of the river stole the black shadow of an Indian canoe.

Mrs. Larned got up from the log and fled wildly back to the house. She tottered through the door, all but finally exhausted, and forgot to lock it behind her. Thank God, the fire was still burning. She had had her lesson. There were savages near-by. It was a sign. She must not go out of the house again. She must wait.

Next morning a cold wind came pouring through the thickets while snow and sleet pattered against the window-panes. She prayed anxiously for strength to endure. Winter had come, and she was all alone. Also—she was running out of flour in the kitchen crock.

Well—there was plenty of *that* in the mill loft. Bags of it were stored on a platform between the rafters, high up away from the mice, she remembered. It was only a question whether she could climb the ladder.

She got a saucepan and a spoon, and hobbling back through the hall to the big door that led into the mill, she opened it with much difficulty, went up a few steps and peered into the place.

She limped to the foot of the ladder and looked up. Finally, after putting the handle of the saucepan in her mouth, and the spoon in her apron pocket, she began to climb. It was painful. But with both hands she held on hard, and resting between rungs, she slowly dragged herself up. The last rung now, all but one . . .

It did seem terribly high up there. The shadowy floor lay miles beneath her. And how was she going to get the flour out of the bags?

At last she pushed the saucepan onto the platform with her mouth, and pulling the spoon out of her apron, she began to jab with it at the side of the nearest bag.

Eventually a small hole appeared. She dug at it some more and flour began to stream out. She shifted the saucepan under it. It soon overflowed. My! This *was* going to be wasteful.

But at that instant her hands were frozen by terror. From the gloom of the depths below her a sepulchral voice said:

"*How.*"

She poised there lightly. Her flour-dusted skirt hung still and drooping behind her like a quiet wing. Her blood no longer whispered in her ears as she listened . . . listened . . . even the sound of flowing water seemed to pause . . .

"*How, mizzy.*"

The guttural voice boomed dismally to crack the silence again.

She looked behind her now. She looked down.

In the shadows at the foot of the ladder stood an Indian holding up an empty bowl . . . holding up a pot . . . There was one white feather in his hair . . . it gleamed.

Mrs. Larned tottered on the ladder and lost her grip. She gasped, and threw up her hands . . .

The flour reached the edge of the platform, poured over, and began to waste into the air.

But Doctor Scarlet did not stay to fill his usual weekly bowl. He left instantly, flitting back through the silent house by the same way he had come.

The door closed furtively behind him, and the mill house stood waiting. Afterwhile, the mice came out again to scamper over the wide mill-room floor. Now and then a squirrel frisked across the roof. It was Sunday afternoon, but Mrs. Larned had forgotten. Only the sound of flowing water babbled on.

23. "Grandma That Art in Heaven"

IT WAS TUESDAY morning when the wagon and the trundler passed through the gate by the artillery gardens without question and took the road for Boiling Springs. Jed drove, and Salathiel rode on Enna happily beside.

They were following the same road that Manoah Glen had covered in the opposite direction only a short while before. But, of course, Salathiel knew nothing as yet of the good miller's fatal journey to town. And it was this state of happy ignorance that had permitted him to look forward with such confident anticipation to a prompt arrival at Boiling Springs. It had been part of a streak of his best luck to have run into Jim Fergus.

Inside the wagon, Bridget sat wide-eyed but demure, swinging her feet nervously. She hoped her Grandma Larned would be like Mrs. McCandliss, soft-voiced, calm, lady-like. She kept putting her hand up to her new bonnet to straighten it. They were *so* near now. Frances was smiling contentedly. She, too, had hopes and cherished dreams of what Boiling Springs might be. But the possibility of her being parted from Bridget was not among them.

In less than half an hour they were rumbling across the stout log trestle that carried the road over the branch at LeTort's Springs. There they were forced to pull up to watch a heavy military convoy turn off the highway for the camp at that much-frequented spot. The main camp of the garrison lay only a few rods down the stream below the log bridge where they were stalled. The engineers were busy there filling in swampy places, a pet aversion of Bouquet's, and pegging new sods down on the bare glacis. There was a good deal going on at LeTort's that would bear watching.

"Get to it, men," he muttered, not without a twinge of nostalgic envy. "Fly to it before Buckey gives you hell."

The camp had long been nearly empty of troops, but was being put in meticulous condition for the return of the units absent with Bouquet.

Before that sorry place, the road to camp and the road to Carlisle parted, or joined, according to how you looked at it, and the cross-roads for a full half acre in front of LeTort's were churned and rutted into a compost of half-frozen yellow mud.

About this infernal tarn, a sad rookery of a village had grown up. In dwellings that were compounded of everything not nice, those who wished to be as near as possible to the protection of the garrison had squalidly congregated. Waiting, wandering, these people picked the last shreds of meat from every bare bone of rumour that was thrown to them from the western wagons at the cross-roads.

Immediately before the gate of the old stockade yard itself, and facing directly on the main road, one Ferdinand, a high yellow of West Indian origin, had set up a shack roofed with bark, old bottles on sticks, and streamers of flapping cloth. Every wind raised the hair on his emporium. Before it, an old kettle hung from a striped barber's pole with a signboard beneath announcing in illiterate and drunken script the presence of *The Barbadgeon Apathakerry*.

Ferdinand was sparse-bearded, had jaundiced eyes, and lived in a gentleman's ancient red velvet dressing gown with a rampant gold crest on it. Apparently, there was almost nothing Ferdinand could not do for, or to, you if you would let him. He told fortunes by reading palms; the future, with two coconut shags. He pulled teeth, cured inflamed eyes, sold love philtres, delivered mares, and bottled herb medicines for man or beast, etc., etc.

All this was not to be gathered from his sign. It was to be heard, however, if you could understand the strange gibberish in "Delaware-

English" from the mouth of his old squaw and woman, who droned out from morning until night the gifts and merits of her lord and master, the father of her five children. They, too, helped loudly, and the combined sound was like that of wind through the knot-holes of a withered oak. It rose and fell. In the evenings, by the light of two pine-knots, a fiddler took the family's place. Ferdinand's was merry after the sun went down. In the day, though, there was nothing so efficacious to drum up trade as an ocular demonstration of the master's skill.

The convoy had made the turn into the camp, and the wagon had started to move forward again. But just as they drove by LeTort's, one of Ferdinand's notable demonstrations was in progress, and Jed drew up by the kettle on the painted pole to let Frances and Bridget see. Salathiel turned back and waited.

It was Ferdinand the dentist who now emerged from his den. He had a young white girl with him, wrapped in a meagre blanket. He rang a bell and began a talky-talk in "Spanish". A haggard crowd rapidly gathered. The bell stopped. A pair of pliers emerged from the dirty folds of the red velvet gown. The girl screamed. The old squaw grabbed her from behind and hugged her like a squat bear. Ferdinand violently twisted out a tooth and held it up for all to see. The bell rang. The girl staggered over and leaned against the painted pole. The tooth was tossed into the pot. Ferdinand came forward and, bowing low before Frances at the back of the wagon, offered to read her palm. She shook her head violently.

" 'Twill be an onlucky day for ye, me foin lady," he shouted after her, as the wagon pulled out.

She thought he had an Irish accent. But how, with such a yellow face? She knew nothing of Barbadians. The wagon rolled onward. An English officer rode up and stopped to look at the girl sobbing convulsively against the painted post. Finally, he dismounted.

"Here, you damned scoundrel," he shouted at Ferdinand, "give me your forceps! You've drawn the wrong tooth!" He opened the mouth of the girl, he pulled hard. Pus gushed out. She began to try to eat handfuls of snow, which rapidly turned scarlet. "That'll do," said the officer. He mounted, and trotted up the road to the camp.

It was Surgeon Boyd. He was on his way back to England via Philadelphia. He was going to retire, and he was glad of it; he was going to retire on a legacy. Ferdinand tossed the second tooth into his pot on the pole above him. It clinked. The crowd laughed. It had been a good show. The wagon continued in its own direction. By such narrow margins do old friends fail to meet . . .

They were soon out in the very middle of the open fields between the town and the forest. On every side small hovels of sod, chinked logs, and fieldstone shouldered up like beavers' huts above the weeds. Mud-and-stick chimneys leaked smoke. Yellow brush fires with forlorn people gathered about their leaping flames dotted the landscape. Even in the fresh winter breeze, the place reeked. Here and there, men or women squatted shamelessly over shallow trenches. A few thin cows, their bells clanging funereally, grazed along the road. How many people were living thus in the ground, waiting dismally, it was hard to tell. But all of these places were not inhabited. Scars and pits of former encampments pock-marked the fields everywhere. The nearer the forest the less of them there were. Salathiel was glad of that. It would be more decent when they came to the woods again.

They took the south fork at the next cross-roads. In a few moments the forest closed over and behind them. The silence smelled sweet. The road to Boiling Springs was quite good, considering it hadn't been used much lately. The harness bells chimed secretly in the solitude. Salathiel felt better and rode straighter in the saddle. Just ahead the water of a small stream glinted through the trees. They must be coming to a ford. Probably a shallow one . . .

Goddam . . . what the devil . . . ?

All the horses seemed to be going crazy at once. Enna reared and walked about on her hind legs. She "trumpeted" with nervous fright. The lead team of the wagon was trying to tear itself out of harness. The others backed and filled. They swerved violently, and the big ash single-tree cracked. Jed had disappeared, and the devil was in all the horses playing merry hell . . . Judas-priest . . . where could he ever get another single-tree like that? And Jed?

"Hey, Jed!"

Jed arose from a ditch full of leaves where he had been neatly cata-pulted, but with enough sense left in his dazed head to snatch at the lead team's bridles and hang on. He began to batter them in the face with his old hat. Salathiel forced Enna to the rear of the trundler, tied her fast, and then racing forward on foot joined Jed in his battle with the frantic teams. It was hard, swift struggling for a minute or two. Finally, he shouted to Frances to toss him out some blankets, which he wrapped around the horses' heads. They stood quiet at last, sweating and trembling but breathing tranquilly.

It couldn't be something they had scented, then. It must have been something downwind, or something they saw. But what the devil was it? A painter stretched out on a limb? He walked down the road cau-tiously. Damnation! That was it—nothing but a white lightning blaze on an old thunder-tree. Horses were the durndest fools, and the single-tree was cracked. Then he saw what Karl and Johann had seen, and began to laugh. To think that *that* had nearly wrecked them.

He ran forward, and leaping the stream lightly, began to cut some young cedars and pile them against the sprawling white blaze on the thunder-tree. Only a stack of green trees stood there now.

"Come on, Jed," he shouted. "Just keep 'em blinded and lead 'em easy. There's nothin' to be skeered of but an old wagon, and it's lyin' wheels upward in the ford."

Nevertheless, he was quite relieved and happy when "the hul consarn", including Enna, finally stood breathing easily as usual, safe on the other side. He took the blankets off the horses' heads and comforted the women. They had taken it well. Frances was more anxious about the cracked single-tree than scared at what had happened. Would the single-tree last, did he think, as far as Boiling Springs?

"Probably," he answered briefly, after inspecting it, but Jed would certainly have to drive slow. He himself would ride ahead now, at quite a distance. The "tree" wouldn't take any more surprises. Mounting Enna thankfully, he trotted ahead. It was not long before he left the wagon well behind him.

The forest road stretched before, curving away easily through the sunny woodlands. There were no fresh wheel marks, he noted. It would be hard to tell how long it had been since the last wagon had passed. The storm had come that way recently. Presently, between the nervous *clip-clop* of Enna's hoofs, he began to hear a sound like a breeze stirring through the forest. It was the sound of ever-falling water. The mill-dam—Mr. Glen's mill-dam at Boiling Springs.

Before him, down a stretch of smooth road covered with tamped river gravel, lay the open space in the forest that was Boiling Springs. A patch of sunshine glinted brazenly on the troubled ford at the far end of the vista, where Yellow Breeches Creek rolled through the trees. The noise of falling water now seemed to accentuate rather than to lighten the silence. The place seemed totally deserted, eerie with the absence of any human noise. On one side of the road stretched a shingled horse shed that ended against a log house. The house in its turn was part of a large mill, stone underneath, with logs in the story above. On the opposite side of the road, a considerable two-story dwelling slept in the cold sunshine, its porch sagging and covered with sodden leaves. A dry bush of many seasons past hung like a skeleton hand of dead hospitality above the door.

A fox trotted across the road and stopped to look at him. Boiling Springs, eh? He scratched his head doubtfully.

The falling water seemed to be complaining about something. The mill-pond trembled slightly, reflecting a wavering picture of the mill with icicles hanging from its wheel. The bare trees that surrounded it were upholstered in white rime-frost from roots to tips. There was no wind in this sequestered vale. A thicket of sumac blazing with red candles hemmed in the race. Enna stamped uneasily.

There was only one sign of life, a blue haze hovered over the top of the chimney of the mill house. Salathiel rose in his stirrups.

"Mrs. Larned," he shouted. "Are you there, Mrs. Larned?"

There was no answer. Perhaps he should have called for Mr. Glen?

The wagon came in sight. He waited for it to draw up and told them to tarry for a minute. He'd like to look the place over himself first. Bridget sat quiet but tense, holding her basket with the kitten in it on her knees. She looked preternaturally neat and vividly expectant. "Granny can't be far away," Salathiel said, patting her hand.

Frances looked up apprehensively. He winked at her, conveying a sense of caution.

"We'll wait for ye," she said.

"Put the horses in the shed, Jed," he ordered, as he tied Enna to a post and crossed the road towards the mill house. "Liken we'll be staying here for quite a spell."

His remark encouraged Frances and Bridget greatly. They already liked the quiet of the place, the cheerful splash of the water.

"Like home," sighed Bridget. "You know, Lissa, I'd almost forgot." Her eyes shone. Frances put an arm about her.

Salathiel walked over to the mill house and knocked at the front door. He waited. He knocked again—then trying the latch, he found the door opened, and stepped inside. The door shut behind him. A small flurry of ashes lifted in the fireplace. There were still some living sparks. A newly shined brass kettle stood on the hearth.

The room was bright. Two large windows overlooked the mill-pond at its far end. The light reflected ripples on the silver-grey ceiling, and the whole place swam. But it was certainly comfortable. Alive. Mrs. Glen's old-fashioned furniture, nicely covered with faded green cloth, looked luxurious to Salathiel. There were books on a hanging shelf. Jars for tobacco and snuff were arranged on a tray with several long-stemmed clay pipes. On the mantelpiece, a shepherd and a shepherdess smiled in gold and blue at either end. A small clock stood between them. It was silent. In a rocking chair, two bone needles thrust upward from a pile of new knitting were still caught in the last stitch. But the room was growing cold.

He went over to the hearth and laid a few sticks of light-wood on the fire and stood waiting. . . .

"Mrs. Larned," he called again. "Mrs. Larned, your Bridget's here!" A squirrel scurried over the roof. . . .

He went down a hall leading towards the mill and looked into the various rooms that opened off it. There were two rooms on each side. The first one was undoubtedly the old lady's. An embroidered counterpane covered the bed in the corner; and a crazy quilt, the little trundle bed next to it. No matter which way he turned, a silly lamb on the window-sill followed him with its smile. A bureau and a small dresser stood with feminine things, waiting. A small table with an embroidered linen cover held a big Bible. It lay open before a half-burned candle that had been neatly snuffed. It looked like an altar, he thought.

He walked to the table and glanced at the back of the Bible. Yes, there could be no doubt of it . . . the whole Larned family tree was there—and Mr. Patton's letter! Very carefully he laid the Book back where it had been, still open at the same place. It was somewhere in Samuel.

He looked at the trundle bed again. It was covered with things that, quite evidently, Mrs. Larned had made for Bridget. They were all too small for her, he thought. But pretty damn dainty, too. And there were some toy clothes and an old doll. There was also a faint stale odour like old white people. He wrinkled his nose and backed out, closing the door.

The other three rooms all had men's clothes in them. One seemed to have been recently lived in. The miller's own, he judged. A pair of wrinkled flour-dusty gloves lay on the stand. That room didn't smell so good, either. Mr. Glen, if it were his, undoubtedly took Swedish snuff. He closed that door, too.

The silence of the house against the sound of water was suddenly overpowering.

No one at home! Maybe the old lady had gone for a visit to the neighbour's to borrow something—or? She couldn't have been gone long. Well, there was one more door.

It was at the end of the hall, heavy and massive, closed. He walked to it and rapped. A scurrying of innumerable small feet on the other side came to him faintly. . . . It ceased. He opened the door and went up five steps.

It was a big place filled with twilight from some windows high up, fogged with flour dust. He was in the mill itself. Mice squeaked, and the water gurgled away underneath the floor. Sometimes it dripped musically. He turned suddenly.

Something dead was close by.

There it was!

He first saw her silver hair shining in the semi-darkness. She was lying at the foot of a ladder that led up into a half-loft on the beams above, where many bags of meal were piled. There was a small saucepan at the foot of the ladder and a high cone of loose flour that must have run out of a sack. Also mice dirt.

She lay crumpled on her left side, her head twisted under her arm, her neck broken. There were no marks on her that he could see. One thing now stood out above all else, the intensely neat part in her smooth silver hair. Her back comb was broken. She was cold, stiff. She had been dead for a long time, he judged. He went hastily and got a candle to see better. It was then that he saw the moccasin tracks in the flour dust on the floor.

They led from the door to the foot of the ladder. One pair of mocca-sins, one person. Whoever it was had turned around in them and walked back to the door again, stepping exactly where he had stepped before. There was no doubt of it. Whoever had come had gone some time ago, and through the house. There were mice tracks over the big rail. The saucepan was half full of flour from a hole in a bag above. He climbed up. A spoon was caught in the threads about the hole.

He thought he could tell now what had happened. Mrs. Larned must have been standing on the ladder, digging into the bag, when she heard moccasins behind her. She must have looked back and seen an Injun. He couldn't be sure of that. Other people wore moccasins. But probably, probably it was an Injun. And ladies from Boston were not used to seeing Injuns at the bottom of ladders. She had fallen? Maybe? He would have to go into that carefully. If it had been old Doctor Scarlet, it would not be so easy for him to keep his fine promise to Jim Fergus, just to say "how". He rose from his knees and blew out the candle. Just now there was Frances to think of first—and Bridget! God ease her little soul! He would have to manage it quickly, somehow or other, now! They were waiting out there in the wagon.

He tied the mill-room door behind him with a thong and a knot that would have to be cut. It was the "death knot" that Kaysinata had showed him.

When he got back to the room, the fire was blazing up brightly. It crackled and talked. That was what really settled the matter for him. He went to the door and called them. "Come in, sweethearts," he cried. "The place is all warm and waitin' for ye. Granny's away, I guess. But she's been expectin' ye. Come and look!"

Frances' eyes veiled with a mist of pleasure as she entered and looked about the room. The fire leaped cheerfully, the brasses glinted.

"Take your bonnet off," she said to Bridget, who had been rushing round examining everything and was now rocking in the chair before the hearth. "I want your grandma to see your pretty brown hair." She combed it back and smoothed it, and looked anxiously at her man. She saw something was wrong.

"Bridget, go into that room and see what Mrs. Larned has made for you," he said. "She'll want you to know."

The child got up and tiptoed to the first door down the hall to which he pointed. "Grandma," she called.

"Go in," he said.

They stood listening to the child's ecstatic cries. "The lamb, oh, the dear, dear lamb . . ."

He took Frances' hands and held them tight.

"Keep her close here. Keep her happy in this place until I can git back."

"What is it?" she demanded.

"Can you bear it?" he asked.

"Yis," she said. "Is it so bad?"

"Terrible," he whispered.

She stood waiting.

"Grandma fell off a ladder and broke her neck. She's lyin' stark and still out there in the mill room behind the house. Can ye keep Bridget here until Jed and I can hide her?"

"Yis," she whispered, and sank down in the rocking chair. The tears sprang out of her eyes now. "Mother of God," she whispered, and crossed herself. She sat looking into the cheerful crackling fire, in misery. A few seconds ago it had seemed to be warming her heart. Now . . .

"Look, Melissa," he whispered, leaning down over her, "I'm not goin' to leave here for a while. We've got no other place to go. And yon is the hearth fire she laid for us. I was just in time to save the flame alive."

"Let it burn then," she said. " 'Tis God's will. I'll beguile the child. You go out and do what must be done, and say a prayer," she said. "Do ye know one?"

"I'll make one," he answered, and left her before the fire. Bridget was calling to Frances as he closed the door.

"Bring two spades from the side-box, Jed," was all he said.

It took small time to dispose of Theodosia Larned. He and Jed got her out of the mill by the back way. He picked a high dry site quite a distance back from the road. They dug a deep grave in the soft red soil, lined it with fallen leaves, and laid her in it, with her face looking east at the house. Jed was not badly frightened. It was bright daylight, and he thought of Bridget's sad case, and wept copiously. Mrs. Larned smiled behind a veil of autumn leaves. Her eyes were half open as though she were quite sleepy. He closed them with two silver shillings, and said a prayer. Jed said "Amen" over and over again, and then prayed himself. They covered her quickly and quite deep. Then they dragged some heavy logs over the spot and went back to the wagon.

Salathiel cleansed himself carefully and changed into his decent blue clothes before he went back into the house.

He nodded to Frances and sat down before the fire. Bridget was nursing her new doll. The kitten lay stretched out, purring. He called to Jed to get some heavy wood for the hearth. Melissa had taken up the knitting where Mrs. Larned had left off. A sleeve on the little jacket was growing longer. She had even started the clock.

Stolen time in another man's house, he thought. He'd explain it, nevertheless. He'd make it right with the miller. Mr. Glen would just have to bear with them. Surely he must have a good heart, if he'd sheltered the old lady. Surely he would understand.

But Mr. Glen did not return. No one came.

It would have been a hard afternoon to pass if they had not turned in to put all to rights in the wagon and the house for staying. Frances made much of it and kept Bridget busy. They were cheerful enough for a while. It was only as the late afternoon wore away towards evening that Bridget became subdued and silent. Everybody was hungry and eager for supper.

They had it on a small table drawn up before the fire. There were three candles. And Jed was proud to show that he knew how to wait on them. He set three places with blue plates and a white cloth. Frances looked at it before she sat down, happily. Bridget went over in the corner and began to drag out another chair.

"It's for grandma," she explained.

Then she stopped. They were all so silent. She saw tears in Jed's eyes.

"Ain't she coming?" she asked finally, and looked at Salathiel.

He shook his head.

"Liken she's gone to be with Mrs. McCandliss," he said huskily. "That's the way it is." He didn't know it, but it was the best way he could have put it.

"Oh," said Bridget, drawing her breath in sharply. She left the chair and came over and sat down, round-eyed. Salathiel said Colonel Chambers's grace. They ate quietly. Melissa began to talk afterwhile about the fine things she was going to make, now that there would be time and a spell free from travelling. There would be a new dress for Queen Alliquippa, paduasoy, with a dash of royal scarlet. Bridget considered this. She listened solemnly.

After supper Salathiel sat smoking before the fire, watching Melissa's scissors snip at the cloth patterns she was laying out. Jed slumbered heavily in a corner. The cat walked about with her tail in the air.

Presently, Frances took Bridget into Mrs. Larned's room. She looked at him significantly as she went out. He heard them undressing together. Then there was a moment of quiet murmuring. He couldn't hear what Bridget was saying. But Frances did.

The child was on her knees and had laid her head in Frances' lap as she always did now. She folded her hands and looked up with tightly closed eyes, but the tears came through.

"Grandma," she began, "grandma, that art in Heaven . . ."

Melissa comforted her as best she could. They cried it out together in the rocking chair. They went to bed afterwhile and left the candle burning. Frances held Bridget close. It would have been too much to try to go to sleep in the dark the first night. Not in the old lady's own room. She looked at the lamb and crossed herself. . . .

Salathiel sat late before the fire pondering. He waited up, expecting Mr. Glen. Time passed with the ticking clock and the sound of rushing water. He whittled, and did a good deal of thinking. He sure was in for it now. How mysterious things were, how unexpectedly they turned out! It was enough to daunt a man. Up there with shillings on her eyes! Did she know? Anyway, they'd *have* to keep Bridget now.

What was that?

Only Jed slipping out to crawl back into the wagon. He didn't blame him. The house surely was kind of . . . kind of strange.

He saw that the candle was still burning in the women's room. Could it be that Mrs. Larned's open Bible might have a message for him? She might have meant it that way. The Word of God! Well, he would see. At any rate, he would outen the candle before it burned to the socket.

He slipped to the door of the bedroom and looked in. Melissa and Bridget lay asleep in each other's arms. Melissa's dark hair streamed down over her shoulders to mix with the brown locks of the child. They were both unearthly beautiful in the candlelight, he thought. White as angels.

Oh, Lord, now *who* had done that? Now wasn't that just like the women! It must have been Frances.

The Bible on the stand was closed.

24. The Triumph of Brigadier Bouquet

THE MUSIC was coming down the great western road, military music. The dull single drum tap of the long tired marches that had marked the weary forest miles all the way back from the Ohio country still ticked off the final paces of Bouquet's veterans returning to Carlisle.

A warning gun boomed solemnly from Fort Lowther.

The music was coming down the great western road, drawing nearer every minute, the music of Brigadier General Bouquet.

All Carlisle bestirred itself instantly. Like the Shawanese towns on the Muskingum, it, too, was being taken by surprise. It was like Bouquet to do the unexpected. He strove to be his own harbinger. It was good strategy at any time. It served to discover the incompetent and disconcert the complacent ones. It amused him, and—after all—he was only ten hours ahead of himself today.

However, that was the reason the commandant at Fort Lowther had fired an alarm gun. *He* was alarmed.

Lieutenant Colonel Asher Clayton had had a beautiful plan to receive the general in right military style and full regalia, every button, even on the goddamned militia, bright and in place. When the news of Bouquet's having reached Shippensburg came in only the night before, he had immediately begun to issue orders. He had even conferred with the Reverend Mr. Duffield and Mr. Tilingham, the schoolmaster, about the erection of a triumphal arch of evergreens with goldenrod and mountain laurel. Twelve little girls from the Presbyterian congregation were to scatter oak leaves and daisies, if there were any. And now! Now, all this was spoiled. The general's music was coming down the great western road, and the devil was to pay.

Boom!

Actually, it was only the commandant who was alarmed. Everybody else was delighted, and they could hear the music for themselves. The best Colonel Clayton could do was to line the square immediately on all four sides with the regulars of the garrison, and even some of his invalids, and to mass the militia by companies at the entrance to the square and down the great western road. And it was well he did so, for the brave news had spread like wildfire. Long before the alarm gun was fired, some people had heard the music and begun to stream in from the fields and down the roads from every direction, and to crowd into the square. Soon there was a solid mass of them between the houses and the thin line in scarlet and white cross-belts that fenced off the rectangular open space kept in the middle of the square. People crowded every doorway and hung out of the upper windows. Even the low shingled roofs were packed with spectators, and the few scraggly trees that rose here and there from dooryards dripped with boys.

The place reverberated with a clang of wild talk, shouts, and a resurgent hum of eager expectation. But to Colonel Clayton's relief, the noise was all good-natured. It was a fine afternoon, and for once the crowd seemed inclined to govern itself. There was a rare feeling of common interest and enthusiasm abroad, a spontaneous undercurrent of satisfaction and loyalty. That was a novel experience for the colonel. It was the first, and, as a matter of fact when he came to recollect it long afterwards, it was the last and only time during his long service in the colonies when all the people seemed to behave like fellow Britons. Even the backwoods characters in buckskins seemed less sullen than usual.

Whether it was Bouquet's personal popularity, the thrill of victory, or the return of the captivated that most moved the various individuals composing the crowd made little difference. In any case, long-deferred hopes were about to be satisfied, and both citizens and soldiery were alike in their enthusiasm. The happy surprise of Bouquet's early arrival was intensely gratifying. That, indeed, was the common interest and uncommon excitement which drew everyone to the square, for there were few residents of Carlisle who would not have some poignant private interest in the spectacle of the brigadier's return.

All LeTort's Springs had poured itself into Carlisle. The hovels in the surrounding fields were left entirely deserted.

By the time the music coming down the road could be heard clearly, as the returning regiments emerged from the forest and approached the town across the open fields, the commandant himself was inclined to feel satisfied. The general's reception seemed to have arranged itself by general consent. There must be between six and seven thousand persons present in and about the square, he figured, probably inaccurately. He and his staff, the mayor, the burgesses, Colonel John Armstrong, and other military and civil notables and worthies were gathered together waiting, as a kind of hastily arranged reception committee, before the west gate of the fort. On the whole, Colonel Clayton felt, the brigadier was bound to be pleased. But like everyone else, as the drums and music came nearer, his gaze and attention were soon entirely detained by the corner of the stockade wall and High Street, where the van of Bouquet's column might now at any moment be expected to appear.

To say that the centre and cause of all this excitement and interest, Brigadier General Henri Bouquet himself, was not interested in how he was going to be received at Carlisle would not be accurate. Undoubtedly he was interested, but he was highly intrigued rather than deeply concerned. Being of an intensely practical and far-seeing turn of mind, he was never indifferent to what properly concerned him and his officers and men. But at the present moment his thoughts were projected into the future rather than amused by the present or bemused by the past. In short, as he rode along with his tired adjutant and a couple of mounted messengers who comprised his modest staff, splashed with mud, and in a faded uniform, he was not in that vainglorious and self-gratulatory frame of mind which, it is said, has at times been known to accompany victorious generals returning home. Such a mood and such an attitude could not be entertained by a man of Bouquet's genius and depth of character. Despite years of professional service under many flags, Henri Bouquet remained an essentially modest, kindly, and devoted man. He was a professional Swiss soldier who had frequently outfaced both death and defeat in hard-won battles, and was therefore inclined to bear his laurels as he had borne intolerable responsibility, patiently, and chastened by an ironic sense of humour.

Oval- and olive-faced, taller than most, he now rode forward about the middle of the column, upon a borrowed government nag and with stirrups too near the ground; a big man upon a little horse, whose choice of the best, if not the most impressive means of always arriving successfully had won him first the grudging respect and finally the devoted affection of all his veterans, regulars and colonials, who now trudged before and behind him. His and their immediate destination was a rousing and grateful welcome at Carlisle, he hoped, but that is not to say he was preoccupied or intended to be overwhelmed by it.

In several ways things might, and in his own opinion, *ought* to have been even better than they were. The balance of his successes and of his disappointments was, he felt, entirely too nice. His cup was full, but it had never run over. He had won all his battles, but in the process lost his only lady love. His promotion to brigadier had arrived unexpectedly, for the crown was slow to recognize merit in foreigners. *Now* he was brigadier and the applause and affection of the Pennsylvanians and Virginians were his; and *now* he would have to leave them all forthwith. For he had also been appointed to the command of the new Southern Department. Headquarters would be at Pensacola instead of at Philadelphia or New York. Another world to conquer, he thought ironically. At a little higher salary, he might soon become the Alexander of Louisiana. There would be fatal fevers, but no Babylons to die in. Heigh-ho, c'est la guerre! "Oh, Richard, oh, mon roi!" He whistled through a few staves of the old tune, his brown eyes widening with speculation on the future, and then narrowing with regret.

Now there would be no settling down on the plantation near Frederick. Peggy Willing would not come home with him as a bride to be mistress there. Ecuyer was gone, that plucky little devil. No hands of whist and no bottles of Burgundy before the fire in the evenings together. Those capable of conversation always died first, exhausted by trying to explain the obvious. And he would have liked to talk it out with S. Ecuyer as a neighbour. In Maryland they might both have cultivated adjoining gardens. But silence would sit before the fire at Frederick now. He shivered with an uncomfortable premonition. . . .

Peggy would not be waiting for him at Carlisle. She would not be watching for him when he marched in. None of her family, not even Ed Shippen, would be there. Colonel Burd, as a dutiful son-in-law of the family Shippen, would be dutifully sulking at Lancaster, glad of an excuse to stay away. A triumph—but no place to lay his head afterward, and no pretty head beside him on the pillow. Well, it would be headquarters again, a military family. But, by God, he'd set himself up well in Philadelphia for a while before he left for Florida. He'd hold his head high, despite Peggy. He'd entertain. Let the men be received with acclamations, they certainly deserved it. But the poor rescued captives would need something more sustaining than huzzas. And he'd see the people he had liberated taken care of. Yes, he'd look after them; see that every last one of them, orphans and all, found work or a place they could call home. After that, for him—Pensacola.

He brought the column to a halt and for the last time rode up and down it, with his hat off, while the men closed up. Another quarter of a mile and they would be entering the town. There was a certain military pathos in thus seeing his small but victorious army all drawn up in familiar formation for the last time. They understood. They began cheering him as he passed. He sent the 42nd Highlanders forward. They deserved the van. The bagpipes struck up "When All the Blue Bonnets Came Over the Border," the drums danced. The column stepped out like one man. A thousand times they had all dreamed of this. In the square at Carlisle the crowd began to roar.

It was due to sheer blind luck, and a little more, that both Salathiel and Frances were in Carlisle the day "Gineral Buckey" marched in. Jim Fergus had come back from Lancaster only the morning before, and, happening to meet Mr. Williams on the square, he had heard about the death of Mr. Glen. Mr. Glen had then been buried but a few days, a hasty funeral attended by some friends but none of the family. For both the Glen boys were known to be away, and so far as Mr. Williams or anybody else knew, there was no one at the mill but two German redemptioners.

No, the wagon had not come back from the mill next morning to get him. Nor had Mr. Williams had time yet to ride out to Boiling Springs. He and his wife had had their hands quite full. Something had to be done with a dead man pretty quick. Well, they had done the best they could. No one even knew where Mrs. Glen was buried. The commandant had "loaned" them a pine coffin, whatever that meant. Who would pay for it? Mr. Glen had been a man of property. But where were his heirs, and who was his lawyer? At least the interment had been Christian. Mr. Williams would not listen to what Jim Fergus was trying to say. He was out of pocket two pounds ten and was not to be interrupted. It was a serious matter for a small grocer like himself, these days, when even dying came so high.

Beyond saying that at least one of the Glen boys would soon return with Bouquet, Jim Fergus had not been able to offer Mr. Williams much comfort. He thought he would not add to the good man's perplexity by mentioning anything about Mrs. Larned, the Albines, and all that. But, good Lord, what *had* become of the old lady? Doubtless, Mr. Honeywell had departed for Boston as he had said, and Jim strongly suspected the German boys had cleared out, too. Had they left the old lady alone or had they fixed her? Had the Albines found her yet? Jim was genuinely concerned. He was a good friend of the Glens'. Also he'd liked Salathiel. He was tired after the trip to Lancaster, but he'd ride down to the mill that evening and find out, just as soon as he could get his mare's off-shoe tightened.

So, ride down he did, and arrived about suppertime. The Albines were there, and he soon heard all about Mrs. Larned, or all that there was to hear. It seemed bad. He was inclined to blame the German redemptioners. He didn't take much stock in the moccasin tracks at the foot of the ladder. Maybe old Doc Scarlet had come in for some meal and found her lying there. Like enough, agreed Salathiel. But the doc had lit out for the mountains. He'd just naturally do that, insisted Jim. Well, there was no way of finding out immejit. They'd have to wait and trace down the redemptioners. Maybe they could? But it would take time. Meanwhile, the Albines were much confused and not a little embarrassed at finding themselves, and no one else, at home at the mill.

Jim Fergus was not so much concerned about that as were Salathiel and Frances. It was a lucky happenstance for the Glens, he argued. They'd better stay on until one of the Glen boys came home. He'd take it on himself to say he thought both the brothers would be pleased. Any drunken fool might come along and burn the whole place down. No, no, they must stay until they heard. All he knew was that either John or Martin would be back sooner or later, and that the old man had made a will by the advice of a smart lawyer. "A man by the name of Ed Yates, practises out of Lancaster, when he ain't ridin' the borders on Penn family affairs." They could get in touch with him if they wanted to. Mr. Yates would be in Carlisle on a land case tomorrow, he'd heard him say only last Tuesday up at Lancaster. Yates had asked him to get him a place to stay at the Williamses', and, by God, he'd forgotten to do it. "Doggone it"—he smote his knee with vexation.

"Well, I'll be damned," said Salathiel. "I'll be double damned!" He and Frances looked at each other. Frances laughed.

"Sure, and it's fate," she said. "I'll be after makin' up one o' the Glens' bedrooms for ye, Mr. Fairgus. Ye're the most welcome body with a soul in it I've seen for many a long day. And it's a koind heart ye have, too. I was beginnin' to think that the rest of the world had been destroyed intirely, sittin' here listenin' to the sound of fallin' water. But it's a snug, sunny little house, and Sal has shot a turkey for supper. Bridget, put your dolls to bed now and do up yer hair. We have company."

Jim Fergus was favourably impressed. The house shone. The supper was excellent. He listened to the murmur of prayers after Bridget went off to bed. Sal Albine had found himself a mighty spry young wife. The Glens were lucky. He'd drop in this way again. The ford was a short cut to Shippensburg. Poor old Mrs. Larned, what a fall she'd had! He yawned, had a nip, and went to bed.

Next morning they were up bright and early. Salathiel put Enna in the Glens' two-wheeled cart and drove off to town with Frances beside him. Jed and Bridget were left to keep house together. They hoped to find Yates at Carlisle and persuade him to come back with them. That, Frances suggested, might not be so hard to do. But what she needed was another woman in the house. A lawyer would not be much help in having a baby, she opined. Salathiel agreed, but drove on steadily. Enna made a good cart horse, he observed.

When they got to LeTort's they heard the general's music coming down the great western road. And Jim Fergus kept riding up behind them shouting out what it was. They were caught in the crowd rushing to town, and if Salathiel hadn't turned Enna off the road and driven the little cart directly across the fields, they might never have got into the square at all. As it was, they were stopped just at the corner of High Street and the stockade by a sergeant of the guard, an old Fort Pitter whom Salathiel recognized, and forced back against the wall. The commandant and his staff were only a few rods away to his right. Luck was still with him. He could see the whole show from here.

"How be the Sweeney twins over at Pittsburgh, sergeant?" asked Salathiel mildly. "Or do ye ever hear from there any more?"

The sergeant came closer. "So, it's yourself," said he, "the little captain's Injun boy turned country gintleman—and the captain's mare, too!" He looked at Frances appreciatively. He winked. "All right, keep your big mouth and your little harse quiet, and I'll niver ask ye how it is ye've lost an ear."

"Now, how *did* ye lose it, Sal?" demanded Frances, throwing herself into the spirit of the occasion.

Salathiel tied Enna firmly, climbed into the cart, and waited. Up the road the bagpipes and drums broke out with "When All the Blue Bonnets Came Over the Border." The crowd roared and stared at the corner —where the cart was tied.

The general's music marched into the square first. The drummers were ragged, hatless, and mostly boys, but they were veterans; and they knew they were good. Their elbows all lifted together while their drumsticks shivered in a rhythmic mist. They stopped. The brass trumpets tossed, shouted triumphantly, and the drums resumed.

The crowd in the square was lifted clean off its feet. Some people began to try to dance and holler where they stood. A happy breeze of feminine voices seemed to breathe through the place. Even little men began to bellow, and the staff horses pranced. The rigadoon continued as the music, drums, fifes, bugles, and bagpipes, marched across the square to the south border, countermarched, and stood playing—more softly now—but ready to burst into new tunes and appropriate flourishes as each regiment or unit turned the corner of the stockade to march in review across the square.

The massed weather-beaten, shot-torn, faded colours of the 42nd, 77th, and 60th royal regiments and Royal Americans and the flags of the Pennsylvania militia battalions appeared next. They were met by a respectful silence, for everyone now craned his neck to see what came next. The drums flourished, the pipes squealed, and the 42nd Highlanders, white knees flashing, kilts and tartans flaunting, marched into the open space and passed before the commandant. The crowd cheered them wildly. There were many people at Carlisle who remembered the Highlanders, the forlorn hope of the frontier, leaving lonely and in the midst of terror and silence, with Bouquet at their head, only two summers before. The general's compliment to the Highlanders was well understood and taken kindly. Even the backwoodsmen were vociferous, remembering how they had charged at Bushy Run.

"What a pity it can't always be like this," sighed Colonel Clayton, who had never found gratitude associated with buckskins before.

It was only when the Highlanders began to march past them at the corner that Salathiel came fully to appreciate what a nice point of vantage accident and the Irish sergeant had conferred upon him. Sitting in the high-wheeled cart, he and Frances could look directly down into the faces of the men in the marching ranks as they turned the corner. Now and then he recognized someone familiar. Ensign Erskine, a lieutenant now, and the four surviving Alexanders replied to his happy yell. Then the Royal Americans began to pass, the old companies from Fort Pitt.

His hands and voice were kept busy. Even the captains gave him a pleasant nod. Well, well . . . they seemed to say, as they smiled and marched on. And now the general was coming. Yes, there was Buckey himself.

He was riding a shaggy-looking little horse. He looked faded and warworn. Captain Ourry was acting adjutant. Bouquet must have brought him along from Bedford. But Ourry was never much on a horse, either. Why, the crowd didn't seem to realize who the general was! Salathiel stood up in the cart and began to roar his name.

The crowd caught on, the place rocked with cheers.

Bouquet passed within ten feet of the cart. He looked up at the tall fellow waving a hat and roaring his name, with an amused smile. That terrible ragged ear—where had he seen it before? . . . but yes! He made a wide cordial gesture, he took off his hat and bowed in his saddle to Frances.

The crowd began to cheer her. It was the proudest and happiest moment of her life. "Oh, Sal," she gasped, "oh, Sal, he really knew ye. Ye'll be after takin' me now to see him at headquarters, won't ye, Sal? The grand, good man! To think that we might have missed him! Oh, I think I'm really married to ye now. Now won't ye . . ."

"I'll take ye," he said.

After that the rest of the procession was bound to be something of an anticlimax to the Albines, but not to the rest of the crowd. What they were most eagerly expecting was the captivated.

Over there, a few rods away, Salathiel saw Buckey being welcomed by the commandant. There was a deal of saluting and hat-raising. People were stepping up to shake hands with the general. My, my, what a powwow! Mr. Tilingham, the schoolmaster, began to try to read a Latin address he had composed but had not had time to memorize, and against the bagpipes, too. Buckey finally patted him on the head like a big dog, and the committee and staff dissolved in laughter. The drums and bagpipes took over. The remnants of the 77th Royal were passing, veterans of campaigns from Cuba to the Ohio. But few people remembered that now.

The big ovation, naturally enough, fell to the green-coated, brown, and buckskin-clad Pennsylvania battalions, especially to the Rangers, and the Light Infantry with bucktails in their hats. The town went wild over the "country troops". Only *they* were really coming home. Friends and relatives began to break through the line of redcoats that held the sidelines, and there was no stopping them. Wives, mothers, and sweethearts found their men. But some were forever absent, and there were cries of anguish mixed with cheers and laughter, and few dry eyes. With the return of the home troops the culmination was reached, and the military precision of the occasion began to disintegrate.

At the corner of the square a hostile roar turned all heads in that direc-

tion, and rapidly bore down the din of cheering with a welcome of
another kind. Three open ammunition wagons surrounded by a company of the 77th with fixed bayonets entered the square at a slow walk.
A threatening silence gradually grew, and accompanied them. Why was
it, Salathiel wondered, that Indians in wagons always rode standing up?

But so they did, packed in solidly, all standing up and looking straight
ahead. Their eyes glittered. So did their beads and wampum finery.
They held their coloured blankets close about them.

A furious tempest of catcalls, laughter, and imprecations burst out
from every side and accompanied the end of their stolid progress across
the square. These were the Indians who would not be separated either
by threats or cajolery from their beloved adopted captives. Despite all
that Bouquet could do, they had followed them and the army downcountry. Now, for their own protection, the general had loaded them
into wagons and was sending them to jail.

Here and there lank-haired men in buckskins ducked under the arms
of the line guards and ran out to menace the wagons, threatening to
combine for mischief. But they were stopped cold by the hedge of
bayonets. And the helpless contents of the wagons were safely lodged
in jail. The grenadiers of the 77th immediately surrounded the building
and prepared to camp there. Bouquet was taking no chances of another
Paxtang massacre—and the renewal of the Indian war.

The captivated now began to arrive amidst enormous tumult and excitement at the south end of the square. There was a universal rush in
that direction.

A line of seventeen wagons interspersed with men, women, and children walking, or in a few cases mounted on the sorriest of nags, forced
its way slowly into the crowd at the bottom of the square. They were
preceded by the remains of Bouquet's Virginia Rangers, whose use of
rifle-butts on the toes and corns of the too curious cleared the necessary
space for the liberated to continue to breathe in, unload their dunnage,
and encamp. The detachment of Royal Americans that had marched
beside them all the way from the western Ohio woods was now withdrawn. Captain Morgan of the Virginia Rangers took charge.

The scene that ensued transcended the powers of several gentlemen
who afterward tried to describe it. Ecstasy, pathos, tragedy, and dumb
disappointment were epitomized. For a few poignant hours all the emotions attributed to heaven, hell, or limbo found their genuine earthen
mix. The long lost, the supposed dead returned. Children rushed screaming to throw themselves on the breasts of parents. Small daughters
grown to be young women in the wilderness laid their cheeks darkened
by far-western suns against the pale cheeks of their mothers and begged
them to repeat the cherished music of their half-forgotten names. Shy
orphans with scraggly feathers in their hair, their naked legs trembling
under ragged blankets, were tearfully examined by hopeful relatives,

claimed ecstatically and borne off. Or they were patted on the head sadly and left to stand waiting, trying to say who they thought they were. "Me Smitty, me 'itty Yon Smitty," one Saxon-looking child kept shouting. But none of the English Smiths knew him. Little Smitty eventually went home to the valley of Virginia with a big Ranger named Ed Tredigar. Old people, captured many years before, for the most part stood together. Time as well as war had lessened the chance of their being found again by kin. It was not likely that grandchildren would know them. And not many young people did stop to inquire. Only Lillian Johnson of Grand Island found her grandpa. She already had two children of her own holding onto her skirts; but she had kept a small wooden fox grandpa had once whittled out for her. He hobbled off with her without looking back, a warm fireside before him and the cold misery of the forest behind. God, what a little wooden fox could do!

But the babies, the babies with Indian beads around their necks and small moccasins with porcupine quills in starry patterns on their small feet—there was a whole wagonful of babies—some standing up and some crawling around, under the care of two Scotch matrons and a couple of Shawano squaws. Bouquet had seen to that. But the babies? It was hard to know who and whose they were. There was a crowd of women about the wagon. But not so many mothers. They had been scalped. Other women came around the wagon, crying, talking together, wondering. People kept coming up and looking into the baby wagon, and then going away again. Some of the two- and three-year-olds were plausibly claimed. Gaunt women looked bloody death at the nursing squaws they envied, and walked away.

All this for an hour or two in the late-afternoon sunlight, and then suddenly, for the fortunate, the era of captivity was over as early twilight came on.

Up and down the tramped-out "streets" between the lonely wagons of the captivated that still waited glimmering whitely in the public square, those who had *not* found what they had come so hopefully looking for still stood talking together softly in dejected groups. A few still wandered alone, or searched in desperate couples afraid to look at each other, hunting amid the wagons, peering into the faces of half-savage children, asking questions, hoping against hope. A continual wailing now came from the baby wagon, one which was not easily to be assuaged. Captain Morgan now had the supper fires kindled and rations issued, after ascertaining that upwards of seventy people still remained unclaimed. He and his men, tall fellows in fringed buckskins, went about carrying what comfort they could, and explaining with bashful embarrassment why it was necessary to tie up some of the captives, especially the younger ones—"jist for the reason that as soon as yer back gits turned, they slip off like wild deer into the woods ag'in and run back to the Injuns that be waitin' fer 'em. Hit's orders, and until their people come or somebody kin work on their speerits, a light leg-iron at night's the only answer."

The supper fires began to dance, and the shadows wavered on the wagon-tops. A Quaker brought two buckets of fresh foaming milk still warm from the cows, and gave them to an attendant squaw.

"Thee will find it helpful," he said.

"Heap heap good," grunted one of the nursing Indian crones. The babies began to quiet down. The Quaker stood watching the proceedings in the wagon contentedly. The bucket yoke now rested lightly across his neck. There should be more milk in the morning, but he would take the two buckets home tonight. It was hard to get iron hoops in Carlisle.

"A very sensible thing, Friend Tavistock," said a quietly contained voice just behind him.

The Quaker turned slowly. He remembered just in time to keep his hat on. "Thee has a firm memory, Friend Bouquet," he said.

"I seldom forget those who come to help the men in the hospitals," replied the brigadier. "They're not so numerous as to confuse me. It was at the City barracks in the Northern Liberties, if I remember right."

"Yes," said the Quaker. "Not many came to help there, 'tis true. But then the smallpox is always so catching—and that was many years ago."

"Nevertheless . . ." said Bouquet. They stood talking while Friend Tavistock waited for his buckets.

The news that the brigadier was come amongst them spread rapidly. The unclaimed captives, the disappointed people who had not found their lost children or relatives, gathered about the big fire that crackled near the baby wagon, looking at the general, and the Quaker in the brown coat he was talking with, curiously. The children and young people gradually edged forward. That was Buckey there, that was the great man who had brought them back over the mountains. They had seen the chiefs, the terrible fierce warriors, humble before him. The long wampum belts had been laid across his knees while the soldiers stood behind him. Many fine speeches had been made. Buckey was strong and powerful. But standing in the warm light of the dancing supper-fire he looked different. He looked tired and had a sad smile. Maybe he would help them now, if somebody would only ask him.

Bouquet felt their eyes upon him, and turned. They were all looking at him. Bon Dieu!

He beckoned to them to draw in closer about him, with a familiar personal word here and there for some of the captives he knew. Tomorrow, he said, they would all be moved out to the camp that had been prepared for them at LeTort's Springs. It had been a heroic march they had made over the mountains from Fort Pitt in the depth of winter. Things would be better in the new huts at the camp. Let those who had not found their own dear people take heart. They might still find them —let them hope on and be patient. To those who had no place to go, and for the orphans, he would see that they were taken care of. There were many good people in Philadelphia, at Lancaster, and in other towns and on farms, who would open their hearts and their homes to the captivated. Good men in the assembly and the governor himself had them in mind. Before he left the province he would promise them that everyone, great and small, should have a decent place and honest work to go home to. He had laid that upon his honour and upon his soul. For those who had been beguiled by their Indian captors and would return to the ways of the wilderness, he asked them to consider well what they were doing. Let them be patient and try to learn.

His voice ceased, but they still stood looking at him standing alone with drooping epaulets in the red firelight, the shadowy Quaker behind him.

"Be ye goin' to leave us, gineral?" asked an old woman in a cracked voice, leaning on a stick.

"The king hath commanded me to far southern parts," he replied. "But I shall still be with you for a while."

A sigh went up from the circle. "God bless you, Buckey," someone said. There were a number of amens.

A five-year-old in ragged deerskins and the fragment of a trade blanket walked out and gravely shook hands with the general. He then presented him with his chief treasure. "Blow it, general. Blow it," the boy said.

Bouquet looked at his gift gravely. It was a long white willow whistle with two red-robin feathers tied on little strings at the end.

"It blows," insisted the child.

"Thank you, my boy," said the brigadier. He put the whistle to his lips and blew hard. He puffed out his cheeks. A splendid squawking squall emerged from the thin tube. The red feathers danced forward in his breath. The crowd was delighted.

He blew on the willow whistle long and hard. . . .

At the bare and quite unprepossessing headquarters in the camp at LeTort Springs, Captain Ourry already had all the marching orders for the regulars laid out on the table, ready to be signed. The Royal Americans and the 42nd were to march early next morning for Lancaster. Some of them were to go in wagons, and it was time to get the orders to the colonels. Also, it was long after suppertime. Captain Ourry was hungry. Jesus, where in the name of the fifteen colonial governors was the general?

There was a rout at the new town hall that night and the brigadier must be there to answer the speeches. Under no consideration was Ourry going to do *that* for him.

At that moment the thin sound of a shrill whistle commenced to sound outside the barrack door. The three clerks sat up, with their plumes behind their ears, listening. The whistle continued.

Now, there are *some* things which even an adjutant doesn't have to stand for. Captain Ourry arose, upsetting his desk stool, and strode furiously towards the door. He flung it open indignantly. . . .

Salathiel and Frances had not joined the crowd in going to look at the captivated. For many reasons it would have been more than Salathiel could bear. Also he was afraid Frances might want to bring some babies home. They sat in the cart after the captivated passed and the crowd broke up about them, rather doubtful just what to do. It was in that way they saw what nearly everyone else had missed. Long after the rearguard had passed and the music had stopped playing at the north end of the square, a lone farm wagon appeared, pulled by a single sway-back nag. There were no less than five ministers seated in it. The Reverend James McArdle and the Reverend Charles Puffin, the chaplain at Fort Bedford, were on the front seat. They looked over the heads of the crowd in the square and into the future with a fixed and enthusiastic expression.

Salathiel ducked. He found it necessary just then to be sure that Enna was firmly tied to her post. The wagon with its holy freight moved slowly forward and disappeared up the road on the other side of the square. Salathiel thought it just as well not to tell Frances who and what had passed.

A few minutes later they were interrupted by the familiar voice of Yates, who stood with his hand resting on the side board and looking up at them quizzically.

"I've just had a good talk with your friend Jim Fergus," he said. "Don't you think it would be a good idea to come across the square to the Williamses' and spend the night there? Mrs. Williams says she'll make room in her own bed for Mistress Albine. You and I, Sal, can roll up in our cloaks in the back hall. It won't be so bad, and I really think you'd better come and talk over the Glen affair. Besides, this will be a memorable night in Carlisle, you know. Bouquet has come home—and the war's over. I suppose you'll be wanting to make plans for moving to the City now."

"That's about the size of it," replied Salathiel.

25. Applewood and Sealing Wax

IT IS DEFINITELY a pity that the title of "counsellor", rather than that of "attorney-at-law", was not the usage of the bar of the Province of Pennsylvania before which Edward Hamilton Yates, Esquire, had the honour to practise; for while he was very much an attorney and constantly at law, it was as a counsellor in the art of conducting life's more serious affairs in general rather than arguing legal cases in particular that he most shone as a lawyer.

And Yates's success in this advisory and admonitory capacity was due not alone to a technical knowledge of the law and statutes but also to a fine sense of justice both innate and cultivated. Add to this, the peculiar flavour of his amused and amusing charm, his disarming smile, and his singular eye; and it was difficult for most people not to accede to, or at least to acquiesce in, any points of law, equity, or logic which he undertook to defend or promote by his dapper and fearless personality.

As a friendly adviser, then, Mr. Yates was like a compass whose true north was the opposite pole of folly. Not occasionally it did take both courage and intelligence to follow his counsels, but few who took his advice were ultimately disappointed. All of which might be summed up in Salathiel's homely remark the morning after Brigadier Bouquet's arrival at Carlisle, to the effect that Ed Yates was a damned good man to have on *your* side, and his cleverness a kind of friendly virtue.

Certainly, the results of the morning were good warrant for Salathiel's assertion, for the affairs of the Albines were straightened out in a manner that seemed little short of magical to Salathiel, and finally forced even Frances to revise her estimate as to the value of having a lawyer and a good friend actually in and about the house.

Even while they were washing together, stripped to the waist, under the frosty water that fell from Mr. Williams's pump, early that morning, Yates had cross-questioned Salathiel. And while they were having their bacon, eggs, hominy, and small beer together later on, he had arrived at certain conclusions as to the exact items which it was advisable to cope with in order to relieve Salathiel's perplexities and settle the Glen estate. Most of his legal cogitations took place while Mr. Williams and his wife kept repeating still perplexing and expensive details of Mr. Glen's mysterious demise. But while Yates picked over his victuals he also picked over what brains there were present, and arose from his breakfast refreshed by certain salient points in an otherwise trivial conversation.

For it was Yates's custom, after breakfast, to retire to his chamber and, after locking his bedroom door, to go through a bit of physical and mental ritual which had to do with two worlds, this and the other one.

First, he cleaned his teeth with a furred sassafras stick and Eccles' Powder of Desiccated Pearls. Then he attended to his left eye, washing the empty socket and the smooth stone Surgeon Boyd had given him in an emollient elixir. After which he tied a fresh black eye-patch securely in place. After that he shaved and did his hair, usually without powder, unless he were pleading a case, and dressed himself carefully, keeping in mind the visible weather and the probable business of the day. He then pulled all the bed-clothes into the middle of the bed, provided he was staying overnight, so that the servant would have to make the bed up new. After which he knelt down, usually over a chair, and addressed a prayer to the Father of Mankind, which somehow embodied a plea for continued mercy, an act of gratitude and contrition, and a hope for the continuance of a sound body and a clear mind.

His mental preliminaries were more leisurely. They usually consisted in setting down in a diary in brief Latin sentences the events of the day before, together with such items of accounting and other factual reminders as he deemed essential. He then pondered the total result, noting keenly the probable effects of the events of the previous day upon the one which lay immediately before him, he made his final preparations for the campaign of the next twelve hours. These always consisted in putting into or taking out of his leather trunk such articles as the exigencies of the current day required, and transferring them to his portfolio which closed with a silver hasp engraved with the ducal arms of the House of Hamilton. He then put his watch, his keys, and the necessary change to see him through the day into his waistcoat pockets, and assuring himself he had *not* left anything behind or anything of value, he locked his trunk, put on his cloak and neat cocked hat, opened the window to air out the chamber if the weather permitted, and descended the stairs.

On the particular morning in question Mr. Yates varied his program slightly. Instead of going downstairs immediately after locking his trunk, he sat down at a small dressing table, and extracting some foolscap from his portfolio, carefully sketched in and then wrote out in fair-hand three formal statements which he felt would hold good in law, to wit: a lease embodying a waiver as a preliminary agreement, a form of indenture for a minor child, and an agreement between certain parties for the hiring and subsistence of a slave. Having checked these for correct phraseology, he again locked the large leather travelling valise, and returned the key to its ring. His plans for the day thus thoroughly in mind, and the documents he had completed and certain other writing materials in his portfolio, he then descended the stairs.

In all the plans Yates had made it would not be precise to say that he had been entirely and professionally averse to considering his personal interests, since he had decided to include himself in the temporary establishment that he now foresaw, for various reasons, it would be advisable to set up at Mr. Glen's mill. Unexpectedly, he found he had to stay for some weeks at Carlisle in connection with certain of St. Clair's land warrants. But what could be more pleasant or convenient, he thought, than stopping with old friends and in good company? And since by doing this he could also accommodate both his friends and clients, and protect the property for which he was an executor under Mr. Glen's will, he had decided to try to perfect the arrangement.

Frances Melissa and Salathiel were probably the only ones who might prove inimical. They were always talking about moving to Philadelphia. But after a short conversation with Frances, she proved unexpectedly pliable and was soon pleading with Salathiel for a delay at the comfortable mill, while the child was coming on.

Having thus opened the campaign for the day hopefully, the only other thing that remained for Yates to do was to get Mr. Glen's son, Martin, and Arthur St. Clair together with the Albines and Williamses in order to accomplish the rest of his plan. To that end he now acted immediately, and putting on his grey cloak, he made his excuses and departed to call upon Mr. John Byers. It was at that gentleman's residence that he confidently expected to find Arthur St. Clair.

Nothing, in fact, was more certain that morning than finding Arthur St. Clair. He was stopping only a few houses down the street with his good friend, the wagon commissioner, and few people slept sounder and no one liked better to linger in bed a little longer when circumstances permitted than Mr. St. Clair. He was, therefore, very much at home but not yet up when Yates sounded his ardent reveille on Mr. Byers's bright brass knocker—and who should come to the door but the Reverend Mr. Muir Craighead, with his bald pate wrapped in a home-made turban—and his features in a cordial smile.

There was a bright applewood fire going in Mr. Byers's snug little parlour, where they were all having breakfast that morning on Mrs. Byers's only and best marble-topped table. But despite the fire, the minister was taking no chances of catching cold. He continued to wear his turban like a Turk, but for a Christian reason. Next to coughing amongst the congregation, he feared a cold in the head most as the Nemesis of good preaching; so that the loss of his wig had been the incessant topic of his conversation for many days past and was the immediate theme of his salutation to Yates, whom he began to question as to the whereabouts of Salathiel almost as soon as he had opened the door.

"The Lard be praised," said he, leading Yates into the parlour. " 'Tis now over a week since John Byers delivered your friend Albine's message to me that he'd found my best bag, and now you tell me Salathiel's biding practically next door. Well, well, *that's* good news! I wonder if he brought the wig with him?"

"I wouldn't guarantee that," replied Yates. "But I'm sure Sal will be able to put it in shape for you soon."

"Will he now? What a help that'll be! I shall drop in on him immedjit. At the Williamses' you say?" He again touched the faded crimson stuff on his head thoughtfully, while Mr. Byers tried to stifle his laughter in a large blue bowl of coffee.

"Sal will be glad to see you again, Mr. Craighead, I'm sure," continued Yates, suddenly struck by a notion. "But if you *are* going over to the Williamses', kindly be sure to rouse St. Clair first and take him along with you. Tell him it's quite important and urgent. There's to be a bit of a meeting, and he'd best not oversleep himself. Sal will be all the happier to see you if you take St. Clair along."

"Now, I'll *do* that," cried Mr. Craighead emphatically, and departed upstairs hot-foot, where he was soon heard banging at St. Clair's door lustily, and getting sleepy replies.

Thus having assured the reasonably prompt attendance of St. Clair, Yates was about to depart, explaining his necessity of finding young Martin Glen. But Mr. Byers would not hear of it. Mr. Yates must sit down. He must have a dish of coffee. One of the coloured boys could be sent with a note to young Glen's captain. His company was camped just outside the town. Mr. Byers would see to it. He would guarantee young Glen would get to the Williamses' in a jiffy. Pompey could leave now. "Martha, pour Mr. Yates a dish of mocha."

So it was that Mr. Yates sat quite comfortably in the Byerses' snug parlour and discussed a dish of steaming mocha with his host and hostess, as congenial a pair of morning gossips as sat happily at their own board for many miles around. And it would have been surprising if amongst the lively small fry of town gossip with which they regaled their visitor, one or two convenient minnows of information had not lodged in the meshes of Yates's net, which he had learned to make small and fling wide.

It was in this way that he learned further details of Mr. Glen's death and burial, his host's concern over the disappearance of Mrs. Larned, the pertinent fact that *both* the Glen boys had been courting the same girl at Conestoga, and, of course, all about the loss and finding of Mr. Craighead's wig. After which, Mr. Byers could not refrain from telling in his most finished humorous manner what *he* had heard had happened at Stottelmyer's stable the first morning after the Albines came to town. There were many versions of the affair going about Carlisle, but Mr. Byers guaranteed that he *knew*.

Hence it happened that about half an hour later, when St. Clair and Mr. Craighead finally did come downstairs, they descended into a gale of laughter. They were even able to join in themselves heartily, once Mr. Byers repeated his story and they discovered that the merriment was not at their expense. Mr. Craighead was now fully dressed in his decent black suit, with a starched clerical stock. And he also held a respectable black chapeau under his arm, ready to clap it down on the India silk handkerchief swathed about his shaven poll, as soon as he went out.

"At least," Yates remarked, "it will prevent you from being taken for a tonsured papist in disguise, Mr. Craighead. I understand there are several priests of the old religion, out of Maryland, running loose amongst these hills."

"Shocking," said Mr. Craighead, looking suddenly nervous. It had never occurred to him he might be taken for a Roman priest. "I'd be consternated if any such report ever got about." It made him all the more anxious to see Salathiel. But it was only decent to let St. Clair finish breakfast, he felt, and to wait for the return of the coloured boy with young Martin Glen. So the talk went on while the applewood burned smoothly, and Mr. Craighead's only sop to his impatience was a rather doubtful twinkle in Mr. Yates's single eye.

Yates was quite content to delay a little. He was picking up a deal of minor information that would stand him in good stead in the meeting at the Williamses' that was soon to follow. He thought he saw the way now to settle the affairs, not only of the Albines but of his several clients and other friends, quite satisfactorily and in the round for some months to come. And it also occurred to him that Mr. Craighead's wig was not the only one at Carlisle that might need attention. And that Mr. Albine, if he cared to, might profit considerably thereby. There were all the regular officers, for instance, whose false hair had been so considerably disarranged by the exigencies of an Indian campaign. Yates chuckled aloud, and he might again have had to explain himself had not Mr. Byers's boy, Pompey, returned with the news that young Martin Glen had been excused from morning drill by his captain and was even now waiting in the Williamses' parlour. "An' he done take de news ob his pappy's death hahd," said Pompey.

"No doubt, no doubt," murmured Mr. Byers. "Poor fellow, I thought he might have heard of it before."

"I think we'd better adjourn to the Williamses' without further delay," said Yates. Thanking Mrs. Byers and his spouse for their morning hospitality, he and St. Clair and Mr. Craighead walked hastily up the street.

Mr. and Mrs. Williams, the Albines, and young Mr. Martin Glen, who had quite evidently *not* yet been introduced to anybody, received the newcomers in the Williamses' best front room. There was no fire there and the atmosphere was not only frigid but sadly constrained; although tempered, Mr. Yates noted, with precisely the proper lugubrious respectability on the part of the Williamses. Mr. Craighead, for one, was so much impressed by it that he forbore for more than half an hour to say anything about his wig, although he did nod hopefully at Salathiel and received an encouraging wink in return. Nevertheless, and despite the fact that St. Clair called for a fire immediately, and got it, Mr. Craighead always remembered the occasion as one which required the exercise of considerable Christian forbearance and patience on the part of a certain clergyman.

The truth was it was a legal rather than a clerical occasion. And Yates moved so skilfully and so tactfully into the arena of action that it was soon a nice question as to whether he or the fire was the more efficient source of the light and warmth that now so rapidly pervaded the frigid gloom of the cold front room.

Young Martin Glen was, of course, rejoiced to see his father's attorney, and to find somebody on his side, as he bluntly put it. But Yates put an end to all taking of sides by immediately expressing with a plaintive twist of funereal eloquence the immeasurable sorrow and horrid sense of shock felt by the united company at the untimely and unexpected departure of so virtuous and kindly a man as the late Mr. Glen. How he would be missed! So phrased, Yates's gentle opening of the case amounted to an elegant bit of threnody, and all who had not actually been moved by the event were now deeply touched by the attorney's kindly and deeply poetic words.

For the first time young Martin fully realized from what virtuous loins he must have sprung. Tears of natural pride rather than a mist of indignation now suffused his eyes. Mrs. Williams herself was not able to refrain from letting fall the damp overflow of a neighbourly heart into the conveniently absorbent lap of her apron. Nor was this aquid tribute to the virtues of the deceased at all diminished, rather it was increased, when she heard the charitable and sensible offices of herself and her spouse celebrated with an unexpected and tender applause. The small expenses which the Williamses had so generously incurred in burying Mr. Glen were now guaranteed to be forthcoming immediately from the miller's estate; and, in addition, as a kind of mortuary bonus and just dividend of appreciation, two fine jet mourners' rings, worth not a whit less than a pound apiece, were apportioned to herself and her husband. To which proposition, since Yates looked at him so fixedly, young Martin was compelled to nod an immediate and solemn acquiescence.

Mr. Yates now swept aside the death of Mr. Glen and the tragedy of poor Mrs. Larned as misfortunes. And he then began to prove to Martin Glen what an essentially fortunate young man he actually was. For, had not the passing of both Mr. Glen and Mrs. Larned occurred in a manner as merciful to them as possible, and more fortunate to their heirs, assigns, and survivors than *they* had any right or reason to expect? How much worse and sadly otherwise it might have been!

Mr. Glen might have died alone at the mill, deserted by his unfaithful servants, and left to be devoured by rats. Instead of which, it had been vouchsafed to Mr. Glen to depart this life on the front porch of pious and kindly neighbours. And old Mrs. Larned, too, might she not also be said to be only the devoted victim of a wise Providence? She seemed to have been providentially sent to replace Mr. Glen at the mill, a faithful caretaker *ad interim*. And scarcely had she been removed, by the mysterious will of God, when those whom she had manifestly been preparing to receive providentially appeared to continue her good offices. "And," said Yates, "is it not the best part of our childish wisdom to take hold of the hand of Providence, which seems to have been so happily extended to us, and to continue to walk in the direction in which we are manifestly being led?

"To that end I thought it well this morning to prepare certain papers to be signed," he added, and turning to open his portfolio, he set out on the table before him an ink-horn, a couple of plumed pens, sealing wax, a sand-box, and several sheets of legal paper with blocks of his small but clear professional script on them.

So that's what he was doing upstairs, thought Salathiel. But isn't Ned going a bit too far? The next thing, he will be trying to show young Glen that his father's death was a special act and favourable dispensation . . . that he ought to be glad. Salathiel, however, was to learn that his friend did not make serious mistakes like that.

"You see," said Yates, "young Martin here finds himself in difficult circumstances in regard to taking immediate possession of his father's estate. He is only one of two heirs. The other, Mr. John Glen, his brother, has probably not yet learned of his father's death, since he left some time ago for Conestoga, in order to get some wrought-iron work done for the mill machinery, I'm told—but I fear he has been detained there for softer work on even more malleable metal."

"Oh, the foxy old polecat!" exclaimed young Martin, and began to sputter. "The last thing John promised me was he wouldn't go poking around Clara over at Conestoga, until the war was over and I came home. That was the bargain between us, if I went to war."

"*H-m-m*," said Yates, "I fear your affectionate brother has anticipated the calendar slightly, although the war may be said to be over."

"But *I'm* still in the service!" exclaimed Martin. "Now look here, Mr. Yates, you've got to help me, sir. If Clara . . . if that derned skunk . . . !"

"I've anticipated your natural feelings under the circumstances, Martin," said Yates. "Mr. Byers has already showed his good offices, and I'm sure Mr. St. Clair will be pleased to aid in expediting your discharge. Your captain, I believe, is a Scot."

"McCalister, Captain McCalister," mumbled Martin without any enthusiasm. "But maybe he'd give me a furlough to Conestoga. Even a couple of days would help, before my discharge."

"I'll do you the service if I can, young man," said St. Clair. "And I know Don McCalister."

"Oh my, oh, sir, if you *only* will," cried Martin. "I'll never forget it, I promise you."

"Meanwhile," continued Yates, "since both of Mr. Glen's heirs will probably be at Conestoga for some time to come, there is the matter of the care of the mill property. It would be most inadvisable to permit it to stand empty and unguarded."

"I don't give a damn—" began Martin.

"No, but as executor of your father's will, I must and do," insisted Yates. "And it seems to me that you could not do better than make an arrangement with the good people who are already providentially occupying the premises to continue to do so, and to look after the place and continue the business of the mill, while you and your brother are settling your, *ahem*, mutual affairs at Conestoga."

"That's just elegant, but what'll John say?" cried Martin.

"I've drawn the lease with an agreement to take care of that," said Yates. "Under your father's will, our two signatures will be sufficient, since it is a matter of preserving the property."

Martin extended his hand for a pen eagerly and would have signed forthwith if Yates had not cautioned him to read the paper.

"You see," he pointed out, "this not only takes care of the legality of Mr. and Mrs. Albine's present occupancy of the mill property, but also gives them tenancy for the full quarter beginning New Year's Day, 1765, they to take all care of the premises and such runs of the mill and other items of business as may come up during your and your brother's absence. The ten shillings a month rent is merely nominal to be sure about the value-received clause. As I expect to board with the Albines for some weeks to come," he added, looking at Frances, "you and your brother can be well assured that the property will be looked after until you settle your difficulties. By the way, Martin, it's about time you formally met your new tenants." He motioned to Salathiel and Frances to come forward. Frances made a grave curtsy to her young soldier landlord.

Thus, with all due formality, the lease on the mill property at Boiling Springs was duly signed and sealed, Mr. and Mrs. Williams being greatly flattered and much pleased at being called up to act as witnesses. The ink on the lease was scarcely dry, however, before Martin Glen was making his excuses and bouncing down the street to be sure Mr. Byers was going to go with him to see Captain McCalister—and would Mr. St. Clair be sure, please, not to forget his promise?

"Not where a lady's concerned, Mr. Glen," said St. Clair, "provided she's one of the truly fair."

"Oh, she's lovely, she's the toast of all Conestoga," shouted Martin. "Clara? My God!" Then he blushed to the roots of his curly red hair and rushed out.

"'Pon my word," exclaimed St. Clair, "I hope that young cockerel does win his girl. I'll see McCalister today. You have my promise, if that's all you wanted with me," said he, rising.

"There's something that concerns you much more nearly, Arthur," replied Yates. "As for young Martin, freshest advices from Conestoga have it that John is not faring so well. But what'll concern you more is the suggestion you made to me at Lancaster that we make a definite arrangement about Jed."

"Ah!" said St. Clair, taking the paper that Yates handed him. "Good! I simply can't have that rascal on my hands any more when I ride the western road, and Mrs. St. Clair is at her wit's end with what to do with him in the City. He's the black Lothario of the second ward. Yet I don't want to sell him. Hmm, yes. This will do well enough, if Albine here will agree. I might rent Jed out to the stone-cutters, but like enough he'd run off." He passed the papers to Salathiel.

It was an agreement by which Salathiel was to provide Jed with board, shelter, and clothes for the next six months, and to receive his services "as a house servant" in return. If Jed ran away, Salathiel would be responsible to the extent of fifty pounds.

Both parties being willing, the bill of rental for a chattel was signed, witnessed, and sealed.

"One thing more," Yates was saying as he picked up the last of the written sheets and looked at Frances and Salathiel. "You young folks who have just come out of the woods into the realm of legal papers, this concerns you both deeply, I'm sure. You know, since Mrs. Larned has gone, you are going to have to do something definite about Bridget. Now, legal adoption is a rather involved matter, and not much indulged in in these parts. Later some of Bridget's relatives may show up. But meanwhile, you won't want to let her remain a waif. To save trouble, I have drawn up an indenture here, binding her out to you, Sal, until she's eighteen. You'll have to produce her before a magistrate and swear to the provisions for her nurture before this can be registered, but you can easily do that any day now, and meanwhile I'd advise you to sign the paper."

"She'll belong to me, too, won't she?" demanded Frances, her colour mounting and then growing pale. She knew that Yates was avoiding a certain marriage difficulty.

"In fact she'll be a child of your household," he answered. "The indenture is a helpful formality."

"Sign it then, Sal," said Frances eagerly. "And I'd like to see anyone that durst try to take her away from us now."

Yates smiled, and Salathiel signed.

"Ah," said Yates, shading his good eye with one hand, "a proper morning's work, I take it. And now—Mr. and Mrs. Williams!"

He shook out some guineas on the table from his ring-purse. "These will reimburse you, my friends, for your expenses in burying your neighbour, and perhaps a little more. The mourning rings will have to come later. It will take some time to probate the will and settle Mr. Glen's estate."

"Naturally," mumbled Mr. Williams, "of course." He cleared his throat as he signed the receipt that Yates extended to him, and turned the money over to his wife.

A warm atmosphere of general satisfaction and mutual gratulation suddenly pervaded the room. Everybody but Mr. Craighead got up and shook hands with one another.

"Bejasus," whispered Frances to Yates, "if iver I find me in a pickle, 'tis yourself I'll be after askin' to pull me out of the brine."

"I accept the tribute—and responsibility too," he added. He took her fingers that showed out of her black knitted half-gloves and pressed them lightly to his lips. "It's a bargain," said he.

"Here, here, Ned, what's going on?" called Salathiel. "If you're thinkin' of takin' my gal for the retainer, it's too high a fee." He put his arm around Frances possessively. "Not that we're not beholden to you more than I can say," he blurted out. "I can't think of a single thing that you've overlooked . . ."

"My wig," said Mr. Craighead, coming forward. "You've forgotten my best Sabbath hair."

"That," said Yates, laughing, "is something you and the good minister will have to settle between you, Sal," said he. "I'm long overdue at the courthouse to file Mr. Glen's will." He gathered up his papers rapidly, and started for the door.

Salathiel now found himself fully engaged with Mr. Craighead. Before he could hoist his colours, the minister was pouring in his broadsides. The Williamses took the opportunity to leave the room. It was Frances who saw Yates to the door. In the hall he managed to put a bee in her bonnet about the fine prospects at Carlisle for anyone who could and would mend wigs . . . "And I'll see you at the mill day after tomorrow," he said, raising his eyebrows.

"That'll be all right—and any day after that, too," she said. "But board, kindliness—and no more!"

"Precisely that," he answered.

He lifted his hat to her and smiled as he went down the steps. In the parlour she found Salathiel reduced to making all but abject promises to the minister. "Before next Sunday, the wig I must have. It's that, or invite McArdle in to preach."

"I'll tell ye what, *father,*" said Frances, causing Mr. Craighead to blanch, "Sal will fix your wig for you, if you'll tell everyone who did it."

"Now, what's all this?" demanded Salathiel.

"Never you mind, I've got my own good reasons." She then addressed herself directly to Mr. Craighead. "Just tell them who done it, and how well it's done. That's all we ask."

"Why, certainly, madam," replied the minister. "I'll do anything to get my hair back." He shook hands then and left hastily. *Father!*—did he really look like that? It was not until he thought it over at the Byerses' that Mr. Craighead began to see the sense in Frances' remarks. "So that's it!" he suddenly said at dinner to Mrs. Byers, causing her to regard him doubtfully. Mr. Byers had just served him the *next* to the largest mutton chop. Was that *it?* she wondered.

In the parlour at the Williamses', Salathiel and Frances sat down on the sofa together and held hands. Presently she leaned against him and sighed happily. He put his arm around her.

"Wal," drawled Salathiel, "I reckon we can go back to the mill house now. Yes, ma'am, we can just about go home!" He took a deep happy breath.

"Not for a little, not yet," she said.

"What?" he exclaimed, and this time he was genuinely disturbed.

She pressed closer to him. "Let's call on your best friend first," she whispered. "The brigadier will be after expectin' you. Oh, Sal, let's not neglict the opportunity."

26. A Day at Great Headquarters

IN THE PERMANENT CAMP near LeTort's Springs, the morning at headquarters had been a busy one, and not without its peculiar irritations. A number of officers, of both the staff and line, had hangovers from the night before. The new adjutant was among the severer sufferers, since rum punch in quantities always gave Captain Ourry what he called an "echo". That is, when anyone spoke to him in even a medium loud tone, the words seemed to reverberate inside his head. With an echo aboard, Captain Ourry tended to repeat what had already been said. Fortunately, the brigadier understood and didn't think him stupid. Even when he repeated his orders verbatim like a sentry, Bouquet only grinned.

Colonel Haldiman, however, roared. And there had been a terrible lionlike interval just before morning mess over a minor mix-up in the marching orders for the 60th (R.A.) and 42nd regiments. But then the colonel, too, had been up most of the night before. And no doubt, being notified shortly before dawn to start marching for Lancaster was something few officers could endure quietly.

Ah well, mused Ourry, the colonel and his gallant men were gone. By this time they were probably trying to ford the icy Susquehanna. Regimental headquarters for the Royal Americans would be at Lancaster, Colonel Haldiman commanding. The Highlanders would eventually go to Philadelphia into their permanent quarters at Camptown in the Northern Liberties.

Captain Ourry thought of this arrangement with considerable satisfaction. The brigadier was mortal afraid of the smallpox, and always made a point of scattering the troops as soon as he could. Incidentally, it relieved department headquarters at Carlisle of a lot of trouble that was purely regimental. Also it gave the adjutant a chance to clean up his headache, a bottle-cold—and various other odds and ends of military troubles that remained after the long western campaign.

Ourry often wondered just why Bouquet had chosen to promote him. He was not so sure it was not a dubious compliment. As aide to the brigadier, he would be responsible not only for departmental administration, but for the general's official military family, too. Bouquet was a Frenchman by nurture, and he liked to live well when he could. Hardships might be condoned in the wilderness, but it would have to be different when they moved to the City. The brigadier would have to live there as befitted his rank. Well, he would try to improve headquarters mess first, and brighten the aspect of the general's table later. Also there was the serious matter of personal finances, his own and the brigadier's; laundry, the general's badly tattered linen; and his own sorry clothes. It would never do to be called "Captain Lazarus" by the damned macaroni subalterns.

Ourry rested his chin on his hand and tried to gaze into the future. Probably they would stay for some weeks at Carlisle, closing out the campaign. The brigadier would have to go to New York to report, and then come back to Philadelphia to set up temporary headquarters there. After that Pensacola in the new colony, West Florida—*Lord!* But all that delay might give him a chance to perfect arrangements and domestic details.

Meanwhile, he took a surreptitious drag out of a bottle of schnapps. He always carried it well. It was the damned Jamaica rum that got him. He took another good swallow. Almost immediately he felt better. It was about time! Noon mess call would sound presently, and there would be a deal of conversation at the general's table which he wouldn't necessarily desire to repeat like a parrot. What a morning it had been!

Not that the brigadier had not arisen cheerful as usual, calm-voiced and self-contained. It was Colonel Haldiman who had done all the roaring. The brigadier had shown no ill effects of his reception at the town hall last night. He had gone to the hall, drunk a toast to the king and another to "the ladies"; answered the speeches of welcome and thanks most affably; shaken hands all around cordially—and departed for a good night's rest. Ourry, of course, had had to stay; it was the part of a faithful adjutant and aide-de-camp to do so.

The rout, the noise and confusion of the small hours had gone on without the general. The adjutant had managed it alone as well as he could. And it was not until the punch bowl had been emptied five several times that any real trouble had started.

That damned fool creole, Monsieur Molyneaux! What was he doing at Carlisle, anyway? Lieutenant Frazier's challenge, quite inevitable under the circumstances, would have to be withdrawn just the same. How had the brigadier ever heard about it? The very first thing he said when Ourry came on duty that morning was "No duels in the militia, captain. Let them learn to dance without quarrelling. Let the officers fight the savages, and no one else. Arrest both the young coxcombs who made that trouble last night."

That was the way the morning had begun, if you disregarded the trouble before dawn with Colonel Haldiman.

The next thing was a delegation of the evangelical clergy. Scarcely had the last troops marched when the ministers drove in. There were five of them, headed by that crop-eared fanatic, James McArdle. As if there hadn't been enough trouble with *him* at Bedford. Why, he'd devilled poor Ecuyer into his grave. The brigadier, nevertheless, had received them quite courteously.

As far as Ourry could tell, the Reverend Mr. McArdle desired to drive a sharp bargain with the general. McArdle's proposition was that he would drop his complaints about dancing and other more delicate affairs provided the brigadier would lend him some tents and a few engineers to help put up prayer-booths for a big field preaching, one which all the ministers had come to Carlisle to attend.

A visitation of the Holy Spirit was about to occur, Mr. McArdle insisted, and he would like to have the loan of some military equipment suitable for the occasion. The brigadier had demurred. There was no warrant, he said, for lending the king's stores, men or matériel, for what he was pleased to call an "evangelical revel". Mr. McArdle was not only shocked at the expression, but indignant at being refused so small a request.

McArdle was angry that two regiments had quietly been sent away to Lancaster that very morning. He had counted on preaching the Word of God to them. "When many sinners are gathered together," he said, "the work of the Spirit is bound to be more efficacious. I have waited long and prepared patiently for this occasion." The four other clerical gentlemen also considered themselves much aggrieved.

It was the duty of the secular authorities to further the Kingdom of God, McArdle then proclaimed. If the brigadier was genuinely interested in furthering the work of the Spirit, he would order the troops back to Carlisle to attend the field preaching. The Reverend Mr. Puffin, the official Church of England chaplain to the garrison at Fort Bedford, agreed. And it was he undoubtedly who had provoked McArdle to drop to his knees and ask God to touch the general's heart to return the troops to Carlisle.

Two *hallelujahs* accompanied McArdle's fervent petition to heaven; and a rolling chorus of *amens* followed. Owing entirely to the phenomenon of the echo, Captain Ourry contributed an inadvertent *amen* himself as a final remark, much to his own chagrin, the general's secret amusement, and the excitement of the ministers. After this Bouquet permitted a short interval of silence to elapse to restore order.

"*Ahem*," resumed the brigadier a bit dryly, for he was quite used to dealing with the unconscious self-righteous effrontery of the frontier— "you seem to forget, gentlemen, the different stations in life to which it has pleased God in His mysterious wisdom to call us."

"I, for one, fail to see the application of any such text, sir," said Mr. Puffin stiffly.

"Ah, *you*, in particular, have failed notably there, Mr. Puffin," continued Bouquet. "I shall take that up with you later. But, meanwhile, permit me to explain myself in my own house. I refer to these humble headquarters." This the brigadier said hurriedly, raising his hand in anticipation of the protests which his assertion about Mr. Puffin now obviously threatened to bring down on his devoted head. "If you please, gentlemen, if *you* please . . ."

Another moment of hard-won silence, not entirely respectful, ensued.

"My point," resumed Bouquet, "is that while it may be your office by divine commission to shepherd souls towards the realm of the hereafter, it is mine by the king's commission, and sundry acts of Parliament, to dispose of the bodies of fighting men in the sinful kingdom of this world, according to my best, although admittedly fallible, judgment. Now, I do not propose to interfere with or enter into your field of the divine, and you should not rashly presume to advise me in my worldly rôle. In my judgment," he continued, "it was expedient to march two regiments to Lancaster this morning, and the orders stand. Frankly, I am not convinced that marching them back to Carlisle would cause them to enlist en masse in the service of the Kingdom of God, even with the advice and assistance of you gentlemen. A visitation of smallpox is as likely to occur as that of the Holy Spirit, and it is my duty to consider the former contingency."

For a moment or two the self-appointed delegates from Beulah Land sat digesting this thought as well as they could.

"He that is not with us is against us," shouted the Reverend Cadmus Thurston, a thin man with a horse face and inflamed red hair. "*Henry Bouquet, you are an atheist!*"

"Tut, tut, *Cadmus*," replied the brigadier, who was long familiar with the Reverend Mr. Thurston's strict Calvinistic doctrine, "I was baptized at the very fountain of our mutual faith in Geneva; and you will not, I presume, have the effrontery to deny the efficacy of baptism by the Mother Church. I," said the general, leaning forward and pointing inward towards himself with his thumb, "I, *too*, am a certified Child of Light, *Mr.* Thurston."

Mr. McArdle snorted. "Be that as it may, general," he said, "and *if* so, as a Child of Light, you might well lend us a few tents to help erect the tabernacle of the Lord in the wilderness."

"I concede your point, Mr. McArdle, since it is now sensibly and respectfully put, and you shall have your tents. Captain Ourry here is authorized to lend them to you. See that some of the less mouldy of the condemned marquees are issued to Mr. McArdle, captain."

Captain Ourry repeated the orders verbatim, while the ministers looked both impressed and pleased.

"But on the same reciprocal basis, Mr. McArdle," continued Bouquet, "you should aid headquarters in checking the lists of the returned Indian captives. Your work as a missionary beyond the frontiers is well known. No doubt you have saved many souls. Will you not, then, help me in seeing that the bodies of these poor souls are now rescued from the savages? It is the Shawanese especially who are to be watched. They have agreed to bring in to Fort Pitt all those who remain in their hands, by next spring. But I should like to be certain none are being secretly withheld."

"I'll not refuse ye," replied McArdle, "but, tell me, what have ye done with the list written upon bark that Albine carried into Fort Pitt at the risk of his young life, when Ecuyer was besieged there? My memory is no longer so keen, but that list was complete. 'Twould be a pity were it lost."

"Have a search made for the bark list, Ourry," said the general. "If it isn't here, send Fergus for it to Fort Pitt. I do remember now of Captain Ecuyer's speaking of the 'bark roll of the captivated'."

"Aye," groaned McArdle, "Ecuyer! Gone where no further questions can be asked him. Gone! And beyond hope!"

"A godless, obstinate little man," interpolated Mr. Puffin, "without marcy on others or upon his own soul. It would be just like him to have destroyed the list to hinder further the work of salvation."

"It would *not* be like him," said Bouquet, the icy calmness of controlled anger smoothing his voice dangerously. "It would be more like *you*, Mr. Puffin. And I will not have the revered memory of such a devoted and loyal officer as Simeon Ecuyer traduced before my face. Saving your cloth, sir, your assertion is a stinking calumny."

No one had ever seen the brigadier so angry. The veins throbbed in his temples, and he was red with wrath. The attack on a dead comrade had outraged him to the soul, and sparks seemed to leap from his eyes, and the tension in the room was intolerable.

A pretty mess, a fine kettle of fish, thought Captain Ourry, who was standing at rigid attention just beside the general's chair. He was flabbergasted. So were the ministers. They sat staring with white faces; all except McArdle, who had gradually been turning brick-red.

That Mr. Puffin should undertake to reply to the general was, therefore, a matter of no little astonishment. Secretly, even his colleagues felt he had gone too far. But they had not supposed he durst undertake to defend himself. At first he was scarcely audible. They leaned forward to try to catch what he was saying.

"A week ago come Thursday," Mr. Puffin began in a half-whisper, while his voice trembled, "in the middle of the afternoon at Mr. John Inman's house by the Arched Spring at Aughwick, there was a visitation of the Holy Spirit. Our prayers were notably answered. At three of the clock that blessèd afternoon, the Spirit of God overshadowed us. Mr. Thurston and myself were both vouchsafed the gift of many tongues. Mr. McArdle prophesied in a tremendous voice. All of us rejoiced loudly together in a new Pentecost. I received a call, a direct revelation that my work lay in the missionary field. In a holy trance the heavens were opened to me. I heard the voice of my Saviour, the very Voice of God. Can you understand what it is to have the call? I have been called to the mission for the saving of lost souls. I am no longer a member of the Established Church of England. I renounce the laying on of hands, sir. I denounce all worldly and ecclesiastical restraints. I am made free, and subject to the Voice of the Spirit alone. Oh, Lord Almighty, oh, Christ in Heaven!" He checked himself, for at this point his voice threatened to achieve the shrillness of a feminine scream. Also, the Reverend Cadmus Thurston had begun to mutter and to show signs of internal excitement. He cried *amen* loudly, and rose up to address the meeting.

"Sit down, sir," roared Bouquet. "This is not a conventicle." Mr. Thurston sat down, instantly. The general kept looking at Mr. Puffin.

"Have you notified your superior, the Bishop of London, of the step you have taken, Mr. Puffin?" asked Bouquet.

"Not yet, sir, but I shall. That is now only a worldly formality."

The brigadier considered him carefully again, and arrived at a reluctant conclusion.

"Let me relieve you of that formality," he said, "—and your appointment as chaplain at Bedford as well. I shall also save you the trouble of writing the venerable Society for the Propagation of the Gospel to cancel your stipend as a missionary. You can rely upon me to relieve you of *all* such minor mundane affairs, Mr. Puffin. In fact," continued Bouquet, "since *all* you gentlemen are in more or less direct communication with the Almighty, I can see small advantage in your conversing any longer with a mere brigadier general. However, permit me to offer you a glass of inspiration." He sniffed—"Now, Captain Ourry appears to have a distinct odour of the working of the spirit within, or somewhere about him. Captain?"

But no one took advantage of the offer. They sat as though confounded, staring. Finally Bouquet waved his hand affably.

"Show the clergy out, then, captain. Perhaps some of the more inspiring examples of divine handiwork outdoors will interest them. There is a noble view of the mountains from the outer barbican."

"We can see the mountains without your assistance, sir," replied Mr. McArdle in an acidulous tone. The general waved his hand again, indicating his release of all claims on the landscape, whatsoever. "But the tents?" exclaimed Mr. McArdle.

"They are yours as I promised," answered Bouquet, and bowed him out.

Somewhat mollified by this concession to shelter religion, Mr. McArdle followed Captain Ourry to the door of headquarters more cheerfully, and, without pausing to observe the mountains, clambered into the muddy wagon after his four colleagues and rattled down the road towards LeTort's Springs. The progress of the evangelical mission along the roads of this world was dilatory. And there was ample time, before the company reached Carlisle, to discuss the finer shades of meaning in the general's remarks, and to indulge in a bit of mutual chiding.

Thus it was that the day at headquarters got under way. The next hour or two was taken up exclusively by the removal of the remaining unclaimed captives from the square at Carlisle, and settling them in the huts at camp vacated by the 60th only that morning. A large crowd of putative relatives and not a few of the curious followed, and insisted upon staying. It was impossible to separate the sheep from the goats without making scenes, and Ourry had capitulated. The wailing from the baby wagon was now transferred to a room in the log barracks.

It was almost time for the noon mess call when Captain Ourry finally sat down at his desk to fortify himself with his antidote for rum, and take further stock for the future. The schnapps had just begun to convince him that the crisis of the day was really over, when he was confirmed in that opinion by what he afterward considered to be a stroke of luck, both for himself and for the brigadier.

"There's a lidy and gen'leman outside in a two-wheeled country cart, sir," announced the sergeant major, saluting. "The man says as 'ow 'e 'as business with the general." Captain Ourry grimaced. "Rather a decent sort, sir. Drivin' a neat little mare."

"One of the town shopkeepers come to protest sending the troops off before pay-day, I suppose," sighed Ourry. "We'll have the lot of them here by tomorrow."

"No, sir. They don't look it," said the sergeant.

"Show 'em in, show 'em in," sighed Ourry resignedly.

The next moment as fine a looking woman as he had ever seen came proudly into the room, and the frame of the door was familiarly occupied by Captain Ecuyer's man: Salathiel Albine!

"I'll be everlastingly damned!" exclaimed the captain, blinking. "*You!* Rat me, if you're not one huge piece of luck come in the nick of time." He took a deep breath and shouted, "What became of the bark list of the captivated?"

Salathiel smiled, and shook hands calmly with the captain. "I thought you'd be askin' that question. You see, we met McArdle and his friends drivin' out. Oh, yes, *quite* an encounter. I'll tell ye about it later. Yes, I've got the list—here," and he pointed to his breast, which Ourry took to mean his pocket. "But I want you to meet a lady, someone who lives with me now. Happened recently."

"My word, madam, headquarters are greatly honoured. The brigadier will be delighted. You can scarcely imagine how fortunate is your advent this morning." Ourry bowed deeply.

"Oh, I have an idea how it is, captain," replied Frances. "When the gineral bowed to us yisterday, I urged Sal not to fail to call upon him. Sal's always talkin' about old days at Bedford."

"And well he might," cried Ourry. "This is an auspicious reunion.

Permit me to mark it. Orderly, two chairs and three glasses. An old military custom, madam. I hope you'll not mind." Frances did not mind at all. From underneath the desk Ourry produced the bottle of schnapps. Alack, it was only half full! The captain had to send to his quarters for another bottle, immediately.

Now, Ourry admired a lady who drank heartily and daintily at the same time, a girl who became softly radiant at the first glass. After the second, his impression that the difficulties of the day were entirely surmounted was confirmed.

A hundred ideas and surmises had been chasing themselves around in Captain Ourry's suddenly clarified head. In the fortunate presence of the visitors before him he thought he saw the possible solution of many of his difficulties in organizing the new department headquarters. The matter of the bark list was only one item. Salathiel, he remembered, had been a combined "secretary and valet" to Captain Ecuyer. Now, perhaps Salathiel could be persuaded to come back and apply what he must have learned from the captain, for the benefit of the new brigadier. Yes, it might, it ought to be, arranged. As for Frances, she might bring that missing touch of feminine elegance into the domestic arrangements of the general's official household which no bachelor aide-de-camp could ever accomplish. The first step was to detain and to get on famously with his visitors. Details could be laid before the brigadier and perfected later. All of this, he, Ourry, saw in a flash.

After all the amenities he could think of were applied—and all the liquid hospitality advisable—Captain Ourry responded to a sigh and a hint from Frances that they ought to be going, and led them both into the other room to present them to the general.

Bouquet grasped the advantages of having the Albines appear so opportunely. He took the words of explanation out of Ourry's mouth by congratulating him on being freed now of any dependence on Mc-Ardle. And he was much amused at Salathiel's explanation that he could "sing" the list from memory. "That'll be music to my ears, whether you're off key or not," insisted the brigadier.

As for Frances, he was charmed with her.

Bouquet was a soldier-courtier with a Gallic flair for clever conversation. In five minutes they were all talking with him as with an old friend. Captain Ourry was reassured; Salathiel carefully consulted and his advice honoured; Frances complimented in a discerning way. For the first time Frances sniffed the keen air of those higher altitudes to which she aspired. Her laughter conveyed a hint of rapture, and her eyes shone like twin stars twinkling in the lacy haze of her cloudy black bonnet.

Bouquet, on his part, had soon learned as much of the story of his visitors as he thought he needed or ought to know. He pondered Salathiel's progress as something to be noted for future reference, and appraised Frances as a beautiful young female, who *might* go far. The interview might easily have continued if the bugle announcing noon mess had not put a natural end to it.

However, the general's invitation to his table also followed naturally. He laid Frances' hand over his arm gallantly, and her great moment arrived—and passed swiftly—as she emerged from the door of headquarters with the "gineral", while the sentry presented arms.

Melissa was walking on air, Salathiel observed. But he did not begrudge her the triumph. His chief concern was that she should walk steadily. But she was doing that. Yet his concern was only natural under the circumstances, for Captain Ourry tended to deviate from a straight military line of approach. And there was no doubt that his tongue wagged more than was required of an adjutant.

That at least was Salathiel's opinion. It was only a few hundred yards across the parade from headquarters to the old log building where the general's mess was temporarily installed, although Captain Ourry did follow a rather zigzag course. But in that short distance, he managed to spill his plans for annexing Salathiel to headquarters, with a completeness and amplitude that a more sober and less sanguine view of the future would have prevented.

Salathiel listened intently but made noncommittal replies. He would be helpful where he could, for the sake of old days and out of admiration for Bouquet. That much he felt was due the memory of Ecuyer. But he also remembered that when he had left the captain's service, he was through forever with being anyone else's man. Whatever he did now must receive its equivalent reward, and that implied a transaction between equals. What he would do, he reserved for time to unfold. He listened to Ourry and replied with smiles. If the captain took them at more than their face value, that was his affair. Frances, he knew, would not fail to make hay in the sunshine, and he was going to leave the reaping of opportunity largely to her.

Ten officers, and the two visitors, for whom chairs were hastily brought, sat down to luncheon at the brigadier's table. Frances, of course, sat next to Bouquet and on his right. As the only woman present, Frances was naturally the centre of constant attention, which she enjoyed greatly and managed to cope with, without neglecting the brigadier. He was delighted with her salty and naïve anecdotes, her quick responses, and her witty replies. The anecdote of Mr. Craighead's wig convulsed the general and brought down the house. The result later that afternoon was a pile of wigs left at headquarters with fervent prayers on paper for their repair. Salathiel was right. He knew that somehow Frances would make hay.

There was no time for lingering at the table that day or for the customary formalities of leave-taking. The brigadier explained that, what with the departure of two regiments that morning and the moving-in of the Indian captives from the square at Carlisle, the camp was in a turmoil, and everyone frantically engaged.

"But there is something more interesting in camp now than drill and parades of soldiers," Bouquet added. "Let us go and have a look at what Ourry here has managed to do with his unfortunates. I think it will be something for you to remember having seen."

Thus, with Frances leaning on the brigadier's arm, and Ourry, who was now much himself again after a full meal, leading the way with Salathiel—they all set forth on an afternoon's stroll about the camp, one that was to have momentous consequences for several people.

Frau Anna Lininger was a figure of woe, and her troubles were so notable that Henry Mühlenberg, pastor, patriarch, and chronicler, made permanent note of them. A score of prominent Pennsylvanians had had to listen to her story. And she had taken to haunting the headquarters of various generals or colonels, whenever a hopeful expedition westward was getting under way.

She was a dumpy little German peasant woman with moles on her face and scraggly grey hair by the time she took to haunting Colonel Bouquet in the early months of 1763; and after he marched west she stayed at Carlisle through the desperate summer of Pontiac's Rebellion. Time could not wither nor old age abate Frau Lininger's infinite capacity for tears. They ran down between the several moles on her apple-cheeked face as between islands of grief overwhelmed in a spate of sorrow. The trouble with Frau Anna Lininger was that she expected someone to *do* something about her tragedy. Bouquet, among others, came to know her story well. But he not only listened, he heard.

In the great immigration of the 1740's Frau Lininger had come from the Palatinate with her young Bavarian husband and settled in Berks County, Pennsylvania. In course of time, three fine children and a profitable farm were the rewards of their labours. Then in the days of the French and Indian troubles, on an afternoon when Frau Lininger was visiting a neighbour, the hatchet fell.

Her husband and eldest son were horribly murdered while ploughing. The house was burned down, and her two daughters dragged off into the wilderness. Their mother heard about them afterward from a man who escaped with scars of fire on him. The older daughter, a girl in her teens, died while on the march westward; the younger, a child of six, had survived. Her name was Regina—Regina Lininger.

Owing to her mother's dedicated labours, Regina's name was remembered by many at home long after she had forgotten it herself in the damp shades of the forest on the distant Maumee.

Among those who remembered was Henry Bouquet. Even in the desperate hurried spring of 1763 he had found both time and sympathy to listen to the old German woman, who had trudged from the Lehigh valley to Carlisle to tell him the sad things that had happened to her ten years before. Perhaps it was because Bouquet understood and spoke a little German, in a Swiss way, that she had put her complete trust and founded her final hope on his success.

Frau Anna had remained at Carlisle. She went to live at Captain William Rainey's log house on Pomfret Street, where she helped the family in the kitchen and the garden. As the rumours of Bouquet's victories were brought back to Carlisle, she seemed to grow younger and to blossom with hope renewed. And when she was shown the name of her lost darling on the list of captives returned by the Shawanese to Bouquet, posted on the gate at Fort Lowther, she became hysterical.

It was not until the afternoon when Bouquet and the army returned to Carlisle, and the captivated were brought into the public square to be recognized, that it occurred to Frau Anna that she might not find the little girl she was looking for. Instinctively she had gone first to search amid the smaller children, and it was only the fact that Regina was *not* there that shook Frau Lininger out of her static dream and forced her to face the reality of fleeting Time.

It was only as the afternoon wore away that hope began to burgeon again and to renew itself in the reasonable expectation that Regina had grown up and was waiting for her somewhere amongst the wagons, a young woman of sixteen. It was only after Frau Anna had counted over all her fingers several times, and *so* slowly, that she was able to understand and to face the conclusion. She was aided in this more by the sympathy than by the logic of one of the guardian Virginia Rangers to whom she appealed. He made out her broken English and German only with difficulty, but was touched by her pathetic appearance and floods of tears.

Sunset was near when the tall Virginian finally understood her difficulty and led her to where eight or ten maidens under twenty were sitting protectively together. Some of their companions had already been claimed, and it so happened that those who remained were Shawanese captives who had been carried away many years before; girls who were young squaws so far as their habits or their language were concerned. Most of them felt a dread of and an ill-concealed hostility towards the palefaces, and despite the honey-coloured hair of several amongst them, they looked and acted like the sullen savages they were.

It was to such hopefuls as these that the tall ranger had led Frau Lininger and then stood waiting expectantly, while she called out the name of "Regina, Regina Lininger" again and again. She stood before them, took her shawl from her head and smiled, making soft German noises persuasively. But nothing happened, except sloe-eyed glances of shy fear or secret contempt from most of them, or at best sullen unintelligible replies from the girls with yellow hair.

This went on for some time, and it was then that Frau Anna suffered a second terrible shock that awful day. It was almost like a physical stroke, the stunning realization that Regina might never be able to recognize *her*. Old Captain Rainey found her thus and led her back to the comfort of his warm hearth and family; and it was in that way that she missed Bouquet when he spoke to the captivated that evening, standing before the supper fire.

Frau Anna remained up late that evening, restless, staring across the square at the dim figures moving in the firelight about the wagons. No one knew what she thought, for she said nothing.

There is a proverb about hope and the human breast, one which Frau Lininger well personified. For next morning when the captivated were moved from the square to the camp at LeTort's Springs, she followed them. At the camp itself she continued to haunt the precincts of the huts assigned to the girl captives, and to walk up and down before them, moving her lips silently. When questioned she mumbled something unintelligible in German about General Bouquet . . .

It was towards the middle of the afternoon when Frau Anna looked up and saw a tall hawk-faced man and the adjutant, Captain Ourry, turn the corner of the log barracks where the babies were. Behind them came Bouquet in his red coat and faded epaulets, with a lady leaning on his arm.

The next thing Frances Melissa knew, an old woman, her grey hair tousled in the breeze, came running up to the general and started to beat her hands frantically on his breast, while she made uncouth noises. Then she tried to put her arms around his neck. Captain Ourry turned with an oath.

"Now, now, Frau Lininger," cried Bouquet, catching her hands firmly between his own and trying to quiet her, "so it's you! Has our good Father Almighty not been merciful to you?"

"Ja, ja, gracious lord general," sobbed the old woman, "she is here; she is near, but she is forever verloren. She does not know me, her mother, nor do I know her. Thou alone canst help, thy august self alone. Have pity on me, serene and exalted sir."

"Come and sit down on the steps awhile, Frau Anna," replied Bouquet, leading her towards the porch stoop before the log barracks. "You are tired. Ah, I can see that!"

"Bitte," said Frau Anna, wiping her eyes. Trotting over to the steps like some subservient domestic animal, she sat down.

They all gathered about her. Bouquet stood directly before her, looking down patiently into her face, one hand twirling a small walking-stick nervously behind his back.

"Now, tell us," said he, "tell us slowly, Frau Anna. Perhaps I, or this lady here, can help you."

At the mention of the lady, the old woman looked up at Frances' face, and so forlornly that Frances impulsively sat down beside her and put an arm about her. Thus reassured and comforted, she managed to speak more clearly, and at last made her predicament clear.

"Good Lord!" exclaimed Bouquet, looking stumped. "That girl is probably even now within a hundred yards of us, sulking in one of those huts down the street. But how to trace her, if she doesn't know who she is; there's the rub."

"I'm sure she's here, sir," said Ourry. "I distinctly remember her name being on the lists, and of your speaking to me about her at Fort Bedford. Yes, yes, *Regina, Regina Lininger.*"

"Ja!" interjected the old woman, "*Regina,* mit der flaxy hair."

"If she's among the Shawanese captives, maybe *I* can talk with her and find her out," suggested Salathiel.

"Do so by all means," replied the brigadier. "Suppose you go along, Ourry, and show him where you've put the young females."

Accordingly, Captain Ourry and Salathiel started down the camp street hastily. Presently, they could be seen going into and then coming out of one hut after another.

"Ach, du Lieber Gott, my poor baby!" exclaimed Frau Anna, and burst into tears again. "Ten years ja, it is a long time." Frances strove to console her.

"But she must remember *something* of her childhood," muttered Bouquet, striking at the grass with his cane, "something that you often did together, Frau Anna: a game you played; a pet she played with, a family dog or cat. The Injuns don't keep 'em, you know."

"No use to bark or meow," muttered Frau Anna despondingly, "no use . . ."

"No, but you can sing, Mrs. Lininger, you can sing!" exclaimed Frances in great excitement, seizing the old woman by her shoulders and holding her at arms' length, while she looked into her face. "A lullaby! A song you used to sing Regina to sleep with at home."

"By God, it would take a woman to think of that!" cried Bouquet. "Do you understand, Frau Lininger? Do you see . . ."

"Ja," she cried, leaping up, hope dawning in her eyes again. "Ja, I remember. I vill sing, *sing!*"

She ran down the street a piece, and then stopped.

"Now pray heaven!" exclaimed Bouquet. "Ah!" Frau Anna had started to trudge down the street, and she was singing, singing with a kind of desperate urgency and tender appeal in her soft old voice, the words of an ancient German hymn.

She trudged on bravely, looking to neither right nor left, holding her shawl wrapped tightly about her, singing ever more clearly. As the plaintive voice continued, faces came to the doors of the huts and peered out. Soon a number of the captivated came outside to watch her. Captain Ourry and Salathiel emerged from the fifth hut down the street and stood watching, too. They had not found Regina. At the bottom of the street Frau Anna turned and came back again still singing. She was now half-way back, coming up the street. The brigadier stopped twirling his cane and waited tensely.

Suddenly there was a piercing scream, and from one of the huts a young woman in a deerskin skirt, with a snood of blue wampum over her light-brown hair, ran out, and falling to her knees clutched Frau Anna frantically about the waist. "Kleine Mutter," she cried in a strange thick accent, "Mutter, Mutter, kleine Mutter."

"Du, mein liebchen, du," whispered her mother, leaning over her and half covering her with her drooping shawl.

People down the street began to shout in various Indian tongues, and to run from one hut to another as the news spread. Bouquet turned away from looking at Frau Anna and Regina. He was not immune to emotion. He saw Frances sitting on the steps with a far, far-away look in her grey eyes and tears trembling on her lashes.

"Well done, madam," said the brigadier huskily.

Frances dried her eyes and smiled at him. "It's like this, sir, I'll be after remimbering *you* in times to come," she said.

"Ah, the days to come," said Bouquet. "I wonder? But better a soft heart like your own than letters traced on granite. 'Tis the living quality of remembrance that lasts. Will it be hearts, marble, brass, or bronze that is chosen—who knows? Fate is a weird engraver. Children are the best of all remembrancers, I suppose . . ."

" 'Twas hard remindin' Regina Lininger," said Frances.

They both laughed.

"True," he said—"but here come Ourry and your long-legged ranger. We stole a march on them this time, my dear. Let's rally 'em about it."

"*Well*, captain," he said, with a mock severity, as Ourry and Salathiel appeared, "how now?"

"Oh, quite as usual, sir," replied Ourry. The adjutant was getting nowhere, when he saw that the general had solved the difficulty. "But Albine at least had a certain success."

"I found someone I wasn't looking for," explained Salathiel.

" 'Tis a talint you're much afflicted with," cried Frances. "What is it you'd better be after tellin' me?" she added anxiously.

"Come, and I'll show you," he replied. "It concerns you more than anybody else, I guess."

Salathiel had now said enough not only to arouse Frances' curiosity, but also to alarm her. A mystery was what she most abhorred.

The brigadier laughed. "Sounds like something you had better investigate, Mistress Albine. I shall count on hearing about it before you leave camp. But the captain and I *must* be getting back to headquarters. You will not forget, Albine, to see me before you go?"

"Lord, no," said Ourry; "the list, you know, the list!"

Salathiel promised, and after the bows were over, and the clicking of rapier scabbards on boots had died away, he turned and put Frances' hand over his arm precisely as Bouquet had done at headquarters. "Madam, permit me," he said ironically, "only a brief stroll . . ."

"Oh, Sal," she said. "Howly Mither, what is it now?"

"Do you remember, yesterday, when we were driving into town from the mill, you said that what you needed was another woman in the house?"

She turned pale under her bonnet. "Oh, my dear," she said, "you'd not be twisting the words out of me mouth the wrong way like that, all for a little jealousy over me passin' the time of day and a bit of blarney with the brigadier? All that I meant was . . ."

"Yes? What was it you meant?"

"Why," she cried, "all I meant was havin' a bit of help in the house, an old woman with a talint with a broom and for makin' beds, or cookin' in the kitchen. Now that Mr. Yates is comin', and Mr. St. Clair, and God knows who else, and we'll be after keepin' house at the mill for another five months at least, before we git to the City, and the baby comin' on, the baby, Sal, *your* baby . . ." Then she saw he was laughing at her. "You rogue, you miserable rogue, to twit me like that!"

"Come on, me love, I've found the very woman you're looking for. An old friend of the Little Turtle. I hope you'll not be jealous of her for that."

"Some squaw, I suppose," she said, tossing her head.

"Come and see," he replied. "She's as Irish as you are."

It was at the fifth hut on the left-hand side of the street that they stopped. He motioned for her to wait and went in. She heard him talking in guttural Shawanese. The voice of an old woman replied. The conversation went on for some time, and then the woman's voice said, "Howly Saints, you big awkward spalpeen, have you left her tied outside like a colt! Ask her to cross the threshold, and twice tin thousand blessin's on her little fate." Frances waited no longer.

The hut was filled with twilight; there was only one small dusty window and the streak of sunshine falling through the open door to light it. Salathiel towered into the gloom, and before him, squatting on the mud floor, sat an old woman in dirty deerskins.

"Frances, this is Malycal," said Salathiel. "She says, since you're not a cold-hearted Englishwoman, she'll go home with you. She had an English mistress once."

"The wolves et the hard obstinate face off her," said Malycal, "and her proud daughter's, too. I foretold them so."

"I hope I'll plaize you, Malycal," said Frances, and filled the hut with a tentative ripple of laughter that shuddered towards the end.

"Stand ye in the sunlight, mistress, and throw back your bonnet over your shoulders. I would see what betides between us."

Frances complied, and the old woman rose stiffly from the ground and

came towards her, crouching a little and making a small sign of the cross
with her little finger.

"Are ye there, Sal?" asked Frances apprehensively.

"Yes," said he, with his head still in the gloom.

"Don't ye be scared," said the old woman. "My Christian name's Mary
Calahan, and I was baptized at Cashel. I'd niver overlook ye. 'Tis only a
dear Irish face I want to see again."

She laid her hands on Frances' shoulders and looked at her with her
small intensely blue and finely wrinkled old eyes. Frances quietly returned her gaze without flinching.

"Ah, the blessed wild soul and the sweet fey face of ye, mistress! 'Tis
a wanderin' angel ye be; and I see the bright sunlight beyond ye, and
the glory of it catchin' in your raven hair."

"Come home with me, Mary Calahan," whispered Frances. "The
house is full of men, and the sound of lonely water. I've only a Presbyterian child and a hathen black boy to help me. And there's a new
baby under my heart."

Malycal laid her head on Frances' breast and said so low that Salathiel
could not hear her. "Why, I'll come home to ye, mistress, and brew
white magic and hot cups of tay before the fire. 'Tis comfort I need
in a lonely land, and comfort I'll bring ye."

Frances slipped an arm around her.

Salathiel was so pleased, he couldn't help showing it, which meant
that he was very pleased indeed.

"It takes the women to fix things up," he asserted twice over, and
claimed thrice that it was a wonderful day.

". . . which is five times as much as ye ginerally say," laughed
Frances. " 'Tis the influence of Edward Yates turnin' you into an orator.
But the wonderful day will soon be over. And Bridget's alone at the
mill with Jed. We must get back now, get back to her!"

"So we must," he agreed. "Malycal, put your plunder up in a bindle.
We'll call for ye with the wagon. Dang it, I wish we could skip goin'
to headquarters now."

"But ye can't," said Frances. "You promised the brigadier, and besides
the wagon's hitched there with Enna gnawing the painted post. I'll
wait here with Mary Calahan till ye git back. Give the gineral me affectionate remimbrance, and for God's sake sing them lists to Captain
Ourry, or he'll be after pestering us all to death. And fix up about takin'
Mary home with ye—and hurry! I guess that's all."

The last items she had to call after him, for he was already striding
away up the street. He felt like running, but the captivated might have
wondered. He was all in a sweat now to get out of camp. He'd forgotten
about Bridget, and his heart smote him.

Too many things had been happening today. Everything was working
out much too well. It was being too nicely wound up. If it hadn't been

for that meeting with McArdle, he'd be downright superstitious about being so happy. Maybe that was where his luck would begin to turn. McArdle gave him the shivers now. The way he'd looked at Frances when they stopped in the road to talk. My God! Did McArdle think he'd ever leave a woman like Frances for a girl like Jane? Just let him try to bring that up. But he'd like to get back to the mill now. He wished he hadn't come to camp after all, just at Frances' behest. Now that they had a house to go home to, he wished . . . well . . . he wished he'd gone home. He'd get over with it at headquarters in a jiffy. God, what a life the military led. He was sorry for the brigadier. In many ways he reminded him of Ecuyer—but a truce to all that. How much faster a man could get things done, when he didn't have a woman along!

None the less, it was a good hour, or more, before he finally got through at headquarters. He copied the lists out himself for Ourry and only had to hum a little now and then. There was no trouble about Malycal. He just signed for her; and Captain Ourry countersigned, without question. So much for that. But the brigadier called him then and had quite a long talk with him. He'd had to admit it was a reasonable proposition that Bouquet asked him to consider. Also that he was tempted by it. Good pay. He'd promise to come back after he'd thought it over. He didn't see how he could do less than that. Besides, Bouquet was so understanding and sympathetic, and a great man! Of course, he could not refuse to repair his parade wig for him. So he'd brought it along with him—and the six others, including Ourry's, that were waiting for him in a bundle of brown paper. Ourry had certainly been grateful, no doubt about it, but too hopeful, he thought. He'd think it over. But home now!

Frances and Malycal were ready when he dashed up to the hut with the two-wheeled cart, but they were alone. None of the captivated came to say good-bye to Malycal. She climbed into the back of the cart with her bundle and sat there cross-legged in the straw. "Sure and it's like gintry you are with a low-backed car and a fine little harse," she said.

"Hold on, for I'm drivin' fast," he warned her.

"I've no teeth left to rattle in me head no more, drive on," she flung back at him, and showed her toothless gums in a happy grin.

He drove fast. It was about an hour before sunset, he figured, when he turned Enna's head eastward at LeTort's Springs. But he'd forgotten the mountains, and the sun sank behind them sooner than he'd thought. It was twilight when they splashed through the little ford where the turned-up wagon lay. He was glad now that he'd piled those cedar boughs against the scar on the tree. Enna didn't even snort. Darkness began to fall as they struck the silent road through the woods.

"We'll be home about candlelight at this rate," he said, breaking a long silence. "I hope Bridget *will* have the fire lighted for us. She's got too much sense to wait in the darkness, or to think we'd leave her alone for another night, don't you think?"

"Yis, I do," Frances replied. "She's wiser than *you* think, Sal—wiser than her years. Belike she's been havin' a foin time playin' mistress of the house and orderin' Jed about."

Frances had been silent all the way through the dark woods; and as usual he'd said nothing, either. Something in her tone now disturbed him. But it was only for a moment. She leaned nearer him, laying her cheek against his shoulder. He slipped an arm about her and drove with one hand. Enna knew the way back, anyway.

"Oh, I'm terrible happy tonight, Sal," she whispered. "I want to thank ye for bein' so good to me." She felt him tremble, as her arms crept about his neck. "I love you—and now we'll be at home togither at least for a while."

"That's how I figured it," he said. Their lips met in a long kiss.

"God, but I'm a lucky orphan," he said hoarsely at last.

"Hush, niver say it," she whispered. "Who knows what's leanin' over us now in the darkness, listenin'? Hear that!"

"'Tis the sound of runnin' water at the mill," he answered, "water talking peacefully. And I see a light!"

"A light!" she exclaimed. "Lights, you mean. Bejasus, 'tis an illumination. There's a candle in every window. Now, what did I tell ye?"

27. The Labours of Hercules

IT IS ONLY in retrospect that the full flavour of a period in personal experience can be roundly savoured and evaluated. Yet most people's lives tend to fall into distinct epochs. There are both chapters and paragraphs in the volume of life which take on in perspective an emotional or dramatic unity of their own. And Salathiel and Frances Melissa were no exceptions. Looking back at their experience together in the mill house at Boiling Springs, it took on for them in retrospect the form of a distinct and memorable chapter in their volume of mutual adventure.

In a diary which Salathiel kept in a calf-bound ledger in his round, carefully shaded, and all but juvenile script, his several entries at *Glens Mills* (*sic!*) run from the sixteenth of November 1764 to the twenty-eighth of March 1765, N.S., closing on the latter date with the remarks:

> Leaving this pleasant place of Glens Mills near Boiling spring this morning at half after five by Capt E his watch, intending for the city of Philadelphia by way of the town of York at E Yates behest, he awaiting us at Lancaster, & the latest advices from the brigadier—with 1 wagon, 1 cart, 6

horses, myself, Frances, Bridget & our people, Maly & the two
black boys, along. We being heavily laden & a long muddy
haul by way of John Wright his ferry, of which some qualms
by last report, & a slow trip expected with Frances growing big
now & oft-times queasy.

£184-6s-5d in hand, with £4-2s-6d due Stott'l'myr for harse
hire. But he will owe me £80 str upon final del'v'y of wagon &
return of the teams to him at Carlisle. Therefore—have this day
to touch or in just expectation 260£s sterling plus 3s & 11d,
with 18£s drawn at sight upon Japson in the City, being the
first advance from the Brigadier sent lately by Capt Ourry in
his last letter. Fair enough, with coins scarce as hens teeth.

A.o.h. X libra r.g. cast bullets; XVI libra bird shot, but small
powder. (6 scalps), pelts new and left over 32, fair to mid'l'n.
Now farewell to the country, may the good Lord prosperous us
in the City.

> "My burdens upon Him I cast
> That shelters lambkins from the blast,
> And hears the new born coddlins peep
> To Him from out the murky deep."

& & &

Here endeth *all* the entries under "Glens Mills", with a grand shaded
flourish in the form of a bow knot and a few inky splutters from a worn
quill; indicating perhaps great haste about half after five that morning
of departure (if one may guess) accompanied by the loud ticking of
S. Ecuyer's indomitable watch.

From which entry, with careful reading, and some scanning between
the lines, a fairly accurate idea of the material condition of the *familia
Albine* upon their eventual departure for the City at the end of March
1765 can be puzzled out.

Three facts stand out from Salathiel's entries: the stay at Boiling
Springs was a comparatively short one; it was happy; and it was memorable out of all proportion to its length. The rest can be gleaned from
Captain Ourry's orderly book; from his letters to Salathiel from Philadelphia; from Yates's cryptic Latin entries in his "Daily Reminder", and
the known course of events in and about Carlisle.

But "the rest" is actually *not* so relevant to this chronicle of character
and feeling; and the time at Boiling Springs could better be expressed
for its emotional and inner meaning in terms of a sustained and quiet
piece of music rather than in the faded and silent entries in old accompts
and diaries. And phrased in terms of moonlight, falling water, the lilt of
applewood fiddles, candlelight, tree shadows on mossy roofs, departed

footsteps, and vanished voices—the themes, grace notes, overtones, dissonances, and harmonies of the Mill House Symphony must have been something like this:

It began with winter, a quiet season, clear, cold, and dry. The streams froze. The sound of water was much hushed under the ice. All about the Boiling Spring stretched the silent, sunny woods and unfrequented roads of the deserted neighbourhood—only fitfully disturbed as yet by some solitary messenger spurring to Carlisle or by a creaking farm wagon returning with a family to their long-abandoned home. Snow fell occasionally.

Once that season the rare Northern Lights came far southward. Hanging on the northern fringe of the horizon one December evening, they smouldered with the cold fire of diamonds in a black vault. Then shaking with sidereal palsy, they died out; only to flash again into distant lightnings: steely white, cobalt, wonderful!—flaming up at last into a climax of S-shaped glory, twin green and lilac curtains trailing faint dripping fringes of pale icy blue.

Frances and Malycal, Bridget and Salathiel saw the Lights. Standing before the open door of the mill house, they watched the show and went in silently afterward, touched by awe and the hint of some unrecoverable memory that hung and flickered like the iris of a watchful eye just beyond the horizon of the mind, cold and fearful—but that closed with the house door—and left them happy and rejoicing together in the shelter of the roof-tree and the warm leaping of the familiar chimney flame.

Jed had seen the Ghost Lights, too. Out in the wagon, where he slept, he lay peeping under the canvas and shuddering under his blankets. That night the comfortable remembrance of the hot suns of Africa withered like flowers blackened by frost-bite and ceased to warm his hope. He knew now he would never get back. "I don't know what you've done to him," said St. Clair to Salathiel not so long afterward, "but Jed's a different nigger. He seems somehow to have been toned down."

"I reckon he's jes wintering through. We ain't teched him," replied Salathiel.

But something had.

Thus, mysteriously for everybody, the winter nights at Boiling Springs began. But the days were quite different. They were cheerful. They seemed to slip away one into another rapidly, smoothly, and timelessly. Everybody great and small was fully occupied. Salathiel, for one, was busy as a beaver with two tails.

There was firewood to be cut and hauled, whole carloads of it. And Jed was not skilful with the hand-axe yet. But he soon learned. They burned stacks of logs that winter; great logs in the chimney place, until the fire-back glowed white hot and beat a genial wave of summer clean down the long hall; and piles of kindling and pine faggots in the kitchen where Malycal revelled in simmering August heat in January, as if her bones could never be warm enough after the icy draughts and aching ground-cold of Kaysinata's gloomy forest hut. And with the mill full of flour, an eternal baking went on in the Dutch oven that also glowed genially with wooden fuel and sent a continuous stream of hot breads, piping meat pies, muffins, corn puddings, and honey cakes smoking and steaming to the table.

So the sound of the wood-axe was frequent. It rang cheerfully in the thickets near-by, and there was a perpetual chopping and splintering of kindling on the big stump just outside the kitchen door. There, too, the bucket yokes hung: yokes that fitted equally well, and so naturally and so often, across both Jed's and Malycal's shoulders, as the numerous pails full of spring water, or "waiting" milk smoking in the inside entry, proclaimed.

Jed was leary of Malycal at first. Gradually he came to like her, but he never dared take liberties. She said her prayers on beads, charmed away warts with burnt feathers, and muttered sight-unseen to somebody who wasn't there. So Jed fetched and carried, waited on the table, plucked fowls, cleaned fish, and drew rabbits diligently—and kept his mouth shut. But above all he chopped wood. All Malycal had to do was to turn the northern lights of her blue Irish eyes upon him, and the hand-axe began to ring.

Chopping, however, was not the only sound that broke the silence of the forest. Many an afternoon, or in the first light of morning, Twin Eyes's sharp bark as a rifle bullet went home; or the brief cough under a light charge of powder, when a cluster of swan shot burst from an old bell-shaped fowling piece of Mr. Glen's—both could be heard near or far along the banks of Yellow Breeches Creek or in the woods and abandoned fields near the mill.

It was small game, "varmints," as Salathiel called them; rabbits, squirrels, and an occasional coon or possum that he was after, and the waterfowl in the quiet back-reaches of the creek.

For that matter, ducks and wild swans came down regularly on the mill-pond just behind the house. And the deer particularly frequented the lonely farm lanes. It was amazing how less than two years of an abandoned country had brought the game back into it again. The wolves came back, too. Foxes were careless, even curious; and he shot a good many, for their pelts were worth something.

Driving the wagon had been small exercise, and to be back in the forest again in the cold sweet air and solitude, with the crisp leaves under his feet, was balm to Salathiel's body and his soul. He soon looked the better for it, leaner and more hawk-like and keen; more himself. And he went back to moccasins, keeping his boots and shoes for trips to town or when company came.

Jed tended the night fish-lines faithfully, and every morning there were chubbs, suckers, or catfish with bacon for breakfast, even when the ice grew thick. What with wheat, grist, oats, corn meal, and fine flour, with which the mill loft was bursting; with fish, game, barrelled salt meat, venison, and wild-fowl, they lived high, wide, and handsome at Boiling Springs that winter. And Mr. Glen's cellar was provided with sundry cider kegs, liquor barrels, and a minor stock of wine bottles; to say nothing of potatoes, carrots, onions, and turnips buried in straw away from the frost. It was Bridget's task to keep the mother of yeast alive and growing in a warm crock covered by a damp cloth in the kitchen. But that was only a small part of her daily round. It no more covered what Bridget was doing than did a few excursions into the woods pot-hunting suffice to explain Salathiel's innumerable activities.

The truth was he had never been so busy and so happy before. And it was all his own work, work which possessed a genuine importance, because it was naturally essential; tasks for the hand, heart, and head. He now got out and set up all of Johnson's valeting and wig-making kit and machinery. He set them up in a shed with a forge in it, next to the mill. Some of the tools he had never used before, but he soon surmised their application and went to work.

Mr. Craighead's "best Sabbath hair" was soon a happy replica of its pristine self. The brigadier's parade wig was a simple matter, for Salathiel was used to the regulation military set for perukes, and the other officers' wigs were in the same case. All these when returned, powdered and in new stow-bags made up by Frances, were samples that generated a surprising and all but clamorous patronage. Yates had been more than right in foreseeing it.

Salathiel charged all that the traffic would bear, from a guinea to five shillings, depending on the state of the wig and its owner's apparent solvency. And there were then more wigs in the country than he could have mended or retrimmed in a year. It was a veritable lode of rich ore he had accidentally struck, and he worked at it hard. If some of his repairs were amateurish, they were at least ingenious. But venting falderal vapours and minor complaints upon a "wig-maker" who frequently delivered his wares with an axe dangling from his belt was something to cause even a peevish personage to ponder gravely. It was better on the whole to look pleased—and to pay promptly.

For Salathiel, it was the beginning of what became for him later a profitable side-line. He brought to it, besides Johnson's initial instruction, a natural aptitude in the use of his hands and a certain ingenious cleverness of invention. Also his skill in the preparation of skins, pelts, and hides, in connection with wigs and in a hundred other ways, was of infinite service and profit to him as time went on.

The aptitude for using tools and weapons that he had picked up and come by naturally during his years of life with those who, even Frances allowed, must have been "ingenious savages" now proved invaluable.

If he lacked some article or item, he generally made it. He could copy almost anything in wood or iron, if he put his mind to it. He had patience and the inherited knack of seeing *how* things were to be done. In the wagon he had accumulated a raft of peaceful tools and a small armoury of lethal weapons. With the former he now went to work in various ways.

It was this manual capacity in Salathiel which Yates could never admire enough. He liked to think that in his own head was the same *kind* of latent cleverness which Salathiel found in his hands. The alliance of head and hand in their friendship was, Yates felt, the chief advantage of it; "highly expedient". But he went further. He was also given to speculating upon whether the combination of the two capacities in one personality was not the ideal of proper character for success in the New World.

So work, and work of many kinds, now went on in the forge shed at the mill. It was soon the shelter for all kinds of minor crafts. Jim Fergus, for instance, brought a curious and, in the end, a dangerously lucrative suggestion. It was for nothing less than the counterfeiting of scalps. And Salathiel was found equal to the occasion.

Fergus traded whisky and new scalps for old with some of the warriors still living in the hospitable protection of the jail. He then turned in the old ones for bounty money. Thus the chiefs retained the replicas of gory trophies to sew back on the fringes of their breeches and lost none of their glory, while Jim profited considerably, and Salathiel shared. The trick, of course, was to copy the old scalps so passably that they would pass muster even when the "chiefs" returned to their own people. And to copy Indian scalps only, for it would not do to have turned in scalps of the inhabitants to the authorities. Some carefully tanned and shaped rabbit hides mounted on willow rings, horsehair tied in the proper knots indicating various tribes, some ink stains, dyes, and a little smoking accomplished the design. Yates laughed heartily, but opined that this was going a little too far. He finally managed to put an end to the episode after only a few transactions, and before any embarrassing questions were asked.

But all this activity at the mill required numerous trips to town—and to headquarters—for Salathiel had succumbed and made certain arrangements there. In particular, he undertook to look after the personal comfort and kit of the brigadier. He also managed to get things done and to see people who could oblige headquarters in local but important personal matters. Bouquet paid him decently, and Captain Ourry proved grateful in various ways. Salathiel came twice a week to camp, and Ourry and the brigadier occasionally rode back to the mill with him for an evening of good company there, a game of whist, and a supper that was always worth going eight miles to get. On several evenings the gathering was notable, and the company rode back to town next day.

Undoubtedly the brigadier appreciated the good fare and the cheerful domestic atmosphere. And this was especially true after the "French cook" came.

It was a Saturday, and Salathiel had hitched up the greys to the big wagon, and with Jed driving, had taken Frances along with him to make the usual rounds at Carlisle. There were no less than six resuscitated wigs to be delivered to various persons at camp and in town, and Frances herself had three bonnets to return after retrimming them. Then there were some imported groceries to be bought, such as pepper, coffee, tea, and spices; and the injured singletree was to be repaired at the blacksmith's, since the forge at the mill had not yet had its bellows repaired. Last, and most important, a final arrangement about the team horses was to be made. Stottelmyer had returned to Carlisle and sent a message to Salathiel about them. With such a calendar of business before them, Frances and he started early and expected to be gone all day.

The advent of the French cook must have occurred during the time when the wagon was waiting at the blacksmith's. In fact, Salathiel learned afterward, although the smith would never admit it, that the man had been working concealed at the forge for almost a month. Probably Jed knew it.

At any rate, it was Jed's fault, Salathiel figured. Perhaps there was a bit more work at the mill now than one boy could well be expected to do. The firewood proposition alone was admittedly quite considerable. And he had heard Malycal driving Jed hard. But even then Jed ought not to have let the man persuade him; or did *he* persuade the man? It must have been what Yates called "a meeting of minds". And it must have happened at the forge. There was plenty of time to have arrived at an understanding. And it turned out that both Jed and this other black fellow spoke the same African tongue. It put a white man at a great disadvantage.

So, while Salathiel was out at the stables settling the delicate matter of the "horses" and while Frances was calling on Mrs. Williams with a new jet-trimmed mourning bonnet to learn all there was to know about how the Glen boys were faring with Clara Garber at Conestoga—it had happened. That was the way it must have been—and now there was another mouth at the mill with about twenty stone of man behind it to feed, and what was much more difficult, to keep shut.

That was the way Salathiel thought about it at first. And it wasn't until later that he began to think that it was a great blessing in disguise.

But as they drove away from the smithy late that afternoon neither of them had an inkling that anything was in the wind; and the simple fact that he had decided to take the reins himself and Frances sat beside him all the way was what made it so easy. The man must have just climbed in the back of the wagon as they left, and sat grinning at Jed all the way to the mill, with his outlandish plunder on the seat be-

side him. Neither he nor Frances had thought of looking behind the
canvas. Why should they? It had been a long and satisfactory day, and
there was a lot to talk about.

All the errands were done and the new purchases piled in the wagon
behind them. Frances had three good Portagee joes for herself, and ten
shillings still coming, for her trouble with other women's bonnets; he
had collected for all the wigs, and the settlement with Stottelmyer was
easier than he had thought.

He had forgotten that he and Stott had fought that passel o' scum
together at Bedford. That helped now. So the teams were his now for
a pound a month apiece, as long as he needed them. And Captain
Jack's nag was to be sent back to the mill at the first opportunity just
for the cost of oats consumed. He didn't know just what he'd do with
that extra horse now, but there was plenty of feed at the mill. The surprise came when Stott had offered to *buy* the wagon! They'd argued a
long time over that. It was worth at least a hundred pounds, Salathiel
thought. But Stottelmyer wouldn't pay more than eighty.

Well, he'd chew the proposition over. He hadn't thought of selling
the wagon. But when they moved to the City it would be of small use
there. And he could never keep four horses. Probably, he couldn't keep
even one! Still he hadn't said "yes" yet; and he hadn't talked it over with
Frances. Stottelmyer had agreed to let the offer stand for a while, and so
he'd let it go at that . . .

It was half an hour after dark when they got back to Boiling Springs.
Bridget met them, jumping up and down in the doorway, and with
all her dolls and the cat sitting before the fire in a solemn company
waiting for supper. He just left it to Jed to bring in the plunder and
put up the wagon and teams, since Jed had had an idle day in town
loafing at the blacksmith's—and half a bit for drink. They sat down to
dinner before a clear fire and three candles, with the comfortable feeling
of a day well spent. Bridget was merry as a grig.

So was Jed. He spilled the peas porridge, ladling it out on the hearth,
and instead of being contrite, made trouble afterward in the kitchen,
where Malycal could be heard remonstrating with him in a high-pitched
voice for turning handsprings past the milk pails.

"What the divil's got into him?" exclaimed Frances.

"A bit of blackstrap, no doubt," surmised Salathiel. "I think tuppence
will be enough next time Jed goes to town. You're like to spoil him,
Melissa, with your constant indulgence."

But the shindy in the kitchen continued, and Malycal finally came
in to say that an elegant corn pudding had just disappeared.

"Jed, you black rascal, come here!" roared Salathiel, whipping off his
belt.

"Where's that corn pudding?" he demanded, when Jed appeared, his
chin trembling. "I want the truth."

"Yas, sah, yas, cap'n, I gwine tell ye gospel. De lil ole conjure man, him done et um spang up."

"Git a lanthorn," said Salathiel.

"Him already done got 'em now," sighed Jed, holding up two fingers. Bridget giggled.

"Lead on!" commanded Salathiel, putting his belt on again and slipping Kaysinata's axe into it—at which Frances sat quite still with her palms down on the table, and Bridget's eyes grew big and round. "Lead me to the conjure man, Jed."

They went out through the kitchen, and Salathiel now saw a telltale crack of light under the forge door. He strode ahead and flung it open.

In the light of the two best brass wagon lanthorns set on the floor conveniently near his feet; and seated on the anvil, with the bowl of smoking corn pudding in his lap, sat probably the mightiest Negro then in North America. He was simply stupendous, not so much in height as in width, and he was black as night.

He laid the bowl and spoon at his feet when Salathiel and Jed came in, and stood up. He showed neither fear nor surprise. He simply stood there. He stood calm, and looked Salathiel in the eyes. Then he bowed civilly and said, "Bonsoir, monsieur."

Salathiel examined him slowly, holding up one lanthorn . . .

A decent blue fustian coat, not so decent now. *A fine cambric shirt,* frayed and filthy. *Good black silk breeches,* still passable. *Red worsted stockings,* badly darned and muddy. *Stout Copenhagen boots,* out at the toes. *One silver earring . . .*

"What have you done with your master's gold watch, Herquelees?" demanded Salathiel.

"Jed, him got um," replied the newcomer.

Salathiel did not make the mistake of taking his eyes off the man. He simply held out his left hand behind him until Jed laid the watch in it. He then slipped it into his pouch. The man muttered something in French. But Salathiel shook his head.

"What do you want here, my very big friend?" said he.

"Amis, oui, *grands* amis!" exclaimed the big Negro, flashing his white teeth. Then he pounded his chest. "Me, Hercule. Me work. Me cook, très bon chef! Make ze hammair go." At which he turned suddenly and seizing the smith's hammer made it ring on the anvil mightily.

Something in the sound of the clanging hammer and the dull answering bell of the anvil moved Salathiel, and settled the business in his mind. He held out his hand to stop the demonstration.

Hercules dropped the hammer and grabbed the hand. He began to shake it up and down in a kind of ecstasy of animal delight at being accepted. He seemed to have read Salathiel's mind. Gradually Salathiel closed his grip on the Negro's fingers.

And then, for the first time in his life, he felt fingers as strong as his closing over his hand, and the muscles of a tremendous arm replying to his own. They stood man to man for some moments in the lanthorn-light, testing out each other's strength, arm against arm. Neither swayed nor spoke, but their ligaments cracked. Jed's eyes bulged while he watched. Neither of them gave. Hercules finally grunted. Salathiel suddenly let go, but the man did not fall.

"Ye can stay," said he. "Understand? Savez? *You*, you Herquelees, stay. *Freeman. Work!*"

"Oui, monsieur," replied the Negro huskily. "Vous, grand ami." He slowly made a fist out of his half-crippled right hand, patted it with his left consolingly, and blew on it.

"You, me, verra fine people," he said.

Salathiel grinned. Hercules resumed his bowl, and sitting down on the anvil again, began to finish his supper with the big iron spoon.

When Salathiel turned to go out, he found Jed doing cartwheels in the shadows, and was forced to take him by the collar to shake a bit of sense into him. With a lanthorn in one hand, he ended by hoisting him through the shed door with his foot, although since he was wearing moccasins, it was not too serious. But he didn't enjoy having huge surprises brought home to him. Jed understood.

"From now on, I guess you'll be working for Herquelees instead of Malycal," mused Salathiel. "And you may have noticed he's a powerful man. I jealoos you didn't figure it that way, did ye, Jed?"

"No, baas," said Jed sadly, "no, ah see ah ain't figured it jes right. But hones' to Jedu 'twarn't de goold watch brat me to it. No, sah, baas. Not dat tic-tic. Hit war de *mnungee* bird!"

"Bird?" said Salathiel. "*What* bird?"

"You come see um," said Jed, showing excitement again.

They went hastily to the wagon, and Salathiel looked in. There were two raggle-taggle bundles on the side seat, and between them was a wicker cage of curious and obviously foreign design. It looked like a miniature hut from some heathen tropical land, and the "native" who inhabited it was of a blue-black complexion. It was a large raven. His eyes burned coal-red as the lanthorn-light flashed upon him, and he fluttered and croaked dismally at having his sleep disturbed. At the sound of the sepulchral voice from the depths of the wagon, Jed retreated several paces and put his hands over his ears. None the less, he was forced to take Hercules his plunder, prophetic bird and all, and make up a shag mattress for him in the forge shed.

Satisfied with these proceedings for the time being, Salathiel returned for a pipe by the hearth and to discuss with Frances the rearrangements of the household.

At first blush, these complications appeared to be more serious than they proved in the end. Frances instantly saw an opportunity to take Malycal out of the kitchen and to install her in the house for her company by the hearth while sewing and weaving, and for a thousand other small tasks. Malycal's being an Irishwoman and a Catholic was a boon to Frances and a firm bond between them. And there was also a certain mystical understanding that underlay and cemented their feminine friendship far deeper than all else.

It was something out of the past that they shared with instinctive understanding and subliminal sympathy. If Malycal was a weird-woman and knew what was toward with both people and the weather, Frances Melissa also had her moments in which the world and immediate surroundings were lost in a suddenly expanded awareness and exquisite sensitivity; times when she became conscious of whole realms and areas within herself where it seemed to her that the past and the future were both present and a fearful swiftness of incalculable activity was going on.

It was true that Frances' new-found happiness and her pregnancy seemed greatly to have relieved and lessened these "spells", as she called them—or so she thought. For, on the whole, the winter spent at Boiling Springs was calm and lit with a quiet happiness and the sense of growth and self-accomplishment, a completion, for which she said prayers of gratitude before Mrs. Larned's holy lamb—but there were also certain other moments. And then, oh, then it was balm to have Malycal in the house. Someone who could understand, and keep the bottle out of her hand! At the mill house she drank hardly at all.

But that evening that Hercules came—she saw her opportunity. "Sure," said she after Salathiel had finished explaining, "sure 'twill never do to be after havin' an African wizard and an Irish witch all in the kitchen at the same time. So, I think I'll just move Malycal into young Martin's room, for that will put her right across the hall, if I want to call her nights. And I'll be wantin' to call her.

"For I'll be askin' her to drop a few beads with me when we say our evenin' prayers, whither Miss Bridget likes it or not; and maybe Malycal knows a few prayers backwards that will keep poor Mrs. Glen's harp quiet behind the door, and the old woman with shillin's in her eyes for spectacles from sittin' in the rockin' chair and readin' her Bible in the moonlight. Aye, it will be a fine thing for me. And the two black boys and yourself can have the run of the kitchen entirely. Whist! I'll have someone besides Bridget to talk to and help me make clothes for me own baby, instead of ilegint fairy costumes for Miss McCandliss' dolls."

These remarks, of course, settled the matter with Salathiel. Indeed, in some respects Frances' eager consent had been flooring, for he could not remember ever having told her that he had put shillings on Mrs. Larned's eyes, and it had never occurred to him that there was anything but affection between Frances and Bridget.

So it was that the coming of Hercules revealed many things in the household to Salathiel, and brought him to a fuller realization of the nature of her who was going to be the mother of his child.

As for Bridget, she had already observed that Malycal said her prayers in the same elaborate and peculiar way that Melissa did. This troubled her greatly.

Hercules and Jed now had full and undisputed run of the kitchen. Or at least Hercules had. Salathiel supplied fresh game with Twin Eyes; and Jed, the fuel for cooking, with his axe. The other viands, potables, and comestibles Hercules had a knack of assembling himself by dint of his own acumen and unheroic labours. That is, either he asked or he took. And so it was after his arrival that the "card-suppers" at Glen's Mill began to prove more and more attractive to certain officers and gentlemen, and a few others, in and about Carlisle and LeTort's Springs; Brigadier Bouquet and Captain Ourry amongst them.

Amongst those who can definitely be traced as frequently present were Edward Yates and Arthur St. Clair, esquires; the Reverend Mr. Craighead; Messrs. Byers, Tilingham, and Williams; Jim Fergus; and both the brothers John and Martin Glen with their ever-memorable friend, "Colonel" Cornelius Vandercliff.

Meanwhile—and that meant the time when February had commenced to roar like March, but not a single bleat of spring had yet been heard—there was many an undisturbed winter night when Salathiel and Frances had the hearth-fire all to themselves while a wig or a bonnet was under way, the wind sang in the chimney, and Bridget, to her dolls.

About this time M. Henri de Molyneaux was released from his bond to keep the king's peace at Carlisle, and having been cruelly prevented by the brigadier and the unfeeling Quaker magistrates from meeting up with Lieutenant Frazier and spitting him on a small sword, began to pursue in earnest his runaway servant and his creoline intention of carrying Hercules in chains back to Martinique.

Anyone *might* have told M. de Molyneaux that taking one Hercules away from another even stronger was not a matter that should be gone about lightly. But no one *could* tell M. de Molyneaux that, or anything else in English. Bouquet had remonstrated with him in French about his madcap challenge, and had eventually been forced to send him to cool off in the town jail.

For "butterfly" was the name for Henri. He fluttered. His coat was wired out from his waist in a graceful Parisian manner. He minced when he walked, and his delicate little behind twinkled in tight doeskin under the wiry tilt of his coat-tails like the nose of a white rabbit under a leaf.

He chattered English like a wren, but never understood its serious import. He was rich, and richly adorned. And he had come to Philadelphia to arrange for the smuggling of sundry cargoes of Martinique molasses up the Delaware, with himself and his tropical estates thrown in as a kind of amatory bonus. For he also fully expected to return to Saint-Pierre with a lily-white and, if possible, a fertile daughter of one of the affluent merchants with whom he did business.

Now there were no major difficulties with the merchants over the molasses. It had started to flow north promptly without *any* customary delays. And M. de Molyneaux had also promptly been bidden to flutter in some of the best drawing rooms in Philadelphia. In fact, he was finally invited to the Assembly. But even belatedly virginal daughters of his mercantile hosts were forced to reflect on what going to bed in Lilliput might be like, if they returned with him to Saint-Pierre. For such a little thing the better half of M. de Molyneaux's northern mission eventually failed.

Thus with a far heavier sensation in both his purse and his heart than when he had arrived, M. de Molyneaux had been forced to stay longer than he had expected at the London Coffee House on Front Street. But even he was at last convinced of the permanent aloofness of northern Dianas; and his stay was unexpectedly and, as it finally turned out, permanently prolonged, by the exasperating disappearance of his valet, cook, and general factotum, Hercules.

Actually, Hercules had not run away at all. He had liked his indulgent and carelessly generous little master well enough. And grooming a butterfly was small labour for a Hercules. But he had been left idle in Philadelphia, and had spent his time loitering along the water-front, picking up an odd job here and there. In this way he had been inveigled one day into loading some especially heavy military chests being shipped westward by wagon-train; and was further indulged with a ride as far as the barracks at Lancaster. There he had tarried for a few days and picked up the raven for his conjuring tricks from an old German woman. It was no great shakes to repeat his wagon performance and get a lift with another convoy as far as Carlisle.

Hercules had enjoyed all the excitement he found under way there, and profited by it. He had no trouble in getting enough small change together to ensure his living. Shortly before the brigadier's arrival Hercules had decided to let M. de Molyneaux return without him to Martinique. And he had about made up his mind that this departure must have taken place, when he was warned one day that his master had come to town looking for him, and that a great reward was posted at the town hall for his apprehension and return.

This put another face on affairs, and he was forced to disappear promptly, for fear he would be betrayed for the five pounds offered. He determined, nevertheless, to remain in the neighbourhood of Carlisle. Besides, it was winter and travelling was doubly difficult. So he made careful overtures to one Josiah Loften, the blacksmith, who hid him by day in his barn and allowed him to work at night by the warm forge fire.

Matters had thus strung along for some weeks, and Hercules might have emerged as a successful Vulcan had not M. de Molyneaux also lingered in the vicinity. And it was for that reason that Jed had finally been cajoled to smuggle Hercules out to Boiling Springs.

It was the "borrowed" gold watch that eventually caused all the trouble. It, and Captain Ourry's mischievous curiosity. Salathiel's sense of property was a strict one. It was still tinged with the colour of Indian customs, but he had his own code, and he stuck to it.

Thus Hercules had come to him as a fugitive asking shelter, and he had made a certain bargain with him and shaken hands on it. Hercules he had come to regard in the light of a chief of his own people, one who had escaped, much as a prisoner of war might escape, and been given shelter at his fire. That Hercules was black had little to do with it. Furthermore, Salathiel now regarded Hercules as a friend, one whose giant strength and primitive but indomitable self-respect he greatly admired. All this had come to pass in a few weeks' acquaintance at the mill. They had been working and out hunting together. That Hercules trusted and liked him, and in much the same way, Salathiel had no doubt. Almost from the first it was thus understood. He would no more have betrayed Hercules for a reward than he would have turned in Bridget's scalp for a bounty.

But the watch was different. It was a piece of property like an item of trade goods that had been made away with unfairly. He had no quarrel with the Frenchman, and he had instantly decided to return the watch when he could. So one day towards the middle of February, when he was working at camp, knowing that the brigadier had locked up M. de Molyneaux over the matter of a duel and the Frenchman's impudence, he had given the watch to Bouquet and asked him to return it when he was released.

He thought no more of it. Both Bouquet and Ourry knew Hercules was at the mill. They had seen him there, but they had said nothing. Their silence as guests was taken for granted. The watch would be returned, thought Salathiel—and thought no more about it.

His perplexity, disgruntlement, and eventual indignation were, therefore, considerable when a few evenings later Yates returned from town with what he described as a "missive and masterpiece of coxcombry", written in French in an exceedingly minute but engraved hand, on a tremendous piece of paper. Upon being read in quite literal translation, and obviously with an all but ribald enjoyment by Yates, what Salathiel heard was that M. de Molyneaux would call on him the next day to get Hercules.

M. de Molyneaux's seal, firmly impressed, disclosed two cupids romping in an infantile but abandoned manner with a crescent moon that was advisedly hiding behind a cloud.

Yates handed the letter to Salathiel, who received it without comment. None the less, he was considerably annoyed.

It was not so much that the visit of the little Frenchman threatened to disturb the happy tenor of the life they were now leading at the mill; there were a hundred ways of dealing physically with such a man as

M. de Molyneaux. But it was quite apparent that both Yates and Captain Ourry had collaborated to bring this coxcomb down upon him out of a humorous curiosity as to what might happen when the little Frenchman set out to capture a giant with a butterfly net. This, Salathiel thought, discovered a certain surreptitious superiority in Yates and Ourry.

So he let Yates laugh alone as he read the letter; and laugh alone all over again as he returned to it to repeat its more memorable passages. "Very large Gentleman of the Forest"—after all, what in hell was so funny about that? He determined to take care of M. de Molyneaux, Ed Yates, and Captain Ourry all at the same time, and to teach them a lesson about what was funny and what wasn't.

When Yates had stopped laughing, therefore, Salathiel quietly took the letter again, thanked him for his trouble, asked him to say nothing about it, and put it in his pocket without comment. He simply did nothing further about it, and he was aware at supper that night that Yates was uneasy and all but consumed with curiosity.

Next morning Salathiel saddled Enna and rode with Yates as far as the ford with the upturned wagon in it. There he parted from him, for Yates was going to town, and for the first time alluded to the letter. "Tell your *new client*," he called out, while Yates was in the middle of the stream, "that you delivered his letter to me, and that I await his arrival *at the mill*." Yates nodded, nonplussed for once, and continued on to Carlisle, where, happening to meet M. Henri on the street, he delivered Salathiel's message.

Salathiel waited at the ford for some time after Yates had left him; a good half hour at least. A fine sunny day, a little misty so early in the morning after a thaw, but the forest was quiet and the water gurgled about the sunken body and through the wheels of the overturned wagon cheerfully. One of the wheels occasionally moved a little, spinning slowly between the current and the wind.

After he was quite sure that Yates was not coming back, Salathiel dismounted, and tying Enna well back in the thicket, went over to the thunder-tree and removed the cedar boughs that he and Jed had so carefully piled over the broad white lightning blaze. The tree was damp underneath, and the white blaze glistened. After that he rode back. But M. de Molyneaux did not appear at the mill at noon. Indeed, no one was expecting him—not even Salathiel.

About four o'clock the same afternoon, however, both the horses which M. de Molyneaux had hired that morning returned sweating, and with empty saddles, to their owner's stable at Carlisle. Some inquiry was aroused, but the little Frenchman had not seen fit to leave word as to his destination or errand. Doubtless the horses had escaped him.

It was already twilight when Yates and Captain Ourry had a decidedly grim experience just as they attempted to cross the little ford. Their horses suddenly went crazy. Ourry was thrown headlong into the mud as his horse tried to bolt, and he was dragged by the bridle. Yates's fine big grey swerved and made a desperate attempt to start back to Carlisle on his own. After a considerable interval of swearing, racing, confusion, grabbing of bridles, and scraping off of mud, they soothed their trembling horses and managed to force them across the stream.

It was while crossing the water that Yates first noticed the man lying in the water face down, with his head thrust through the spokes of the wagon wheel. He had small doubt as to who it was and what had happened. Further examination disclosed that it *was* M. de Molyneaux, and that he had been pitched forward so violently that his head had broken one of the spokes in the wagon wheel. Yates then ascertained for himself that the big white blaze on the tree, which he had never noticed before, was a genuine freak of nature, while Captain Ourry dug clay out of his features and swore.

Much chastened in spirit and somewhat further matured in experience, Yates and Ourry brought the news to the mill long after supper that night. Nothing was said about it to Frances, at Salathiel's earnest request.

"Why, of course not," said Ourry. "I simply can't understand it."

"Act of God," suggested Salathiel, looking gravely at Yates. "I waited here all day for your client, Mister Attorney, but he never turned up."

Yates nodded sagely and said nothing about the legal aspects of collaborating with the deity. It was his fault, too, he felt. He would not underestimate the Very Large Gentleman of the Forest again.

Hercules was given unexpected instructions by Salathiel next morning, and buried his master on a small hillock in a sumac thicket overlooking the ford, while Salathiel cut down the thunder-tree.

But the gold watch, and sundry other small pocket trinkets of M. de Molyneaux, had now returned to the mill. These Salathiel gave to Yates and suggested that he dispose of them *properly*.

Mr. Yates did so. The watch was water-stopped but still of some value. He gave it to a stone-cutter at Lancaster with instructions. The other trinkets, a diamond pin, some gold buttons, keys, and the cupid seal ring, he sent to the governor of Martinique on the same ship that was to have conveyed M. de Molyneaux home, with a discreet statement of the tragic circumstances of his late client's demise. The stone-cutter, after a month or two, carried out Yates's instructions, and for over a century afterward it was well known to certain farmers and hunters in the neighbourhood of the little ford that in a small thicket overlooking the water stood a neat headstone.

Salathiel, as in the case of Taffy's hand, smoked over the letter thoughtfully, preserved it in confidence, and as usual, said nothing. Nor did Hercules, whose freedom was founded henceforth on silence.

Life at the mill house continued happily in its domestic round. Before the end of February, Bouquet departed for New York and Captain Ourry, to set up new headquarters at Philadelphia. Spring showed signs of coming in early. The inhabitants of the country about Boiling Springs began to return confidently to their long-abandoned farms. Business at the mill gradually resumed. The ice was broken and the wheel turned.

Only the preparation for the colossal field preaching under way at Carlisle prevented and delayed a major exodus from that still much thronged and troubled borough. James McArdle and his inspired colleagues were preparing the town and the countryside for miles around for a visitation of the Holy Spirit. They prayed and preached fervently, with the twelfth chapter of Isaiah like fire on their lips, proclaiming "a joyful thanksgiving of the people for the mercies of God". As February began to turn into March, the spiritual excitement mounted—and "Colonel" Cornelius Vandercliff rode into town on his famous white horse.

28. The Fifth Horseman

NOW, THE WHITE HORSE of "Colonel" Cornelius Vandercliff was greatly feared in all that part of Cumberland which marched on the west with the mountains; and from Ephrata on the north to York on the south, and down into the borders of Maryland, as the sign of evil and a portent of disaster to the Shepherds of the Lord and the bleating of sheep they gathered amongst the hills, against the Day of Judgment.

The name of the horse was Mahar-shalal-hash-baz, or Baz for short, and his master, Cornelius Vandercliff, was an atheist whose geniality was stentorian; a son of Belial, who prayed negatively with a mighty voice that was at once the envy and despair of every itinerant evangelical roarer from Philadelphia to those valleys called the "Shades of Death" amidst the Alleghenies.

The horse was tall, white, narrow, and bony. He was ribbed like a skeleton; and his countenance was zebraic, with yellow teeth and fawn-like eyes. A mane like blanched seaweed waved behind him; but he shaded off into yellow towards his hocks, beneath which the mark of evil was plainly laid upon him. For the hoofs of Baz were not as the hoofs of the nags of Christians. They were spatulate like the war-horse of Julius Cæsar; and when he trod in the dust he left the marks of two toes behind him, sinister as the cloven trace of the Devil himself.

Nevertheless, Baz was the bad apple of his master's evil eye, and he paced off the parasangs between camp meetings with a soft padding sound, instead of the healthy *clop* of iron shoes, which lent his approach a stealthiness that some held to be unearthly. Indeed, even a rare advance glimpse of Baz with his black-cloaked, spade-bearded master, slipping along through the sumac thickets shortly after twilight, making towards the red glow in the sky and the shouts and songful clamour amongst the hills, which marked the site of some hopeful preachment, was about as welcome to the pastors of a mountain flock as a cockroach scuttling amidst the sprays of a bridal wreath is to a bridegroom—and almost as disruptive of the ceremony. For the arrival of Cornelius Vandercliff at a stump preaching in the forest was nicely timed and so precisely managed as to take the ministers at the height of their own demonstrations of the power of prayer, and turn the rough scale of their previous success into the exact measure of their undoing.

Colonel Vandercliff prided himself upon two major ways of timing his disruptive arrival successfully. There was the appearance dramatic, and the approach subtle. But for small affairs, it was the former that he had found more effective.

The appearance dramatic consisted in riding Baz directly out of the night of the forest into the smoky ring of torchlight around the pastors at the very height of holy enthusiasm. When the bench was full of mourners, and moaning sinners were beginning to sway and press forward to take shelter in the outstretched arms of ministerial grace, then the bony white horse and his black-cloaked rider would appear, usually from somewhere behind the pulpit.

After allowing a few seconds for the silence to sink in, the colonel would rise in his stirrups and shout, "Lost! Lost!" with the voice of a siege cannon, while he pointed to pillars of the congregation who had already testified as to their heavenly future, and quoted horrid prophecies from Scripture as to the wrath in store for such tall Pharisees and hypocrites. And if this artful dodge did not suffice to break the spell of holy oratory, he would himself dispute with the ministers, attacking the orthodoxy of their faith and the authority of their particular brand of salvation. And he would end by challenging all the ministers present to a test of their faith in the efficacy of prayer. Let them pray, and let him pray; and let the Lord judge between them. This was the colonel's top offer. "And I'll kiss anybody's white tail if it ain't a fair proposition," he would sometimes add, fishing for sisterly giggles.

Now, in this bare but provocative offer lay the devilish cunning and the demoniac strategy of Colonel Vandercliff's attack. For the crowd was always eager for a contest, even though they were on the side of the ministers; and the ministers durst not refuse without denying the sincerity of their own belief in the power of prayer.

For it was only the mercy of the Lord that the ministers could invoke; at most they might ask that He should forgive all their enemies, and for Christ's sake save Colonel Vandercliff. Only thus by innuendo could they indicate he was bound for hell's fire. While he, when his turn came, he prayed for lightning, *now*.

Naturally, it was those nearest to the colonel who usually began to leave first. But this was not always so. Sometimes mere spectators on the outer verge of the gathering early took advantage of their open line of innocent retreat. As the first fervent requests for lightning ascended on high, they could be seen by ones, twos, and threes sneaking for the hitching-trees on the edge of the camp-ground, untying or cutting their horses loose, and making off into the country beyond as anonymously as possible.

If, in the end, no lightning actually followed, still the triumph of the ministers who stood to abide the result was a lonely one, since there were few save the most obstinate of the elect who cared to remain to give praise to the Lord that it was His mercy rather than His vengeance that had finally prevailed.

Most exasperating of all was the colonel's sudden and humble concession of his defeat, while standing upon the field whence all but him had fled. After which he would blithely turn the head of Baz towards pastures new, and ride off into the sheltering night.

Yet behind him lingered the fear, likewise the anticipation that his fearful prayers for levin might still be answered. In this sense, the colonel's dreadful reputation stretched into the past and extended witheringly into the future. The great moment of his life had been experienced on the borders of Virginia, when during a preachment that had shaken the spiritual foundations of the lower Valley itself, thunder had gathered behind the mountains, red lightning had flowed along the Blue Ridge, even while the colonel was intoning; and the assembly had been scattered by a furious shower of pelting rain and hail. This incident was long and vividly remembered.

Nothing caused the Reverend James McArdle or his inspired assistant, Mr. Puffin, more serious thought in the spring of '65, when the great field preaching was getting under way, than the sinister news that Colonel Vandercliff and his apocalyptic steed had undoubtedly been seen passing through the streets of Carlisle.

That was in late February after Bouquet and Ourry had both left Carlisle. But as nothing more was seen there of the man on the bony white horse, and there was no further rumour of his immediate whereabouts, the anxiety of the ministers was gradually allayed, and the fervour of their exhortations mounted.

Meanwhile, the north wind switched into the south and became a kind of gulf stream of the air, day by day. Winter vanished like the receding memory of a white sin. Save for the groanings and travailings of minor spirits in preparation for the coming of the Great One, the season advanced happily, rapidly; and proved a peculiarly lovely and peaceful one. The Indian war was over. March came early, imitating May. Spring arrived lushly and all at once.

Salathiel had never seen anything like it. Spring along the Ohio had come in less abundantly than this; more reluctantly. There the winter chill died slowly. Here the very skirts of the Season herself seemed to swirl overhead as she strode swiftly northward, her ivory ankles flashing briefly amidst the dogwood as she passed. Boiling Springs was in the direct path of the great bird migration from the Atlantic coastal swamps up the valley of the Susquehanna. The sky overhead was alive with restless music; the earth beneath replied with rustlings and snatches of delirious song. Everyone at the mill house heard it.

Indeed, they were not *in* the mill house any more. The doors were now thrown wide and the windows propped open. The fires died down, and they leached the piles of white ashes in the yard. The smell of new leaves—and a lost fawn wandered in through the open door. The child began to move faintly under Melissa's heart. There were six new kittens in Bridget's basket. Malycal grew plumper and less inclined to predict unpleasant things. The water-harp was touched with new fantasies of melody, and Frances washed her black tresses in vinegar and soft spring water and sat in the beating sunlight to let them dry.

No man can keep any promise as fully as every woman would like him to, but Frances Melissa felt for a while that Salathiel had more than lived up to his word about bringing her "home". There was one week of quiet living in pure ecstasy, with the sound of wings on window sills and a stir of life within and without her, when she understood why a plant struggles through all its other stages just to bloom. That was before many people and the farm wagons began to pass by.

Salathiel and Hercules were much afield together that early spring. They hunted with bow and arrow and with guns. The larder lacked for little. They ploughed five acres to keep the horses fit and last year's seed wheat from moulding. They cleaned sedge and cress and water-weeds from the race and sluices. They sludged down the wooden engine that turned the mill. The stone house shook and shuddered now to its muttered thunder. The raven fluttered and ran croaking to the end of his pegged string. Jed would have liked to let him go. Perhaps there was a black she waiting for him in the woods, he speculated. His mind ran much upon such matters that spring. He hoped they would all be going to the City soon. He was sorry for the *mnungee* bird. The country, for all its newborn beauty, irked him.

Not the least lovely aisle in that forest was the tree-arcaded strip of sandy and river-gravelled road that led past the mill-house door down to the ford over Yellow Breeches Creek. In the summer the road was like a long tunnel with the yellow waters of the river streaming past the end. It was overarched with tall red maples that Mr. Glen had planted, and in the spring the lacy shade along its red-velvety floor was intricately wonderful.

There Bridget danced now in her new moccasins and took her dolls out for promenades, while cardinals whistled at her down the lane. There the empty inn on one side of the road had long stared silently at the face of the mill house just across the shadowed way. The porch of the old tavern was sagging in, but a change now came across the resigned expression on its weathered face. Wagons began to pass up- and downcountry, splashing across the ford, with chiming bells. The old place seemed to listen. The wheel ruts in the red dust of maple buds grew frequent. Farmers' carts came to gather before the mill door. About the time that violets nodded over Mrs. Larned's secret grave, Conklin Drake, the erstwhile proprietor of the deserted ordinary, returned, sniffing business in the warm southern trade wind.

He swept the leaves of two autumns off the porch floor, opened the doors and shutters on their screaming hinges, and hung a new bush over the door. In another week cross-eyed Jenny Greentooth was back serving beer over the bar, and stronger liquor if you asked for it. And it was just about this time that John and Martin Glen with their fascinating new friend, Colonel Cornelius Vandercliff, came riding along under the new maple shade and put up temporarily at Mr. Drake's badly weathered establishment, pending the lapse of Salathiel's lease on the mill.

The Glen brothers had compromised their mutual difficulty over Clara Garber in a way that was perhaps more complimentary to them than to her. They had tossed a coin one evening to decide who should have her, and young Martin had won. Whether this was more satisfactory to Clara than if tails had come up for John, being a sensible girl she would never say. Indeed, it was her reticence that had brought about the coin tossing, combined with Colonel Vandercliff's advice. For he had been staying in the same ordinary at Conestoga with the Glen boys during the time of their double wooing. And he hated to see two such fine fellows embarked on what he considered to be a gratuitous quarrel. The world was full of pretty girls waiting to be wived, but where would either of the boys get another brother?

Fraternity having been thus, on the whole, happily restored again by the toss of a coin, and the course of true love made clear, it had been settled that Martin and Clara were to be married in June at Conestoga. Meanwhile, both Martin and John had come back home to advise with Mr. Yates as to the final disposition of their father's estate and the equitable division of the mill property between them.

Colonel Vandercliff had included himself in this happy return of the brothers to the vicinity of Carlisle almost inevitably, or so it seemed to them. As a man of considerable, albeit somewhat mysterious means, who always paid in coin, he was deeply involved in several schemes for western trade and settlement, amongst them St. Clair's "colony" at Ligonier. Both he and the Glens, therefore, had business to transact with Mr. Yates. And what could be more practical and natural than to find him riding back with them from Conestoga and taking rooms at Mr. Drake's ordinary at Boiling Springs, with bed, board, bar, and stable; with Mr. Yates, the Penns' land attorney, just across the road, and with Arthur St. Clair himself a frequent visitor?

Why, it was convenience in a nutshell, the colonel told himself, even if the inn *was* a bit unsound in its upper story. But surely Mr. Yates had not meant any more than exactly what he had said in recommending its upstairs chambers as "quarters perfectly suited to a gentleman like himself". No, no, ambiguity was an inherent quality of English which every good lawyer must abhor. And Mr. Yates was an attorney whose opinions were always delivered gravely. Clever, no doubt, and a bit of a wit, too. But it was not to be supposed that even *he* could as yet suspect the compelling reason that actually brought Colonel Cornelius Vandercliff to board at such a place as Drake's ordinary—or the unparalleled opportunity for the exercise of his peculiar talents that was about to be afforded him at Carlisle.

The news of the great field preaching being prepared at Carlisle had as inevitably attracted Colonel Vandercliff to the vicinity as honey does a fly. He and Mahar-shalal-hash-baz had come a-riding. In this case, however, owing to the size of the assembly, Colonel Vandercliff had decided when the day came to try the approach subtle, rather than the appearance dramatic. At Boiling Springs he now awaited only the time appointed for the descent of the Holy Spirit.

29. Retrograde Procession of the Paraclete

EDWARD YATES, who was in many ways an epitome of the Age of Reason, was peculiarly sensitive even to a slight haze of bats flying about the loftiest of belfries. Also, he was a close observer, and from the very first he had sensed in Colonel Vandercliff a something extraordinary. He was, therefore, quite content that the colonel had taken his recommendation of the shaky upper story of the inn as a fitting place of abode literally, for he opined that the whimsical Cornelius had thus been prevented from becoming another guest at the mill house with the Albine family, for whom Yates now felt a high moral responsibility, since he lived there himself.

But that is not to say Yates was not considerably intrigued by Colonel Vandercliff, or that he did not take the trouble to find out in what particular direction his obliquity lay.

His conclusion, after an evening or two as *amicus curiae* before the bar, with Jenny Greentooth assisting spiritually behind, was that the colonel and the Reverend James McArdle were both afflicted by the same kind of bats, although by hostile varieties. And since Cornelius finally became confidential and eloquently outlined the nature of his mission to liberate mankind, with emphasis upon his plan for scattering the coming field preaching at Carlisle, Mr. Yates began to view that evangelical occasion from another standpoint, and revised his decision not to be present at what now promised to be a diverting and informative scene.

The chances of the colonel's drawing down lightning at any given time and particular spot were, he felt, negative, or at most constituted a risk he might cheerfully take as a purely passive spectator of the event. For this time he was determined to remain neutral. The colonel might prove to be the prince of harlequins and a past-master of divine fooling, but Yates had had his lesson with the little Frenchman as to just how tragic comedy can be; and God, lightning, and Mr. McArdle were a triumvirate which he thought it expedient that the colonel should undertake to try to tease all by himself.

In this sentiment he found himself completely at one with Salathiel, who desired nothing less than to bring down on himself and Frances the meddling or indignant attention of James McArdle. That day when driving out to headquarters he had encountered the angry ministers in the wagon, Mr. McArdle had addressed him in the tones of an ancient Hebrew prophet, and it had been all that he could do to restrain himself. Another time, and he might not be able to do so. After all, there were distinct limits to what he could take quietly. And so he, too, had determined to stay away from the field preaching, when the arrival of Jim Fergus and Arthur St. Clair for an overnight stay on their way to Philadelphia caused him to change his mind. Fergus had brought him a letter from McArdle.

Salathiel's indignation upon reading this unexpected and unwelcome effusion was unbounded. McArdle alone could strike at his happiness so nearly; and what gratitude he felt for his former "preceptor and spiritual guide" was now cancelled by the unbounded claims of the man himself and his fanatic and pious threats. It would now be necessary to take immediate measures to see that Mr. McArdle minded his own business. Plainly, in one way or another, here was an end of peace and quiet home-keeping at the mill; and equally plainly, this letter could not be answered in the direct and practical way in which he had "replied" to that of M. de Molyneaux.

Mr. Yates also was alarmed, for fear that Salathiel would resort to some simple violence. He was soon relieved of that apprehension by Salathiel himself. But his sympathy for his friend, and his natural repugnance to meddling fanatics, prompted him to sit down the same evening that Jim Fergus brought the letter and go into a careful conference over what he now called their mutual affairs. Both of them now admitted it had come to that, and they now for the first time put their heads together as partners to work out a solution of their difficulties in a partnership that was to prove perpetual.

They both agreed that in view of Frances' delicate condition, it would never do to have McArdle come and make trouble at the mill. After a long talk, and a careful weighing of means of defence and offence, and all the possibilities involved, they determined to act in advance upon the advices in the letter, and so take McArdle at the disadvantage of his own terms. "Nothing," said Yates, " is so disconcerting to those who undertake to disturb the repose of whited sepulchres as to find them occupied by wasps."

So it was arranged that he and Salathiel should both ride up to Carlisle together and appear in the field at the great intercession—but take Colonel Vandercliff along with them.

"Of course, we shall all have to avoid being converted," said Yates, "but the chances of that do appear to be small. And this will let Mr. McArdle see the face of his belovèd pupil, and thus prevent his coming to the mill. If the colonel and Baz scatter the ranks of the faithful, we can then suppose that the Reverend James will be provided with sufficient troubles of his own to detain his attention; if not, we can still outface him, deny the validity of the marriage, and threaten him with the law of slander if he talks.

"As to the alleged marriage, I'll be frank: McArdle might make his contention good as to the legality of the ceremony. It is unfortunate that your girl has that piece of bark with the signatures on it and her ring. But I do not think there are any living witnesses left. And in any event, we can contend that this marriage was never consummated and that you did not and could not understand at the time what the ceremony implied. Therefore, no consent and no consummation. But I hardly think it will ever come to trial. Having lost his plea to your emotions, Mr. McArdle is not the kind who will take an appeal to the law. I think I can shut his mouth, since he is not able to shout 'bigamy'. You see now why I always felt it best to let your living with Frances remain a matter of common law. After the child comes, you can both consider further. But meanwhile, only the girl herself, now at Cresap's, could make real trouble. And you will always, unless she dies or marries, have to abide that chance. But we'll meet that when it arrives. Mr. McArdle we can outface now on his own ground by pulling it from under him. If nothing else, we can certainly admonish him to keep away from the mill."

Salathiel agreed, although he did not care much for Colonel Vandercliff as an ally. He also felt it a good opportunity to tell Yates that he thought it high time to arrive at a final understanding with the Glen boys, to tell them that he would not enter into any further arrangements with them as to occupying or running the mill. "I intend for the City," he said; "I always did, and Frances is content as soon as I can make decent arrangements there."

"I'm glad to hear it," Yates replied. "I was diffident of trying to persuade you to leave, since we've been so snug and comfortable here. But both the reason and the convenience of your stay in your journey to the metropolis are now over." Here Yates reached down and knocked his pipe out on the hearth, where the fire was beginning to burn low.

He continued, refilling his pipe and drawing on it comfortably. "Your arrangement with St. Clair will soon be over, and I'd advise you to terminate it. I happen to know he'll not be able to start any new settlers westward until well into the summer. Also, let me remind you of a certain promise you made one evening at Patton's to help me in settling people on *our* land."

"*Our* land?" inquired Salathiel.

"Yes, yes," insisted Yates. "For I'll tell you what, if you'll come in, I'll make it amount to that. I haven't had a chance so far to go into the result of that little card game with Lieutenant Grant, but we came off well. Yes, sir," cried Yates, "damn well! I've put Wully's papers through, and seen to all those important and nasty legal details, and the result is two considerable tracts of land, one in the province of New York and the other in East Florida. But we'll have to occupy them both some way or other in the near future. Now, I've plans under way to do that; if you and your former acquaintance, Friend Japson, can get together in Philadelphia and undertake to work with me. It's a grand scheme, and you'll be needed at first in the City to help see it get under way. It's nothing less than our mutual fortune, mayhap!" Yates snapped the patch on his eye.

"Now, that's one thing. The other is that I think you do well *not* to try to enter into business with the Glens. Martin is going to bring his bride home to the mill house this summer, and you wouldn't want to board Frances and have the child born at Mr. Drake's ordinary, which, as I pointed out to Colonel Vandercliff, is infirm. No, I am sure you wouldn't want to do that. Milling isn't your permanent career. And if you do move, move to the City.

"Ourry is mighty set on having you and Frances come over to Philadelphia to help conduct domestic headquarters for the brigadier. If I were you, I'd settle *his* mind about it. So far you've avoided saying yes or no, but it would be, if nothing else, a fine chance to get started in the City, and provide Frances respectable quarters to settle down in for having the baby. To be sure, Ourry hasn't thought of that. But let be! You would have at least a stipend to start on, and the helpful influence of the general. I'd not delay. St. Clair and Fergus are going to the City tomorrow. Why not send a note on with them to Ourry? You could write it tonight. I'm due in Lancaster on land business, and later to go on to the City myself, but I'll stay over and help outface the Reverend James McArdle on behalf of a client. You and I and the colonel can all ride over and watch the spirit descend. As far as that goes," he added, "if you can get ready in time, you could come by Lancaster and pick me up on your way to Philadelphia. Why not?"

Salathiel sat considering all this for some time. Finally he reached over and knocked his pipe out on the hearth, too.

"I'll do that," he said. Yates nodded.

That was the reason that shortly afterward on a Friday morning five horsemen, the two Glens, Salathiel, Edward Yates—and Colonel Vandercliff, all set out together, bound for the great field preaching at Carlisle.

The natural scene, human strategy, and the divine event of the great field preaching at Carlisle took place essentially as follows: Inwardly, within the minds and hearts of the multitude who had been drawn to the spot; outwardly, upon a level field about a mile outside of town with the trade sheds of *Boynton, Wharton & Morgan* along the road at one end and a clump of high and still noble pine woods at the other, which last provided a convenient grove for the retiring cabins of the ministers, and a place to tie innumerable horses.

Between the woods and the sheds, along two sides of the approximately square area kept free for the grand congregation for mass preaching, Mr. McArdle and Mr. Puffin had erected the marquees which they had begged from the brigadier to be used as prayer booths and rallying points for the flocks of the twelve ministers who were "joined together as members in Christ for the revival and reawakening of religion along the western borders in a great beseeching of grace to be holden at Carlisle". Although the total number of the ministers was purely accidental, it had not failed to receive some arch comment, and was the cause of professional persiflage even amongst the ministers themselves as to which one of the "twelve apostles" would prove Judas.

The canvas marquees, however, were not the only shelters along the east and west sides of the grassy square. There were also booths roofed over with green boughs in a Biblical manner, rustic sheds for the purveying of meat and drink, pits for roasting, hitching bars, and the lines and spaces for covered wagons, which lent the scene of the great preachment a bowerlike and pleasantly rustic appearance, which the assembly of God's people in a tabernacle in the spring woods might justly be expected to show.

The centre of all pious comment and attention was the mighty pulpit and platform for the divine oratory of the ministers, erected in the heart of the field. Stairs ascended to it on every side in the centre. It was built of strong logs and rough-hewn planks and meant for mass exhortation. As many as four ministers could exhort from it at the same time, each facing his own cardinal portion of the listening crowd. A choir of the faithful sat upon it in the middle to lead the multitude in psalm and hymn singing. The newly converted climbed the steps to testify. It was surrounded at a little distance by poles with iron baskets for cressets and rings for pine torches, lit and renewed frequently during night preaching. And day or night, the pulpit was a mighty instrument to be played or danced upon by the ministers, even as David played and danced before the Lord—albeit with more attention to raiment.

There was something impressive and memorable about the scene itself; a sense of fitness and of apt design with purpose, as though a modern Moses had pitched God's tabernacle in the wilderness and paused in the years of journeying to rest and refresh the people of the Lord. The mountains looked at it, the sky overarched it. And quite suddenly it was indubitably there.

Like many other things, however, this impression of ease of achievement of the miracle of being was apparent rather than real. In one sense the tabernacle was the culmination of the life-work of the Reverend James McArdle, who was looked upon as the Moses of the occasion. And it was he who was now expected to strike the rock of indifference with the rod of inspiration and bring forth the gushing waters of salvation. It must be remembered, however, that James McArdle had spent many years in both the location and the preparation of the Rock. And in the end it was his devotion that had gathered about him, and in some cases converted, a band of inspired apostles for the preaching of the Word to the multitude at Carlisle. He was now regarded by many as a prophet, and in some sense a martyr to the faith.

The mission of James McArdle to the people and the savage tribes of the Alleghenies, "God's country", now extended backward into time for well over a quarter of a century. He had started preaching to the Indians before Salathiel was born.

James McArdle was firmly persuaded that Indians were the lost tribes of Israel, ignorant of the coming of the Messiah. And he had tried valiantly to bring them the news of salvation and gather them into the Christian fold. In the process he had lost both ears, but in compensation, the power of making other people listen had been added to his tongue.

Bitter experience in having his Indian converts murdered by the white settlers, eventually gave Mr. McArdle pause, although it never changed his opinion. He had gradually, during his own captivity, changed the object of his ministrations from the Indians themselves to the white captives he had found amongst them; and upon his deliverance and coming eastward, he had continued to preach the Word and to hold revivals and prayer meetings in the settlements along the frontiers.

Gradually, he had gathered about him the ministers of certain mountain flocks. The accession of the Reverend Mr. Puffin at Bedford, by conversion, had given him a Joshua to match his Moses. And it was this group of devoted ministers with whom he had worked and held pentecostal meetings, until they were all as one, fanatically enthusiastic and irretrievably inspired.

It was their great ambition to hold a mighty mass prayer meeting or "Beseeching", as they called it, at Carlisle. McArdle had long felt his powers were being wasted in working with single converts or in small meetings lost amidst the hills. He was now for conversion by multitudes; for the bringing in of the millennium, if possible, at one stroke. And in the state of mind to which he and his colleagues had attained, almost anything seemed possible. They held that where two or three are gathered together, what they ask shall be given, as the Scripture promised —and what they asked was the descent of the Holy Ghost.

Such a boon was not, of course, lightly to be asked nor easily obtained. Long and arduous preparation had marked their early meetings together: searchings, repentance, and open confession; abstinence, fasting, and days and nights of continuous prayer. At last, a final beseeching for grace by all of them praying aloud together.

Then, at last, the moment would arrive. Often it was late at night, usually when it seemed that the weak flesh could stand no more—a power would shake them as the wind shakes leaves. It would come pouring down upon them. It was this enormous experience which bound them together, in faith confirmed by the event. And it was this supreme moment which, as good evangelists, they strove to repeat in bringing down the power of the Spirit on a crowd.

After the success of their own meetings, they had held Beseechings with each other's congregations. Then they had ridden about in groups of three or four to larger assemblies. Finally, after several years, they had all combined for one culminating meeting at Carlisle in which the whole countryside was to receive the baptism of the Spirit en masse. That, at least, was the ambitious goal of James McArdle, who was now in such a mood of high exaltation that it prompted him to think he might be capable of hastening the date of the millennium all by himself.

To him, it was now a matter of indignation, or at best mysterious chagrin, that many of his regularly ordained brethren held aloof. And if they did not openly denounce, at least passively opposed him. The Reverend Mr. Craighead was one of them. Also many of his brother Masons were not to be moved. Mr. Byers, who was of high degree, gave him the gate. As for the gentlemen and the gentry, lawyers like Mr. Yates, and the conservative members of the old churches, with a few exceptions, they were plainly not with him at all. Only a few of the merchants contributed. In short, there were two minds at Carlisle as to whether the Great Beseeching was good for trade or not. People who came in wagons and camped, usually brought all their "fixin's" with them.

All this, for a man of James McArdle's spiritual sensibility and exalted state of mind, was hard to bear. Wheedling contributions in kind from the faithful was also a sordid and difficult burden. During the preaching, he and the other apostles would live in plenty; but afterward, he and Mr. Puffin would be reduced again to Mr. Inman's oval-wheeled wagon and the tired old horse.

It was a combination of these petty anxieties and annoyances that had prompted the letter to Salathiel. For James McArdle had not only met Jim Fergus on High Street one morning, and had to listen to his gossip about how well Salathiel was doing at the mill—a few minutes later he had run into Dr. Craighead, in his newly restored wig, and had to listen all over again to the merits and talents of Salathiel and Frances, as well as to Mr. Craighead's scarcely veiled menaces about tampering with his flock. They were, he claimed, already in "a reasonable state of Grace" and had fully accepted the Atonement. Did Mr. McArdle *not* think the Atonement sufficient?

Now, this was quite a poser, and in the heat of the ensuing argument Mr. McArdle had found great difficulty, among other things, in refraining from telling what *he* knew about Salathiel; and his somewhat fiery vein at parting from Mr. Craighead had been continued into the letter.

Mr. McArdle did not permit any small opposition to abate the fervour of his preparations and exhortations preliminary to the final event itself. He and the other eleven had continued to preach and to visit and exhort in all the countryside about. People now began to pour in from all sides, even from distant towns and hamlets. On the Sunday preceding the Beseeching there were almost as many people in overwhelmed Carlisle as there had been a few months before when Bouquet marched home. Day after day family wagons and lone horsemen continued to arrive.

At last the great day dawned, Friday morning. Before sun-up McArdle gathered his colleagues and in a cabin in the pine woods next to the tabernacle they prayed together. The rumour that the white horse of Colonel Vandercliff had been seen stabled at Boiling Springs was more like fuel to their enthusiasm at this point than water on the fire. Promptly after breakfast a drum sounded solemnly from the platform. The Welsh choir began singing, and the people gathered in from all sides. Looking across the fields still hazy with the mist of morning, the multitude now saw the twelve ministers advancing towards them from the woods. A loud exultant shout went up to heaven. The preaching and praying and beseeching began.

No, there had never been anything quite like it. And long afterward those who followed the progress of evangelism westward, in what were later on called "revivals", harked back in memory to the great original Beseeching at Carlisle. It was James McArdle's genius and devotion, his very fanaticism that had brought it about. There were more people gathered at other places later, but never a greater fervour, such loud hosannas or more overwhelming excitement. Excitement, excitement, excitement—it began in the morning; it mounted and climbed and reached minor crests through the afternoon. It attained a delirium of repentance, a triumph of conversion, and a peak for the Spirit to descend upon in the wild fiery hours of the torch-lit night.

It was a warm spring morning. The breeze kept blowing from the south. Even by ten o'clock the ministers and the congregation were sweating. The heat of the noonday began to wear them down. It had been McArdle's plan to spend the morning in thanksgiving for the blessings of peace restored, the afternoon in repentance, and the night in purifying prayer. The beseeching itself and the hopeful advent of the Spirit had been planned for Saturday. But the rising tide of emotion now began to outrun the schedule of Mr. McArdle's plan. This was plainly apparent even before noon.

After a morning of hymns, songs of thanksgiving, and an outpouring of praise and gratitude, ending in an acclamation of universal joy and a storm of hosannas, time was taken out for the noon meal. Buckets of boiled meat and potatoes were passed around, chunks of bread, and certain liquid refreshments.

During this mundane interlude Mr. McArdle imparted to the other apostles that it had been revealed to him that the Spirit would descend that night. This apocalyptic news flew from lip to lip. Sinners realized that they now had less time than they had counted upon in which to procrastinate; the joy of the elect was unbounded. And the entire assembly gathered about the pulpit platform to hear the clarion call to repentance from ten ministers, who succeeded one another without pause, except for the singing of the choir.

Mr. McArdle and Mr. Puffin were saving themselves for the great and final beseeching in the evening. They had carefully planned the strategy of the night attack between them. Mr. Puffin was to hold forth upon the mercy, the love, and the free fountain of salvation. He was to preach his great sermon, now perfectly memorized with appropriate gestures, upon the unparalleled sufferings of the Lamb of God. It was a masterpiece of forensic rhetoric, which he had been practising and revising ever since the days of his long-past but inspired youth. With it he had brast many a brazen heart in twain.

That night there was to be a middle moon. It would appear about meridian at sunset and glide slowly down into the west. Mr. Puffin was to preach it halfway down the sky. Mr. McArdle was then to take up the tale of God's mercy and paint the horrors of the pit, for those who refused to accept what was freely offered. When the moon dipped, that was to be the crucial moment. Then would go forth the call for the Spirit to descend and lighten the darkness.

Meanwhile, neither of the two leaders was idle. During the afternoon they divided and visited between them the twelve tents, where for the most part bands of women awaited praying, preparing themselves for the great event. Some were already torpid from their long vigils; others were hysterical from apprehension. The former the two ministers roused again to a sense of spiritual crisis, the latter they calmed with extended promises of hope.

Outside, the tumult of continuous preaching, shouts of glory, and shrieks of despair, wild psalm singing and uncontrolled weeping marked the afternoon hours, as they swiftly unrolled with ever-mounting excitement, until the shades of evening began to fall. As the moon appeared directly overhead, the twelve bands of women emerged from their tents on either side of the square and were marshalled towards the platform, while the crowd burst into glad hymns and hallelujahs of welcome. The torches and cressets were now lighted, while Mr. Puffin waited for a calm moment in which to begin.

It was just at this juncture that the five horsemen from Boiling Springs approached the assembly. Evening, they knew, would be the height of the holy spectacle. They rode their horses along the dusty South Road through the dusk of twilight and tied them under the platform of the trading sheds. There Baz could be well concealed, and a modest fee of sixpence assured the others from being lifted by sinners anxious to flee from the wrath to come. Without attracting any attention, they took their places upon the outskirts of the crowd. Gradually Yates and Salathiel worked themselves forward until they stood close under the platform. Mr. Puffin arose, and quieting the multitude with a prayer, began to preach.

The great appeal, the original reason for Christian hope and sympathy went home. Mr. Puffin related the suffering of the Saviour Himself. He detailed the scenes at the stations of the Cross, and the great defeat and triumph at Calvary. No one who was not feeble-minded remained unmoved. Mr. Puffin was sincere. He suffered. The crowd suffered with him. Tears ran down from the single eye of Edward Yates. Salathiel stood transfixed with amazement that all this had been suffered and borne patiently for him. Mr. Puffin preached the moon halfway down the sky. He ended with the despairing words of the Divine Man on the Cross, "My God, my God, why hast thou forsaken me?", and held out his arms to the multitude, begging them to accept the salvation so dearly bought.

Oh, if it could only have been left like that! The crowd sighed as one man, and moved forward unconsciously two or three steps as though to receive the boon. Many were weeping, many distraught. It moved forward—and found itself, almost magically, it seemed, in the flaring shadows of the torches, confronted by the grim earless countenance of James McArdle.

Here and there arose shrieks of startled and anticipatory terror from the women. A great groan went up. In the midst of this, Mr. McArdle began.

"And He descended into Hades" was his text and theme. Steadily, unrelentingly, and convincingly, he pictured the obscene horrors and writhing torments of the pit. He quoted Scripture, line by line. The field of McArdle's labours gibbered and seethed in ripples of fright. The breath of vengeance seemed to strike down and wither the crowd in wilted spots, where the people writhed and lay moaning on the ground.

Thus it was that James McArdle preached the moon down to the western horizon. The great moment of his lifetime was now at hand. As the branches of the distant forest began to finger the silver bottom of the moon, he paused. Darkness was rapidly coming on. The noise from the multitude before him was like the sound of a herd of buffalo caught fatally, and wallowing in a bog. Men bellowed, and women shrieked to be saved. In another moment the time for the universal beseeching would have come. But at that instant the man on the white horse rode down the aisle of terror and dismounted before the platform. The horror was so great that it seemed the Devil in person had come. In the universal and overwhelming silence, the spade-bearded and black-cloaked figure climbed to the platform and stood outlined in the smoky red glow of the sputtering pine knots.

He threw his cloak back with a confident gesture, and stepping to the low rail of the platform just as the moon finally sank and darkness swooped, he roared, "Lost, lost!" like a sudden double clap of thunder from the surrounding murk.

But the effect was quite different from what the arch-atheist expected. Mr. McArdle had already been so successful that terror could do no more. And it was the minister alone who responded. He came forward and laying his hand familiarly on the colonel's shoulder, leaned out over the rail and shouted, "See, good people, here is the great doubter himself come to be saved. Oh glory! Glory be to God in the Highest! Let us pray!"

The revulsion came. A babble of indescribable relief, a shout of joy at this visible miracle of mercy, rose from all sides. The stricken leapt to their feet with new hope and began to prance. The colonel's prayer for lightning went unheard. Indeed, those who saw him praying thought he was giving thanks. A vast and wallowing excitement ran in waves through the crowd. Colonel Vandercliff realized that he was undone. His failure weakened his knees and struck him like a blow somewhere in the back of the neck. In fact, neither he nor McArdle had control any longer over the crowd roaring below.

A wizened little fellow, a discharged militia drummer, with a head shaped like an eggplant and small burning eyes turned back in his head, emerged with a line of rocking and swaying people, arms on shoulders, following behind him, beating an imaginary drum with flailing hands, and roaring over and over again in a harsh voice:

> "A rat-a-tat-tat, the dog and the rat,
> A rat-a-tat-tat, the dog and the rat."

To this fascinating rhythm the crowd now began helplessly to respond. It swayed to and fro; it trembled and it stamped.

Some people leapt high into the air. A Samson of a man howled exultantly that the Spirit was upon them. On the edge of the encampment, boys rocked back and forth in the boughs of maples and whooped to one another gleefully. Women were mowed down in windrows. They lay gasping on their backs with their legs apart and their eyes turned back into their heads. Mr. Yates, who went to the assistance of one of them, was sternly repulsed by the girl's husband.

"Leave her lay where Jesus flanged her," the man roared, and then rising, tore his handkerchief loose from between her teeth, and went jigging off after the little drummer, beside himself with spiritual glee.

James McArdle, with his hands before his face, was now kneeling on the platform and praying earnestly that God should not mock him, that this cup of gall and stupendous failure should be removed from his lips. His prayer was answered. He looked up from where he was kneeling and saw that Colonel Vandercliff was being converted. He looked upon him in the very throes of the act. The colonel began to prance to the roaring chorus of the crowd. He could not prevent himself. The drummer's song lifted his feet into the air one after the other. He bowed and swayed. And then the miracle occurred.

The Spirit descended, and the gift of tongues was upon him. To Cornelius the power seemed to be coming from behind. It rained down into the crowd. He could see in the wavering torch-light patches in the crowd before him that seemed to be struck as by puffs of wind on the surface of water. The power poured into the people, and everywhere they ceased shouting about the dog and the rat and began to gibber in a new, a holy dialect, and a hundred strange languages. Each was given his own heavenly tongue. Colonel Vandercliff was lifted by his neck to the rail of the platform. He stood upon it. He meant to pray for lightning. But he began to prophesy.

As he ended he tottered, threw up his hands with a great cry, and pitched forward from the rail, diving head-foremost into the crowd. Someone had hamstrung Baz, and the tormented cries of the white horse rose above everything, until the wild clamour of those who had found salvation drowned his moaning in a prolonged gurgling and chortling of the peace that passeth understanding. . . .

Hours later Cornelius Vandercliff came to in a tent, surrounded by triumphant ministers. As their prize convert and chief exhibit, they now ministered tenderly to his extreme bodily wants. He looked about him. He remembered. He understood what had happened. But he said nothing. He was sick in soul and body, and he slept intermittently for two days and nights.

Yates, Salathiel, and the two Glens returned together to the mill. They had not waited after the fall of their friend, Colonel Vandercliff. They emerged from the babble of tongues without making any comment themselves, mounted their horses, and came home.

"Thank God for the cleanness of the dawn," said Yates. Salathiel agreed. He felt that he had escaped from a foul quagmire, but still felt the mud caked upon him. He took a swim in the mill-pond, and at breakfast began to talk to Frances about getting ready to move to the City. He said nothing about what he had been through at Carlisle. Such things were not for a sweet woman like his common-law wife to hear. He had kept trouble away from her. McArdle, he knew, would never come to the mill now. He would be too busy with his converts and other plans.

At Carlisle the Reverend James McArdle's triumph was complete. His cup ran over. He had seen the face of his pupil stricken with repentance in the midst of the crowd. It was enough. He was now preparing to carry the message of the gospel westward. He hoped to take Cornelius Vandercliff along, and regretted the loss of the white horse.

At Boiling Springs all was haste and hurry in the days that followed. Captain Ourry had sent back a note by Fergus urging that Salathiel and Frances be on hand to meet the brigadier when he returned to Philadelphia from New York. Convenient quarters in one of the most respectable boarding-houses in the City had been found. General Forbes had been buried from that house, after being laid out in the parlour. And no better assurance of convenience and respectability could be desired. Yates laughed; and left for Lancaster, where he would wait to be picked up when the wagon came through. He would be at Colonel Burd's house, he said—not the one that Colonel Burd was building at "Tinian" in the country, but the big one on the square. At which Frances pricked up her ears. Perhaps Bridget could see that house, after all. It was the mansion which Mrs. Patton had thought of at Lyttleton as being so "very, very genteel".

Heigh-ho, who could tell? Respectability, gentility, and possibly affluence now lay before them. Frances Melissa hurried about her packing in the old mill house contentedly, while Malycal and Bridget excitedly helped. Whatever else it might be, Frances was certain a move to the City was a move in the right direction.

Let the rest happen as it might.

The City in the Dawn

Prelude

IN THE EAST the morning star still hung alone in the dawnlight like a last spark struck from the anvil of hope. Here and there along the city water-front, where the massed rigging of many ships traced a black spider web against the quickening glow in the sky, watchmen quenched the fading yellow stars of their lanthorns, sounded their rattles perfunctorily, and turning homeward with echoing footfalls, proclaimed with sleepy voices that it was a fair spring morning—"and all's well."

Certainly April the fourth 1765 was a fine spring morning—and, as far as most contemporary eyes could see, affairs in the City of Philadelphia went well enough.

The tender green of early April had flushed the formal gardens of the great houses with a haze of opening buds and starry shrub blossoms. Cherry trees already dressed like brides. The noble proprietary forest, called the Governor's Woods, that stretched from the Schuylkill to the environs of Central Square, was laced with white dogwood thickets, and delirious with bird song. It swam with dreamful green and yellows and chattered with insect delight.

As Salathiel Albine and Edward Hamilton Yates, with the big wagon and a small baggage cart behind them, rode from beneath the trees into the cleared, level common of Central Square, a fiery sun sailed up out of the dark Jersey woods across the Delaware and began to lay a disturbing wand upon the low-lying river mists of the water-front scarcely five miles away.

Faintly, from the barracks at Camptown in the Northern Liberties, came the shock of the sunrise gun. The riding lights on his Majesty's frigate *Coventry* were instantly lowered and doused. The distant mutter and jolting thunder of heavy drays along the newly cobbled water-front began. In the tented wagon, Negro Jed's raven began to croak and snap its beak with a kind of premonitory excitement.

Across the heavy green turf where a number of cows were quietly grazing, the wagon and cart followed the two horsemen in a short cut. On the eastern side they struck the green, but heavily rutted lane, known officially as High Street, but more familiarly as "Market Way," and proceeding now at a somewhat slower pace, they continued to press townward.

It was not long before they became part of a lively and ever-growing stream of vehicles, fed by farm wagons and carts of every description on their way to market, a quaint rural traffic that kept pouring into the Market Way on either side from the country and villages near-by.

Immediately before them a blue-and-scarlet wagon led the way like a gaudy chariot of plenty, the bells of its two pony-like horses clanging harshly. On a side panel, in German and in German script, the legend "Stuppelheimer, The Hog Butcher, nach Doylestown" was displayed in gilt. Confirming this, two newly dressed hogs, with carrots in their writhing jaws, were laid out hairless and pink on a bierlike counter in the wagon's midst, while links of sausages of all kinds swung on hooks from the latticed racks of the vehicle, which in turn supported a light hipped roof painted a vivid cerulean.

Within this fence of dangling sausages, like Christian martyrs cast into a cage of wriggling serpents, sat the bearded, black-clad, shovel-hatted farmer and his sombre, poke-bonneted wife, as close together on the driving seat as propriety permitted. Behind them, looking out from the rear of the cart, and swinging their sturdy clogs and calves over the dropped end-gate, rode the farmer's twin daughters, pink and white, flaxen braided, smiling under their starched linen caps, and prinked out in their market-best.

Plain people as the Stuppelheimers were, and shy Mennonites at that, it was not quite possible for them to conceal a certain worldly curiosity as to the nature and errand of the interesting travellers in the "cavalcado," which now followed them so closely behind. There was considerable turning about and surreptitious craning of necks in the Stuppelheimer cart, together with some speculative appraisal in Low German dialect. In fact, Papa Stuppelheimer, his name famous in the annals of the Philadelphia market for fine scrapple and sausage, continued for quite a distance to glance behind him as if to oversee the conduct of his daughters or the state of his wares. Meanwhile, Mamma's black straw bonnet seemed to be reversible, as though on the head of an owl, and her twin daughters, Bertha and Gertrude, were overtaken by spasms of ill-concealed curiosity ending in wriggles.

So many bright, saucer-blue German eyes staring at her from under the even deeper blue of the ceiling of the sausage cart caused the lady riding beside a huge black man driving the big tented wagon to smile back with good-natured amusement—and the little girl who sat beside her, with a tabby cat looking out of the hole in the lid of its basket, to wave her small handkerchief amicably. A dapper, one-eyed gentleman clad in elegant grey, riding a beautiful grey horse, winked at both Bertha and Gertrude at the same time with his one good eye, and grinned. This was too much, and the wriggles of the Stuppelheimer twins now became one with the nervous danglings of their papa's sausages.

Farmer Stuppelheimer at length spoke sharply to his womenfolk about their unseemly conduct, and whipping up his little team he pressed on down Market Way. He had a deal of fresh pork to dispose of that morning, and it would never do to be late for market with raw meat in his cover crocks, and the weather getting so unusually warm.

But Farmer Stuppelheimer was by no means so dull, or even so simple, as he looked. And he had already arrived at the conclusion that the gentry must be the family of some official, perhaps a high military officer, returning to Philadelphia from the western frontiers. And for this not entirely incorrect conclusion, he had his own good reasons.

In the first place, the gentleman in Bedford grey, with the patch over one eye, wore a lawyer's wig; and in the second place, the horse with the fine Arabian head was undoubtedly a scion of the proprietary stud at Pennsbury. Any Bucks County farmer would know that, for there were no other horses like them in all the colonies. *Ergo*, the one-eyed lawyer was a family retainer of the Penns.

But the other horseman, the tall man with the piercing grey eyes and hawklike countenance—it was hard to place him. He might be an officer? He was dressed in a decent suit of black with pewter buttons. He wore heavy riding boots with brass spurs, a white scarf, and a large but flimsy cocked hat that drooped a bit over his right ear. Yet his hair was most correctly powdered, and brushed straight back from his forehead into a meticulous, military-looking queue. Also he rode in a military saddle with double holsters marked with the brass monogram R.A.—60.

Yet, for all that, his air was familiar and native instead of foreign and military; free and pantherlike, rather than stiffly precise. Somehow he bestrode his horse, a nice roan mare that minced in her gait under his mighty bulk, more like a savage than a soldier. And there was a bright little moon-shaped hand-axe in a leather sheath—it might be a tomahawk—slung from his saddle bow. Perhaps he was a ranger? Possibly a lucky Indian trader turned gentleman? Or one of those fierce Injun-murdering Paxtang rebels! Ach, you could never be sure about these tall fellows from the backwoods and the frontiers! Besides, to a mere Stuppelheimer, the wagons, horses, and harness of the cavalcado were far more interesting than the people. "*Property, property, property,*" all the horses' hoofs seemed to say as they trotted along.

Du lieber! He had never seen anything to equal the big ark with the green canvas tent for a top. Heavier than a Conestoga, it was more like a barge on wheels. Such massive wheels, with heavy shrunk-iron tires and brass-bound hubs! It would take hard labour on many a fertile acre to support that style of travel. As for the horses, they were sleek heavy greys with shaggy fetlocks, regular Belgians, powerful. And there was a chime that must be the sweetest north of Virginia. Silver bells! And what was that trundling behind, if not a neat artillery cart on two wheels? You might suppose all this would be enough to carry any one man's worldly plunder. But no, the trundler was followed by still another baggage cart driven by a young Negro servant with an old white woman in a shawl and sunbonnet sitting beside him.

Both looked contented and happy, but you could easily tell the crone had been worked much too hard. Such a wise and weazened old face he had seldom seen. Doubtless these gentry got all there was to get out of their people, old or young. Grinders of the face of the poor! He spat out of the side of his mouth . . . That proud, worldly woman riding on the big wagon seat, for instance, the mistress—ach, she was a one, no doubt!

Still there was something so preternaturally trim, so practical and self-sufficient, about everything he had been examining that without knowing it, and pious man that he was, Farmer Stuppelheimer broke the last commandment on the spot. He was filled with envy.

How some people did get along in this wicked world, and not God's plain people either! The lady on the big seat was beautiful. Also, in his humble opinion, she was handsomely dressed in a flame-colored bonnet and a great black shawl embroidered with flamboyant roses. Her little girl looked out of her own bonnet, a miniature of her mother's, with a face like the bud of a rose just beginning to open. The giant black man driving, who was almost as big as the hawk-faced white man on the little mare, had arms like gnarled oak roots. He tooled his four horses along with one hand, as though they were a single team. Rich people paid one hundred pounds, and more, for a slave like that. A hundred pounds sterling worth ten miles of sausages! All for a servant! At this point Farmer Stuppelheimer suddenly made up his mind—irrevocably.

This vain show of solid worldly prosperity must be the fruit of sin and much hard dealing. Mere solid labour and honest sweat would never do it. No, it must be the result of usury and of frequent going-to-law. Doubtless, the natty one-eyed attorney was the chief begettor of the whole cavalcado. Farmer Stuppelheimer grunted with convinced satisfaction at his own deductive acumen. As for himself, he was one of the Plain People, virtuous from hard labour; poor, but a child of God, bitte— and such cogitations would never get his own goods to market.

"Look out, papa, they're *against!*" cried Bertha in alarm. While he had been dreaming, the big wagon had almost caught up with him. So they would pass him, eh! He leaned forward and lashed his little horses viciously.

The sausage cage on wheels surged forward dangerously. Bertha stifled a scream. Papa was late! Papa was angry! He did not like the friendly people who were following them so closely. The whip cracked again and again. But for all that the two horsemen and the big wagon kept overtaking him whenever he relented.

The lady smiled and the little girl waved her handkerchief. The four grey horses trotted forward into the morning, their harness bells chiming together softly and solemnly. The broad iron wheels rumbled and followed relentlessly after the two horsemen, as though they were all long practised and determined travellers together, adepts at following the roads of this world and arriving somewhere on time.

1. The City in the Dawn

THEY WERE NOW passing rapidly and smoothly through a level champaign interspersed with low, gently rolling hills and wide, well cultivated farms and pastures. It was dotted with a few outstanding country houses, the new estates and "belvederes" of Philadelphia merchants, who, in the short course of two generations or even less, had built up substantial fortunes in the prosperous seaport that had so rapidly become not only the metropolis of colonial North America, but the second city of the British Empire as well. Here and there patches and rounded clumps of primeval forest still remained, frequently upon the tops of knolls, where huge maples, oaks, poplars, black walnuts and not a few mighty evergreens continued to overlook the surrounding landscape in undisturbed dignity.

These, with the rich brown plough-lands that stretched smoothly about them, lent an island-like and semi-classic aspect to the landscape that was vaguely beautiful and yet inherently memorable to all those of sensibility who then passed through it. Indeed, it was this finished and domestic, yet wide and magnificent perspective of smooth cultivation mingled with the majestic remnants of half-subdued wilderness that was already giving another twist and a new North American meaning to the much-vexed term "romantic".

Suddenly, from a small rise not far west of State House Square a panorama of the City of Brotherly Love, "from horn to horn," lay stretched before them. Not only was the sudden completeness of the view astonishing, there was a further element of surprise in the very projection of it. For contrary to all reasonable expectation, from this point on, the plane inclined sharply upward to the riverbank, and the City situated along the high bluffs of the Delaware stood out sharply against the sky in startling silhouette with the light behind it.

Here most travellers approaching Philadelphia from the west were given to pause involuntarily, while the more eloquent among them would invariably take time to expatiate on the view. And this tongue-tripping trick of the landscape having been remarked by the more reticent Quaker residents of the neighbourhood, the low crest of the road at which travelling orators so invariably paused had long been known locally as "Mount Philosophy."

The travellers in the cavalcado that morning proved to be no exception. When the two leading horsemen reached the verge of the crest, they checked their mounts and paused to admire. But it was Salathiel Albine who exclaimed impulsively "Godamighty!" Philadelphia, the city of his hopes and longing, at last lay before him.

It extended along a great bow in the river for two miles or more, a medley of roofs, mellow brick house walls, white steeples, and hazy kitchen chimneys lost amidst blowing treetops. There was a tangle of ships' rigging that grew black near the middle of the town towards which the Market Way they were travelling seemed so precisely headed. On either flank of the City itself, villages and even smaller clusters of dwellings had begun to invade the countryside westward. These hamlets punctuated the scene with pleasant marks of human interest, while along the farm roads from every direction the white tops of wagons and the glint of farm carts slid marketwards through lanes bordered by trees.

Perhaps the most arresting, certainly the most illuminating element in the entire view was the perpetual flash of silver light reflected upward from the broad and tranquil river in the east. It was felt rather than seen, for it lay for the most part just below and beyond the natural horizon and the darker line of the City itself.

Yet it was this all but subliminal and overpowering impression of "light just beyond" that transfigured and dramatized all the countryside. Against the diffused reflection from the Delaware, the outlines of both man-made and natural objects in the vicinity stood out with a boldness and sharpness of profile that conferred upon them both order and character at the same time.

Thus, out of a half-wild and still pastoral countryside, the new City seemed to have forced itself suddenly upward into the light of day, as in fact it had, and there was both vigour and a beguiling and perpetual promise in the quality of the morning light that surrounded it.

"There lies your dream!" said Yates to Salathiel, with an inclusive and familiar sweep of his hand across the outlines of the City before them. "Now we'll see what you can make of it. For myself, I do admit that I'm more than a bit content at getting back to town. Well, Master Little Turtle, how does it appeal to you?"

Salathiel swallowed hard. This was the fulfilment of many years of determined scheming to go downcountry, to escape from the forest and claim his inheritance as a white man. And now the City lay just before him. In a few minutes he would actually be there! There, too, were the ships he had so often dreamed about. To him they seemed the greatest

wonder of all. B'God, he'd go aboard one that very morning! As for answering Yates—he could only swallow his emotions. Consequently, his
Adam's apple, quite a large one, went up and down several times.

Yates laughed. "Beyond eloquence, eh? Well, most strong private
emotions are. Let's just contemplate for a moment or two."

So they halted for a pause, and for the wagon to catch up with them
at the crest of the height. They sat there close together, letting their
horses breathe-in the sweet morning air. Yates laid his hand impulsively on his friend's mighty arm.

"One thing," said he, "I must warn you against. Take no offence
here from any man lightly. Keep your heavy hands to yourself. Violence
will get you nowhere in town. And recollect that for a while, at least,
you will be a stranger in a strange land, and must earn your welcome."

Recalling certain violent passages in the not remote past, Salathiel
felt the wisdom of this friendly warning. He nodded solemnly, and was
about to reply, when the wagon suddenly caught up with them. Frances
Melissa, at the sight of the City, rose from her seat. She rode standing
up dangerously, gesturing with excitement, and calling out to him, "How
do ye loik it, Sal; how do ye loik the fine, brave town I've beguiled
ye to?"

He motioned to her violently to sit down. Sometimes he thought he
cared more for the child she was carrying than she did.

"I like it fine!" he said, riding up close to the wagon, "but do be
careful, my fancy. We be so near now. Let nothing untoward happen."
She promised, coloring with embarrassment at having forgotten her
plight. But there were still tears of enthusiasm on her lashes, and she
smiled at him with the sheer happiness of a fulfilment that was beyond
mere content.

Holy Saints, the long years of forest wandering and bound-out slavery
were over! No one need ever know about them now. She would be a
lady in town. She would soon make a place for herself—and the rest
of them—in the City. Often she had thought she would never win her
man away from the wilderness. Again and again he had seemed upon the
point of returning. But now they were going home at last, going to town.

She sat on the wagon seat between black Hercules and Bridget as they
drove along, pondering. Casually she wondered what Madame Graydon,
the mistress of the fashionable boarding establishment for which they
were headed, might be like. Doubtless, Captain Ourry, as a good adjutant, knew what he was doing in setting up headquarters at the Slate
House. Doubtless, it would be a fine place for the brigadier's new military family. And as for General Bouquet, the brigadier himself, she felt
she had a way with him. Had he not especially asked for her? Besides,
in the dim and remote past in Cork, which only she need recall now,
she had had considerable experience with the keepers of boarding-
houses—and other establishments of entertainment. Even if Madame

Graydon proved to be a harridan, she still might be managed. At worst, it would be an opening skirmish in a long campaign, which she, Frances, did not intend to lose. Well, she would soon know now!

The big grey horses were trotting steadily toward the City again, down the Market Way, following Yates and Salathiel, who were riding along only a few yards ahead. The silver bells and the rumble of the wheels made a happy symphony for Frances Melissa. But there were other happy occasional notes in it, too. Behind her she could hear Malycal chirping cheerily to Jed in the baggage cart. The old Irish crone was beside herself with excitement at getting back to town again. As for Jed, he was calling out to every young colored wench he saw. Next to Dahomey, Philadelphia was home for him. He and the mungee bird, in the back of the wagon, were making more than their fair share of noise. But she did not feel inclined to restrain them now.

It was Bridget who sat most quiet, riding along with the cat basket on her lap, intent on all the sights of the road and on their imminent arrival. She was ready to descend at any moment now and begin housekeeping. She kept staring ahead with all the calm gravity and assurance of childhood. Perhaps she was staring into the future, thought Frances, slipping an arm about her more to reassure herself than the child.

It would be a comfort to have a little body like Bridget in the house to depend upon. And you could depend upon Bridget McCandliss. She could even manage Salathiel, when she wanted to. When the new baby came, Frances told herself, Bridget would have something to mother besides her cat and her dolls. Frances Melissa counted on that. Bridget was like a small mother already.

Frances began to reckon up the weeks and days still left her. Sometime about the middle of summer, she guessed. Probably about the middle of August. For one thing, she did not intend to nurse the child any longer than she had to. No, there were other things she would be more needed for—and Bridget and Malycal both liked to stay in the house.

Where would that be? she wondered; and what would it be like? She leaned forward impulsively. She wished that Yates would press on now, instead of deliberately lagging, as he appeared to be. What was the matter? Yates had slowed down almost to a walk again and was talking earnestly to Salathiel, talking with gestures. What an eloquent tongue the lawyer man had. How it did run on! Frances sighed with sheer impatience.

2. The Last Mile and the First View

YATES, however, had his own precise reasons for slowing down. From the start he had catered in every way to the natural impatience of the

Albines to get to Philadelphia. But, what with spring freshets and the heavy wagon and extra cart, it had taken them all of two days and the better part of the night before—no, the *best* part of it in his estimation, the early morning sleeping hours—to cover the distance between Lancaster and the Middle Ferry on the Schuylkill. Also, in Mr. Attorney Yates's always legal opinion, three o'clock in the morning was much too early to rouse anybody, even a ferryman. In this the entire Byrne family, who kept the ferry, had unanimously concurred with sonorous snores.

So it had taken the devil of a shindy, with Salathiel pounding on the barred door of the ferryhouse with his gunstock to waken old Joshua Byrne and his two sons, and to get their necessary interest and attention enlisted in the task of easing the big wagon across the Schuylkill on the ferry barge. After that they had to come back twice for the horses, the extra plunder, and the baggage cart.

Of course, the ferry gear had fouled dismally in midstream and had to be profanely untangled by starlight. A Spanish milled dollar, a full jug of the best Cumberland rye, and about twice the usual fare had been required to soothe the too-early aroused feelings of the Byrne boys. And there would probably have been further argument, and even more to pay, if Salathiel had not kicked young Sylvester Byrne into the river on account of his foul mouth before the women. That had at least cooled Sylvester off.

None the less, it was all of five o'clock and beginning to lighten when they started to hitch up again on the western bank. Five o'clock, seven miles, and about two hours to go.

That would time it just about right, Yates figured, to please their prospective hosts in the City. Seven o'clock would be a fairly auspicious hour for arrival there. Most people, even the guests at the Slate House, would by then have had their breakfasts. And Mistress Graydon, he remembered, was always more affable after her matutinal pot of chocolate. As for himself, he did not intend to stay at the Slate House with the Albines, not at first. He planned to give Frances and Captain Ourry a chance to get Bouquet's official family well under way at the new headquarters before he applied for a room there. He might even wait until after the brigadier himself returned from New York. On the whole that would suit his own plans much better. He had had a long and difficult sojourn on the frontiers and a little gay bachelor life in the City would be restorative. Besides, he had numerous accounts to settle with both John and Richard Penn, and it would be much wiser to stay at first with the Shippens, who were close advisers to the Penns and where provincial politics were ever part of the air. Yes, the Shippen arrangement would be best.

He was taking a letter from Colonel William Burd at Lancaster to the colonel's father-in-law, William Shippen, in the City. And Yates had a pretty good idea that the letter contained a request for a loan.

Colonel Burd was preparing to move away from Lancaster. He was about to build himself a fine new country house to be called "Tinian," on the banks of the Susquehanna near Middletown. "Tinian" was to be a country seat that in every way would befit the colonel's dignity as the commanding officer of all the militia of the province and a son-in-law of the Shippens. But no doubt the colonel had again run into his perpetual "temporary difficulties".

In fact, Yates was practically sure of it. He would therefore be the bearer of unwelcome tidings, and there was no use arousing the good merchant betimes to hear them, especially if the bearer expected to get an invitation to stay in the house. Too much haste in covering the last seven miles might, therefore, prove embarrassing at the last minute. William Shippen was by no means an early riser, and not much of a man to talk to until he had had a dish or two of java. Afterwards he could be affability itself and hospitality personified. And he was quite partial to Scots.

So Yates decided he would arrange to arrive *after* the morning coffee. He would first get his invitation to stay, and *then* deliver Colonel Burd's letter. Consequently, he now looked at his watch thoughtfully, deprecated Salathiel's haste, and slowed their horses down to a walk. And while they rode on thus, leisurely, between ploughed fields where the early morning mist was still rising from the hollows, he purposely began at some length to instruct his rude friend from the frontiers in the urbane art of a timely arrival in town. . . .

Having thus delayed the caravan for well over two miles, the young Scotch lawyer took another peep at his watch, sighed, and glanced at his tall friend to see how he was taking it. Belated market carts were now sweeping around and past them with German imprecations, spattering April mud. But Salathiel's expression did not change. His face cleft space like the cut-water of an Indian figurehead and he rode forward at a walk with the same grim look and as silently as he had lately ridden at a trot.

Now this at the moment was enormously disconcerting to Yates, and he was annoyed. "Well?" he said, clearing his throat eloquently. But there was no reply. He was just about to begin another homily on the failure of great silent men to achieve humanity, when Salathiel spoke.

"I take it your Honour feels we're getting to Philadelphia a mite too early this morning to suit your Honour's honourable friends," he said, imitating the clipped tones of a military orderly. "Or is it you calculate as a philosopher that the City is like to be there for a long time to come?" he added in his natural voice.

"Both," admitted Yates, "but may the devil take you! As usual you cramp my style by merely stating the heart of the matter. But 'tis true. Neither Master Shippen nor Madame Graydon will be apt to welcome us before the market carts, and certainly the City will abide. It is earlier than you think. Listen, what have I been saying—there goes early guard mount at the barracks only now. Some of our old friends of the Forty-second Highlanders must be there." Over the fields, much mellowed by distance, came the skirl of bagpipes and the thud of drums.

All that Yates had been saying faded away. Salathiel could see the new Highland guard wheeling into place, the flash of the officers' clay-mores in salute. Just then the far-off bugles joined in the march, lifting their golden shout in a world of triumphant dreams—lifting him clean off his horse and back to Fort Pitt on another spring morning years be-fore . . .

A wave of memories engulfed him, washed clear over his head like the wind in the treetops of the forest. He was homesick for its green silence, for the days that passed one into the other like folds in the silken fabric of time. It was not often he succumbed to visions of the past like this, but when he did he plunged deep. Memory entranced him, and the familiar drums and bagpipes sounding over the fields from Camptown had torn back the curtains of the past.

The infinite vistas of the long forest road he had travelled over the mountains seemed to rise and fall before him again. But now the silence of the woods was filled with many voices. It became a green tapestry woven with many scenes: Ligonier, Bedford, Lyttleton, Chambersburg, and Carlisle; forest, fort, village and farm. He was searching for some-thing. Suddenly the infinitely sweet face of his first love, Phoebe, rose before him bathed in the mists of his dissolving dream. He could hear the beloved tones of her soft voice dying away with the blood of his own heartbeats whispering in his ears, "Darling, darling. Lost, lost." He could hear the Juniata singing it to him dirge-like in the moonlight of that summer night at Bedford two years ago—"lost"—dinning it musically into his ears, "lost, lost."

Godamighty, poor mateless he!

Then he was engulfed in an infinite sense of self-pity and of helpless doubt. And then, instantly, he was back at the very beginning of things for him, at the ultimate bounds of what he could remember.

In the secret light of the forest the beautiful face of his dark Irish mother bent over him, haloed in a shaft of afternoon sunlight. She was whispering with the voice of the leaves those words of abysmal comfort for her baby, words he could never quite recall. But he was a child again. He put his chubby hand up to feel the smooth curves of her cheeks. What was she saying, what words? Only the tender tones of her voice came through, and presently she would scream. Oh, yes, he knew that. She always did. The Injuns would get her.

This was his ultimate nightmare and he began to struggle against it in the direction of the present. This morning he must save himself from hearing that despairing scream.

There was something in the present that would save him from that banshee scream of terror out of the past, a new comfort, balm for the shuddering mind. Ah, this was it. After all, God was kind to him.

He heard the soothing sound of falling water and saw himself in the peaceful firelight of the room in the old mill house on Yellow Breeches Creek near Carlisle. Bridget and Malycal were talking somewhere in the house. He could hear the old woman and the child laughing together. Frances Melissa was seated sewing on a baby's shift before the fire, the steeple clock ticked on the mantel while time flowed on peacefully. Yes, here he had found peace at last. Frances began saying something in her familiar rich Irish voice. She began to rock and sing softly, and it was then that the revelation came to him. Balm of Gilead! He remembered! Frances and his mother had the same voice.

He gave a half-articulate cry of joy and relief. Why had he never realized that before this morning! And that must be Frances calling to him now to look . . . to look at . . .

3. The Slate House

"LOOK at the grand town clock!" she was saying. "Did you ever see the loik?" He struggled back to himself. He looked out over the points of his horse's ears down a long street into the present.

It was swarming with wagons, riders, and people. On his right hand was the largest building he had ever seen, red brick, with a great squat clock tower on the gable-end nearest him. It must be the State House and State House Square through which they were passing. Automatically he followed Yates's example, and taking Captain Ecuyer's silver watch out of his pocket he set it by the big clock. Twenty-seven minutes before seven by the big dial—and from now on he would be keeping city time!

This must be the back of the State House they were passing, judging by the long line of white hitching posts and the big bell tower rising on the opposite side. On his left were open fields with trees, ponds, a few benches here and there, and paths worn in every direction. Before him Chestnut Street ran directly down towards the river with a welter of ships' masts against the sky at the far end, and houses, houses, houses that finally blent into two continuous walls of buildings without an apparent break. People swarmed. They seemed to be coming out of the doors like ants.

A moment later as they passed the east end of the State House he smelled fire, cooking flesh, and raw Indian. It was a familiar combination. And sure enough, in a big shed against the State House wall several squaws, while a few braves lay about on trade blankets smoking, were boiling an entire leg of beef in a huge iron cauldron. The un-

severed hairy hoof of it stuck up out of the pot into the air. Delawares
or Mingoes, he guessed, chiefs on some mission to the governor, or beg-
gars and guests of the honourable house of assembly. There they were!
He grunted audibly as they passed and made Yates laugh.

Then, almost instantly, they were down into Chestnut Street and
closed in by houses and fenced gardens on every side. Evidently more
people rose early in Philadelphia than Yates had led him to think—and
they were not all of the lower classes either.

To be sure, it was now comparatively late, almost seven o'clock. Already some ladies were hurrying home from market. They were dressed
in high bonnets, hoop skirts, and long gloves, and followed by barefoot
black girls carrying their heavy market baskets. You could tell the
Quaker dames by their grey dresses and demure walk, and by the sign
that they always carried their own market baskets. For all that, they
managed to look dove-like and no less elegant than their more worldly
sisters. Their faces and their satins shone alike. Every block there was a
great public pump, where scrambling for water was going on amongst
the black wenches with buckets and pitchers surrounding it. The creak
of the pumps and the constant gushing of water mixed with the shouts
and laughter of gay Negro voices accompanied them all down the street.
It was the universal morning noise of Philadelphia.

On the sidewalks bound-servants were down on their knees scrubbing
brick with brick, but they stopped flourishing their brooms a moment to
stare at the big wagon as it passed. Only they were silent and sullen.
But Frances Melissa, who well understood why, felt her heart go out
to them in a flood of sympathy, while at the same time she praised her
saints that she no longer shared their lot.

No, she would never forget what it had been like to be a poor bound-
out thing. When some of them spat in the gutter as Jed called out to
them in ill-timed merriment, she could not blame them. It was the only
reply they dared make. But nothing, she knew, so irritated these white
drudges as the happy pampered niggers of rich folks. "Black bastards,"
they muttered. "Wait!"

Salathiel, however, saw none of this. That certain people should labour or be miserable, and others happy and comfortable, seemed all in
the order of nature to him. That every man had his status, he took as
much for granted as he did the hierarchy of rank in a military garrison
or the presence of prisoner slaves, labouring squaws and idle chiefs in an
Indian village. What surprised him, and disappointed him considerably,
was that the City was not all city. It was not quite the solid and unmiti-
gated town he had read of in books about London and other European
places. He expected it to be all bricks and one solid front of shops.

But it was not so. They were now well into Philadelphia, only a few
blocks from the water-front, and yet the country kept intruding itself.
Eighth and Seventh Streets seemed scarcely more than lanes with a

few houses strung along them, and you could see out into pasture on every side. Cows and pigs were being driven out to graze. Indeed, Chestnut Street itself was not without a certain rural aspect.

It was lined on either side all the way down from State House Square not by brick buildings and shop-fronts, but by a succession of low, rambling houses surrounded by broad verandahs. They were set in fields and gardens with their dooryards fenced in with neat white palings. Sometimes several neighbours were joined together by a stretch of common green lawn and there were patches of vegetable gardens, thickets, and every now and then a stream or swampy place dotted with ponds which ambled off into an eccentric vista of sloughs and wood patches, where wild fowl and domestic poultry mingled in friendly flocks. Ducks paraded and geese honked. Off to the right on a hillock a great house with many chimney pots and marble-silled windows stood up, conspicuous from every direction. Chestnut Street rose and fell. Over the creeks there were wooden bridges or brick culverts. At other crossings pedestrians and vehicles alike floundered through the mud. At such places the brick sidewalks were interrupted by stepping stones. Then they would pick up and go on again.

But above all Philadelphia seemed to be the city of porches and verandahs. As he rode down the street that morning, Salathiel could look in through dooryards and gardens at "everything that was going on".

At one house they were serving breakfast on the porch. It was a rather grand family. A merchant's, he supposed. The father in a silk dressing gown and a morning turban instead of a wig sat opposite his wife, who presided at the other end of the table over a tall silver coffee urn, wearing a high laced cap on her towering coiffure. She sat very straight and stiff in a whaleboned bodice, her voluminous skirts sweeping about a stately chair. Between the parents on either side a row of small yellow heads were bent low over the table. Father was saying grace.

Behind him a barefoot black girl stood bowed forward, too, but holding a large smoking silver tureen, while stopped in her tracks she waited for the end of the morning prayer.

Upstairs he could see them making beds. Women holding pillows under their chins while they pulled on fresh slips; women dusting furniture and hanging mattresses out of the windows to "sun off". In almost every yard coloured servants were carrying jordans to the outside privies, some of them star-shaped and all decorated with elaborate lattices and scrollwork. From and to these, members of the family of all ages could be seen hurrying back and forth. In fact, it was just the time for such offices which on a warm spring morning became almost a social occasion. A few moments later as the ships at Carpenters Dock at the end of Chestnut Street began to come into view, a medley of bells from all over the city began to toll seven o'clock. A wild answering clangour of ships' bells swept along the river-front. As if at a signal, the whole city now seemed suddenly to spring into life. Everybody and his clerk or servant seemed to have urgent business along the water-front.

Gentlemen emerged from gateways in chaises; gentlemen passed them mounted on horseback. Schoolboys in blue aprons, carrying satchels, dashed out of doorways and took off together shouting down the street. Once a great coach-and-four crowded them to one side and passed with a cracking of whips. Mr. Chew's, Yates said, the attorney general's. It was the only coach they saw and there was nobody in it. At one place they passed a whole flock of little girls in white dresses and blue ribbons being herded along to dame school by two harassed-looking English nurses. Bridget nearly jumped from the wagon seat and held up her cat basket to be admired. At this the wagon was all but stopped and surrounded for a moment by the children and that peculiar silver gale-like sound that only admiring little girls can make.

"I am going to school, too, Melissa," insisted Bridget, as the wagon disentangled itself and they went on again. This possibility had never occurred to Bridget before. Frances said she might. It had not occurred to her either. But why not? They were in the City now. Anything might happen!

Certainly a good deal was going on. They were stopped now by a crush of drays making for the water-front, and a long string of pack horses coming up the street from the docks in the opposite direction. The horses were laden with chests, small barrels, and bales marked with the broad arrow of the king.

"Whar ye bound for?" asked Salathiel, as the drive-master in charge drove by.

"Upcountry. Fort Loudon, I guess," the man added, drawing rein. "Specs I'll git my final orders at Carlisle."

"Happen ye pass through Chambersburg, make my compliments to Colonel Chambers. Tell him he can reach me in the City at the Slate House."

"I'll do that, sir," said the man, touching his hat. "But who shall I say . . . ?"

"Tell him *Mister* Albine," said Salathiel, and repeated his name to make sure, with no little satisfaction at having added the handle. It was something to be a mister at last, and no one to laugh at it.

"Mister Albine . . . to Colonel Chambers—I got ye," said the driver, touching his hat again. After which he took off after his string of horses. Meanwhile, they still stood waiting at a crossing for the last files of the convoy and rear escort to pass.

"It's really a big convoy," remarked Yates, "supplies for the western forts, fresh arrived from England. Bouquet is good at that. You can depend on him not to forget his garrisons. Man, look at the rum! There'll be high jinks at Bedford and Ligonier, amongst our friends. But for all that, I'm glad we're going the other way this morning. We're almost there now. This is Fourth Street, where the City really begins. You'll see what I mean in a minute, as soon as the last of these packers get by."

Fourth Street! Something pulled a trigger in Salathiel's head. "Doesn't Friend Japson live hereabouts?" he asked.

"Why, yes, he does," said Yates, "but how the devil did you know that?"

" 'Fourth Street betwixt Chestnut and Mistress Nicholl's racing stables, the house farthest in.' 'Tis the first city address I ever learned, years ago at Ligonier one morning. Japson told me."

"You're a strange one," observed Yates. "Fancy remembering it all that time. Well, *thee* is correct. That's Friend Japson's house down there," said he, pointing. "And we'll be seeing him soon enough, I opine, when he learns what's in the wind about our land deals. But here's the last of the demned pack horses now."

The rear guard, an escort of five mounted men and a sergeant, Royal Americans of the 60th Regiment, in the new grey field uniform into which Bouquet had only recently put them, now rode by after the last of the pack horses—and Chestnut Street lay clear and open before them from Fourth Street to the docks.

"This is it!" exclaimed Salathiel. "Look, Melissa, not a single damned tree!" he shouted. And so it was.

Frances Melissa stood up again to look. A cobbled street lined solely with houses, shop-fronts, and a forest of bright painted signs overhead swept before them clear to the water-front, where the drays could be glimpsed passing constantly. It was a human ant hill; the sidewalks were thronged with people. Yes, this was certainly it! Bridget began clapping her little hands in excitement and Jed seemed to be crowing like a rooster.

They were moving forward right into it now. A few people had stopped to wipe off the mud, which the pack horses had spattered on them. But nearly everybody else was hurrying toward Front Street. Several drays that had been dammed up behind them now rattled and pounded by. Doors opened and gentlemen in wigs and cocked hats came out and joined the throng. A jangle of bells from all parts of the city marked the new quarter hour.

Everybody began to hurry even faster. Clerks began to run. No one paid any attention to the big wagon and its two outriders or to the noisy and seemingly ecstatic Negro driving the cart. They were all taken for granted. They had become a part of life in the City. The bells ceased ringing, and time went on again as usual. But it was different now for every one of them in the cavalcado. For each in his own way time had changed. They were there!

In fact, just at that instant they had crossed Third Street and left the workhouse on the left side of Chestnut Street behind them. There an unusual number of unfortunate slatterns were scrubbing the brick walks and the steps of the doorways. One woman rose, and tossing the tangle of her unkempt hair back from her eyes to look at the wagon, pointed at Frances with a tragic gesture and laughed. Frances shuddered and looked away. Then they were by, and she caught a brief glimpse to her left down a long alley past the Presbyterian Meeting House and into the swarming market on High Street beyond. Yates called out a warning to black Hercules and they swerved suddenly at the next corner, turning south into Second Street. Here, too, the houses were close and there were many people.

A half block farther, and there was the Slate House.

No doubt of it! It had a—in fact *the*—slate roof of the town. There was a splendid stand of immense white pines in the garden behind it. And Yates did not need to point it out as their destination, as he did, for it was precisely the kind of house to which Frances hoped and expected he would take them. She realized that fully even as they were drawing up before it, and she smiled at him as he looked back and nodded.

The Slate House was old, sedate, and massive. It had something of the combined public splendour and the quaint domestic piety of the seventeenth century about it, much as though King Charles II had good-naturedly consented to stand for his portrait in a broad Quaker hat. It was like a brick cottage that had somehow been inflated into a mansion, and, as the process continued, had just stopped short of becoming a fort. It stood at the corner of Norris Alley and Second Street and the alley side was prolonged by a high brick wall which extended indefinitely towards the water-front in the rear.

The main front on Second Street itself was composed of two ells, veritable military bastions that intruded onto the front sidewalk. They frowned. In the central or curtain wall between them the entrance façade was retracted from the street all of eighteen feet. Now in the middle of this front section there was a large double-panelled door at exact street level painted Saxon blue. It had a low arched fanlight clear across it, and there was a memorable brass knocker all to itself in a smaller panel painted red. On either side of the blue door was a large oblong leaded-glass window.

The effect of the entrance façade was thus inevitably that a pair of old-fashioned gold-rimmed and square-lensed spectacles had been draped over the blue nose of a genial but cross-eyed old gentleman. He undoubtedly smiled. Yet if any stranger were unduly encouraged by his squinting smirk, and concluded to take liberties with the knocker, one glance upward was sufficient to admonish him to desist. For on the vast expanse of dull slate roof adorned with a forest of swallow-haunted chimneys, precisely in the middle, and exactly over the front door, one lone dormer window glared malignantly at all who dared to approach, like the protruding eye of a cyclops. It made even innocent passers-by uncomfortable and seemed to follow them suspiciously down the street.

Nor was all this a piece of mere rhetorical fancy. Part cottage, palace, and fortalice that the building undoubtedly was, the Slate House, as if by the force of internal will power constantly and powerfully exerted, triumphantly combined all its separate and distracting features into one memorable and imposing personality. It was the personification of the dignity of virtue, and the permanency of respectability softened and dissolved in a quaint and mysterious charm.

No one who was at all familiar with the Slate House ever forgot it. On various of its distinguished inmates, from travelling English noblemen to French spies, it laid a permanent spell. Children who grew up in its vicinity spoke of it affectionately in the memories of their later years. The legend that William Penn himself had once lived in it and that for one summer the Slate House had also been the State House of the infant colony was inevitable, but it was also true. General Forbes, a canny Scot and a patient and able strategist, had chosen the Slate House to die in and achieved from its north parlour the most notable and impressive military funeral that Philadelphia ever saw. The example of the Scot had been more advisedly followed by other British officers and various high personages to the extent of living in it. Its present chatelaine, known to all her military clientele affectionately, but respectfully, as Desdemona, or "Desdy," and to the rest of the world as Mistress Graydon, was a handsome, affable, and sophisticated widow with a courtly manner. Nothing more impressive could be said of her than that, since taking over the management of the establishment about a year before, she had already succeeded in adding to the prestige and social laurels accumulated by her predecessor, the memorable Mrs. Howells. In the late winter of 1764 General Henri Bouquet had chosen the Slate House in which to set up the temporary headquarters of his new Southern Department and as a home for his entourage and military family. He could scarcely have done better. The brigadier, himself, was then absent on official business in New York, but his adjutant, Captain Ourry, was in residence, and although in bed at the moment, he had expected hourly the arrival of the rest of the brigadier's military family, who at that moment, seven twenty-five ante-meridian, were actually driving up before the blue door in the street below.

One glance at it, and even Frances Melissa was satisfied. Although at the moment she was all but a mental glutton for respectability and well-founded elegance, still the Slate House had surpassed even her fondest expectations, and the smile she conferred on Yates was one not of understanding alone, but of genuine gratitude.

He on his part acknowledged it with an easy wave of the hand, and although the gesture became a part of the same signal with which he also brought the caravan to a halt, his reply had not been lost on

Frances. It was typical indeed of the manner and of the kind of communication that frequently went on between them; significant of a subtle semi-humorous, half-gallant, and yet enduring and mutually respectful sympathy. Each understood the other's predicament and knew not only when, but how to be helpful. And, if in the process Salathiel was sometimes ignored, it was only upon occasions when he was unaware of it. That was where part of the humour came in. And yet the joke was never at his expense. Usually it was for his benefit. This was a delicate balance, yet it could all be conveyed by a smile and a wave of the hand.

Yates and Salathiel were dismounting. The wagon and the cart with Jed still chuckling loudly had come to a halt. Sensing something of a free spectacle in this arrival, a number of people, young and old, now stopped to watch and loitered on the sidewalk opposite the Slate House.

Yates was halfway up the walk to the blue door when it was violently flung open and a schoolboy with his book satchel dashed out, leaving the door swinging open behind him. "What! Late again, Alec!" said Yates. "Mr. Yates? You!" cried the boy, sliding on the bricks and stopping before him just in time. He then stood transfixed with astonishment at the sight of the wagon and horses.

Brief as the moment was, young Bridget McCandliss never forgot Alec as she first saw him that morning, arrested suddenly in full flight, leaning forward slightly like a fencer from the waist. He stood there sensitive and vibrant in every limb and feature. A tangle of brown curls was caught back from his handsome freckled little face by a ribbon of black satin. His dark eyes sparkled with excitement. A fine youngster in the morning sunshine, there was something at once delicate and intrepid about him. So Bridget always thought. Then he saw her and blushed scarlet.

He dropped his satchel, turned without another word, and boy-like rushed back into the house. They could hear him calling out with excitement, "Mamma, mamma, they're here! Mother, do you hear? The general's people are come!"